WAY OF GODS

A *Buried Goddess Saga* NOVEL
IV

RHETT C. BRUNO

JAIME CASTLE

JOIN THE KING'S SHIELD

Sign up to the *free* and exclusive King's Shield Newsletter to receive early looks and new novels, peeks at conceptual art that breathes life into Pantego as well as exclusive access to short stories called "Legends of Pantego." Learn more about the characters and the world you love.

Did you know we have a Facebook group too? All the same perks as the email readers group plus instant interaction with Rhett and Jaime! The Official King's Shield Fan Club.

__The Bruno/Castle parental units respectively__—Thanks for all the love and support and for not being as terrible as all the parents in this series.

BROTLEBIR
BREKLIODAD
THE DRAGON'S TAIL
hornsheim
THE GLASS KINGDOM
fettingboroough
YAOLIN CITY
PANPING
THE BLACK SANDS
nahanab
saujibar
LATIAPUR
THE BOILING WATERS

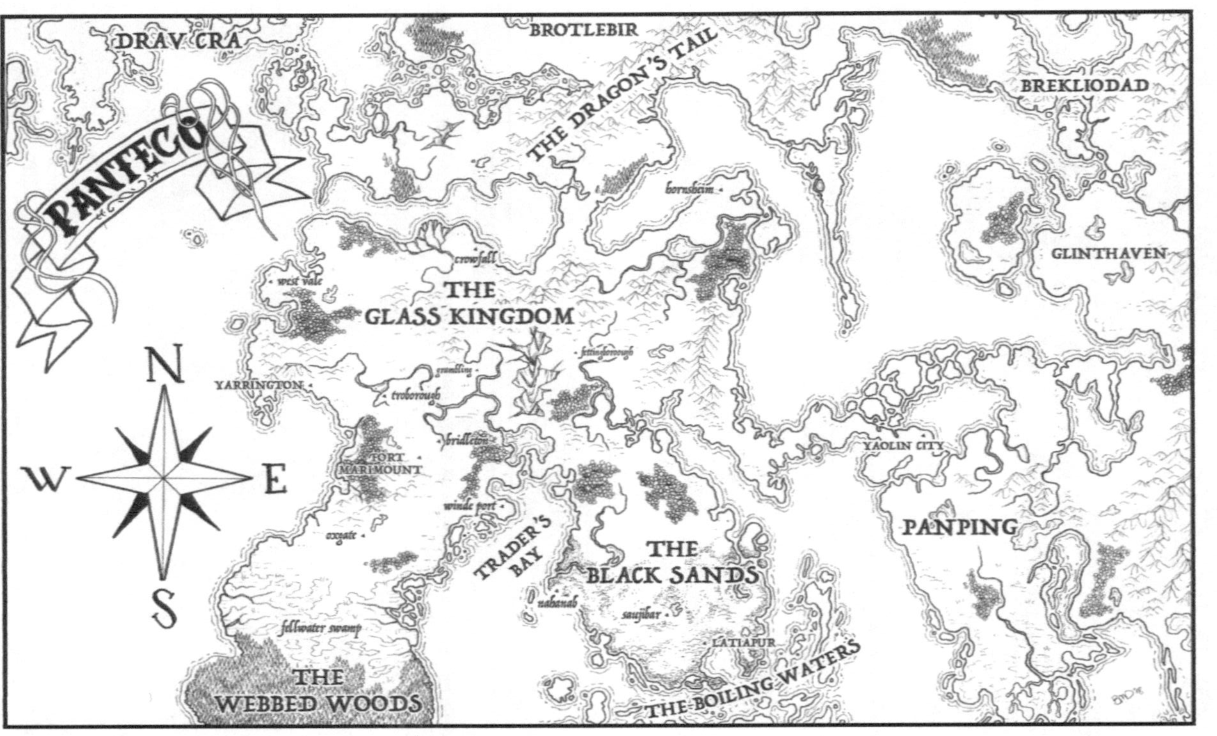

PANTEGO
DRAV CRA
BROTLEBIR
THE DRAGON'S TAIL
BREKLIODAD
hornsheim
GLINTHAVEN
crowsfall
west vale
THE GLASS KINGDOM
fettingborough
crumbling
YARRINGTON
troborough
bridleton
YAOLIN CITY
FORT MARIMOUNT
winde port
oxgate
PANPING
TRADER'S BAY
THE BLACK SANDS
nahanab
saujibar
LATIAPUR
fellwater swamp
THE BOILING WATERS
THE WEBBED WOODS
N
W
E
S

PROLOGUE

Drad Mak the Mountainous, of the Fyortentek clan, swung his mighty battle-axe, cleaving the tusk of a zhulong as it slipped on a strip of sand turned to ice by a warlock. The vibrations of the blow made Mak's hands sting, but he held firm, and the force sent the beast to the ground. Its rider, legs crushed beneath the zhulong's weight, raised his hands in surrender as Mak hefted his axe high. The blade ignored the dying gray man's pleas and sunk into his chest.

Mak's father had given him the axe, and his father before him, and so on. A thick human skull served as the socket for the dual blades and dated back so many generations, none could remember to whom it belonged. All Mak knew was that brothers feuded over the dradinengor title of his clan and the winner got the axe. Stories claimed the weapon thirsted for blood as an upyr of Breklian lore. If that were true, this day, the axe was fully sated on Shesaitju blood.

"Drad Mak!" someone shouted.

Mak spun around and looked into the eyes of a Shesaitju warrior. The man had his fauchard raised, ready to plunge it into Mak's back, but collapsed and dropped the weapon instead. Sir

Nikserof, King's Shieldsman and co-Wearer of White stood behind the attacker, his white helm covered in blood. Mak wore a matching helm, signaling that he was a joint-leader of this allied army, although his wasn't made from glaruium as Nikserof's was. Before following King Pi's orders to end the Black Sand's rebellion once and for all, Hovom Nitebrittle, the Glassmen's lead Smith, had quickly and crudely fashioned the helmet to fit the mammoth man's head.

Mak and Nikserof exchanged a nod, then Nikserof returned to a wall of shields and his advancing forces. The campaign into the Black Sands had been a success thus far. Even the infamous Afhem Muskigo Ayerabi, "the Scythe," didn't know how to handle the Glass Army and Drav Cra working together, and many of the Shesaitju people refused to join him, including any afhems and their substantial naval forces. Nikserof and his flower pickers hid behind shields and spears while Mak's men, hardened by lifetimes of bitter cold, slaughtered Muskigo's ground troops.

"Retreat!" Shesaitju voices carried on the hot air. "Fall back!"

Mak crushed a corpse beneath his boot and watched as Muskigo's army responded to the command to fall back behind the high walls of Nahanab. The rebellious afhem himself was the last to heed the command. From atop his zhulong, he slashed down and gashed a Drav Cra warrior. Then another. A nearby warlock sliced her palm and sent a fireball hurtling at Muskigo, but he deflected it with his blade, embers and sparks bathing him in harsh orange light. Then, he grabbed a spear from the chest cavity of a fallen soldier, and launched it through the warlock's heart.

Muskigo glared across the haze of heat, blood, and sand straight at Mak and Nikserof. His eyes were dark, full of rage. Mak's grip tightened on his axe. For a moment, Mak thought the rebel might charge, that, finally, he may face a foe worthy of staining his axe. Then one of Muskigo's commanders grabbed him and convinced him to retreat.

"The cowards fall behind walls!" Mak exclaimed, thrusting his axe into the air. "Tonight, we shall feast in the name of the Buried Goddess!"

Night was a relief for Mak and his people in this arid region. They camped at the edge of the M'stafu Desert, where the Wildlands gave way to black sand. The heat was unbearable under the beating daytime sun, even with warlocks summoning ice to keep them cool while they marched. But at night, a chill ran on the south-bearing breeze, as if Nesilia's loving embrace arrived to comfort them. The Glassmen sat around their fires and huddled in blankets, but Mak's men needed none of it. They welcomed the cold.

Drums beat in celebration. Warlocks sat in a circle, mounds of bone in the center upon which a goat lay—a sacrifice in the name of their Lady.

"Louder, my people!" Mak laughed as he downed a horn filled with southern ale. The stuff was weak, but he planned on drinking deep into the night. "Celebrate. While the grey men cower behind walls, we will strike fear into their hearts. Louder!"

Soft green nigh'jel light from within Nahanab glowed on the horizon. It was a highly defensible city, surrounded on two sides by the black stone cliffs bordering the Wildlands, and on the other, Trader's Bay. A wall stretched between the eastern cliffs and the bay, with a single gate—the only entry from land. And Mak knew well the skill of Shesaitju archers. Despite how far they'd been beaten back, the blackwood barbed arrows had claimed more of Mak's people than anything while the Glassmen hid behind their shields painted with the Eye of Iam.

A siege was in order.

In the same manner Mak's raiders would leave Northern

Glassmen to shroud themselves beneath the shadow of tall cathedrals, they would take Nahanab. In the North, the Drav Cra raiders could easily ride in and slaughter them all, but instead, they take joy in watching as the flower pickers stew in fear until they willingly surrender anything of value. Only this time, Mak had no interest in valuables. After the Shesaitju starve themselves out, the Drav Cra and Glassmen will enter, steal the heads from Shesaitju shoulders and claim Nahanab as their own.

Sir Nikserof had called for a new wave of warships to moor off-coast and block Afhem Muskigo and his men from retreating into the bay. Drav Cra longboats, already dispatched from what was left of Winde Port, had initiated the blockade. All while the army cut off all trade to the land.

Within Nahanab, Muskigo and his rebels would, indeed, starve in time. And they would know that the might of the Drav Cra couldn't be resisted. And soon, Prime Minister Redstar would command the ear of the Glass Kingdom's boy-king, and the Buried Goddess' will would fall upon Pantego before anyone could stop it.

Mak grinned and raised his horn in cheers as Nikserof and a handful of Shieldsmen strolled by. The Glassman returned a reticent nod. He and his ilk were fine warriors, but in time, only one would wear the White Helm, and Mak knew who that would be.

"Join me for a drink, Shieldsman!" Mak shouted.

Nikserof stopped. He firmly gripped a piece of parchment, a letter probably freshly delivered by one of their galler birds. *The soft fools. Still taking orders from far-off kings and advisers.* Once a Drav Cra force was dispatched, they were trusted to do what was asked of them. "Defeat the rebels and bring glory to our Lady's name," was all that Redstar, the Arch Warlock needed to ask.

"I would love to, but I have a siege to prepare," Nikserof replied. "Care to join us?"

Mak scoffed. "All these talks and plans. Today is a time for celebration. The Buried Goddess carries us to victory! Perhaps, she truly did lay with your Iam, eh? We make quite a pair." The others seated with Mak chortled.

Nikserof bit his lip but didn't give in to the goading. Ever since setting out from Yarrington, the Shieldsman hadn't been much fun. "Then at least try and keep it down so we can focus," he said. "It is *time* to rest. Victory is not yet won. Muskigo has proven time and again to be full of surprises."

"Where can they go! Their fleet can't stand against what's coming, and the rest of their people have refused to aid them in breaking the blockade. They're titrats in a cage now, waiting to be squashed."

Warlocks interrupted them, chanting in Drav Crava as blood leaked from the goat's throat and into bowls carved from human skulls. Nikserof winced and averted his gaze, soft man that he was.

Iam's favored weaklings.

"Have a good night," Nikserof said, then he and his men clattered off in their heavy armor, wrapped in Drav Cra furs as if a chilly desert night was something to fear.

Mak extended his horn, and one of his men filled it before he commanded it. Once full, Mak tipped some over the edge to feed the earth before bringing it to his lips.

Mak's eyes shot open. He saw the shape of a face above him, then felt cold all over. It didn't hurt, but he couldn't breathe, and the man gripped a short sword covered in blood. Mak's blood.

Mak lashed out and seized the assailant's skull, crushing and twisting, breaking the man's neck in an instant. Mak then grabbed his own throat. The man had cut it, but Mak's neck was so thick with muscle the blade hadn't gone too deep. Still, blood leaked from between his fingers even as he applied pressure.

His blurry eyes darted. All over, tents burned with men both in and around them. It was early morning, the light of sunrise just beginning to touch the horizon. At first, Mak thought Muskigo had gotten the jump on them, then he realized that fire only rose from the Drav Cra portion of the camp. Fully-armored Glassmen stood above his people, slitting their throats as they slept. Simple arrows rained down upon them from all sides as well.

Mak attempted to shout orders, but he couldn't. A Shieldsman charged him through the smoke and Mak pawed for his axe. He found it and swung it upward, catching the man beneath the jaw and killing him instantly.

Mak then tore the furs off his shoulder and wrapped his neck tight to stem the bleeding. He stood, legs woozy from the loss of blood and a night of drinking. He wouldn't last long in such a state.

"The Glassmen betray us!" voices of his men shouted in Drav Crava all around him, lost amongst the yowls of the dying. Warlocks were killed quickly, not allowed to bleed out, but one held on, consuming Glassmen in magical fire and vines even as he died.

Nikserof was smart, hitting them first, but he couldn't get all of them.

A handful survived and chanted in a circle. Great waves of fire crashed down in a large swathe, guarding Mak and a portion of his army from the Glassmen's advance. Arrows crumbled to ash as they neared. Those caught outside of the flaming wreath were slaughtered like pigs—their screams like a cruel symphony. Most didn't even have a chance to raise their weapons.

"Drad Mak!" Drad Ugosah, shouted. "Sir Nikserof has betrayed us."

Mak gurgled in response. Just speaking sent him to his knees.

Blood had turned the furs around his neck deep crimson, almost black. He just stared up at the mustached dradinengor, eyes growing bleary.

Drad Ugosah barked orders at one of the warlocks. While the others kept the Glass army at bay, one of the remaining warlocks knelt at Mak's side. Mak could barely hear now, and tendrils of darkness closed in around his vision.

"You must survive," the warlock said, only her voice wasn't her own. It was deep, ephemeral as if the Buried Goddess herself spoke through her lips. Her eyes rolled back and showed only the whites. "Your work is not yet done."

The warlock slit her own throat, and as she bled, she placed a hand over Mak's throat. The next thing he knew, the warlock was a shriveled husk at his side, and all that remained of his wound was a grisly scar.

Ugosah tried to help Mak stand, but received a shove as Mak grabbed his battle-axe and shouted, "I'll kill them all!"

"You heard our Lady's command," Drad Ugosah said.

Mak glared through the blaze, seeing the silhouettes of Glassmen, ready to slaughter them all. Only a few hundred of his men might have survived their cowardly betrayal, each of them ready to die in battle, backed into a tight circle. Sir Nikserof and his army stood beyond the flames, staring back at Mak. Mak couldn't help but wish Muskigo had charged the day before. At least then all these brave Drav Cra warriors might not have died at the hands of traitorous cowards.

Mak grunted and shoved Ugosah toward their mounts. "Retreat!" he shouted. It pained him to his very soul to say it. "Fall back in the name of the Buried Goddess, and we will slaughter these cowards another day!"

The warlocks' fire shield had managed to protect the zhulong stables filled with the giant creatures they'd stolen from the Black Sands. Beastmasters commanded the caged dire wolves with them to feast, and beasts chased beasts as the warlocks lifted the veil of fire.

Mak and the survivors charged through the Glass ranks, heading north. Mak grabbed the fur of his own dire wolf, Trite, pushing him forward as Mak mounted one of the zhulong. Smoke and ember singed his brow, sweat poured down his back, but he charged ahead, his axe carving a bloody line through the cowards.

By the time Mak reached the ridge looking down upon the camp and escaped the smog of smoke, he glanced back and saw that the Glassmen didn't give chase. Instead, they cheered, raising spears and swords in the air as if they'd won a great victory. A few even continued firing arrows to keep the Drav Cra running.

Mak yanked on the zhulong's thick, orange mane to stop its retreat and watched as his people rushed by. Bloody, exhausted, terrified… he'd seen his warriors be many things, but terrified was never one of them. Even the few warlocks who'd survived looked as though they'd seen Skorravik, his people's eternal plane of rest, and Nesilia wasn't there. They rode on the backs of hard-scaled zhulong, slouched, drained of too much blood and on the precipice of death. They'd need water, food, and all their supplies were burned.

From so high up, Mak could see beyond Nahanab into the shallow cove where it was located. The longboats his people had lent to the war effort were full of activity. Some burned, others flipped, and he could see the shadows of his own people being tossed overboard. Betrayed.

The very sight sent a chill up Mak's spine like never before. He wanted to roar and crack open the earth. Glass warships were on the way, and now, in the night, they'd stolen Mak's ships so they could keep up the blockade on Nahanab. As if theDrav Cra had never been a part of it.

A piece of parchment blew by, signed on the bottom and still spitting ash. Mak snatched it. He couldn't read the Glassmen's language too well, and the top half of the message was missing, but he put things together.

REDSTAR HAS BEEN PROVEN A DECEIVER AND SLAIN... THE DRAV CRA ARE EXPELLED FROM YARRINGTON… THE ALLIANCE IS BROKEN… CLAIM THEM BEFORE THEY CLAIM YOU.
—SIR TORSTEN UNGER, MASTER OF WARFARE.

An arrow soared across the sky and stuck into Mak's shoulder, blood spattering the parchment. He barely flinched, just gritted his teeth, snapped it in half, and then crumped the letter, throwing it on the ground where Trite sniffed at it.

"Drad Mak, we must go!" Ugosah ordered from atop a zhulong of his own.

All those Glass townsfolk he'd spared in the Far North… now Mak wished he'd butchered them all. The Arch Warlock was dead, murdered by fools who prayed to a foolish god who had forgotten them. Forgotten everyone.

Mak reached up, tore the white helm from his head and stared at it. He thought about slamming it down but instead placed it in his lap. He'd worn it in the name of an alliance Redstar promised would be fruitful. No longer. Now, the man who'd caused so many of his brothers to die, floundering and afraid, would pay. Mak would force the helm upon Torsten Unger's head, and crush his skull within it. Every coward who worshipped Iam would die screaming… in the name of the Buried Goddess.

I

THE THIEF

Flames raced through the air, one after another like shooting stars. The heat bore down on Whitney like a rabid wolf as sweat poured from his brow. His back and neck were sore, arms burning from exertion, but he couldn't stop. Wouldn't stop. Children were counting on him.

"Five, four, three, two, one." They all counted down together as they'd been doing for what felt like an hour. Finally, Whitney caught the torches, two in one hand, one in the other, then bowed with a flourish, hands out to his sides.

"Good show, Master Fierstown!" called a voice from the crowd.

Whitney looked down at the still-burning torches, then dropped them headfirst into a bucket of water. Steam rose like smoke from a dragon's nostrils as the fire sizzled out.

"Thank you, kind people of..." He leaned back to one of his fellow performers and whispered, "Where the yig are we tonight?"

"Grambling," one of them replied.

Whitney returned to the crowd and shouted, "Grambling! It was an honor performing for you this evening."

The crowd was filing out even as he spoke. He heard *clinks* as a humble few autlas landed in his cup.

Once all the Gramblites who'd come out for a show dispersed, Whitney picked up the container and gave it a shake. "Good show," he scoffed. "Not good enough it seems. Ungrateful…"

For as long as Whitney could remember, he'd wished to be a part of a traveling troupe, performing night after night, soaking up the peoples' applause and hard-earned coin like a cotton towel on a rainy day. He'd even run with a group early on in his thieving career, but truth be told, he'd done little more than carry the actor's props.

Presently, he sighed, rolled his head back, and tried to recount the events that led him to this mud-sodden town just west of the gorge. As he did, he tried not to remember the fictitious-but-all-too-real-to-him six years he'd spent living in Elsewhere, tending his parents' farm with Kazimir the Breklian upyr. He tried not to remember being so close to Sora after all that time only to watch her torn away and whisked back to whatever hidden mystics she'd —apparently—found in Panping. He tried to forget the sight of his only friend, Torsten—gods he hoped no one ever heard him say that out loud—blind as a bat, lying in bed and waiting for Iam to see fit to spare him the misery of life.

The Webbed Woods and the terrors of the spider queen Bliss seemed so distant now. So trivial. So pointless. Shallow, even, the way most of his life had been. The World's Greatest Thief was no more. Now he was merely Whitney Fierstown, a man obsessed with finding the woman he loved.

That meant traversing the entire world from Yarrington, where that damnable portal had spit him out on the top of Mt. Lister, all the way to Yaolin City where he had to assume Sora still would be. All he had was the vision of her in a stone-walled room filled with frightened looking Panpingese men and women garbed in the robes worn by mystics in paintings.

He removed his mask, the brand of the Pompare Troupe. It was a dark gray and purple fragment of wood that covered the left half of his face, part of the mystique, the show.

Whitney had always said, "A good disguise hides a thief better than shadow…" It was lesson number eighty-two that he wished he could've taught Sora. She'd played the role of his apprentice, but she was so much more than that.

If only he'd told her.

Still staring down at the measly coins, Whitney fought the temptation to snatch a coin purse from one of the fine citizens of Grambling or even one of his fellow performers. But that was the old Whitney Fierstown thinking. *He* was a thief. The new and improved Whitney was not. At least, not at the moment.

He'd done a lot of thinking since his time spent in Elsewhere —what else does one do while stuck in their own personal exile within the supernatural confines of Troborough?

He'd done even more thinking when the troupe passed through the real Troborough a few weeks prior. The village remained in ruins, most buildings burned to ash and cinder, but the church stood proud and intact. Torsten would've called it symbolic, a church of Iam withstanding enemy attacks. Whitney just figured it was the only building in that shoghole, Iam-forsaken town made out of stone instead of thatch and wood.

There's no such thing as divine providence, Whitney thought. *Just luck and shog.*

Lately, Whitney felt like he lived more on the shog-end of things. Luck had been his lady for years, but not since he'd met that dreadful dwarf, Grint Strongiron. It seemed so long ago when Whitney'd sat in the Twilight Manor, drinking and enjoying himself, minding his own yigging business.

"Steal from the King," that little piss of a dwarf had said. And Whitney had been stupid enough to take up the challenge. From there, it was downhill. He'd been imprisoned more times in the last months than his whole life combined, and that wasn't counting Elsewhere.

Alless was there in Real Troborough. Quite a bit older now, but still pretty in her particular way. In Fake Troborough, Whitney and Alless flirted some, although his love for Sora made sure it never went any further. But the real Alless, like everyone else at the Manor—which they'd done a damn fine job rebuilding—didn't remember him any better than Haam had all those years ago in *The Lofty Mare* in Old Yarrington.

All those years ago, Whitney though. *Gods and monsters, it was only a matter of months on this side of Elsewhere.*

And that's the way his life had been. The whole world had barely passed a season, suffering only months under the torment of a warlock named Redstar and the petulant little child, King Pi. But Whitney: he'd had years to grow and mature only to be thrust back into a Pantego that now barely felt familiar.

That was part of why he knew he needed to reach Sora, besides how terrified she looked when the mystics tore her out of Elsewhere. He imagined that maybe, just maybe, a few moments with her would help him feel like he belonged again.

"I'm on my way, fast as I can," he whispered. Then he packed up his things and headed for camp. Trinkets mostly. Since joining the troupe, he'd been given precious-few opportunities to act. Instead, the Pompares, the overfed wretches they were, had him doing the sorts of magic tricks and feats of dexterity a life as a thief teaches a man.

When the other performers also working the south part of town and the ogling crowds had wholly abandoned the area, Whitney clicked his tongue a few times. From behind a stack of crates by the general store, a small, brown reptile scurried out. She stuck out her tongue as if tasting the air, then scampered over to Whitney.

"Good job lighting the torches and not burning my hands this time," Whitney said, bending over to scratch the wyvern, Aquira, behind the frills on her neck. "I know you preferred Sora, but I think you're great, too."

Aquira showed up just a week or so after Whitney had set out from Yarrington to find Sora. He woke up to the wyvern's big eyes staring at him while she perched on his chest, damn-near giving him a heart attack. He had no idea why she was there, but no matter what he did, she followed him like a shadow.

He was certain that with all her clicks and squeaks, Aquira was trying to tell him what had happened, where Sora was, and why Aquira wasn't with her. He was also certain that made him crazy, thinking a wyvern could communicate on such a high intellectual level… but she was, except Whitney didn't know how to understand her. For the weeks they'd been together, Whitney had tried everything to develop a form of communication they could share. But so far, nothing worked.

He looked down once again at his cup. There weren't even enough coins inside to pay for his place in the troupe. Hadn't been for a few stops now. It wasn't Whitney's fault; that yigging, half-naked Glintish dancer kept stealing all the attention! She and her mother, the bard.

He spotted them, bidding farewell to a crowd in the Grambling Inn, a rat-infested dump if he ever saw one. *If I could just swipe a few silver autlas…* but he couldn't. That would only leave them short. If Elsewhere taught him anything, it was how every rotten thing he' ever done affected somebody, even if he'd never realized it.

His selfishness had caused more trouble than ever he could've imagined. Before Elsewhere, he'd only heard stories of his parents' deaths. But there, even if they weren't his real parents, he'd watched his father suffer and die because of decisions Whitney had made. He watched his mother grow old without Rocco there to take care of her, and ultimately, he watched everyone in his hometown die at the hand of sharp-toothed, red-eyed demons.

It wasn't much different in real life, though. The demons from the Black Sands had brought the fires of Elsewhere with them when they decided King Liam's death was worth the lives of a hundred more.

Whitney wasn't used to thinking about others. He wouldn't admit it out loud, but it felt good. Sometimes he imagined that after he retrieved Sora, maybe, together, they could go back to Troborough and help rebuild things once and for all. They could dig up all the stolen trinkets and priceless items buried throughout Pantego which he'd stolen over the years and either return them to their owners or sell them, giving the gold to the less fortunate.

Maybe Torsten, in his disabled state, would settle down there as well. Perhaps there was something prophetic about Whitney's time spent in Quasi-Troborough, where Torsten had been the local priest. Whitney could see his stubborn friend fathering the masses. Yig, he wouldn't even have to burn out his eyes like Wren the Holy. His were already gone.

Maybe providence wasn't all hog shog.

Whitney regarded the darkening sky. It wasn't the deep purple of Elsewhere, but the blue and green skies spoke of the rain that would be coming. Springtime in Pantego was the time of rain and storm, and thus far, it did not disappoint.

You're here, he reminded himself, as he often did when his musings wound up far too reminiscent of life in Elsewhere.

A brisk wind blew in as if to further remind him, and Aquira nestled up against Whitney's neck. She was warm, but also kind of itchy. Whitney pulled his cloak tighter between him and the wyvern. The Glintish performance troupe had him decked out in beautiful clothing from their homeland of Glinthaven. They were flashy folk, with a lust for intricate design—especially Benon and the rest of the actors. The lot of them walked just ahead of Whitney, leading the way back to their camp just outside of Grambling, each one dressed in sparkling clothes meant to draw the attention of the simple people of these simple towns.

Whitney didn't think it was altogether fair. There were so many Glintish, so few Grambling citizens and even less coin to go around. That each of them, including Whitney, had to pay the same for their spot in the caravan was an injustice. *Nobody would pay to see me strip down and dance.*

He stopped himself; he was starting to sound like the noble he'd pretended to be. A man had to earn his keep, no matter the cost.

But the cost was so high. He absentmindedly shook the can again.

"Hey, don't worry about it, Mister Fierstown," said a small voice from behind him, moving quickly to his side.

Whitney turned to see a young Glintish boy garbed in purple and yellow robes. His head was covered with a bandana of the same colors, and coins and charms cascaded down from it in a ring around his skull.

"How'd you do, Gentry?" Whitney asked.

"No better than you," he answered. "Modera Pompare will take into consideration the state of this town when collecting dues. Don't worry. Most men here went off to war, they say."

"It's not Modera I'm worried about," Whitney said.

"What? Fadra? Fadra Pompare is a… what is the word? Stuffed animal?"

"Sure. If stuffed animals were known for fits of anger and drunken rages."

"Oh, he's not that bad," Gentry said, dismissing the idea with a wave. "I know you're new to the troupe, but Modera and Fadra have taken good care of us for decades."

"Us?" Whitney asked. The boy wasn't even two decades old himself.

"Sure," Gentry said. "The Troupe. You know, everyone."

"And you?"

"Awhile," he said, but that was all. The boy was rather secretive about his time spent with the Pompares. Whitney had his suspicions why but kept them to himself. Gentry was his only real friend out here. The only one he could trust who hadn't seen enough of the world to know backstabbing was the way of it.

They walked together down the main stretch of Grambling. Whitney's eye fell upon a small establishment a few doors down from the inn. Its walls were brick, with vines growing up the front, purple flowers beginning to blossom. Its shutters were the color of a morning sky with a door to match.

A memory of the place hit him like a deluge. To him, it was more than six years ago when he and Sora sat down at that very chowder house on their way to Winde Port. To the rest of existence, it was mere months.

He closed his eyes. He kept trying to ignore thoughts of Elsewhere, but he couldn't. His brain hurt when he considered the implications. Had he aged six years more than everyone else? Did his physical body age—hair, bones, teeth… heart? He had to imagine it had. If his mind retained all the memories and lessons he'd learned, and his muscles, thick and firm from years working his twice-deceased father's farm, hadn't disappeared, then it was only fair to believe he was six years closer to the grave.

Aquira shifted on his shoulder, but Whitney hardly registered the movement.

Gentry must've noticed Whitney eyeing the chowder house because he said, "Don't worry, Ms. Francesca will have something good for us to eat back at camp. We'll have to finish it quickly if we hope to avoid getting rained on, though."

"It's not that…" Whitney started, then said, "How long until we reach Myen Elnoir?" He immediately felt stupid asking a boy so young to judge the distance to a city so far away. The troupe was headed there for some Glintish festival. Yaolin City was on the way, which was why he'd chosen to travel with them in the first place. It was his only option considering he hadn't even a bronzer to his name after leaving Elsewhere. Moving south and east across the seas was far too dangerous with the Shesaitju at war. And stealing a horse and traveling alone across Pantego wasn't in the cards. War brought the worst sorts of people to the roads, from greedy bandits to mule-headed Glass soldiers—not to mention rumors of marauding Drav Cra and Shesaitju east of the Jarein Gorge.

In these uncertain times, traveling with a group was the best way to ensure he'd reach Sora alive, and he had to.

"One thing you gotta learn about the Glintish: we're never in a hurry," Gentry said.

"So I've seen," Whitney groaned.

"A month?" Gentry guessed. "Two? If everything goes all right."

Whitney grunted. He liked the kid, reminded Whitney of Torsten, and not just for the color of his skin. For all Torsten's piousness, he was kindhearted and selfless. Gentry, no matter how young, shared those same attributes. Whitney knew Torsten had never stepped foot in the home of his heritage, having been born in the South Corner of Yarrington, but he wondered if all Glintish men were kind.

Then he remembered Fadra. Whitney didn't know the man's actual name. At first, he thought it was Fadra, but after some time with the troupe, he learned the word Fadra meant Father and Modera, mother. Modera and Fadra Pompare were the leaders of this ragtag team of performers. Whitney was lucky enough— which, considering the circumstances was a horrible thing to say —that the group's juggler died from rioting cultists in Yarrington and they needed a replacement. Lucky as well that he'd always a knack for juggling. He taught himself with farming tools as a child when his dad thought he was working.

They'd only been traveling for two weeks or three—it was easy to lose track of time on the road—but Whitney kept finding himself lost in the fun of it. It took the not-so-gentle reminders like the chowder house to break the once-carefree Whitney Fierstown from his meditations and force his attention back to the mission.

Find Sora.

What he knew was Sora *had* been there in Elsewhere. She wasn't just contacting him through some strange mystics. They'd kissed, *actually* kissed, though who knew if that meant anything? A kiss while surrounded by the demon-hounds of Elsewhere wasn't much of a romance.

None of it even made sense. Whitney had been in Winde Port when he... died. Then, he was in Troborough after a brief voyage across the Sea of Souls where he was attacked by a giant sea monster called a wianu, and then, finally, somehow, he wound up back in Yarrington beside Torsten.

If there were one person who might understand, it would be Kazimir. But that damnable upyr disappeared along with everyone else. For all Whitney knew, Kazimir might still be in Elsewhere suffering for all his monstrous murdering. Even though the two had forgiven each other their debts, maybe even become friends, Whitney sort of hoped that was the case. The moment he woke up back in Pantego, he remembered how it was Kazimir's fault any of them were in these situations to begin with.

Some friend...

If not for Kazimir, Whitney would've been together with Sora in Panping, scouring for mystics. Torsten might've still had his sight for all Whitney knew. It was a farfetched thought, but still— who knew how many things would've gone differently if not for that vile upyr.

Then Whitney had another thought: Kazimir wouldn't have come to Winde Port in the first place had it not been for that tub-of-lard Bartholomew Darkings. None of his years in Elsewhere altered his regrets for not just murdering that arrogant bastard in cold blood.

"Must be some daydream," Gentry said.

"What?" Whitney replied.

"Oh, I dunno. I've been talking to you since the middle of town, and now we're at camp, and you've been quiet, like I wasn't even here. You're never quiet."

Gentry told the truth on all accounts. Whitney stood before a camp of about a dozen tents and three covered wagons, and he'd not heard a thing the boy had said to him since he'd begun thinking about Sora and the events that had unfolded since their unfortunate separation. He could see his tiny abode in the distance on the other side of the fire.

"Sorry, I just…" Whitney said.

"Don't sweat it, Mister Fierstown," Gentry said. "You hungry? Let's eat."

They passed tents, some bigger than others, but all made of the same worn canvas. A few bales of hay—food for the horses—acted as benches and circled a blazing fire above which Francesca absolutely did not disappoint. The smell of roast pheasant with garlic and onions permeated the countryside from the pot hanging above it.

Francesca was a pretty woman with the face of a girl. She wore her hair like many of the Glintish women did, pulled up on top of her head like a tall tower. From her ears, a series of medallions hung, jittering and clattering as she moved about.

Whitney went to take a seat.

"No time for sitting tonight," Francesca said. "Here's a dish." She handed him a tin bowl. "And a bit of bread for the lizard. Just don't go telling the Pompares. Go get ready for the storm."

Whitney grabbed the chunk and tossed it up to Aquira who gobbled it up in one bite.

Whitney looked at the darkening sky again. He'd weathered far worse, but not without solid walls and at least a thatch roof. Maybe she was right. "Thanks, Franny," he said. "It smells wonderful."

"Off you go."

Whitney turned to Gentry and tossed his hand up. Gentry returned the gesture as he grabbed his own plate and headed toward his tent in the opposite direction.

Plodding forward, Whitney took a bite of pheasant and moaned. "Yig and shog, that's good," he said to himself since no one else was around. "Reminds me of mother's…" He didn't finish, as the first vision to pop into his head was one from Elsewhere's version of his childhood home.

Whitney absentmindedly kicked a small stone around the camp as he ate. Aquira screeched and took flight. Whitney watched as she made a straight line for their tent.

"Goodbye, then!" Whitney called, then shook his head and laughed. "Mind of its own, that one. Just like her master."

He continued walking at a reasonably slow pace, enjoying his meal when he heard music emanating from one of the larger tents. Inside, he could imagine Lucindur the bard playing her odd Glintish *salfio*, a sort of percussive lute instrument he'd never seen before.

She was always the main attraction at any town they'd passed through so far. The Glinthaven bards weren't like the other types Whitney had seen throughout Pantego. Glinthaven was said to be the birthplace of the bard, and within their songs were untold magics. Though, he was sure it was all merely a trick or illusion. Otherwise, Lucindur would be doing something far grander than traveling with some amateur troupe.

Before he knew it, he found himself drawn before the tent by the melody. As he stretched out his hand toward the flap, it fluttered open and Talwyn, Lucindur's daughter—also known as the half-naked dancer—stepped out.

She was not half-naked then. She was fully clothed, and even still, Whitney couldn't deny her beauty. Her long, raven-dark hair, so much like Sora's, fell well below her shoulders. Her eyes, spread wide on her face, were a unique shade of green.

"I'm so sorry!" she said, startled.

"No, it was my fault, "I—"

"Don't worry about it. We were both clumsy."

Whitney laughed. "Yes, I guess we were. We haven't officially met, have we?"

They'd been traveling together since Yarrington, but it seemed as soon as her performances were complete, she was gone, into her tent without a word. Whitney never even spotted her eating Francesca's fabulous meals.

"Talwyn," she said, extending her hand. "I'm afraid that's my fault. I prefer to keep to myself between towns. Helps me perform better."

"So what brings you out tonight then?" Whitney asked, shaking her hand.

"I—I dunno. I guess whatever Francesca's cooking smelled too good to pass up." She looked down.

When she didn't say anything more, Whitney spoke up. "Whitney Fierstown, "World's Grea—" He cleared his throat. His rehearsed introduction had started without even a thought. "Whitney Fierstown."

"I've caught glimpse of your performances.," Talwyn said. "Quite talented with your hands." Although the words themselves sounded flirtatious, the way she said them did not. She was beautiful, indeed. But there was an innocence about her that was far more appealing. Again, like Sora.

"I should be going," Whitney said.

"Were you coming to see my mother?" Talwyn asked. "I was just leaving. She's inside."

"Ah, yes. Thanks."

"See you around, Whitney Fierstown."

He watched as she left, her lithe frame swaying as she ambled toward Francesca and the delicious pheasant. When Whitney turned his head back, he was staring into the face of a man. Well, he was staring at the spot a face would be on a normal-sized man.

"What do you think you're doing?" Conmonoc was three hundred pounds of muscle and about a quarter-pound of brains. The perfect combination for entertaining beleaguered townsfolk with feats of impossible strength.

"Thought I was enjoying a bite of pheasant and a sunset stroll before the storm came in," Whitney said. "But suddenly, I've lost my appetite. Do you smell something?" Whitney leaned toward Conmonoc and sniffed the air. "Oh, yes. That's you. Hope there's plenty of rain, and perhaps a bar of soap."

"Think you're funny?"

Whitney shrugged.

"I saw you talking to my girl," Conmonoc said.

"Ah, you *are* as stupid as you look," Whitney said. Conmonoc just tilted his head. "If by *talking* you mean we ran into each other in this rather small tent community, then yes. However, I'm not sure she would rather like the sentiment of being called *my girl* by such an execrable brute as yourself."

Conmonoc grabbed Whitney by his cloak with one hand and reared his other back, ready to strike. Even with the strength he gained working in Elsewhere, Whitney couldn't do anything about it.

"I don't know what that word means, but I'm sure you ought to take it back," Conmonoc growled.

Whitney reached out to the air, grasping frantically. "I'm so sorry. It doesn't seem I can grab hold of them."

"Boys," said a matronly voice from just behind Conmonoc. "Everything okay?"

"Splendid, I'd say," Whitney answered.

Lucindur stepped out from behind the big man's shadow and said, "Conmonoc, why don't you let Whitney go before we have to mend his cloak or your skin."

"Huh?"

"She is implying that you are out of your league, zhulong breath," Whitney said.

Conmonoc gave Whitney a shove and grunted, "Stay away from her," as he took a step away.

"I hope you are not referring to my daughter, Conmonoc," Lucindur said. "We have both made it very clear you are out of your league in that regard, as well."

Conmonoc practically roared and stomped away. Once he was out of sight, Whitney turned to regard Lucindur.

"You know he would have smashed you to ground beans, right?" she asked him.

"Oh, without any doubt," Whitney said with a bow. "My gratitude is yours."

"Come inside; the wind is getting a bit nippy."

They pushed their way into the tent and Whitney was amazed. They'd only just settled into the countryside near Grambling that morning, and where Whitney's little tent was a drab beige bit of canvas propped up on sticks, hers was an indubitable palace. Rainbow colored streamers cascaded down the walls, and multi-hued bean cushions covered the floors.

"I love what you've done with the place," Whitney said.

"What can I do for you, Mr. Fierstown?" Lucindur strolled across the tent and lit two candles, then shook out the match.

"Straight to business, then? Fine. I hear you have a special talent."

"We all do, Mr. Fierstown. Otherwise, we would not be in a

troupe." She sat down on one of the cushions in the middle of the room.

"I'm sure you know what the rumors say. Are you truly one of them?" Whitney asked.

"There is a storm coming. We do not have time for such mysteries. Speak plainly or go."

"Are you a lightmancer?"

Lucindur looked at him, unblinking.

"Too plain?" Whitney asked.

"No," she said. "But I have not heard that word for some time. Where did you hear that?"

"I heard a couple of the boys chatting by the fire last night," Whitney said. "Asked Gentry about it and he didn't say no or yes, and you know that boy can't tell a lie."

"All too well." The woman's eyes narrowed, creases forming at the corners. She drew a deep breath. "That gift has been long-forgotten by most, especially after Glinthaven became part of the Glass. Tell me, what do you think a lightmancer does?"

"Here I thought we were short on time?" Whitney said, edging further into the tent.

"If you would rather leave…"

"Fine. Fine," Whitney said. "May I sit?"

Lucindur motioned to one of the cushions, and Whitney plopped down, crossing his legs.

"When I was in Glinthaven a while back," he said, "I heard rumors of bards that weren't *normal* bards. Bards whose music commanded light like it was a dog. Some even said they didn't just create illusions, but could transform light into something… physical. Tangible. The rumors say lightmancers can show you people or places far away. It's no secret, your performance is the star of the show around here, and I don't think its just because of your daughter's beauty."

"Ah, so you think Talwyn beautiful?"

Whitney smiled. "That is what you took from this?"

"It might be true, Whitney Fierstown, this kind of magic did exist. But it is long in the past. Ever since Glinthaven found itself a part of the Glass Kingdom, magic has retreated into the depths of history for fear of retribution like that which was faced at Yaolin City or Latiapur. So, no, I do not possess such a gift."

"Do you think I am a knight of the King's Shield?" Whitney said. "Biding my time for you to slip up and drag you to the dungeons? Or maybe you think I'll burn you at a stake?"

"Knight or no," she said, "there's nothing here but an old woman and her salfio."

"Lucindur, please—"

"You must go now, Whitney Fierstown. Prepare for the storm."

Lucindur stood and showed him the exit.

On his way out, Talwyn pushed through the tent flap, soaked to the core. What was previously a modest gown was now transparent and left nothing to Whitney's imagination. She didn't seem to care.

What the yig goes on in Glinthaven? He wondered, and also how he'd missed it in his travels there.

"Sorry," Talwyn said, smiling.

Whitney stumbled over a response before continuing past her and out onto the plain. The sky neared black, whether from the night or the storm. Celeste and Loutis couldn't be seen but for a faint glow behind a storm cloud. Rain came down in buckets. Whitney lowered his head and pushed his way toward Modera and Fadra's covered wagon.

As he drew closer, he heard the shouts coming from within. Modera was always shouting. When he was right outside, he could tell they were disciplining Gentry.

"This is the last time you come up short!" Modera yelled.

"There was not enough to go around," Gentry argued.

Whitney heard the unmistakable sound of flesh against flesh. Abandoning caution, he entered the wagon. It was tall enough inside for even Torsten to stand upright. It made Lucindur's tent look like Whitney's in comparison. They lived in luxury—feather mattresses and pillows, warm blankets, solid floors, and half-walls—while the rest of them mudded it.

Gentry was on the floor, tears streaming down his cheeks.

"Gentry," Whitney interrupted.

Modera Pompare was a woman whose dark face was hard, but the rest of her was soft as a sponge. Fadra wasn't much different. Big, bushy eyebrows grew like weeds above eyes, wide-set like a frog. The man never said much, but Whitney was sure it was his hand that disciplined poor Gentry. Both Pompares wore exquisite clothes and even more exceptional jewelry. Gold and silver dangled from both their ears and jingled like chainmail.

Whitney didn't hate them for it; this was their business, and everyone who traveled with them was free to leave whenever they pleased—but striking a boy for not earning crossed a line.

They all spun toward Whitney and regarded him as if he wore a negligee as see-through as Talwyn's sodden dress.

"How dare you enter unannounced," Modera snapped.

"I'm sorry, Modera Pompare," Whitney said, bowing slightly. Then he turned to Fadra and said, "Fadra. It's just that Gentry dropped this back at the campfire and I wanted to make sure he got it."

As Gentry climbed to his feet, Whitney tossed the boy the coins he'd collected from his juggling act. It wasn't much, but he was sure it would pay Gentry's dues when added to what the boy already had.

Gentry gaped down at it, his eyes lighting up. "I wish I could take credit, but—"

"You did a fine job out there today," Whitney interrupted. He cocked his head to the side ever so discreetly and narrowed his eyes, a warning to Gentry to accept the gift and ask questions later.

"Why didn't you tell us you had more, you fool boy?" Modera said, reaching out and snatching the coin purse. She dumped it into her hand, counted it and added the contents to Gentry's small stack.

"Fine," she said. "You can go. Next time, bring it all at once, you hear?"

"This isn't—" Gentry began.

"I'll get him in line next time. Sorry, Modera." Whitney clutched the back of Gentry's shirt and pulled him out of the room before he could get himself into any more trouble.

Whitney turned to leave as well, but a strong hand on his shoulder stopped him.

He turned to see Fadra, tall and wide. He wore a thick goatee, mostly gray but the few dark brown hairs told of an earlier time when the man was probably better looking.

"And where is yours?" Fadra asked.

"I left it in my tent," Whitney lied. "So, sorry. The rain must have me confused. I'll go get it now."

Both troupe leaders eyed him charily but said nothing. Technically, he still had hours left to pay his dues before they could call them late. They didn't need to know he'd just given Gentry the only coins he had to his name.

"A storm is coming," Modera Pompare said, "You'd better make it quick."

"Surely. I wouldn't want to get wet now, would I?" Whitney said, flicking a bit of water from the brim of his hood as he drew it up.

"Maybe you should tell jokes instead of playing juggler with that lizard? Maybe then you could pay your dues on time. I'm sure plenty would love to take your place, Fierstown."

"Yes," Whitney said enthusiastically. "Listen to them beating down the door! Oh wait, that's thunder."

Fadra took a hard step forward, and Whitney fled without another word. The rain fell harder now, in blankets instead of buckets, making it difficult to see very far in front of him.

From within the gray, Gentry approached.

"You didn't have to do that!" he said.

"It's no sweat, kid, really. You'd have done the same for me."

"But now you don't have a single coin. If you don't pay them double in the next town, they'll leave you behind. They don't get it, there's just no money here."

"Over-fat lords and ladies rarely understand the plight of the worker ants," Whitney said. "Anyway, it's getting pretty late, and this storm is going to be bad, I can tell. You should get inside before you blow away."

"Yeah…" Gentry said, eyeing his little tent. It was even smaller than Whitney's and probably repelled even less water.

Whitney lifted his face into the rain. Cold water pelted him, and he shivered. Then, he turned his head back to Gentry said, "Say, kid… you ever stayed at an inn?"

II

THE MYSTIC

Sora's eyes snapped open. Her head felt foggy like it was stuffed with enough thoughts to burst. Her chest heaved, sweat-soaked like the rest of her. She'd woken from nightmares before, but none like this. Blood and screams flashed through her mind. And that voice. That deep, airless voice speaking for her. Speaking from her own mouth, through her own lips.

She squeezed her eyelids to drive it all away, then opened them again. A creaking wooden ceiling greeted her. She was on her back on a bed so soft it made those in the Red Tower seem like stone—the softest bed she'd ever felt. Red, silk sheets with golden trim covered her. The bed of a king.

She looked to her left and the sight nearly startled her off the mattress. It was a King's bed indeed. Grisham "Gold Grin" Gale, king of the pirates and scourge of the seas, lay eyes closed and facing her. Half the Glass Crown rest crooked atop his head and the stray hairs above his lip wavered as he snored. Sora's gaze tracked down in horror as she realized that none of the blankets covered him. He was on his stomach, completely nude, all the disgusting hair on his back matted with sweat.

Sora swallowed hard, but still nearly vomited. She lifted the blanket slowly and saw that she too wore nothing. Scars stared back at her from her chest where the bar guai once was, and from her arms, earned from calling upon Elsewhere's power to open the door to the Well of Wisdom. If seeing Gold Grin didn't rouse her out of bed, the sight of her own naked body next to him did.

She hit the floor, slipped, and scrambled back against the wall. Gold Grin muttered something in his sleep, then rolled over and pulled a bundle of blankets close like a child clutching a doll. Sora got a good look at more of the pirate king than she'd ever wanted and forced her eyes shut. Trying to steady her breathing, she thought back to why she was there. More blood burned through her thoughts, then a cackling, loud and sharp. A wicked, unnatural laugh so like the one she'd heard from Bliss in the Webbed Woods.

She opened her eyes before it overwhelmed her, then searched from side to side. Her kimono lay draped over the nightstand. Sloppy, like she'd torn it off in a fit of passion and thrown it aside. Slowly reaching for it, careful not to make too much noise, she grabbed it and scampered for the door before her arms were even in the sleeves.

A moment was all she'd needed to collect herself before finding herself rushing through the halls of a place she now recognized: the *Reba's* lower quarters. The Captain's Quarters were separated by the Crews' Quarters by a long empty corridor. The ship swayed and bowled her back and forth. She took the bumps against her shoulders in stride and let the momentum carry here to the stairs.

When she reached them, she heard a voice thundering in her head. "Stop fighting, Sora." It made her temples throb, and she had to lean against the wall to keep from falling. A grubby hand fell on her shoulder, and she whipped around to see Hestor, one of Gold Grin's crewmen. Half his teeth were missing, and his hair and ratty beard were knotted from the salt of the sea. An orange glow caught the color of his tanned skin.

Sora looked down and saw embers floating around her hands. She wasn't bleeding, and she didn't feel the haunting of Elsewhere, yet there it was: fire at her fingertips.

"You are willful, my dear," the sultry voice spoke in Sora's head. "Close your eyes. Let me back in, and I'll take care of everything."

"Nesilia?" Sora said out loud. Now she remembered. The mystics, littering the floor like garbage. Cut open. Aihara Na on her knees, begging for her life.

"H-Hestor, Lady Sora. Ye be all right?" the pirate asked, voice trembling.

Sora's vision snapped back into focus, and she saw him with his hands raised, eyes bright with fear. She ignored him and swept up the stairs. Cold rain whipped across her face like a hundred tiny needles and the hatch slammed hard behind her, caught by the wind. She turned her cheek and pushed through until she stood looking at nothing but gray clouds and gray sea.

The ship dipped to the side and sent her stumbling into another crew member. He tried to catch her, but Sora's hand wrapped his forearm, and he squealed from the heat of her touch.

"Get off me witch!" he howled and shoved her away.

He promptly earned a backhand from Fortist, Gold Grin's first mate. "Cap'n catches ye addressing her like that, ye'll be drinking sea water," he said, having to raise his voice over the heady winds, driving rain, and waves. He turned to Sora. "Milady, ye shouldn't be out here."

She spun around. The crew was hard at work keeping the deck clear of water. It was a losing battle, but they had discipline. Men swung from the sails as they turned them to catch the wind. Another climbed up the foremast like a worker ant; a knife clenched between his teeth.

"Where is *here*?" she asked.

The first mate's brow furrowed. "The Torrential Sea, Lady Sora. We're a few days away from Yarrington, just like you asked."

"Like I—" Confusion caused the words to trap in her throat.

"Ye should go back below deck until this storm passes."

She ignored the warning and walked toward the ship's prow. Rain soaked her kimono through. Her hair dripped, sticking to her skin. She felt eyes on her from every direction and shuddered.

"Lady Sora, watch out!"

She looked right and saw the boom of a sail swinging toward her. She ducked just in time and staggered against the rail at the ship's front. An unseen force kept her from flipping over and straightened her back. She peered down into the icy depths of the violent waters below—a raging, foaming wall of blue, desperate to reach out and sweep her off her feet.

"Careful now, my dear," Nesilia spoke within her. "We have so much to do together, and I won't suffer another prison."

"Get out of my head!" Sora snapped, grasping the sides of her head.

"It's our head now." The words echoed, all around her. Sora spun as if she'd see the goddess standing there, beautiful and terrifying at once, but all that greeted her was more of the endless sea. Her hand's squeezed the rail as she squinted off into the distance. No land in sight, no end to the storm that blotted out even Celeste's bright light.

A pair of burly arms wrapped around her. She looked down at the hands covered in an assortment of jewel-emblazoned rings, and green tattoos, then turned to see the face of Captain Grisham "Gold Grin" Gale. He smiled, his golden teeth shimmering from the light of the lantern hanging over the bow.

"Ye should come back to bed," he said. "This be no place for a lady, even a mystic such as yerself." He gave her an all-too-familiar squeeze. It made her skin crawl. She liked the man's company but not enough to…

"Did you think your first time would be special?" Nesilia said. "Trust me, my sweet Sora. Love is overrated."

"What are you?" Sora was speaking to Nesilia, but Gold Grin paused. The way he looked at her… she'd seen that glint in a man's eye before. The drunkards back in Troborough regarded Alless, the barmaiden at the Twilight Manor, the same way.

"Something wrong?" Gold Grin asked.

Sora tried to respond, but words didn't come. The ability to control her own body waned. Suddenly, she looked through her own eyes, but the view was distant. Her arms extended, wrapping the pirate's thick neck as she pulled herself close.

"Nothing at all," her mouth said. Why was she talking? She didn't want to be talking. "I must thank you again for the passage to Yarrington."

He flashed his famous grin. "Anything for the Queen of the Reba."

"Perhaps I should *show* you again *how* thankful I am." Sora leaned in and pressed her lips against his. Sora shouted in defiance, but the words never came out. She did, however, gain control of her arms enough to push Gold Grin away. Embers swirled around her hands. She expected him to respond with fear. Instead, he bit his lower lip.

"Want me back in the sack already, do ye?" he said.

Sora fought to keep her lips sealed, but doing so gave over control of her body. She watched as she took his hand and pulled him back toward the cabins.

Sora's vision flickered. She smelled sweat, heard moaning, felt skin rubbing, and bodies gyrating. When she saw clearly again, she lay beside Gold Grin in his quarters once more. She was upright in the bed, wearing nothing and not shy about it. The pirate was back to snoring, and a fresh layer of perspiration glistened on his forehead.

"What do you want from me?" Sora asked before realizing the conversation was in her own head. She was present, but not, seeing through her own eyes as if looking through the Well of Wisdom.

"To give you what you've always wanted," Nesilia answered.

"I don't want any of this!" Sora shouted. Gold Grin shifted slightly but didn't wake.

"Do not forget, my dear, I see all within you—your deepest longings. Together we can make them all come true. You want a family, to belong? I will make all the world bow and call us 'mother.'"

"Just leave me alone!" Sora was able to gain control of her arm and swung it toward the nightstand. Her knife—Wetzel's knife—was so close but her fingers halted near the handle and hovered over it.

"Careful, my dear," Nesilia said within. "You aren't thinking clearly."

"I'll carve you out of my head. Get out!" Those final words escaped her lips, and Gold Grin woke with a startle.

"Do ye ever sleep, girl?" he grumbled. He threw his arm over her waist and pulled her close. Sora couldn't fight it. Upon his touch, she felt herself sinking away, losing any semblance of control as she had in the chamber of the Secret Order.

"Relax, Sora. I'm taking care of everything…" Nesilia spoke. "Redstar failed me, but his servants belong to me."

And then, once more, Sora was gone. Watching from somewhere deep within herself, silent, frightened… alone.

III

THE KNIGHT

"Y ou mustn't look away, Your Grace," Torsten said, not missing the irony of his words. He patted King Pi's shoulder, then slid his hand up until he was able to touch the boy's jaw with his thumb and forced his attention toward the square.

"I thought we've had enough blood?" Pi asked, his voice small and frail again. With Nesilia's influence over him vanquished, he was a mere child again. Every bit the sweet twelve-year-old boy he truly was, except he wore the crown of the Nothhelm line. And that circlet of jewel-encrusted glass, although infused with glaruium now, was as fragile as the kingdom he ruled. Even still, being the king of Glass meant being the king of the most powerful nation on Pantego.

Torsten exhaled, giving Pi's arm a reassuring squeeze. "Iam make that true one day. But for now, the people need closure. Wren the Holy's death has left a deep chasm in the hearts of our people. With none yet selected to take his place, we have to offer something."

"She's so fair… beautiful even now that the paint is stripped away. How could she be guilty of such heinous acts?"

"The dark magic of disgraced gods make wicked those who fall for their lies. You don't have to worry anymore, Your Grace. Neither she, Redstar, nor any of those Drav Cra heathens unwilling to see the light as your mother has can hurt you any longer."

Torsten couldn't see Pi's throat bob—a month had passed since he'd lost the use of his eyes due to Redstar's vile blood magic—but he heard the boy swallow. Pi seemed fully back to his old self—the one Uriah and Oleander always spoke of, that curious, kind boy with a craving to devour books as if they were sustenance. Yet, Torsten couldn't imagine the scars that filled Pi's mind from everything he'd suffered. Being cursed, brought back from the dead, possessed—the very fact he still seemed sane was a sign that Iam's blessing was with him.

Torsten offered the king another reassuring pat on the shoulder, then continued by. He scratched the mottled skin around his eyes that burned with a deep itch as it often did now.

"This way, my Lord," said the squire who took Torsten's arm.

Torsten bit his lip as he allowed the young Shieldsman-hopeful Lucas Danvels to guide him across the castle's outer parapets. He hated being led around like a dog, and he was getting handy with a cane, but atop the walls and before so many of the kingdom's citizens, he couldn't risk any mistakes.

Nobody could.

The Glass had endured much at the hands of Redstar the Deceiver, as he'd come to be known. Enough to rattle the peoples' faith in God and Kingdom. An inability for the Church of Iam to quickly choose a successor to Wren, in addition to the continuing war in the South with the Shesaitju and Drav Cra marauders in the East didn't help, but things were coming around. All the violent ripples of the great Liam Nothhelm's passing were beginning to settle.

"Here you are." Lucas guided Torsten's hands to the lip of the wall facing out over the Royal Avenue. Torsten grunted, then forced a nod. He never meant to be rude to the new recruit, especially since Torsten had been the one to name him a squire in the first place.

"The streets are full," Lucas said. "All the way from Pike's Crossing to Cathedral Square. This was a fine idea, Sir."

"I long for the day when it wouldn't be," Torsten replied. "Though I imagine I'll be long gone by then. Above, or below."

"She did this to herself. With what they caused in Dockside..."

Torsten could practically feel the young man's anger. He'd become good at sensing these things since facial expressions were of no use to him now; good at noticing the tiny inflections in voice and tone which accompanied certain emotions.

"Careful, Lucas," Torsten said. "I know you hail from Dockside, but to be the King's Shield, is to shield *all* of the kingdom. Where we come from or who our parents are... those are irrelevant details."

"Is that why things never get better there—in Dockside?" Lucas replied.

A brief silence hung on the air between them, made tolerable only by the constant chatter of the hundreds below.

"I'm sorry, Sir. I meant nothing by it," Lucas said.

"I know, but you're right," Torsten said. "I neglected a great many things when I was Wearer."

"You did all that you could."

"If only that were true," Torsten growled.

"Your Grace!" the familiar voice of Sir Austin Mulliner shouted up from within the battlements. "The Queen Mother sent me to inform you that she will not be attending." With the current Wearer of White, Sir Nikserof Pasic, along with many other Shieldsmen, still fighting Afhem Muskigo in the South, Mulliner was the most experienced man left in Yarrington who still had eyes.

The news reminded Torsten of his surroundings as grumblings from the Royal Council rose behind him. So many of them were strangers to Torsten as the mess Redstar left behind was rectified. However, they were worthy men invited from high posts and loyal houses throughout the Glass.

Lord Kaviel Jolly, Sir Wardric's older brother and the new Master of Ships summoned from Crowfall, hushed them. He'd been extremely eager to honor Wardric's sacrifice by serving his kingdom in a meaningful way. When Oleander, the Queen Mother, recommended him for the new Royal Council based on a longtime friendship, he was already visiting Yarrington to lobby for himself.

Torsten turned back toward the castle. Sight wasn't needed to know its direction. He wasn't sure, but he thought he could *feel* Oleander's presence on a balcony high up on the tallest spire, watching from afar where people couldn't see the wounds she felt made her a monster.

"That's her watching, isn't it?" Lucas said. "She's never visited Dockside. Is she as beautiful as the legends say?"

She was, Torsten thought, then cursed himself. Oleander agonized daily over the burns which now coated half her body, more gifts from her brother, but Torsten tried not to allow her dour spirits to affect him. To him, she remained that tortured beauty who, after so much failure, finally stood up against Redstar atop Mount Lister as the champion for her kingdom, who finally proved herself worthy of the light Liam saw in her.

"She is," Torsten said.

"Did she really have Sir Langley hang all of those people?" Lucas asked.

"Redstar's influence blinded us all, from kings to peasants. Now, today, we wipe the stain away for good."

"Not a moment too soon."

The crowd broke out in moans and cursing. It grew louder and closer, a wave of loathing unable to be contained.

"What's happening down there?" Torsten asked.

"They're leading her out," Lucas said.

From the Castle's deepest dungeon, Redstar's pet warlock, Freydis, was being escorted to the gallows. She screamed in Drav Crava as the guards shoved through the crowd to bring her to the platform set halfway between the Yarrington Cathedral and the Glass Castle. There, she would stand trial for helping murder and manipulate Wren the Holy and so many others. It was all a formality.

"What of the crowd?" Torsten asked.

"People from all corners it looks like," Lucas said. "Guards have her surrounded though; they can't get close. Windows within arrow range overlooking the area are all barred as you requested."

"Good. What about up the street, toward Old Yarrington and away from the mob?"

"Bunch of nobles in their fancy trousers," Lucas replied.

"Anyone worth noting?"

"I… I'm sorry, Sir. I didn't meet many men of their class back home."

Torsten withheld a sigh. He was so used to scouring rooms for any sign of danger to the Crown or men with agendas. It was hard to let go of that part of himself. There were other, more capable men, to stand guard. Torsten remained a King's Shieldsman, but per Pi's request, a new position was added to the Royal Council for him: Master of Warfare. Torsten couldn't stand the title, though he accepted graciously. He longed for the day when such a position was no longer necessary.

"Spotted someone shady," Lucas said. "Valin Tehr is here. Do you know him?"

Torsten's stomach lurched at the thought of the crime lord

who ran Yarrington's most infamous brothel, the Vineyard. There was a time when he tried to shut the place down, but Valin had a way of sticking around like a cockroach, as well as having the support of unnamed nobles who frequented his establishments to unwind in ways Iam dare not see.

"We've run into each other before," Torsten said. "I'm from South Corner, remember?"

"Right," Lucas said. "Well, he's nestled in with the common folk, but I'm pretty sure it's him. I'd recognize his creepy Breklian assistant's white mustache and fake eye anywhere. Used to show up at my father's shop every month demanding tribute."

"These affairs bring out the worst Yarrington has to offer."

"Should I have someone keep an eye on him?" Lucas asked.

Torsten shook his head. "He's a cockroach, but he's no danger to the Crown. He likes to play in his own fiefdom." Torsten believed what he said, though he couldn't ignore the thought in the back of his head that something was off. It had been many years since he'd dealt with Valin in the name of the Crown, and suddenly the man popped up again, even helped Rand free Torsten from the dungeons. Torsten understood how the Drav Cra savages with their refusal to use coin could have harmed all the businesses Valin owned. However, now he was doing something far beyond his nature: showing his face outside of Dockside.

"Lucas, when this is all over, remind me to finally pay Valin a visit in Dockside," Torsten said.

"For?" Lucas asked.

Torsten ignored him. It had been a month, and until that moment, thanking Valin for helping Rand free him from Redstar's prison had never crossed his mind, what with learning to be blind and tending to the Crown's affairs. Rand and his sister had vanished from Yarrington after saving Torsten, not a soul knew where. Torsten spent weeks having Rand searched for until he feared the boy and his sister were killed in the riots and lost in the piles of bodies carted away.

It was then that Torsten informed Oleander and Pi what the former deserter had done, though he purposefully left out Valin's part in it. Rand's was hailed as a story of redemption under the Light of Iam. Without him and what he'd become—thanks to Redstar driving Oleander mad—the Drav Cra would have never been defeated.

It was the least Rand the Redeemer deserved after all he'd been through. Only, now that Valin Tehr's name had come up again, Torsten couldn't help but wonder if Valin had helped him disappear… or worse, *made* him disappear. From all Torsten remembered of him, Valin preferred the anonymity of the shadows. Rand telling his story and tying him into saving the kingdom would bring far too much attention.

No. Rand's redemption is what the Glass needs now.

Lucas went quiet for a good while before saying, "The warlock is arriving at the podium. She's gagged."

"A precaution against her using her teeth to draw blood."

"Why would she do such a thing?"

Torsten made an unintelligible sound.

"His Grace was right, out of her rags, the witch is actually quite attractive. Looks like one of the women in the Vineyard…" He cleared his throat. "Not that I ever frequent there…"

"Iam's not judging you today, kid," Torsten said.

"I thought he always was?"

Once again, Torsten didn't bother responding. The screaming amplified as Freydis was led up to her position. Fruits, vegetables, and Iam-knows-what-else slammed against the wooden stand. She screamed in Drav Crava, squealing like a cornered boar through the gag.

Torsten pictured it: her laid, bare on her back so only Iam could witness her, like so many criminals before, body doused in the incandescent paint worn on faces for the Dawning. A symbol of hope that Iam may find mercy for even the most wicked on Pantego, and offer a chance at light before damnation to Elsewhere.

"Sir Mulliner is stepping up," Lucas said. "He's wearing a hood. Do the Shieldsmen who pass sentence always wear those? It's not like we don't know it's him; what's the point?"

"We dare not steal the attention of Iam from the accused," Torsten said.

Sir Mulliner stood in since Sir Nikserof was absent, but it was usually the Wearer of White who stood as executioner in the name of the King, as Rand Langley had for so many—though things were often more civilized than slinging men and women over the wall to dry in the sun.

If anyone deserved that treatment, it was a warlock like Freydis. Hers was an execution Torsten wouldn't have minded seeing, but he knew it was that sort of thinking, that lack of grace which allowed the Glass to fall into such dark times.

"She should be drawn and quartered for all they did," Lucas said.

"Let *them* be the savages," Torsten said. "It's bad enough we have no High Priest here to offer her absolution."

"Then let me be the first to say I'm glad the selection is taking so long."

Freydis's muffled, rage-filled screams pierced the crisp, spring air as her ankles and wrists were fastened to the platform. Guards had been instructed to form a tight circle around Freydis, so no blood was drawn by airborne projectiles, but mistakes happen. One droplet of her blood could've meant destruction.

"Your Grace, it's time," Torsten said, looking in the King's direction. As he did, he felt a gust of cool air that reminded him of the long winter past. A cold droplet of rain splashed on his shoulder. Iam weeping for the fallen.

"Go on, Your Grace," Lord Kaviel Jolly instructed.

The sudden change in weather caused even more of a stir amongst the crowd, but Torsten heard Pi's small feet shuffle forward. Many things may have changed—even the crown he wore itself—but the Throne of Glass, the kingdom, and the Nothhelm line which founded it still commanded respect. The citizens quieted upon sight of their king standing atop the ramparts. Pi cleared his throat and fumbled through a few welcoming words, unable to project.

"You'll be fine, Your Grace," Torsten said. Redstar-possessed Pi had no issue speaking, but a riled-up crowd like this could've stricken fear in anybody whose name wasn't Liam. "Don't look away. Show them who you are. Show them you stand on your own, apart from the memory of your father."

It had grown so quiet, Torsten heard him breathe. Only the sound of a drizzle pelting stone and Freydis' incessant objections sounded.

"People of Yarrington, my people," Pi began. His gentle voice grew in verve with each passing word, but it was still no match for his father's. "It is a somber affair that brings me before you today under the watchful gaze of Iam. I take no joy in sentencing anyone to death, even one so wicked as her."

"Burn her at the stake like the witch she is!" someone in the crowd hollered, received by a swell of applause.

"Gut her for the gallers!" cried out another.

"Silence!" Torsten roared, pounding his fist on the parapet. He regretted it immediately. Pi needed to learn to assert himself before the people. It did, however, have the desired effect of instilling silence.

"Today, on the first day of Tresholm, I, King Pi Nothhelm, son of Liam Nothhelm, sentence Freydis of the Ruuhar clan to death," Pi said. "The servants of Iam's Holy Church may be absent today, but Iam watches you still. Speak your last words, declare your desire for forgiveness, and perhaps Iam, in his infinite wisdom, will grant it."

"Sir Mulliner is removing her gag," Lucas whispered. "Is that wise?"

First, there was quiet, then Freydis began to cackle. The sound made all the hairs on Torsten's neck stand on end.

"You come down here and swing the axe yourself, and maybe then I'll beg for mercy," she hissed. "You're cowards, all of you. Drad Redstar should have slaughtered you all when he had the chance. Burned your bodies to ashes for the Buried Goddess!"

Torsten heard enough and raised his hand in the gallows' direction. The signal was to inform Sir Mulliner to gag her again. Most who were to be publicly executed begged, groveled at the foot of the High Priest, claiming they were changed, reformed. Torsten knew she wouldn't number among those.

"Don't touch me!" she howled. "Your reckoning is coming! The Buried Goddess will devour you all!" The rest of her screaming grew muffled again, but then a gasp came from the crowd.

"What happened?" Torsten asked his aide.

"Blood's pouring from her face," Lucas said. "Nobody touched her, she just… she spat the gag at Sir Mulliner along with her tongue. What's wrong with these people?"

Lucas merely sounded disgusted, but he didn't understand what she was capable of. How could he?

Torsten shoved the boy aside as he stormed across the ramparts, not caring who else he rammed into. "Kill her!" he shouted. "Kill her now!"

Armor clanked as guards closed in around the gallows. Then Torsten heard the soft *thunk* of metal meeting wood. Screams of horror rang out from the crowd.

"Vines! Vines are growing out of the ground," Lucas said,

finally sounding as nervous as he should. "One tripped Sir Mulliner. They're grabbing guards. Sir, should I go down—"

"I need your eyes." He turned toward the Royal Council. "Get Pi back inside immediately and seal the gates." He grabbed Lucas's arm. "Lead me down."

Lucas guided him down the steps and through the gate, speeding up after Torsten yelled at him once for acting like he was some fragile thing prone to breaking. Bodies of fleeing civilians slammed into him. After all Redstar had done, he didn't blame them. But Freydis could do nothing alone.

"The guards have her surrounded, but she has the axe," Lucas said, panting. "Her vines are keeping everyone back and slapping down arrows."

"And Sir Mulliner?" Torsten asked.

"They pulled him to safety, but she cut another Shieldsman's chest. Can't tell who. Just missed his throat."

"Freydis!" Torsten bellowed. "Stop this. Your fight is over. You lost."

Something thorny touched Torsten's ankle, then wrapped it tight. He was heaved up into the air so fast Lucas couldn't keep hold. Wind and rain slashed at his cheeks. Freydis couldn't scream, but the gurgled hissing released from her tongueless mouth was a thing of nightmares.

"Enough of this!" Lucas said. "Drop him!" Lucas' sword rasped as he unsheathed it. Then Torsten heard the crack of something whipping across Lucas's feet and the thunk as he hit the ground.

"Stay back!" Torsten shouted as he was jostled through the air. "Let her tire—" The pressure on his ankle suddenly went slack, and he plummeted. His back slammed hard against the cobblestone street.

"Are you all right, my Lord?" someone asked, his Breklian accent thick as Glintish syrup.

"I think he'll live, Codar," someone else said from behind. "It's time for us to go."

Torsten lay for a few more seconds, listening to the turmoil from around the gallows. Fire crackled—a sound with which he was all too familiar. He imagined it, now extended from Freydis' hands. He could feel the heat and hear the sizzling of embers despite the intensifying storm overhead.

"Sir!" Lucas shouted as his arm wrapped under Torsten's back. "Is that you?"

"I'm the one who can't see, damn it!" Torsten barked. "Take her down."

"The storm… It's so dark… She…"

Torsten heard it before he said it. The driving rain suddenly ceased, leaving water to gush across the cobblestones. Glassmen groaned, whispering about what had happened.

"What is it?" Torsten asked.

"The warlock, she's…" Lucas stammered.

"Out with it, boy!"

"She's gone! Vanished into darkness."

Torsten exhaled through clenched teeth and patted at the wet stone. A thorn on the unnatural vine pricked his thumb. At first, he expected to be angry, then a wave of relief hit him.

"Let her run," he said. "The Drav Cra are our concern no longer."

"But everyone saw what she did," Lucas replied.

"All the more reason to hurry up the stubborn priests in Hornsheim. Torsten stood, and Lucas took his arm. Torsten removed his hand. "No, help the injured here. I can make my way back alone."

IV

THE DAUGHTER

ahraveh Ayerabi stood, silent, disciplined. Her eye followed the line of a blackwood arrow nocked in her short bow, the string pulled tight and aimed toward a pit lizard. The beasts weren't often found wandering the sands alone, much less this close to the rocky southern shore. Mahraveh could still see the hazy outline of Saujibar, the oasis town she called home between the Black Sands dunes and the coast. If she could manage to drag one so large back to the village, she knew how proud her father would be.

The pit lizard flared its neck flap and flicked a half-a-meter-long, forked tongue. Mahraveh's eyes darted from side to side, wary for its kin. One of the man-length reptiles, with their dagger-sharp teeth, she could outrun, even with her little legs, but if the pit lizard's mate showed up, she wouldn't be so confident.

A yellow eye blinked on the side of its head, and she focused the tip of her arrow on it. Her chest shuddered, a deep, steadying breath entering her lungs. The sun's heat bore down. The base of her thick dreadlocks itched, and sweat trickled into her brow, threatening to break through to sting her eye. Mahraveh ignored it all, exhaled, and let the arrow loose. The barbed end glimmered in the sunlight, rotating toward its intended target.

"Mahi!" a voice shouted from behind her. The two-meter long lizard skittered away just in time, and the arrow nestled harmlessly into the soft, black sand.

Mahraveh swore. She knew the voice. She'd only just entered the desert on the outskirts of Saujibar, and already they were trying to bring her back to an "environment more suited to a Shesaitju lady."

Farhan, one of her father's commanders, crested a tall dune flanked by three others. He was young—though not nearly as young as little Mahi—and handsome. Backdropped against the sun, his gray skin appeared like pitch, the expression upon his face, unreadable. But she knew it would be anger.

"Mahi, you should not be out here alone," he scolded.

"Should I rather stay safe in my father's house sewing headdresses or scarves?" she replied. Without turning to him, she started to thread another arrow. The bold reptile had stopped only a short distance away to scour for insects.

Farhan slid down the sandy dune, his fingers creating snaking trails behind him. Coming to a stop beside her, he wrapped a hand around her bicep, and the arrow fell through her bow as she yanked her limb away. She hated how all her father's men felt they could treat her as if she were their own daughter merely because they worked for the afhem.

"Your father—" Farhan said.

"If my father wants me back at the manor so badly, he should have come himself!" Mahraveh interrupted.

At that moment, a new shadow appeared atop the dune. Now the pit lizard scurried away, lost forever to the dark sands. Thick muscle and bright white tattoos laced the man's body, which could be made out even against the blazing sun.

"*Does this make you content, daughter?*" *His voice carried like distant thunder.*

"*Father,*" *Mahraveh whispered, falling to her knees. Muskigo Ayerabi, her father, was one of Caleef Rakun's afhems—warlords whose spirits provided tabernacle for the God of Sand and Sea.* "*I am sorry. I just wanted to—*"

"*Mahi, you know this is no place for you,*" *Muskigo said.*

Farhan gently pulled Mahraveh to her feet and guided her up the slope into her father's arms.

"*You are still yet a child,*" *he continued.* "*You belong in the manor learning everything you can from Shavi.*"

Mahraveh glanced around at her father's men. Each was covered in tattoos, like him, but none wore them upon their bald heads. Only Afhem Muskigo Ayerabi carried that honor.

Farhan's hand returned to Mahraveh's arm. She tried to pull away again, but he resisted, and his grip tightened.

She let out a sharp breath and said, "*I am not a child, father. I am twelve; nearly a woman grown. I don't wish to lead with a broom, but a sword, like you.*"

"*You dream of bloodshed—a noble dream—but women do not spill blood except in childbirth. So many, though they are honored to serve our people, would give all for a chance to be served. You throw away a gift, my little sand mouse.*"

There was a time when hearing her father's voice speak those words would have caused Mahi to blush. But now, it felt so much like an insult. She was no sand mouse; she was the snake, ready to strike and devour its prey. If only he'd let her.

"*Now, come, let us put aside this foolishness and return to the safety of home. Shavi is making zhulong stew, and it smelled wonderful.*" *Muskigo motioned to one of his other men, Impili—she hated Impili most of all with his broken front teeth and neck scar. Impili grasped her bow and spare arrows. She glowered at*

*him, hoping his hand got cut on the arrows' barbs, but their eyes
never met.*

"Someday," Muskigo said, "Saujibar will need you."

Mahraveh wasn't sure why her mind was drawn to that moment,
which was just one of so many times she was forced back home,
but she was. Perhaps if her father had let her go out on her own
even once in her life, she might've been more prepared for things
now that he was the one in need of saving.

Presently, she stood at the base of Caleef Sidar Rakun's
golden throne. Surrounding her were frightening men. Scarred,
tattooed, and calloused men. Shesaitju afhems and their closest
advisors, arms flailing as they shouted at one another.

Serpent Guards lined the walls like armored statues, still as
stone. They held no affiliation to any afhem, only to the Caleef.
They were trained from birth by the masters of the Tal'du
Dromesh to be his personal guard after—as mere children—their
tongues were taken. Solid gold masks covered the top halves of
their faces, scales and ridges forming the visage of a snake. Each
one was a physical specimen, corded muscles and rock-hard
abdominals like they could have been chipped from the Pikeback
Mountains. After the Caleef was taken prisoner by King Pi of the
Glass, some had broken ranks and gone with her father, Muskigo,
to fight to free their Caleef. The rest stayed behind in the Boiling
Keep.

Nigh'jels painted the room in green light, coruscating off the
golden walls, reflecting across the hall like poison moonlight.
Shavi, the head handmaiden of the Ayerabi house, used fire for
cooking, and Mahraveh always wondered why her people didn't
use simple torches instead of luminescent jellyfish in glass and
bone cages. Her father, Muskigo, told her when she was much

younger, he preferred the product of the Boiling Waters to the creation of man. That they were a gift of the God of Sand and Sea. Mahraveh still thought fire would be brighter and warmer.

On a relief sculpture along the back wall, above the throne, a Shesaitju sand snake wrapped itself around a zhulong. The grooves were old; black but not tarnished. Each scale of both snake and zhulong was meticulously carved—each one the pride of her people. The zhulong were powerful and loyal, but not a beast to be crossed. The snakes were vicious, sure death to any who were unfortunate enough to stumble upon one—just like the Shesaitju, at least, how they used to be before the Glassmen made them bend the knee.

Mahraveh crossed the room, disinterested in the complaints of men who were grown enough not to be acting like children. She'd only been to the capital city of Latiapur one other time—in the arms of her father—but she'd never been in the throne room. She'd heard stories of the gaping maw in the center of the floor, an open door gazing down into the choppy Boiling Waters far below.

As she inched closer, the sound of the wind and waves grew louder. Her knees shook, but she pulled it together.

You are the snake, she told herself.

There was no ledge, no wall separating the sturdy golden floor from certain death, just a massive round hole. And below, she could imagine dorsal fins swarming in the waters.

Without a second thought, she backed up and felt a hand against the small of her back.

"Mahi, you should not be so close."

She turned to see the handsome face of her father's right hand, Farhan. He'd only recently returned to Latiapur after a brutal loss in Winde Port that sent Muskigo and his rebel army into retreat. They were now surrounded by the Glass Army in Nahanab, under siege, while her father begged for other powerful afhems to heed the call of rebellion and come to his aid.

Farhan had snuck out to carry his message and fight in the upcoming Afhemate Trials after the tragic passing of Afhem al-Tariq when a storm struck his ship out at sea. The man commanded a sizable fleet but kept to fishing around his island in the Boiling Waters after a critical loss to Liam shamed him and his afhemate.

Mahraveh harrumphed and stepped back toward the mass of arguing afhems.

"Do you propose we stand before the waves and petition the Lord for a new vessel while ours yet lives?" one afhem said.

"I propose we do something instead of wait around while our land is further destroyed," said another.

"Our lands are in far better shape than that of the Glass," Farhan said, stepping into the fray. "And our waters are rife with fish to keep our bellies full. What we must do is assemble our respective armies and march to Afhem Muskigo's aid before the Glass take that too."

"What you are calling for, *Commander*, is open war against a new king," Afhem Babrak Trisps'I spat the word commander as if there were spoiled zhulong stew upon his tongue. He was not nearly as physically fit as Mahraveh's father, but what he lacked in muscle he made up for in sheer mass. Mahraveh had always detested the man, whose late father's rivalry with her own was well-known, but he commanded the largest fleet in the Black Sands. Without his support, it would be difficult to gain any from the other afhems.

"Their 'king' is a baby," Farhan said, bending two fingers on each hand with the word king. "Liam the Conqueror is dead. His mighty sword earned our respect and loyalty. It is our way. But should we kneel to a son who has won nothing? Muskigo saw this coming and refused to bow to weakness. Thousands rallied to his call and rode out to earn freedom for our people while you would all stand here arguing."

"Muskigo raised an army of fools who believed in the legend of the man and not the man himself," Babrak said.

"He acted on his own," added another afhem. "And his actions led to the capture of our Caleef and so many dead in Winde Port. He blocked our tribute to the Glass for years of his own volition as well. If the Caleef were here, he'd throw him through the Sea Door for his insolence!" the afhem pointed to the opening in the floor, and merely the thought of her father near it made Mahraveh cringe.

"But he is not here," Farhan said. "Perhaps you are right, and Muskigo acted out of line, but it was Liam's son who locked up the Caleef, regardless. And it was he who was so weak he allowed Caleef Rakun to escape into the wild."

"And do we know for sure these aren't rumors spread by the Glass?" Babrak asked. "To root out unloyal afhems and further weaken us?"

"Because he was there!" Farhan pointed to the gaunt-faced Glassman seated in the corner. "He set our Caleef free and saved my afhem's life at Winde Port."

"Bah," Babrak bellowed. "More Glassman games. This Yuri Darkings claims to have helped free the Caleef, yet the Caleef is not here."

Yuri stood to his full height, staring down at all of them over his hawkish nose. His form-fitting tunic was threaded with gold, and he wore more jeweled rings than any man ought to. Ever since he'd arrived alongside Farhan, his presence made Mahi's skin crawl. He was like a ghost, from his pale skin to his smooth, gliding gate. He seemed to represent everything her father had taught her not to trust.

"I did what I could under the circumstances," Yuri said. "Perhaps you think it easy to betray a Nothhelm, even an inferior one.

I told you, your Caleef is being escorted as we speak. If you want to send men out to search for them, that is your choice. I have done all that I can."

"So we should trust a man who'd betray his own people?" one of the afhems said.

"I served Liam because I respected him," Yuri responded, voice filled with accusation. "Just as your people bent your knee."

"You will watch your tone Glassman!" an afhem barked.

"History is already written, my friend. Neither you nor I can change it. But Liam's greatness died with him. His wife would have hung me over a wall like dried meat for speaking my mind. And their son?" he scoffed. "He's crazy as a sick boar. Betray my people? I'm saving them from a generation of madness."

"So you say," Babrak said.

Yuri stalked right up to him. Their figures couldn't have contrasted any more. Except for their height. It wasn't often a Glassman stood so tall. "Do you think I enjoy helping you people kill my own? I thought the Child-King would die and end this rotting dynasty, and then he rose from the dead, or so they say. I would have killed him myself if I could've gotten close enough, but now, the more the Glass unravels, the clearer my people will see that the time for a new line of kings has come. They'll do it for me."

"I am certain the pile of gold and shoreside villa Muskigo offered you doesn't hurt either," Babrak said, pointedly turning his back to the Glassman.

"Villa?" Yuri scoffed. "I gave up more wealth than you'll see in a lifetime to help him. My family, beyond my son, will be ostracized. Besides, I'd hardly call a home by an oasis 'shoreside.'"

Babrak turned back to face Yuri.

"Had I thought Muskigo's peers would rather squabble like fat lords," Yuri continued, patting Babrak's bulbous stomach with the back of his many-ringed hand, "perhaps I would have backed a Panpingese rebellion."

Babrak stomped forward, his bulging gut pushing Yuri back. "Perhaps if you were an afhem, you could lead an army yourself. The tournament to find a new one to rule the al-Tariq Isle nears. I'd give you a minute lasting on the sands."

"You gray men," Yuri clicked his tongue. "I've been on the Royal Council since before many of you were a twinkle in your father's eye. You've grown soft. For generations, all the Shesaitju ever cared about was fighting, and now that you can, you'd rather let one of your own die because he didn't *ask permission*."

"Do not presume to know our ways. Muskigo brought war and suffering to more than his afhemate... without our knowledge or the Caleef's. That betrayal cannot be tolerated."

"Or maybe all of you fear what might happen when you lose all the wealth and food serving the Glass brings. The annihilation of the Ayerabi afhemate leaves ample room for others to grow in power."

"Muskigo made his choice. I take no pleasure in it."

"I've read stories about Shesaitju bravery. So far I've seen one brave man amongst a sea of cowards."

Babrak lashed out and grabbed Yuri by the arm. His hands shook. "You are lucky it is a bad omen to kill invited guests. If what you say about your new king is true, then why should we sacrifice thousands when they'll destroy themselves?" He released Yuri and turned back to his people.

"Every corner of this land is filled with fools," Yuri spat, then stormed down the long golden hall and out of the room. He passed Mahi on his way by, and they made eye contact for a moment before he studied her from head to toe. It gave her a shiver.

Farhan cleared his throat and said, "If we do not heed Muskigo's call, what will we do?"

"We should keep our heads down and wait until this blows over," Babrak said. "If Caleef Rakun escaped the clutches of the Glass, he will return to us."

"And if he doesn't?" Farhan said.

"Then the God of Sand and Sea will claim a new host from the depths to guide us." The big man took several steps forward, placing himself in the center of the afhems. "Who are you, Commander Farhan Uki'a? You are no afhem. Lord Darkings was invited, but do you even have a place in these halls?"

The others murmured in agreement.

"I am here representing the Ayerabi afhemate, as is custom when an Afhem cannot be present," Farhan said. "Surely, I do not need to recite to you our customs?"

"I thought that's why the girl was here?" Babrak pointed at Mahi, who tried to look like she belonged.

Farhan's shoulders dropped ever-so-slightly, but he quickly straightened and said, "When was the last time you swung a sword, Babrak?"

Mahraveh was impressed. Farhan was both handsome *and* brave. All her childhood, he'd had helped keep her from exploring the dunes, hunting on her own. She'd never realized he wasn't much older than she, and whatever had happened in Winde Port had changed him. She could see it in his eyes. It was said a Shesaitju boy wasn't a man until he gripped a blade in battle, and Farhan was clearly now a man.

"When was the last time any of you wielded your blade against someone without gray skin?" Farhan said, looking around the room. "We've been pissing on each other so long, we've forgotten we are all slaves to the Glass."

"We are slaves to no one!" shouted a tall afhem, every inch of his head bald covered in tattoos like Muskigo's.

"We are slaves to anyone who wishes us to be!" Farhan snapped. "Yuri was right. When was the last time free men paid tribute to a king not their own? Look out that window," he said, pointing. "How many Eyes of Iam do you see in those streets? Is Iam our God? No! But we are forced to endure his temples within our city walls, all so the men in this room can grow richer and fatter. Meanwhile, our God is absent from our people, his chosen vessel dead for all we know."

"Caleef Rakun is not dead," a sultry voice suddenly spoke from behind Mahraveh. She'd appeared out of nothing and nowhere. She stepped forward, hips swaying, causing the strings of shells and seaweed draped across her naked body to rattle.

Mahraveh had no idea one of the Sirens would be present. She'd never seen one of the strange, ageless women so close. They lived alone on the far islands of the Boiling Waters, listening to the waters for guidance. They usually stayed in their far-off homes until a new Caleef needed to be drawn from the sea, but with Sidar Rakun missing, there were rumors they'd begun to make their presence known again.

The woman's hair was knotted, discolored—green, as if she'd spent her life in the salt water. Her gray skin was creased, not the way old skin wrinkled, however, but smooth furrows like drift-wood, small bits of coral growing from the cracks. Her beauty was unquestionable, and her eyes were bright as Celeste hanging in a pitch-dark sky.

And Mahraveh knew she was deadlier than any warrior within these walls.

The Siren cleared her throat. "Do you not know that the very stars would fall from the sky upon the death of Sidar Rakun, calling us home to shore?"

Mahraveh had never seen anyone capture the attention of a room like the Siren had. Secretly, she'd always fantasized of being one. To be free to travel as they pleased until the God of Sand and Sea summoned their souls back to him. Little more was known about them, and Mahraveh loved the mysterious.

"The oceans would roar and tumble," the Siren continued. "Their froth billowing, rising so high this room would fill from the Sea Door. "The sun would fail to rise, and the moons would go black. I assure you, our Caleef yet lives."

"Then tell us, voice of the deep sea, what we should do?" Babrak said.

She closed her eyes, eyelids flickering. "We should be patient. The Caleef returns to us in the hands of Glass traitors. Twin towers made of steel with crimson beards. We mustn't act without his blessing, unlike one of you whose death is now secured." Without so much as another word, the oracle dissipated into sand. Her essence flowed through the open Sea Door and caught on the wind.

The men murmured, but Mahraveh stared. Stories of the Sirens claimed many things, but seeing one in person turn to black sand on the wind was entirely different.

"Even the Sirens see the folly of Muskigo's ways," an afhem said, addressing Farhan.

"Would you ignore their sage advice now as well?" Babrak asked. "Muskigo made his selfish play for power, and we all pay for it dearly."

Another afhem shouted, and the arguing began again. Farhan didn't back down, and his deep gray skin went a shade darker as he waged war with his tongue. These sorts of arguments usually led to conflict between afhemates, like the one long ago which claimed Mahraveh's mother when her father loved whom he shouldn't have and won a war he should never have fought.

Mahraveh took a staggering step forward. Her heart felt like it was in her throat, and she was sure the words wouldn't make it past the lump.

"My father," she began, then cleared her throat. "Afhem Muskigo is off fighting a war you were all too fearful to fight."

Babrak spun to face her, scowling. "Enough of this! Your

father is a rebel against both Crowns. He has acted of his own volition to bring our time of peace and rebuilding after Liam to an end."

"Peace?" Hearing the word emboldened her. She stepped up the first gilded dais of the empty throne, bringing herself eye level with Babrak. There were a few inhalations at the sight of not only a non-afhem, but a woman at that, sullying the dais of their god-king, but most listened with rapt attention. "Since when do we care of peace? Yuri spoke the truth. You've grown soft as your belly, Babrak."

The other afhems laughed, and she gained more confidence.

"These ancient lands have been home to our people for generations longer than those pasty-faced pink men have been away from the tundra," she said.

"And they should have stayed there!" one of the afhems cried out.

"Be that as it may," Mahraveh continued, "they did not. And they were not content to stay beside their mountain."

"They will be put in their place," Farhan agreed. "Our fathers may have failed to defeat them, but we can."

"Who? This slob?" Mahraveh knew she might be pushing it, but Babrak just continued staring at her. They could disagree with her father all they wanted, but she knew they respected and feared him. He who had never lost a battle in any feud amongst their people or otherwise... until Winde Port—who'd claimed the Ayerabi afhemate in the Tal'du Dromesh after King Liam killed his predecessor.

"Are you too afraid to step outside these gilded walls?" she questioned. "My father—"

She felt the sudden sting of Babrak's hand on her cheek and then hit the cold, golden floor. Blinking twice, she rolled to her back. Cries of protest arose, Farhan's voice loudest amongst them all.

"Stay back, Commander," Babrak warned, drawing his scimitar. "Or you will join her. This is a place for men to discuss war, not for pampered children to exercise their voices."

"That is the daughter of an afhem," Farhan said, rushing to Mahraveh's side to help her up. "When her father returns from Nahanab, victorious, you will answer for this, and you know what Muskigo is capable of. Or do you not remember your last feud?"

"Muskigo's victory amongst our people was a fluke," Babrak said. "If that sandstorm hadn't hit, he would've been food for the gulls."

"The God of Sand and Sea favors him," Mahraveh bristled as she stood. "He defeated you to claim my mother, outnumbered four to one. Do you dare believe the Glassmen are stronger?"

"Pazradi was to be my wife! He had no right to her, just like he had no right to start a war. Can't you all see how that man believes he can do whatever he wishes?"

"At least he isn't blind."

"The Siren has spoken," Babrak said. "Muskigo's favor with the Sands is lost. We must wait for the guidance of Caleef Rakun."

"Afhem Babrak," Farhan said. "This war can be won. Don't be a coward."

"Perhaps one day soon it will be, but it will not be by *him*. He is the coward who turned his back on this circle, and so we shall do the same." Most of the afhems grumbled in agreement, though a few remained silent—Afhem Tingur of the Jalurahbak numbered among them. Mahraveh took note of each. "Now, take this impudent child and run back to your master, little Farhan. And watch out for sand snakes. We wouldn't want Pazradi's beautiful child to suffer the same unfortunate fate as she herself."

Babrak shoved Farhan, smiling. Mahraveh couldn't stomach the disrespect any longer. She punched the fat man without thinking twice, but her hand recessed into his belly like it was made of sand. He shoved her down again and walked away, skirting around the Sea Door and the waters beneath.

Mahraveh was the first to rise again, but she froze upon seeing what Farhan did next. He rushed toward Afhem Babrak like a rabid zhulong.

"Farhan, stop!" she cried, and as she did, Babrak turned to see Farhan charging him. He stepped to the side, grabbed Farhan by the tunic and launched him through the portal into the violent, shark-infested waters.

"No!" Mahraveh screamed, but it was too late. Nobody could survive that fall lest they be named Caleef. "Farhan!"

She'd come so far, and now, she was left all alone amongst the real snakes.

V

THE KNIGHT

Torsten spread his hands across the parchment, feeling every wrinkle, the subtle bumps of dried ink. The message had only just arrived by galler bird from the front lines where Sir Nikserof, the Wearer of White, battled to put down the Shesaitju rebellion led by Afhem Muskigo Ayerabi.

Torsten remembered that day in Winde Port when the winds of war shifted, the fire, the blood—his duel with the afhem which almost claimed his life. He'd never felt as helpless as when he'd cracked through the ice into the cold waters of Winde Port's grand canal. He'd never felt as broken as when Muskigo beat him. He remembered how Redstar used that failure to climb and manipulate; to take the Glass Kingdom for his own.

Worse even than the day Liam had finally passed, the worst day of Torsten's life, yet he longed to return to it. Because on that day, he could see, which meant on that day, he could fight; he could serve his kingdom the best way he knew how.

"Lucas, what does it say?" Torsten asked, flapping the letter to his right. Torsten scratched the tender skin around his eyes as he listened to the young man flatten the parchment across the heavy oaken desk in his quarters.

"It's addressed from Sir Nikserof, dated Freefrost, twenty," Lucas said. A period of silence passed between them.

"Do you plan on finishing the rest, or having me guess?" Torsten asked.

"I… uh, sorry, sir. He writes to inform you and the King that, and I quote, 'News of Redstar's fate allowed us to get the jump on Dradinengor Mak in their sleep and ravage the united Drav Cra horde. It left our position in the South weaker and exposed the Wildlands to what's left of Mak and their raiders, but with the Glass army at my command, and the ships quickly dispatched from Crowfall thanks to Lord Jolly taking command, I have surrounded Afhem Muskigo in Nahanab and have him under siege. Spies in Latiapur inform me that other powerful afhems hesitate to throw their support behind Muskigo, whom they believe acted outside the best interest of their people. When Muskigo is defeated, I feel that peace will be within our grasp. Many of the Shesaitju blame him for what happened with the Caleef; that he pushed us too far.' End quote."

"This could have all ended at Winde Port," Torsten interrupted. "Cut the head off the snake. I hope he can do what I failed to."

"Sir, there's a postscript," Lucas said. "Would you like me to continue?"

Torsten nodded.

"'I heard what happened to you, Sir,'" Lucas read. "'I hope the heathen suffered when he died. And know that I never wanted to wear this helm. Upon my return, it's yours. If you want it back. You don't need eyes to lead; you only need to see.' End quote."

Lucas rerolled the letter. "That's it, but for the seal of the Wearer of White," he added.

Torsten's fingers squeezed the edge of his desk. He could feel the wood beginning to divide as his grip hardened. More than anything, he wished he could be there with the men he'd neglected for so long. He didn't care about leading them, only standing at their side in battle. It was where he belonged. Now, he'd merely weaken the Shield.

"Sir, shall I draft a response?" Lucas asked.

Torsten drew a slow, grating breath, then released his grip. "Tell him to push Muskigo to the brink. The Shesaitju respect only martial prowess. It was how—"

"Sorry, sir. I need a moment."

Torsten grumbled under his breath as Lucas gathered supplies. The young man fumbled through a drawer, then Torsten heard a clattering followed by a curse.

"Sorry, Sir. Spilled the ink. Just a—yes, there we go."

The moment Torsten was released from the physicians, Shield Taskmaster Lars brought him a new pool of Shieldsmen recruits from which to choose an aide. Lucas was a member of the city guard who hailed from Dockside and was there when the Buried Goddess cultists rioted. He had luckily been stationed by the city's southern gates that night and ignored orders not to open the portcullis in fear of losing the Caleef permanently. Hundreds were able to escape fire and death thanks to his deed. And after, he went down to the street to help direct scared citizens to the opening when smoke and night had clouded their vision. A handful even claimed he'd saved them from cultists, killing three with his own blade.

All the while, his parents lived and worked in a Dockside bakery. They'd, luckily, survived by hiding in a cellar, but the shop suffered much damage. Lucas could have abandoned his post like so many others had that chaotic night, choosing instead to help them, but he didn't.

Torsten wasn't exactly sure why he selected the boy over any of the others. After all, no matter what happened, Lucas had ignored orders that could have allowed the Caleef to escape Yarrington. But war and the Drav Cra insurrection had weakened the Order, so there were many ambling for positions. Humble origins in the poorest part of South Corner, parents with nothing left, the ability to see what was right despite orders—Torsten had a soft spot for men like Lucas.

"I'm so sorry, Sir." Lucas gathered everything, and Torsten heard the *thud* of the supplies scattering atop the table.

"I hope you're not this nervous on the battlefield," Torsten said.

"I… I won't be."

"They all say that until they're there. You hesitated the other day at the execution. It isn't always as easy as cultists slaughtering the helpless. And time is rarely on the Shieldsman's side."

Torsten turned in the direction of the young man's breathing. At first, atop Mt. Lister, he could see blurred shapes and shades, but now there was nothing. He remained blind as a priest of Iam. A knight who couldn't wield a sword… useless.

"Now, where were we?" Torsten said.

"'The Shesaitju respect only martial prowess,'" Lucas recited to the tune of a quill scratching across parchment.

"Yes." Torsten continued, speaking slowly so the boy could jot it all down. "That was how the late King Liam got them to kneel to our sovereignty. It is why so many of them cower now after their loss at Winde Port."

"It is why so many of them…" Lucas repeated under his breath.

"Beat Muskigo down," Torsten said after a moment to allow his squire to catch up, "no matter what it takes, and this will end. Allow him no quarter and be ruthless in your siege. Only through strength shall the bonds of peace with the Black Sands be reforged."

Torsten cleared his throat. "Regarding your postscript, I am in no need of sympathy or charity. I embrace the will of Iam, and it is clear he wishes for you to wear the white helm. For your prowess at the battle of Winde Port, there is no man more quali-fied to lead our army through this difficult time. I will support your efforts from the capital as any good knight would. The King's mind is clear now, and with you away, I have his ear as Master of Warfare. Whatever you might need to support this campaign, ask, and I will do what I can. Iam guide you."

"Is that all?" Lucas asked.

"Yes. Bring it to the Master of Rolls, and he'll have it sent with our fastest galler."

"Sir, apologies, but who is the Master of Rolls now?"

Torsten exhaled. It was a reasonable question. The Council seemed to rise and fall as quickly as the sun and moons.

"Master Caspar Brosch. He's a good man. A bit eccentric. And hurry. In war, haste of communication is everything. It was a lack of it which led to our defeat at Fort Marimount."

"The men say it was 'Redstar the Deceivers' fault," Lucas said while sealing the letter.

"It is good to hear him bear a name other than 'hero' or 'sav-ior,' but fault never lies in a single pair of hands. We all missed what was right before our eyes."

"But, Sir, how could you have known—"

"I'm not wallowing, Lucas," Torsten said. "I'm instructing. You will take the vows of a Shieldsman one day. A man from South Corner, just like me."

"With all due respect, Dockside makes the rest of South Corner seem like paradise."

Torsten let a chuckle slip out. "That may be so. And if men from either wretched place learn anything, it is how to do so from failure."

"Yes, Sir."

"Taskmaster Lars Kesselman tells me that while your marks in your studies are exceptional, your swordsmanship lacks."

"I'm trying, Sir. I've been in plenty of scraps back home, but they're less refined. I'm used to the street and the dirt."

"You handled those cultists well enough."

"They weren't trained to fight and I... I was so angry that night, Sir. I honestly can't remember much of what I'd done until they were all dead."

Torsten reached out, and it took a few seconds for him to find the young man's shoulder. "I understand. We aren't brawlers though. We are a shield, and if a rivet in the wall of metal fails, so shall the wall itself. Worry less about me, and more about yourself. They say the Shesaitju Serpent Guard are the greatest warriors in our world, but I hope to prove them wrong once again."

Torsten stood, nearly tripping on the leg of his chair. He caught himself on the desk and straightened his back.

"Here you are, Sir," Lucas said. Torsten felt a cane placed into his hand—just like Wren the Holy used to use before he too died thanks to the heathen, Redstar.

Torsten snatched it away. "I told you to worry about me less."

"I was given strict instructions to help you around the castle."

"Help yourself. That's an order." Torsten extended the cane and tapped it along the wall to find his way. He remained living in the old Wearer's Chambers which Redstar had sullied so. New quarters for Sir Nikserof and the future Wearers had been established at the other end of the castle, nearer to the Shield Hall this time, but without the man's presence in Yarrington, they had remained empty.

Torsten could have stayed anywhere else. However, he preferred the reminder of what happens when evil is allowed to fester. He couldn't see the bloodstains from Redstar's wicked rituals or the cracks on the walls where Oleander suffered at the Arch Warlock's hand, but he could still smell the copper tinge of blood. Feel the taint on the air.

He tapped along the carpet and stone walls to find his way to the Western Tower. Soft footsteps tracked behind him.

He stopped. "Were my orders not clear, Lucas?" he said.

"Yes, Sir," the young man replied. "Sorry, sir. Oh, and my father intends to seek audience today, if you remember. A rival stole a shipment of flour, and the Dockside captain is too busy to hear about it. They have their shop up and running again thanks to some help from friends, but supplies remain slim."

"Right, I remember." He scratched his upper cheek. "Well, we'll hear their claim like any other. No special treatment."

"Of course, yes. I... Thank you, Sir."

He scurried away in the other direction, and Torsten couldn't help but smirk. He was young, eager like Torsten had been after Liam first brought him on as a squire. Eating food that wasn't spoiled, turning a corner without getting a whiff of shog—a chance to live anywhere but grimy South Corner had seemed like Iam's greatest blessing back then. Probably even more so now that the cultists of Nesilia had ravaged the district so.

If there was one reason he was glad to have lost his sight, it was that he didn't have to witness that gruesome affair. While he thwarted Redstar and the Drav Cra's plans to revive the Buried Goddess, the cultists Redstar emboldened threw the poorer districts of the city into chaos. They made the Drav Cra seem civilized as they burned and slaughtered—women, children... anyone who got in their path. With the Drav Cra sent home, they too were dispelled and forced back underground where cultists belong, but the damage was done.

Young Lucas Danvels emerged from that chaos, and would soon learn the pressures that came with serving a higher calling. Training for the Shield would either grind a man down and spit him back from whence he came or mold him into one of worth. He'd handled his first crisis with Freydis well enough, but that was nothing compared to what the kingdom had seen. One

Shieldsman died—Iam comfort his soul, another a near mortal wound to the chest, and Sir Mulliner suffered a gash on his arm that would take some weeks to heal.

All Torsten could do was vow to be there for Lucas and all the other recruits if they needed guidance. For any Shieldsman, really. To help turn the order back into something to aspire to, something above reproach. Warriors forged from honor and duty to King and Iam.

Torsten tapped the first step up to the highest level of the tower, then found footing. He leaned on the rail with his other hand, then climbed the spiral stairs. He went until his cane pushed out and found no opposition.

"Sir Unger, let me help you," spoke the familiar voice of Sir Austun Milliner. No Shieldsman had seen Torsten's failure in greater clarity than he had, riding to Torsten's aid atop Mount Lister because it was the right thing to do. But Torsten didn't deserve Sir Mulliner's forgiveness for what he'd done. Yet there he was, like so many others, offering a helping hand to the poor, blind former Wearer of White.

"I've got it," Torsten said, brushing Austun's hand away, feeling the sling on his arm. Torsten tapped the cane a few more times, then found balance. Austun quickly wrapped his healthy arm through Torsten's to guide him.

"I said I'm fine." Torsten brushed him off again, then tapped the side of the arched portal leading into the Royal Avenue.

"There's no need to be stubborn," Lord Kaviel Jolly said, apparently at Mulliner's side. "The slayer of Redstar 'The Deceiver' shouldn't need to struggle."

"We can all do to struggle a little more," Torsten replied. "Even you, my Lord."

Lord Jolly chuckled. "I suppose that's true."

"His Highness sent me to retrieve you both," Mulliner said.

"You should be resting," Torsten said.

"It's only a scratch. I'm just ashamed we couldn't put that witch down. We should've thrown her off that mountain."

"She was Redstar's hound, that's all. She can't harm us any longer."

"Tell that to Drad Mak and his raiders, running wild in the east."

Torsten twisted his lip, then nodded. "Is the King prepared for the public audience?" Torsten asked.

"More than. He seems eager, really."

"He won't be after dealing with the mob of terrified citizens concerned about the black magic they've just witnessed," Lord Jolly said. "We're used to it in the North. Damn warlocks."

"I don't know why you don't all move south," Mulliner said.

"Home is home, but, alas, the Crown calls and here am I. I can't let my brother be the only one to have died with glory after all."

Torsten's heart sunk at the memory of his brother. And he was not surprised to find a bit of anger rise at the casual way Wardric's own brother spoke of the event. Perhaps he hadn't seen Wardric cut open and left to bleed by the traitorous Darkings', but it was his brother nonetheless.

At least Lord Kaviel had called it glory but was hardly the word for it. Torsten wished the hard-nosed Shieldsman was still here. Wardric wouldn't have babied him for not being able to see.

"Can you both inform King Pi that I'll meet him at the throne shortly?" Torsten asked, changing a subject which Lord Jolly often so flippantly brought up.

"She's not going to come," Lord Kaviel said. "I was just with her. I think I snuck one laugh out of her. Progress." He gave Mulliner a playful jab in the arm, probably too self-absorbed to remember the Shieldsman was injured. Sir Wardric Jolly, the man was not.

"These audiences were her idea," Torsten said.

"Even so. I'm glad to see things around here are changing, but the world never changes too much. I've known the Queen Mother a long time. She's a hard, stubborn woman. Worse even than you, if you can imagine."

"I'm aware," Torsten grumbled. Lord Jolly was also not shy about reminding people of his longtime connections with Queen Oleander, having known her since she was a teenager housed in his castle after Liam tore her from the Drav Cra and attempted to subjugate the savages.

"When she wants to be seen, she'll be seen," Lord Jolly said. "She can't be forced, never could. You think Liam took her as his against her will? Even back then, if she hadn't wanted him, she would have torn out his throat with her teeth."

"Or hung him out their window," Mulliner added under his breath.

Torsten bit back a response.

Lord Kaviel sighed. "Such ferocity is both a blessing and a curse, I fear. When Pi truly needs it again, I know she'll do the right thing. For now, he has us."

"He needs *everyone* he can get. Just wait for me while I talk to her." Torsten tapped by him, then stopped. "Oh, Sir Mulliner. Would you mind offering a little extra attention to Squire Lucas at weapons training today."

"Found another favorite, have you?" Mulliner replied.

"No," Torsten said, shaking his head, "but we need more men like him. Ones who are here for more than just themselves."

"I'll see what I can do." Torsten heard the rattle of his armor as he bowed. "Sir Unger."

"Sir Mulliner," he replied, returning the gesture. Then, "Lord Jolly."

Torsten continued slowly down the hall, using his cane to test the walls for doors. Luckily, as former-Wearer, he'd spent so many years in the castle and so much time catering to its royal inhabitants, he knew each door and who'd resided behind them without needing sight—at least on this floor. Below, the new Royal Council was beginning to take shape, and he barely knew where to find the new Master of Rolls.

Master Caspar Brosch hailed from Lilith's Mill in the south. Once a small town, it had grown in stature until it suffered under the Shesaitju attacks that started this war. His time serving in their library—one of the most complete in all of Pantego—made him a perfect choice for the job.

Weeks ago, Torsten had sat with the young King and Oleander to discuss those from great houses around the Kingdom who were worthy and may've been able to provide support in valuable ways. Oleander may never have been a great leader, but apparently, she paid attention to all those who came and went; who seemed trustworthy. Finally, as the weight of Liam's shadow distanced itself from her, she was coming into her own.

All that remained now was choosing a Master of Coin and a new High Priest. The former was difficult, considering what had happened with Yuri Darkings, the traitor who yet-remained at Muskigo's side. Icarus deToit, Darkings' first replacement, mysteriously disappeared after Yuri had been reinstated. That should have been Torsten's first indication something was amiss. The latter's selection was beyond the will or influence of the King.

Torsten's cane clattered along the ridges of a carved stone frame until he stopped, inhaled through his teeth, then rapped on a thick, wooden door.

"Is that you again, Kaviel?" Queen Oleander snapped.

"It's me, Torsten," he said. "I came to inquire if you might consider joining us in the Throne Room, my Queen." He heard the bed frame squeak, then feet dragging along the stone floor.

"So, they can see what's become of me?" Her voice was closer now, just on the other side of the door.

"So they can see what evil we faced, and yet face, my Queen."

"My son does not need a monster by his side."

"Then show them how far from one you are."

Oleander swung open the door. Torsten's cane, still resting against the door, slid into the hinged side. As the heavy door came around, it tore the cane from his hands. He staggered forward into her arms. Even as large as he was, her tall, Drav Cra frame allowed her to support his weight, especially now that he no longer had need to wear his armor.

"I'm so sorry, Torsten, I…" Oleander helped him upright and leaned him against the wall. She slid his cane back into his grasp, her long fingers stopping, wrapping around his. If he'd still had sight, he'd have seen her stark white digits intertwining with his dark flesh in perfect contrast. Even the thought was a not-so-gentle reminder of how different they truly were.

She tightened her grip. Her skin was cold, but he welcomed it and covered her hand with his.

"You need never apologize to me, my Queen," he said.

"Then you're the only one," she said.

"You're King Pi's mother and the wife of his great father. You should be at the boy's side, just like you should have been when we cleansed Yarrington of Redstar's stain once and for all."

"That's not what I hear. I hear *Freydis*…" Oleander spat the word from her mouth like foul-tasting milk. "…vanished into thin air. That witch who helped my brother attempt to destroy us, gone into the world. What were they thinking giving her a chance to escape like that?"

"It was handled per my instructions, my Qu—"

"Then you should have known what she was capable of!"

"You're right, but let her run home to her tundra," Torsten said. "The time of warlocks in Yarrington is finished. The time of Pi is now. He's coming into his own with your brother's influence broken. Like a sponge, he absorbs every bit of history he reads."

"Good. Then he doesn't need me there."

"You're his mother. Every child needs his mother. Even a king. He needs to grow in confidence after everything he's been through."

"If you could see me, you'd understand," Oleander said. Her voice quavered ever so slightly. "I'm a walking reminder of the horrors we suffered at the hands of my brother…"

She pulled away. Torsten felt her turn, but he drew her back. Finding her arm, he used it to reach up further and locate her face. He lay his hand over the mottled, burned skin now covering half of her body from her chest up to her forehead. Even her once luscious, silvery hair grew bountifully from only one side, the rest consisting of patches of thin wisps and cracked skin.

Oleander had locked herself away in her quarters ever since Redstar's magic nearly killed her. She wasn't driven mad as her son had been when the Drav Cra Arch Warlock had forced him into solitude, but her door remained closed for all but King Pi, and Torsten… and apparently, Lord Kaviel.

Torsten heard a quick movement and imagined she turned her face away.

"At least now my appearance mirrors that which they've always seen in me," she said, voice quaking. She covered her head with a shawl when around the others, but not for Torsten. He was the only one. Why bother hiding what he couldn't see?

"That isn't true, my Queen," Torsten said.

"Now that we're being honest with each other, Torsten, I would prefer it if you did not lie. And for the last time, please stop calling me that when we're here alone."

"Oleander," he said softly.

"I've told you many times that I am keenly aware of how the people have talked about me for years. 'Monstrous shrew,' the

'Whore Queen,' and my personal favorite "Liam's Leftovers." Even the Dockside brothel wouldn't take me now."

"We all made mistakes in the face of their evils, Oleander, but life is long. Iam is forgiving. There is still time to do some good with these lives we cling to."

"Forgiving?" Torsten heard her long nails scratch at her burns. The sound made him cringe, then reach for his own burns to satisfy an imagined itch. "He is just," she said. "My face was all that I had. It was what my Liam fell in love with. It was—"

Torsten grabbed her hand and placed it back at her side. "It was your ferocity he fell for, trust me," he said. "You are so much more, Oleander. More than a pretty face. Opening the halls to common folk as the kings of old once had… that was your idea. Your recommendation for Lord Jolly as Master of Ships proved crucial in expediting our fleet's support of Sir Nikserof. It may very well be the reason we win this war."

"Those of us from the North are hearty aren't we?" she said, a hint of playfulness entering her tone just for a moment. "Even if he's only from Crowfall."

"Truly," Torsten said. "And one day, Pi will be a great king. For now, he needs all our help, his mother's most of all. The people will forgive you if you open up to them. You only need to forgive yourself first."

"Sweet, loyal Torsten. If only you could see me, you'd know how foolish you sound. Now, go and help my boy fix the mess we left him after *I* allowed my wretched brother to steal his mind, and wasted all our riches on festivities so our people might think of me as more than a 'whore.'"

Torsten wasn't sure how to respond. He'd never consider that as a reason for why she had been so loose with autlas after Liam fell gravely ill, each month throwing masquerades and feasts that put royal weddings to shame.

He felt her hand on his side, applying enough pressure to shift his position. The door slowly closed, and before he knew it, he stood alone in the hallway once more. Rubbing his temples between his thumb and forefinger, he bowed his head. He'd tried. Every day, he tried to get her to leave, and he wouldn't stop.

Things changed on Mount Lister. Finally, he'd seen the woman she could have been if not for her brother's games or her insecurity over Liam's many infidelities. He'd seen her cast herself at wickedness without a thought for her own safety—a den mother protecting her cub.

Liam may not have treated her like the flower he claimed her to be. He may not have known how. Liam was a man of war, not romance. But he'd always had an eye for talent. Always, Torsten hoped there was more to him picking her as his wife than beauty, and on Mount Lister, Torsten saw what *that* was.

Pi needed her as more than a voice locked away in a castle chamber, and as much as Torsten never expected to admit it, so did he.

VI

THE MYSTIC

A naked woman wrestled against Sora's body, shoving her, slapping at her. Her odor was pungent, like she'd spent years in a dungeon. Rotten food, blood and worse coated every crease of her.

Sora couldn't recall how she'd gotten here, wherever here was, or who the woman was. She imagined the sudden struggle and smell had yanked her out of the darkness within her own mind. Nesilia grew stronger every day, and Sora found herself increasingly unable to exact her own will. She refused, however, to sit idly by while someone—even a goddess—possessed her body.

Sora released the strange woman and attempted to scream. The sound never escaped her lips in the real world, but she could tell her effort bothered Nesilia.

"Quiet!" Nesilia spat with Sora's tongue. Sora wasn't sure if she was speaking to the stranger or to her. "Be still."

Freydis stopped moving, and her eyes went wide. *Freydis?* Sora knew this woman's name. She didn't know how, but she knew her. She was Freydis, a Drav Cra Warlock of the Ruuhar clan; Redstar's clan.

Then, Sora realized where they were. They stood between two buildings just off of Port Street in Yarrington. Freydis' stench apparently wasn't all that stirred her. They were in Dockside, and the air was unlike anything Sora had ever smelled—rotten fish, salty air, and refuse.

"Daughter of the earth," Nesilia said. "I am here to help you."

Freydis' features darkened, then she hissed and leaped at Sora's body. They collapsed to the cobblestone, blood pouring out of Freydis' mouth. Flakes of dry, white paint filled the creases of her fingers which she wrapped around Sora's neck. Fire burned at her fingertips, searing Sora's flesh. She could feel the intense burning, wanted to scream, but couldn't.

A vine wrapped around one of Freydis' wrists and wrenched it backward, then the other. In seconds, Freydis was thrown back against a wall, held in place by the vines which had grown through the stone as if it were soil. The warlock hissed again and sent a burst of flame down her forearms, but the mystical plants didn't burn.

Sora's body stood, and she bent her neck, the burns instantly healing. Freydis pulled at the vines, attempting all manner of magic—more fire, then ice to freeze them. She summoned vines of her own to attempt to tear them off of her; then she turned them on Sora's feet. The thorns dug into Sora's angles until she looked down at them and they turned to ash.

"You are strong, daughter, but you have a lot to learn," Nesilia said.

Sora's arm extended toward Freydis' face, but Sora finally gained enough control to stop it half-way. The arm trembled, the muscles tensing.

"What are you doing?" Sora asked Nesilia.

"Saving the damned and the forgotten," Nesilia replied. "Stop fighting." The arm edged closer to Freydis.

"No!" Sora yelled. She willed the arm to reel back so hard she crashed onto her rear. She realized at the same time that her scream had come out of her physical mouth and echoed. "Get out… Get out!"

"Hey, what's going on?" a man asked. "City's on lockdown with that witch mis—"

"Quiet!" This time, Sora knew it wasn't her yelling. Nesilia's voice thundered, and Sora's arm shot out in the direction of a guard standing outside the alley they were in. The man didn't have a chance to answer. His helmet squeezed so tight it drew a line of blood, then he was hurled against a wall. His neck cracked and he was dead before he hit the street.

"No," Sora whimpered. "Why would you do that?"

"You are strong," Nesilia replied within Sora's head. "Both the blood of kings and powerful mystics runs through your veins, but I am beyond your world. Stop resisting, or more will die who don't need to. Embrace the quiet of darkness, and I will make you all powerful."

"I don't want—"

"You don't know what you want, child."

A shadow moved nearby, and Sora once again lost control of her body. She turned to find Freydis watching her. Vines no longer held her in place, but she neither ran nor attacked. Her head remained cocked as if she could hear the conversation between Sora and Nesilia within their shared head.

"Ah, so there is more to you than pet hound," Nesilia said. "Do you recognize me?"

The wild-haired warlock opened her mouth, and blood poured out as she flicked a stub of her tongue which had apparently been cut out.

Then, Sora's own hand reached toward the warlock. Her fingertips slithered into the warlock's mouth like serpents. Power left her body. Intense, inexpressible power. It made how Sora had healed Torsten in the Webbed Woods seem like a parlor trick.

After a few seconds, the warlock lurched in pain. She dropped back into a fighting stance. Garbled words came out, half in Drav Crava, half in common. Freydis grasped at her jaw, then flexed it. She stared down over the ridge of her nose, awestruck, as a fully-formed tongue filled her mouth.

Sora was equally awestricken, even though she could do nothing but watch. She'd seen many miracles in the Red Tower, read or been told about others while under Wetzel's tutelage. She knew wounds could be healed, but not that body parts could be regrown like a lizard whose lost its tail.

Sora sauntered toward Freydis. The warlock didn't retreat but remained in shock as Sora's hand lay upon her cheek.

"We cannot have you handicapped, Freydis of the Ruuhar clan," Nesilia said. "We have work to do."

"It's you, isn't it?" Freydis said, her voice distorted as she still got accustomed to her reformed tongue.

"Shhh," Nesilia whispered. "You needn't say aloud what you already know."

"So Drad Redstar didn't fail?"

"He failed at everything!" Nesilia snapped. "But there were others who didn't forget me. Other vessels more powerful than that fool." Sora stroked her own arm, down toward the crease of her elbow, marveling at how smooth the skin was.

Freydis leaned in close and sniffed like a wolf sniffs its prey. She glared straight into Sora's eyes. All Sora wanted to do was cringe. Warlocks were terrifying, but this woman didn't need her face painted to appear like a nightmare. It was in her very expression, radiating hate and anger.

"You aren't alone?" Freydis said.

"Another forgotten soul needs my help," Nesilia answered. "Together, we can do great things."

That last phrase seemed directed inward at Sora rather than at Freydis. She'd heard the vile creature Kazimir say it to her once and remembered how fear gripped her. But he was small, focused only on himself. The power now coursing through her body was capable of things she couldn't imagine. Fear of what Nesilia might consider great made the bile within her rise up and burn her throat.

"Please… let me go," Sora begged into the darkness.

"That's all up to you," Nesilia replied.

Freydis seemed satisfied with the answer. She fell to her knees and turned up her palms in worship. At the same time, Sora felt an internal force pushing at her, driving her back into the recesses of her own mind.

She saw black, then white, then nothing at all.

VII

THE THIEF

Thunder cracked outside, and flashes of lightning kept illuminating the little room that served as the fellowship hall for the Grambling Inn. Townsfolk stood shoulder to shoulder inside like rats in a cage. What's more, people kept packing in, trying to stay dry. It was clear the reason the place was called the Grambling Inn was that it was *the* inn in Grambling. As in, only one.

It hadn't taken much to persuade the innkeeper to give Whitney and Gentry a room in exchange for entertainment for the evening. Leof Balleybeck had no way to predict the night's events would lead to his tavern being filled to capacity, and thus, hadn't prepared any talent or enough food. Getting people drunk was the answer, and drunkards did so love to be entertained. Whitney had traveled enough to know a good storm meant good business for these types of establishments. Distracted drunks made the best targets—but Whitney wasn't a thief anymore. No sir, he was a stand-up citizen content to entertain the masses.

Presently, however, it was Gentry doing the entertaining, performing the trick he was known for: swallowing a sword. There was no illusion. No trick. It was a dangerous act, and

Gentry did it masterfully. The sword was hilt deep into the boy, and his arms were stretched wide, showing the crowd he wasn't hiding anything. The trick was met with a round of applause, and Gentry carefully pulled the blade out. He coughed twice, but that was to be expected.

Whitney felt bad sipping the sour ale while the kid did all the work, but Gentry was adamant about repaying Whitney for the coin purse he'd used to bail Gentry out with the Pompares. Although Whitney didn't feel it necessary, he knew what it was like to feel indebted.

As if to further push guilt upon him, Aquira rubbed up against his leg after having snuck in through a window. Having such a rare and expensive creature at his side may have been a problem had he been alone, but with the Pompare Troupe, it added to his act. She'd pop up and light the torches, earning *oohs* and *ahs*. Sometimes, she'd even dart through the air between them and really got crowds going.

But at night, when she nestled up next to him, all she did was remind him of Sora. Whitney didn't think there'd be enough time in his life to pay Sora back for everything she'd done for him. He'd probably have gotten himself killed by Redstar and his Drav Cra buddies back near Oxgate if Sora hadn't shown up. Beyond that, she'd practically saved him from himself. She'd taught him what it meant to care about something other than Whitney Fierstown.

He took another sip. Then a gulp. He didn't want to think about her or his feelings any more this evening.

Gentry continued the show until the moons, Celeste and Loutis, rose so high they had to begin their inevitable nightly descents. Whitney was proud of him, performing so many things beyond his typical tumbling act—things Whitney had been working with him on since they'd departed from Yarrington. He was a fast learner; would make a fine thief.

Whitney shook the thought from his head. There was no way he was going to drag that poor boy through the same puddle of shog he'd been trudging through his whole life. Gentry had real talents, usable talents. He could perform for kings one day.

Gods that sounds boring, Whitney thought.

When Whitney was Gentry's age, he was skipping stones down at the Shellnak River with Sora. "River" might have been a bit of an exaggeration. By the time the arm of the Shellnak reached Troborough, it was little more than a dried out creek.

Stop thinking about Sora!

He peered up at Gentry. The kid was young. It made Whitney wonder how he'd ended up in Yarrington with these other Glintish folk. He'd spent enough time with the boy to know he wasn't related to any of them. At least not in any other way than heritage, no more than Torsten was related to Gentry, or Whitney was related to King Pi.

When the final, stumbling couple made their way up to their room, Gentry hopped off the foot-high stage and plopped down on the seat next to Whitney, exhausted.

"Great job, kid," Whitney said, placing a hand on Gentry's shoulder. It sometimes scared Whitney how much Elsewhere had changed him— wanting to teach Gentry to better his life without it being about Whitney's name attached to him as an apprentice? Who was he?

"Someday, people are going to say, 'Hey, you're that kid Whitney Fierstown mentored, aren't you?'" Whitney said. He couldn't help himself.

Gentry laughed.

"So, what will you do about your dues?" he asked.

"The Pompares?" Whitney said, taking a sip of his ale. "They'll be a problem for tomorrow. Tonight, we sleep on something softer than the dirt before we hit the road."

Whitney shoved his ale toward Gentry.

"Really?" Gentry asked.

"Sure, you're what like fifteen?" he said.

If Gentry's skin could have turned red, Whitney was sure it would have.

"I don't know," the boy said.

Whitney's eyebrows raised. "That sounds like a tale."

Gentry took a small sip from the mug and gagged. "That's awful." Leof, the bartender looked over but said nothing. "Is it spoiled?"

It was Whitney's turn to laugh. "No, it's actually pretty good. Most of it tastes worse than this. Call it an *acquired* taste."

"I don't think I want to acquire a taste for that."

"Smart boy," Whitney commented. "So, how is it you've come to join this little group of misfits? You still haven't told me."

"It *is* a tale… and a long one."

Whitney motioned to the empty room, and as he did, thunder boomed outside. "We're not going anywhere."

"I don't remember a lot of it," Gentry said, slumping back in his chair. "You don't want to hear about me."

"I certainly wouldn't have asked if I didn't. Come on, kid. Tell me."

Gentry smiled and sat up straight again. "I grew up in Myen Elnoir… the capital of Glinthaven. That place we were in back in Yarrington…"

"South Corner?" Whitney offered.

"By the docks? Yeah. There's nothing like that in Myen Elnoir, not at all. Have you been to Glinthaven?"

Whitney considered telling the boy how he'd once been in the old Glintish temples when gold flakes fell from the heavens, but instead, he merely said, "Once, a long time ago, but never Myen."

"It doesn't matter," Gentry said. "The whole kingdom is like that. Like Myen. Beautiful. Clean. Proper."

"Far cry from Yarrington, I'd say."

"Yarrington's not bad. Just kind of… dirty."

"That's a word for it," Whitney chuckled.

"People in Glinthaven aren't used to kids like me: barely three years of age and living alone underneath the Gilded Bridge," Gentry said. "At first, people didn't even notice me. When you never see vagrants or vagabonds, you don't really know what to look for. They probably just thought I was up early and out late playing."

Gentry lifted the ale to his lips, gave it a whiff, then put it down. Whitney snatched it back.

"Eventually, one of the sentries—you really should see them if you haven't," Gentry said. "All of them are impossibly tall, with gold armor. Their helmets have these plumes at the top, gold as well. Thing is, the sentries are mostly for show. No one commits crimes in Glinthaven. The Glass barely even needs fortresses there."

Whitney knew that to be true. During his time spent there, he found himself nearly incapable of stealing. It was as if magic compelled him to behave, but really, the place was just so peaceful he didn't *want* to disturb anything. It reminded him of his first year in Elsewhere. Awful.

"We have no enemies, no rivals," Gentry said. "We, as a people, merely live under the Glass's rule. Happy really. We didn't even have need for a ruler they say, until the Glass put Warden Quilarez in control of our lands. So, when something as strange as a boy beneath a bridge stirs the attention of the guards, it stirs the attention of the whole land. I was a bit of a centerpiece for conversation."

"You boys need anything?" Leof called over.

Whitney raised his pint. "Good for now." The man turned, and Whitney stopped him. "Maybe water for the boy?"

Leof nodded and returned to the bar.

"When I stood before the Warden," Gentry continued, "he asked where my parents were, but I couldn't answer. It wasn't because I didn't know. Everyone assumed they died, but they didn't. They did that which was most aberrant in Glinthaven. They'd brought me to that bridge, hugged me, and left. To this day, I don't know where they went. I didn't answer because I had no language."

Leof set the water on the table and went back to doing what all bartenders did: cleaning mugs and wiping down counters while drunks made a continuous mess of them.

"You mean you couldn't talk?" Whitney asked.

"I was only three years old and had no one to teach me," Gentry said. "I'm not sure how long I was under that bridge. Really, I don't know how I survived. I think back and can barely remember how I kept myself fed."

Whitney couldn't imagine. When he was three, he didn't have a care in the world. His parents might have been…

"Looking back," Gentry continued, interrupting Whitney's thought, "I realize I was an embarrassment. I thought, at the time, I was being done a kindness when the sentries sent me away with the Pompares. Told me I was meant to see the world and not be confined to the borders of Glinthaven—but they just didn't want their peaceful land marred by an abandoned child."

"You've been with the Pompares since you were three?" Whitney asked.

"I got lost once," he said. "I don't know how long I was missing. Got beat pretty bad that day. Fadra has a bit of a temper, right?"

Whitney's face grew hot at the thought.

"Where are your parents?" Gentry asked.

"My dad is dead," he said before thinking.

"And your mom? She's alive?"

Whitney was shocked at his own answer. His mother was

dead too; at least, his real mother was. But he'd spent so long living in Fake Troborough that he often thought about Lauryn as the living, breathing, plump woman he'd left there just a month ago. Even so, no one, fake or not, survived the demon attack.

"She's dead too," Whitney said. "That one's just harder to verbalize." Then, before Gentry could respond, he said, "I have a friend who's an orphan. Her parents died in the Third Panping War."

"Glinthaven has no wars," Gentry said.

"Maybe a stupid question to ask a kid—no offense—but I've been to Glinthaven. I could barely manage to draw my knife from my belt. It's like some god or magic keeps violence at bay. How then, did Liam manage to conquer it?"

"Only things I know I know because I've heard the older folks talk about it. I've heard them say the only thing Liam asked of them was for them to pay tribute and claim to follow their God."

"People have destroyed realms over far less," Whitney said.

"Sure, but when you're a people who care nothing for gold or gods, you do what it takes to keep the peace."

"Sounds like fairy tales to me, " Whitney scoffed. "I've never heard of a people who care nothing for gold or gods. Only liars who claim it."

"Francesca said once that you could throw a dagger at the Pikeback Mountains and you're like to hit a vein of gold. You remember the streets, right?"

"Shimmered like gold at sunrise," Whitney said.

"And that's what they *walk* on there."

"Okay, but I've been to the temples nestled in those same mountains."

"Tradition, from what I hear," Gentry said. "I've been with these folks my whole life, and I've never heard one of them speak of gods or goddesses."

"Sounds like a place no one would ever want to leave."

Whitney raised a finger to the bartender. When the man arrived with Whitney's ale, Whitney said, "One more for the night and then we'll take our room."

"I'm sorry, sir," Leof said sheepishly.

"For?"

"I… uh. Please don't get upset," he said, placing the ale down and taking a step away from the table. Aquira stuck her head out from beneath the table, but Whitney shoved her back with his foot. "Turns out, I.. uh… I just sold our last room."

"You did what? But we had a reservation," Whitney said. "We performed all night in exchange."

"Yes, yes. But…"

Whitney stood. "No, *buts*. You took a reservation."

"I did… I took one, but he offered so mu—we no longer have a room is all," Leof said with a forced sternness. However, it seemed he immediately lost his resolve when he stuttered, "I-I'm sorry."

Whitney grabbed the man by the collar. Aquira whipped up from under the table, and slid across the top, her talons scraping up the varnish. The man looked like a mouse: pointy nose, bushy eyebrows, balding head. He wasn't exactly fat, but he definitely tipped the scales more toward the higher end.

"The whole point of a reservation is to *reserve the room*, you shog-faced triss," Whitney said, blood boiling. "Anyone can *take* a reservation. You're supposed to *keep* the reservation."

"I didn't expect so many folks willing to pay tonight," the bartender said.

"You're going to have to kick someone out."

"P-please, Mr. Fierstown, you have to understand."

Whitney looked over at Gentry who stared, horrified. Whitney cleared his throat, then let go of the man, smoothing his apron as he did.

"Thank you, sir," Leof said. "It's just… a noble came in just before the young boy finished his act. Demanded a room—you know how them lords can be."

"Mmmm. Payment then," Whitney said, holding out his palm.

"Excuse me?"

"Payment," Whitney repeated. "To me, and my associate for… oh, let's say six hours of work apiece. That'll be…" Whitney pretended to do the numbers on his fingers. "I think twenty-five silver autlas would suffice."

"Mr… Sir, I cannot authorize that kind of payment. I—I'm just an employee."

"It seems we have a bit of a problem, then, don't we?" Whitney said.

"Okay, look. I have a spare room down in the cellar. There're even a couple of beds. Not the most comfortable things, but they'll do for a night. It'll keep you dry at least." The man was sweating.

"Breakfast in the morning?" Whitney said.

"What?"

"Breakfast. In the morning," Whitney repeated, slower this time.

"Yes, yes, fine. Of course."

"Hot?"

The man groaned. "Yes. Hot breakfast. Toast, eggs, and bacon."

Whitney smiled, reached out and shook the man's hand. "We've got a deal. A room for the night. Hot breakfast in the morning. Coffee. Lots of coffee. Oh, and we want to perform again after breakfast. Isn't that right Gentry?"

"Absolutely!" the boy blurted, spitting out some water mid-sip.

The bartender coughed into his hand, nearly choking. "Tomorrow? But I've reserved the stage for the famous solo bard Fabian 'Feel Good' Saravia to stop on his travels to the Glintish festival."

"Funny thing, reservations," Whitney remarked.

"Please, sir. He comes highly recommended and is performing a new song about the Slayer of Redstar the Deceiver."

A laugh snuck through Whitney's lips. He plopped back down and took another sip of his ale.

"What's so funny?" the bartender asked.

"Torsten saves the kingdom, maybe the world, and he doesn't even get his name on the title. Now I definitely don't plan to let the man play until I say we're leaving. Right Aquira?" He gave her a scratch under the chin, but her sharp, yellow eyes never left Leof.

"Okay, you're right," Leof said, swallowing hard. "A fine deal. Please, follow me."

"C'mon, Aquira," Whitney said, leaning down. The wyvern crawled up his arm before he stood.

Together, the three followed Leof Balleybeck down a short hallway, walls lined with bags of flour and sugar. Wooden barrels were stacked everywhere, even on the stairs themselves as they delved into the cellar. Cobwebs hung from every corner and Whitney was sure he'd seen a rat the size of a dire wolf pup scurry across the floor.

"Sorry about the mess," the bartender said. He pushed aside a crate with his leg, then motioned toward a doorway on his right with a lit lantern. "Right this way."

"I've slept in dungeons with less rat shog," Whitney whispered. That drew Leof's attention, but he kept walking, occasionally peering over his shoulder, nose twitching nervously. It took a few seconds for Whitney to realize it was because he'd just admitted he was a dungeon-faring criminal. People didn't visit such places for leisure, after all.

The lantern cast eerie shadows in the unfamiliar place, and Whitney placed his hand on Gentry's shoulder. Then, after clearing his throat said, "Come on, kid. Don't fall behind."

Leof showed them to a couple of hay piles stacked in the corner with bedrolls covering them. It reminded Whitney of his parents' barn in Fake Troborough, where he and Kazimir spent many nights.

"I'm sorry, it's all we've got," Leof said.

"It's all you've got *now*." Whitney corrected.

"Here," Leof said, shoving a small pouch at Whitney. "Least I can do."

Whitney shook it. "Yes, probably." Sounded like a few autlas. It was impossible to tell what kind they were without opening the bag, probably bronzers, but it was the man's own coin.

The loud crack of thunder aboveground made Whitney think about the meager tents he and Gentry would've been sleeping in. His clothes were dry; his bones were warm. Whitney tossed it back. "Keep it," he said. "Leave the lantern, and we're even."

"Th-thank you, sir. Good night." Leof didn't wait around for Whitney to change his mind. The little mouse-man handed over the light, then scuttled up toward the tavern. Whitney didn't blame him. He couldn't decide why he'd thrown the bag back either.

Aquira zipped to one of the bedrolls and curled up. "Guess that one's mine," Whitney remarked.

A nasty-looking spiderweb draped between the corners of the walls right above it. He'd seen enough spiders for a lifetime. He broke it up with one hand, closing his eyes in case the spider fell on him. Then he put the lantern down on a crate and began unlacing his britches. His boots came off next. He sighed, relieved that his feet could breathe again.

"What are you waiting for?" he asked Gentry.

"I… well… it's dark," the boy stammered.

Whitney grabbed the lantern and handed it to him. "Watch the sides. They'll be hot."

As Gentry took the light and moved toward his corner,

Whitney was left in near-complete darkness. Darkness had become the way of things for Whitney Fierstown: dungeons, spider-infested woods, dank sewers beneath Winde Port, Elsewhere. At least he knew this time the only threat was a storm up above.

He plopped down on the bedroll. It wasn't soft. He suspected there were crates beneath the thin layer of hay it lay on. But, as he'd told Gentry: it was better than wet dirt.

Whitney sighed. Aquira purred and moved into the nook of his armpit.

"Goodnight," Whitney said to Gentry.

"Goodnight," came the boy's reply.

He started snoring almost instantly. Living on the road in tents since he was three, Whitney wasn't surprised. But he'd been a traveler for most of his life, too, and ever since Elsewhere, Whitney'd found sleep hard to come by. He'd just picture those last moments with Sora on repeat, wondering if he could have done anything differently to bring her back with him. He thought about the demon which claimed to be Nesilia, and the mystics hell-bent on controlling her, until, eventually, the gentle rumblings of the storm above lulled him to sleep.

VIII

THE DAUGHTER

Afhem Babrak snapped his fingers, and two Serpent Guards broke ranks to come to his side. An unusual sight for sure, but nothing like Mahraveh watching as her father's most trusted commander and selection to fight for the al-Tariq afhemate was heaved into the open Sea Door like so little trash at the end of a long day. No, not trash, excrement. Like he was nothing more than someone's waste.

"Remove her," Babrak said, then stroked her face with the back of his hand. "Don't hurt her if you can help it. It would be a shame to damage one so pretty. Besides, her father is brash enough to do something else the whole kingdom would regret."

"Don't touch me, pis'truda!" Mahraveh cursed.

"I can find my own way." Mahraveh regarded the Serpent Guards standing silently at his side. "Are you sure you wouldn't like them to kill me as well?"

Babrak smiled again, then turned his back and continued speaking with the other afhems and dignitaries as if Mahraveh was just a minor inconvenience.

The Serpent Guards walked one step behind her as she

stepped through the large, golden doors and into the bright Pantego sun. Behind her, the doors slammed with a metallic *clang,* and she was left more alone than ever. It wasn't as if she'd have considered Farhan a friend by any means, but at least with him, she wasn't a scared girl alone in Latiapur for the first time since she could walk.

Not a girl, she told herself. *A snake.*

The courtyard was a long stretch of pebbles, smooth as only the Boiling Waters could do to rock. Blackwood palms rose like wild-haired beasts, and their long shadows provided a scant reprieve from the brutal sun. The city was beautiful, but to her, it all looked red. The black sands were red. The blue waters were red. The gray faces of the many guards were red. Anger coursed through her like a storm.

She didn't even want to leave Saujibar with Farhan to begin with—especially not with Yuri Darkings in tow—and now she felt like she'd caused Farhan's death. What was she thinking, calling out his name? Babrak wouldn't have been injured by Farhan's attack, but perhaps he wouldn't have been able to use Farhan's momentum to cast him to his death.

It wasn't her fault. She knew it wasn't. It was that pis'truda, Babrak. That worm. 'Babrak had hated her father ever since her mother chose Muskigo over him. As if he didn't have' so many other wives and concubines already. Now he had all the afhemates believing her father was a traitor rather than a hero.

She took off through the courtyard, drawing the attention of several Serpent Guards whose hands fell to their leather hilts. But they just watched as she crossed onto Golden Bluff. She looked over her shoulder at the tall gilded walls of the Caleef's palace. Tall columns made the blackwood trees look miniature.

As she turned back, the vast sea spanning before her, sharp rocks and breaking waves, she felt the weight of it all against her chest. Her father was several day's ride away, even on the back of the fastest zhulong. There's no way she could get there by sea; transit had all but stopped since Winde Port was lost and the Glass Kingdom shifted over a greater naval force.

She felt a heavy drop of rain against the back of her neck, and it sent her spine shivering.

Farhan was a good man. If the sky could open up at his loss, so could she. But she wouldn't. She wiped away the beginnings of a tear, lifted her head against the wind and budding rain, and started down the bumpy, pebble road.

"And I thought the Royal Council argued too much instead of getting things done," Yuri Darkings addressed her. He stood just outside the palace grounds, leaning against a palm, slicing a bellot fruit with a knife.

"You know nothing about us," Mahraveh snapped.

"Perhaps." He moved into her path. "But I do know a lot about arguing. Your father won't last long without reinforcements. That was Farhan's great plan, so now what?"

"Nothing you can help with." She went to pass him, but he shifted to block her. "Move."

"I grew up in Winde Port, girl. And this war destroyed half of it. If your father dies, I go with him. And I don't plan to die for a long time yet. So you'd better help me think of a way to gain support."

"Isn't that your job? I said 'move.'" She shoved by him and continued down the road. For as long as she could remember, all she'd ever wanted was to be left alone, but she didn't mean like this, or with *him*. Anyone but Yuri. Who did she have now? Shavi? Shavi would be at home, and Mahraveh didn't even know how to get home. She racked her brain, thinking of anyone she knew in Latiapur that could help, but no one came to mind.

Before she knew it, she was at the bottom of the palatial cliff.

The city was as peaceful as if a war wasn't raging and their people weren't dying. She figured that was always the life of those who lived in the capital. No thoughts, no worries.

Stall owners and vendors stared at her as she pushed through a crowd in the marketplace. The swarm of people looked more like a school of jewel-toned fish weaving through coral in the Intsti Reef.

She knew it was the tattoo on her neck which drew the attention, bright white against her gray skin, marking her as a member of the Ayerabi afhemate. Each had its unique brand. The Ayerabi afhemate, hers, wore a twisted root which wrapped around the back of her ear at the top, and at the very bottom of the tattoo, which was currently covered by Mahraveh's teal, satin sarong, the root ended in a droplet of what looked like blood, but it wasn't. Saujibar, her father's settlement, stood proudly in the middle of the harsh desert plains, an oasis amidst black, and the only source of water for days. That root and drop of water represented everything her people knew.

Lost in thought, Mahraveh bumped into an older woman garbed in a plain white sarong balancing a broad basket of wares on her head. The woman stumbled and cursed, but she didn't stop. Mahraveh apologized, but the woman paid no attention.

The smell of salted fish and flatbread hit her nostrils as she rounded the corner. She could hear hot oil spattering over an open flame.

"Bellots! Fresh bellots!" cried a fruit vendor, and Mahraveh considered buying one until she realized she had no coin. Everything she had with her in Latiapur now beat against the sharp, hard stone at the bottom of the Sea Door in the Caleef's throne room. Farhan had carried it all—a pouch bulging with coin. He was supposed to be taking care of her while they made their futile attempt to garner support for her father.

Now, she was alone.

Snakes don't live in packs, she reminded herself. She straightened her back and strode toward the bellot seller.

"Give me one and charge it to my father, Muskigo Ayerabi," she demanded in Saitjuese.

"Get out of her, girl!" the man shooed.

She reached up and pulled back her collar, revealing her tattoo fully. The man stared at it for a moment, then laughed.

"Can't charge anything to a dead man," he said.

"Muskigo Ayerabi is the most fearsome afhem in all the Black Sands," Mahi said. "When he returns, you will wish you'd taken up arms in his defense."

"And join all those fools like my brother who ran off to die beside him? Go back to your pond, girl."

Mahraveh glared at him. Back home, she would've never been talked to in such a manner. Before Winde Port went so horribly wrong, her father was a legend amongst the people. It was how he raised such an army of commoners and lesser afhems to march west. He was the man who'd stood against Babrak and impossible odds in a feud to claim Mahi's mother, and won, who'd battled in the arena to take his name without suffering so much as a scratch. An unbeatable warrior and master of the black fist.

How quickly the tides had changed now that he'd lost.

"I'll tell you what, girl," the trader said when she didn't budge. "Take a token for your loss and for the man your father used to be until he brought pain to so many."

He reached below the stand and pulled out a bellot, more brown than yellow. He then took a cleaver and chopped it in half, then quarters, before holding out one of the slices for Mahraveh.

"He's not dead," Mahraveh said defiantly, then looked down at the fruit. She thought about refusing it out of principle, but her stomach outargued her pride. Snatching it, she turned back toward the crowd.

"Don't worry," the man said, causing her to look back. "The Ayerabi afhemate will soon pass on to a more worthy warrior. It'll be nice to have another contest soon. Good for business! In the meantime, there's plenty of work in the brothels for orphan daughters like you."

Mahraveh felt her jaw tighten and the red return to her eyes, but just as she was about to respond, a hand touched her shoulder. Like his hand, the man's face was as gentle as the waters of the Saujibar oasis. Serene, calming, peaceful. And his tattoo was the same as hers.

"Let it go, Mahi," he said. "The fool speaks only from the lies the other frightened afhems spin."

"Jumaat, what are you doing here?" she asked.

"Saving you from a rotten meal it seems?" He pointed at the discolored bellot. "Put that down. I will buy you something more fitting for someone of your station."

"Salted fish?" she asked.

He bowed. "Whatever you desire, Lady Ayerabi."

"Stop that," she said with a hand wave.

She followed him to the other end of the market. Jumaat had moved to her father's afhemate a few years back after a particularly destructive sandstorm season claimed his parents' home in Avassu. His parents said they wanted to live a slower life, but the way Jumaat's father followed Muskigo around, Mahraveh knew it was more. Lucky for him, it was just a couple ten-days before his first hunt—where the men are taken into the dunes to prove their worth. Should they return alive, they are branded. Had they waited, he would forever bear the mark of a traitor—like his parents.

Her father's influence had grown with the common people throughout the Black Sands. She knew it was part of why the other afhems resented him. They were the sons and followers of men who'd bravely fought and lost to the Glass Kingdom. Happy to serve and respect their conquerors, as if what Liam did was some everyday feud between afhems. They gave her people a bad name—the scared, fat, cowards.

Mahraveh couldn't help but feel sickened by all those going about their lives like nothing was wrong. Her father had spent her entire life telling her how they needed to become stronger to prove to the Glass they weren't to be ruled over. He thought he'd inspire the whole region in taking Winde Port, but when it burned to the ground with so many Shesaitju warriors inside, all that progress died.

"Come, let us talk somewhere more private," Jumaat said, stirring her from her thoughts. He held two servings of salted fish and flatbread.

Mahraveh nodded, but not before snagging her share and taking a bite. She licked a salt crystal from her lips. It was delicious. If only her once-mighty people fought as well as they cooked.

Jumaat led her through the winding streets while they ate. She saw him eyeing her, and she flicked her dreadlocks over her narrow shoulder. "Did you follow me here?"

"Follow you?" he said. "I didn't even know you were here. It is typhoon season, remember? That means nigh'jels aplenty, stirred from the depths where their light is most needed."

"I'm still unsure why we can't breed them in the oasis."

"They require salt waters—if we could, we would not be able to drink from the pool. A fair trade, I'd say."

"Here for trade… you sure that's all?" Mahraveh lowered her chin slightly, looking up at him playfully.

"I swear it on the sand and sea." He grinned impishly. She nudged him in the side, then brought another bite to her lips.

"How are your parents?" she asked, mouth still full.

"Mother is fine. My father, same as yours," Jumaat said. His smile made the words go down easier. Mahraveh had forgotten that his father marched with hers. Otherwise, he wouldn't be in Latiapur fetching nigh'jels. Jumaat hadn't yet reached his sixteenth year so he couldn't join them. But an afhemate's strength was more than it's warriors; it took everyone.

"Let me guess, you are planning to go back with Farhan to help your father or something insane, like always?" Jumaat said.

"I... Farhan is dead," she blurted out.

Jumaat stopped. "What?"

"Farhan," she said. "Afhem Babrak Trisps'i killed him. Threw him straight through the Sea Door."

"That is not... How could he? There is no way the others will be okay with it."

Mahraveh took another bite of her meal, surprised she still had an appetite. But that was the thing about growing up in the Black Sands. Death was all around. It was part of life, not just the end of it. She knew Farhan's spirit would be caught upon the eternal current of the sand and sea.

"They were fine with it," she said after swallowing. "It was technically self-defense."

"Farhan attacked Babrak? What was he thinking? Babrak is more zhulong than man; he's an animal."

The thought of the big man made her stomach flip more than the thought of poor Farhan. "He was defending my honor."

Jumaat's face scrunched and his eyes slid shut. He reached out with both arms and took her by the shoulders. Mahraveh flinched.

"I'm sorry," they both said at the same time.

Jumaat reeled his hands back. "I should not have been so presumptuous," he said.

"No, it's okay. I've just had a traumatic day."

It was then that Jumaat must have noticed the bruise on her

cheek. He stretched his hand out, slower this time, and brushed her face. "He hit you?"

"Hit me. Shoved me. You said it; he's an animal."

"That no good son of a zhulong shog shoveler!" Jumaat's hands squeezed into fists.

Mahraveh grasped his wrist. "There's nothing either of us can do about it now."

"Well, we will see how tough he is."

Mahi raised an eyebrow. "*We?*"

"Of course. What could you possibly do without the fearsome Jumaat!" He stuck out his chest and, considering how stringy the young son of a nigh'jel trader was, Mahi couldn't help but chuckle. He laughed with her. He had a knack for making the world seem brighter.

He wiped his lips. "Are you full?" he asked. "Would you like more?"

"I'm fine," Mahraveh answered. "I really should get going. My father's symbol is not as welcome here as it once was."

"I could go with you. I just need some time to gather my shipment. We could travel together. It would be safer. After we drop off the nigh'jels to my mother, I could go with you. Wherever you're going. Nahanab. Brekliodad even. Anywhere in the world."

"That's sweet," she said, probably blushing. "But really, I'm okay. I need time to think."

"Nonsense. We will travel together. Your father would kill me if he knew I let you travel the dunes alone. My father's taught me a bit about how to handle a sword too, you know."

Mahraveh began to formulate an argument, but Jumaat said, "Just let me be the gentleman for once. I know I am not Farhan. Not in looks nor in strength, but I am your loyal friend… always. Plus, I would appreciate the company on the trip home."

Although he might've been right about not having Farhan's

strength, Mahi had always found Jumaat handsome. In a town known for fearsome warriors, he was something different. There was warmth and kindness in his eyes. He'd have to fight one day, as all Shesaitju men did. She only hoped that their occasional sparring sessions back home would prepare him for what it meant to be a man.

"Fine," she said. "Only so you're not lonely. But why don't we let me handle the sword."

"Deal," he said, laughing. "It should not take me long at the shore. Do you have Honey here?"

Mahraveh's zhulong Honey, named for her creamy, golden coloring, wasn't the biggest zhulong, but she was the toughest. "Always. She's tied up at the hub."

"Get her and meet me at the north gates at dusk. If we start off later, we can avoid more of the hot sun. I will see you soon."

He took her hand as if to kiss it, released it first, and bowed awkwardly. Mahraveh smirked as he then took off toward the shore.

She would have a couple of hours before midday and nothing to do in the city. She'd heard so many stories of the capital, and it wasn't terribly far from Saujibar, but now that she was older, this was her chance to see it; really see it.

Latiapur was an ancient beauty. Older than any city in Pantego, except perhaps Glinthaven's capital city of Myen Elnoir or the mysterious Brekliodad. It stood the test of time and only became more beautiful with age. Most buildings were short and squat, made from hardened black clay and blackwood, but just off the coast—the cove—stood an edifice it seemed only giants could have erected.

The Tal'du Dromesh.

The blood of countless Shesaitju warriors had stained its hallowed sand.

Mahi stared at the incredible structure, which sunk from

where she stood to the rocky coast of Latiapur. It curled into the cove—the grand arena. Her ancestors had long ago piled stone to build a dam against the sea and carved stands into the natural cliffsides surrounding a pit filled with sand. Sea-water and coral seeped in along the edges. Caverns sunk into the sides and led to the undercroft, impossible to tell whether they were natural or manmade.

Alternating levels bore golden statues of fierce zhulong. Nigh'jel lanterns hung at intervals in the arches sculpted into the tops of each cliff, then built up with black sandstone above them. The lanterns were nothing like the ones Jumaat's family sold— these were massive globes filled with water and dozens of the creatures in each. They cast a tremendous amount of light, even in midday.

"Incredible sight, isn't it?"

The salted fish floated back up to Mahraveh's throat. Babrak stood beside her, arms crossed over his bare, tattooed chest.

"How dare you speak to me after what you did!" Mahraveh turned to him. Her nails pressed into her palms and she squeezed her fists. It took all her willpower not to charge him.

"You will be the one who watches how you speak, girl," he said, leaning in. His rotting teeth were inches from her face. "When your father fails—and he will—and the Caleef returns, your precious oasis will be offered up in that hallowed arena and you along with it."

"You're sick," Mahraveh said.

When an afhem died without a living male heir, the afhemate tournaments were held where a warrior presented by each afhem would fight to claim the leaderless afhemate as their own.

That was where her father had supposedly earned his nick-name "the Scythe." Caleef Sidar Rakun held such a tournament during King Liam's birthday after the conquering they called an alliance was complete. Warriors presented from all over the south fought, but Muskigo, much younger then, stepped into the sands as well.

King Liam watched as her father sliced down ten men in the final round with nothing but his scimitar to claim the name of Ayerabi. It was said her father then looked up at him, pointed his blade and said, "You're next, my king." Liam supposedly laughed in adoration of his fire. It didn't take long for warriors and travelers to flock to Muskigo's side, and—like Jumaat's parents had—abandon their afhemates for his.

"I believe you'll come to appreciate my…" Babrak yanked her in close, her arms touching his sweaty stomach, "…power."

"My father will return, and he will make you eat your own manhood—if you even have one," Mahraveh said. "Perhaps that's why my mother chose him."

"It won't be long until you know for sure," Babrak said, wearing that same smile he'd shown her in the throne room. "Be careful, little sand mouse; the snakes lurk beneath the dunes."

Despite the heat, an icy chill washed over her. The nickname only made her think of her father and bolster her resolve. Babrak let her go.

She rubbed at her wrists where his sweaty palms had just been.

"Soon, the battle for Afhem Awn'al al-Tariq's land and horde of ships will begin. I wonder, with Farhan gone, who will your father have stand? Perhaps that skinny, trader's son who follows you like a dog."

"Don't you dare speak of him," Mahraveh spat.

"A shame. Whoever it is, they don't stand a chance." He nodded to the towering, stack of muscle behind him. A single strand of dreaded hair draped down from the back of his head to below his waist. Boiled zhulong-hide armor covered his torso and one side of his neck, the other remained revealed to proudly display the mark of the Trisps'I Afhemate. "Rajeev has been training all of his life to claim an afhemate. He won't fail."

"Will you then turn your back on him like you did my father?" Long before Mahi was born, Muskigo fought under the mark of the Trisps'i before being entered to compete in the Tal'du Dromesh by Babrak himself. The fat afhem couldn't handle being outshined after his great victory.

"Unlike your father, he knows his place." He forced a bow and walked away before Mahraveh gathered thoughts enough to respond.

She hadn't the opportunity in her life to meet many people to loathe, but she did him. She'd encountered him a few times back home, and with her father around, he'd behaved. Now he strutted around Latiapur like a king. The bad taste in her mouth from the throne room which Jumaat helped alleviate returned in full force.

She made her way to the bluffs adjacent to the palace so she could get some fresh air. A path led down to a promontory over-looking the Boiling Waters. To the north, she could see the sands of the Tal'du Dromesh, tiny dots of warriors training upon them. Even so high up, salt sprayed her as the waves crashed into the rocks. She found it refreshing. And even though the waters were violent, the sound was rhythmic. Relaxing.

Gulls cawed overhead, singers in this melody of the sea. She closed her eyes, and for the first time in a while, tried to think of something besides her father and how she couldn't do anything to help him. If she'd been born a man, maybe the fools in the palace might have listened to her. Perhaps she'd have an army of her own.

But she wasn't, and she didn't. Babrak was right: her father had no sons, nor wives to bear them. When Mahi was very young, the mother he'd fought for died at the venomous bite of a sand snake, and Muskigo vowed to take on no other wives, instead, dedicating himself to Mahi and the sword.

Look where that got you, Father, she thought.

She opened her eyes and sighed. Trying to force herself not to think of him only made her do it more. Instead, she sat quietly and let her mind take her where it may, just like how the waves rose and fell. She watched the sun glitter over the foaming crests until the color grew reddish from dusk. A few times, her mind even cleared of worry, but the vision of Farhan careening over the lip of the Sea Door kept returning.

Squeezing her eyes tight, as if forcing the thoughts away, she turned her head, opened them again, and glanced down at the shore where tiny men and women rushed around on floating platforms, loading and unloading things from large ships. She wondered if Jumaat was down there still, but she couldn't tell from such a distance.

Finally, she stood. Jumaat had said dusk. It was time to meet him and see where the winds would blow. It was clear she couldn't accomplish anything waiting around in Latiapur. She needed to do something herself.

"I'll find a way to help, Father," she said to the sea. "Just keep holding out."

The rain that had been threatening all afternoon began in true force. She headed down from the bluff, across the bazaar, and found herself staring at the Tal'du Dromesh once more.

If she'd had her own army, she could help her father. If only they'd allowed women to fight. The thought of Jumaat battling within and losing his head to Babrak's huge hands gave her a shudder. But he wasn't old enough, regardless.

She turned away from the arched upper level of the arena to the stable where she'd left Honey. As she moved toward the zhulong, the stable master glanced over, no doubt anxious for coin.

"We've gotta make this quick," she whispered to Honey. Keeping an eye on the stable master, she slowly untied the zhulong, patting her on the neck. The stable master looked away for a moment, and she wasted no time hopping on and spurring Honey into a gallop.

"Come back here!" the man screamed, taking up the chase but ducking back inside as the rain poured over him. "Thief!"

"Bill my father!" she cried back. "He'll be back." Then she whispered to herself, "I hope."

IX

THE MYSTIC

Sora felt the sway and rushing wind. She felt the heat of flames and heard the crackling of wood being devoured. She smelled the salty air and acrid smoke. As her corporeal senses began speaking to her again, she listened to the death cries. For a moment, she thought she was back in Troborough on that fateful day when everything she had became lost to her, and she chased after Whitney Fierstown. An act she didn't regret as much as she knew she should. There was nobody else in Pantego she wanted to see.

But as her vision sharpened, she saw the chaos for what it was. Blood spattered in a wide arc as a blade clenched in her own grip lashed out before her eyes. She heard a laugh that didn't belong to her but sounded just like her.

"Nesilia! Stop this!" she shouted.

"The fun has just begun!" Nesilia replied.

"I've never seen ye this way, Sora," said a gruff voice next to her. Sora's head turned, and she found herself staring at Gold Grin, skewering his own Glass soldier with his gilded scimitar. "I like it!"

"Well, I did promise you wealth beyond your wildest dreams, pirate, did I not?"

"Ye did!" Gold Grin chortled as he ripped his sword free and parried the attack of another Glassman. "But that's only for me men. Only riches I need are under the covers." He grabbed the attacker's spear, snapped it at the shaft and drew a long gash across the soldier's neck.

If Sora could've cried, she would have right there, standing aboard the *Reba's* deck, surrounded by the chaos and din of battle. Instead, her sword lashed out again, wreathed in magical fire. No matter what Sora did, she couldn't manage to control her own limbs.

Freydis, the Drav Cra warlock they'd recently taken on board, darted across the ship, her hand raised, face twisted with rage. Large chunks of ice erupted from her palms, slamming hard into armored soldiers. The shards exploded on impact, leaving devastation in their wake.

Sora's eyes regarded the headless soldier at her feet. She saw her own body, nearly naked, covered only by leaves and vines. They were woven into a beautiful, preternatural pattern, but she noticed, for the first time, how cold it was.

Sora suddenly found herself soaring through the air. Vines extended beneath her body, frigid wind burned against her flesh. In an instant, she stood at the top of the crow's nest looking down upon the *Reba*. Two Glass galleons bobbed in the water beside it, both on fire, both half sunk with their bows sticking up. Beyond that was the vast and frozen Drav Cra tundra. Sora had never seen the place before, but she was no fool. There was no mistaking the stark white of the land north of Winter's Thumb.

Below, Gold Grin stared up at her in disbelief. The distraction nearly caused him to be speared by a Glass longsword.

Sora's lips curled without her controlling them, and her hand stretched forward. She fought the impulse. Her muscles seared in pain as her arm shook from the internal battle.

"Would you let him die too?" Nesilia asked.

"I..."

The hesitation caused Sora's focus on blocking Nesilia's control to break. Her arm swept from side to side, and then a great gust of wind tore through the air, catching the ship's sails. The Glassmen were flung from the ship. Gold Grin and his crew tumbled safely to the deck, all but one who slipped off his perch and into the icy depths. Freydis flew off over the bow, but turned the spray of waves to ice, allowing her to climb back onto the *Reba* as if they were stairs.

Nesilia whispered, barely audible but she might as well have been screaming. "You are about to be part of something so much bigger than yourself, my dear Sora." Sora's arms spread out, embracing all of the Drav Cra from their perspective. "Welcome to your new world."

"Why are we here?" Sora asked, desperately trying to ignore the flailing arms of the drowning Glassmen surrounding them. "Nesilia, I won't give in."

"How long are we going to keep at this, girl?" the goddess said. "Aren't you growing weary?"

"Aren't you? Why don't you find a new body? Why not the warlock? I'm sure she would enjoy it."

"Strong as she is, she is but an insect compared to you."

"Just let me go!" The words exploded from Sora's physical lips. At the same time, she regained temporary control of her muscles. She jerked left, then plummeted off the crow's neck. In seconds, freezing water enveloped her, filling her mouth and lungs. It felt like a thousand tiny knives scraping her skin.

As she thrashed involuntarily, she realized that neither her nor Nesilia were in control. It was instinct; her body clawing for survival. She felt fear, not just her own, but an overwhelming, primordial sense of dread in every fiber of her possessed being. Nesilia was scared as well.

She's bound to my body, Sora discovered.

Sora felt all those years, buried beneath a mound of dirt at the bottom of Mount Lister. She experienced the helplessness of being bound by her very own creation. Anger welled up in her heart when her head popped out of the water.

"Foolish, girl!" Nesilia roared. The water rippled outward, separating itself from them until they floated within an air pocket. Sora had never seen anything like it. Her arms were extended, the magic of Elsewhere holding dark, churning seawater at bay. She could see the shadows of flailing legs from the soldiers within it; some already sinking like frozen stone dragged down by armor.

"You can't resist me," Nesilia said. By then, Sora had lost control of her limbs again and slowly, their air-pocket rose through the sea toward the surface.

"And you can't escape me, can you?" Sora said. Time had grown immaterial to her in the recesses of her own mind. It was neither like Pantego or Elsewhere, but for the first time in however long it had been, she felt a hint of satisfaction when Nesilia didn't reply to her.

Sora's body emerged from the waves. Freydis, Gold Grin, and all his crew stared over the edge, terrified.

"Aye, there!" Gold Grin shouted, pointing at Sora.

He ran for a rope, but Freydis shoved him aside. Five skinny vines sprouted from her fingertips, winding into one another as they draped off the ship and found Sora's hands. Then, without so much as a thought, Nesilia forced Sora to climb up them and over the hull.

The battle, pushing back the sea, fighting Sora, it was apparent now that Sora's mortal body limited even a goddess.

Gold Grin grabbed her by the shoulders and heaved her up.

"Sora, my dear, ye be all right?" He ran his hands through her hair and leaned in to plant a kiss on her.

"Get off me!" Nesilia barked. She threw him against the ship's mast so hard the wood cracked.

Ignoring everything else around her, she stormed into the ship's cabin. The darkness enveloped her until she thrust out her hand and a fire erupted in Gold Grin's hearth. The icy water steamed off her flesh. But as she leaned against the wall to draw a deep breath, her limbs started to shiver from the cold and Sora felt fire burning on the inside of her now.

"I'm buried, but not forgotten," Sora said to Nesilia within, taking note of how mortal a thing it was to shiver. "Whitney and—"

"Will never see you again!" Nesilia snapped. She banged on the wall, and a chunk of wood cracked off. "Make no mistake, Sora. Fight me as long as you want. Resist if you must. But time forgets everyone."

Sora tried to respond, but she felt the familiar sense of being pushed back down. Only this time Nesilia worked harder to do it. The color drained from Sora's surroundings, and it was like hands wrapped her throat as she was buried beneath an avalanche of darkness, struggling to breathe.

X

THE KNIGHT

"Sir Unger, there you are!" Pi exclaimed. Torsten heard tiny feet patter across the floor, then felt the boy's skinny arms around his waist.

Torsten rustled his hand through Pi's long hair, feeling the sharp points of the Glass Crown atop his head. He still felt strange every time Pi embraced him, but the young king had taken a liking to him ever since being freed from the Buried Goddess' influence.

Torsten never knew him as an exuberant child eager to learn, though Sir Uriah always used to describe him that way. The boy Torsten knew was first a hermit whispering wickedness in the dark, then a dour, ruthless soul—Redstar's puppet. Torsten's last visual memory of Pi was him levitating in the air under the dark magic's influence.

It seemed now his rebirth was finally complete, but it would take Torsten longer than these past weeks to trust it. He prayed nightly to Iam that it was true, then wondered if his God even listened any longer. Torsten allowed evil—which led to so much despair—onto their doorstep. He couldn't help but feel that the church's inability to agree on a new High Priest was partly his fault.

"I read about my father's battle at Latiapur today," Pi said, pulling away. "Is it true; was there truly a cavalry of ten thousand zhulong under the command of the Afhem Babrak there?"

Torsten shook away the raw feelings. "Of course it is, Your Grace. I was there." He smirked. "Maybe only nine thousand. But your father was smart. He knew we couldn't charge a force like that, led by one of their more powerful and experienced afhemates. And our ships in the Boiling Waters had been repeatedly repelled by their superior naval experience. But you would be remiss to forget that because of that day, there's a new Afhem Babrak."

"But I thought you said they only respect strength?"

"Strength in victory. Not stupidity. Do you know what it takes to feed a herd like that? We retreated, and feinted, spending months cutting away their supplies until the larger of the beasts were too starved to remain obedient. Mounted archers picked away at their forces, our ship's continued to sting their fleet and keep it distracted, and only once they were weak enough did we charge by land. It was the lengthiest, most expensive campaign Liam ever led, but it earned the respect of the Babrak Afhemate. Their leader accepted his defeat, and his son took over, having borne witness to our abilities."

"The scrolls said their afhem was executed?" Pi asked.

Torsten nodded. He remembered that day under the beating sun when Uriah parted the man's head from his shoulders. Many afhems joined him in surrender, including the Ayerabi afhemate, which Muskigo would go on to claim in their Tal'du Dromesh after its leader took his own life in shame."

"In an arena battle?" Pi said, incredulous.

"That is their way," Torsten said. "When an afhem fails in such grandeur, their life is forfeit, and their afhemate handed either to a surviving son of proper age and ability or the winner of their sacred tournaments."

"Like the jousts father used to host?" Pi asked.

"I believe he got the idea from them. Only the Shesaitju prize is more than mere renown—theirs is wealth and the loyalty of an army."

"An entire army?"

"Depends on the name. They are a strange people, my King. But we must study our enemies if we ever hope to defeat them."

"I thought only some of them are our enemy?" Pi asked innocently.

"But we must study our allies as well. Seasons change, as do allegiances. Leaders pass on, and sometimes their descendants forget what is best for their people."

"I'll never forget."

"I hope not," Torsten said. "Now, come. Enough questions. Let us see what *our* people want from their Crown." Torsten extended his cane to find the nearest bundled column bearing the weight of the high, vaulted ceiling and the glass spire. From there, he figured out his position and followed the footsteps of the young king toward the throne.

Liam was often too busy to hold public court, where any soul from the kingdom could stand before the Glass Crown and beseech their monarch. His wars to unite Pantego took up much of everyone's time. In his later years, as his health declined, he avoided being seen altogether. For a time, Queen Oleander would receive guests, dignitaries, and representatives from all walks of life, but her ruling was harsh as the tundra from whence she came, and soon, it stopped altogether.

Presently, Oleander had surprised Torsten with the idea to have Pi hold court weekly, building his rapport with the people. She'd hated it so—dealing with the "rabble" as she once called them—but the kingdom knew Pi only as the Miracle Prince and then Cursed King, not as the young, capable boy he seemed. Torsten didn't know him either, and was coming to find that, while he wasn't Liam, neither was he dull, or ordinary.

"Is mother coming?" Pi asked as he plopped down on the Glass Throne, then slid back on the oversized chair.

"No, she still needs rest," Torsten said. He found the groove of the dais and stepped up, then made his way around the throne, careful not to stand beside it, but slightly behind. No mere Shieldsman should have been permitted so high, only the Wearer of White, but Pi insisted when he'd named him his newly-created position of Master of Warfare—the chief military advisor. Torsten could do nothing but accept the will of his king.

"Will she ever stop resting?" Pi asked.

"She's lucky to be alive, Your Grace."

The doors at their backs creaked open. Torsten heard a few members of the Royal Council shuffle in. Then the clanking of armor as Shieldsmen formed an arc around the rear of the throne, and Glass soldiers lined the hall.

"Do you really remember nothing of what happened atop Mount Lister?" Torsten asked, keeping his voice low. Pi didn't respond, but Torsten heard the boy's collar brush against his chest. "I can't see your head movements, Your Grace."

"No," he said. "It's like I told mother: everything since uncle Redstar came to my room so long ago is… it's like a dream. I remember the color red, then darkness, then light again… snow… it's all—"

"It's okay, Your Grace. All that matters is you're here with us now."

Pi grew somber any time those dark days were revisited. Torsten couldn't imagine what it would be like to have endured so much and remembered so little. At first, he thought Pi was blocking the memories, but the Buried Goddess' curse clearly ran deep.

Perhaps it would be better for him not to remember in detail what it was like to leap from a balcony or wake up in a grave. Or how he'd instigated Muskigo's sacking of Winde Port and allowed Redstar to usurp the kingdom. One day, Pi would figure it all out, but for now, while he learned what it meant to be king, Torsten and Oleander told him they'd made those decisions together. Peace of mind was the least they could offer for how they'd failed him.

The doors of the Throne Room swung open, echoing as they banged against the inner wall on their way around. Torsten turned his head to try and better hear who was coming through. No armor clanking toward the throne was always a good thing.

"A Sister from the Hornsheim Convent," Caspar Brosch, the Master of Rolls, whispered in Torsten's ear.

Torsten nodded. By law, Lucas wasn't permitted beside the Glass Throne to help him. Pi would, however, probably have allowed it had he asked, but Torsten wanted to appear strong at the boy's side in so hallowed a place.

As the sister grew nearer, he could smell the familiar scent of charred pine on her. Hornsheim was nestled in the frigid North-lands overlooking the Yevet Cove. It was there that priests took their vows of sightlessness, and that monks and sisters offered their service to Iam's holy church. For sixty years, Wren had served as High Priest, long enough to have crowned Liam himself beneath the Eye of Iam.

Now it was time for a new one, and all the priests in the kingdom were locked in Hornsheim for the sacred selection. And they wouldn't leave until a majority settled on their next High Priest, when it was clear Iam showed them the proper path. Considering all the recent troubles and the rise of the cult of Nesilia, a decision was taking longer than usual. Priests from all over Pantego felt they knew what was right, what was needed.

Torsten knew that without a High Priest, decisions came

slower, with less conviction, and the people who'd come to fear so much would start to question. Freydis' execution was made public to distract the people—a decision which backfired. Every day that a sister or a monk showed up without news, full recovery from Redstar's betrayal was delayed.

"Your Grace," the sister said. "My Lords. I have come to inform you that a decision has yet to be made."

A chorus of groans sounded behind Torsten.

"Are they any closer to a verdict?" Pi asked. For a boy not even yet in his teens, he had remarkable self-control and aplomb in smaller settings, not to mention the vocabulary of a scholar— nothing like the possessed version of him, prone to lashing out after long bouts of silence.

"It appears not, Your Grace," she said. "At this period of great consequence, there is much deliberation."

"A king should not sit upon this throne without the full support of the Church of Iam," spoke Lord Kaviel Jolly. "Especially one so young."

"Wren the Holy served for a long time," the sister explained, "but he was in fine health. His passing was unexpected, and there is a great deal of concern over who might be—"

"What is your name, sister?" Torsten interrupted. He stepped forward.

"Nauriyal, sir," she answered.

"By your voice, I can tell you are young. I doubt there are many who yet live from the day Wren was chosen. But I hear he was young and unexpected, known to his flock for speaking bluntly. He arrived in Hornsheim to support another more renowned priest, and in speaking on that man's behalf, won over the entire convent."

"That is indeed what they say," Nauriyal agreed.

"They called it a miracle, same as they did the waking of our king. Can we not expect another? I fear this wait has to do with scared men deliberating, and not closing their minds and listening to Iam."

"Perhaps that is true, my Lord. It is not my place to say. I merely deliver the news."

"The people grow anxious without the priests to offer morning Light," Pi said. "That warlock's escape reminded them of their fear. I agree with my Council. Please, ride back and inform the clergy that a decision must be made soon for the sake of our kingdom."

"I will try, but the affairs of Iam cannot be rushed," Nauriyal said.

"Or are these more of the Darkings' games?" Lord Kaviel Jolly remarked.

Torsten heard the breath catch in the sister's throat.

"What do you mean, Lord Jolly?" Torsten questioned.

"I recognize the sister here from a trade meeting with the traitor's son, Bartholomew. I'd remember a face like hers even with her head shaved as it is. She is the granddaughter of Yuri Darkings, the bastard who murdered my son!"

Murmurs of disbelief broke out behind Torsten. He couldn't tell who from.

"Those who take the cloth forsake their names, you all know that," Torsten pronounced, raising his hand to instill silence.

"She might know what her father did with the Caleef," someone blurted out. Much of the Royal Council was new to Torsten, so he couldn't identify all of them merely by the sound of their voices, especially not while in a group.

While men argued, Torsten heard Nauriyal slide closer to the throne. "Your Grace," she addressed Pi, "my father, Bartholomew, banished me to Hornsheim before all of the horrible things they did, all because I helped a lost soul when he wouldn't. I have not spoken with them since, and I don't plan to again. My faith is in Iam alone."

Pi took a few seconds, then replied, soft and gently, "I believe you. If we ever hope to find the Light again, we must all learn to trust each other once more. Return to Hornsheim with word of our urgency. And do not worry. We will find the traitors in your family, and they will pay for everything. For now, be glad you left that vile name behind you. Darkings no more, Daughter of the Light."

"Thank you, Your Grace. Many speak of the miracle that is your life, but not of your kindness."

Torsten heard the soft pucker of her kissing the foot of the throne, then she shuffled out of the room. Another week, another lack of decision.

At least this one came with some excitement.

"Why do they not just send a galler if their news is no news at all?" asked a voice that sounded as if it could have been Caspar Brosch.

"I figured she vanished with the rest of their house," Lord Kaviel said ignoring the first. "Your Grace, your leniency is welcome, but could we not use her to expose them? It's the least they deserve."

"If they sent her off to Hornsheim, they either did so out of bitterness or protection from their devious plans," Torsten said.

"You were there, Sir Unger, when her family betrayed us all," Jolly said. "Murdered my brother in cold blood. Who knows what they were up to."

"If we punished every child for the sins of their father, we'd all be dead. The Darkingses will pay when the Shesaitju fall, but young Nauriyal's fate is out of our hands now. She's made her choice to serve Iam, as they have made theirs to forsake him."

Bastards and disappointing daughters were sent off to Hornsheim to serve as sisters and monks all the time, leaving their houses and their loyalties behind. As much as Torsten may have wanted justice for all those the Darkings family had wronged, including himself, maintaining a tight bond with the church of Iam was in the Crown's best interest.

"Sir Unger is right," Pi said. "My father fostered harmony with the church of Iam throughout his rule. I will do the same."

"As you wish," Lord Kaviel said, and Torsten couldn't mistake the bitterness in his tone. Men from Crowfall grew up hard and distrusting; being in the shadow of murderous Drav Cra raiders and greedy dwarves was bound to have that effect. Another time he might have scolded the new Master of Ships for his attitude, but he knew they needed men like him during this great transition. His experience defending against Drav Cra longboats at Winter's Thumb made him invaluable.

"A just cause, Your Grace." This time, Torsten was sure the voice belonged to the Master of Rolls, Caspar Brosch.

There was a shuffling movement behind him as a door squeaked open. After several whispered exchanges, Lord Kaviel Jolly said, "Your Grace, if I might be excused. We've just received word that two Glass galleons went down near Ice Deep."

"Drav Cra?" Torsten demanded.

"I shall report back when we are sure it was the result of an attack and not just an unfortunate accident with icebergs, Master Unger."

Torsten still wasn't used to being called Master, and he didn't like it.

"Thank you, Lord Kaviel. You're dismissed. Sir Unger can accompany you if needed."

"My place is here until we have more information, Your Grace. Let us continue." Torsten said.

Waving in the direction of the great doors, Torsten beckoned forward the next guest of the Crown. His muscles tensed involuntarily every time. He knew guards and Shieldsmen surrounded them, but he was trained to be ready in defense of his king. The boy's age hardly mattered; he was king and Liam's heir.

Torsten had a knack for spotting untrustworthy visitors—at least, he thought he so when spotting could still be done with his eyes. But then there was the Darkings debacle.

Feet shuffling across the marble floor tore Torsten from his thoughts. Knees slid. "Your Grace," a withered old voice said. "My name is Murray, and I'm here on behalf of the South Corner. My baby boy was murdered, and my wife scarred by the cultists who ran rampant this Dawning past."

"You have my eternal condolences," Pi interrupted. "In the name of Iam and all the former kings of Glass, we will make those monsters pay more than they already have."

"Thank ye, Grace," Murray said. "But I'm here to request only that the Crown send more builders to help with repairs. Winter breaks, but there are still so many without beds to sleep in."

"Between the war in the South, repairing Winde Port, driving back Drav Cra raiders, and the selection of a new High Priest, the Crown's resources are drawn thin, sir," said the new Master of Masons after Pi allowed some time to pass in silence. Young Lord Leuvero Messier was the son of the governor of Westvale, who'd returned just in time from an apprenticeship with dwarves to be named to the post.

"The Young Master of Masons is correct," Torsten said. "Until the South is returned to order, income from trade has slowed considerably. We will do what we can to help fix South Corner, but for now, that is all we can do."

"I'd ask that ye'd please consider more," Murray implored. "We are yer people too, Grace, and it was *ye* who invited the Drav Cra here. Who gave the cultists power and—"

"You dare speak to your king in such a manner?" one of the Council spat. "I suggest that you leave before you get yourself hanged."

"I… I meant no offense," Murray stammered. "It is merely the truth. Please, Grace—"

"The Lord is right," Torsten said, embarrassed he knew not which. "I assure you that South Corner does not go forgotten. You have our sympathies for your family, but we are doing all we can."

"Well, do more!" Murray barked, and Torsten heard the sudden clatter of armor. Then the gasp as the pommel of a sword struck the man in the gut. "Ye brought the devils here!" he screamed as he was carried away. "They took everything!" His enraged shouting echoed out into the greeting hall.

"He's right, Torsten," Pi whispered after a brief period of silence, voice cracking slightly.

"You were not *you* when Redstar came," Torsten assured, leaning in toward his king's ear. "None of us were. He twisted and cursed these lands like his own playground. But he's gone now."

"What he did will never be gone…"

"It will, Your Grace. Magic can be a wretched thing, but your father survived all the attempts of the Eastern mystics to unravel this kingdom before their own people turned on them. So shall we."

Torsten waved again toward the doors. One by one, dozens more citizens of the kingdom arrived. More displaced people from South Corner and witnesses of Freydis' magic, fearing for their lives. People came asking about war or the Church of Iam or for Pi to settle a meager dispute between traders. Lucas Danvel's father even showed up over the stolen shipment of flour. Unfortunately, there was no proving that the rival he'd indicated was behind it. Crime festered in the district with so many homeless—and starving people were known to turn to crime to survive. All Torsten could do was offer his personal apologies.

Then came the raving loons—more of them than anything, as usual.

Dwarves from a Northwestern trading post arrived, suffering from the Drav Cra presence wherein protection was an arrangement Liam had established long ago. A diplomat from Glinthaven as well, the small province north of Panping from where Torsten's worthless parents had hailed, which had long ago bowed to Liam without a fight. Their duke sought to renegotiate their rate of taxation. Pi wisely requested they wait until a new Master of Coin was appointed. Torsten and others agreed.

Eventually, the flow of visitors slowed to a trickle. A few more angry citizens were hauled away, but getting through court without anyone hanged or sent to the dungeons was a success. Oleander rarely had such successful days when she'd received guests. And Liam seldom lasted so long before he was drawn back to the practice grounds or Shield Hall to study war strategy.

None were complaints that indeed required the Crown's involvement, but Torsten knew it was necessary for the people to see Pi as more than a legend, especially since he couldn't yet fight at their side. Maybe he never would. Torsten had yet to see any indication he possessed the heart of a warrior; he'd yet to even join a hunt as the cold thawed and animals stirred.

During what seemed to be the first prolonged period of silence they'd experienced all day, Torsten stretched out his sore legs and cracked his neck.

"Are we done yet?" Pi asked, exhaustion setting in.

"I think so, Your Grace," Torsten replied. "I know this isn't easy, but you are a natural. To think I ever doubted you—I deserve Iam's punishment for it. Your mother will be proud."

"She won't care."

Torsten was mid-response when the great doors creaked open once more. Murmurs from the Royal Council broke out as another guest arrived, and this time the soldiers lining the hall joined them.

Torsten heard the clack of his gold-topped cane first, then his name uttered from the mouths of the Yarrington-born men behind him. Valin Tehr had arrived, showing his face again. Tehr was selfish, cruel, ruthless—there weren't enough foul adjectives to describe the self-proclaimed King of Dockside. Unlike Redstar, though, he wasn't a deceiver. He wore the monster he was plainly on his sleeve.

"Who is that?" Pi asked as the clack of Valin's cane grew closer. The young king didn't sound as frightened as he should've been. Nobody knew for sure how Valin lost the use of his mangled leg, but legends abounded. Some said he was born a cripple, others that he sold a part of himself to demons for wealth, others still that it was ravaged in the underground fighting arena he supposedly operated.

All Torsten knew for sure was Valin never did anything for free. It was why he'd refused to acknowledge Valin's role in helping Rand help him publicly. Owing Valin Tehr was the last place anyone with power wanted to be. Torsten hadn't thought about him in a long time, the affairs of the Glass stealing his focus, but he'd seen first hand once how the man leveraged anyone he could.

"Your Grace," Valin said as he stopped. "I am Valin Tehr, a fair and loyal servant of the Crown hailing from Dockside." His district remained in shambles, yet he smelled like fresh lavender. Torsten was sure that he also likely wore a tunic fit for a prince.

"Bow before your king," Lord Messier demanded. If he were more familiar with Yarrington politics, the brash man would have sounded more cross.

"I could, but I would ask for you to consider allowing me to remain standing." He patted his gnarled excuse for a leg. "Going down is easy, but rising again isn't so simple a task for me these days." He laughed under his breath. False humility. False self-depreciation.

"I manage," Torsten said, unable to mask his venom.

"Ah, Sir Unger, I'd heard they found a new role for you advising the king," Valin said. "What was it, Master of Warfare? It's been too long since we've seen each… Ah, forgive my carelessness with words."

"Long enough," Torsten said, softly. "Now kneel before your king, or leave."

"That's all right, Sir Unger," Pi said. "I won't ask a crippled man to do anything more than bow."

"He is no cripp—"

"Thank you, Your Grace," Valin said, cutting Torsten off. "Your generosity knows no bounds. I'm glad to see the throne receiving our fair people again. Rumors said you weren't healthy, but I never believed them. I know better than most that looks mean very little in this cruel world."

"Why are you here, Valin?" Torsten questioned. "Don't you have your own throne to attend to?"

"Is that the thanks I get for instructing my man Codar to risk his life helping you in the square the other day? Vines growing through the streets like the arms of giants, was that how you intended the execution to go?"

Torsten breathed a sigh of relief when Valin referred to the square rather than Codar springing him from jail. The last thing he felt like dealing with was why Valin's role in the defeat of Redstar was kept quiet. Not even Oleander knew.

"Watch your tongue," Lord Messier said.

"I don't judge lack of trust for those outside this room," Valin said. "Not after everything. I am here, however, to offer help to the Crown."

"I think we can do without your brand of 'help,'" Torsten said.

"Let him speak, Master Unger," Pi said.

Torsten bit his lower lip to keep from snapping. Pi couldn't have known anything about the wretched lord of the Yarrington underworld. All he saw before him was a skinny cripple leaning on a cane, the same thing he probably saw when he regarded Torsten—an invalid. It was how Valin always got away with so much. Looking pathetic, and providing pathetic sinners with power was what they wanted.

Valin drew a deep breath, then said, "With so much trouble throughout the kingdom, the royal coffers wither. You needn't deny it. I know it to be true. Between rebellions, fires, and the traitorous Darkings family."

"We deny nothing," Torsten said. "And it has nothing to do with you."

"Am I not a fine, upstanding citizen of the Glass Kingdom?" His cane tapped as he paced before the throne. "Over the years, I have amassed a great fortune."

"Off the backs of the suffering." His rise to power coincided with Liam raising Torsten from South Corner, but Torsten had heard enough stories; dealt with enough poor saps who claimed to have been wronged by Valin. Somehow, the cockroach always skated by untouched. No evidence, no witnesses. He had the entire area under his thumb.

"Without me, Dockside would be a war zone," Valin said. "Especially now that the cultists had their way with it."

Torsten couldn't help but know that was true as well. Growing up, South Corner and especially its Dockside district were riddled with gangs openly warring over their turf. When bodies filled the streets, Valin and his cronies scared everyone straight.

"I'm not here to point fingers like some of those before me," Valin said. "I am here to offer solutions. I can offer Dockside and South Corner much, but the Crown owns all the land of Yarrington, and without your permission, I dare not overstep."

"Lord Tehr," Pi said. Torsten cringed at the title. The man was no lord, but Torsten couldn't help feeling proud of Pi for his diplomacy. "If you are worried that we will stand in the way of repairs, I assure you, I wish to see all of Yarrington prosper."

"I would expect nothing less from the miracle son of the great Liam Nothhelm, Your Grace. I am merely here to make a proposal which may further that goal."

Torsten cleared his throat, earning the room's attention. He reached out, searching for the arm of the throne, and when he found it, he leaned down to Pi's level. "Your Grace," he whispered. "Valin Tehr is not to be trusted. I advise you ignore any request he makes."

Silence greeted him, then Pi's tiny hand fell upon Torsten's. "Thank you for your wisdom, Master Unger," he said, "but would it hurt to listen? South Corner can't be any worse off."

"Your mother asked the same question before the last snake entered this castle. Redstar nearly ruined us."

"As you said, we cannot live in fear."

Torsten grumbled under his breath, then returned to his post. He could imagine Valin's sneer as he watched the exchange.

"Go on, Lord Tehr," Pi said.

"I would be honored if you would allow me to fund the restoration of South Corner personally," Valin said. "From Dockside to Province Avenue, excluding all churches of course. Iam has no need of gold."

"In exchange for what?" Torsten muttered.

"Excuse me, Shieldsman?" Valin said.

"Nothing from you comes without recompense, so what is it this time? A brothel for you in Old Yarrington? New whores from Panping for your Vineyard?"

"You think so lowly of me?" Valin feigned hurt. "There is worth to our little corner of Yarrington, as you know Sir Unger—or is it Master now? No bother… the last two Wearers of White, including yourself, hailed from there. As does the boy who I saw helping you around in the square when my man saved your life. So many from such a *worthless* place. Perhaps its time we treat South Corner with the care it deserves?"

"I'm not sure we can count Sir Langley as a Wearer," Master Amon Fenwick, Master of Husbandry remarked, "regardless of how he changed his ways before disappearing."

"Even so," Valin said, "a cleansing fire struck our humble home, and as fire helps replenish forest, so it does cities. I see no reason why the terror South Corner endured cannot lead to something… greater."

"Careful, Valin," Torsten said. "Talk like that might make me believe that you invited the cultists to riot. You do so enjoy blood sport, or so I hear."

Valin's cane clacked nearer, and Torsten's grip squeezed tighter around his own.

"I come, offering gold, and you dare insult me with such insinuations?" Valin asked.

"I'm sure Master Unger meant nothing by it," Pi scolded, sounding a bit too much like he had under Nesilia's influence.

Torsten remembered that he needed to stay on the king's good side to avoid another situation like Redstar. Possessed or not, he was evidently susceptible to manipulation, as any child would be.

"Of course not," Torsten replied. "So sorry, Your Grace."

"It has troubled me in my studies of this city, that our waterfront suffers from poverty and despair even though that is where our people first settled," Pi said. "To think, Autlas' Inlet… my ten-times great grandfather would roll in his grave if he could see the state we've allowed it to fall into.

"I could not agree more, Your Grace," Valin said. "I have lived there my entire life; nobody knows this better."

"Then I would be honored if you would help hasten the restoration of this city. The Crown will reimburse you when it is able. When a new Master of Coin is instituted, you may negotiate terms of interest."

More mumbling broke out from the Royal Council, no doubt amplified by the young King's eloquence on matters of coin.

Torsten's heart skipped a beat. He knew South Corner deserved better. When he'd become a Shieldsman, his heart's desire had always been to help the place. But that was before the entirety of the kingdom took precedence. Perhaps Valin Tehr kept the peace, even Sir Uriah Davies had once said as much, but Valin only helped prosper the things which filled his own pockets. He was a godless gold-monger.

Just then, the doors behind the throne opened once more.

"Ah, Master Jolly," King Pi said. "You've just missed Lord Tehr's generous offer to help rebuild South Corner and Dockside until such a time as the Crown can pay him back."

"You mistake my intentions, Your Grace," Valin said. "This is not a loan. I require no compensation for helping my home. I have spent a lifetime saving gold for a worthy cause. I can think of no better use for it."

The murmurs at Torsten's back turned positive. *Why wouldn't they?* The offer seemed too good to be true.

"Surely you want something, Valin?" Torsten said.

"Commoners don't grow wealthy throwing gold around," Lord Jolly said. Torsten didn't know the man well, but he was beginning to feel he had an ally on the council who shared certain points of view. He hoped there was a lot of Wardric in his fallen friend's brother.

"I'll admit, my businesses in Dockside struggle under these circumstances," Valin said, injecting a bit of solemnity into his tone. "But while I will survive, so many others won't—employees at my harbors or in my taverns."

"And brothel," Torsten added.

"Yes… people find pleasure however they will, it is not for me to judge. I have made many mistakes in my life as I'm sure every member of this esteemed council has. It is not too late to embrace Iam's light."

"How da—"

"Your proposal honors me," Pi said, raising his voice to quiet Torsten. "The Crown will be happy to work with you on the reparations of South Corner, and I will personally find a way to repay your generosity when our affairs are in order."

"The honor is all mine," Valin replied. "This is your city after all, and I am but a humble servant. I only feel that if we, your people, stand with the Crown with all our hearts in improving this great kingdom, what happened on this Dawning past will never happen again. Thank you, Your Grace, for all of this. A king shouldn't stay locked up behind stone walls, away from his people."

The sound of Valin's cane and footsteps distanced as he backed away.

"Is that all?" Torsten said knowing nothing with Valin came free. Even if he made Pi's agreement sound like charity, it was gold from Valin's own pocket that would be used. Torsten remembered the last time he'd owed the man a favor, a long time ago, and shuddered.

Valin stopped. "Come to think of it, there is one more thing."

"As I suspected."

"My eyes throughout the kingdom tell me that the Caleef was spotted heading south in a trading caravan."

There was a collective gasp.

"That's not the richest of it," Valin said. "He was accompanied by Bartholomew Darkings."

"Why didn't you tell us that earlier?" Lord Jolly snapped. Torsten would have asked the same if the news didn't rob the breath from his lungs.

"I'm telling you now," Valin calmly replied.

"Where were they last seen?" Torsten managed to say.

"East of the Jarein Gorge. The Shesaitju man they were with wore nothing, and so I cannot confirm if it truly was the Caleef. Avoiding all postings and the Drav Cra raiders now ravaging the

Wildlands under Drad Mak will have slowed their progress if it's really them. It's possible they might yet be found before reaching the Black Sands."

Torsten turned toward the throne. "Your Grace, I'm not sure I trust this man, but if that's true, we cannot hesitate. I will send gallers to Sir Nikserof and every fortress north of Nahanab and tell them to dispatch scouts to stop every carriage. If the Caleef reaches Latiapur, it might inspire more afhems to join Muskigo's rebellion."

"You may go, Sir Unger," Pi said. "And thank you Mister Tehr for this information."

Torsten used his cane to find his way down the dais. He knew the direction of the Shield Hall where he could privately disseminate orders by heart, but he wished he could move faster.

"Yes, thank you, Tehr," he said as he passed. "But next time you claim to uncover information like this, don't wait until you need something to tell us."

"My apologies, Sir Unger," Valin answered. "Secrets can be so harmful, as you know. With all the madness we're dealing with in Dockside, it slipped my mind. I do hope you find them posthaste. Farewell, Your Grace; my Lords."

Torsten reached a column and the side aisle, and then Lucas suddenly arrived to take his arm and guide him. He preferred moving on his own, and he also preferred trusting his sources of information. But there was no time to be picky.

Finding the Caleef could provide the last bit of leverage to end Muskigo's rebellion once and for all.

XI

THE THIEF

hitney brushed aside a strand of tangled branches. The light of Pantego's moons could barely pierce the thick canopy, leaving the world impossibly dark. Even the torch he held had difficulty casting light across the brush of the Webbed Woods.

"Of all the places to wind up," Whitney grumbled. He walked straight into a vine without seeing it. "Yig and shog!"

Shoving it out of the way, he went to pass, but the trees it draped between seemed to grow closer until Whitney was sideways, struggling to force his body through. He was about to curse but yelped instead when the vine slithered around his neck like a snake and squeezed.

He pawed at his hips for his daggers and found nothing. Then, he turned his attention to his throat. Digging his fingers under the thick vine, he tried to pry it loose but the more he did, the tighter it became. His feet lifted, and he kicked at the trees on either side, but his boots merely dragged along, peeling away dried bark.

"Help!" he cried, the air barely managing to squeeze through his crushed throat. Just then, Aquira swooped down and landed on his shoulder. "Help…" he rasped again. She stared straight into his eyes, screeched, then flew away.

Now his whole body thrashed. The world grew more and more dark as his air gave way, until he heard a familiar voice, all at once callous and welcoming.

"What are you doing up there, foolish thief?" Kazimir asked. A blade hummed through the air, slashing the vine.

Whitney fell from the canopy, screaming erratically, but before he knew it, he was on his back in the Troborough square. He searched from side to side, frantically patting his body and wondering how he wasn't a pile of shattered bones.

"I can't keep fixing all of your problems," Kazimir said.

Whitney flipped over and saw the white-haired upyr sitting on the edge of the well. He calmly gazed off into the sky, but there was no mistaking the shimmer of fresh blood dripping from his lips like cleaning it was too much of a bother.

"You?" Whitney gasped. "Are we—"

"Dead again?" Kazimir said. "You tell me."

"I…" Whitney stood and brushed off his pants. He was about to start cursing the upyr when he noticed how quiet Troborough was. The Twilight Manor didn't have a soul inside. Not a chimney in the town smoked. "It's different."

"Is it?" Kazimir lowered his gaze. "I hadn't noticed."

"What, did you do—devour them all this time?" Whitney asked.

"I suffered more than half-a-decade with you because I pushed the Sanguine Lords' patience. I take only what is meant for me now."

"Aren't you a special little goose?" Whitney scoffed, then made his way to the well and took a seat beside the man he'd never had any desire to befriend.

"So, you didn't get out?" Whitney asked.

"Didn't I?"

"Always riddles with you," Whitney complained.

"Eternity is relentless, Fierstown. An upyr never escapes. But I have seen that which cannot be mine. Have you?"

"What are you talking about?"

Kazimir's arm lashed out. Before his fingers touched Whitney, Aquira landed on his arm.

"Aquira!" Whitney exclaimed. "Come here, girl." He reached for her, but her curious eyes suddenly went fierce. She bit his hand before scurrying up Kazimir's arm. The upyr snatched her by the neck. She squealed and kicked, scratching Kazimir, whose wounds healed almost immediately.

"Let her go!" Whitney shouted. He too pounded on Kazimir's chest, but the impossibly strong upyr didn't budge.

"Do you really think you can still help her?" Kazimir asked. "That she's just waiting in that tower for you? She's gone, Whitney. You angered the wrong people, got yourself killed, and because of it, she's gone."

"I said, let her go!" Whitney shouted.

"You can't help her now. You can't help anybody."

"Stop!"

Kazimir squeezed, and Aquira stopped squirming. "What wasted potential." He sighed and tossed the wyverns limp body into the well. "You can't help her, Whitney. Nobody can."

"No!" Whitney screamed. He shoved Kazimir to the side and leaped headfirst into the well, falling, endlessly, without a splash.

———

"No!" Whitney screamed, lurching upright. Aquira was already awake, perched atop some crates and staring down at him and chirping. Sweat drenched Whitney's forehead as he caught his breath.

"Just a dream," he whispered. He went to crawl off his bedroll, and his palms landed in a shallow pool of water.

"What the—"

It wasn't sweat drenching his body. Massive drops of water splashed along his legs, then face until finally, Whitney woke up enough to understand.

"Gentry! Up! Up!"

"Huh?" the boy said, sitting up and rubbing his eyes. They went wide when he realized his hands were damp.

Whitney didn't wait. He snagged Aquira and sprang out of bed, then clutched Gentry by the arm and dragged him through calf-deep water toward the other side of the cellar.

"What's happening?" Gentry asked.

"That bastard forgot to mention his basement floods!" Whitney said. "I knew I should have taken him for everything he's got."

"Taken him?"

"Nothing," Whitney said. "We've got to move. Let's—"

An earsplitting *bang* sent them stumbling into the door. It frightened Aquira so much her claws dug into Whitney's shoulder hard enough to draw blood. The sound of wood splintering followed, like Torsten's heavy boots snapping the twigs that littered the floor of the Webbed Woods.

"Gentry!" Whitney grabbed the boy and fell back into the stairwell just in time to avoid being crushed by the collapsing cellar roof. Rain slashed in, and Whitney had a straight shot up through the heart of the inn, where a portion of the roof had been rent by a falling tree.

"C'mon!" Whitney yelled. He pulled Gentry up the stairs before more of the first floor split open to smash them like mashed potatoes. Whitney thought he heard screaming upstairs, but it could easily have been the susurrus of the wind. Gentry shouted something and even right next to the kid, Whitney had trouble hearing him.

"Just stay down, cover your head; it'll be over soon." Whitney wasn't at all sure that was true, but he had to say something.

A few steps up the staircase, another crash made them both duck and wince, as if that would help. Gentle sobs came from beside Whitney, and he felt Gentry's gyrations.

"You'll be fine," Whitney said, slowly putting his arm around the boy. Comforting others had never been his strong suit.

Gentry yelped as a wooden plank swept across the doorway above and slapped hard against the adjoining walls. "I don't want to die!"

"You're not going to die!" Whitney promised. "Keep it together!"

Whitney grabbed Gentry's arm again, but the boy dug in with his heels and refused to budge.

"We've got to go!" Whitney said.

"Go where?" Gentry said. "Up there? We'll die!"

"I have a good plan for how I'm going to die this time, and it isn't like this. Let's go!"

"This time?"

Aquira screeched on Whitney's shoulder before Whitney could answer and flew to the banister at the top of the staircase. Whitney used the distraction to drag Gentry up with him. When they reached the top of the stairs, rain pelted Whitney in the face.

"All right!" Whitney shouted. "On my mark, we make a break for the exit, okay?"

Gentry didn't respond.

"Okay?" Whitney repeated.

Finally, the kid nodded. Whitney clutched his arm tight, taking a few seconds to realize he was likely cutting off the boy's circulation. Watching as branches and mugs and anything else in the tavern flew by the doorway, it was impossible for him not to be terrified. Sure, he'd braved a storm or two at the tip of the Yevet Cove where they were worse than anywhere south of the Pikeback Mountains. And yes, he'd endured the Webbed Woods and Elsewhere, but he was no knight.

"Ready, Aquira?" he said, voice shaking. He swallowed the lump forming in his throat, then pulled his cloak up over his face and took off through the Grambling Inn. The rain whipping through the broken roof felt like tiny knives stinging any part of him left exposed. And the cold... even in spring, the water was frigid as Kazimir's sallow skin.

The inn's great hall was in shambles. Branches, tables, and ruptured floorboards covered the place. The barrels of ale behind the bar had all been overturned, cracked, and were leaking down through the portion of the floor that had collapsed into the cellar.

At least I'd have drowned drunk, Whitney thought to himself.

He hopped over a part of what he thought had once belonged to a chair. As he did, he felt Aquira's claws pry loose from his shoulders.

"Aquira!" he yelled. He lowered his cloak and spun around, but the rain beat against his eyelids, and he couldn't see anything. He tripped, skidding with Gentry into the bar.

Wood split like thunder and a ceiling beam came loose and swung down. Whitney didn't think. He grabbed Gentry and tossed him out of the way. Right before the beam knocked Whitney straight back to elsewhere, Aquira swooped in and unleashed a stream of magical fire. Ash coated Whitney as it vaporized the wood, but the inferno continued.

Even the rain couldn't squelch it before it reduced a pair of columns to ash. The second-floor walkway collapsed inward, a mess of charred wood and Whitney heard a patron of the inn shriek as the floor of her room joined it. The woman slid out through the door, crashed through a table, and the failing floor threatened to splatter her.

"Aquira, help her!" Whitney shouted.

The tip of the wyverns wing sliced Whitney's neck just below his scarred ear as she whipped around and turned the falling chunk of floor to molten slag before it crushed the woman. The soot poured down, narrowly missing her. Whitney bolted over and dragged her upright. Again the fire consumed everything it's way before the rain doused it, burning a hole in the exterior of the inn and devastating the second floor.

"Whitney, c'mon!" Gentry shouted. He'd made it to the front door by himself.

Whitney took the frightened, dazed woman under the shoulder and ran for the door. Aquira slashed over his shoulder, looping in and out of harm's way as more debris soared around the room, fearless.

Whitney didn't feel like he could breathe until they made it through the door. His tired legs gave out, and they collapsed, sloshing through the town's muddy, main road. Wind and rain continued to beat against his face, but it seemed to calm enough for him to lift his arm to his brow and survey the town.

Dark clouds swarmed overhead, but it was light enough to see. He'd slept long enough for morning to arrive, and beyond the heart of the storm, in the distance, the sun rose, and calmer skies approached.

Around them, the inn wasn't the only building in Grambling to have suffered the wrath of the storm, though it was by far in the worst condition thanks to the huge, fallen tree protruding through its roof. Everywhere else had porches and pieces of roofs blown away. Carts were overturned. Whitney even saw what looked like a tent from the troupe caught in a tree, flapping like a frightened galler with a clipped wing.

Whitney's gaze froze on the chowder house where he and Sora had eaten lunch together so long ago. The sign swung loose from a thick post in the ground, and the shutters were long gone;

however, the brick building stood in near perfect condition. Almost like… like there was some higher power trying to tell Whitney everything would be okay, Sora is still out there.

Shog. I'm beginning to think like Torsten. It was just well-built. Sturdy. That's all.

"Where is everyone?" Gentry said.

Whitney didn't have the breath in his lungs to answer. He continued searching the ravaged town until he noticed a man hunched over across the street, blood covering his face and chest. A long shard of broken wood pinned him against what little remained of the general store. He had to look away.

"Talwyn!" a husky voice echoed. "Talwyn?"

Whitney whipped around and saw the silhouette of a figure running down from the Grambling church. The structure was quaint, but being made from stone meant it could weather any storm. Even the Eye of Iam sculpted within its spire stood true.

"Whitney?" a weak voice said, coughing.

Whitney looked down and saw that the mud-and-ash-covered woman he'd saved from certain doom was none other than Talwyn. He'd never seen her in such layered clothing before. Even staring right at her, face covered in soot, hair disheveled, he hardly recognized her.

She wrapped her arms around him and kissed him on the cheek. "You saved me," she said, accentuating each word with another kiss. "You saved my life." Try as he may, Whitney couldn't get her off him. Even Aquira had to wriggle free of her position pinned between them.

"Gentry, you're all right!" Lucindur said. "And Whitney. If I keep seeing you and my daughter like this, my mind might begin to wonder." Whitney glanced up to see her smiling amidst the barrage of freezing rain.

"It's not like that, I assure you," Whitney said.

"That's too bad," Lucindur said.

Talwyn lay below him, looking up at Whitney like he was a war hero. Whitney cleared his throat, broke free of her hug, then helped her to her feet. "Where is everyone?"

"Come," Lucindur said, taking Gentry's hand. "The town offered us shelter in the church alongside anyone who needs it."

"What in Iam's name were you doing in there?" Whitney questioned Talwyn as they shielded their eyes and ran for the church. He couldn't believe how much he sounded like his father, scolding her.

"Looking for you two!" she said. "Pompares rounded up everyone to get inside, and you were both missing."

"And they sent you? Not Conmonoc?"

"They didn't *send* anybody," Lucindur hollered back. "You two are the fools who left camp with a grasslands storm brewing. You know better, Gentry."

"I…" the boy replied, but she yanked him faster through the gate into the courtyard of the church before he could answer.

"So," Whitney said, "I guess, technically, I didn't save you, did I—Whoa!" A loose branch zipped at them, and Whitney took Talwyn and spun. Aquira snatched it out of the air and crunched it in half.

"No, I suppose it was your friend," Talwyn chuckled from a position like Whitney was dipping her for the grand finale of a dance. Even in the face of all the chaos, she batted her long eyelashes and grinned.

"Aquira is quite the hero, true," Whitney said, spinning Talwyn back so they could continue on their way to the church.

"Open up!" Lucindur shouted and slammed on the doors.

Whitney reached them next and pounded even harder. "Hurry up!"

A few seconds later, the great church doors swung open, and they piled inside. Someone sealed them with a plank of wood across the bars, leaving them to rattle against the relentless wind.

The entire troupe was inside, along with many of their supplies. The horses were hitched to the pews, stomping in place and whinnying with fear every time the storm made the doors and shutters groan. Tents were folded up in the corner, carts were by the nave, and in the center of the rearranged pews. A couple of them had even started a fire to keep things warm and played a soft tune.

But it wasn't only Whitney's merry, traveling band who were displaced. He saw the faces of Glassmen, townsfolk wet with tears and mud, driven from their homes at the risk of being crushed in their beds. A mother and three little girls sat by the altar, whispering prayers together since there was no priest around, all of them in Hornsheim, trying to choose a new High Priest or something, it was the same in every town they'd passed through.

Whitney couldn't imagine how anybody could want to talk to Iam or one of his servants after he'd ravaged their homes. Though, it was his own house of worship that saved them. *A building made by men,* Whitney noted, for good measure.

"Talwyn you're okay!" Conmonoc shouted. He shoved through the crowd and hugged her, though her arms didn't reciprocate. A few more members of the troupe greeted her and Lucindur, though not a soul addressed Whitney or Gentry.

"No thanks to you," Whitney muttered.

"What was that?" Conmonoc said. The giant man stomped over in front of Whitney. Aquira promptly threaded Whitney's legs and crawled up to perch on his shoulder, letting loose a low growl.

"That's okay, Aquira," Whitney said. He was exhausted, but he didn't care. He'd suffered enough muscle-bound oafs with brains the size of walnuts in his life. He plucked Aquira off and set her atop a crystal candle holder.

"I said if you were worried, why didn't you go out there?" Whitney said.

"I told her to leave you and the boy out there to swim, instead," Conmonoc said.

"Would you stop this?" Talwyn said.

"Wow, you're a natural Liam the Conqueror, aren't you?" Whitney said to Conmonoc, then laughed. "If I only had a daughter. Let me tell you… I'd hope to Iam you were her suitor."

"Think you're a real tough guy, huh?" Conmonoc said, edging closer until their noses were only a few centimeters apart.

"If you only knew the things I've seen."

"I can show you the underside of my boot," Conmonoc threatened, taking a step forward.

"What exactly is your problem?" Whitney asked.

"You. You're my problem." Conmonoc poked Whitney in the chest.

"Conmonoc, quit being such a fool," Lucindur said. "The night was rough for us all."

"He's not even Glintish, and he comes into our troupe, steals our money, our children." Conmonoc turned his gaze to Talwyn and studied her from head to too. "Our women."

Whitney groaned. "This again? I suppose you think I summoned this storm too with my magic powers." Whitney wiggled his fingers like he was performing a spell.

Conmonoc shoved Whitney with his full hand this time, causing his back to slam against the wall. That got a growl out of Aquira incensed enough to make Conmonoc wince, but Whitney held out his hand to keep her at bay.

He chuckled a bit under his breath. "Don't do that."

"Do what?" Conmonoc said, shoving Whitney again. "This?"

Whitney clenched his jaw and repeated himself a little harsher. "*That.*"

"Oh, alright. What are you going to do, though?" Conmonoc

went to shove Whitney again, but Whitney stepped to the side, grabbed the big man by the wrist and bent it in the wrong direction. Conmonoc screamed out, but Whitney just pushed harder until the man was on the ground, face against the stone floor.

"I said, 'Don't do that. But you don't seem to care what anyone else says, do you, Conny? I said, 'Stop.' Now, I'm going to give you one final warning…" Whitney wrenched the wrist further until Conmonoc was frantically tapping on the floor with his other hand. "Mind your business."

"What's going on here?" Modera Pompare said.

"Oh, we were just playing around, Modera," Whitney said, releasing Conmonoc and rising. "Isn't that right, Conny?"

"That outsider had Gentry out in the storm," Conmonoc said through clenched teeth. "Nearly got Talwyn and Lucindur killed!"

"I assure you, my daughter and I are perfectly safe," Lucindur said, bowing. "No thanks to either of them."

"But he—" Talwyn began before Lucindur lay her hands upon her shoulders and guided her toward the fire.

"Come, dear, let's get you dried off," Lucindur said.

"But—"

"It isn't your problem."

Talwyn looked at Whitney, then her gaze turned to the floor as they walked away.

Conmonoc made a whimpering noise from the ground, then said, "Modera, this man has no respect for us!"

"Oh?" Modera answered. "Because what it looks like is that our 'world's strongest man' just got bested by this frail Glassman."

Gentry couldn't contain a snicker, but a glower from Modera quieted him in a heartbeat.

"Sorry, that we weren't with everyone, Modera," Gentry said. "We were trying to earn extra and used some to get a room at the inn and stay dry."

Yigging exile, that boy needs to learn to tell a lie, Whitney thought. "Some good it did," he said aloud. "Apparently, the inn was built by a couple of blind dwarves who can't nail a beam."

"Spending *your* autlas on a room when he owes you dues?" Conmonoc said to Modera. "You provide us fine shelter. He deserves the back of Fadra's hand."

Modera scratched her chin, then sighed. "It seems today, we could not. So, I see two of us who were working hard, far beyond what was required to pay their debts." She knelt in front of Gentry. He sunk backward, and to Whitney's surprise, so did Aquira. "Thank you for your honesty, boy. And you…" She turned to Whitney and Conmonoc. "Your initiative is appreciated, but break our strongman's arm, and you'll be performing for two."

Whitney found himself backing away. He wasn't sure he even wanted to, but the hard lines Modera's face made even the Spider Queen Bliss seem inviting.

"Rest," Modera said. "We leave for Fettingborough as soon as the storm breaks. We'll need some supplies after what happened to our camp. You and Gentry can help with some of the extra autlas you scrounged up."

"But I thought—" Whitney began. Modera raised a single finger, and again he froze.

"If you're a Pompare, you share," she said to Whitney for what must have been the thousandth time since their first meeting.

"Unless you're you," Whitney muttered.

"What was that?"

"Nothing ma'am."

"When you earn like Talwyn," Modera Pompare said, "then you get the right to complain. Get up, you fool." She gripped Conmonoc by the ear and dragged him away and back toward her and Fadra's carriage which, miraculous, appeared utterly undamaged.

"Uh, Whitney," Gentry whispered once she was gone.

Whitney glanced down. Aquira was curled up in Gentry's arms like a cat, which was odd, considering she rarely let anyone but him even pat her.

"What?" Whitney asked.

Gentry turned out his pockets, and only water dripped out. "I think I forgot everything we made in the cellar."

"You, wha—" Whitney bit his tongue. This was why he always preferred to work alone, because he rarely disappointed himself. But, Gentry did a yig of a job that night, and not everybody was prepared to handle nearly dying properly. "It's fine." He rustled the boy's hair. "We'll make it up somehow."

Gentry blew air through his lips like he was relieved. "We're an unstoppable team," he said.

"Yeah," Whitney said as Aquira clambered up his arm. "We sure are..." he sighed, being reminded of Sora. He recalled the early days of their partnership when her raw power caused Bartholomew Darkings' Bridleton manor to go up in flames, how he'd pushed her to go after him, which then caused Kazimir to pursue them, and their lives to be upturned.

I had a teammate, and I ruined it...

"Mr. Fierstown?" a man said.

Whitney turned to one of the pews and saw Leof Balleybeck sitting, his leg bouncing nervously.

"You're here?" the barkeep said.

"Why wouldn't I be?" Whitney said. "Why are *you* here and not at your inn?"

"When the storm picked up out of nowhere, it was so strong I saw Mrs. Potter's chickens—gods-damned chickens!—flying down the street. A tree hit the roof and caused flooding. We emptied the inn and took refuge with most of the town here."

Whitney stared at him, mouth agape.

Leof put a hand through his hair and said, "Were you not… oh… yes… I'm sorry. I must have—"

"First, you give away our room," Whitney said. "Then you *forgot about us?"*

Aquira blew a small spout of flames over Whitney's shoulder, and the barkeep hopped back.

"I'm sorry!" Leof cried, "Really, I'm so sorry. It slipped my mind."

Whitney clutched him by the collar, and by the way the man cowered, there was no doubt he'd had seen how Whitney'd handled Conmonoc. Though, Aquira baring her teeth and snarling right beside his face certainly didn't hurt.

"We were nearly crushed in that shog heap you call an inn, and we 'slipped your mind?'"

"I… I… it was I who told your friends you might be there," he stammered.

"Oh, so it didn't *slip your mind,*" Whitney said. "We simply weren't worth a trip to the cellar."

Whitney reared his first back, and Leof turned his cheek. But Whitney didn't strike, even though the idea of physically intimidating people was one of the most exciting discoveries of his life.

"Gentry," Whitney said.

"Yeah?" he replied.

Whitney grabbed the barkeep, rifled through his pocket and removed an autlas pouch. "I think I found a way for you to impress the Pompares."

"Mr. Fierstown, that doesn't belong to us," Gentry whispered.

"Doesn't it?" Whitney squeezed Leof's shirt and drew him closer. "You nearly got me, Aquira, and a kid killed."

"Take it, boy," Leof said. He opened his eyes and shooed him. "Go on. You earned it."

Gentry circled Whitney's hand and studied the pouch from all angles, like taking it would make him spontaneously combust. Whitney snatched it and put it in his pocket.

"I'll hold this one lest you leave it in another cellar," Whitney chided. Then he turned to Leof and said, "I hope you enjoy what's left of the inn." He shoved the barkeep away. The man's gut hit the back of a pew and knocked the wind out of him.

"What do you mean 'what's left?'" Leof groaned once he recovered.

"You'll see."

Leof's eyes went wide. "Out of my way!" he shouted, suddenly gaining the courage to push by Whitney. He shoved and squeezed his way by everybody else, knocked the lock off the door, and burst through.

"No!" he howled, so loud it made the storm seem quiet.

Whitney exchanged a sidelong glare with Gentry.

"Stay here with him," Whitney told Aquira before taking off after the barkeep. Somehow, she understood what he'd said enough to listen.

When Whitney emerged, he found that the heart of the storm had passed. Clear skies were near, and all that remained was a light drizzle and a heady breeze. Many of the locals who weren't hiding in the church had begun to emerge from their homes, weeping at the devastation.

"By Iam, what have we done to deserve this!" a woman pleaded. Whitney saw her kneeling before the body of the old man who'd been gored.

"Even his priests abandon us!" someone else cried out.

But none wailed louder than Leof Balleybeck, who stood before the wrecked inn.

"My inn!" he screamed. "My beautiful inn!"

Whitney walked up beside him and surveyed the scene. In the brief time since they'd escaped, more of the roof had caved in. Only a quarter of the two-story structure was left standing, portions of the wall still peeling off. The rest was a heap of debris as tall as a man, most of it soaked through by rainwater, but there was no mistaking the charred ends thanks to Aquira's heroism.

"Your inn, huh?" Whitney said. "I thought you were 'just an employee.'"

"I lied!" he shouted. "I lied and this was all I had in the world. Iam smote me for lying." The man dropped to his knees and sobbed into the mud. "This was everything. And now it's gone."

Whitney reached down and helped him back to his feet, but the man shoved him away.

"No!" he yelled. "It's not worth it anymore."

Leof grabbed a sharp shard of broken wood and held it to his wrist. He was just about to slice when Whitney tackled him to the ground.

"Gerroff me!" he yelled.

"You lunatic!" Whitney shouted as they rolled back and forth in the mud. "You're not killing yourself over a bar."

"It's my life," Leof grunted. "I want to die!"

"You don't want to go to Elsewhere!" Whitney wasn't sure what came over him, but this time, he reared back and punched the man in the nose. The tumbling stopped, and the barkeep blinked several times, blood leaking from his nostrils.

"You punched me!" he yelped.

"I... I did," Whitney said. He closed his eyes for a moment and saw the dark purple sky, and Kazimir seated along Troborough's well, gazing thoughtfully like he wasn't a monster, because in Elsewhere, nothing was as it seemed. "I'm sorry. It needed to be done."

Whitney grabbed the shard and stood. Leof sat up in the mud.

"I've lost everything..." he wept.

"So, rebuild."

The man blew out. "Like it's that easy."

"It is," Whitney said. "Trust me. The second time through

always makes a lot more sense. Maybe you'll build a roof that doesn't break and a cellar that doesn't flood."

The man threw his arms up in anguish. "For Iam's sake, Fabian 'Feel Good' Saravia is supposed to be here, and there isn't even a roof. "The barkeep slid forward on his knees and lifted a piece of wood, blackened on the end from Aquira's fire. "Was it struck by lightning to come apart like this?" he said.

Whitney covered a cough. "Must have been."

Leof's hands fell into his palms. "Oh, Iam has surely cast his Light from me."

Whitney bit his lip, then exhaled slowly. He reached into his pocket where he still had the man's autlas pouch and tossed it at the man's back for the second time in as many days. He hated doing it with every fiber of his being—the man had swindled him after all—but he couldn't help himself. He felt guilty over Aquira helping turn the place into rubble even though it was Leof's fault. At least, that's what he told himself to feel okay about losing the autlas he needed to keep the Pompares happy and stay with the troupe.

The impact of the pouch seemed to knock Leof out of a state of shock. He groped through the mud, found it, then stared up at Whitney, incredulous.

"You need it more than me," Whitney said.

"Oh, bless you, Mr. Fierstown. Bless you." He sloshed forward and took Whitney's hand.

Whitney pulled away, then shook the mud off himself. "Don't make me regret it."

"If you ever return to Grambling, I'll give you my own room if I have to… once it's rebuilt."

"If I'm ever back in this dump, kill me."

"Yes, yes." The man stood, stomping over the debris as if it weren't still wet and rainy out. Whitney winced, worried the rest of the floor would cave in beneath Leof's feet. "I can extend the great hall, put in a massive hearth and… and a taller ceiling! Really make the sound carry."

"It'll be grander than the Cathedral of Yarrington," Whitney said, voice dripping with sarcasm. The barkeep didn't seem to recognize it.

"Grander than the Glass Castle itself!"

Whitney shook his head. "Just make sure to ask this great Fabian fellow to write a song about the hero you left to drown in your cellar. He won't have anything else to do." With that, Whitney turned and headed back to the church, taking a moment to survey the town again now that he could see. So many homes needed repair. It reminded him of how Sora had lost everything when Troborough was burned down by the Black Sands, though at least storms didn't burn the skin off men alive.

The clouds broke on the plains to the east. More supplies and fabric from tents were sprinkled haphazardly over patches of dying grass.

Whitney breathed a sigh of relief. If the troupe hadn't acted so fast in finding real shelter—and forgot to locate Whitney and Gentry in doing so—they might have had to stop traveling for a few days or even a week to repair.

Whitney couldn't spare that. He needed to keep moving east, and his years of adventuring had taught him never to traverse the roads east of the gorge alone. There were far too many bandits and vagabonds, and now, rumors of Drav Cra raiders to add to the Shesaitju rebels after the alliance with Redstar broke. And those were just the bad guys. The Glass soldiers posted to defend against the Black Sands had a knack for taking advantage of citizens. After all, the only difference between a Glass soldier and a bully was that one wore a sigil.

Whitney found Gentry in the church, hugging Aquira like his favorite blanket. She'd even fallen asleep, judging by the puffs of smoke lifting from her snout. At least traveling with the group,

Whitney continued on, could continue to watch over the boy. *Iam knows he needs it*. He was a good kid, even if a bit too honest, and Whitney was excited for Sora to meet him.

He just needed to earn some autlas at their next stop and fast, before the Pompares kicked him to the curb. Especially after even his most genuine attempt at stealing some went up in flames.

XII

THE DAUGHTER

"*Aim just above the ridge of the head.*" *Muskigo pointed over Mahraveh's shoulder.*

A large, male pit lizard laid out in the sun, drying after a dip in the oasis. It was rare the creatures came so close to Saujibar, but not unheard of. After all, even the desert-dwellers needed water to survive. Its yellow eyes were closed against the bright day, totally unaware of its potential fate should Mahraveh's aim be true.

"I know how to aim, Father," Mahraveh said. She straightened her shoulders, squinted one eye slightly, then reopened it and let the arrow loose.

It missed spectacularly. She groaned, lowering the bow and her eyes followed it to her feet. Even though she didn't look at him, she imagined the way her father rubbed his bald head when he was frustrated.

"You didn't aim at the ridge," Muskigo said.

"No, I didn't," she whispered.

"If you insist upon sneaking away to hunt these creatures, you must know how to kill them. If you want to shoot it through the eye, you must aim above the eye. If you can hit your target

without an arch, you are too close. And if you miss, it will kill you. Nock again."

The pit lizard hadn't even flinched when the arrow dropped.

"Now, aim for the top of the skull, pull back, and wait," he said. "Steady your breathing. You must strike hard and fast like the snake."

Mahi could feel his hot breath against her neck, and it gave her goose pimples. She closed her eyes, drew a deep breath, then opened them again.

"Release," Muskigo said softly.

The string thrummed, and the arrow soared, arching slightly and then dipping. The barb bore deep into the beast's eye. The pit lizard twitched several times, rolled over onto its side, and flailed, spraying sand every which way.

"Ah ha!" Muskigo wrapped his arm around her and shook. "That is how a warrior provides for his village. I mean her village."

Mahraveh smiled proudly but didn't let Muskigo see.

"Now, go retrieve it," he said and gave her a gentle shove.

She crossed the rocky ground, no longer worrying about the rocks crunching beneath her sandals. She looked down at the pit lizard's lifeless body, easily twice her size. She'd seen the village men carrying lizard's half the size in pairs, but she grabbed it anyway and pulled. Its scales were so razor sharp. Sharper than she'd expected and with a yelp, she yanked her now-bloody hand back.

"Careful!" Muskigo called. As she peered over her shoulder, she could see him smiling and walking toward her.

She sucked her forefinger where the deepest of the cuts were. The taste of iron on her tongue made her thirsty.

"Let me help you," he said when he neared. Muskigo grasped the lizard by the heavy end and pointed toward the other. "Grab it there."

Together, they hefted it and began dragging it into town.

"Let this be a lesson to you, sand mouse," he said. "Even in death, your enemies can be dangerous."

Mahraveh spent most of the journey back to Saujibar reliving old memories of her father. She'd never been sentimental, but she'd also never faced the thought of her father's mortality. Muskigo had always been greater than death, unable to be killed. But now, so many voices claiming he was as good as dead had her thinking. What if word returned from Nahanab that her father's head now stood upon a spike?

She glanced over at the oasis, at the exact spot she'd killed that pit lizard all those years ago. She followed the trail to the fire pit where she and her father dressed the beast and cooked it over an open flame. With so little wood available, her people hated wasting fire on anything but cooking. Blackwood was for arrows and posts. They much preferred the soft glow of the nigh'jels, and would probably cook with the luminescent jellyfish if it were possible.

"Mahi," Jumaat said, drawing her away from her memories.

"Oh, sorry, what?" she said, looking over at him. He looked strange with a sheath hanging from his side. It didn't belong near his skinny arms, even though soon she knew he'd have to learn to wield the blade hidden inside.

"I thought I lost you there for a minute. I must have said your name a dozen times."

"Yeah," she said. "I was just thinking."

"About Farhan?"

The accusation made her feel guilty. She hadn't been thinking about the man who'd given his life for her. Truth be told, she hadn't thought of him much at all throughout the afternoon. No

Shesaitju was a stranger to death, after all. A good death meant an eternity at sea with ancestors, and death in battle, however short Farhan's was, was worthy.

She looked at her friend, Jumaat, her eyes telling all they needed to.

"Your father, then?" he asked.

"My father," she said, her head sinking.

"He is going to be fine, you know," Jumaat said, placing his hand on her shoulder. "He is the strongest afhem alive; my father always said so. Said he watched him in the Tal'du Dromesh the day he claimed the Ayerabi afhemate. Said he was like a god of the sand."

"Well, he's not in an arena anymore." She didn't mean for the words to come out so harsh, but the way Jumaat's lip twisted made her think she'd been too brash.

"Come on," Mahraveh said, changing the subject. She gave Honey's mane a tug to get her moving. "I'm starved."

Nigh'jels hung from the corner of every home in Saujibar and posts lining the walkway. It was still hot, even at night, but it was no different from any other hot night. They passed by the unlit village fire pit, where several older men sat talking. She knew there wasn't one amongst them that wouldn't have been by her father's side had age or ailment not kept them in Saujibar. Everyone loved Muskigo, and they trusted him, no matter what.

In the distance, Mahraveh could make out the string of nigh'-jels that lined the roof of her father's adobe manor. As relieved as she was to be home, the pit in her stomach over her father wouldn't go away. Being back only made it worse. All the memories they shared; fear that she might not see him again.

They climbed the three steps leading to the door of her home.

"I should be getting back home with these," Jumaat said. He thumbed back at the bundle of nigh'jel filled jars draped over his zhulong's hind-quarters and the cart it pulled.

"You aren't going to get me all the way inside?" Mahi said. "Some gentleman. Didn't my father tell you to protect me before he left?"

He smirked. "Fine." He brushed the curtain of the door aside and beckoned Mahraveh inside. "After you, milady."

The interior of the manor was dark, but the comforting green glow permeated the room. Muskigo kept a modest but inviting home, but really it was Shavi. Most afhems had a harem of wives to care for them, their home, and their progeny. Muskigo had Shavi. She'd traveled with him to Winde Port, along with the other women who chose to help serve the army, but he'd sent her home with Farhan after they were driven out. Mahraveh imagined, probably, to keep her from doing something stupid. She had more fire in her belly than half the men in that army.

"Who's there?" Shavi called. She popped around the corner of another room. "It's pretty late to come calling—oh, Mahi!" The old lady's wrinkles deepened as she smiled. "Welcome home. Where's Farhan?"

Shavi's lips straightened, likely at the sight of Mahi's own. "Snake?" she asked.

"You could say that," Mahraveh answered.

"Babrak killed him in cold blood," Jumaat interjected.

"Pis'truda!" Shavi said. "Sit down. Sit down. I will get you something to eat, then you can tell me about it." She swore again as she shuffled into the next room. "He's never forgiven your father, that wretched man."

Jumaat helped Mahraveh with the pack on her shoulders and set it down next to the door. Then, he turned, and she did the same for him. He unbuckled his sword from his belt, and she tossed her short bow and arrows into the corner. Maybe women weren't supposed to fight, but she never traveled the Black Sands without it.

Mahraveh rubbed her sore neck and then her backside. Honey

made the trek without a problem, but she was still young and didn't have the smooth gait more experienced zhulong had.

They sat down on a plush, brown cushion and Mahraveh sank into it, letting out a long breath.

"So, what next?" Jumaat asked.

"I don't know," she said.

"I know what you are thinking, but there is not an afhem of worth left to beseech on his behalf."

"You don't know that," Mahi said, louder than she'd meant to.

"My father is there as well, in case you forgot."

She hadn't forgotten, and she hated when anger entered his tone. Before she could respond, Shavi returned with a tray of food and set it down on the table before taking a seat herself.

"Tell me what the coward did," she said.

Mahraveh told the story, including how he'd approached her by the arena.

"I'll kill him," Jumaat said, having heard the full story for the first time himself.

"No, you will not," Shavi said. "But Muskigo probably will when he returns."

"Do you think he will be okay?" Mahraveh asked.

"Do you think I am too stupid to know you are planning to make sure of it?" Shavi asked with a smile.

"I—"

"It's okay, Mahi. I would expect nothing less. Just know this: your father is perfectly capable of handling this. He's the only one who is."

"Then why did he need to go to that despicable Glassman, Darkings?"

"I was there in Winde Port," Shavi started. "I can tell you; your father wouldn't have survived the attack without that man's help."

"That's not comforting," Mahraveh said.

"It should be. It tells me that he is not only the fiercest warrior our people have ever known, but he is wily, and the God of Sand and Sea is with him."

"The God of Sand and Sea is either locked up in a dungeon somewhere in the Glass," Mahi argued, "or roaming the planes like Yuri, and the others claim."

"Do you think us so stupid that we would serve a God who can be so easily locked up?"

"But the Caleef—"

"Is little more than an ornament at the end of a hilt. He is not the blade, sand mouse. Your father, he is the blade. He is the Scythe."

"Shavi," Jumaat whispered, "that is blasphemous."

"How old do you think I am?" Shavi asked.

"I… I do not feel comfortable answering that question," Jumaat said.

"Smart boy," Shavi said, turning to Mahi. Mahraveh sniggered. "I am old enough to have seen three Caleefs come and go. I watched as my own father thrust himself into the Boiling Waters in hopes that our God would choose him. Do you know what happened at the drowning?"

They both shook their heads.

"He, along with two hundred other healthy men did just that… drowned."

"You don't believe the God of Sand and Sea chooses the Caleef?" Mahraveh asked.

"I did not say that," Shavi answered, taking a sip of tea from a cup on the table. "But after three Caleefs, I've never seen a single one of them raise a sword in defense of our people. Your father, on the other hand, battles for our freedom. Which of these two men would you believe our God supports?"

Mahraveh remained quiet, watching the gentle coruscation of nigh'jel light against the far wall.

"I can promise this," Shavi said. "When your father is through, the Glass will beg to stay alive long enough to lick his boots. Now, why don't you get some sleep? You've had a long day."

"Yes, Shavi," Mahi said.

With that, Jumaat took his leave, and Mahi retired to her quarters with a lot to consider. Unfortunately, she'd have to do so another day, for she'd no sooner fallen back onto her bed than exhaustion from travel caused her to fall asleep.

Mahraveh's father walked so fluidly it looked as if he were floating. The spray of the sea spattered against his face and corded muscles, glistening on his gray skin. The sky was so dark—shades of red, crimson, and sometimes violet. The sea beneath him mirrored the hue, but the waters were smooth as glass.

He walked along steadily as purple hands reached up from beneath the surface, scratching and clawing at his ankles and calves. The skin was torn away, nearly to the bone, but if he noticed, his face didn't show it. Soft moans emanated from below.

His scimitar was drawn, swinging at his side in steady rhythm. A flick of his wrist occasionally sent it twirling.

From all directions, Glassmen charged, breaking the peacefulness of the serene sea. Like puddles, the ocean splashed beneath their feet, but they made no noise. There were so many that a massive, rolling wave began to form behind them. But still, Muskigo pressed on.

A giant, winged creature descended upon the mass of Glassmen, spewing flames from its maw and turning them all to ash on the wind. It swooped back up and out of sight, and the scene was calm once more.

Muskigo smiled, although his legs were now raw to the bone.

The surface roiled before him, and it rose like a bubble then fell, revealing a familiar, yet putrid looking face.

Farhan Uki'a emerged, skin melting from his body like hot wax. Seaweed and barnacles covered his arms and legs, and there were open, bloody sores like a thousand tiny fish had made a feast of his flesh.

But it was as if Muskigo didn't even see him.

From the air, like magic, Farhan pulled a blade and drew it out in a slicing motion. The tip found Muskigo's throat, and his lifeblood spilled out into the salty sea.

Mahraveh awoke screaming, sweat pouring off of her like fountains. She caught her breath.

Her bedroom curtain swung open, and Shavi stood there, bathed in green light. Mahi wasn't sure how long she'd been sleeping when she heard the cry sounding from outside her window.

"Attack!" Shavi whispered. "We are under attack!"

XIII

THE KNIGHT

Cobblestones scattered like frightened ants beneath Torsten's cane. Lucas walked at his side, occasionally taking his arm when they reached a turn or a carriage blocking passage, only to be shaken away. Eyes or not, Torsten knew these streets—he'd grown up on them.

"Watch out, my Lord," Lucas said. The tip of Torsten's boot caught on a bit of debris and would have sent him to the ground if Lucas hadn't been there to catch him. Torsten steadied himself and drew a deep breath.

"Perhaps I don't know this place as well as I thought," Torsten said.

"It isn't your fault, my Lord," Lucas said. "South Corner has changed much recently."

That was true enough. In every direction, Torsten could hear hammers pounding away and lumber being sawed. The scent of burning wood still lingered in the air, even a month after those Nesilia-and-Redstar-worshipping-cultists had done their damage to the district. If there was any benefit to the riot, it was that it made the stench of shog less prevalent.

"How bad is it?" Torsten asked, allowing Lucas to hold his

arm and lead him along without protest. The embarrassment of having an escort was far more preferable to the humiliation of falling face first into a pile of shog.

"Better than yesterday," Lucas replied. "Valin hasn't wasted any time living up to his promise. Streets are being swept. His men hand out food from storefronts and taverns."

"Fronts for something more devious, no doubt. We've been so worried about threats from the outside, I fear we're letting one fester in our own backyard."

"You really think Valin is a threat to the Crown after all this time?" Lucas asked.

"I think Valin Tehr is a weed. Growing under the cracks. Pulled here and there, so nobody notices the infestation, but never exterminated until one day, the floor is so feeble it breaks."

"Why hasn't the King's Shield thrown him behind bars then?"

"Because he makes things easier for us here," Torsten admitted. "And we're fools."

"Sir?"

"One crime lord of Dockside is better than twelve greedy bastards fighting over scraps. Valin keeps the southern harbor operating efficiently and the Crown happy. But he's up to something now, I know it. All this aid will extend his influence across all of South Corner. He'll have all the other Yarrington gangs lapping at his feet."

"Sir Knight, please, some autlas to spare?" a woman said suddenly. Torsten felt a tug on his hand.

"Back away, ma'am," Lucas ordered.

"Please, I beg you. I'll do anything."

"I said away!"

Lucas released his grip on Torsten to deal with her, but she refused to do the same. She yanked as hard as she could, and Torsten fell to one knee.

"My children, they're starving, please!" she implored.

"Away from the Shieldsman you worthless skag!" Torsten heard the clattering of a city guard jogging over. "Be gone!"

The man tore her away then sent the woman sliding across the street. The sound of children crying accompanied her own after she slammed against something hard. Torsten winced.

"So sorry, Lord Unger," the guard said as he and Lucas helped Torsten back to his feet. "Docksiders, never happy with their lot in life. As if that madness could have happened anywhere else in the city."

Without thinking, Torsten lashed out and grabbed the man by the throat. He pulled him close. "That is not how men of the Glass treat our citizens!"

"Better than hanging," the man said, barely audible.

"What was that?" Torsten's grip tightened until the man gagged. In the castle, people treated him like a delicate flower. It almost made Torsten forget the reason he'd been imprisoned by Redstar—or rather, the reason he'd deserved it. How he'd been driven to kill another Shieldsman outside Winde Port after Redstar the Deceiver drove him to rage.

"N... noth... ing," the guard rasped. Torsten could feel the man's windpipe beginning to collapse beneath his massive hand before he pushed the guard away. The man coughed a few times, then spat.

"By Iam," he groaned. "We're all on the same side."

Turning to Lucas, Torsten said, "Lucas, Help her up."

"Lucas?" the guard said. "Lucas Danvels? Is that you?"

"It is, Captain," Lucas replied as he helped the woman up, whispered to ask if she was all right.

"Well paint the shog gold," he swore. "Personal aide to the Master of Warfare himself? Ignoring orders sure does have its benefits, don't it? I'm impressed."

"Thank you, Captain Henry, I... Thank you."

"A captain?" Torsten said. "You'd do well to set a better example for your men."

"With all due respect, *Sir*, we're walking targets out here," Captain Henry said. "I do what I must to keep the peace."

"Do better, Captain. You can start by taking this woman and her children to the market and buying them a loaf of bread."

"Generous, my Lord," Captain Henry said, voice still hoarse. "Unfortunately, I have to meet my men down at the docks for a routine inspection. A few traders just arrived from Crowfall."

"I gave an order."

"Which I'm happy to carry out if you insist," Henry said. "But we can't be too careful these days, what with warlocks vanishing midair. Surely, you'd rather me make sure there aren't Drav Cra smuggled aboard, or something worse. You want to help her, they give out food to sorry sacks like them at the Vineyard this time every day."

"Valin Tehr does?" Torsten asked.

"Someone has to."

Torsten grit his teeth then sighed. "Go."

Captain Henry's armor jostled as he saluted. "With haste, Sir. And Lucas, give your parents my best. Man, I miss those pies."

Lucas muttered an inaudible response. Torsten listened to Captain Henry leave, barking for another beggar to clear the street like he took joy in it. He wasn't used to such insubordination, but a lifetime in Dockside made most men crass.

"You served under him while you were here, did you?" Torsten asked. Lucas didn't answer at first, so Torsten nudged him to get his attention.

"I—yeah, I did," Lucas said. "He gave me a good scolding for opening that gate against orders. He's a real piece of shog."

"When you get a chance, start preparing a list of worthwhile replacements."

"Me, sir?"

"You know the guards in this place better than me. Who's loyal and who's locked away in some crime lord's pocket. We have to do better. We keep treating people here like shog, they'll never stop thinking they are."

"I'd be honored, sir."

Torsten turned in the direction of the beggar woman's heavy breathing and still-rattled children. "Now, ma'am, the captain said something about Valin Tehr giving out food?"

"Aye, down at the Vineyard," she said. "Line runs down toward the Grove Street Church midday, every day. Sometimes past it. They won't be servin' by the time we get over there today."

"He's not a man to be relied on," Torsten said. "Lucas, you said your parent's bakery was up and running again?"

"For the most part," Lucas replied.

"Where is it?"

"Just around the corner."

"Take us there," Torsten said.

"Sir?"

"Take us."

His young aide didn't protest further. He led them around to the next street. An enchanting aroma immediately greeted Torsten's nostrils. He wasn't experienced with his olfactory sense enough to know what it was but found it as delightful as the white cake occasionally served to King Pi.

"This way," Lucas said.

He pushed through a door, and the smell overwhelmed Torsten. It was almost enough for him not to notice that the bakery was without customers.

"Mum. Dad!" Lucas hollered.

"Lucas, honey," his mom said, opening a door.

"What are ye—" Four sets of knees hit the floor. "Lord Unger, by Iam, what an honor," his father said.

Torsten traced his eye sockets with his fingers. "The honor is all mine."

"Please, let me fetch you something. Supplies are limited, but there's a new sweet I've been working on that will delight your taste buds."

"Dad, we're not—" Lucas started, before his mother cut him off.

"Oh, quiet, son," his mother said. "It's not often the man who saved Yarrington pays a visit."

Torsten raised an open hand. "Please, madame, it's fine. I'm not hungry, but I'm hoping you might consider offering something to this poor family?"

Lucas' parents whispered between themselves. Then his father said, "I'm so sorry, Sir, but things the way they are, we can't afford to give anything away. Customers are… few and far between."

"My Lord it's quite all right," the woman said. "We'll eat tomorrow."

"But I'm hungry…" one of her children whined.

"Shh. We'll queue up at the Vineyard before sunrise."

"Stop." Torsten reached into the satchel on his belt and removed a few gold autlas. It was far more than the cost of a loaf of bread or pie, enough to cover their earnings for the day at least, but Torsten realized that he never had to pay to eat. The castle provided. "Lucas, please give this to your parents."

Lucas hesitated.

"Please," Torsten insisted. "It should cover the cost of feeding them and anyone else who comes by today." He turned toward the woman and her children. "Eat and know that the Crown does not forget you, milady," he said.

"Iam bless you, Sir Shieldsman," the woman said. "Blessings. My family, we will never forget."

Finally, someone took Torsten's hand and closed his fingers

back on the coin. "This is too generous, Sir Unger," Lucas' mother said.

"I apologize we couldn't do more about what was stolen," Torsten said, opening his palm and ensuring she took the money this time. "But places like this are what makes Dockside special."

"Ye are too generous. At least stay then, my husband will whip up something." She took Torsten's arm and led him forcefully toward a table.

"That's quite all right." Torsten struggled to pull himself free.

"I insist. And Lucas, dear. You look famished."

"Mum, we're fine," Lucas snapped under his breath.

"Lucas, listen to your mother," his dad said, voice stern and proper. "The man paid good money, and you know I don't believe in handouts. Someone has to eat for it."

"Unfortunately, your son is right." Torsten was finally able to slip free of her unexpectedly strong grip. Baker's hands, from kneading dough, he imagined. "As much as I would love to stay, we have business in which to attend. Feed this family twice for us if you must."

"Then ye'll come back another day," she said, sounding heartbroken. "Horace will prepare his specialty pie, won't you honey? I swear, the royal chef used to order it for feasts back when Liam was king. Didn't he, dear?"

"He did," Horace said.

"I look forward to it with all my heart," Torsten said. "But feed others first. Whatever you're able."

Lucas took Torsten's arm and rushed him toward the exit like he was ashamed.

"Lucas, say goodbye to your mother," Horace said sternly.

Lucas stopped and inhaled in through his teeth. Then he released Torsten to go and plant a kiss on his mother's cheek. "Bye, mum," he said. "Treat them well."

"Visit soon?" she asked.

"Of course. Bye, dad."

"Get some meat on those bones, boy, or the Shield will toss you out!" Horace hollered.

"I'll have a talk with the barracks," Torsten answered. Lucas had his arm again in seconds and led him back outside.

"I thought you said no special treatment," Lucas said once they were a few meters away.

"These people need to know that it isn't only Valin Tehr who looks after them," Torsten replied.

"Is that true though, my Lord? You can't pay for every beggar in the district to eat like nobles. You can't see, but they're already gathering, wondering why that family is eating, and they starve. Only Valin Tehr has enough scraps for all of them."

Torsten stopped. He didn't respond. He only faced the direction of Lucas's voice and glowered.

"Apologies for overstepping, my Lord," Lucas said. "It's just, growing up here, my father had a saying: 'Beggars are like vultures. You feed one, they'll come circling until they pick you dry.'"

"That doesn't seem to be affecting Valin Tehr," Torsten grumbled. "Now come on; we don't want to keep him waiting."

Lucas continued leading him through Yarrington's poor district, explaining what he saw as they went—per Torsten's instructions. His parent's shop miraculously seemed like one of the few intact. People did love the sweeter things, however. Even if they couldn't afford it, the smells made the world bright. And the deeper they delved into Dockside, the more the salty, fishy stench of the Torrential Sea overpowered everything.

The coming of spring meant a lively harbor; traders arriving from all over the kingdom where war didn't touch, fishermen returning and gutting their hauls. It provided plenty to do for Docksiders lucky enough to have the skills. The rash of repairs needed added work for others, though it would end soon enough, and Dockside would go back to how it was: overcrowded, rife with crime and starving people.

Liam used to say that "even the healthiest body has sores" to describe the grime of Yarrington, that there was no way to avoid places like it in the cities throughout the Glass Kingdom. When Torsten joined the King's Shield, he didn't believe that, couldn't. He'd wanted to turn South Corner into a prosperous, safe neighborhood unlike any other—then he dealt with Valin Tehr and grew up.

War, trade, famine—these were issues that affected the entire Kingdom. One forgotten corner of it could never be his focus.

"It's strange, seeing the Grove Street Church like that," Lucas said.

"What did those monsters do to it?" Torsten asked.

"Stone doesn't burn easily, but all the glass is shattered. The artwork inside is sliced, the pews overturned. Parts of the roof are caved in from where they tried to pull down the Eye. The front doors, blown off their hinges."

Torsten's hands balled into fists. "Animals." He stopped, released Lucas, and tapped his way to the church stairs, whispering a solemn prayer.

"Nobody will touch it until the High Priest is selected," Lucas said. "Even monks and altar servers stay away rather than help."

"The people here must fear they speak only with the darkness." Torsten took one step up, then heard something fall over inside and tiny feet scurrying across the wooden floor. He'd been blind long enough to know they belonged to children and not rats.

"Perhaps not so useless after all," Lucas said. "I've lived in worse places than a rundown church."

"Even in the darkest times, Iam's light still shines," Torsten said. "And to think, there was a time I nearly lost hope." Torsten backed away from the church and continued along the street, Lucas rushing to his side.

"You, Sir?" he asked.

"Rotting away while Nesilia's pawns ran this kingdom into the ground has a way of doing that."

"How did you find it again? Hope," Lucas asked meekly. "If you don't mind me asking."

"You wouldn't believe me if I told you."

"It wasn't easy growing up around here and still holding belief in anything."

Torsten snorted in agreement. "The Queen."

"*Our* Queen?"

"The 'Flower of Drav Cra' herself. Rand Langley may have freed me from Redstar's prison, but she showed me that Iam's light shines in the most unexpected places. That we can, all of us, find redemption when we lose our way. That he is not law and order and bindings, but love. From a killer to the most potent mystic, Iam is forgiveness."

"Maybe you should be the High Priest."

Torsten laughed and patted Lucas on the back. "Maybe not that forgiving, boy. Besides, the King needs me."

"And what about them?" Lucas stopped, forcing Torsten to as well. It was normal for the lane leading to Valin Tehr's brothel to be paved with beggars, but now it sounded as loud as the Yarrington markets. Only there was no spirited bartering, no shopkeeps barking about their wares. There was, however, coughing children, shivering mothers, and desperate fathers making promises to their children they could not keep.

"Stay close to me, my Lord," Lucas said.

"How many?" Torsten asked.

"That woman undersold it. Hundreds. Some look like they've been camped here for weeks." Lucas led Torsten forward and shouted, "Move aside, by order of the King's Shield!"

Torsten felt hands patting at his arms and legs, and the tightness of Lucas's grip as the boy pushed through the crowd. From every direction came pleas for food or spare autlas. Torsten had dealt with beggars plenty of times before, and though they usually gathered in the largest crowds by the churches, using children to earn more—like traveling troupes—this was on another level. Fingers pried at the edges of his armor as if they wanted to tear it from his flesh.

"Back away!" Lucas ordered. A rasp sounded as he slipped his sword halfway from its sheath. His voice betrayed a quaver of fear, and Torsten knew the young man was out of his depth. He'd been a city guard, but it was clear Captain Henry hadn't taught his men how to handle the worst parts of South Corner.

They stopped moving.

"I said, out of our way," Lucas said, sliding his sword out a bit further.

"Why?" a gruff voice responded. "You gonna feed us like that wench down in South Corner, Lord Unger, or is my face not pretty enough?"

"You will liste—"

"Hey, I know you. You're Lucas, Horace's boy." The man cackled. "Look at this, a new pet of the Crown."

"King's Shield," Torsten said. "And you will do as he asks, or you'll suffer the consequences."

"What, because I don't have a plump bosom I don't get special treatment?" Torsten wasn't sure how the man paraded around after that statement, but judging by the chorus of laughter around them he was sure it was lewd.

Lucas released Torsten, and Torsten could hear the boy spin in place, facing the rabid horde of beggars, breathing heavy.

"All of a sudden you lot care for us?" the man said.

"Yeh," a woman chimed in, sounding like she was missing a few teeth. "Wun't enough to let them masked shogs burn our homes. Now ye gunno starve us?"

"Just a pinch 'o gold'll do, like ye just gave to the Danvels.

Won't tell nobody, will we?" It was the man's voice again, and he was closer now.

"You will back away as you are commanded!" Torsten said.

"C'mon, lil Lucas," the man said. "Yer Dockside through and through, not like this Glintish oaf. Got bread from yer mum and dad just the other day and their prices haven't dropped a bronzer since before the Dawning."

"They need to eat too," Lucas said.

"Ye yigging liar. They've got the Crown's support now, dun't they? I might want to go back and get what I'm owed."

"Don't you yigging touch them!" Lucas's sword slid fully free. Torsten's heart sank as, for a moment, he expected to hear the squelching of metal on flesh, but the young man didn't strike. "You're going to rot in the dungeon for that."

"Good. They probably serve better food there than we get here."

"Then you can starve, Murray," a new voice said, smooth, distinguished. Torsten hadn't even realized he'd been dealing with the same poor man who'd beseeched the king only a day earlier.

The ground suddenly shook so hard Torsten swayed, then again, like it was the footsteps of a… giant. The crowd surged in the other direction, filled with nervous chatter. Chain's rattled loudly, links stretched, then dragged along the cobblestone street. The grating sound made Torsten cringe.

"Baaaad maaaan," the deep, cavernous voice of what was unmistakably a giant filled the air. Then came a stench like Torsten had barely even experienced in the Winde Port tunnels— rotting fish, meat, and worse. The troublemaker Murray yelped and then his protests grew distant. By the time he had his wits about him enough to curse Lucas, he was far-off, voice drowned out by more thunderous footsteps.

"Thank you, Uhlvark," said Valin Tehr, approaching through

the now parted crowd, his own cane clacking. "You may sit again."

"Eaaaat?" the giant replied.

"Not until later. Now sit."

The giant's sigh felt like a sudden gale. Then he lumbered away, and more chains rattled behind him as if he were a dog leashed to the Vineyard.

"I do apologize for that," Valin said, drawing nearer. "Always helps to have a giant to keep the order when the guards are so busy elsewhere."

"Added to your collection, have you, Valin?" Torsten said.

"I assure you, I have all the proper documents. Poor Uhlvark is slower than most, wouldn't do any good with a hammer. And he's allergic to dust, if you can believe it. No dwarven tunnelers will take him. Imagine what his sneezes might do."

"Lucas Danvels, my boy," Valin said. "It's good to see you again. How are your parents?"

"Doing well, all things considered," Lucas replied.

"Of course. I miss the simple times."

"What?" Torsten said. "When the only monsters we had to worry about were men like you?"

"By Iam, your Lord can hold a grudge," Valin said. "I received your message that you wanted to talk, Sir Unger. It's been some time coming. Follow me inside, and we can do just that."

"Where you can ply me with your ungodly pleasures?"

"No. Where it's quiet. The Vineyard is a haven for the weary and the hungry until Dockside is healed."

"Forgiveness, my Lord," Lucas whispered in Torsten's ear. "If the Queen can earn it…"

Torsten ran his hand over his bald head, stopped to itch the shriveling skin beneath his brow, then sighed and urged them along. Not a single beggar dared even to extend their hands for autlas now with Valin present.

Lucas told Torsten to watch his step when they reached the entry, but now he was set on making his own way. His cane got stuck in a knot in the wood once, but he yanked it free and made it to the landing. That was where he smelled porridge. Valin's men, gangers and cutthroats, were on the porch handing out bowls one at a time to the poor. Valin's giant had returned, apparently stirring the massive pot, his chains constantly chattering.

"Weapons," requested a man with a thick, Breklian accent. No doubt Valin's right-hand man Codar, who'd saved Torsten twice now. Torsten knew next to nothing about the foreigner, who'd likely been too young back when Torsten was a low enough rank to have dealt with lowlifes like Valin.

Torsten heard Lucas start to untie his sheath but grabbed his arm. Silence passed between everyone until Torsten's skin began to itch again.

"Yes, of course," Valin said. "Apologies, Codar still has trouble with our culture. These are men of the Crown. Of course, they may retain their weapons."

"As you wish, Mr. Tehr," Codar replied.

Lucas went forward first, and Torsten followed close behind. He heard Codar at his back, his footsteps quiet as a mouse. The Breklians were known for their assassins, among other things such as their high fashion and ability to barter a man's last fish for a bronzer. Torsten had dealt with a member of their famed assassins guild, the Dom Nohzi, not too long ago in Winde Port. Operating so far south meant their boldness was growing with Liam out of the picture and Torsten didn't like it.

"My office is just downstairs," Valin said.

"If it's all right with you, I'd rather speak up here," Torsten said.

"Are you sure? It's still so noisy," Valin replied, no doubt referring to the same din of coughing and suffering as outside. Torsten had been to the Vineyard a few times before, with the air rank with sex, sweat, and ungodly things. Now it was stale with a tinge of iron, like a medical tent after a battle.

Valin Tehr, purveyor of whores and bloodsport, now played caretaker of refugees. Torsten could hear moans of starving men and women through the tarps of the rooms along the second-floor balcony, where women used to take lustful men. A few had tried to tempt Torsten when he was a younger man.

"I was fortunate," Valin said, then took a long breath as he sat. "Having Uhlvark outside kept the cultists away. Only a few broken windows."

"Business must be hurting," Torsten replied. Lucas took his hand and led him to a couch where he slowly took his place on the very edge, refusing to get comfortable.

"The girls are happy for the break," Valin said. "What happened here shook us all, and they're doing well helping those in the worst shape. They're naturally generous, you see."

"I can only imagine."

"Where are my manners." Valin clapped his hands. "Codar, would you mind having Abigail fetch us wine. She can choose the vintage."

"I don't imbibe," Torsten said.

"Are you sure? Abigail is new here, but she has a palette unlike any other."

"Not me."

"Of course," Valin said, sounding only a little perturbed. "Well, if you don't mind, I find it easier to converse if I indulge a little. This place earned its name for a reason. Finest wine collection this side of the gorge."

"Enough pleasantries, Valin. In all my time in the Shield, I rarely saw you venture to Old Yarrington but to improve your control over the Southeastern docks, let alone twice in two days."

"I carry the plight of the Greater South Corner district with me."

"Save it. You're making yourself visible at just the right time. I may no longer be able to see, but I can see through you, Valin. The city is in shambles after all the horrors. The kingdom is scrambling to keep up with too many concerns to count. Dockside isn't enough for you? You want all of South Corner too?"

"If we're being frank, Sir Unger. Your sight must have failed you earlier because South Corner has been mine for a while now. Perhaps the people didn't realize, but they do now."

"Have you been reduced to a braggart?"

"I speak only truths," Valin said. Torsten heard him shift in his chair. "That's why I always liked you in our past dealings. We're the same that way."

"We're nothing alike. I don't kill innocent women."

"Iam's light, Torsten, neither do I. Don't let one misunderstanding long ago cloud your judgment."

"Trust me, my judgment is clear as ever."

"Then you sit there and tell me that I'm not what's best for South Corner?" Valin asked. "That I don't keep the peace, your peace, in exchange for what? I keep the public docks humming, and ask very little of the Crown."

"Except for us to look away," Torsten said.

"I never asked."

"A threat is enough!" Torsten slammed on the table sending silverware clattering to the floor.

Valin sighed. "Will our dealings with the Shield ever go civilly, my dear Codar?"

"Manners are a lost art in the west, it seems," Codar said, voice as cold as Breklian ice. "Sir Unger should be thanking you for helping free him from the castle dungeons."

Lucas released a sound, whether of shock or disgust Torsten wasn't sure.

"That is the only reason I'm being so civil in coming here now," Torsten said.

"How does this bottle look, Mr. Tehr?" a young woman asked.

"Ah, what a year," Valin replied. "I believe that was when the great Liam took Crowfall from his brother and ended the last of the extended Nothhelm line."

"You forgot the part where his brother tried to usurp the throne," Torsten said.

Valin scoffed. "Nobles."

"Sir Unger?" the young woman who'd brought the wine asked. "Sir Unger, is that you?"

He turned toward her, showing his lack of working eyes. "I apologize, who is that?"

"By Iam, the rumors about what happened to you are true. I'm so sorry, my Lord. It's me, Abigail Crane. Remember, from Fellwater Swamp. You saved me… twice."

"Abigail…" Torsten could hardly get the name out. He remembered her now, the girl he found shoveling shog for Muskigo's army with other enslaved Glassmen. He'd freed her from there and sent her to warn Oleander about the Black Sands' threat, only to return and find her slammed behind dungeon bars, where he freed her again.

"Abigail, stop bothering our guests and hurry back up here!" one of Valin's men called down.

"Oh, shut it, Curaldo," she hollered back. "I'm bloody coming. Here you go, Mister Tehr." A small bit of wine filled his glass, then he took a slurping sip, licking his lips like it was finest he'd ever tasted.

"Excellent," Valin said. "Thank you, Abigail. Leave it." She was about to respond when he grabbed her wrist. "And what did we say about acting more respectfully?"

"That the highborns like it," she said, wincing.

"And that means…"

"More gold."

"Good girl." He released her and slapped her bottom with the back of his hand.

She seemed to be doing her best to mask her pain. "Sorry, Mr. Tehr." She stopped by Torsten and ran her hand along his shoulder. "It's good to see ye again, Sir Unger. I hope to see more of ye."

Torsten wasn't sure how to answer. He merely smiled and nodded. When he'd helped her, this was the last place he imagined she'd wind up. But he remembered her being petite, and pretty in a homely sort of way, even though her fair skin and blonde hair had been matted by mud and worse. She'd lost everything to the Black Sands rebellion; the exact type of girl Valin Tehr preyed on.

"You know, she told a story about how a Shieldsman saved her down south when I hired her," Valin said.

"You never can believe what the new ones say," Codar remarked.

"But isn't the truth so beautiful?"

"It is." Codar lifted the jug of wine and poured Valin a full glass. "Are you sure we can't interest you, Sir Unger?" Torsten shook his head. "Or your ward?"

"No, thank you, Mr. Tehr," Lucas said. "I have a weakness for the stuff, and I'm in training."

"Ah, what vices sons learn from their fathers. Good for you, my boy. You'll make a better Shieldsman than the last one from Dockside."

"Don't speak of him," Torsten snapped. "If you truly want my thanks for you helping Rand free me, start by telling me why you did it."

"Let's just say Iam spoke to me."

"The truth," Torsten growled.

Valin snickered. "Goldless men like the Drav Cra are a dying breed. Impossible to deal with. I was near ready to surrender Yarrington and relocate to Westvale when Rand the Deserter—or rather, Redeemer now, I can't keep up—showed up on my doorstep begging for my help in setting you free."

"That's impossible," Lucas interjected. "Sir Langley fought the Drav Cra jailers himself to save Sir Unger."

Torsten glared back in the direction of the voice. "It's the truth," he said softly. He heard the sound of feet sliding backward.

"Incredible," Valin said. "A wench tells a ridiculous but valid story, and a knight of Iam bends the truth."

"The world is truly changing," Codar said.

"I let the people believe the story they needed to hear," Torsten said, making no attempt to mask his venom. "I didn't think you'd want any credit."

"Relax, I don't blame you," Valin said. "Besides, who would have believed that my friend Codar arrived just in time to help?"

"Not a soul," Codar said.

"Truth is, I wouldn't have wanted the attention," Valin said. "But Rand, he was willing to give everything to save you. Did you know that Sir Unger? He believed Iam *chose* you to free us from Redstar's corruption. He believed it with such vigor that I nearly started to believe it too."

"Then I'm glad I didn't fail him," Torsten said. "He deserved better than what he got, from me, from you—everyone. I saw the look on his face when he and that Breklian cutthroat arrived at my cell, Valin. What part of his soul did you make Rand sell for you?"

"We helped each other save you so you could remove Redstar. Neither of us wanted to see our ways of life die. Surely, you could understand that? In exchange, Codar helped me arrange passage for him and his sister to Brekliodad."

"And I assume you haven't told him that the Shield has

forgiven his transgressions and invited him back." It was a statement as much as a question.

"I couldn't tell him, even if I wanted to. Brekliodad is far away, and it's his life to make there. He refused all of Codar's connections. Better to truly disappear and be grateful he no longer needs to suffer for Queen Oleander's wanton rage. He was done with this place."

"You know nothing."

"I know being lost in the wild is better than hanging from a noose," Valin responded, "or being forsaken by his own people."

Torsten expected a curse to roil within him, but the words never came. After everything, Rand Langley deserved to be free of the demons which plagued him in Yarrington. Being shipped to a faraway land when he hadn't ever traveled outside Greater Yarrington explained Rand's expression that day. Brekliodad was a hard place, filled with rigid people who'd seen enough death to fill the Torrential Sea. But it was a place where he could finally disappear.

"Just hope he gets there alive," Torsten said. "The boy's suffered enough."

"I'm no expert on cross-Pantego travel," Valin said, "but, what would you say, Codar? Another few weeks before he arrives?"

"It has been a long time for me as well, but that sounds reasonable," Codar replied.

"If I hear word of his arrival, I will make sure you know," Valin addressed Torsten. "Sometimes, it can be hard to find Iam's light, but in the end, I think Rand the Redeemer did what he set out to do."

"Stop, Valin." Torsten waved his hand dismissively. "You have my gratitude for helping Rand free me, and for freeing him, but you've proven time and again how *wholesome* you are."

Valin released an exaggerated laugh. "See, Codar. I told you the old boar would eventually come thank us. He just needed some time."

"Pride slows even the greatest Shieldsman," Codar said.

"It's the last time you'll hear the words from me," Torsten said.

"That's more than enough," Valin said." And don't worry, I'll keep our little secret about how you really broke free. The kingdom needs heroes like you and Rand now more than ever."

"Just tell me, why make yourself so visible now?" Torsten said. "No lies about your generosity or desire to help South Corner because my vow to Liam is a vow to his son. I won't allow another snake near him."

Valin took another long, slurping sip of wine. "Do you know what this place used to be before I bought it?"

Torsten didn't answer.

"A broken-down old tavern," Valin said. "Better off burned to the ground than serving ale. I took everything I saved from begging on the streets, working the docks until my hands were raw, running favors for thugs and used it to buy this place. Now, I have more gold than the Crown."

"Earned off the backs of women and blood," Torsten said. "Or do you think I've forgotten what goes on downstairs, or how bodies get in the harbor?"

"Well, I don't know anything about bodies, but we all do what we must to rise when we aren't born into sunlight. You did the same. Followed your *great king* here and there, killing whoever he targeted, bending knees. The only difference between us, Torsten, is that I gave the orders. These women choose to be here because here is better than anywhere else they could reach. The men who venture downstairs choose to fight because they're tired of waiting on Iam's light to shine down on Dockside. And Iam…" Valin Tehr laughed a despicable sounding laugh. "He abandons us, leaving his churches derelict while a bunch of men in robes argue about who should wear the whitest one. I've spent a life-time trying to make South Corner more, and it took me watching cultists tear the place to pieces to realize it was impossible to do from our quaint little spot on Autlas' Inlet. So, do you know what I want, Shieldsman?"

There was a long, silent couple of seconds where Torsten imagined Valin took a sip of wine. His assumption was proven correct at the gentle sound of the goblet touching the table again. Then, with a commanding tone, he said, "Respect."

"You can't get that through threats and bribes of the flesh," Torsten said.

"I can't get it no matter what I do from here. Look at you. A lowborn Glintish boy from South Corner rising to be Wearer of White and still, when the slightest doubt came into their minds, your men watched some Drav Cra savage slam you behind bars without a word in protest. Us and our false, small names, who gives a fiery shog in Elsewhere? No, it's time for me to give this rotten place a voice worth a damn and you're going to help me do it."

"Me?" Torsten asked.

"Yes, you," Valin said, "who after all your failings somehow still holds the ear of the king. A *'bribe of the flesh'* with his mother perhaps."

"How dare you!" Torsten started to rise, then heard Codar and Lucas shifting behind him. Metal scraped against leather, and Torsten wasn't sure whose weapon was being loosed.

"Everyone calm down," Valin said. "I can only speak of what rumors I hear from so deep underground. If you deny that, then I believe you. Despite what you may think, I want us to be friends. And not only because you're from South Corner, but because you were born here. You know what the people need. So do I. Food, water, work, entertainment, God—all the things to keep us from tearing each other to pieces. It all comes with gold, and nobody on this great world of ours is better at that than me. Even Yuri Darkings was an amateur in comparison, Iam save his soul when he answers for his betrayal."

Suddenly, it was all coming together. Torsten felt his throat go dry and his stomach knot. He couldn't will himself to ask, but Valin answered for him after another lip-smacking sip of wine.

"You're going to recommend to the king that I be named his new Master of Coin," Valin said. "Someone fresh, with perspective. Someone who grew up outside of pampered castle halls. Someone who hasn't been bought—who *can't* be bought."

"Why in Iam's name would I ever do that?" Torsten questioned. "Your deal to free me was with Rand, not me. I owe you nothing."

"Agreed, and if I felt differently, I would have already approached you or made that fact public. But I do think it proves that I have no desire to see this kingdom or the order it brings to our chaotic world burn."

"It proves nothing," Torsten said.

"You love the Glass, Torsten, and you know there is nobody more capable than me. Don't deny it. You would have shut me down a decade ago if you didn't see why Yarrington needs me."

"Something I still regret."

"Help me help it," Valin said, "and in exchange, Codar here will help me hire the finest Breklian mercenaries to eradicate the Drav Cra marauders causing so much trouble east of the Jarein. I hear they've sacked another town, though, nobody in the castle seems to want to talk about it."

"Mercenaries, rebuilding the city, spies in the east; how deep do your pockets go, Valin?"

Valin laughed. "We can find out together."

It was meant as a joke, but that didn't matter. Torsten jumped to his feet, not worrying about finding anything to keep his balance on first. "I would die before I ever let your filthy hands near that position, Valin," Torsten said, blood boiling. "Do you hear me? Keep your army, keep your gold, and keep to your little corner of Yarrington, or we will turn a blind eye no longer."

"The mercenaries will be hired either way," Valin said. "You can either claim responsibility as Master of Warfare or hand it to me. I don't really care. I asked you here as a formality, to make things easier because despite what you think, I love this kingdom too. I love what it stands for and how it has allowed men like us to rise. Rags to proverbial riches. That is why I helped rid us of Redstar's scourge."

"You did it to line your pockets. That's all!"

"If you insist on being stubborn, well…"

Torsten used the table to make his way toward Valin and heard Codar's stance shift again. This time Lucas remained still, likely unsure what to do. "Are you threatening the Crown?" Torsten demanded, seething.

Torsten listened as Valin calmly drained the rest of his wine. Imagining his grin, Torsten wanted to smack him. Then Valin said, "Not at all."

"Good. I'll march the Shield in here and put an end to your kingdom of dirt before you take another breath," Torsten said.

"March soldiers on a man who offered free service to the King himself? On a haven for refugees when war rages in the South, enemy kings go missing, and raiders pillage in the North and the East. And they wonder why the coffers are so drained, Codar."

"Such a shame," the Breklian replied.

"Perhaps stress has clouded your judgment," Valin said. "Might I recommend a night here to relieve yourself. Your friend Abigail is masterful with her hands and seemed awfully interested. On me, of course."

Torsten bit his lip, then whipped around. Lucas barely had time to catch up and help guide him through the warren of furniture and displaced Docksiders. "You won't see the walls of the Glass Castle again," Torsten hissed.

"B… bye, Mister Tehr," Lucas said before Torsten grabbed him and pulled him away.

"Give your parents my best, young Lucas," Valin called out. "And talk some sense into your master. If you can't, there's always a place for you again here."

Once outside, Torsten slammed the door hard enough to earn a drawn-out "Quuuiiieeet" from Valin's giant protector. Lucas tugged on Torsten's arm, and Torsten stopped. The young man was about to say something when Torsten grabbed the boy by the wrist.

"What did he mean by that?" Torsten said.

Lucas stammered for a response before settling on, "What?"

"'A place for you… here… *again*.' How well do you know that bastard? Did he place you at my side?"

"Y… y… y…"

Torsten's grip hardened.

"You chose me," Lucas cried.

"How do you know him!"

"I worked for him in the arena as a boy. And I… well, fought there once before I joined the city guard. Fists only though, and not to the death, I swear. My parents had a rough year. They just needed some autlas."

Torsten found it easier to read men when he could look into their eyes but feeling Lucas's pulse throbbing at his wrist helped. He let go, and Lucas doubled over, clutching his arm.

"I'm loyal to the kingdom, Sir," Lucas said. "I want to be a Shieldsman so I can be the one to save my home next time."

"I know, boy." Torsten helped him upright, realizing how odd it was not to be the other way around. For the first week or so after he lost his vision, he'd fumbled around like an infant learning to walk. Lucas had been there to deal with his frustration, to help him up countless times.

"Forgive me for… that," Torsten said. "He's always had a way of getting under my skin and after helping me get free… I fear what it might mean to owe that devil anything."

"I understand, my Lord," Lucas said.

"I wish you'd have told me you worked for him before I found out like this."

"I didn't think it relevant," Lucas whispered. He cleared his throat and found his voice. "When you were here, growing up, maybe it was different, but nowadays there isn't a boy in Dockside who hasn't done something or other for Valin Tehr. But I didn't know he'd worked with Rand."

Torsten sighed. "Perhaps I should have told someone. Pure redemption seemed such a better tale."

"Favor or not, he *did* save you and help defeat Redstar. And you said it yourself, he keeps the peace here. Why do you hate him so much?"

"Any man of honor should."

"Maybe," Lucas said. "It just seems more… personal."

"It's everything," Torsten said, terse.

"Am I going too far in asking what he did to you? Something many years ago?"

Torsten drew a deep breath. As selfish as it was, he worried if perhaps his ire was fueled by the fact that, if not for Valin Tehr, he would've failed his kingdom and allowed Redstar to bring the Buried Goddess back from Elsewhere. But it wasn't just that. In the depths of his mind, he could hear the pounding of footsteps like drums on a fateful day long ago when Valin helped show him the darkness of the world he hadn't known existed. Of the body he'd left floating in the harbor.

"You are," Torsten said, pushing the memory back down. "Valin is right though. We can't get rid of him right now and risk how it will look. We must show the people of Yarrington that the Crown cares for them—more than anyone or anything. More than war or old feuds."

"How?" Lucas asked.

"We'll figure that out after you get me back home. I doubt Valin will help us pass through his wall of refugees this time."

"Hold your breath then."

"Lead away. Oh, and Lucas. Not a soul is ever to know what Valin Tehr did to help Rand. The kingdom depends on it."

"Yes, Sir. Of course, Sir. But what if he starts spreading rumors now that you refused him?"

"Unless those close to the Crown claim it to be true, it will join a thousand other Dockside rumors dripping in the shog. I suppose he knew that from the the start."

XIV

THE THIEF

The following few days passed uneventfully. The troupe salvaged what they could from the fallout of the storm and set off on their way to Fettingborough.

The spring rains didn't cease. Nothing like that storm hit again, but the clear skies that followed were soon enveloped by gray once again. Whitney was soaked to the core. Water dripped from his clothes and hair and coming off the worst winter he could remember, the bite in the air could still be felt.

They'd lost a covered carriage to the storm, so only the spoiled Pompares now rode in luxury. Talwyn and her mother shared a horse, but even they had to travel exposed to the rain.

Whitney's little show of strength meant he walked with Conmonoc, night and day, in the back of the troupe, heavy supplies slung over their shoulders. Poor Gentry too, as little as the boy could carry. And Conmonoc, the biggest of them all, hadn't stopped whining about sore feet and blisters since they'd left Grambling. Whitney was amazed he didn't join the bastard. In fact, he was surprised at how he didn't mind serving as a human mule at all. Feeling his muscles burn with soreness again made him feel like he was back in…

Whitney froze.

He spotted a large boulder on the side of the road. To anyone else, it was a red rock, but he recognized it even all these years —*months*—later and bit back a flood of emotions.

It was the very spot where he'd hidden while Sora performed her finest solo act as his thieving apprentice. He was stopped in the middle of the road at approximately the location where she'd lain, waiting for that shog-sucking dwarf Grint Strongiron and his mercenary crew. Whitney had convinced her they were rotten so he'd have a chance to steal back his half of King Liam's old crown.

"You coming, Mister Fierstown?" Gentry called back.

Whitney cleared his throat. "Yeah, I'll be right there. And for the last time, it's Whitney!"

"Well, hurry up, Whitney!" Gentry called. "We're almost to the bridge."

"Almost" was far from the truth, but Gentry was right, the bridge could be seen from where they were. It was still a stark white blotch in the distance. The massive stone towers could be made out, reaching up into the sky like the swords of two great warriors.

This was Whitney's least favorite part about traveling. He knew that within the hour, he'd be standing before over-confident, puffed-up soldiers like Torsten. They'd want to check each one of them, study all their belongings, make sure nothing untoward was being smuggled into the eastern Wildlands before Panping. Out there, beyond Fettingborough, there were few towns and even fewer guards. This would be the Glass Kingdom's last chance of ruining anyone's fun.

"Coming!" Whitney called and broke into a light jog.

He tried to put the memory of Sora and Grint Strongiron's caravan behind him, but it was difficult to shake. How he wished he and Sora hadn't turned south at this road, and instead, continued east over the bridge. Then Winde Port and Kazimir and all of those unsavory things never would have happened. *What was I thinking, taking to the sea? That's what rushing things gets you... dead.*

"How's Aquira doing?" Whitney asked Gentry when he'd caught up. The wyvern had taken a peculiar liking to him. Plus, he didn't have his shoulders weighed down by enough supplies to tire a horse.

"Fine, I think," Gentry said. "She really likes these nuts I found in the cellar of the inn."

"Peanuts," Whitney offered.

"Not very good," Gentry said, pursing his lips.

"You have to break the shell away first," Whitney said, laughing. "They can't be found just anywhere you know. A bit of a delicacy anywhere but the west. Save some for Panping, you might be able to make a barter or two."

Aquira growled as if in protest.

"Don't worry, girl. There's plenty." Gentry shoved another handful toward Aquira's snout and the wyvern gobbled them up.

"Would you two shut up?" Conmonoc said as he trudged by, sacks slung over his shoulders and massive arms. "Listening to you two is going to—"

"Make you stupider?" Whitney finished for him. The man's mahogany cheeks went a deep shade of purple, and then Whitney took a hard, aggressive step at him, earning a flinch. After a lifetime of sticking to the shadows to avoid brutes, Whitney couldn't help but feel a bit of pride at joining them.

"Why you!" Conmonoc threw the bundles off his shoulders and charged Whitney. Whitney ducked under the bear paws Conmonoc called hands, then darted ahead in the line of troupers.

"Enough, you two," Lucindur snapped as they passed her horse. The sound of her voice made Whitney's legs stop instantly.

Conmonoc slammed into his back, tripped over a loose rock and he splashed face first into a mud puddle.

Conmonoc pounded his fist on the ground and judging by his face, planned to fight until Talwyn chuckled. Conmonoc bit his lip, stood, and shoved passed Whitney on his way back to the rear of the troupe.

"Where did you learn to fight, my savior?" Talwyn asked.

Whitney's gaze fell upon her, hair wet and dress see-through. She wore it so naturally. So unashamed of her beauty, unlike cagey western women.

"That one was an accident," he said.

"The accidental warrior. What a song that would be, wouldn't it mother?"

"Yes, dear," Lucindur said, rolling her eyes.

"I should, uh…" Whitney shook his head and turned his attention up the road toward the great spires framing the White Bridge. The Pompares' carriage rolled to a stop at the foot of it, and one by one, the line of performers slowed down. "…Probably go up front now. Handling guards happens to be my speci-al-ity."

He didn't get his foot planted before Talwyn spoke again and stopped him in his tracks.

"Isn't it beautiful?" she said.

Whitney choked on his next breath. "What's that?"

"The Gorge."

Whitney joined her in staring off to the left at the great gash in the earth which cut Pantego in half and made traveling a pain in his ass.

"Breathtaking," Whitney said, though he'd never once thought of the massive hole in the ground as beautiful. It was said that ancient gods had created the rift during the God Feud. Of all the ludicrous legends Whitney had ever heard, that one was the most believable. The gods, from Iam to the lowest of them, seemed obsessed with making men's lives a living Exile.

"I can't wait to see Panping," Talwyn said. "That's where you're headed, right?"

"Supposed to be," Whitney said.

"I've never been. Have you?" Then before he could answer she said, "And I'm so excited to see it *with you*."

Whitney drew a deep breath. He wanted to be kind to Talwyn. She was a young girl who was clearly smitten with him—and who could blame her considering his new physique to go along with a charming personality? But there was an added sting at the thought of Panping being his and Sora's destination before everything went south. And the fact that all he had to go on that she was still there, or even still alive, was hope.

"Yes, yes. We are all together, aren't we? Even your mum is here!" Whitney flashed a smile to Lucindur, who looked back and stroked her daughter's hair with pride. As Talwyn nestled against her hand, Whitney jogged a little bit further ahead until he too stood at the White Bridge.

Modera and Fadra were being helped out of their carriage by a pair of acrobats in what was quite the ordeal. The floor was so high up since they were parked on a hill, the performers had to cup their hands like stairs. Whitney could see them struggling not to wince in pain as they supported the heavy weight of their benefactors.

Guards lined the pass, each one bearing a long polearm. Blue and white flags flapped at the tops of the towers on either end, dripping with rain. They stood proud, half-embedded in the rock of the gorge, and what was exposed was made from perfectly cut, white stone. Stained glass at their tops portrayed the Eye of Iam, and at the crests of the pointed spires, glass dust shimmered. On sunny days without rain, they shined bright enough to be seen for miles, a beacon for those who found themselves lost on the winding roads of the gorge.

"Halt!" one guard said, stepping forward with another from the western tower. "State your name and purpose."

"We seek passage east, on our way to our homeland," Modera said.

"I wasn't asking you," the guard spat.

"What was that?" Fadra said, a harsh edge creeping into his tone. The chubby man stomped toward the guard, his jowls jiggling. For a Glass soldier who saw more ruffians pass by than anywhere else in the world, it must have been the least threatening thing imaginable. The Glintish were peaceful by nature—Conmonoc excluded, but Whitney was starting to think the brute had some Glassman in him—and Fadra was so big he couldn't catch a boar with no legs.

"We mean no trouble, Sir," Modera said, stepping in front of her husband. "The Pompare Troupe is renowned from Westvale to Brekliodad, sir."

"So's what's between my legs." The guard chortled, his partner joining him. "I don't care who you are, ain't no crossing without paying the King's Tax."

"And what's that?"

The guard scratched his chin, then craned his neck to examine the size of the troupe, and probably get a peek inside the Pompares' ornate carriage. "For all you... hmm. Hundred gold'll do, right Bover?" He gave his partner a nudge and they exchanged a smirk.

"That's preposterous!" Fadra said.

Modera stuck out her arm to block him again. "That can't be right, Sir. That's as much as we earn in a month."

The guard shrugged. "I don't make the rules. War going on in the south, rebuilding Winde Port... Kingdom's got a lot to pay for and you Glinters are a wealthy bunch."

"Streets paved with gold, eh?" the other guard snickered.

"Nobody is that wealthy," Fadra said.

"You're welcome to head north and try the Dragon's Tail," the guard said. "I'll tell ye though, winter ain't broke up there and judging by how weak you all look, half of ye will freeze to death."

Modera exhaled. She seemed calm, though Whitney could see by the way her jaw tightened that she was anything but. She reached into her autlas pouch.

Instinct kicked in. Whitney lashed out and grabbed her wrist, which meant that Fadra instantly clenched his. Whitney cleared his throat. If there was one thing he never could abide, it was pig-faced guards who treated people from other lands, like Sora, as if they were less than dirt. Sure, he knew he couldn't do anything to change that part of how the world worked, but these men were usually of the sort Whitney'd robbed blind before the Webbed Woods.

"I've got this," he said, braving Fadra's scowl. The guards didn't know that the fat man packed a yig of a backhand.

Whitney didn't wait for an answer. He strode forward, puffing out his chest. "Sirs, we bring joy and happiness to the kingdom. Surely the king values that over mere taxes."

"Rules is rules," the guard said. "Who're you, anyway? You don't belong with this charred lot."

"Oh, well that's a long answer… My name is Whitney Fierstown. Yes, yes, the very same of Westvale fame—"

"Oh, shut it," the guard snapped. "You'll all pay same as anybody else."

"In that case, as fact would have it, my troupe and I are seeking reparations for the damages done to our camp by the storm, and we thought you fine men would be able to set things up."

"Reparations from whom?" the guard asked.

"Whom. Oh, how proper! Well, the King, of course!"

"The King!" The guard laughed. "What did the King have to do with damages to your camp?"

"It happened in *his* Kingdom," Whitney said as if the answer were obvious.

"You think because the storm occurred within the Glass that somehow the King is responsible to pay for your losses…"

"Very well. We take payment in the form of silver and gold. Or the Pompares," Whitney turned around and waved his hand for the Pompares to join him up front, "have a manifest, and itemized inventory. It will clearly outline what we've lost. Modera!"

The guard was preparing a response when Modera and Fadra Pompare stepped forward again. Whitney had never seen their features so bright. So many years of managing a troupe, they'd probably forgotten what it felt like to perform themselves. Whitney too felt his heart racing. In Elsewhere, all he'd ever been was the boring farmhand from Troborough.

"Modera, you'll be pleased to hear these fine soldiers are going to provide, from the royal treasury, reparations for what was lost in the storm." Whitney said.

"Now, listen here—" the guard began.

"That is great news!" Modera said.

"Fine news, indeed." Fadra clapped his hands.

Whitney grinned but the guard's face turned red. "You are not being compensated by the King for your loses!" he snapped. "This foolishness is wasting my time. If you aim to pass through the Gorge, then pay what's owed or turn around."

"Oh, well." Whitney shrugged at the Pompares. "Misunderstanding I suppose. How about we pay… say… fifteen gold autlas, and call it even."

"Fifteen?" The guard laughed. "One more smart remark and I'm throwing you in a cell, is that clear?" He stalked forward, his fully armored, towering figure meant to make Whitney and any other passer shrink. Only, Whitney had a problem with backing down.

"Man, the kingdom has gone downhill since Liam died," Whitney said. Fadra grunted in agreement. "Fifteen. It's my final offer."

"You're final offer? That's it—"

"Take it, or I'll head back to Yarrington and have a talk with my friend Torsten Unger."

The guard froze. "The Slayer of Redstar?"

"The very one. Happens to be a very close friend of mine."

The guard bit his lip, then started laughing hysterically with his partner. "Yeah, and I'm the King's uncle."

"All right, I guess I'll have a talk with him." Whitney spun on his heels and headed back the other way, flashing Modera and Fadra a wink. He also didn't realize that the entire Troupe had gathered behind them, watching, dumbfounded. His gaze met Talwyn's for a moment and he lost his train of thought. The last person who'd stared at him like that was Sora.

"How do you know him?" the guard asked.

Whitney gathered himself, then whistled. Aquira leaped from Gentry and soared onto Whitney's shoulder. He spun back toward the guards.

"Old Torsten?" Whitney said. "You heard the story of how he braved the Webbed Woods and the monstrous Spider Queen Bliss to help break the curse on King Pi?"

"Who hasn't?" the guard said, nervously eying Aquira now. "Brought Redstar right back to Yarrington to face justice too, where the dastardly warlock cursed everyone. Caused—"

"And killed him there," Whitney pointed out. "Saved the kingdom and all that. Well, he didn't survive the Webbed Woods alone. *Lord* Whitney Blisslayer helped him, which just so happens to be one of my many monikers."

"Yeah right," the guard scoffed. "He did it all alone."

"I heard he used a master thief," the other guard chimed in. "Had him steal Redstar from right under Bliss's nose."

"Bullocks."

It took all Whitney's willpower to hold back his glee. He knew from the road with Sora that hundreds of story's about the Webbed Woods had come out after they returned, all telling a different tale. Some that Redstar bewitched Torsten there so he could rise to power. Others still, said Torsten was in cahoots with Redstar. He hadn't, however, heard one which talked of the master thief who'd helped Torsten.

His name included in the tale or not, Whitney found it hard to complain. Men like him rarely made it into legends as anything but the villain.

"Your friend there heard the truth," Whitney said. "It was I who helped defeat Bliss and bring Redstar to justice the first time. Saved Torsten's life a few times too."

"You're lying."

Whitney strutted forward. He felt like he was walking on air. "Perhaps," he whispered. He sauntered in front of the guard who'd heard the more preferable—and accurate—version of the legend. Aquira gave a snarl for good measure, as if reading the situation and joining in on the performance. "Then again, maybe not," Whitney said. "You know, Torsten's Glintish like these folk, isn't he? The most famous in the kingdom I reckon. I wonder what he'll think of a king's soldier treating his people like this."

The rude guard stumbled over a few words, then tugged on his partners sleeve and pulled him aside. They exchanged some heated whispers, then the leader sighed. "Fine, fifteen will do."

Whitney turned and reached into Modera's pouch himself. The scowl he earned from her gave him chills. *Haven't earned that much favor yet.* He removed his hand, and she placed fifteen gold autlas into his palm.

"Ten," Whitney said. He plucked out ten and shoved them in the guards gut. "Because you really upset me."

The man gritted his teeth. Whitney had passed the bridge many times before. The tax was reasonable when people weren't being taken advantage of. A few silver autlas usually, maybe a gold in times of war. King Liam did want to *unite* the world after all—though his subjects never seemed to care.

Finally, the guard took the gold. He and the others were making a tidy profit exploiting foreigners anyway.

"Move along," the guard said, waving the troupe forward. "And keep an eye out for raiders in the Wildlands. I hear Redstar's savages are running rampant out there after their defeat, pillaging, killing." His gaze turned toward Talwyn and her mother. "Raping the pretty ones." Then to the Pompares. "Ugly ones too."

"Thanks for your concern," Fadra said with no small amount of venom in his voice.

The guard looked back to Whitney. "I wouldn't want a *hero* such as yourself to wind up skinned like a doe."

"I faced Bliss herself, how bad could some savages be? You just worry about your bridge." He patted the man on the cheek, then continued on across without waiting for a response.

"You're full of surprises," Modera remarked as she and Fadra waddled by, not bothering with getting back into their carriage yet. Her husband even offered a nod of approval.

"Is all of that true?" Gentry whispered as he went by.

"Maybe," Whitney said softly. "And maybe not." He winked at the boy, and shrugged his shoulder to coax Aquira over. She did and made herself comfortable.

Gentry returned the wink, though his expression revealed his confusion. Reading between the lines wasn't one of his strengths. Instead, he started whistling a tune the troupe had played around the fire last night and tossed a peanut up for Aquira.

"Well done," Lucindur said as their horse clopped alongside Whitney. "A performance for the ages."

"Right, a performance..." Whitney said.

Talwyn didn't say a word, but she let her hand graze over Whitney's arm on her way by. Whitney unconsciously watched her pass as they moved forward. Then he felt something solid connect with his back. He stumbled forward several steps.

"Eyes off, you little piss," Conmonoc said. "You got lucky. It won't happen again."

"Do you really want to lose another scuffle, right here, in front of the Glass army?" Whitney asked, gesturing to the line of soldiers posted along the bridge. "Thought so."

Conmonoc stopped and ground his teeth in frustration. It took him a few seconds to come up with anything to say in return. "Out of my way!" he grunted, shoving Gentry and spilling the peanuts before stomping off.

Aquira was so fixated on the nuts, she didn't snap at him but Whitney knew she would have. One of them flew over the side of the bridge. She dove off after it and into the bottomless gorge before swooping around on the other side and startling a guard.

Whitney chuckled. "Just don't get her fat, kid."

Gentry's eyes went wide. "No more, okay?" he said, sticking his finger into Aquira's face when she returned. She nibbled at his finger. "No." He stowed the bag, once again taking Whitney's words at face-value. "Nothing to worry about, Mr. Fierstown!"

"Just, Whit—" he sighed. "Don't let her go hungry either."

Gentry offered a firm nod.

As Whitney crossed the bridge, he took in the structure as if for the first time. Perhaps it was his time spent in Elsewhere which made him begin to appreciate the land of the living, or maybe it was what Talwyn had said, remarking on the beauty of the Gorge, but the bridge was a serious feat of engineering.

Spanning across the massive Jarein Gorge, white, sparkling

almost, the bridge rose up several stories on both sides with slots carved out in various shapes: galler birds, swords and shields, and of course Eyes of Iam. In its center, a large arch crossed overhead. Gleaming white statues crested its peak, each one representing a kingdom Liam had conquered. When he caught the others at the east end of the bridge, he realized the sky was turning a sickly shade of green. He knew they wouldn't have long to get to Fettingborough before the light rain they'd experienced all day turned into a deluge. And they were still at least a couple hours away.

"We should pick up the pace," Whitney said to Modera. "This storm could be as bad as the last one." She and her husband had stopped as soon as they'd reached Pantego soil again so they could be helped back into their caravan.

"That was excellent work back there, Mr. Fierstown," Modera said. "But we'll get there when we get there."

"But—"

"And Whitney." Modera stuck her arm out of the carriage and waved him over. She grabbed his hand when he got close, and when she removed it, Whitney found the five extra autlas he'd spared them in his palm.

"Your debts from Grambling are forgiven," Modera said. "Keep it up, we may convince you to stay with us after Panping." She drew her curtain closed before he could answer.

A few actors who'd overheard scowled at him but said nothing.

Except for Conmonoc. The big, ugly brute just couldn't help himself as he shouldered Whitney and said, "Shog-eater."

"What is his problem with you?" Gentry asked.

"Well, when you're born as ugly as he is, it's difficult to deal with the ravishingly handsome."

Gentry laughed.

"What's funny?" Whitney asked, straight-faced. Then he gave

the smallest hint of a smile until he found Talwyn watching him. He straightened his collar and tried not to look back.

A crack of lightning in the distance put some pep into the troupe's step as they rounded a wrinkled rock-face. Whitney matched their speed. He took a long stride and when he brought his foot down, it didn't immediately connect with the ground. He felt the wetness of the mud as high up as his thigh. Gentry stifled a laugh and helped Whitney out.

"You know," Whitney said, "I thought this whole traveling performer thing would be a lot more grandiose." He shook off his leg.

Gentry leaned over to help him.

Around the bend, the Eastern Wildlands greeted them, with barely a tree to be found on the horizon. Whitney rarely spent time in the region. It was tough to sneak about without trees.

"First, Fettingborough. Then, the Wildlands."

XV

THE DAUGHTER

A hard thunk *reverberated in Mahraveh's ears as her spear spun out of her hand, and she brought her other arm up to block her face from the imminent attack. The attack never came.*

"I don't understand why I have to fight with this," Mahraveh said when she'd opened her eyes and saw her father standing before her with that smirk on his face she'd come to despise. The one that said, "I know better than you, sand mouse."

"Stop laughing at me!" she shouted. "Give me my bow and I'll show you what I can do."

"A bow might be fine for killing lizards and snakes, but it will do you no good in a real fight."

Mahraveh's brow furrowed deeper. "Why not a sword, like you?"

"You are small. Every opponent you fight will have a greater reach. This is called evening the playing field."

"More even if I shoot them dead from a distance," Mahi argued.

"Fine," Muskigo said. "Go get your bow." He pointed to the

right, behind a tree where Mahraveh's short bow rested along with a few arrows. There were always arrows there.

She stared back at him, unsure what angle he was playing.

"Go."

Even as his daughter, Mahraveh knew when Muskigo gave a command, you listened the first time. She scampered over and grabbed her bow, then returned to him. Before she'd made it back, Muskigo clapped his hands. Two of her father's men were on top of her without her even registering movement.

"Please, show me how your bow will help you?" Muskigo said.

Mahraveh grunted as the men dug their fingers into her arms. She fought and struggled, but the bow fell from her grip. Her boot met one of the warrior's shin, and he winced but didn't let go.

Muskigo approached her and she waited for her punishment, closing her eyes.

"Open your eyes, sand mouse," he said.

Through her eyelashes, she regarded him and saw a different sort of smile.

"You do not know what gift you have here in Saujibar. Anywhere else in the Black Sands and you'd be punished for even asking to touch a weapon. Here, you've mastered your bow, and now I've presented you with this." He held out the spear she'd dropped. "Its blade is fine and sharp—balanced without rival— yet you complain that I train you in its use."

"I am sorry, father." Mahraveh's head hung to her chest. She felt a finger against her chin, lifting her head. She opened her eyes and Muskigo's stared back at her.

"Take it," he said, referring to the outstretched spear. "You never know when you will find yourself in need of the protection it provides." He nodded to his men and they let her go. She considered lashing out at them, mostly from embarrassment, but instead, she grabbed the weapon from her father's hand.

"Now, let's try this again."

———

Shavi didn't stick around longer than to see Mahraveh spring from her bed.

What is going on?

Beyond the black mud walls of her home, she could hear familiar sounds. Metal against metal. Angry cries as well as anguished ones. There was a battle going on in Saujibar.

She hadn't even yet taken off her boots from the trek with Jumaat from Latiapur.

Jumaat! she thought. He wasn't a fighter, not really. No one left in Saujibar were fighters. She heard screams in Saitjuese, and her first instinct was blaming Babrak. He saw his opening and now could complete his revenge against her father for being the better man.

"For Oxgate!" came a shout outside from a Glassman. And then, "Bridleton!" and "Troborough!"

Mahraveh didn't know what any of those words meant, but the voices belonged to Glassman. She darted across the room and hefted a long object wrapped in a simple silk scarf. She laid it on her bed and carefully unwrapped it, revealing a long, wooden shaft topped with a sharp triangular blade. Lifting it, she turned it over in her hands a few times to find its balance. She grabbed its scabbard hanging from a hook on the wall, then laced it over her shoulder.

Despite the coming of spring and the hot days, a chill wafted in through the open window, remnants of the south's coldest winter Mahi could remember. She ran to it and peered outside. She couldn't see any of the Glassmen from her room. As she ran through the open curtain, she grabbed her short bow and a few arrows.

The benefit of adobe homes was they didn't burn easily. Even the blackwoods were stubborn and took more than a little effort to catch. So she knew the raid wouldn't be as easy as throwing a few torches and waiting for the Shesaitju to burn alive or flee into waiting blades.

Her room was upstairs, and her window faced away from the town and the oasis, but her father's room overlooked the whole place. She crossed the hall and came to the only room with a solid door. She expected it to be locked, knowing her father rarely permitted anyone into his quarters, but it wasn't. She flung it open and immediately, the voices of the Glassmen grew louder, coming through the window.

She sneaked in the darkness and sidled up to the side of the opening, then glanced out. Below, men in silvery armor and swords lined up the villagers near the fire pit. Amongst them, she now saw Shavi. Mahraveh swore.

She continued scanning the line. To her small relief, there was no sign of Jumaat. But there were at least a dozen Glassmen, and even more moving from structure to structure, ransacking, searching for more Shesaitju.

She noted their armor, recalling her father's teachings on its strength, but also that a well-placed Shesaitju arrow, barbed as they were, could pierce through. She couldn't take a chance of one bouncing off harmlessly and giving away her position. Only one of them wore a helmet, but large fins protruded from each of their pauldrons to block sideways attacks.

The one wearing the bright white helmet began speaking. "Listen close, gray men."

At that, several children began to sob. Some of the older folks did too. A sour feeling stirred in Mahraveh's stomach.

"Your behavior over the next few minutes could be the difference between life and us burning you alive as you did to so many of our friends and family."

"Burn them all, Sir Nikserof!" shouted one of the other soldiers.

The one in the white helm, called Nikserof, raised his gauntleted hand, and silence followed.

"We are not animals, Sir Porthcombe. We, unlike they, have a merciful God. Although we can't simply ignore the transgressions of their afhem, we are smart enough to know the difference between him and his ilk. These are common folk, old men, women, and children. Except… this one." He stopped at a particularly young man with only one leg and pulled him to his foot by the scruff of his neck.

Mahraveh could feel red-hot anger rising from within her. Before she knew it, she was nocking an arrow against the string of her bow.

Calm down, she told herself.

"What are you doing here while real men are off at war?" Nikserof asked him.

The man's mouth stayed shut like stone.

"Show mercy, he only has one leg!" Gah'ra, one of the Shesaitju called out. He was immediately met with a backhand for his efforts, and the rest of the town sucked in air.

Nikserof dropped the young man back to the ground and sauntered over to the old Shesaitju who'd just been downed. Nikserof glared at him. "Mercy? Do you know how many of my men died in Winde Port at the hands of your master?" He plunged his sword down into the man's chest. Gah'ra groaned as he grasped at it, and the sound of his bones crunching was covered by Mahraveh's people's sobs.

My people. The thought sparked something within her. If her father wasn't here, and Farhan was dead, who was left to rule them? To serve them?

Mahraveh stepped fully into the opening and brought her bow up.

"We didn't start this war!" Nikserof yelled. "Your master did. Now I don't know how you people live down here, but if you give me the answer I need, you may yet continue in this humid wasteland. Does Afhem Mosquito have any family, and are they here?"

"*Muskigo*," Mahraveh growled under her breath as she steadied herself and drew back. Perhaps she couldn't kill Nikserof, with his helmet and armor, but one of his men, the one called Porthcombe, the one who'd called for every last one of her people to be burned alive stood with his back turned to her. The base of his skull was uncovered and open to attack.

When she looked back to Nikserof, he had his sword to the neck of one of the children—Branethra's daughter—while Branethra cried and shouted from somewhere down the line. "Which is the afhem's house, little gray-skin?" Nikserof asked.

Porthcombe stepped forward when the little girl refused to speak. He drove his sword through Branethra's left shoulder, and the woman screamed out.

"Hey!" came a cry from behind Mahraveh at the same time.

She spun to see one of the armored Glassmen, already in the house, charging her. She stepped aside, hoping he'd barrel through the open window, but he saw the move coming and ground to a halt. Mahraveh drew her spear, causing the man to take a step back.

"In the name of King Pi, lower your weapon and your judgment will be swift," he said.

"Of what do I have to be judged? By you nonetheless, pink-skin?"

"Crimes against the Crown, including treason!" He thrust his sword. Mahraveh easily parried the attack, knocking it aside with a downward swipe.

"Is it a fight you desire then?" the Shieldsman asked.

"There doesn't appear," she started, blocking another attack, "to be a choice." She was backed against the wall. The Shieldsman underestimated her, reaching out with his gauntlet to apprehend her. She punched forward with the butt of her spear and connected with the man's nose. Blood poured down his face and erupted into his eyes. She had him temporarily blinded, and this was her only chance.

He shouted, and as he did, another soldier appeared in the doorway—one of the ones from downstairs. That meant there'd be more. She didn't hesitate, couldn't waste the opportunity and brought the sharp end of the spear around. It sliced the attacking Shieldsman's neck. He gurgled as he collapsed to the black floor, a puddle of blood pooling beneath him.

"You bitch!" the other Shieldsman growled as he entered the room.

Picking up her fallen arrows and bow, she slung it over her shoulder and climbed out the window before the man could grab her. He leaned out, screaming at her and at the men below.

She tossed herself over the flat roof, using the short wall for cover. Mahraveh knew these men weren't stupid and it wouldn't be long until she was surrounded. She popped up, aimed for the top of a soldier's head, and let an arrow fly. His skull shattered from the barbs, and he dropped. She didn't even wait for him to hit the ground before she fired another arrow. It pinged off another Shieldsman's armor.

She tossed the bow aside, out of arrows.

She heard shouting from below her, likely the Shieldsman following her up to the roof. If she didn't act fast, she would be stuck up there with Glassmen on every side of the manor. She ran to the opposite edge, the same side her bedroom window was on. The men weren't down there yet. She'd climbed up from her window enough times in her life, and there was a blackwood palm she knew she could scale down. But what about Shavi? Jumaat? Could she just leave them to die at the hands of the pink-fleshed devils?

As she began her descent, she heard the clattering of armor as the Shieldsman in pursuit pulled himself over the lip of the roof. "They're all going to die now, and you're going to watch!" he shouted, breathing heavily. Climbing down, Mahi wished she'd saved an arrow for that man's throat.

"I am Muskigo's mother!" Shavi shouted from the front of the house after Mahi hit the sand. "Take me and leave them be."

The breath caught in Mahraveh's lungs. It wasn't true, though she may as well have been. A younger Shavi had been presented to him as a gift when he won the Ayerabi afhemate. He never laid a hand on her or made her one of his wives. He merely allowed her to chose to serve his family.

Mahraveh rolled and looked up. The Shieldsman on the roof stared back toward the oasis where the news had likely caused a commotion. Mahraveh scrambled to her feet and ran that way when the unmistakable sound of horse hooves pounding against sand met her ears. Two men on horseback raced around the corner toward her, the steeds barely slowed by the black sands.

"Stop running, and we will show you mercy!" one yelled.

Mahraveh was no fool. She knew her only choice would be to outrun them or fight and she couldn't outrun a horse without Honey. Stopping, she turned and faced the men.

"Good choice," the soldier said. "Now make this easy and follow us back to town. You are, what, the afhem's wife?"

Mahraveh said nothing.

The man tilted his head and said, "Daughter?"

"No," she whispered. "I am the snake."

One of the Shieldsmen chuckled. "Funny, girl. But whatever you are, the Wearer wants to see you."

"I will show you no mercy, you know that, right?" Mahraveh asked.

Both men laughed in response. The other Shieldsman lifted

his sword and said, "Our swords are bigger than yours, little gray girl."

With a quick flick of her wrist, Mahraveh's spear spun within her hand, and she brought it down, jabbing it into the sand.

"Cute move," the Glassman said. "And a smart one, too. You'd have lost no matter what."

Mahi's heart pounded against her chest as the two men closed in on her, now so close she could see the sweat dripping from their brows. She took in a deep breath and fell into the black fist pose.

Again, the Shieldsmen laughed, but this time there was very little mirth. She could tell they were confused and possibly scared.

The two continued forward, apprehensive at first. One reached out for her, and with blinding speed, Mahi kicked out, and the arch of her foot met with the connecting joints of armor at both the men's knees in quick succession. One dropped to one knee, but the other stayed upright. Taking advantage of the downed foe, Mahraveh used every bit of training she could remember. Her father had been relentless in teaching her every form of combat he could. Although she'd been best with a bow, he'd let her train with Dorgrom, a tongueless ex-Serpent Guard.

"You're going to regret that, wench," said the Glassman still standing.

Few knew the reason the Serpent Guard's had no tongues, but Mahraveh knew it was to keep them from the distraction of conversation both in daily life and in combat. She lashed out with an open fist while the man finished his taunt and caught him in the throat. He clutched at his neck, but it would do him no good. She'd crushed his windpipe, and he'd be dead in a matter of minutes.

She turned back to the second soldier, still on one knee, struggling to get up. She'd likely broken his leg.

"Stop," he said. "Just go. Let me live. I'll tell them you escaped. I promise." He waved his sword at her to keep her away.

Mahraveh turned back to the dunes, picked up her sword and bow, and walked into the darkness of night. Behind her, she could hear the man breathing, relieved. But she hadn't been running away in the first place. She stopped at a spot just beyond two palm trees, both scarred and chipped from years of use in Mahi's training. She bent over, retrieving an arrow from a reserve her father kept for her target practice.

The Shieldsman still struggled to stand, now screaming for help, hoping one of his comrades would hear him. No matter, he wasn't paying any attention to her as she raised her bow, accounted for the arch of flight, and let the missile go.

The barb struck the man through the mouth and exploded out the back of his head. He fell over in a heap.

Mahraveh slung the bow over her shoulder and returned her focus to Saujibar, her home. She ran, flanking the dead soldiers. She stopped when she reached her house, and sneaked around the side. She peeked out around the corner.

The soldiers were gone, but the town square was littered with her people's headless bodies. While she'd fought those men, the Glassmen went back on their word like the monsters they were and slaughtered all of them.

"Shavi," Mahraveh whispered, unsure if any Glassmen remained. "Jumaat."

Mahraveh clutched back a cry as she walked amidst the corpses. The sight of a headless child made her retch and look away. She fought through the pain of it all and stood, scanning the remains for Jumaat and Shavi. She quickly found Jumaat's mother and younger brothers, but neither Jumaat nor Shavi were there.

Looking across the pond to his home, she started off toward it. His cart was in pieces; his zhulong slaughtered. On the backside of the house, a soft green line glowed in the black sands, barely perceivable. Below a thin layer of sand, she found a blackwood hatch. She bent to open it, and the doors flew open, knocking her on her backside. A small dagger pressed against her throat. The hand it was attached to belonged to Jumaat.

"Mahi?" he whispered, then fell on her, embracing her and crying.

"Jumaat! What are you doing? How are you alive?"

"Shhhh," he warned.

"They should be out here somewhere!" came a shout in the distance. "They went after that child with a bow."

Not all the Glassmen had left after all.

Jumaat pulled himself together and grabbed her by the hand. Together, they climbed the stairs down into the cellar.

It was a large room. The walls were hard blackwood and mud and were lined with nigh'jel lanterns of all sizes. An opaque layer of blackish gray dust permeated the cellar.

She heard a clattering noise and looked back to see Jumaat barring the hatch behind them.

"They won't find us in here," he said.

"I did," she said. "You can see the nigh'jels glowing through the cracks."

Jumaat swore, then pointed to a stack of tarps in the corner.

"Quickly," he said, "help me cover the shelves."

As quietly as they could manage, they did as he said until the room was black as pitch.

After a few moments, Mahi laid down, experiencing the truth of her exhaustion. Jumaat sat next to her.

"I am so sorry," he said.

"For what?" Mahraveh sat up and looked toward the sound of his voice, although her eyes still hadn't adjusted enough to see his face. "You didn't do anything. Those monsters, they..." She didn't even have words.

"I am such a coward. I… I saw them taking my family. I saw them. I saw it all, and I chose to hide."

"You chose to live, Jumaat. There is no shame in that. You could not have done anything."

"I could have died with honor." She could almost sense his chin lowering to his chest.

"That is stupid."

"That is what our fathers teach!" Jumaat said, louder than was smart.

"Then what our fathers teach is stupid!" she said just as loudly. "This way you live to fight another day. Why die with them all? Who then will avenge their deaths?"

Quiet filled the room but for the gentle lapping of water within the lanterns.

"Lie down next to me," she told him. "It's cold beneath the sands. We have to stay warm. In the morning, we will decide what we will do, but for now, this is the safest place in the whole town."

Jumaat didn't respond verbally, but she felt him lay down beside her. She softly stroked his hair until the soft sounds of snoring filled the room. She wasn't sure if she was trying to comfort him or herself. Now that her adrenaline had slowed, her chest felt so tight she could barely breathe.

"Tomorrow," she said to herself, "the Glassmen will pay."

XVI

THE MYSTIC

Sora couldn't say how she got where she did when her senses returned. Nor could she say what had spurred her cognizance. Every moment in her timeless, empty prison, she fought to take control. If not control, to at the very least, see. She drew on the lessons taught to her by Wetzel and Madame Jaya. Even though she no longer had the Bar Guai, or even Wetzel's dagger to slash her skin, they had taught her how to manifest the powers of Elsewhere.

But this was so much more than Elsewhere. Worse or better, she wasn't sure, but it felt like Nowhere—that was the name she'd given it at least. Like she was floating it a soundless, weightless, colorless room.

While on the *Reba,* on the rare occasions Sora managed to peek through her own eyes, it was easy to sense the passing of time. She could see where they were, compared to where they'd been. But this time, as she looked, she saw only ice and snow all around her.

Drav Cra.

Explorers said that the maps couldn't properly capture the tundra's enormity as no ships had ever been able to sail all the way around it without being sunk by ice-caps. And on foot was suicide. Many had tried, but none had returned. There were rumors of a vast, magical world beyond its borders, with lush vegetation and marvelous creatures—but Sora figured they were just that, rumors.

Her body tread barefoot through the snow, Nesilia controlling the gentle pendulum swing of her legs. Cold powder sifted between her toes and the feeling was invigorating rather than deathly cold, as if she'd been reunited with a long-lost friend. Perhaps that was what had stirred her.

She considered confronting Nesilia again, trying to regain control, but every time she did, she found herself stuffed back into Nowhere within minutes. The Buried Goddess was too powerful. So instead, Sora remained quiet and watched. She imagined Nesilia could feel her spying regardless, but she didn't care.

Beside her walked Freydis, the Drav Cra warlock. Sora could feel the evil emanating from the woman. It wasn't just the magic of Elsewhere, not the power she'd felt stirring within herself so many times. It wasn't even what she'd felt in Aihara Na or the other mystics in the Red Tower. The warlock had a darkness swirling inside—it reminded her of Redstar.

The thought of Aihara Na and the other mystics—Madam Jaya, Master Huyshi among them—had bile roiling in Sora's throat. She'd killed them all except Aihara Na. She'd seen the blood on her own hands. So many times, she'd tried to convince herself that the act was no different from the acts she'd performed with Gold Grin under Nesilia's possession, but she didn't *want* to sleep with Gold Grin. Somewhere, deep inside, she was glad those mystics were dead for all they'd done. She hoped they suffered in Elsewhere.

Sora could barely remember what happened to Aihara Na before they departed on the *Reba*. Clear memory of the Ancient One stopped at the woman pleading for life. After that, Sora retained flashes of the mystic and Nesilia discussing quietly rebuilding the Mystic Order and seizing anyone with a strong enough connection to Elsewhere for training, with no fear of risking being caught by the Glass Kingdom. That was it. No details, just plans and glimpses of the past.

Then, the now-familiar feeling of Nesilia's power overwhelming Sora blocked out everything until she blinked awake aboard the *Reba*, sharing Gold Grin's plush bed. But even presently, Sora felt herself taking deep breaths to fill her own lungs, and finding no relief.

It was like the Buried Goddess knew her thoughts, relished in them. The freezing air coursed through her nostrils and into her lungs. An icy finger traced her spine.

Sora's head turned to regard Freydis once more, Nesilia still in control. The warlock had painted her face with the blood of the Glass soldiers they'd murdered—two stripes from the roots of her fiery-red hair to below her eyes and one long smear across her lips. Sora hadn't seen her do it, but she knew it because Nesilia knew it.

"It is good to walk upon these grounds once more," Nesilia said out loud.

"I still cannot believe it is truly you," Freydis replied. Only then did Sora realize that Nesilia and Freydis were conversing in Drav Crava, and that she understood every word just as she had Panpingese after encountering the goddess in Elsewhere.

"Believe," Nesilia said. "Faith is all that has kept me from the darkness of Nowhere."

Sora noted how Nesilia used the term she'd invented. It seemed their shared memories and thoughts didn't only go one way.

Then she worried the name wasn't her own creation but a fragment of Nesilia's own thoughts.

"For all my life, I have worshiped you," Freydis said. "Strove to honor you with my very breath, and now you walk beside me, in my own land, like any other." Then, as if she realized she'd said something wrong. "Not that you are like any other."

"I understand your meaning," Nesilia said, flatly. "Curb your weakness, it will not benefit us where we go. You may accept me for who I am, but the others will not at first. They see only what they can with their eyes." Nesilia raised Sora's hand and examined it from both sides. "Not what lies beneath."

"Surely, that can't be true. They will worship you as I have. They will hear our words and understand."

"And are you so sure you've not just been duped by a Panpingese mystic talented in the arts of illusion?" Nesilia asked.

Freydis thought for only a fraction of a second before saying, "Never. I have felt your presence so many times. I felt it with Redstar. I felt it with King Pi. Now, it is the same only… so much more."

"Good."

"Though I can't understand your fascination with the pirate," Freydis said. "He fulfilled his role. He got us here, drew the Glass off our scent by making them think their ships were attacked by mere pirates. Surely, he's better off at the bottom of the sea now."

"Perhaps. Perhaps not. Only time can say. But while I inhabit this grotesque form, I should at least sample why you mortals revel in physical contact, and not a soul in this tundra would dare touch this… heathen body for pleasure unless they meant to harm it too."

Suddenly, Sora recalled. Gold Grin was anchored just off the coast, he and his crew had been ready to join them. He'd asked if this was where the infinite riches Sora had promised were, and Nesilia told him to wait for her return. He argued, but a kiss on his cheek and a tender stroke up his arm silenced him.

He was a plaything for Nesilia, every bit as much as Sora was. Sora felt a twinge of pity for the man. He'd been kind to her before Nesilia took over, and now lust had caused him to chase her across the world. Dragged along like a pet dog. He could pretend he was after treasures all he wanted.

The gleam in the man's eye at the mention of *Sora's* return was enough proof to trust he'd be anchored to that spot with no plan to move. It was more than likely Gold Grin would die there, slaughtering any crewman who even suggested they pull anchor, frozen by the cold.

Any question that Nesilia was the beautiful, pitiful, heart-broken thing Sora had seen within the chamber beneath Lord Bokeo's shop; any question of her being Iam's lover, and a lover of creation, was gone.

"There," Nesilia said. Sora's arm rose to point toward great, sheer cliffs rising from the ice ahead. They were cold, gray slate, bleak but so beautiful. As they approached, the walls created a natural pass that shielded them from the harsh winds and whistled a gentle melody. Black-furred dire wolves stood out against the white sky, watching from atop the cliffs, and following them from up high down the pass

"It is the time of Earthmoot," Freydis said after a long spell of silence. She looked up, wide-eyed, at a sky so white and bright, it appeared like daytime. "The moons are high. Celeste is full, is she not? Redstar will be replaced by a new Arch Warlock."

"That is precisely why we are here, daughter," Nesilia said.

Sora could see pride wash over the warlock's face at the title.

"You will claim the throne that is rightfully yours, then?" Freydis stated.

"No. The Drav Cra needs a new, mortal Arch Warlock to serve me. It needs you."

Freydis was stricken to silence. Sora felt her own lip curl. Since Nesilia entered her, she'd shared thoughts, memories even. Sora had a full understanding of what had happened in the God Feud so many years ago—or at least she understood what Nesilia *thought* had happened. But regarding Nesilia's plan here in Drav Cra, there was only black, empty space.

They walked in the quiet until a soft pounding filled the air. At first, it could have been mistaken for hoofbeats in the distance, but soon, Sora noticed the rhythm. It swelled as they walked, growing ever-closer. When the cliffs tapered off to meet the ground, Sora's breath caught in her throat. In all her years being told of the harsh, wild North, she'd always pictured it as nothing more than snow and jagged ice, but what stood before her was a beautiful forest, trees topped with fresh snow, red and blue berry bushes.

It was… *beautiful.*

Even with the limited time she'd spent around the Drav Cra people—especially Redstar—Sora expected their land to be a place of death and darkness. But the woods teemed with life. Birds chirped and soared above. Even a white-furred deer skittered into the thicket when it saw her, powder kicking up behind it.

"Home…" Nesilia said after a long breath. As if in response to her voice, a strong gust of wind tore through, shaking boughs and sending more birds to flight.

"The Buried Hollow," Freydis said.

Together, they walked beneath the canopy of the Buried Hollow, but it wasn't dark like the Webbed Woods. Here, Sora felt a strange sensation: hope. Her body practically glided through the trees at the will of the Buried Goddess, each root and branch bending to allow her unhindered passage without her even having to exert her body's gifts. Even those same dire wolves arrived, nestling against her thigh and letting her stroke their backs. Sora knew they wouldn't harm her, terrifying as they might appear.

The power—raw and unadulterated—was exhilarating. For a moment, and it was only a fleeting one, Sora had forgotten the violation being done to her. Then she wanted to scream.

"Just enjoy it," Nesilia said internally, feeling Sora's torment. "Let the pleasure of this place flow over you. Eyes like yours have never fell upon this sacred place, where Iam once proclaimed his love for me before he forgot me… like Liam and so many have forgotten you. Even your friend, the thief, I can't feel his essence anywhere."

"No…" Sora whimpered, then felt pressure against the back of her neck and she suddenly became weak. Although she felt her body moving, in her mind, she was curled up into a tight ball, nothing but darkness all around her. In Nowhere.

The next thing Sora remembered, they were deeper into the woods. It was now night, but the sky was bright and colorful. She'd never seen anything like it. Celeste was there, full, and this far north, her light must have been brighter. It burned with such ferocity it felt like daytime. Loutis was also full, however, he was just as haggard as ever. Surrounding them though were all shades of green, purples, and blues, but Celeste's orange light overpowered them all. It reminded Sora of the fireworks in Yaolin City, but these were not manmade, nor were they made of magic.

As her eyes and ears adjusted to the world around her, the soft thumping of drums became deafening.

Nesilia smiled and said, "Are you ready?"

Sora began to respond until she heard Freydis.

"For what, my Lady?" Freydis asked.

"To become all you're capable of being."

Without waiting for a response, Nesilia carried Sora's body in long strides. Moving forward, Sora noticed the orange glow she'd mistaken for Celeste's were, instead, massive fires burning in huge basins just beyond a jutting outcrop and a break in the forest. Once she passed the escarpment, she could see them, and beyond those, the source of the driving beat.

In a long line, at least a hundred Northmen stood shoulder to shoulder, wrapped in furs, covered in trinkets, faces painted and pounding on drums.

Beneath a blanket of leaf-bare branches, she saw what could only be described as a temple cresting one of the foothills. Colossal stones, old and gray, sat in a tight circle with a roof overhead that came to a sharp point. Each was entirely covered with glyphs inscribed in a language that seemed to pre-date Drav Crava.

In addition to the six bonfires—easily rising ten meters into the canopy above—there were hundreds of smaller flames burning on torches. Little figures moving throughout the hillock came into view, each stumbling through the trees.

Where there should have been snow, there was now dry ground, the snow melted and the waters licked up by the flames. The heat was so intense, it felt like summer in Troborough. Nesilia let her hand pass through one of the flames on her way by, the fire circling up her arm in loving embrace before puffing away in smoke and embers.

Silver goblets were everywhere, some turned over in the throes of passion, a liquid, red as blood, leaking from them. Drav Cra men and women were engaged in sexual acts in open air, no regard to those around them, and seemingly no discrimination toward gender. Sora had never seen such wanton lust in her life. Men and women alike, exposing their most private areas, everyone moving in rhythm with the drums, and the sounds. Moaning, flesh slapping against flesh, made her uncomfortable, but no one else seemed in the least bit bothered.

Some bit each other, drawing blood and drinking as if it were wine. It stole her thoughts back to Kazimir, although these were no upyr. Branches descended from the trees to wrap the many painted warlocks as they bled, lifting them into the air as if the trees were alive. Embers burst forth from their eyes when they moaned in ecstasy.

Nesilia sauntered through the place like nothing was wrong. Where Sora would have turned her head or shut her eyes, the Buried Goddess stared intently and thus, Sora was forced to do the same. Freydis still flanked her, but drifted several times to momentarily involve herself in the surrounding revelries. Sora suddenly found herself glad everyone was otherwise preoccupied. A Panpingese woman in the midst of all these Drav Cra, dressed in nothing but sticks and leaves, would have stuck out severely.

It soon became clear that Nesilia intended to walk directly to the top of the hill and into the circle of stones itself. For the first time, Sora longed to sink back into Nowhere. She emptied her mind, stopped resisting, but the blackness didn't come. It was as if something was keeping her alert this time.

"You mustn't look away from this," Nesilia said, answering Sora's thoughts. "This is life as it's meant to be. Raw. Natural."

"Please, Nesilia, I don't want to be here," Sora replied. "You said you would help me. This isn't help."

"You've been blinded by the world Iam left behind. A world of rules, of order. Walls, with those behind them and those beyond. Everyone afraid of being watched."

"I thought you loved him?" Sora asked.

"He lost his way without me. And when the other gods abandoned him too, he looked to order for answers. Order, the things the light touches, that can be seen, understood. He forgot everything I taught him about the wild nature of our creations, just as he forgot me!"

Sora could feel condemnation pouring over her like hot oil. If she'd never dabbled in the magics of these people, she wondered if she'd have still been in this situation. Her own people, the Panpingese, dealt with magic through an internal connecting to Elsewhere, not the bloodletting of these savages. Bloodletting she once performed.

The stone circle loomed over them like a mountain—Sora

didn't at first realize how far away the primeval temple was, how large a construct it was—so much larger than Sora could describe, bigger even than any cathedral to Iam she'd seen. It wasn't as tall as the Red Tower, but what it lacked in height, it made up for with its imposing nature.

Eye's of Iam were arranged before each pillar, made from wood with men stretched out across them and crucified. Some still wheezed. They all bled from being nailed down through their wrists and ankles, defacing the holy idol of the Drav Cra's sworn enemies. The blood slowly trickled into bowls, to be used by the savages to paint their faces. Sora knew this because Nesilia knew this.

From each corner of the roof beyond hung bones tied together with rope and vines. Sora saw skulls from various animals and some that definitely looked human. They clattered ominously in the wind, somehow able to be heard even over the driving drums. In the center of a platform, a man stood behind a stone table—or an altar—and a single flame cast light which reflected from silver discs hanging in a smaller circle around him. A dead deer laid before him, its throat cut and the blood running through a trough into another bowl.

The man, heavily robed, hood casting black shadow over his face, had just finished drawing a deep line of red across his forearm. His own blood poured out and mixed with the blood of the slain deer. He lowered his blade as he looked up, and with his other hand, gripped a gnarled, wooden staff, the end of which housed a skull with two glowing green gems set into the eye sockets.

"Freydis of the Ruuhar?" he whispered, hollow and cold as the ice surrounding them. "We thought you were dead."

"But here I am, Oracle," Freydis said, drawing her fingers down her lithe form. "In the flesh. And look who I've brought with me."

The man lowered his hood. His head was shriveled and old, almost devoid of hair on his scalp or chin. Liver spots dotted his flesh and his eyes were black as night, but as the light played over him, Sora noticed those same hieroglyphics on the stones carved into every inch of his body. He took a step forward.

"And this is?" he said.

Freydis looked at Nesilia—at Sora. "Do you not feel her power?"

"I told you," Nesilia said.

"Power? Did you bring us a mystic?" the man asked.

"I… no… I…" Freydis stammered, looking straight into Sora's eyes. "Oracle Rathgorah, this is the Lady herself."

Rathgorah tilted his head. "Freydis, what did you suffer at the hands of those warm bodies?"

"Nothing," Freydis protested. "When Drad Redstar performed the ceremony atop the mount, our Lady entered the world through this vessel, far away. I cannot say how it happened, but it did."

"Drad Redstar failed us," Rathgorah spat. "He ignored my advice and has put us in a position where none of us desire to be: needing a new Arch Warlock so soon and questioning the truth of his decade-long endeavors to piece together a story I warned him was the lie of Iam's acolytes. And now you bring this… *knife-ear* mystic to our land and call her the Lady?"

Nesilia remained quiet. Sora's blood boiled upon hearing that insult once more. She'd grown used to at least being accepted in Panping for the way she looked.

"Oracle, surely we do not question…" Freydis turned to her goddess. "My Lady, show him as you did me."

"If he already believes me to be a mystic, no amount of tricks will change his mind," Nesilia replied out loud.

"My tongue," Freydis said. "The southern devils cut it from me, but she healed it."

"That is enough!" the Oracle boomed and slammed the

bottom of his staff, causing the bones and chimes all around them to rattle. "I don't know what you were thinking, bringing this one here—at the time of Earthmoot nonetheless. Have you led the flower-pickers to us as well?"

The question seemed to catch Freydis off guard. Rathgorah bent over, dipped his fingers in the fresh blood drawn from both his arm and the deer, then pointed with his staff. Freydis flew back against one of the stone pillars.

Nesilia still did nothing. Freydis' head turned to the side, her jaw clenching. She looked like she was being crushed.

"Redstar proved we cannot align ourselves with them!" Rathgorah said. "Drad Mak roams their grasslands, the head of a slaughtered army, betrayed by cowards."

"No, Oracle Rathgorah," Freydis groaned. "I'm here to indwell, by command of our Buried Goddess, buried no more."

"Indwell?" the man said.

He returned the staff to his side and Freydis crumpled to the ground, panting. Sora had seen her ferocity firsthand, and memory of it through Nesilia as well, but in the face of this Oracle she seemed timid. The answers of who he was came to her from Nesilia's well of knowledge almost immediately. If the Arch Warlock was the public face of Nesilia's will, the Oracle was her memory. Stories, old as time, were inscribed in his flesh. He'd lived for an eternity in this temple at the heart of the Buried Hollow, given life by the sacred forest and never to leave. It was he who blessed all warlocks and named the new Arch Warlock—a guide for those to come, and those who came before.

"I'm afraid that is not possible, Freydis," Rathgorah said.

"I was Drad Redstar's second and a warlock, embraced by you upon my first bleeding," she said. "It is custom all warlocks indwell."

"You were dead. How is it that you survived, yet all the rest with Redstar did not, unless you are a traitor?"

"Our Lady intervened!"

Nesilia strode over to the man, and he watched her eerily. She let Sora's finger glide over the crest of his ear. Then she whispered, "It is my will she become Arch Warlock of the Drav Cra."

Oracle Rathgorah cleared his throat. "The will of mystics carries no sway here," he declared. "Only the earth may choose the Arch Warlock."

"And it shall choose me," one of the warlocks said. He stepped forward into the torchlight. His face was painted white with a dripping black handprint in the center and blood over his lips. Unlike many of the other warlocks around, he was a young man, barely older than Sora. Sora imagined without all the trinkets, paint and tattered robes he may have even been handsome.

"Kotlkel of the Dagson Clan," Freydis said, voice dripping with venom. "Our Lady would sooner choose a tick."

"Our Lady is wise. She's learned from the mistake that was Redstar. Who among us spoke against him most? Told that all his dreams would lead us to was death and despair?" Many of the other warlocks within earshot voiced their agreement. "A new age is upon us."

"And you think you'll be the one to lead us? With your help, perhaps Redstar would live and the Glass Kingdom would remain ours. But you hid here like a weakling. You turned on your faith."

"And you have brought this foreign girl to this sacred place. You're lucky we don't kill you now."

"Silence!" Rathgorah banged the end of his staff again. From between the stone pillars, painted faces appeared, black eyes glinting with fire. At least a dozen warlocks raised their hands, fresh blood dripping from their palms.

Thorny vines twisted up Sora's ankles, then up around her waist to her chest. One found her neck and tightened until even Nesilia struggled to breathe. But she didn't fight.

Nesilia settled in. Sora could feel the goddess' power ebbing beneath the surface. Her lungs began to fill again, and a sensation like fire roiled. That's when Sora realized it wasn't just a sensation, *like* fire. From the basins beyond the confines of the structure, long tendrils of flame curled. Sora could feel Nesilia coaxing them, willing them toward Rathgorah. They licked at low-hanging branches.

Sora's eyes closed and immediately, the vines released their hold of her body.

"What…" Rathgorah asked.

"You have clearly lost your way," Nesilia croaked to Rathgorah. Behind her, the warlocks shifted uncomfortably.

"What is the meaning of this?" Kotlkel shouted.

"Someone stop her!" shouted another.

Sora's whole body spun toward the sound. At the same time, she felt a hand on her shoulder. Her arm batted a painted woman aside. The resulting *crack* as her body shattered against the stone wall brought quiet to the rest of them. The female warlock groaned, bringing Sora a modicum of relief that she hadn't just been party to another murder.

Nesilia brought her around and the vines followed. They whipped across the other warlocks, sending many staggering. There were tens of them now and with a raising of Sora's other hand, the grass grew up around the savages' feet, then twisted over their whole frames. Some fought against it; others even fell as they tried desperately to break free.

Nesilia returned her focus to the Oracle standing before her. "Go, my children," she said.

At her words, the fire from the basin roared as it darted toward Oracle Rathgorah. The heat of the flames crackled as they passed over Sora, engulfing her but causing no damage or pain.

Rathgorah cried out in pain, louder and louder as the heat grew around him. Then, so did Sora. "Stop!"

The magically infused fire stopped a finger-length from melting the Oracle's face.

"How dare you!" Nesilia snarled inwardly.

"You won't keep using me to do your dirty work," Sora said. She wasn't sure if it was out loud or in her head, but she spoke with a confidence she hadn't had for a while. She refused to watch herself kill someone else, no matter who it was. No matter how perverse this entire scene was.

"My Lady?" Freydis said, answering the question of who now used Sora's physical mouth.

"Rathgorah," Sora said. "Go."

The Oracle looked as confused as anyone would have if they'd been there, watching contradictory behavior coming from the strange Panpingese mystic.

"I don't…"

"Go!" Sora snapped.

"Stop her," Rathgorah commanded and the warlocks immediately responded.

"What is happening, my Lady?" Freydis asked.

"My name is Sora."

"Kill her!" someone shouted.

Sora was more in control than she'd been in days, but that control was quickly fading under the hate-filled glares of the Drav Cra men and women—warlocks all—who now surrounded her.

Hands grasped her as ice crusted around her ankles, spewed from the fingertips of one of the warlocks. Sora snapped her head toward the woman. She thrust her hand out as she'd seen Nesilia do so many times and watched as energy burst forth from it and slammed the warlock in the chest, knocking her back several steps and into a clumping of angry Drav Cra.

She could only imagine what it looked like, a Panpingese woman amidst all these porcelain-skinned blood warriors. But after that outburst, suddenly, she could no longer feel the over-whelming sensation of Nesilia's essence resisting her.

"Yes…" Nesilia taunted. "Do it. Kill them all. Give in to your rage."

It was apparent only Sora heard the goddess. Her arm trembled, fire wreathing it, hissing like snakes surrounding their feeble prey. She knew then that she had the power to do it. Nesilia's essence mixed with her royal mystic blood… she could turn the entire temple into cinder.

"No." Sora lowered her hand, accepting her fate as the Drav Cra closed over her. For however long she was in control, she refused to keep killing. Even if that meant dying herself. She remembered Nesilia's fear as they nearly drowned. Perhaps, Sora might take the Buried Goddess with her. What a story that would make to tell Whitney when he inevitably met her back in Elsewhere.

"Stop it!" Freydis demanded. "You are making a mistake. That is the Lady herself. You'll both burn!"

Sora stayed silent, hoping her actions would bring a swift end to her and the horrible being that dwelled inside of her. Then a thought struck her: what *would* actually happen to Nesilia if Sora died? What if her spirit could leap into one of the others… Freydis. Then there'd be no stopping her. What if this was what she wanted.

Sora fought to free herself again. "Unhand me… children," she said, affecting her voice to sound like Nesilia had.

"What are you doing?" Nesilia questioned. Her fear was unmistakable now.

"She tells the truth," Sora said, ignoring her. "I am Nesilia, Buried but not forgotten!" Sora focused outward, and a surge of energy blasted the Drav Cra off her, allowing her to stand.

XVII

THE DAUGHTER

Muskigo sat, mounted on his zhulong at the front of his men, only Impili, the toothless dog who rarely left Mahraveh's father's side, and Farhan directly beside him. Hundreds of men armed with swords and spears stood in ranks behind him, waiting to march. Mahraveh ran, bow in hand, spear strapped to her back.

"Father!" she called out as she ran toward him. Still talking with Impili, Muskigo turned toward the sound.

"Sand mouse," Muskigo said. "What are you doing here?"

"I've come to join you," she said without pause.

Muskigo hopped down from his mount, but Impili stayed on his zhulong, looking down.

"Mahi, you know you cannot come," Muskigo said.

"Why, because I am a female?" she spat.

"No," he said, "because you are too young, just like Jumaat. Stay here with him, help him refine his skills and keep Saujibar safe."

"Then why does Shavi get to come!"

"She's patched up more than a few of your scrapes over the

years. We need healers. What do I always tell you? An afhemate is more than it's warriors."

"I can best nearly every man in this army," she argued. She looked up at Impili who merely smiled, more gums than teeth, then to Farhan. "Ask Farhan."

"I was going soft on you," he said, cheeks going a darker shade of gray.

"That's zhulong shog, and you know it. I can help!"

Muskigo took her by the shoulders. "Of that, I have no doubt. You are skilled with both bow and spear."

"I am better with my fists," she said.

Muskigo smiled and bent down, kissing Mahi on the cheek. "Next year, sand mouse. After I have the Glassmen on the run."

When dawn came, and Mahi and Jumaat pushed their way from their basement hatch, the air stank of death. Carrion birds pecked at the remains of their friends and loved ones, and the once-beautiful homes of Saujibar were husks of their former selves.

Jumaat ran to the bodies of his family and fell over them, weeping. Mahraveh scoured every corner of the town, searching for Shavi and shouting her name. She was nowhere to be found. Nor were the Glassmen Mahi had killed, probably taken so there'd be no proof they'd done this horrid act. With no survivors, they probably hoped to turn us against each other, pitting afhem against afhem and causing further unrest.

Mahraveh grew faint and had to lean on her father's house. The Shesaitju may not have been strangers to death, but no one could've prepared for this.

"Mahi…" a woman groaned.

"Shavi?" She ran toward the sound and found Branethra

beneath a cart. She'd lost so much blood the sand beneath her was purple. Mahraveh pushed the cart off her and cradled her.

"Nobody spoke of you," Branethra rasped. "We stood brave as your father taught us."

"How could they do this?"

"Because we are Ayerabi, and we are strong." She coughed up a gob of blood.

Mahraveh pulled her close. "Did you see Shavi? Is she alive?"

"They believed what she said and took her... Think's she's his mother—your grandmother. I heard them say they were going to use her to help break Muskigo. They might have gone after you if she hadn't... ungh!" She clenched her jaw.

Tears filled Mahraveh's eyes, but she knew what she had to do. Many women learned the healing arts; what herbs and insects to put in wounds. Mahraveh left that to Shavi while she learned to fight. If only she'd done what she was supposed to, she might have been able to help Branethra.

"Just look at me, Branethra." Mahraveh laid her head back in the sand and stared into her eyes. With one hand, she brushed her hair. "They will pay for this, I swear it."

She moaned. "My daughter. Is she?"

"She'll never have to suffer again." Mahraveh stabbed an arrow into the woman's heart. Branethra embraced her and squeezed until all the life fled her arms and she fell slack. A breeze blew a light cloud of sand over her face.

"May the eternal current carry you," Mahraveh whispered, then closed the woman's eyes.

She stood and returned to Jumaat, who'd closed the eyes of all his family. He sat beside his mother, head hanging.

"I..." he swallowed back tears. "I should be with them."

"Then you'd be dead," Mahraveh said.

"Better than being a coward." She watched as he rose and crossed the village to his home. After a moment, she followed.

Giving him distance, she waited outside but heard him rifling through things, throwing other belongings aside.

"Jumaat," she said, knowing he wouldn't hear.

Finally, he returned carrying a scimitar and a suit of leather armor still too large for him.

"What are you doing?" she asked.

"What does it look like? I am going to fight like my father and his father. I am going to kill them all." He went to walk by, but she grabbed his arm.

"All by yourself?"

"If that is what it takes. Today is my birthday, or did you forget? I always figured you were counting down the days until I was a real man. I'm supposed to fight."

"Jumaat…"

"You can come with me or not. It is up to you."

"Would you stop! I…" She took his hand. "You think I don't want revenge? They took Shavi. They're going to torture her. But she gave herself up so they'd stop looking for me. I won't lose you for nothing too."

He looked to the ground. "Then what? Where do we go?"

Good question. She turned and stared out at the devastation filling the place where she'd spent most of her life. It was no sprawling city, but the oasis had been a good home filled with kind, loyal people. If those in Muskigo's army all died as well, there'd be nothing left. A broken afhemate… left just as it had been before Muskigo took it over by winning in the Tal'du Dromesh and brought it to such heights.

"We fight as my father did," Mahraveh said.

"What? I just said—"

"You're of age, and Farhan was supposed to fight in the tournament, but now our afhemate has no representative."

"Mahi, I am man enough to admit I am not man enough for the arena."

"Well, we don't have a choice." She groaned. "I wish I'd thought of it while we were still in Latiapur. The al-Tariq afhemate boasts enough ships to break the blockade and give my father a way out."

"Mahi, you know I cannot win. You just said you do not wish to lose me."

"Well, I can't fight!" She whipped around, panting. "I would if I could. I may be of age now, but a woman has never taken to the sands. They won't allow it, especially not for my father. We don't have long, but I can teach you everything I know."

She saw all the bravado Jumaat had only just boasted fade. His cheeks went nearly as pale as a Glassman's.

"You said you wanted to fight," Mahraveh said.

"I did. I do."

"Then this is the way." She approached him and took both of his hands. "You may think yourself a coward, but I know you're not. We can change everything. I'll help you. Father taught me, and he's better than all of them."

His throat bobbed. He didn't say anything, but he slowly nodded. She threw her arms around him and pulled him close.

"We can do this. My father was nobody too… until he won. Gather everything we need. We have to go before it's too late."

She backed away, and his thousand-meter-gaze aimed toward the oasis, near where most of the killing had occurred. The water was darkened as blood spilled across it. Gallers and other carrion cawed overhead.

"What about them?" he said. "Will they receive a proper burial in the sea?"

"We can't…"

"They're my family."

"Then let us honor them," Mahraveh said solemnly.

"By allowing them to rot in the sun. What will happen to their spirits? What happens to those who are not returned to the sea?" Jumaat asked.

"They will aimlessly roam the sands until they stumble upon the waters. Jumaat, I promise… we'll tell people at Latiapur what happened so they can send carts for the dead. And if they refuse, when you win that fleet, we'll ship them out ourselves. But we need to go."

A few more beats passed in silence, then he eyed her and said, "I'll see if any zhulong survived."

"I'll gather supplies." He started walking, but she called out his name to stop him. "Thank you."

XVIII

THE KNIGHT

Torsten breathed in the warm air as he listened to the recruits for the King's Shield training in the castle bastion. He couldn't remember the last time he was able to stand outside without wearing long sleeves—the past winter felt like an eternity.

Sir Mulliner led them, and his injury at the hands of Freydis had him extra ornery. He guided them through stances and formatting techniques, often breaking to berate one of them. It was no surprise considering how raw they were. The order remained desperate for numbers to ensure snakes like Redstar and Valin Tehr could be kept down.

"Lucas Danvels!" Sir Mulliner barked as he stomped across the grass. "We never break rank without word from the commander!"

"I… I didn't break," Lucas stammered.

"Our shield is only a wall if we stand together. A half-step too far is breaking. It reveals a chink in our armor, and that is what our enemies will use, be it Sandsman or another. Tell me, soldier, do you want to die?"

"Of course not."

"Then quit acting like it and show your kingdom what you're worth!"

Torsten heard the clang of Sir Mulliner ripping the shield out of Lucas's hands and slamming it on the ground.

"Ease up, Sir Mulliner," Torsten said.

"Ah, Master Unger, I wasn't aware you'd be watching today," Sir Mulliner said.

"Listening, my friend." Torsten stood and approached the men, using his cane to push aside any stray stones or weapons. He stopped where he'd last heard Sir Mulliner. "May I?"

"Of course," Sir Mulliner grumbled, stepping aside.

"Listen up boys," one of the recruits at the back of the formation whispered, with a haughty accent that spoke of Old Yarrington royalty. "He'll teach us how to catch a whiff of our enemy's shog." A few of his mates snickered.

"Quiet," Lucas snapped. "He killed Redstar the Deceiver, or did you forget?"

"He let him in too," the other recruit countered, voice getting louder. "Or did you forget that while you strolled him around helping him piss?"

"I'll show you piss!" Lucas warned.

Torsten stuck out his cane, holding Lucas back before he could do anything stupid.

"You will watch how you speak to our Master of Warfare, Marcos!" Sir Mulliner growled. He and Torsten had never been close, but the man was a fierce defender of the Order.

"It's okay, he's right," Torsten said. It wasn't the first time Torsten heard how many people still perceived him. He knew Mulliner shared many of the same feelings. Despite putting an end to Redstar, he knew if he'd been stronger at the start, none of what the Drav Cra had done would've been possible. None of those who'd died could ever be brought back.

"I have made mistakes and paid dearly for them, as I'm sure

all of you will," Torsten said. "I let my faith be shaken, and our Order suffered for it. Because it is not only on the battlefield that we must be as one. We lost that. We let heathens cloud our judgment and invited a wolf into our midst.

"As Wearer, that was my failure. But it will not happen again. Look to your brother on your right and your left. Protect them. And know that they will protect you, too. Trust. That is the essence of the Shield." Torsten tapped the ground a few times with his cane until he heard a metallic *clink* of Lucas's heater shield. He groaned as he bent to lift it and hand it over.

"Now, form ranks," Torsten said. "And remember that instruction from Sir Mulliner is the same as instruction from any Shieldsman." Torsten turned in Sir Mulliner's direction and nodded.

"Shield wall!" Sir Mulliner shouted, each word succinct and echoing across the courtyard.

Torsten listened to the chorus of banging metal as the men did as he asked. He could picture it in his mind, the shields coming together in front, not a finger's span between them. The second row, longswords and spears at the ready to stab through and repel the enemy. He could picture himself in so many battles as just another cog in the wheel, and then in Winde Port when Muskigo's treachery broke the wall. Broke him.

He inhaled slowly and paced across the formation, head low, so his ear was aligned with the top center of the shields. He wasn't sure what he was listening for until he heard it. The clamor from the other end of the bastion was louder through the right side of the formation, where Lucas stood.

Torsten extended his cane under the shield and drew a line until it bumped into Lucas's left foot first. It was so close to the recruit beside him that when Torsten pushed and disturbed Lucas's balance, they knocked each other.

"Watch it!" the other recruit snapped.

Torsten reeled in his cane. "You favor your left side, don't you?" he asked.

"I suppose," Lucas said. "Always helped my father kneed the dough on that side."

"Soft-fingers," the recruit called Marcos muttered under his breath.

"Iam makes us all differently," Torsten said. "The trick isn't molding into the wall. It's finding your place in it. If you must favor that side, I suggest moving to the other end of the formation where your footwork won't be as obtrusive."

"You heard him!" Sir Mulliner shouted. "Move."

Torsten backed away just in time for Lucas to rush by and switch positions with someone else. He whispered, "Thank you" on the way.

"Thank you, Sir Unger, for your wisdom," Mulliner said. "Marcos, Yulniz, Bali, come to the front. I want you to give this wall everything you've got. Break them, and you'll get extra rations today. Everyone else, fail to hold the line, and you'll be out here until Iam's light fades!"

Torsten smirked as he walked back toward the castle, remembering his days in training, back when Sir Uriah and old Taskmaster Lars put them through Elsewhere and back to forge them into warriors worthy of leading King Liam's armies. He wondered when things changed for the worse, and everyone grew lax. *Probably when Liam got sick.*

No longer.

"Sir Unger!" a small, eager voice shouted for him at nearly the moment he entered the castle's Great Hall. "Sir Unger, there you are."

"Your Grace, is everything all right?" Torsten asked.

Pi stopped before Torsten, panting. Torsten heard the clamor of armor as the two King's Shieldsmen watching over Pi came to a halt a short distance behind him.

"Yes." Pi drew a deep breath. "I just had a question."

"Did you try asking your mother?" Torsten said. He'd been pushing Pi to visit her as much as possible, knowing he was the only thing in Pantego she gave a real damn about. If anybody could get her to leave her room and be the Queen Mother Torsten knew she could be, it was him.

"Lord Jolly is with her."

"Doing what?" Torsten asked, cursing himself inward for how that news made his heart momentarily sink. When no answer came, he said, "Did you shrug? Remember, Your Grace, I cannot see."

"Sorry… I'm not sure. Just talking, I think. I don't like him."

"Did he say something to you?" Torsten asked.

"No, he's just… He's always grumpy. Like father used to be."

"Men from the North usually are. They've lived harder lives than us."

"Then they should all move down here," Pi said innocently.

"Indeed." Torsten chuckled and rustled Pi's hair. His thumb caught a point of his crown and drew blood, but he didn't let the pain show on his face. "So, Your Grace, what was your question?"

"You're of Glintish descent, aren't you?" Pi asked, though his voice and footsteps were now a bit distant. The child had a knack for moving along without telling Torsten first and leaving him scrambling with his cane to keep up.

"I am," Torsten said. "Why?"

"I've been reading the tomes about my father's conquests. Is it true they're the only people who didn't even try to fight back at first before they surrendered."

"From what I hear."

"Weren't you there?" Pi asked.

"I was still a boy living on the streets of South Corner when the Glintish Alliance was forged."

"Oh…"

"But I've heard many tales of it. How King Liam strode alone into their capital, right up to their *swinlars*—their equivalent of a king or queen, I suppose, but there are many of them. Maybe more like a council of sorts—but not like the Panpingese…"

"Yes, I read of it."

"Ah, of course. Well, the story goes that your father went in alone, unafraid, and convinced them to lay down their arms in exchange for peace in the name of Iam." Torsten felt the kiss of brisk, morning air, and the sudden chirping of robins come to roost in the castle's western courtyard. Water from the dragon fountain transplanted to Yarrington from a square in Yaolin City trickled as the pipes within thawed.

"Why do you ask?" Torsten said. "Aren't you supposed to be studying the military exploits of your father? If you grow up as strong and wise as him, we'll never have to deal with another rebellion."

"I don't think that's true."

"You don't?" Torsten's cane found a bench leg, and he tapped along it to find the seat. "Sorry, may we sit? You're getting harder and harder to keep pace with. Growing inches by the day, it seems."

"I'm sorry Sir Unger," Pi said as he hopped up onto the bench beside Torsten. "I've just always enjoyed the spring."

"Me too, Your Grace. Iam's light may not shine brightest in the months after the Dawning, but the warmth it brings is unlike any other." Torsten shifted his position to face the boy. "So, why do you think rebellion will come regardless?"

"Well, it's just… after my father inherited the crown from my grandfather, the Glass Kingdom was at war for so long. He conquered other kingdoms in the name of Iam, made alliances, and since he started, every single one of them has taken part in some sort of rebellion or betrayal. Even if only in small groupings like this Afhem Muskigo."

"There has been much peace in Panping—" Torsten started.

"Yes, but with them being so cut off from the rest of the Glass, it's only a matter of time before Governor Nantby loses control."

"They are not cut off, Your Grace," Torsten argued.

"Call it what you will. Once they realize there's very little keeping them from reverting to their past way of life. They will. It seems history often repeats itself."

"People are rarely pleased with what they have in life. They can't see how much worse life would be without the light we bring. Take the Shesaitju, for example, they have a history of warring amongst each other, slaughtering entire towns, women and children alike. Regardless of what they believe about the glory of battle, since they bent the knee, their population has grown vastly. It's what has allowed them to now fight us so effectively."

"Not Glinthaven."

"What do you mean?" Torsten asked.

"Of all the places father brought under our banner, they've never bred rebels. They've never been late on a payment of tribute, even after Masters of Coin denied them better terms, like they currently ask for through our duke."

"How do you know this?"

"I had the new Master of Rolls bring me all of Yuri Darkings' records of our dealings with them."

"You read through all of it so fast?" Torsten said, incredulous.

"Father and Mother were always busy when I was little. Sir Davies had to deal with the city. I spent a lot of time teaching mother's handmaiden, Tessa, to read. I think I got good at it."

"I see…"

"What happened to her, by the way? Mother's new handmaidens, I can't remember any of them, and they don't like talking."

Torsten nearly choked on his next breath. He pictured poor Tessa's slight body swinging from the castle parapets, being pecked at by ravens after Oleander had her killed out of rage. Her new handmaidens were distant because everybody was distant from Oleander after what happened, and now she rejected even Torsten's company.

"She was released of her service and went home," Torsten said. He hated to lie—Iam's teachings expressly forbade it—but the truth was too ghastly for a boy Pi's age, king or not. And he was sure Pi had heard enough whispers throughout the castle about what had happened after Redstar drove his family to madness.

"I see," Pi said solemnly. "I hope she's teaching her people to read there."

"I'm sure she is. Now, about the Glintish. You're sure about what you read?"

"I can't find any instance of even a formal complaint anywhere in the archives," he said. "They've been at total peace."

"Well, unlike me, my ancestors have always favored the brush over the sword," Torsten said. "Perhaps, unlike the others, they have seen the grace of Iam."

"Their churches to Iam experience fewer worshippers than any throughout all the lands in the Glass Kingdom—even the Shesaitju."

"And how do you know that?"

"I wrote a letter to the priests who serve that province while they're all gathered in Hornsheim. A galler with their response showed up just yesterday."

"You did all of this on your own?" Torsten asked. He heard the boy swallow hard.

"Is that all right?"

"You're the king, Your Grace. Of course, it's all right. I'm merely suggesting that you could have requested help."

"I… I prefer to have all the scrolls open at once in my room."

The image of Pi, surrounded by candles, standing in a room with heathen symbols scrawled in blood on the walls passed through Torsten's mind. Then, so soon afterward, the boy's mangled body at the base of the West Tower, cradled in his mother's arms. Torsten shuddered and fought to bury the memory, reminding himself that it was Redstar's curse acting, not the real Pi.

"To see all angles at once, yes?" Torsten said. "Your father did always say that studying history was much like battle. So, is there something you want from Glinthaven? I must admit that despite the color of my skin, I have no connections to that place."

"I think they can help us," Pi said.

"I'm sure I needn't remind you that in the forty so-odd years since Liam and their swinlars agreed to peace, they have raised no army to speak of. It is a nation of artists, poets, and bards. So, if you wish to take advantage of our relationship and hire mercenaries to deal with the Drav Cra marauders under Drad Mak, I fear that won't be possible."

"I don't mean like that." Pi hopped to his feet, and Torsten listened as he paced through the garden, running his hand along the budding flowers. "I just mean that maybe all the wars father fought are the problem. It's all anyone seems to think about, yet the Glintish are happy to just… live. They don't need Iam or armies to control them. They don't need anything."

"I… I'm sorry Your Grace," Torsten said. "I don't know what you're trying to say."

"That maybe it's time we stop fighting. If the Black Sands don't want to serve us or Iam, then maybe we stop forcing them. Let them find light in their own way." His voice grew softer as he spoke.

Torsten sighed. He stood and followed the sound of Pi's footsteps until he could rest his hand on the boy's shoulders. "You are wise beyond your years, Your Grace, but you have seen so very little. Your father made as many mistakes as any man, but fighting to unite Pantego wasn't one of them, and very few are like the Glintish. They resist change, even for the better, and they cannot convince with songs or pretty pictures. We had twenty years of unprecedented peace when your father's campaigns waned, and now, there are even some dwarves who see the light of Iam."

"And yet, here we are, at war." Pi moved ahead to the next patch of flowers and Torsten was left behind, speechless. The way Pi spoke of change, like it was effortless—Torsten knew it was his youth, but he also envied it. And then he wondered what would happen if he listened; if he and the Wearer of White pulled their army out of the Black Sands and let Afhem Muskigo go, let them sort things out for themselves.

"Mother!" Pi yelled suddenly.

"My precious boy," Oleander replied, her smooth, sultry voice carrying across the courtyard.

"Your Grace," spoke Lord Jolly.

All the thoughts bouncing around Torsten's head were squelched when he heard the voice of Oleander Nothhelm out of her quarters for the first time in a month. He spun too fast and caught his cane on a vine, but tore it free and followed the path toward them.

"My Queen, you're here?" Torsten asked.

"Why, I suppose I am." She cackled. "Foolish Torsten, did you forget where you are?" Torsten felt a gentle slap against his chest. Then he smelled it, wine coating her breath like poison on an assassin's blade.

"No," Torsten said. "You're just… not in your room."

"I wanted to see my son," she said. "You're the one who keeps telling me to show myself. So, look at me birds! Here I am! Let the flowers turn their colorful heads and look upon my grotesque face!"

"They see only your masquerade mask, Oleander," Lord Jolly laughed.

"By Iam, you're right. Look away, my son. Sir Unger, can you please break this in half?"

Before Torsten could answer, he felt the porcelain and crystal mask Oleander had worn to so many of the extravagant parties she'd thrown as distractions for both herself and the kingdom after Liam grew ill.

"Go on, Torsten," Oleander goaded.

"Are you listening, Sir Unger?" Lord Jolly laughed again. Torsten heard the gentle sloshing of liquid as Kaviel Jolly presumably raised his glass of wine to his lips. "She said break it."

"Your Grace, this was your favorite mask," Torsten said as he ran his fingers along the bumps of the crystals set along its brow. "A gift from Liam after his visit to Myen Elnoir."

"Yes, and now it will keep me looking beautiful forever!" Oleander was drunk enough that her words came out almost incoherently. Torsten found himself wishing Pi was far away.

"Your beauty was never in question, Your Grace," Lord Jolly said. Torsten then heard the pluck of the man's lips against her fingers.

"Mother, since you're here, would you like to go to the stables with me like we used to?" Pi asked, tugging hard enough on her sleeve to get her attention that Torsten heard it.

"Damn it, Pi," she snapped. "You made me spill."

"I'm sorry, Mother. I—"

"Why don't you run on ahead yourself. You know I don't want to visit that ghastly place now that Sora is gone."

Torsten found himself startled by the name at first, forgetting for a moment that the Panpingese White Oleander used to ride shared a name with Whitney Fierstown's blood mage friend.

"Please, Mother?" Pi insisted.

"Your Grace, why don't you head up to your room and continue with your studies?" Torsten interrupted. "I think whoever we select to be our new Master of Coin will be very interested in your analysis."

"What an idea!" Oleander exclaimed. "Yes, my sweet child. Run along, and later I'll be up to brush your hair and tell you stories about your incredible father." She then whispered to Lord Jolly, "I'll leave out the good parts."

Whatever Pi said next was squelched when she pulled him into a tight embrace and kissed his head too many times to count. "Now run along," she said. "Be a child for Iam's sake!"

Torsten wasn't sure where the boy was, but he nodded assuredly and hoped it was in the right direction. Then he heard Pi stomp off, and the snap of a branch as he broke one off a plant or tree.

"Oleander, do you know how long he's been waiting for you to come downstairs?" Torsten said.

"Oh, don't be such a bother, Torsten," Oleander said. "I have a lifetime to spend with him. Who knows how long I have to catch up on old times with Lord Jolly before someone else in this forsaken castle dies."

"I didn't realize you two were that close."

"She spent a great deal of time in my castle when Liam drove back Drad Ingriztt... how long ago was that again?"

"Too long," Oleander said.

"Indeed. What a rare treat it was to host a noble that enjoys the harsh, cold life of Winter's Thumb."

"I was no noble yet," Oleander said. Then she spun and clapped boisterously "Speaking of cold. Clarice!"

"Yes, Your Grace?" said one of her young handmaidens.

"Fetch us some more wine and bring another glass for Sir Unger here."

"My Queen, are you sure this is a good—"

"Lord Kaviel said he remembers you from back then," Oleander said. "A brave Shieldsman defending his lands against the savages. Oh, whoops." She snickered. "My people. That you were a brown dot amongst the snow, killing anyone who got in your way. And what is it you remember saying to Sir Uriah Davies from atop the wall?"

"That if ever there was to be a next Wearer of White, it was you," Lord Jolly said. "Even over my own brother."

"And then you handed the white helm over to someone else. Sweet Torsten. When will you learn that you never hand back power when someone is foolish enough to give it to you?"

"Perhaps when I can see again," Torsten said, biting his tongue. This was how Oleander used to get while Liam was sick, drunk and cruel. Like the bitter cold of the place she was born. Dump a glass of wine into her, and she knew how to cut through the heart of any man.

"Oh, Torsten, don't be bitter," Oleander scoffed.

"I'm not bitter, my Queen, just blind. How is it Lord Jolly managed to convince you to visit the gardens," he asked, changing the subject.

"I reminded her that she needn't care what others think when they look at her," Lord Kaviel said. "There isn't one of them who wouldn't trade places to live here."

"They need us, Torsten," Oleander said.

"Who?" Torsten asked.

"All the rabble outside these walls. We help give their lives purpose, so why should I fear what they'll think of me?"

Torsten lifted her mask, still in one piece. "Then you won't need this?"

She snatched it out of his hands. "No. I like the way it looks." She snapped in half and flung one side halfway into the bushes. Then, Torsten listened as she fussed with her hair to secure what remained over the scorched side of her face.

"Radiant as the day I met you," Lord Jolly said.

"Kaviel Jolly, you lie like no other."

He laughed. "In that regard, I think your brother was ruler of the proverbial roost. We men of Iam are honest folk. Isn't that right, Sir Unger?" Lord Jolly nudged Torsten in the side.

"My brother," Oleander hissed. "Damn that man."

"At least now he suffers in the lowest level of Elsewhere," Kaviel said.

"It's still too good for him," Oleander said.

"Your Grace, here you are," Clarice said. Torsten heard the timid footsteps of the handmaiden as she approached, then the gurgle of wine filling Oleander's glass. "Lord Jolly," she said as she turned her attention to his glass.

She finished and back away.

"Aren't you forgetting something?" Oleander said, a harsh edge to her tone. "Sir Unger would like a glass."

"My Queen, it's fine," Torsten said. "It's hard enough to walk without a stomach full of wine."

"That's because you haven't tried it yet!" Lord Jolly slapped Torsten on the back like they'd known each other for years. Apparently, wine also transformed him from a grump to a lush. Torsten preferred the grump.

"Please, Oleander," Torsten implored. "You know I can't."

A few moments went by in silence, with Torsten left struggling to figure out if Oleander was angry with him. Finally, she barked at Clarice, "You heard Sir Unger! Leave us. Go on! My bedchambers haven't been washed in ages."

Wine splashed on the pathway as the young women hurried away.

Oleander sighed. "Where has good help all gone?"

"Who knows," Lord Jolly agreed.

A vision of Tessa swinging from the walls crossed Torsten's mind's eye once more. He shook it away and said, "Oleander,

Lord Kaviel, I hoped I might have a chance to speak with you about something I worry cannot be ignored much longer. Valin Tehr is a scourge, and I think we should reconsider—"

"Work, work, work," Oleander groaned. "Is that all there is to you?" She poured what had to be the entirety of her glass down her throat. "For the first time in a month, I feel like myself again."

"And I couldn't be happier seeing you down here, but—"

"Torsten, stop. Do, you know what I want? I want to walk out of the gates and have my people look upon me and know that I'm as strong as ever."

"And they will see that, Your Grace," Lord Jolly said. "For there is nothing else to see."

"Then, it's time for Yarrington to witness her Queen again. Torsten, will you be joining us?"

"I… My Q—Oleander, it's still dangerous outside of Old Yarrington."

"Then have some of your men follow us," she said. "For Iam's sake, Torsten."

Torsten heard her glass shatter against the ground, then the sharp *clack* of her heels as she set off back toward the castle. "Are you dullards coming?" she asked, then hiccuped.

"How much wine did you give her?" Torsten asked Lord Kaviel, sticking out his cane to slow him.

"No more than she needed, and no less," he replied. "Turns out, all she needed to leave her room was to be treated like a human and not a glass sculpture."

"I thought you said to give her time?"

"I tried a new strategy," Lord Kaviel said.

Torsten tugged on his sleeve. "Did you only come here to honor your brother and serve your kingdom?"

"Relax, Sir Unger." Lord Kaviel patted him on the chest. "The Jollys have pledged fealty to the Nothhelms for centuries. I know where my loyalties lie. But a strong woman like Oleander doesn't deserve to be alone for the rest of her life. And all she's surrounded by here are weak flower-pickers—if you'll excuse the phrase—and Shieldsmen married to God."

"I said let's go!" Oleander hollered back.

Lord Kaviel got a head start before Torsten caught up. Men from Winter's Thumb, especially Crowfall, were a proud bunch. It came from a lifetime defending their homes against raiders and surviving winters worse than Elsewhere. It took a lot to get a noble like Kaviel Jolly to consider moving south, but now Torsten knew what he really had his sights set on, and it made his skin crawl.

Valin Tehr wanted to own the Crown's coffers, Lord Jolly the Crown's mother, and all without a voice of Iam to be found.

XIX

THE THIEF

Fettingborough didn't look much better off than Grambling, though that had nothing to do with the storm overhead. It wasn't as destructive, leveling buildings and felling trees, but in the Wildlands, trees, rocks, and buildings were like lightning rods. Bolts flashed in every direction, striking near the same point multiple times. Which meant that tall, iron posts rose at intervals throughout the large town, absorbing the strikes.

The troupe took up temporary shelter in the stables outside of town. Modera slid her legs off the carriage, her husband a bulbous shadow behind her.

"Where are we going to set up, Modera?" Conmonoc asked.

"Set up?" Whitney said. "Here? This season? We'll be cooked before breakfast."

"What're you scared?" Conmonoc said.

"No, I just have a brain."

Lucindur glared at the two of them, but to Modera said. "I know you hate staying in the same place there's money to be made."

"It ruins the mystery," Fadra remarked. "The allure."

"Yes, but, I have to agree with Mr. Fierstown on this one," Lucindur said, "especially with so many supplies needed."

"I agree as well," Talwyn said softly.

"Same," said Gentry. A few others also agreed, especially those who, like Whitney, had the luxury of the troupe's worst tents.

Modera pursed her lips, then said, "Fine, but I expect everyone to cover the cost of lodging."

There was a quiet grumbling throughout the group.

"Mr. Fierstown," Modera said.

"Uh… yeah?" Whitney stuttered, amazed that his proposal went over so well. That was one of the first things he'd learned about the troupe: how the Pompares' loved to camp outside of the towns they passed through, and send performers in one at a time, as if they'd suddenly appeared out of Elsewhere.

"You seem to like inns," she said. "Find the best one and get us a deal. I could use a night outside of a carriage."

"My specialty," Whitney replied, neglecting to mention that a night in the Pompares' luxurious carriage was nothing to complain about.

"How many specialties do you have?" Talwyn giggled.

A witty, inappropriate response died on the tip of his tongue upon realizing who'd said it. "I'm still finding out," he said instead.

"Conmonoc," Modera said.

"Yes, Modera," the big oaf replied, hurrying to her side like a hungry, stray dog.

"Head to the markets with Lucindur and start replacing what we lost back in Grambling."

His features darkened at the task and said, "Yes, Modera."

"And do try to look intimidating, so she gets better deals. The rest of you, get to work! We've got a long night ahead to make things even after buying new supplies. A town like this, just north of the war, they'll be desperate for a few smiles."

"Yes, Modera," everyone chanted.

Whitney motioned for Gentry to follow him and set off into town. Aquira swooped down from the roof of the stables and landed on Whitney's shoulder. He scratched her neck with his knuckles.

"You know, for a fire-breather, you sure like rain," he said.

She screeched in approval.

"Though, I guess you do have scales," Whitney added.

Whitney and Gentry walked the town's unimpressive streets, more mud than cobbles with all the rain. The place was quaint and not too busy. Despite what Modera said, making a killing would be as easy here as it was in Grambling. The town was filled with mostly the elderly, and mothers with too many children to deal with alone. Here too, war had robbed the place of most of its working-age men.

They better win at least, Whitney thought. He hadn't a care for the wars waged by nobles and greedy men, but the Shesaitju deserved it for what they'd done to Troborough and Winde Port, not to mention all the other little villages like Oxgate. Slaughtering so many innocent people like sheep—savages.

Whitney searched for the best of several inns—which, again, wasn't saying much. The Grasslands were a place for country bumpkins, like Troborough spread across an entire region.

The Five Round Trousers had ten rooms available—more than sufficient accommodations for the troupe. After confirming with the Pompares that it would meet their posh standards and negotiating a rate by promising that Whitney and Aquira would only perform in that inn, Whitney procured the rooms and had the owner prepare food. The long-bearded fellow's eyes lit up like he hadn't served so many paying customers in years.

Whitney took off water-logged boots and plopped down at a

table by the inn's hearth. The place was almost entirely empty save for a few haggard, toothless old-timers yammering about better days. Even though it wasn't evening yet, Whitney didn't expect it to get much better. Aquira curled up in a ball by his feet, nearly inside the fire.

"Shouldn't we find spots to start earning?" Gentry said.

"We've been on the move for days, kid," Whitney said. He slapped the table. "Take a load off; eat a bit. Modera loves me after all."

Gentry's eyes darted nervously from side to side as if the Pompares were watching. They weren't. They were too busy in their luxurious carriage by the stables counting the gold Whitney'd saved them.

"C'mon, we'll make a killing tonight," Whitney said. "Work together again."

"Fine," Gentry said. "But no more ale."

It didn't take long for the rest of the troupe to file into the tavern since they weren't always under the watch of the Pompares in a camp. Even performers needed some time to unwind. It was still early.

Whitney turned toward the hearth and breathed in the hot air. It felt good, drying Whitney after day's worth of rain. As he turned away, he realized that they all smelled like mud and sweat after traveling. They all needed a hot bath, though, this wouldn't be the kind of place they'd find one. They'd barely get hot food.

"Did someone order the shoe leather sandwich?" Whitney asked, spitting out a piece of the meat he was served.

"I've had worse," said Benon, the lead actor in the plays the Troupe put on in the larger towns. The actors kept to themselves mostly, like acrobatics and feats of strength were below them—*stuffy bastards.*

"I bet you have too, huh, thief?" Conmonoc said. "You think I didn't hear you with those guards? What's dungeon food like?"

"Conmonoc!" Talwyn scolded. She didn't sit at the same table as Whitney, but the one next to it, facing him.

"What? He said it."

"He helped us pass," Talwyn said.

"It's okay, Tal," Whitney said, taking a sip of ale. "Can I call you that? I've lived a long life for my age, and I've done things I'm not proud of. Then again, I've done plenty of things I'm damn yigging proud of too."

"So, it's true then? You're a thief?" Talwyn asked. To his surprise, her eyes lit up like Whitney had just become even more desirable.

"*Was* a thief. And a yigging good one. I once stole the Sword of Grace—"

"This man is an admitted thief, and we still keep him around?" Conmonoc said, addressing any of the troupe who would listen. "Gives us all a bad name."

"Please," Whitney scoffed. "If Conny had been in charge of getting us lodging, we'd be in the stables sleeping on piles of shog."

A few of the members of the troupe who weren't busy with their own conversations laughed.

"I don't have to take this," Conmonoc said. "This is about him and his thieving ways. I bet he's just waiting for his chance to rob the Pompares blind."

"No, he only wants to reach Panping alive," Gentry said, honest as ever.

"Sure."

"Conny, why don't you tell everyone what you did before joining the troupe?" Lucindur spoke up, apparently listening even though she was busy tuning her salfio.

Conmonoc actually growled and shoved his chair out before storming off and out the front door into the rain.

"That didn't seem called for," Benon remarked.

"I tire of his complaining," Lucindur said.

Whitney took a bite of his… whatever meat it was. "So, what was it?" he asked through a mouthful.

"What was what?" Lucindur said.

"What was the sack of muscle doing before joining up?"

Lucindur looked to Benon and a few others. "It's too late now, Lucy," Benon said. "Or isn't sharing secrets what you do?" He cleaned his mouth, pushed off and followed Conmonoc out the door. The rest of the actors joined him. Their act took the longest to set up anyway.

"Well, you can't leave me waiting now," Whitney said. "I told you mine."

"I too would like to hear, Ms. Lucindur," Gentry said.

She sighed, then started talking without any more prodding needed. Whitney now understood Benon's accusation toward her. He also, with every day, was getting more clarity into all the little quarrels amongst the troupe. Modera and Fadra may have been tough, but without them, it seemed the troupe would've fallen apart in an hour.

"We found Conmonoc working for a man by the name of Valin Tehr," Lucindur said. "Ever heard of him?"

"Who hasn't?" Whitney said.

Nearly everyone who stuck around their tables raised their hands, mostly the younger members like Gentry who hadn't been around long enough to know every detail about every member down to the way their breath stunk in the morning.

"Really?" Whitney said. "I figured he was famous all over. Guy runs all of Dockside and South Corner in Yarrington. A real no good shog. I heard he's got some underground fight club where people can make money fighting against big, nasty… wait, shogging exile. Conmonoc was a fighter?"

Lucindur nodded.

"Exactly. He's got some nerve harassing Whitney for his past when he himself was a killer!" Talwyn said loudly.

"Keep it down," Lucindur admonished. "We don't need the whole town knowing."

"I doubt anyone in this cesspool cares," Whitney said.

"He was such a good boy when he'd first joined," Lucindur said. "So thankful to be a part of something that wasn't illegal. Something, noble and of his own people."

"What happened to him?" Gentry said.

"Some men can't leave their pasts behind."

"Nah," Whitney said. "Men just do crazy things for love. Or go crazy." He chuckled at his own joke.

"Love?" Lucindur and Talwyn said at the same time.

"Oh, please. Don't you see it? The guy is sick over you." Whitney pointed at Talwyn with his dinner knife.

Lucindur seemed appalled. Talwyn choked on a sip of water.

"*Interested*, maybe," Lucindur said. "Like many others have been. But he's not *in love*."

"Suit yourself," Whitney said, shrugging.

"Whitney, you did a fine job with this inn," Lucindur said, changing the subject. "I thought for sure we'd be spending the evening in a barn."

Whitney wasn't used to being praised. He was more often the screwup. He just shrugged again and kept eating.

The barmaid approached Whitney's table, clearing it of dirty plates. "Are you finished?" she asked Whitney, bending over lower than necessary and batting her eyelashes.

"With what I can stomach," Whitney said, pushing the plate over.

"She's up to something," Talwyn said after the barmaid was gone. "I don't like her."

Lucindur smiled and regarded Whitney but kept eating. "Talwyn, why don't you go to the tavern across the way, see if there's more of a gathering. This is a great town to practice your return for the real show next month. Tired people are hard to entertain.

"I'm having fun here," Talwyn argued.

"We've had a long day and an even longer week. Please don't argue."

"Fine," Talwyn said. She stomped out of the tavern, and there was no mistaking the stares a few of the older townsfolk offered her as she went by.

"Speaking of, I guess it's time we turn this place into the talk of the Wildlands?" Whitney said, patting Gentry on the back. "We'll start out front, try and get people inside where Aquira can jump into the fun."

Aquira let out a deep sigh as if in response.

"A fantastic idea, Mr. Fierstown," Gentry said. "I'd rather not fall behind again."

Gentry stood, and Whitney was halfway up when Lucindur said, "Whitney, do you mind if I speak to you alone for a moment?"

Whitney swallowed his suddenly dry throat. "But Gentry—"

"Is a far more experienced performer than you, young as he is. I'm sure he can handle things alone for a few minutes."

Whitney gave Gentry a look, but it seemed to go right over his head.

"I can handle it," Gentry said.

"Good. Great," Whitney said through clenched teeth. How could the boy know about the kind of conversation that happens when a protective mother gets a chance to talk one-on-one with a man her daughter is spending too much time with?

"It's down to us," Whitney said to Lucindur. He chuckled nervously and retook his seat.

"So it seems," she replied.

Whitney reached all the way across the table and pulled Benon's untouched ale toward him. He took a healthy gulp.

"So, who is she?" Lucindur asked.

Whitney choked on the ale and said, coughing, "Who's who?"

"The girl. My daughter is practically throwing herself at you yet you're looking for a lightmancer. Who is it you wish to spy on?"

"Spy on? That's absurd." Whitney took another sip. "Just find."

"Ah. The one who got away, then?" Lucindur asked, smiling.

"Not quite that either." Whitney finished Benon's ale. "I'm gonna need a lot more of these to talk about that." As if the barmaid had overheard—which Whitney then realized she hadn't ever strayed too far from their table—she brought two more pints and set them down.

"Thank you," Lucindur said.

Whitney took another sip, then a bigger one.

"How'd you know?" Whitney asked, burping. Lucindur scrunched her nose in disgust but didn't back down.

"When Talwyn was five years of age, I found her in front of our home taking silver coins from pink-skinned little ones in exchange for kisses," Lucindur said. "The line of boys—and some girls—wrapped down the street."

"And you let her?" Whitney said.

"Things are not so restrained where I'm from. Your priests say Iam wishes to spread his light, yet all of you cover up so... dutifully. When I discovered Talwyn's line, I told her she was a fool not to charge gold."

Whitney wasn't sure how to respond, so he lifted his mug and bowed his head respectfully.

"You're one of the few men we've ever come across who has shown no interest. Even fewer still whom she has shown interest *in*."

"What can I say. I'm picky."

"A thief, picky? This tells me that either you don't fancy women…"

"That's not—"

"…or, there's someone else."

Whitney ran his hand through his dirty blonde hair. "I'm still not sure there's enough ale in this building to help me talk about it."

"What if I told you I could show her to you?" Lucindur asked, leaning forward.

"I knew it!" Whitney said, slapping the table, upturning a goblet and making the tableware rattle. Several parties glanced their way. Whitney wasn't sure when the shoghole had started to fill in so much.

"I knew it," he said a little softer.

"I never said I was a lightmancer," Lucindur said.

"And I never said there was someone else." Whitney smirked.

Lucindur nodded her head appreciatively. "You will need to tell me a bit about her if I'm to help."

"That simple? What's the price."

"No price," Lucindur assured him.

"Please. There's always a price with this troupe."

"Perhaps. Yet, despite what you may think there is love between us all, even when we fight. You are troubled, Whitney Fierstown. You may not show it, but I see beyond the façade into the music of the mind."

It was Whitney's turn to lean in this time. "C'mon, *Lucy*. You're not the only one who can see when someone's hiding something."

"My daughter fancies you and this troupe has been good to us in every way but for a man worthy of her."

Whitney laughed. "Well, that ain't me; trust me."

"Maybe, maybe not, but I won't be around forever to protect her. A man like you who can handle himself could keep her safe in the troupe. But you are intent on leaving for this other person, so I'd at least like to know why so that Talwyn may know the truth."

"There we go," Whitney said. "Honesty. Was that so hard?" Whitney lifted his ale and threw it back, and before he knew it, the mug was empty. He checked for the last few drops and clanked it down.

"Her name is… is Sora…" He had to force it out, realizing he hadn't uttered her name to anyone after Elsewhere except for Aquira. Upon hearing the name, the little wyvern perked up and was up on an empty chair, staring at Whitney in a heartbeat.

"Sora what?" Lucindur asked, eyeing Aquira.

"Just Sora," Whitney said. "She's an orphan. Refugee after the Second or Third Panping War, I can't keep track."

"Ah, I see." Lucindur frowned. "That makes it a little more difficult."

"Shog," Whitney swore.

Lucindur held up a hand. "Difficult, but not impossible. You should watch your language around women, especially those who are your elders."

"Elders… you can't be a day over thirty," Whitney said, adding his own brand of charm.

"Yes… I surely was ten years of age when I gave birth to my daughter. Flattery stops working once the hairs turn gray, Whitney Fierstown. I'd have thought you'd know that by now."

"I'm a slow learner."

"What else can you tell me?" she asked.

"She and I grew up in Troborough after she was taken in by a healer. We were separated for many years but were reunited about six years—I mean six months ago."

Lucindur raised an eyebrow. "Which was it? Years or months?"

You tell me, he thought.

"Months," he said out loud.

"Where did you last see her?" Lucindur asked.

Whitney couldn't very well say, "in Elsewhere," or Lucindur would think he was insane. But that was the truth. He'd spent countless nights wondering if he'd hallucinated it all—everything —the years in Elsewhere with Kazimir, tending his parents' farm. His father's injury. The demon attack. Being surrounded by ghostly mystics calling out for Sora.

Now that he'd been on the road for a couple of weeks, he'd wondered if he'd imagined Torsten being blind since no gossipers spoke of a blind knight now in charge of guarding the Glass Castle. Whitney honestly didn't know what to believe anymore.

"In Yaolin," he lied.

"'I take it you don't plan to continue on to Glinthaven if you find her in Yaolin when we stop, then?" Lucindur asked.

"No," Whitney admitted. Eyes on his pint. "Maybe. I haven't really thought of what I might do after I find her."

"So you saw her in Yaolin last? How long ago?"

"About a month." As soon as Whitney said it, he realized all efforts to not seem mad had just gone out the window.

"You saw her in Yaolin a month ago, traveled to Yarrington, and now you are traveling back to Panping? Did you fly on the wings of dragons?"

"You have your secrets, lightmancer," he said. "I have mine."

To Whitney's relief, Lucindur accepted his response. "Final question: Where in Yaolin did you last see her? Specifics help. Street names. Shop names. Anything you can remember."

"It's a bit complicated," Whitney said. "I wasn't exactly *there* with her."

"Oh?"

"I saw her, in a sort of vivid vision."

"A vision… like a dream?" Lucindur asked, skeptical.

"No, not a dream. I was awake. Too awake. I'm afraid the

story is very long, and I honestly don't think you'd believe me even if I told you."

"I can bend light at the willing of my fingertips," Lucindur said, wiggling her digits. "We have all night and plenty of ale. Why don't you tell me your story so I might better assist you?"

"I…" Whitney glanced over at Aquira, who titled her head and blinked her two sets of eyelids at him. He blew air through his teeth, then pushed away from the table. "I promised Gentry a joint show," he grumbled. He wanted to tell her, tell someone, but knew anyone with half a brain would think he was crazy. *He* thought he was crazy.

Lucindur grabbed Whitney by the hand. "I think Gentry can handle himself." She tapped her ear, then pointed to the door, where the sound of clapping and a few cheers could be heard. "Trust me."

Whitney pulled away. "I don't trust anybody. It's nothing personal."

He started toward the door when she said something that stopped him in his tracks, "You're afraid, Whitney."

"Now look here. You may play a mean tune, but you don't know me. I'm not afraid of anything. You told me the other night you weren't a lightmancer, so let's just leave it at that."

"Lie to me, but do not lie to yourself. You're afraid, Whitney. Afraid of what you will see, and that she might be gone, or worse, over you. That all you went through might have been for nothing."

Whitney masked the wiping of his eyes as sleepiness. "How do you know I went through anything?"

"Because I'm not a fool."

"All right." Whitney slid his chair back out, purposely making the legs screech across the floor. "I'll tell you, and you'll help me pay for a night's work lost."

Lucindur's eyes narrowed. "You forget that I am helping you."

"Fine, then you'll give it to Gentry because of all the *love* you hold for him. And he'll owe me."

Lucindur stretched her neck back as if to hide her expression. When she lowered her chin, she nodded Whitney along. Aquira was now perched on the table as well, like she was eager to hear.

"Well," Whitney began, dragging a second mug of ale closer to his face, "it all starts in a cell in Yarrington. No, wait… it all starts with a shovel-headed dwarf in Troborough."

As more townsfolk filled the watering hole, Whitney recounted the whole story of his and Sora's reunion to Lucindur. Gentry brought his act indoors at some point, and beyond offering Whitney a confused look, said nothing. He knew better than to question the business of an elder trouper like Lucindur.

Whitney told her everything from Grint Strongiron's foolish challenge, to each and every imprisonment, going back from time to time to detail his childhood with her. He'd told her of Bliss, the spider queen, and Lucindur listened with rapt attention. She had a few questions about the Webbed Woods and the battle at Winde Port, but when he reached the part about Elsewhere, she didn't speak… not even a word.

When he'd finished, she stared, eyes squinted.

"I knew you wouldn't believe me," he said, finishing his—he wasn't sure how many—ales.

Lucindur swallowed. "I did. I do. I do believe you. I have seen that realm. Many times in my playing. Only one who has seen Elsewhere could so aptly describe it."

Whitney wasn't sure she could understand how much of a relief that was to hear. Sure, by then he'd drank so much he saw two of her, but it took every sip for him to eke out what seemed insane just to speak."

"But there is a problem," Lucindur added, making his heart drop.

"A problem?" Whitney said, his voice slightly slurred.

"There's no way I could show Sora to you if she is in the Red Tower."

"A red tower? Who said anything about a red tower?" Whitney asked.

"Not *a* red tower, *the* Red Tower," Lucindur clarified. "Where you saw her... she was in the mystic's hold. The Red Tower on Lake Yaolin."

"That dilapidated old sundial?" Whitney asked, having been to Yaolin City many times in his travels. "I've heard Liam had that place locked up decades ago."

"It may look rundown from the outside, but I assure you, the Tower is filled with powers unknown anywhere else in Pantego. There's no way I can show Sora to you if she is still in that place."

Whitney's head drooped. It might have been the ale, but he finally gave in to his emotions. "So, I'm right where we started." Tears welled in the corners of his eyes, and he allowed one to dribble down his check for the first time in as long as he could remember.

"I am sorry, Whitney. Truly, I am."

"It's fine." He hiccoughed. "At least someone believes what happened."

"Come on, let me help you upstairs. We can discuss this again at a more sober time." Lucindur circled the table and wrapped her arm around his to help him.

"No, you've done enough." He pulled free and stumbled into the next table.

"Watch it!" A dwarf in a hooded cloak glared up at him, having spilled some ale onto his red beard.

"Sorry, my tiny friend," Whitney slurred. He attempted to perform a flourished bow but stumbled again, and Lucindur helped him stand. He smiled up at her, straightened his collar, then patted her on the shoulders. "Thank you, but this isn't my first drunken night."

"Sleep well, then, and know that hope is not yet lost. I will spend the night looking for Sora."

"You're as sweet as your daughter." Whitney pecked her on the cheek before she could get out of the way, then made his way to the stairs.

"Are you okay?" Gentry whispered, pausing his performance.

"I'm fine, kid," Whitney said. "You're doing great."

"Whitney, you need to earn."

Whitney slapped his hand over the handrail of the stairs up to the rooms. Aquira landed atop the post at the same time, causes him to yelp in fright. He clutched his chest and chuckled nervously.

"Aquira will earn for me," Whitney said as he pulled himself up the first stair. Aquira started to follow. "No," he said. "Stay with him."

Aquira's eyes narrowed, but as Whitney continued pulling himself up, she didn't follow. He knew it was probably the alcohol, but he wanted to be alone, and that included her. After telling his story, he needed a break from everything that reminded him of Sora and Elsewhere.

The same dwarf shoved past Whitney on the stairs.

"Hey, you watch it!" Whitney slurred, stumbling down a step or three.

Gentry shouted something after him, though he wasn't sure what. And he heard Lucindur calming the boy before he rounded into the top of the hall. He tripped on the top stair and caught himself on a wall painting depicting five fat men in the largest pairs of trousers he'd ever seen.

"So that's where the name comes from, eh?" he said. He

laughed at himself, then staggered over to the door of his room and fumbled to find the key.

"A lightmancer, right," Whitney scoffed. "What a joke. That's about as likely as…"

Whitney found the rest of his words muffled as blackness closed in around his head. He found the taste and texture of dirty cloth against his mouth. Then something hard smashed against the back of his head.

"Got ye, thief," someone whispered in his ear before he passed out.

XX

THE MYSTIC

Despite Freydis' attempts to dissuade the crowd, and Sora's own insistence that she was, in fact, the Buried Goddess, she and Freydis now stood before Oracle Rathgorah and the other warlocks. Kotlkel sidled up to Rathgorah and whispered something to him. Even Nesilia knew little of the man beyond what he and Freydis had discussed since he was so young, but it didn't take a reservoir of memories to know that his past vocal opposition of Redstar gave him sway over the other warlocks and that he was favored to claim Redstar's title.

They stood in the place where the Earthmoot would take place in mere hours, which Sora knew because Nesilia knew. A circular pit, east of the temple and beyond the revelers and orgies was filled with soil, four log benches bordering it. Strung high above, hanging from ropes tied to branches, were the carcasses of a hundred hoofed animals. From some, blood still leaked out and into the muddy dirt below. Others were bone dry. The steady dripping sounded like a gentle rain.

"Oracle Rathgorah, please listen to reason," Freydis said.

"What you are asking us to believe," Kotlkel Dagson interrupted, "is that this Panpingese woman is our Lady? That's preposterous in every form of the word. What happened to you under the possession of the Glassmen?"

Freydis regarded Oracle Rathgorah. He returned a look that said, "Answer the question." Freydis then looked to Sora, who she still believed to be Nesilia.

"Go on," Sora said, feigning the confidence of the Buried Goddess. Inside, she could feel the goddess's anger brewing and hoped Nesilia had been just as uncomfortable feeling Sora's every emotion. Being out of control. "Tell them exactly what had happened in Yarrington."

Freydis recounted the story of Redstar's thought-to-have-been-failed attempt to bring Nesilia back to the physical plane. She told of how she'd been caught and brought for trial, explained that she'd escaped by biting off her own tongue.

Rathgorah laughed, then said, "You speak well for one without a tongue."

"The Lady… she restored it," Freydis said. "As I've already told you."

"The Panpingese mystic performed magics of her pantheon of lesser gods, you mean," Kotlkel offered. "Those shunned by both Iam and Nesilia."

Freydis sighed and looked to Sora again, who offered a smug grin, trying her best to mimic the exact facial expression she'd felt Nesilia make. It was disturbing to know that someone else could make a face so foreign to Sora using her own muscles. Having never seen it, she hoped it was right.

"I am no fool," Freydis spat. "I have felt the presence of our Lady, just as each of you has. It has carried on the wind, saturated our furs in the rain. I have tasted her in the dirt of the field, and in the blood of my enemies. Never before have I been so sure of anything. This vessel… it is just that—an empty husk but within that frail form is Lady Nesilia in all her glory."

Kotlkel clapped slowly. "Beautiful words, Freydis. Convincing. Just like Redstar was before he got so many faithful killed. It is time we worry only about our own lands."

"They are more than mere words. You are not Arch Warlock yet, Kotlkel Dagson. Don't you dare presume to lecture me like I'm some child. I am Freydis of the Ruuhar Clan, and Arch Warlock is my destiny."

"No one is questioning who you are, but it is clear the ways you've learned are not the best for our people. Death, bringing foreigners here—what might you do next?"

"Kill you for starters," Freydis hissed.

There will be no Drav Cra blood spilled in this sacred place," Oracle Rathgorah said. "We should be preparing for the Earthmoot instead of listening to this insane babbling."

"Just as I am saying, Oracle. It is clear she might have been… tainted. We all felt it on the air as she entered the forest. And it is clear Redstar's mission was a farce. All that time spent—for what?"

"*You* waste their time." Freydis spun and pointed to all the gathering warlocks and Drav Cra men and woman. Sora hadn't realized how many had gathered around the temple by then. "We all know the Earthmoot is a formality. Redstar chose me as his second because he knew my power. The same reason he rejected you as a child, Kotlkel. Are you still bitter?" "Bitter?" he scoffed. "I'm glad I wasn't manipulated as you when my mind was weak as you'd been."

"I followed because I have faith. You indwelled me yourself when my time came, Oracle. I am a warlock, chosen by Redstar. Perhaps I might die, but you cannot keep me from the earth."

"This is nothing to take lightly. Even if the Lady speaks—" Oracle Rathgorah said before Freydis cut him off.

"*If?* Kotlkel Dagson is a boy! Has he ever looked into the eyes of our enemies and burned them out? All of these…" She motioned to the other warlocks prepared for indwelling. "*Chil-*

dren! You would trust a child to rule us all? Who are we—the Glass? Are we no better than those fools?"

"If this is our Lady, tell me: why does she just stand there?" Kotlkel asked.

It was a good question. Sora had so many memories to dig through to try and figure out what was going on. She couldn't help but watch. So few in the world knew anything of the Drav Cra's ways.

"Why not call forth the mountains to rise from the sea?" Kotlkel went on. "Why does she not demand the gallers return from their migration and blot out the sky with their flapping wings?"

"I do not hold power over the Buried Goddess," Freydis said.

"Ah, yes. Of course. Well, you've been away, Freydis. You do not understand. With all that has happened in Yarrington and beyond—"

"I don't understand? I was in Yarrington. Or did you forget that while you and your ilk were here dreaming of flowers and warm winters, I was there? I saw the Goddess rise from her dirt tomb. Watched as all of Elsewhere responded to her voice. She has called me to this. And she will not—*I* will not be denied."

"Ah, a bit of truth in her words," Kotlkel said to the gathering. "So concerned she is with her own position. Why should we not believe this to be some kind of trick?"

"I've heard her voice—"

"Freydis," Oracle Rathgorah leaned in, his eyes drifting to Sora, and whispered, "I am not convinced the foreigner's voice can be trusted."

"That is blasphemy," Freydis said taking a stride toward the man. Near a dozen hands grabbed her and pulled her back.

"Redstar failed. It's time to move on."

"If he were here, he would separate your head from your

shoulders, that smug face and all. You say he failed, but I—who was there—not only tell you he didn't, but bring proof of it."

"I've heard enough," Rathgorah said. "Without an Arch Warlock, we have no one to make this decision. Never in all my centuries have I been so perplexed. I'm sorry Freydis, but in past, present, or future there is no precedence for this. The risk of giving you power when you may be a spy for the enemy is too great."

"I'm not—"

"I propose she be locked up and bound until the Earthmoot is complete. Maybe then we will receive an answer from our Lady."

"So, you would deny me my right as a warlock?" Freydis could no longer restrain her voice. The veins on her throat.

"If the Light of Iam has tainted her, we risk tainting the whole ceremony. This is not right."

Oracle Rathgorah scratched his chin with the top of his staff. Then he turned to the gathering of warlocks. "What say you, people of this holy tundra?"

There was a mixture of responses ranging from moderate support to outright refusal.

"Oracle, may I?" one of the female warlocks said, stepping forward.

Rathgorah motioned in affirmation.

The woman had wild hair and clothes even sloppier, like the mad witches in storybooks the mothers of Troborough used to read to children. Of course… the witches in Wetzel's stories were real and horrifying. She stepped so close to Freydis' their noses touched. It was difficult to tell her age with her face covered in chipped paint, but she was clearly older than Freydis.

"Freydis?" the woman said quietly.

"Sahades, it is me," Freydis replied. "I am not crazy, nor am I tainted. It is I who you held as a girl."

Sora watched as the warlock called Sahades lifted her hand

and placed it behind Freydis' neck. She stared into them a moment, then their lips met. They stayed that way several seconds before Sahades pulled away, panting. Her eyes went wide, and she said, "Freydis," again—softer this time.

Sahades turned to the Oracle Rathgorah and Kotlkel Dagson and said, "She's not tainted." Then to the other warlocks, she said, "This is the Freydis we all knew. Of that, I have no doubt. She must indwell."

More arguing broke out. Sora could hardly keep track of it, and she realized as she watched, that her life depended on how convincing Freydis could be—of all people, a woman who served as Redstar's own right hand.

"Even in control, you are out of it," Nesilia said to her within. *"Why bother trying?"*

Sora squeezed her temples between her thumb and index finger. Holding Nesilia back was draining on her. Her head pounded. Her muscles stung under the strain.

Oracle Rathgorah paced around his stone table. He had his eyes closed as if listening to the tune of the rattling bones around him. He ran his finger around the rim of the blood-filled bowl. Bring it to his lips, he chanted in Drav Crava and swept his hands across the air.

Specs of pure darkness exploded from his mouth, swirling about above him before taking the shape of Freydis herself in shadow. Seeing the display cast silence upon nearly everyone but a few. Shadow Freydis shot through the air, plunging through real Freydis' chest. The warlock lurched as if struck by a club, then gasped for air. The blackness spewed from her mouth, then vanished.

"Skorravik has spoken," Rathgorah said finally, listening to the spirits. "Freydis will indwell. If the Lady has chosen her, she will rise like any other. If not, she will perish, and with her, this one she claims to be our Lady will die as well."

"And if she is our Lady, she cannot die," Sahades added.

Rathgorah looked into Sora's eyes, expecting a response. She wanted to say "No," but she couldn't. Nesilia resisted and held her mouth shut. And before she gained back total control of her muscles, Nesilia forced a nod.

"Look what you've done now," Nesilia said within. *"Put our life in the hands of... what do you think of them? Savages... So cruel, from a girl with enough scars to compete with any of them."*

"Is it agreed?" Rathgorah said.

"This quim licker kisses her, and suddenly all our minds are changed?" Kotlkel said, gesturing to Sahades.

"This *quim licker* has served the will of the Lady twice as long as you have," Sahades said.

"She is a liar like Redstar!" Kotlkel said. "The Ruuhars cannot be trusted."

"Enough," Oracle Rathgorah said. "It is decided by those who came before, for we in the present are shortsighted. We should celebrate the return of our sister from the dead until she forces us not to."

"Bareese mista u lafe!" Kotlkel swore and flapped his robes as he stomped off. A warrior at his back greeted him, and they exchanged a few heated words. She was a woman, gray of hair, but the largest woman Sora had ever seen. She wore fur armor and had an axe on her back.

"That is Haral, Dradengor of the Dagson clan," Nesilia informed Sora. *"She is Kotlkel's mother, and one of the greatest warriors in all the tundra. Why do you fight us? Here, a woman can be anything... even king. Better than being forgotten."*

"Quiet!" Sora whispered to herself, earning a few confused glares from those nearby.

"Let him go," Rathgorah said. "He will cool down before the Earthmoot, or he will be the first to breathe in the dirt and enter into death. Either way, the Lady will have spoken."

"If she even speaks at all," said one of the warlocks eliciting several grunts of agreement.

"On this, the day marking when her Lady gave her life only to be forgotten beneath the holy soil, you dare question her?" Freydis said.

"It is okay," Sora said, once again doing her best to mimic Nesilia's tone and cadence. "They will learn the truth."

Oracle Rathgorah stepped forward and placed his hand on Freydis' shoulder. "Freydis, go. Prepare yourself with the others. You're right. I buried you here when it was your time to siphon the Lady' power from the earth into your blood. I should have given you the benefit of the doubt. We all should have. Don't make a fool of us."

"I won't, Oracle," Freydis said. "But what of her?" She nodded toward Sora.

"I will be bound," Nesilia said out loud. Sora was so focused on figuring out her surroundings, she hadn't even noticed Nesilia had gained control again. Sora pushed but failed. "If you do not rise," she said to Freydis, "they will crucify me just as they would any other foreign intruder."

Sora screamed, "*No!*" but Nesilia's smirk had already returned. Her voice never emerged, echoing endlessly in Nowhere. Sora's heart sank. She knew Nesilia's heart, and now it was clear. Nesilia had never intended to kill Rathgorah, the keeper of legend in the Buried Forest. She teased Sora with control, merely to show her how out of control she truly was.

Freydis' turned to Rathgorah for an answer.

"She speaks the truth. She will be bound, and if you fail, she will join the Glassmen in Exile. Her blood shall wet the earth, feeding our new warlocks. Her power will become our power."

Freydis glanced back at Nesilia. Concern twisted her features.

"*Any of them can suffocate down there,*" Sora said within. "*She can die.*"

"Not if she's worthy," Nesilia replied to Sora alone. *"You think I don't want this body? I assure you, my dear. There's nothing I do without reason. Freydis is nothing compared to you, daughter of Kings and Ancients.*

Rathgorah turned back to his stone table and hunched over it. He seemed exhausted from all the arguing and exhaustion. "Whether this Panpingese woman truly is touched by our Lady is yet to be determined," he said to Freydis without looking back, "but one thing is true: she believes in you."

XXI

THE DAUGHTER

Thankfully, the Glassmen hadn't bothered with the zhulong tied up in the town stables, having only killed Jumaat's and a few others who hadn't yet been put away for the night. Mahraveh rode Honey and Jumaat another beast whose owner would no longer have use for.

It was discouraging for Mahraveh to be back on the road to Latiapur, especially since the word "road" held no true meaning. It was one dune after another followed by yet another. The endless sea of black sand constantly shifted with the wind.

It was a few days ride, and every time they had to take a break, they trained. In the beating sun of daylight, in the cold winds of night. Jumaat was small, like her, so she could teach him to fight the same way.

"Ouch!" he yelped as Mahraveh accidentally sliced his hand. His spear dropped to the sand.

"Pis'truda!" Mahraveh yelled. "You have to keep your guard up, Jumaat."

"I am trying," Jumaat groaned.

She clenched her jaw. "I know." She kicked the spear toward him. "Again."

He groaned again as he bent to lift it. As soon as he got his hands around the grip, she struck, forcing him to act quickly.

"I'll tell you the same thing I was told. 'You're small, and you always will be compared to your opponent,'" she said as they stood in lock.

"Who said that?" he asked.

"My father the first time he gave me a spear." She whipped around, and he got his shaft up just in time to parry. She followed the blow with a flurry of strikes, which he blocked, but the final knocked him off balance. She didn't finish the move.

"Use their weight against them, she said. "Deflect, evade, and strike when they least expect it. Be the sand snake."

Jumaat swung at her, but his hips revealed his movement before his hands did, and she ducked. Her leg swept his legs out from under him. His back hit the sand, and her spear tip aimed at his neck, but she felt something poking the inside of her calf—Jumaat's spear.

He grinned, at least until she stomped on the blade to wrench it from his grip. "Better."

"Better? We've been traveling for two days, and the best I can do is stab you in the leg!" Jumaat stood and walked over a dune, staring into the distance. Green specks of nigh'jel lanterns hung from posts throughout the sands like a giant fan pointing toward Latiapur and the seat of the Caleef. Wayfarers left them so the Shesaitju could always find the Boiling Waters.

"The other men have trained all of their lives for this," he said. "I am going to die the second I step in. I will fail everybody."

"You won't," Mahraveh said. "Every warrior in there is going to ignore you."

"Oh, thanks."

"I mean, they won't think you're a threat. You don't need to fight every combatant to win; you only need to survive long enough to take out a handful. You may not be strong Jumaat, but I've seen you run. You're fast."

"Great. I will hide from them to death." He turned back. "It should be you, Mahi. They would not stand a chance. Is there any law against it?"

"Those men are arrogant fools who don't give a zhulong's dangle for what is or isn't law. They care only about their pride, and pride would dictate there being no positive outcome for them by allowing a woman to participate in the arena."

"If they were to lose to a woman," Jumaat said, realizing what Mahi meant, "live or die, they would wish for death for all the ridicule they'd suffer."

"Winning would be even worse!" Mahi said. "Imagine being known as the afhem who could only win because he faced a 'weak, puny' woman in the arena?"

"How about your father, being the man who won in front of King Liam and threatened him, only to be left to die for keeping true to his words?"

Mahraveh closed her eyes and nodded. "Nothing's fair. But I saw it, Babrak has all the others on leashes. He won't risk looking bad, whether I was to win, or lose in the first round. It has to be you." She extended her spear. "Now, again. And remember, we aren't the zhulong. We are the snake."

The morning sun was hot. Jumaat was so exhausted from training she had to waste a bit of their water on his face to wake him. Lati-apur was a hazy blotch in the distance sticking above the sand, beginning to take shape.

"I can practically hear the sounds of the Boiling Waters," Jumaat said, breathing in.

"I can nearly taste salted fish," Mahi said.

"I'm starved. Is there any more dried bellot?" He reached for their bag.

"No food until after you fight!" She fired an arrow right in front of his face. It startled his zhulong, which shook him off. She leaped off hers and swung down at him, but he rolled out of the way, using the beast to create a buffer.

"Smart," she said. "Use the entire arena to your advantage. Every rock."

"Are you trying to kill me?"

She came at him again before he could grab his spear from its hook strapped over his zhulong's back. "They all will be."

"I'm unarmed!"

"Then you'd better get armed."

She'd learned enough from her father to be able to determine her opponents' advantages and weaknesses. Jumaat had many of the latter, but of former, he was skinny. That made him faster and harder to hit. Judging by the size of Babrak's champion, the warriors he faced would tower over him. And he was agile. Working on the nigh'jel harvester ships wasn't easy. Not only were the creatures faster than most fish, but they were easily startled. It took small, one-or-two man vessels to sneak up on a grouping enough to trawl. That meant working the boom, the rudder—everything by oneself.

"Nothing trains you for war more than life," Muskigo had once told her. That a man could spend a lifetime training, but a true warrior fights in every breath. Seeks perfection in everything they do.

"Watch it!" Jumaat shouted as Mahraveh swung at him, with as much reckless abandon as his opponents would. He rolled over Honey's back, but Mahi didn't relent. High, low, she came at him from every angle, and without a weapon, all he could do was dodge. Her father would have made an attempt to disarm, and so did she, but Jumaat kept evading until Mahi stopped for a break. She too hadn't eaten yet.

"Good," she said, panting, and lowering her weapon.

He went to approach her, then hesitated.

"Sorry, I'm done," Mahi said.

"By the God of Sand and Sea, was Muskigo this hard on you growing up?" Jumaat asked.

"Not until I begged him to be."

"I think you might be insane." Hints of a smile betrayed his words.

"I just want to give you a chance."

"And in two days I already have a much better one than I did when you got me to agree to this. But I still might fail. Then what?"

"If we think like that, you've already lost," Mahraveh said.

"I am serious, Mahi."

"I don't know, okay?" She threw up her arms in frustration and walked back toward Honey. "I'll gut Babrak in the streets if I have to. Maybe then someone will listen to reason. Or maybe I'll marry him since, apparently, that's all someone like me is good for."

Jumaat's hand fell upon her shoulder. She leaned toward it, nestling for a moment before controlling herself.

"Then I will not lose, Mahi," he said.

"Good. Then eat." She pulled a bit of dried fruit from the pouch slung over Honey's back and laid it in his hand.

"What a treat, Master."

She brushed her hair across her face to hide her grin, then took some for herself. She wasn't sure why, but as she watched him walk by, sweat glistening off muscles she'd never realized he had, she felt a tiny flicker of hope that their crazy idea might work.

Mahraveh and Jumaat stopped before the gates of Latiapur. The sun hovered at its zenith, beating down on her shoulders. The stench of death which hung over them was masked only by their sweat.

"You're sure you still want to do this?" Mahraveh asked. She turned and noticed him staring at a group of warriors, covered in scars.

"No," Jumaat said, "but what choice do we have?"

"You're as strong as any of them," she said.

"You should not lie to your students."

"I'm not," she said. "They're not fighting for anything. Only for power, always power."

"And what do I have to fight for?"

"You'll figure that out." They exchanged a smirk, then Mahraveh urged Honey onward through the main gate.

With so many people, it was difficult to push their way into the city. All the talk was of the coming tournament, and it appeared people had journeyed from every afhemate in the Black Sands to participate in the festivities—except Nahanab. Mahi forced every distracting thought from her mind and pressed on.

Traders flowed in and out, mostly women and old men who couldn't wield the sword any longer. Warriors from different afhemates traveled with them, letting Muskigo lose while they enjoyed a tournament, Though it was their leaders Mahraveh blamed.

Then there were the inhabitants of Latiapur who affiliated with no afhemate and instead helped to build the wealth and resources of their people. Some called them the markless, others, the Caleef's afhemate. Mahraveh couldn't imagine drifting without a group to call family, without being bound by honor, in peace or war to serve her afhem—even though it was her father.

The Glass invasion had left more markless than ever as they dreamed of a life like their conquerors.

They were the worst of all. Barely Shesaitju. Spineless. Any of them could have decided to heft a weapon and fight.

She turned to the magnificent palace built into an arched outcrop of rock—the Boiled Keep. The last time Mahraveh had traveled to Latiapur, just a few days ago, her mood was brighter. She'd been convinced that she, Farhan, and Yuri Darkings would've been able to convince at least one of the afhems to aid her father in Nahanab before Farhan took to the tournament to try and become an afhem himself. Now, she was absolutely sure they were all cowards. There was only one way to ensure both revenge for what was done to Saujibar and reinforcements against the Glassmen at Nahanab.

"What is wrong?" Jumaat asked. Mahraveh didn't know her face revealed so much. Her anger must've been written upon it like ink on parchment.

"While my father fights for his life and their freedom, these pis'trudas revel, and party."

"Familiar customs are always easiest to follow in dark times."

"Easy for them," Mahi said. "They haven't lost anything yet. Their family, their homes." Mahraveh peered over and saw tears welling in the corner of Jumaat's eyes. She urged Honey closer and lay her hand over his thigh. "Sorry… our fathers… They still live at least."

"Yours does. I have not heard a word from mine." He stopped and scanned the colorful Latiapur marketplace. "We came here all the time on the way to the shore—stopped at that stand for palm root juice. I suppose he should have taught me more about fighting instead."

"That's why you have me."

"I hope he is dead," Jumaat said at the same time. Mahraveh's breath caught in her throat.

"Why would you say that?" Mahraveh asked.

"How am I supposed to tell him that I let them all die? That I hid in the cellar like a coward."

"You'll tell him at the head of a fleet," she said. "While we're saving their lives. There is nothing either of us could have done against those men."

Jumaat sniveled, then wiped his nose. "How are you so strong?"

"I'm just a good actor. Come." She gave his foot a kick and guided Honey through the bazaar. Once they passed, shoving through the crowd became a more straightforward task, their zhulong doing most of the work.

The Tal'du Dromesh loomed below them. In only a couple days, the tournament would be held for one member of every afhemate to battle for the right to rule over the al-Tariq afhemate. The tournament would also serve as an official funeral for Afhem Awn'al al-Tariq. It wouldn't be a grand thing like those for afhems who'd died in battle, but, unlike her own people, he'd be properly drowned and sent off to the seabed with his ancestors. Then, his city on a small island chain out in the Boiling Waters, which boasted a rather sizable naval fleet, would be fought for by any who stepped forth to claim it by sword or fist.

"Stable master!" she called to the same shop-owner from the other day.

"You!" he barked. The man was angry and had every right, but Mahi raised her palm, pushing the air forward as if to beckon him to calm down.

"I apologize for yesterday. Here."

When she raised her other hand, it held a small pit lizard skin pouch and jingled when bounced. The man's face contorted into something more pleasant. She'd taken it from her father's room before they left. He wouldn't mind.

"It contains payment for my time in your stables as well as a gift from House Ayerabi for your distress," she said. "There will be another when my father returns."

She tossed the pouch to the man, who greedily opened it and began counting.

"Is that enough?" she asked.

"More than, my lady," he said. "More than!"

"I know you are busy today," Mahraveh started.

"Yes, busy, busy. The whole city is busy." He spoke but never looked up from his treasure.

"I was hoping you'd have room for Honey here and my friend's zhulong?" She pointed toward Jumaat.

The stable master nodded his head. "For the daughter of an afhem, we will make room."

Mahraveh waved Jumaat over, and they waited while the man tied the zhulongs with a loose rope to the stables. Mahraveh patted honey, whispered a goodbye into the beast's ear and turned to thank the stable master.

Jumaat patted the zhulong.

"Does he have a name?" the stable master inquired.

"A name?" Jumaat repeated.

"Yes, your zhulong. Does he have a name?"

"Morkesh," he said after a short pause. "My father's name."

The stable master gave him an odd look, then said, "You two have a fine afternoon. I will take care of your mounts."

Jumaat bowed to the stable master. Always respectful, Jumaat was. It made Mahraveh smile. When she looked back toward the arena, her smile faded. Packs of huge men gathered outside every archway.

"Those are the other challengers and their supporters," Jumaat said, having attended one such event as a small boy. Mahi hadn't been there when Afhem Qui'sili died. Her father hadn't permitted her to join him. She'd stayed with Shavi while her father went off to attend. He said Qui'sili's land was a pile of zhulong droppings and would be better off cast into the sea.

The thought brought back the sickening memory of Shavi, missing from amongst the headless bodies in Saujibar. If that was their fate, what would 'Muskigo's mother' earn at the hands of the pink-skinned monsters?

"Well, I guess we will have the smallest of them," Mahraveh said. "Just you and me."

Jumaat's face twisted into what Mahi assumed was supposed to be a smile, and she grabbed him by the hand and dragged him toward the arena. The closer they got, the bigger the challengers became—each of them easily twice the size of Mahraveh and even bigger than Babrak in some cases.

"There's still time to back out," Mahraveh said.

Jumaat laughed nervously. "Well, in that case…"

"Don't be a coward," she said. She took his hand and towed him along. "Come on."

They pushed past some of the multitudes to the covered arcade wrapping the top of the arena where the presiding afhems were presenting their prized fighters. There was no greater pride for an afhem than when one of his own warriors, trained from birth, claimed another afhemate. And there was no better way to gain new allies or expand armies. Or in Babrak's case, new enemies. When her father won, Muskigo refused to bow to a man he considered crass and cruel.

Presently, Babrak sat sprawled on a beaned cushion in the shadow of the arena's highest concourse. Two stunning women fanned him with palm leaves while another fed him. When his eyes met Mahraveh's, they opened wide, and Mahi's stomach lurched.

"Spectators enter through the North entrance," he shouted over the din of the gathering.

"We're here to fight," Mahraveh said.

Babrak stared at her for a moment, face blank. Then, he broke out into a roaring laugh that jolted Mahraveh and those around. Several looked over. Many joined in for fear of upsetting the large afhem.

When he was through, he waved his hand dismissively and said, "Move on, little sand mouse. This is a place for warriors, not children."

"I am not kidding," she said, straightening her spine although her knees shook. "We will fight for our afhem, my father."

"You?" he scoffed. "A woman?"

"No, him." Mahraveh pulled Jumaat in front of her. "Right Jumaat?" He'd been eclipsed by a mountain of a man—Babrak's hulking champion, Rajeev.

Jumaat shifted weight between his feet. "I will…" his voice cracked, and he cleared his throat. "I will conquer that arena and walk away with al-Tariq as my own."

"Exactly," Mahraveh said. "Then we'll sail his many ships to Nahanab, and turn the tides of battle in my father's favor. And I will have no one to thank out of the lot of you cowards."

Jumaat elbowed her hard at the last statement, knowing that any response from Babrak would be acceptable after such an insult.

The big man looked between her and Jumaat a few times, then broke out in hysterical, rolling laughter. If Babrak's earlier laugh startled the crowd, this one reached the depths of the seabed and startled the dead. All the men surrounding them joined him, even the women fanning him. And it wasn't a courtesy to their afhem this time—they all stared at Jumaat and his skinny frame.

Babrak held up his hand, trying to speak but struggling through laughter. "Oh, girl, thank you. I haven't had a laugh like that in ages."

"This is no joke!" Mahraveh snapped.

"This is your father's grand plan? Send this puny whelp into the sands? I figured Muskigo was desperate after everything he did… but this?"

She took a step forward. "You have no idea who he is. Jumaat has been trained by my father himself." Jumaat shot her a withering glare, and she knew she'd gone too far.

"That boy, trained by the Scythe?" He and Rajeev exchanged a chuckle. "Have his balls even dropped yet? Can he even fight?"

"He's of age to march with our afhemate, if that's what you mean. Champion of the Ayerabi."

Babrak swayed backward once to build enough momentum to get to his feet. He stomped toward Jumaat. For what it was worth, her friend did his best not to cower in the giant's shadow. Not that he could've backed up anywhere, Rajeev's immovable frame right behind him.

Babrak lifted Jumaat's chin and turned him one way, then another. He gave his side a slap, like he was appraising a prize zhulong bull. "Strong arms, I'll admit, but you haven't even filled out yet. You will be slaughtered. Look around you. These are strong men, violent men. Veterans of many battles."

"So skilled in battle, yet none could be bothered with fighting for the freedom of our people?" Mahraveh remarked.

Jumaat bit his lip.

"Go home, boy," Babrak said, more serious this time. "You too, Mahraveh. This is no place for children."

"We're not going home. We have nothing to return to," she said. "The Glassmen you refuse to fight brought their hammered fist down upon Saujibar last night."

Babrak looked to Jumaat, and Jumaat corroborated her story with a resigned nod.

For a moment, Mahraveh thought Babrak was going to show some sense of decency, but instead, he said, "That's what happens when an immature afhem foolishly leaves his afhemate. Clearly, the bellot hasn't fallen far from the tree."

The red returned. Everything red. The fat pis'truda killing Farhan flashed before her eyes. "The Ayerabi are fighting in this tournament!"

"That isn't up to you, girl," Babrak said with a tone of finality. "Your friend is too young. Too weak. You will not make a mockery of this ceremony with such a pathetic tribute."

"I'm of age," Jumaat squeaked.

Babrak leaned in, his head twice the size of Jumaat's. "Law doesn't count for everything. Spectator's entrance is on the North side," he said again before turning back to his fellows beside him. "Enjoy the show."

"Then why don't I fight?" Mahraveh said.

Babrak rolled his eyes and waddled back toward his cushion. "You are relentless, girl. We will not sully the sands with the blood of a child bearer, even if you are the daughter of a traitorous afhem with no loyalty for the family that helped build him into what he was."

"You're just afraid. Afraid I'd cut your man here to ribbons."

Babrak fell backward and made himself comfortable. "Even I am a victim of circumstance. Leave things to the adults, girl."

"Coward." Mahraveh's hand reached up to grip her spear shaft, but Jumaat pushed her aside and stepped forward.

"I am going to fight," he proclaimed. "By the doctrine of the God of Sand and Sea, you cannot stop me. I will fight for the honor of my father and my family.

"You will die before you step out onto the sand," Babrak said. "But if that's what you wish, then I suppose the Ayerabi have their champion. I'll prepare the boat for your funeral."

"You'll be making one only for yourself, pis'truda," Mahraveh cursed. She took Jumaat's arm and pulled him away, hearing Babrak and his sycophant's laughter echoing, louder than even the waves crashing against the Latiapur cliffside.

XXII

THE KNIGHT

"Sir, what in Iam's name is going on?" Lucas asked as he led Torsten out of the castle gates. They had to move fast to keep pace with the drunken queen made bold and brash by liquor.

"The Queen Mother decided that today was a good day to visit her people," Torsten said. "Keep up with her!" Torsten shouted back to the Shieldsmen and recruits who'd followed them out of the city. Maybe he'd seen Oleander's redemption, but he imagined there were plenty of common folk who thought of her and remembered only the bodies she'd left swinging from the walls, or the extravagant parties she hosted and drained the kingdom's already-suffering coffers.

"Isn't it good she's finally out of her room?" Lucas said.

"Not in this state," Torsten said.

"You!" Oleander shouted at someone on the Royal Avenue. "What are you all murmuring about? Yes, it's me, your 'whore queen,' seared like venison at a Dawning banquet!"

Torsten pulled free of Lucas and hurried ahead, not taking enough care along the treacherous cobblestones. He stumbled, but Lord Kaviel was there to steady him.

"Lord Jolly, you have to put an end to this before she goes too far," Torsten whispered, seething.

"She has *already* gone too far," Kaviel replied. "Many times. Now it's their chance to see her as a human, not a monster hidden in a tower."

"She's in pain," Torsten said. "Can't you see that? You should have consulted me before—"

"Take no offense, Sir Unger, but you know only the widow. I know the woman, ever since Liam plucked her from the tundra. She needs this."

Torsten swallowed the lump forming in his throat and slowed down a bit. He and Oleander had grown close over the last year, especially after Redstar took over, but the Lord from Crowfall was right. Before Uriah went missing and Torsten inherited the white helm, he was just another face in a crowd of servants to Oleander. She'd gotten his name wrong as often as she got it right.

"Am I not as beautiful as you remember?" Oleander hollered. So many footsteps cleared out of the way of the royal escort, Torsten could no longer make out which direction she was yelling, though it sounded to him like it was at the drunkards who usually wasted the day away outside of the Lofty Mare.

"More beautiful, Your Grace," Lord Kaviel said. "For you have survived what so few could have and came out stronger for it."

"Lord Jolly, you flattering, northern croon, I didn't ask you," Oleander said. She stroked his arm loud enough that Torsten could hear it, and her hand slid lower toward his hip. "Is that your autlas pouch?" she asked. "The people need their Queen!"

"What are you—"

Coins rattled, then Oleander laughed as she flung a handful of coins into the air. They bounced along the street, and immediately, a fight broke out. Crowfall wasn't known for its wealth, but a man like Lord Kaviel Jolly was sure to have gold autlas on him rather than bronzers or even silver.

"Am I not your most generous Queen?" Oleander said. Again, coins clattered, and Lord Kaviel was left muttering curses under his breath.

"I suppose now he's getting what he bargained for," Lucas whispered into Torsten's ear as he caught up and retook Torsten's arm.

Torsten couldn't help but chuckle. "She always has been a handful."

"You!" Oleander barked. "Buy your wife a new dress." More autlas sprinkled the street. "By Iam, it's been long enough since mine's been torn off by a real man."

Torsten coughed in shock. Lord Jolly very likely did the same. But a few of the onlooking citizens laughed in response and applauded, something Torsten never imagined would happen in response to Oleander after all she'd done.

"She's nothing like I expected her," Lucas said.

"She's rarely how any of us expect her," Torsten replied.

"It's just... the way men in Dockside taverns talked about her all my life..."

"Trust me, it was the same in the castle, and I'm ashamed to say I was among the naysayers who didn't think she belonged. But to come from Drav Cra, to face what she has—she's a remarkable woman. I see it now, even if no one else can."

"If you say so, Sir," Lucas said. "Throwing gold out to the masses certainly won't hurt though."

"No. No, it won't. Especially when it's his."

"You don't trust Lord Jolly? The men talk about his brother Wardric all the time."

"Our king is still too young for me to trust anybody completely," Torsten said. "I know Lord Jolly loves this kingdom, but—"

"Nothing affects a boy like a father's influence, for the good or bad," Lucas interrupted, clearly having perceived Lord Jolly's intent. "Before mother straightened him out, every time my father came home from the taverns he'd tell me men like us could never be more than Docksiders. I love him and mum, but he taught me exactly what I didn't want."

"Father's do have a knack for that," Torsten agreed. "Why do you think I won't drink, even when the Queen asks me to?"

"Because Shieldsmen aren't supposed to dull their senses," Lucas said as if reciting from a rule book.

"Plenty have before me and plenty more will after I'm gone."

"Ain't got no gold for us?" A nearby Docksider said. It was easy enough to tell by his accent, and judging by how far they'd walked, they were near the street that led down through South Corner toward Dockside.

Oleander's heels tapped as she lost her balance for a moment. "It appears my Lord's pouch is empty," she said, then hiccuped. "See?" Cloth rustled as she turned it inside out.

"Figures. Only Valin Tehr's got our back, not ye lot!" The Docksider spat at their feet. Torsten now recognized him as the troublemaker Murray. In an instant, guards were upon him and slammed him against the street.

"That's right," he groaned. "We're just filth to ye highborn."

"Let him go," Oleander said. The men listened, though not without offering the poor beggar a few blows to the stomach. "Here. This silk coin purse is probably worth more than you've ever seen and it won't quite fit over my head to cover my face." She slid it across the street, the metal tassels scraping.

"Now roll on back to your filth, skag," Lord Jolly said.

"With this?" Murray protested, lifting the coin purse. "This gonna put food on our table or fix our roof."

"I'm from Crowfall, lad," Lord Jolly said, a harsh edge creeping into his tone. "Don't have a roof? Build one yourself.

The Crown keeps you safe enough. Least you can do is shut your trap and work harder."

"This gonna bring my son back?" Murray shouted.

One of the guards grabbed Murray and hauled him away. Before he could say anything else that might guarantee him a spot in the dungeons, a woman stopped him.

"Murray don't," she said.

The Docksider named Murray grunted and shook her off. "Gods-damned nobles! They'll get theirs. Iam's forsaken us all!"

"Are you okay, Queen Mother?" Lord Jolly asked.

"Okay?" She laughed. "Hearing the people whine about gold again is music to my ears! Like everything's back to normal. I was beginning to worry I was in a nightmare."

Back to normal, Torsten thought as they continued down the streets of Yarrington. Now that was a sentiment he could agree with. Beggars were better than foreign invaders, cultists, and fallen gods. No matter how the kingdom rose, even at the height of Liam's reign, there were always those whose fortunes faded. It was the way of the world. And though he wished Iam's blessings fell upon all, he didn't dare question the wisdom of his God in making Pantego the way it was.

"Torsten!" Oleander hollered. "Torsten, get over here, now!"

Torsten found himself speeding to greet her call without hesitation, leaving Lucas in the dust. He'd served Oleander closely for so long, he wondered why being called upon then made his heart race so.

"Yes, my Queen?" he asked.

"Torsten, my dear Torsten," she said. "I'm used to seeing the markets filled with savages. Now, it thrives again." She took Torsten's hand. "Go, fetch me a new dress worthy of my son's new crown."

"Your Grace, you donated all of the autlas we had," Lord Jolly interceded. "Shall I send a courier to fetch more?"

"I'm Oleander Nothhelm, you dolt. Any designer in the Glass would pay to have me slip into their handiwork." She guided, then releases Torsten's hand so that his fingers brushed along the curve of her hip. He wondered if it was intentional, his mind wandering back to that night in his chambers…

"Then perhaps there is someone more suited to the task than a blind man?" Lord Jolly said. He turned to Torsten and whispered, "No offense intended."

"Like you?" Oleander scoffed. "I'm sure in Crowfall that sorry smock of yours could be mistaken for high fashion, but not here."

Torsten smirked. Oleander's favor was often fleeting, and it was a relief now to be on the other end of it whether she was drunk or not.

"Lucas will help me fetch something in your favorite color," Torsten said. "Perhaps you can wear it to the next public audience in the Throne Room? A dress by the people, to show you're one of them."

"How lucky the people would be," Oleander said.

Torsten nudged Lucas and had him lead them down into the Yarrington markets. The warming weather had them bustling even though night was nearing, like citizens never expected the snows to break. Even folk from Old Yarrington wandered down to throw away autlas on trinkets and exquisite clothing just because they could. Torsten could recognize them by their pompous way of speech.

"Sir, I have no idea what she likes," Lucas whispered, voice shaking.

"Worry not, my friend," Torsten said. "There is a modiste shop on the corner run by a Panpingese seamstress the nobles favor. They're always more than eager to dress the Queen Mother."

"And if she doesn't like it?"

"She won't hang us," Torsten said. "Don't let rumors make a coward of you, Lucas. We are King's Shieldsmen."

"Not if I don't survive training. I'd rather face down an army of Sandsmen than her."

Torsten chuckled. "Trust me."

Lucas took his arm tighter as the crowd thickened. A thousand different smells assaulted Torsten's nostrils, all of them welcome. Anything was better than a horde of grimy Drav Cra camped in the square or the flocking beggars in Dockside. Traders from throughout the kingdom and beyond peddled wares: dwarven jewelry from Brotlebir, lutes and other instruments from West-vale, paintings from Glintish artists. When Liam set out to unite Pantego, Torsten imagined this was what he dreamed of. Though he doubted any Shesaitju were around presently, all sorts of people could be found in Yarrington square.

"Sir Shieldsman!" a trader shouted. "Sir Shieldsman. Surely a man of your size must be hungry. You've never tried stew like this."

"Pardon me," Lucas said, pushing through a group with Torsten in toe. "Move aside."

"Sir Unger, I believe?" said another trader, popping up directly beside Torsten. "Yes, it must be you. He who felled Redstar the Deceiver. Is it here? Do you have Salvation here? I'd love to glimpse the blade. Bless you, brave Shieldsman!"

"Step aside," Lucas demanded, but the assertive trader didn't listen. Instead, he nudged his way to Torsten's frontside.

"There it is," the trader said, awe in his voice, although it sounded false. "A man with such great taste in weapons… I have here an axe forged by the legendary Brike Sledgeborne. You'll be able to cut clean through dragon scale, hew through a stone wall!"

"What use do you think I have for an axe, friend?" Torsten asked, gesturing to his useless eyes. He couldn't help but scratch an itch around them as well.

"Then perhaps your aide?" the trader shoved in closer and broke Lucas's grip on Torsten's arm. "Could you not see yourself with this grand weapon, young man? You'll be the envy of the entire castle."

"Would you shog off!" Lucas shouted. He pushed the trader out of the way, causing him to trip on cobblestone and drop the weapon. The way the blade *clanged* and reverberated, it sounded like little more than basic iron. Dwarven smiths would've never crafted something so rudimentary.

"Badgering scum," Lucas cursed. "Worse than beggars back home."

"Relax, Lucas." Torsten patted him on the back. "It's nice to see the swindlers back at it. Better than heathens."

"I can't stand liars and embellishers. It's hard enough for honest workers like my parents to make a living."

"Worry, not. Iam sorts the true from the rubbish." Torsten lifted his chin and inhaled. He caught a whiff of flank cut from his favorite butcher off on the left, a chubby fellow from Winde Port. The modiste shop stood adjacent to it. Even without eyes, he knew Yarrington from a lifetime of patrolling its streets.

Things had been chaotic, but it buoyed his spirits to be out in the din of it all. To experience his city as it ought to be, a melting pot of peoples who saw the worth of Liam's vision.

"That's the shop," Torsten said, pointing. He could picture it in his mind, the street sign outside, the grubby butcher who set up his stand at the corner to try and get lords and ladies to think his meat was somehow worthier of their palate than any others. Success in the Yarrington markets was as much a war as that with the Black Sands… but at least people didn't die.

"You're sure you know what to choose?" Lucas asked.

"I watched her handmaidens come and go with every extravagant outfit she ever wanted so that she could stand out at her masquerades and balls," Torsten said. "I'm sure I can—"

"Thief!" a woman howled. "Thief!"

A man blew between Torsten and Lucas. Lucas absorbed the brunt of the blow, getting knocked off his feet while Torsten stumbled.

Aye, back to normal, Torsten thought. *As the traders flock, so do the thieves.*

For a moment, he worried that Whitney Fierstown was back to his old ways despite everything he'd been through. The thief who never seemed to disappear wasn't heavy enough to hit with such force, however, even at full speed.

"You have to pay for that piece, you Docksider rat!" the woman screamed. "He stole a golden locket. Guards, help me!"

"Piece of sewer trash, get back here!" Lucas barked. Torsten heard him scramble to his feet, push someone out of the way and give chase.

"Lucas, leave him!" Torsten called.

"I'll stop him, Sir!" Lucas shouted back, not listening. "Gives us all a bad name!"

"Youths," Torsten sighed. Chasing thieves was below the station of a Shieldsman, but Torsten couldn't blame Lucas. How could he after all his dealings with Whitney? And the young recruit had only just served as a city guardsman in South Corner. Old habits were hard to break.

Torsten extended his cane to walk on his own and tapped toward the shop's direction. He actually found the crowds easier to traverse without a guide. People recognized him more readily, and bowed out of the way, offering blessings for how he'd stopped Redstar the Deceiver. He wished they'd all do the same for the others responsible, like Sir Mulliner and Oleander. But he knew—only he who drives the blade through the heart of evil ever winds up in bard's tales.

He found the walkway and had begun to follow his nose toward the shop when he heard a shriek. If he'd had any hair on his bald head, it would've stood on end. Torsten knew that sound. He'd heard it from Oleander's mouth after Pi threw himself out of his window.

"Lucas!" he shouted, but the young man's chase had taken him out of earshot.

Torsten couldn't wait. He took off toward Oleander's voice, using his size and armor to shove through citizens. He plowed through a vendor's stand and apologized profusely as he sped by.

"Ah, I see you changed your mind, Shieldsman!" the weapon's trader said, forcing himself in front of Torsten again. "Even a blind man couldn't lose with a weapon like th—"

Torsten flung the man to the side and rushed ahead, ignoring all the curses at his back from those he'd hurt or pushed aside.

"You ruined it!" Oleander screamed.

"Queen Mother," Lucas stammered. "I didn't mean—"

"You ruined everything!"

"Oleander, what happened?" Torsten questioned as he neared her. He immediately regretted using her name so casually, but it wasn't the time to worry.

"My Queen, calm yourself, it was an accident," Lord Kaviel said.

"Calm myself?" Oleander bristled. "He broke my mask… You sniveling cur. Look at me! Look at this revolting face. I should have you hanged!"

All around, citizens had begun to murmur about how she was at it again, and Torsten physically cringed.

"I was chasing a thief. It was—" Lucas said.

"Liar!" Oleander roared. "You wanted to see the face of your wicked, 'whore queen.' You wanted to look upon me and laugh!"

Torsten heard the explicit sound of the back of a hand across Lucas's face. He knew well how her rings stung, and how easily they broke the skin. Torsten's cane crunched a piece of Oleander's mask as he hurried closer, his foot another. He cringed. The glass and porcelain shards scraped stone, as terror-inducing a sound as a barrage of Shesaitju thorn-arrows.

"Oleander, stop!" Torsten bellowed as he placed himself between Oleander and Lucas. The silence that ensued was like all the city had suddenly vanished, and with Torsten's lack of sight, it may well have.

"I swear, Sir Unger," Lucas stammered. "I didn't mean to knock into her."

"I know," Torsten said. He extended his open hand and took an uncertain step toward Oleander. "My Queen, I think it's time we returned home."

She didn't answer. More whispering broke out around them as the attention of the market-goers found them. Torsten knew how the situation must have looked. The Queen Mother stooped over another servant of the Crown, tall and fierce as the land from whence she came.

"So, it is true," a citizen said.

"Look at her face," said another.

"I heard, before he died, her heathen brother cursed her to be as ugly on the outside as within."

"Should have tossed *him* over the wall instead a long time ago."

The murmuring was relentless.

"Oleander," Torsten whispered, struggling to drown out all the chatter. He only hoped that it was his heightened senses which allowed him to hear the voices so clearly. "Please."

"Yes," Lord Jolly said, finally growing stern. "Maybe it is time we cut our fun short."

Again, Torsten stepped closer. He hoped Oleander remained in front of him, but as the throng of spectators grew, and the Shieldsmen fanned out to keep them at bay, he couldn't even perceive Oleander's breathing anymore.

"Oh, Torsten," she cried. Her arms wrapped around his broad

frame and she collapsed against his chest. "How hideous did the monster make me? What did he do to me!" Her legs grew wobbly, and Torsten helped her to her knees.

"It is a mark only of your bravery," Torsten whispered. "You saved your son, our king."

"You promised never to lie to me," Oleander said. "This reflects how they all see me. All of you!" She stood and screeched at the top of her lungs, saliva spattering Torsten's face. "And they should! They deserve a better queen and my son a better mother. Liam should have wedded that Panpingese witch instead!"

"Oleander, you've simply had too much to drink," Torsten said. "Your son loves you, and all your people will learn to do the same when they glimpse you for who you truly are and not what Redstar's treachery made you become."

"This *is* the real me."

"Torsten," Lord Jolly said. "Let's get her bac—"

A crash sounded up a way by Southern Court. Horses whinnied, and their hooves clopped into the distance. Iam-knew-what bounced loudly along the road next, causing a few citizens to squeal in fright. Torsten squeezed Oleander close. With his other hand, he grabbed Lucas's leg and dragged him over.

"What in Iam's name is going on!" Torsten asked.

"A wagon wheel just gave out on a carriage coming up from South Corner," Lucas said. "Looks like a food delivery from the docks for the castle."

"Someone, get up there and help them clear the way!" Torsten ordered. A few soldiers took the orders and started to jog up the hill, boots crunching as they passed.

"Back off, filth!" the wagon driver shouted. "This food belongs to the Crown."

"What is it now?" Torsten asked.

"Docksiders," Lucas said. "They're flooding out of the corner church. That same beggar from earlier and dozens of others. It's like they planned—Torsten, we need to get the Queen Mother to safety!"

"They got 'nuf, dun't they!" the Docksider Murray replied to the wagon driver. "How 'bout some for us ye left to die."

"Should be ours!" another one yelled.

"The rest of you, fall around your Queen Mother!" Lord Jolly ordered. "We must return to the castle; let's move."

"Drop that, you ingrate!" one of the men Torsten sent up ahead barked. "Or Iam help you—" Something blunt smashed against his face. Nothing else could illicit that hair-raising sound of bone cracking.

"Iam has forgotten us!" Murray screamed. Those words were echoed by a few more as the racket from their violence grew to deafening. More footsteps from the direction of South Corner pattered as more poor citizens mobbed the broken wagon.

Torsten tore free of Lucas. "Lucas, get up there and help them break this up!" he demanded.

"What a perfect time those ungrateful whelps picked to raid a food cart," Lord Jolly said. "All right men, let's push through—"

Lord Jolly grunted, and warm blood splattered onto Torsten's face, tasting like rusting bronzers. Oleander shrieked.

"Watch out!" Lucas crashed into Torsten's side, knocking him and Oleander to the ground. Arrows whizzed overhead, clacking against a shop wall.

"We're under attack!" a Shieldsman shouted.

"Where is that coming from?" said another.

"Shield wall!" Torsten yelled. "Protect the Queen Mother." Armor and shields rattled as they fell into formation around Oleander, Lucas, and Torsten himself. "Push toward the castle."

"Lucas, be my eyes," Torsten said, barely able to hear anything over the burgeoning chaos. The growing mob of rioters from South Corner erupted into such a frenzy, they flipped the wagon onto its side. The crash sent all those near it into a panic.

"The arrow came from the rooftop," he panted. "Lord Kaviel is injured, maybe dead… I…"

"Focus, Lucas." Torsten shook his shoulders.

"They're throwing crates and supplies all over the street," he said. "They're—duck!"

Lucas yanked on Torsten's head, and the feather of an arrow fluttered by, burrowing itself in the flesh of one of the Shieldsmen.

"Sir Hystad!" one of them shouted as the man collapsed against Oleander, earning a slew of curses like Torsten had never heard as he caused her to trip and snap her heel. She dragged Torsten down with her and his face smashed against the ground.

"Torsten, what is happening!" Oleander shrieked.

Torsten tried to focus through the clamor, but it was all too much. Things breaking, feet stomping, men and women yelling in both fear and rage—he felt like he was drowning in the Grand Canal of Winde Port again only this time, he wasn't sure of the way out.

"Out of our way, in the name of your king!" a Shieldsman demanded.

"The king has forgotten us!" Murray yelled up ahead.

"Torsten!" Lucas said. "Torsten, we have to get out of here!"

Torsten dared not move from shielding Oleander, but, finally, he turned his head and focused in on the voice of his aide. The blade of an arrow glanced off a nearby shield, bounced beside Torsten's hand, and made him wince. He couldn't remember the last time battle had that effect on him.

"The road is jammed!" Lucas said, hardly able to breathe. "We can run back through the markets while the Shieldsmen clear the protestors."

Torsten felt Oleander's shaking body beneath him as he

stretched out and grasped the stray arrow. He ran his thumb along the blade and over the bumps of an engraved pattern in the steel, then down toward the fletching, fashioned from the tail feathers of a waldrooth pharimon.

"Torsten!" Lucas shouted.

"The markets are too exposed," Torsten answered. "Those arrows… angry Docksiders can't afford anything like this." He wasn't sure who could; the craftsmanship was almost dwarven in quality, and the waldrooth were only found near the Pikeback Mountains in the Northeast. He went to lift it, but one of the Shieldsmen in formation was pushed back by the swelling mob and cracked it in two with his feet.

"Watch it, you buffoon!" Oleander yelled as another stomped on her hair. Torsten gave her a tug free, and the Shieldsman's legs went with them. The man stumbled back over them, and at the same time, Torsten heard the *squish* of a blade through flesh, and the gargle of a dying man.

"Ass… assin…" the Shieldsman rasped before the end, voice so low and quavering that only Torsten likely heard it.

"Get off of me!" Oleander squirmed, pushing away from Torsten and letting the heavy man fall between them with a *thud*.

Torsten could think of a hundred groups which might've wanted Oleander dead, but it didn't matter who. Perhaps whoever it was had purposely sparked this riot when the markets would be at their busiest, at dusk, after the craftsman stop working. Maybe they'd been lying in wait for months for Oleander to leave the castle. All Torsten knew was if they didn't move fast, one of the arrows would eventually find purchase in *her* throat.

"We have to get off the streets, now!" Torsten shouted. "Lucas, take her."

"What about you?" he asked.

"I'll follow!" Torsten took Oleander by the shoulder and pushed her in the direction of Lucas's voice without asking permission. "Go!" He shouted as he patted the street for the shield of one of his fallen comrades. When he found the edge, he lifted it and pushed through in the Queen's direction. Her incessant complaining made it easy to follow them.

"You expect me to go in there with him?" she scoffed. "The house smells ranci—" An arrow jammed into wood, and judging by how quickly Oleander was silenced, far too close for comfort.

"Oleander, just listen to him for Iam's sake!" Torsten shouted.

"Come, Your Grace!" Lucas said as a door creaked open.

Torsten rushed in after them, back first, feeling out every step. The rioters still chanted about how Iam and the Crown had forsaken them, even as Shieldsmen and guards pressed through the chaos and began arresting them. Torsten exhaled slowly, from his position in the doorway, focused on drowning the entire world out.

Iam, let me hear true, he thought. *Oleander may have done dreadful things, but she sees your light now.*

Torsten suddenly perceived the thrum of string, and a blade slicing through air. He raised his shield, and an arrow *banged* off the top. He staggered back, heard another arrow, and lowered his guard to block it.

"Stay in the corner!" Lucas shouted.

Young girls, likely the home's occupants, cried and pushed furniture aside, the grinding, grating sound unmistakable.

"Torsten, what is going on?" Oleander asked. "Whoever that is was aiming at me."

"There's no way out the back, Torsten," Lucas said nervously. "Just a wall."

Torsten raised a finger to his mouth and took a few, slow, deliberate steps across the squeaking floorboards.

"Torsten, what are we doing in here!" Oleander barked.

He ignored her and approached the townhome's stairs. Then

he heard it. The *whoosh* was subtle, but someone had entered through the upstairs window.

"Run!" Torsten pointed to the front door.

"I can do it myself," Oleander snapped as Lucas attempted to grab her.

Torsten felt the air as they ran by, then heard another squeak of wood.

"No!" He raised the shield high and deflected a projectile. He expected an arrow, but judging by the weight and the way it sank into the floor, it was a throwing knife. The assassin reached into his jacket and flung another. This time, Torsten was too slow. The grip just barely brushed his leg on its way by.

"My ankle!" Lucas yelped as he slammed down hard on the front porch.

Torsten screamed and with all his considerable strength, flung the shield up the stairs at the assassin. Then he turned for the exit. His hands groped frantically for the wall but found a table instead, which he purposefully knocked over, and then fell through the entry. The air had grown noticeably chiller in just the short time indoors. That meant the sun had dropped below the rooftops.

"Torsten, he shoved me out of the way," Oleander said from on the ground beside Lucas. "He did—"

"What any Shieldsman should've done," Torsten finished for her. They were certainly not the words Oleander was going to use.

"I'll hold them off," Lucas groaned. "Get her out of here!"

Torsten grabbed Oleander and yanked her free of Lucas. "We have to get you back to the castle."

He didn't wait for a response to move. He found the steps down and nearly tripped on the lip before his boot met the street. South Corner rioters continued to cause a mess under Murray's lead while hysterical citizens fled for their lives.

"Oleander, you need to lead me," Torsten said.

"If you didn't weigh so much I could," she snapped, tugging on his arm.

Glass shattered. Someone dropped onto their feet behind them, and Torsten knew by how soft the landing was that it had to be the assassin. Lucas screamed and pushed himself off the porch to tackle the assassin. A throwing knife shredded the side of Oleander's dress.

"Oleander!" Torsten exclaimed. He patted at her legs but found only ripped cloth and smooth flesh.

"Assassin!" Lucas yelled, this time enough outside of the chaos that others heard him. Lucas released a primal scream as he, presumably, tackled the assassin because the next moment, Torsten heard them wrestling on the ground. He also thought he heard teeth rend flesh, followed by another scream and then a fist crashed across one of their faces. Torsten hoped it wasn't Lucas's.

"Feel me up another time, Shieldsman," Oleander said to Torsten. She pushed off him and said, "Seize that man!" to a soldier who could see.

"Halt, Breklian!" a Shieldsman who'd heard Lucas's cry demanded. "Drop your knife!"

The man answered in Breklian, accent thick as soup. Torsten didn't understand a word of it, but the assassin did as requested. More Shieldsmen approached, having dispelled many of the rioters by then who weren't scared off by news of an assassin.

"Now discard all of your weapons," the Shieldsman ordered. "That's right."

Torsten positioned himself in front of Oleander and turned his head to listen for the man. He also heard Lucas's breathing. It rattled in his chest, but the boy was alive.

I can't believe even Valin would stoop low enough to send Codar. He knew of only one Breklian in Yarrington who could fight like this.

"Codar, do as they ask, and we won't blame you for your master's bidding," Torsten said.

Metal struck stone as the assassin dropped more weaponry. Then the man's knees hit the street.

"Take him!" Oleander hissed. "This one deserves to hang."

Torsten kept his arms spread wide in her defense as the Shieldsman marched toward the killer. "Get off the recruit," one said. "Hands where we can see them."

"The blood pact is written," the Breklian said. The moment Torsten heard him speak common, his heart skipped a beat. He knew what Codar sounded like, and this man had an accent so thick it was like he'd never stepped foot in the West before.

Torsten recalled his time back in Winde Port when Whitney was on the run from a blood pact Bartholomew Darkings made with the Dom Nohzi. That was the only time he'd heard that phrase before.

The mysterious assassin's guild in the northeast reaches, which the Breklian Oligarchs refused to condemn, rarely targeted kings and royalty. But stories of ancient times, before Liam united so much of the land, spoke of times when their order was forgotten and no longer haunted the dreams of children... that they returned in unforgettable ways. Liam's own Great Grandfather Tarvin the Terrible was said to have died at their hands, though there wasn't a soul in Pantego who didn't want him dead. His cruelty made Oleander's spell of hangings seem tame.

"Kill him," Torsten said. "Kill him now!"

As soon as the words left his lips, Oleander screamed in horror. Torsten heard no sounds of metal clashing, just grunts of surprise, followed by flesh tearing and blood and entrails gushing out onto the stone. Before a soul knew what happened, three bodies collapsed.

"Blood must be spilled," the assassin said.

Torsten stuck out a hand, and a throwing knife cut a long gash across the top of it. The change in direction probably saved her life.

"Where did he go?" she asked, terrified.

"Oleander, I want you to run," Torsten said, squeezing his teeth to hold back the roar the sharp pain in his hand made him want to unleash.

"What about you?"

"I'll be right behind you. Go!"

He gave her a shove, and she took off. One step and she tripped over her one remaining heel but tore it off. With Torsten's help, she scrambled back to her feet and started running out in front of him.

"Move aside for your Queen!" Torsten screamed as they approached the remaining protestors, guards, and curious citizens who'd left the Royal Avenue a mess. "Move, or you'll be held in treason!"

"She ain't no queen of mine!" Murray the Docksider spat back.

"It's the 'Whore Queen,'" said another who was busy trying to fend off a guard who had him pinned.

"Let me through, you worthless runt!" Oleander snapped.

"Whatcha gonna hang me over the wall?" Murray asked.

A guard released a mouthful of air as something hit him, then Oleander screamed, "Let go of me!"

Torsten rushed toward the voice, seized Murray who'd grabbed her and punched him. His fist hit the man's face like an anvil, but as Murray twisted onto the ground, he tore Oleander's dress up the seams.

The sight of it and the ensuing gasp silenced everyone nearby. Torsten had touched the burns which coated half her chest and arms, but now they were bare for all to see. He imagined her like the moons, beautiful on one side, shriveled and haggard on the other.

"Unhand the Queen Mother!" one of the Shieldsmen barked. What sounded like a small army of them climbed the hill, one pair disappearing at a time followed by massive bodies tumbling. Torsten had fought against armies beside fewer than one hundred Shieldsmen, and this Dom Nohzi assassin cut through them like they were mere children.

"Behold, the witch in her true form!" Murray shouted from his place in the dirt.

All the rioting and crazed chanting stopped, replaced by solemn mumbling about the "grotesque queen."

"Stay back, demon!" a Shieldsman ordered before a gurgling tipped off Torsten to his condition. Soon, there'd be no one to hold back the assassin.

"I've got you, Oleander," Torsten said. He wrapped her with his arms and pushed through the crowd. "Out of our way!" Now, nobody dared stop them. He could only imagine the people staring, thinking they knew anything about the woman Oleander dared to be.

"Torsten…" Oleander wept, barely able to speak.

He hushed her. "They'll hold them, Oleander. You don't have to worry any longer. I'll prot—"

"Sir Unger?" spoke a woman up ahead. As thick as the assassin's Breklian accent was, this woman sounded like a proper, Dockside lowborn. Sometimes, those who never left the area of the docks may as well not have been speaking common.

"Whoever you are, move aside in the name of the Crown," Torsten said.

"Already forgot me, eh?" the woman said.

Torsten stopped. He'd rarely visited the darkest corners of Dockside after he'd become a Shieldsman—rarely went back home. Her brogue was distinct enough to recognize, and he couldn't believe it.

"Sigrid?" he said, incredulous.

"Ah, so ye din't forget bout us?" she replied.

"Forget? I looked everywhere for you and your brother after the madness. Why are you here? Is he alive?"

"Who knows?" she said with casual dismissal.

"She is armed with a bow and has the bodies of guards at her feet," Oleander whispered into Torsten's ear. The fear in her tone was palpable now.

"Let 'er go, Sir Unger," Sigrid said. "I ain't here for ye."

Torsten swallowed, his throat suddenly dry as the Black Sands. He slowly positioned himself fully in front of Oleander. "What do you want? Where's Rand?"

"He was gunna live happily ever after with that handmaiden, Tessa," Sigrid said. "Til yer Queen destroyed 'em that is. She took 'em from me. She dun't deserve no castle."

"She was deceived by her brother," Torsten said. "Driven mad. We all were."

"She let him in."

"Sigrid, think about—"

"I won't ask again!" Sigrid screamed. Her bow snapped, and an arrow soared over Torsten's ear. The string continued to thrum. He'd heard that same sound earlier, and knew now that the Breklian wasn't the only one after Oleander.

"I know you're in pain, but your brother is alive," Torsten said. He slowly released Oleander and stepped toward the girl, making his body as big as possible like a lion protecting its cubs. "He's traveling to Brekliodad. Weren't you with him?"

She cackled, and Torsten noted how unhinged she sounded. Nothing like the overbearing but loving barmaiden Torsten knew before. "That what they told ye?" she said. "The Rand I knew disappeared long ago. Left me with monsters to die, he did!"

"Let us pass, and together we can find out where he is," Torsten said.

She answered by letting another arrow fly. This one didn't miss. It slashed across Torsten's shoulder, just above the pauldron.

"Torsten!" Oleander called out.

"You dun't get to pretend ye care, witch!" Sigrid screamed.

Torsten wasn't sure if it was the pain, but he only heard two footsteps before Sigrid had somehow closed the distance to them. She slammed into Oleander, knocking her through the gateway of the South Corner church's front courtyard. The Queen Mother bayed in agony.

"She's biting her!" a frightened woman yelled.

"She's possessed!" shouted another.

"Get off her!" Torsten growled. He lunged at Sigrid, but before his mighty fist met her face, Sigrid lashed out with a single hand and grabbed his wrist. His bracer wilted under her strength even though it was made of glaruium, and she tossed him like he weighed nothing at all. He crashed through the church's wooden doors, splinters snapping off as the bulk of them crashed down to pin Torsten. He struggled, pushing with all his might to break free, but he couldn't figure out the size and shape of the doors atop him, and bright lines of pain raced down his arms. All the while, Oleander's shriek intensified. She sounded like a hog who'd survived a butcher's first attempt at slaughter.

"What are you doing to her?" a man shouted from the street.

Sigrid pulled her mouth free and hissed.

"Get off her!" someone else yelled. Whoever it was charged them, but Sigrid broke free and Torsten perceived the cracking of the man's neck and cringed. He knew the amount of pressure required to snap the spine and couldn't imagine the lithe barmaid possessing the strength to produce it.

"Are you done toying with your food, apprentice?" That same Breklian assassin asked. Now that he wasn't fighting, he sounded more refined. The accent remained thick, but it reeked of Breklian nobility.

"Not until she suffers," Sigrid said.

"She already has. Now get up."

Sigrid grunted as she was torn free of the Queen. Oleander no longer screamed; she couldn't. All that was left were her tears. Torsten pushed through the pain and finally removed the broken door with the help of a brave citizen inside the church. His mind raced in confusion. A Breklian assassin from the Dom Nohzi order and Sigrid knowing each other—none of it made any sense. But they were both after Oleander.

Torsten slid Salvation from his back-sheathe and charged. "Unhand her, you filth!" he bellowed.

The Breklian sighed, then before Torsten knew it, the man was across the courtyard, and Torsten felt a blow to his stomach. Even wearing his armor, all the air fled his lungs as he doubled over, the sword of Liam Nothhelm slipping from his grasp. He'd never been struck so hard in his life. It reminded him of when the rebel Afhem Muskigo had punched him in Winde Port. But this…

"Help me," Oleander wept. "Torsten, help me!"

"How's it feel, nobody answerin yer cries?" Sigrid said.

"Enough, girl," the Breklian said.

"Enough? This is what she deserves, ain't it!" she shouted for all to hear. Torsten could still barely breathe, let alone answer. "There ain't one of ye who wouldn't do the same. And now, her reign ends."

As Torsten clutched his chest, he listened to Sigrid's grip tighten around the shaft of an arrow, then the blade driving down-ward. He wished he hadn't spent time honing his hearing so he wouldn't know, but he did. The tip plunged toward Oleander's chest, only, right before it struck, the Breklian grabbed her wrist, the sound of flesh on flesh.

"What're ye doing?" Sigrid said, struggling. "Ye said the blood pact is made!"

"The Sanguine Lords will have what is theirs," the Breklian said.

"Then let me finish it."

"Focus, young one. It can't be personal for us, and it can't be about hunger. I learned that the hard way. Clearly, you aren't yet ready for what Dom Nohzi means."

Torsten listened to the argument with rapt attention, still unable to move or breathe.

"I am ready!" Sigrid protested. "I opened my eyes from Elsewhere faster than any before me, you said so yerself."

"I don't blame you, Sigrid. It took me centuries here and years in exile with that feckless thief to truly understand. We are the hand that guides this world from the shadows. The sculptors of life and death."

"Ye promised me she was mine," Sigrid said, softly.

"Only the Sanguine Lords make promises. You will make your mark. For now, sate your thirst on one of them. Your eyes, I can see it. You hunger. It's okay, my child. The early days are hardest."

"No, she's mine!"

"I will not warn again!" the Breklian's voice thundered. A thud sounded, and Sigrid's body slid across the courtyard, bashing through a fountain-statue of Iam's eye in the center before stopping somewhere near Torsten.

"Now, fair, Queen Oleander," the Breklian said, his tone immediately calming. "It has been ages since the Sanguine Lords have accepted the demand for royal blood. Be honored. In your death, we rise again."

"Torsten…" Oleander wheezed.

He could feel her staring at him, heartbroken. It helped him muster the strength to crawl toward her and make one final attempt at thwarting the assassin. His hand landed, wrapping a loose stone from the church's doorway, but before he could pry it free, Sigrid's tiny hand fell atop it, her flesh felt as cold as the flattened peak of Mount Lister.

"He left me alone with them, for ye," Sigrid said, seething.

"Sigrid, you have to stop this," Torsten said. "We can stop this."

"No one can."

A pair of fangs sank into Torsten's neck. Cold surged down to his chest like icicles. He knew what was happening. Parents told stories about the upyr, blood-sucking fiends living simultaneously in both Iam's domain and Elsewhere. In some legends, they served amongst the Order of the Dom Nohzi. In others, they were a sickness born from the Culling of ages passed when evil allowed the dead to roam the world. Now he knew the truth.

Sigrid's tongue lapped at the wound. She groaned in ecstasy.

"Let Sir Unger go, girl," a man shouted. His voice was Breklian as well, only Torsten remembered it from a few days before in Valin's Vineyard. Codar, truly arriving this time.

Sigrid dropped Torsten against the cold stone. Blood oozed from the fang marks, but he couldn't move to stem the flow. It felt like a tree made of ice, spreading its roots throughout his body, making him numb everywhere.

"Grandson," the Breklian assassin said. Oleander released a bloodcurdling cry as he stopped doing whatever he was doing to her to address Codar. Torsten hoped not drinking her as Sigrid had been him. "I wondered if you'd show."

"I had to get you back here, Kazimir," Codar said.

"Hundreds every day wish for the death of their kings and queens. Never content. Few come to us, yet the Sanguine Lords have rejected altering the fate of men in such a way… until now."

"You…" Sigrid snarled. "I'll kill you!"

"Sit down!" the man called Kazimir bellowed. Again, Sigrid flew back and landed beside Torsten. She groaned as she struggled to return to her feet.

"Somehow, I always knew you'd serve a purpose for us," Kazimir said.

"My purpose is here," Codar replied.

"You could have served at my side for millennia. Instead, you reject immortality, like your father, to what, play house here with crime lords?"

"With Valin, I was no longer a shadow," Codar said.

"No, just a coward."

Metal rasped from Codar's direction.

"Put those silly knives away before you hurt yourself," Kazimir said. "You made your decision, Codar. Now, have you come here to watch us work?"

"I've come to stop you," Codar said.

"It's too late for that."

"You are a perversion of our people's dark past, Kazimir. A monster leftover from the Culling, nothing more. I knew you'd come, and now I will end you, and our once great family which you destroyed will be remembered again."

Kazimir laughed. "History is for those who didn't live it. You think books tell anything about what I did? Go along and play with your master."

"No," Codar replied. "Your time is finally up."

He charged, and all Torsten could do was listen.

Sigrid shouted, "No!" grabbed her bow, and let an arrow fly. Kazimir said the same right before Codar collapsed at his feet.

"What have you done!" Kazimir roared. "Codar, Codar." Torsten couldn't see where he'd been hit, but judging by the way he struggled for air, his lung was most likely punctured.

"Now... you... serve our purposes, grandfather," Codar forced out.

"You knew she..." Kazimir caught his breath.

"Still struggling... to raise your children... I see."

"Impressive, boy," Kazimir said.

"Don't make me one…" Codar begged. "Please."

"Never," Kazimir said. "When you find your father in Elsewhere, tell him—"

"Tell him yourself in eternity." By the sound of it, Codar suddenly stabbed himself in the chest with one of his own daggers.

"Kazimir, he was going—" Sigrid began before Kazimir clutched her throat. They were so far apart, the man must have moved like lightning.

"Do you know what you've done?" he questioned. She couldn't answer. "The pact is broken. I should have left you behind in Brekliodad!" He released her, and before she got a chance at her first breath, smacked her across the face.

"Foolish, rash, girl!" he yelled. "You wanted vengeance for your brother? Well, take a hard look at her, at the wretch whose time has yet to come. Enjoy it, Queen Oleander. Whether the Sanguine Lords come calling again or not, you are not long for this world."

"What?" Sigrid cried. "No, she destroyed him!"

There was a tussle, and it sounded like Kazimir grunted as he hit the ground. Footsteps skidded past Torsten. He was too dizzy to know exactly which way. Then came the *creak* of a bowstring pulled tautly, then released.

"Stop, girl!"

For a second, Kazimir's voice echoed, louder than anything. Then it was gone. Sigrid's presence vanished with him, her bow clattering to the ground. At the same time, far above in the church's spire, its bell began to chime.

XXIII

THE THIEF

"What are we going to do with him?" a man's voice said as Whitney started coming to.

"What do ye mean?" another replied. As drunk as Whitney was, the accent was unmistakable. It belonged to a dwarf who'd spent too much time amongst Glassfolk, and now was barely understandable to either.

By Iam, I'm starting to hate dwarves.

"We have enough shog stirring with the raiders out here, and with 'our *friends*, and now you *kidnap* some two-bit thief?" the man said. "How about you leave well-enough alone! We're so close."

The dwarf grunted. "No one asked ye to follow me." Something broke, but all Whitney could see was light and shadow through the thatching of burlap.

"Two-bit thief?" Whitney slurred, voice muffled by the bag over his head.

"Shhh, I think he's wakin up," the dwarf said.

Whitney 's head pounded—whether from ale or the conking he'd received, he didn't know. He heard a shuffling and then loud footsteps approached him. The dwarf grabbed hold of the bag and tore it from Whitney's head, taking some hair with it. Cold rain pelted his cheeks.

"Ouch!" Whitney half-shouted before the air left his lungs. The ugly mug which greeted him was unmistakable as well. Lump for a nose, ruddy cheeks the same color as the man's wild hair and beard, and one eye that never quite aimed the right way.

"Shut up, ye damned fool, or I'll cut out yer flappin tongue," Grint Strongiron threatened, the very dwarf who'd caused Whitney's simple life of thievery to unravel. "We don't need the whole yiggin town hearin ye."

Whitney was dumbstruck, looked around. "Grint-shogging-Strongiron, you—what? You kidnapped me, took me..." He cringed upon noticing he was surrounded by... tombstones. His vision swam. A short distance away, he could see the back of the Fettingborough church, Eye of Iam high above the rest of the town as if looking down with harsh judgment.

"We're still so near town?" Whitney asked. "What is this your first time bagging a man? Did you even think this through at all?"

Whitney then regarded the man accompanying Grint. He wore no armor, but there was just something... Torsteny about him. The hard look in his eye directed toward Whitney maybe, like he recognized him. Whitney's first thought was that this was the town's constable out for one of the many bounties on Whitney's head, not realizing his name had been cleared. If nothing else, he was a soldier.

"I thought glass soldiers were supposed to be smart," Whitney said. "What sort of lies did this rat-beard tell you about me?"

"As did I," the other man said, confirming Whitney's suspicions. His eyes turned toward the dirt, brimming with shame. "But I haven't done a smart thing in longer than I can remember."

"Quiet, both of ye!" Grint barked as he paced between tombstones. "I need to think."

"Something you, perhaps, should have done before breaking into my room." Whitney shifted. He was seated, back against something—a post? No. "You tied me to a grave? Yuck!" He looked down and figured he was sitting precisely six feet above a dead body. His legs were straight out in front of him, tied at the ankles. They were in the Fettingborough cemetery, located down a muddy trail through tall grass, just north of the town.

"You do realize that I have an entire troupe that'll be looking for me?" Whitney said. "I'm practically family to them now."

"Final warnin," Grint said.

"Is this still about the crown? For Iam's sake, you stole it from me first."

"I said last warnin!" The back of his furry hand crashed across Whitney's cheek. Dwarves were small, but generations of mining left them stout and robust. The blow was hard enough to cut Whitney's cheek.

"What in Elsewhere are you doing?" The soldier seized Grint's hand before he could strike again and shoved him away. It started to drizzle, and a bolt of lightning flashed, briefly illuminating the man's face as if it were daytime.

Realization hit Whitney like a ten-ton hammer as he stared up at the soldier. The last time he'd seen him, he was looking up at him as well, after a hard-fought battle. It only took watching the man act like a savior for Whitney to realize that he was more than just a soldier or constable—he was a Shieldsman.

"You're Ralph!" Whitney said, the fog of inebriation fading a bit. "You're Torsten's guy. The bastard who caught me in Troborough with the Glass Crown!"

Grint stopped pacing and turned to Ralph the Shieldsman. "Ye were there?"

"Doesn't matter," Ralph said. "It was a long time ago."

"Oh, don't sell yourself short, Ralphie!" Whitney exclaimed. "That was some mighty good soldiering you did that day—well, except for the fact that you were too late and let my home burn down." Whitney lost his train of thought for a moment when it struck him that he'd referred to Troborough as his home.

"At least you got the crown though," Whitney said, recovering quickly. "It would have been too tough for King Pi to have a new one made… oh, wait…"

A boot banged against Whitney's thigh after Grint broke through Ralph's blockade.

"His name is Rand, ye dolt—"

"Whoa!" Rand said, seizing the dwarf by the beard this time. "You didn't need to tell him that! This was your yigging idea. You've dragged me into this enough already."

"Ah, yes," Whitney said. "Rand Luney… Larily… Langley isn't it! Wearer for a week. You're the one who hanged all those fine, innocent folks. I had the pleasure of seeing their corpses swinging from the parapets upon my return from being a hero. Guess this… kidnapping is right up your alley, hmm?"

"Of course not—I—you." Rand released Grint; the dwarf flattened his beard. Rand then ran his hands through his hair and over his face before letting out a frustrated growl. "What did you do, dwarf!"

"This little shog-eatin thief nearly killed us all when he and his dirty witch of a woman left us stranded at the gorge!" Grint argued.

"Excuse me," Whitney accused. "*You* started this whole gods-damned yigging thing with your rock-brained challenge to *steal the King's crown.*"

Rand tilted his head toward Grint, eyes going wide. "The crown? You were a part of that?"

"Bah!"

"No," Rand said. "Not bah. What is he saying?"

"I was minding my business in Troborough when fire-crotch

over there waltzes over and challenges me to steal the King's crown," Whitney said. "Called the great King Liam a 'prick who deserves his come-uppings' if I'm remembering. Dwarves always sound like they've got a mouth full of shog."

"Who'd have thunk ye'd actually do it!" Grint said. "Ye were just some braggart who needed a dungeon."

"For starters: I'm not a dwarf."

Grint fought Rand to hit Whitney again, but this time the Shieldsman stood proud. At his full height, even Whitney had to admit he was rather imposing.

"Stop," Rand said, a harsh edge creeping into his tone. "So, it's your fault all of this happened."

"It ain't me fault the stupid thief got caught," Grint said. "I just wanted him to shut his *farmboy* trap."

Rand turned away. His shoulders heaved as he drew long, beleaguered breaths. "I killed people," he said softly. "I murdered. And it all started the day I caught this waste of breath holding the King's crown and earned the Queen's attention. No... it all started when you..." Rand released another frustrated growl and took a hard step away.

"I'm sorry for interrupting this... moment... but what's the plan here?" Whitney asked.

"Shut up!" they both shouted at Whitney together.

Hushed arguing continued between them for a while. Whitney picked up on bits and pieces. Rand accused Grint of being the reason he was left in charge of Yarrington when Torsten was temporarily exiled, and Grint claimed Sir Torsten Unger, the famed slayer of Redstar, would have left no matter what.

"Look, Rupert—can I call you Rupert?" Whitney spoke up after he could listen no longer. They were arguing in circles because it wasn't really anyone's fault. They were just two fools who'd gotten in too deep and expected the world owed them something. If Whitney had learned anything for sure in Else-where, it was that it didn't.

"My name is Rand," he said, seething.

"Okay, sure… we all make mistakes, *Rand*. This one was yours. It was a stupid, big, giant, dumb-as-shog-in-a-barrel mistake, but it *was* a mistake. Everyone deserves another chance. You let me go, and we let bygones be bygones. I really can't afford to be in this place another day. The troupe is moving at dawn."

"We ain't lettin ye go, thief," Grint said.

"So, then you are going to kill me?"

Grint punched a tree trunk, causing a bird to flee its nest. "Ye ruined me life, thief!" he howled.

"I ruined *your* life? It's *your* fault I stole that crown. *Your* fault I got caught. *Your* fault I lost Sora!" That wasn't wholly true, Whitney realized. If not for Grint and his stupid challenge, Whitney never would have reunited with Sora to begin with. It was Barty Darkings' fault he lost Sora. Darkings' fault he ended up in Elsewhere with the personality-challenged Kazimir. It was Darkings whose throat would be split if Whitney ever found him again.

"Who the yiggin shog is Sora?" Grint asked, then one of his bushy eyebrows lifted. "That Panpingese witch who helped ye steal my company carriage?"

"Doesn't matter," Whitney said as he tilted his head, trying to crack the kink out. "What happened to the two big brutes you always had with you?" Whitney asked, desperate to change the subject from Sora. "And the fat, pouty trader. Oh, and the gray man? Did you tie them up somewhere and leave them for dead too?"

"What is he going on about?" Rand asked, a hint of nervous-ness in his tone. "Gray man?"

"I have no idea," Grint said.

Just then, another crackle of lightning struck nearby, and thunder boomed. From the south, a shrill scream erupted from Fettingborough. Then another. The strengthening rainfall drowned them out fast along with the now constant rumbling of thunder.

Whitney couldn't turn his head all the way, but it was enough to see beyond the graveyard's sole, lonely tree—now with a Grint-fist-shaped hole in it. He couldn't spot anything other than the rooftops and a field of bovines.

"What was that?" Rand asked.

"I'll go check it out," Grint said. "Stay here with the thief. Ain't finished with him yet." Grint said.

"We need to return to the others. Enough is enough."

"Just stay." Grint started off through the headstones toward the town, hand on the grip of his axe.

"What is it?" Whitney asked.

"Keep quiet, thief," Rand said with a finger to pursed lips.

"Oh, c'mon, you're the reasonable one. Just let me go. I'm not worth anything, and Torsten Unger will vouch for me. I did my duty to the kingdom after you caught me. If anything, he owes me."

"Trust me," Rand said. "Torsten doesn't want to hear from me now."

"What—"

"Just be quiet."

Whitney watched, sobering more and more by the second. He wasn't sure what was happening, but fear gripped him and refused to let go. He'd heard enough screaming recently to last the rest of his life. The last time he'd been tied up and heard shrieks like that, he'd had a noose around his neck, and the Shesaitju invaded Winde Port right in front of him.

He winced. Then his mind flitted back to Elsewhere, and he

imagined the winged demons from that place hovering above Fettingborough. He could practically see the beasts tromping through the streets, teeth tearing chunks from the many citizens.

I really should talk to someone about that... he realized, desperate to bury the memory.

"See anything?" Rand called out to Grint in a raised whisper.

A *zip -thunk,* preceded a dwarven grunt just before Grint dropped like so many rocks from a cliffside. He was impossible to see in the tall grass surrounding the clearing for the cemetery outside of Fettingborough.

Rand swore and drew his longsword, looking around frantically. As Rand moved toward Grint, Whitney hissed, "Untie me, Shieldsman! You're going to leave me to die? We're under attack."

The Shieldsman shifted his weight between feet, turned his head several times.

"What are you waiting for!" Whitney said. Rand disappeared behind him, and Whitney clenched his jaw. He waited in silence until suddenly the impact Rand's sword made against the tombstone sent reverberations through Whitney's entire body.

Whitney leaned forward in the mud, the ropes falling off of him. The world spun a bit as he stretched out the knot in his back. A year earlier, he would have been gone into the darkness of the night before Rand had a chance to say anything.

Presently, he took his time to think. Gentry, Lucindur, Aquira, and the others were all still back in town, clearly in danger. Reaching Panping where Sora hopefully remained was the most important thing in his life, but making it there alone now seemed impossible. After years working on his own, he'd grown used to traveling partners. Plus, if he reached Sora without Aquira, she'd kill him on the spot.

A groan from Grint signaled that the insufferable dwarf was alive and stirred Whitney from his hesitation.

"Go ahead, thief, leave," Rand spat.

"Leave?" Whitney said. "And go where? My friends are still in town."

"This is your chance to just go; run away," Rand said, darkness coming over his features.

"You think I don't know anything about you? I'm not the deserter here." In light of what Rand had been through, Whitney winced. It wasn't a shot at the man's integrity, but maybe that's what he deserved. Whitney had heard talk in towns lately that Rand Langley had redeemed himself and saved Torsten, but Whitney knew it was all hogwash. He was there atop Mount Lister when Torsten ended Redstar's reign, and Rand was nowhere to be found.

Redeemer, Whitney scoffed at himself. It was probably a story the crown let out to make themselves seem heroic and forgiving. Torsten probably hated every second of it—someone getting unmerited praise. There's no redemption for slinging the innocent over walls like dried meat, no matter how powerful the person is who demands it.

"Now get down," Whitney said to Rand. "Or did you forget there's an archer out there?"

As if his words willed it, another arrow whizzed by and stabbed the ground behind them. Whitney quickly exaggerated a fall as if he'd been shot. He grabbed Rand and pulled him down too. They splashed in mud, then skittered behind a gravestone.

"Stay low. It came from over there," Whitney whispered, thumbing over his shoulder. "Follow me."

"Who's the Shieldsman here?" Rand said.

"Not you, anymore." Whitney didn't wait for a response before he started crawling on his stomach, using the many headstones as he pushed toward the east where the arrow had come from. "Cemeteries, spider lairs. Why can't I ever crawl through a palace?" he complained to himself.

Grint continued to groan and writhe in the grass.

"We should get him," Rand said.

"He'll be fine," Whitney said. "And if he isn't, he yigging deserves it. Now hush before you wake the dead."

They crawled through wet dirt until they reached a small, dilapidated undertaker's shack on the outskirts of Fettingborough. Whitney imagined it was filled with shovels and bones. Using the building as cover, he stood and peered around the corner. He could see the owner of the bow whose arrow had taken down the loud-mouthed dwarf. His weapon was high above his head as he waded through the waist-high grass, looking for Grint who still laid prone.

"Drav Cra," Rand said with venom. "Damn it. We've been trying so hard to avoid them in the Wildlands."

"So, we'll take him together," Whitney said. "He appears to be alone."

Rand raised a closed fist. A woman's scream echoed over the storm, though this time closer. "That's a scout for Drad Mak's larger raiding party I'm guessing. Where there's one savage, there's always more."

Whitney instinctually reached for his dagger that wasn't there. He turned to question Rand, but the Shieldsman held the blade by its tip, hilt extended toward Whitney.

"I could kill you with this," Whitney warned.

"You won't," Rand said. "You flank him on the right. I'll take his left. We'll try to get him alive and see if he speaks common enough to tell us where his friends are."

Whitney and Rand exchanged a nod, then held eye contact as they flanked the Drav Cra. Rand was too noisy, and Whitney was disgusted with himself for being grateful for the series of louder screams which suddenly emanated from across Fettingborough keeping them from being discovered. All of that plus the storm made it impossible to tell what sounds came from where.

Whitney signaled Rand to stop. He pointed to himself, then to the Drav Cra, then to Rand, then back to the Drav Cra. Rand offered a puzzled look.

"Shieldsmen," Whitney shook his head and whispered under his breath. He then shouted, "Hey, ice breath!"

The Drav Cra warrior spun toward Whitney and reached for an arrow, but Whitney was faster. He threw his dagger; it spun end over end. The hilt bounced almost harmlessly off the Northman's fur and leather armor. The warrior looked down, incredulous, then back up to Whitney with a smirk. He nocked an arrow and pulled back slightly, but couldn't fire it before Rand's longsword buried itself so deep in the man the hilt slammed into his ribs. The blade protruded out the other side. His lifeless arms let the bowstring go, and the arrow arced a couple of feet in front of them as he crumpled into the grass.

"I said to take him alive," Rand scolded.

"Iam's shog man, you're the one who killed him!" Whitney replied. "Why'd you do that?"

"I was saving your life."

"I had him right whe—"

"I'm over here, ye dolts!" Grint moaned.

Whitney and Rand stopped arguing and followed the voice. When they got there, Grint was already standing, using a gravestone as a crutch. His head could barely be seen poking up over the tall grasses. The arrow was caught in his bicep, but only superficially. The dwarf's ego would remain wounded far longer than his body.

Grint reached up and cracked the shaft, wincing. Then, after dropping the feathered end, he pulled out the other end and dropped it too.

"You okay?" Rand asked.

"Bah!" he grunted. "Only thing worse than ye flower pickers are Dravs."

A chorus of screams carried on the wind.

"Do you hear that? We have to get back to them, now." A hint of urgency came over the Shieldsman's voice. Whitney could see the fear in his eyes as the frightful screaming and clamor from the town grew louder.

"Let's go kill some Northmen then," Grint said. "Sooner we're done, the sooner I dun't need to ever see a blade of grass again."

"Aren't you a Northman?" Whitney asked, bending over to retrieve the dagger he'd thrown. Grint ignored him and started toward the town again, bouncing a two-headed axe in his palm.

"Fine, fine, ignore me."

Grint spun on Whitney. "I don't know why my *friend* there untied ye," he said. "It'd been me, I'd of left ye to out there to feed their dire wolves. So, shut your lying, thieving mouth afore I split it with me axe."

"Testy," Whitney said.

"Would you two stop arguing," Rand said. "We need to get the Cal—everyone, and get out of here."

Whitney stifled a reply. They pushed forward. By now, the screaming had died down, and Whitney wasn't sure that was a good thing. The structures along Fettingborough's main avenue stood in a neat line with their backs facing Whitney and the others in the open fields, the church the most prominent and the closest. Narrow alleyways fit snuggly in between each building.

"Look, over there," Whitney said.

Silhouetted in one of the alleys, two figures wrestled. One was large, and wearing furs, the other, small, slight, and shoved against the wall, whimpering.

Without warning, Whitney snatched Rand's sword. The Shieldsman protested quietly, but it was too late. Whitney was already halfway to the alley. The Drav Cra was distracted with hiking up his victim's dress against her will. He didn't even see the longsword stab through the side of his neck. A spurt of blood covered the young lady, and she squealed before collapsing to the ground, sobbing.

Whitney lowered the sword down and wrapped his arm around the Glintish girl. "It's okay," Whitney said. "Franny," She was the troupe's cook, who he'd admittedly probably never said a word to away from the campfire.

"Oh, thank you, Whitney," Francesca said, throwing her arms around him.

"Are you hurt? Why are you out so late?"

Francesca sniffled and shook her head slowly. "I saw them coming. I was... I... he... he... grabbed me."

"You're fine now. Where is everybody else?" Whitney asked.

"Still at the Five Round Trousers, well... except for Madera and Fadra. Nearly the whole town was there watching Gentry perform."

"All right. Just stay here; we're going to get everyone."

"Whitney..." She sniveled, grabbing his arm. Whitney flinched. He wasn't used to anyone relying on him, especially those who were basically strangers. He hated it.

Is this what Torsten went through every day?

"Just stay here and hide. Trust me. And if anyone else comes, you run fast as you can and don't look back."

She reluctantly followed his instructions, and a moment later, Grint and Rand stood behind him.

Rand picked up his sword. "Don't do that again," he said.

Whitney pulled out his dagger and waved it around. "I needed something longer." With that, he bent down and snagged a short bow and quiver from the dead Drav Cra as well as what looked like nothing more than a shapeless piece of metal sharpened to a fine edge. Then he kicked the man for good measure.

"What can you see?" Rand asked Whitney who was closest to the alley's mouth.

"Do ye see the big'uns?" Grint asked, trying to shove his way to the front.

It was too dark to see much, but there was commotion down the road, toward the Fettingborough square. Whitney squinted, then a bolt of lightning struck a lightning rod atop a building at the edge of town.

"There's twenty of the Northmen, at least," Whitney said, quickly analyzing the scene. "They have zhulong-drawn wagons. Huge things. The size of small houses. Big cages built onto the backs of them and they're piling the people in, one at a time." Whitney had never seen Drav Cra with the southern-inhabiting beasts, but he assumed that they were stolen after their defeat in the south.

"I counted a few dead bodies, but not many," Whitney went on. "All town guards outside the barracks looks like. Your big brutes are locked away, Grint, not putting up much of a fight I might add."

Grint swore.

"The Drav Cra usually come in hard and burn things," Rand remarked. "This is careful for them. Quiet. Twenty can't be all that's left after Sir Nikserof drove them off, so this can't be all of them." He turned to Grint. "Do you think they know who we…"

"How could they?" Grint said.

"This shoghole doesn't have much to fight back with," Whitney said, half-ignoring them. "We make it so damn easy."

Whitney squinted. It was dark, and there was very little light. For once, Whitney missed the green glow of the nigh'jels the Shesaitju carried in Winde Port, at least then he could better make out what he was looking at.

"Talwyn…" Whitney whispered.

"Who?"

"My troupe. There's Lucy, Benon… They're all there already. Shog!" A dire wolf circled them, snarling, leaving them no choice but to get in a wagon. Just the sight of one of the terrifying beasts sent a chill up Whitney's spine. He tried to ignore it and scanned the area, searching for Gentry and Aquira. The wyvern wouldn't go into a cage for anyone, which had him fearing the worst.

"It's a relief they're not dead," Rand said. "The savages aren't known for their mercy. Let me see." Rand pushed down on Whitney's shoulder so he could get a better view.

"Do ye yigging see him?" Grint asked.

"Not yet. You foul-mouthed, pint-sized piece of…" Rand groaned in frustration. "If we don't get him back safely, my sister…"

"Enough of yer sister," Grint said. "There's a pile of gold bigger than a giant's scrotum waiting on the other side of this delivery."

"Sigrid is worth all the gold in the world!" Rand said.

"They're gonna hear us," Whitney said. "I'm trying to count how many of them…" his words trailed off as amongst the darkness and the Drav Cra prisoners, he spotted one ugly mug being imprisoned that he'd never forget.

"Darkings," Whitney whispered, voice dripping with acid. The man who'd ruined everything, Bartholomew Darkings stood a hundred yards away, being prodded at by a fur-clad Drav Cra warrior.

"What about him?" Rand asked. "Wait, how do you—"

"I'll kill him!" Whitney started forward, but a steady hand on his shoulder held him back and pushed him against the wall.

"Stop," Rand said. "He's with us."

"Why would ye tell him that?" Grint said.

Whitney's face went slack. "Uh-ph… I… you… uh-ph," he stammered.

Rand merely stared at him.

"You're working with the worst family on Pantego," Whitney forgot to whisper, and Rand covered his mouth.

"I'm not *working* with him. Just stop."

"You don't get to order me around anymore. If Torsten knew about this…" Whitney let the warning hang in the air a moment. "You're in trouble. Yeah. Shog-deep kind of trouble. What the hell could you possibly be doing with him? Moving their traitorous gold? Taking him to his father. Is he really working with Muskigo like the rumors say?"

"Cut it out, thief. You don't get to judge," Rand warned.

"Cut it out? Next, you'll tell me you all are sneaking the missing Caleef around." Rand glared but said nothing. "You know what? I can't believe I'm saying this, but you should turn yourself in when this is over. And Darkings."

"Stuff it," Grint grumbled, throwing his hands in the air.

"No, I'm serious—he owes it…" Whitney turned back to Rand. "You owe it to the Crown, to Torsten. You owe it to *yourself.*"

Rand looked aghast. "Sure. Turn myself in. Better yet, why don't I just walk out there right now? Give myself up to the slaughter. Then my sister can die for my failings."

"Again, with the sister," Grint groused.

"It's your gold too," Rand addressed the dwarf. "This is all your fault. If you hadn't gone after the thief, we could have protected them."

"*My* fault? I didn't tell ye to follow me. This was my business."

"I'm in charge of this expedition," Rand stated.

Grint got up on his toes in front of Rand, and his hands balled into fists. "Is that so."

"Quiet," Whitney said. "Both of you."

Rand and Grint turned to him simultaneously and snapped, "What!"

"All your complaining gives me a plan," Whitney said.

"I'm not turning myself in," Rand replied. "We need to find out who the savages have and free them. Everything depends on it. You can help us, or you can run like I told you."

"Run, now?" Whitney said. "I've been waiting a long time to have words with old Barty. So, let's go save him too."

XXIV

THE DAUGHTER

Mahraveh's spear *clacked* against Jumaat's. They sparred on that same promontory by the cliffs where she'd waited for Jumaat on her last trip into Latiapur, where the lapping of waves hid the sounds of blackwood against blackwood. All the other combatants trained within the distant Tal'du Dromesh, but Mahraveh didn't want to reveal any secrets yet. That's what she told herself at least. Mystery was better than them saying how small Jumaat still was. How raw.

She went high on her next stroke, but he ducked by and stabbed. She twisted out of the way, and before she could stop herself, rammed a knee into his gut. Jumaat gasped for air and folded forward.

Mahraveh cursed. "I'm so sorry." She knelt at his side as he gathered his breath.

"Don't be," Jumaat said. "That Rajeev beast will hit way harder."

Mahraveh lifted him and patted his chest. "The spear isn't the warrior's only weapon. Their entire body is."

"I know. I just… I thought you wanted me to avoid fighting?"

"For as long as you can. But you'll need to fight eventually.

My father taught me this strategy. Now, remember, aim for their legs first, slow them down, then the neck, right here." She brushed aside a braid of hair to reveal her neck.

"With the tip of my blade only, I know," he said.

"Why?"

"Because if I get too close, they're stronger," he said.

"So, we weaken them first. A predator hunts the weak and wounded first."

"Isn't that always me?" Jumaat asked, an awkward laugh tinging his words.

Mahraveh swung at him with no reservations. He ducked just in time, then rose, aghast.

"What was that, Mahi!" he shouted. "You could have taken my head off."

"They never target the fastest either. Know your strengths."

"I know them, all right." He threw his spear down.

"Jumaat… I."

"I need a break, okay? Just for a little." He hopped down a few rocks and sat, staring out across the Boiling Waters.

Mahraveh thought about joining him, then stopped. He hadn't been the same since they ran into Babrak and his men at the arena. He trained harder but grew frustrated quickly. Probably because he knew that somewhere out there, in the water, was the sea-bound afhemate that might save their people—her father.

They'd been training for nearly a week now, and he was admittedly much better. His anticipation had improved even if his own sword-work remained adequate. *Is it enough?* All the other combatants had been preparing for the sands for their entire lives. They were hand-picked warriors. The best. She knew that because they'd seen them outside the arena.

"Is this really your plan, girl?"

Mahraveh whipped around to see Yuri Darkings standing upon the path, looking down at her.

"I don't see you helping," she said. "Isn't that why you're here?"

"That arrogant bastard, Babrak, has no need for gold. But when the Caleef arrives, Babrak and his ilk will have to listen to him. I imagine he won't be keen on letting the Glass get away with this."

"If or when he arrives," Mahi said, "my father might already be dead."

Yuri sighed, and climbed to join her. He needed to use his hands for balance even though it wasn't steep—the rich pampered Glassman.

"I know you don't trust me," he said.

"I don't," she replied.

"I don't blame you. But I'm on your father's side now. I have to be. There has to be a better plan than sending that poor boy into an arena to die. I'm a student of gold, not war, but I know a poor bet when I see one."

"You want to earn my trust, Lord Darkings? Your people attacked my village in the night like cowards. Slaughtered everybody. Use all your great wealth to send carts so the dead may be put to rest in the Boiling Waters like all worthy Shesaitju."

"Haven't you told anybody?"

"Who? Babrak laughed it off like my people deserved it," Mahraveh said.

"You should have come straight to me," Yuri said.

"How dare you?"

"Learning that the Glass murdered innocents could help sway some afhems to our cause."

"They left no proof," Mahraveh said. "It could just as easily have been raiders."

"You underestimate the power of rumors. I will do as you ask, and spread news about this atrocity. This can be exactly what we need."

She glared at him. "My people dying, you mean?"

"A poor choice of words. But perhaps, they will not have died for nothing. I'll focus there. You try to win this insane tournament with that… child."

"Unless my father could get another man out and here in time, our best chance was Farhan. Jumaat's all that's left."

"I'm sure Babrak knew that too." He lay his hand upon her shoulder but backed away when it earned a scowl. "I won't pretend to understand your culture, or why a fleet can be earned without riches, but winning *is* the smart move. Place that responsibility in that boy's hands if you must but in times of crisis… drastic measures are sometimes needed."

"Says a man who probably hasn't worked a day in his life."

"Do not assume the only work that can be done is done with hands. I made good choices, right decisions. Until that day I chose to betray my kingdom before it rotted from within."

"How brave."

Neither said anything for a few seconds until Yuri changed the subject. "I received word by galler from Nahanab. They're still holding out, but don't have the supplies to last more than another month under siege. The Glass aren't risking an attack. They'll wait your father out."

"Or break him with Shavi."

"Who?" Yuri asked.

"It doesn't matter."

"Then I hope you're doing the right thing, placing your faith in the boy. Just like I hope I did right trusting my son to accomplish anything. The return of the Caleef could sway many."

"The Caleef is weak." Mahraveh couldn't believe she was echoing the words of Shavi. She wondered if the old handmaiden spoke like that around her father, or if he too believed her.

"My people don't seem to think so."

"Your people don't know anything."

He chuckled softly. "You have fire, like your father. It's too bad you were born a woman."

She didn't bother offering a response. Instead, she stared down at Jumaat, who now was pretending to thrust with a spear. She could read the frustration all over his face, even from far away. It was easy to talk about stepping onto the sands until the moment loomed. Dozens entered, most died, only one claimed anything.

When she turned back, Yuri Darkings was gone. Off to lurk in more shadows. There was no question what he'd been implying, but she couldn't trust a word he said. She wondered if it was him all along who'd convinced Muskigo to attack the Glass Kingdom without the support of the Caleef or any powerful afhems like Babrak or al-Tariq.

"Mahi, are you ready?" Jumaat asked.

She spun back around and saw her closest friend bending down to retrieve his spear. He twirled it in his hands, and pointed it at her. His smirk spoke of brashness, but his eyes told a different story.

Mahi forced a grin as she brandished her own and threw back her head to get her braids out of her eyes. Her heart sank as she saw his future right in front of her eyes. He was trying his best—trying to be the warrior all Shesaitju men were supposed to be—but if he stepped into that arena, he was going to die.

"You must eat this," Mahraveh said to Jumaat as she entered the chamber he'd been summoned to in the bowels of the Tal'du Dromesh's caverns. Each warrior was kept there on the eve of battle, alone, to make peace with the God of Sand and Sea. Seawater rose calf high throughout, natural stalactites hanging all around. Baby nigh'jels filled the shallow waters. Their green bioluminescence didn't come in until they reached adulthood, so they remained white like a starry night sky.

"How did you get in?" Jumaat asked as he readjusted the bracers of the armor he'd been given, ignoring her. Every combatant wore the same, a scaled zhulong leather cuirass with a tasseted skirt, sandals suited for sand, and golden bracers with colorful coral from the Intsti Reef inlaid in bands.

"That's none of your business," she said, forcing a smile. Mahraveh had claimed to be a gift from her father on the eve of battle for his champion. The fauchard-wielding guards upstairs had been happy to allow a woman down to please one of the champions. Why wouldn't they? She had to hold her tongue as they snickered, studying her from head to toe.

"Now, like I said, eat this." She shoved a large clamshell filled with still-hot zhulong stew into Jumaat's gut. "You need to keep up your strength."

"Right, thank you." He dipped his fingers in and fished out a chunk. Mahraveh tried not to stare as he did.

"Are you ready?" she asked.

Something thundered above, causing a bit of sand to spray from the ceiling. Jumaat looked up. His hand trembled as the crowd came to life overhead. He tried to hide it by shoving his fingers back into the meal.

"As I will ever be," he said. He gave a tug on his cuirass with his free hand. "If only father could see me now."

"He'd be as proud as I am." Mahraveh slid closer to him. "Who'd have thought that little Jumaat would be our last chance."

"I am not so small anymore."

"No," she chuckled. "You're not."

Jumaat swallowed another mouthful of his meal, then turned, his eyes boring into hers. "Thank you for believing in me, Mahi."

"I always hav—"

Jumaat suddenly leaned in and pressed his lips against hers.

She recoiled, eyes going wide. It wasn't because she didn't care for him—she did—enough to not want him to be the one to die. It was because of what he had in his mouth. She spat.

"I'm so sorry," he said. "I didn't mea…" he coughed, then his eyes drooped. "I…" He looked down at his hands. "What is go… ing… on?" The shell-bowl slipped through his fingers and shattered on a stone. He joined it soon after, rolling off the bed and splashing in the shallow water.

Mahraveh fell to his side and propped a pillow under his head. His lips trembled as he struggled to speak.

"Shhh." She placed a finger over his mouth. "I'm the one who's sorry, sweet Jumaat. But it's my father's afhemate. It's my responsibility."

His eyelids flickered, then his head rolled to the side. He'd survive. It was only a bit of laca cactivicus leaf. She'd seen Shavi use it to keep injured warriors unaware during treatment for amputations. He'd wake up in a few hours, unable to stop Mahraveh from what needed to be done.

As she dragged Jumaat's body into the corner, out of clear sight, she recalled those many years ago, dragging pit lizards back to Saujibar.

It was strange, stripping him down of his armor after they'd just shared their first kiss. He'd been her friend since childhood, and while she'd never really thought of him that way, watching him train the last week changed things. Even her father might finally approve of the boy who he felt lacked 'true Shesaitju spirit.'

Adjusting the armor on her frame, she thanked the God of Sand and Sea for Jumaat's lack of muscle. It wasn't a perfect fit, but it was enough. She also thanked Him for her age and the relatively flat chest it afforded her.

A knock came at her door while she was in the midst of tying her braids atop her head so they'd be hidden by the full, nasal helmet Jumaat had chosen to wear, so he'd appeared more mysterious and frightening.

"Ayerabi, it is time," a guard said.

"Coming," she replied, doing her best to imitate Jumaat's voice. It wasn't too deep, so as long as she kept her words short, she'd be able to pass for him. She lowered the helmet over her head and made sure none of her hair showed, then went to the door. Drawing a deep breath, she opened it.

The guard looked her over once, then turned to lead her through the arena's underbelly. The ground beneath her shook with the gathered crowds' roars. Battles had already begun, and she could smell the blood in the air, pungent as the salt of the water.

She'd never been inside the arena, much less the caverns beneath. As they made their way toward the sounds, a loud rumble made the black walls quake, and dust dropped from above, making Mahraveh sneeze. The guard eyed her appraisingly. She thought she'd blown it, but he turned, and they continued.

At the end of the hall, she reached a large, nigh'jel-lit cavern filled with men, each of which more impressive than the next. They were all covered in tattoos, except on the crowns of their heads—a spot reserved for afhems. Straightening her back, determined to look like she belonged among them, she forced her way through, careful to not make eye contact with anyone.

A row of weapons lined the back wall. Mahi approached and reached out for a spear when she felt a hand snatch her wrist. She looked up to the ugliest face she'd ever seen. The man was huge, both tall and wide, but little of his girth was fat. Dark eyes stared out of darker sockets. His head was tipped low. He had giant earlobes, the kind a man would spend years stretching.

"Don't touch my weapons, pis'truda," he said.

"I'm sorry," Mahi started. She cleared her throat and lowered her register to sound less like a woman and more like Jumaat. "I'm sorry. Thought I was to choose."

"Did I call your name?" he asked.

"No."

"Then don't touch my weapons."

Mahraveh turned and started back toward the far side of the cavern where a giant portcullis opened up into the arena. From there, she could see the crowd in all its raucous glory. More people attended than she'd ever seen in her life. Enough to dispel the Glass Army without breaking a sweat. Several levels up, a balcony with a long walkway extended out over the lower stands. Mahi could see Babrak seated amongst the other afhems. In the middle of them sat a man in gold robes and a tall, angular hat. Behind him stood two Serpent Guards.

Above the center of the black sand pit hung a glass globe the size of a fully grown pit lizard and filled with nigh'jels. So many that even during the day they painted the arena in a greenish, vacillating hue that almost made it seem like they were among the weeds on the seabed. Colorful coral, like that in her bracers, helped form the cage which held it, and thick ropes held it taut, stretched to the arena's upper cliffs in equal intervals.

Two men fought. One was huge, but not as big as Babrak. The other was thin but agile.

The big man swung, his bandaged fist aimed at his opponent's head. The thin one brought his shoulders up. The blow connected with his upper arm, no doubt hurting, but doing a fraction of the damage, it would have had it met its intended target. The big man menaced toward his opponent, limping—Mahi missed the part where he'd been injured.

He had a flat nose, jaw like an anvil, and skin the color of burnt zhulong skin.

The smaller of the two recovered just in time to intercept another punch. Skinny as he was, he managed to counter and return with a punch of his own. It didn't even faze the big one. The small warrior shook his hand, tilted his head back and forth, loosening his neck.

That would have been Jumaat, she thought.

Mahraveh wondered where their weapons were just as the thin man rolled and retrieved a long sword from the sand, bringing it up to bear.

One of the contestants sidled up to Mahi.

"Who you rooting for?" he asked.

She cleared her throat. "Not sure, you?"

"Sands and sea, of course, I'm hoping the little one wins. I don't want to fight that giant, do you?"

Mahi snorted. "I suppose not."

The big combatant smiled and circled his opponent. He was holding back, waiting like a sand snake for the little one to attack again. The size difference was laughable, half-a-meter in height, easily. It dawned on Mahraveh that the thin one was likely still taller than she was and probably twice as strong.

It didn't matter. She'd been trained by Muskigo himself.

"What's your name? Afhemate?" the man asked.

"Mah—Jumaat. Ayerabi."

"One of the rebel's own?"

The accusation brought a twinge of anger, and then pride. "The bravest of all afhems, yes."

"You have my deepest sympathies for what happened at Saujibar."

"You heard about it?" Yuri Darkings wasn't lying when he said he'd spread the word about the attack, considering a man confined to the arena somehow knew.

"I've heard a few rumors," the man said. "Glass or not, traitor or not, no afhemate deserves to have their women and children butchered so."

"A good afhem would have been there to defend them,"

Rajeev said, stepping up beside them. Mahraveh built her distance away from Babrak's man, realizing he may recognize her up close. She also quelled the sudden desire to slit open his throat.

"Not everyone is born into the Trisps'I afhemate, Rajeev," the man she'd been speaking to said. "I thought about forsaking all to march with Muskigo, Jumaat. My father died fighting the Glassman."

"Whose didn't, Khonayn?" Rajeev said.

"Well, mine still fights," Mahraveh said. "For all of you."

"For a fool. When I am afhem, Babrak and I will show the Black Sands our true destiny."

"To cower here underneath a Glass boot?"

Rajeev whipped around, but Khonayn was in his way.

"Well, the Jalurahbak afhemate may be small," Khonayn said, "but I'll prove we groom the best warriors."

"Not if you face me," Mahraveh said. She may not have been to the arena in her life, but she knew men. Knew how they poked and bragged and goaded when it came to fighting. It was all part of the process.

Khonayn laughed. "Gone with civility, I suppose."

Back in the arena, the thin one lunged, and the big man side-stepped, then brought a heavy fist down onto his opponent's bare back. The thud was loud enough to echo throughout the crowd but was drowned out by hundreds of voices gasping.

The smaller one was tough. He took the hit, rolled, and bounced back to his feet before the big man even had a chance to bask in his triumph.

"Dracir is going to lose this I think," Khonayn said.

"The big one?" Mahraveh asked.

"He may be big and strong, but he's already growing tired."

A hard kick exploded into the back of Dracir's bad knee, dropping him to a more manageable height. Dracir breathed heavy, his chest heaving.

"I can't watch," Rajeev said, then laughed. "Do it, Amoud!"

The thin one who Mahraveh now knew was Amoud brought his long sword up high over his head and jabbed it down hard into the base of Dracir's skull, the tip exploding through the big man's throat.

The crowd roared, and Amoud pumped his fist high as he kicked Dracir's corpse to the sand, relieving his sword at the same time.

Mahraveh glanced up at the stands and saw Babrak whispering to the man in gold robes. She now recognized him as one of the Caleef's personal council. A eunuch, robbed of his manhood so he could want for naught but serving the Caleef. The eunuch stood, then walked out onto the walkway. When he reached the end, the crowd grew still and quiet.

"Latiapur!" he shouted. The crowd erupted in response. He pumped his hands to quiet them. "Amoud of the Avassu, victor!"

Avassu? Mahraveh thought. That was Jumaat's afhemate when his father and mother had chosen to leave to pursue greater endeavors amidst Muskigo and the Ayerabi. It was rare that one abandoned an afhemate for another without repercussions or war, but Jumaat's father was persuasive, and Muskigo's legendary victory on these very sands inspired many men to do the same.

"Well done, Amoud. Well done. We honor your brethren. May his soul find it's way along the eternal current." The entire crowd recited those words in Saitjuese, and Mahraveh found herself doing the same. "For your great victory, we have chosen a fitting beast."

"Now what?" Mahraveh asked Khonayn.

"Have you never been here before?" he replied.

As if in response to her question, a gate to a cavern on the other side of sunken arena cranked open, and a giant zhulong charged out.

Amoud dove out of the way, and the beast slammed into the

sandy wall, making the very floor beneath Mahraveh shake. Amoud rushed it as it was dazed, leaping and driving his spear into the fatty area above its shoulders. The beast squealed but didn't go down. She'd never seen a zhulong so massive.

With the spear lodged in, it gave a mighty shake and sent Amoud flying. His knee smashed on one of the many rocks littering the sands. He flipped over it and hit the ground, but couldn't stand. He crawled for a war hammer seemingly dropped by his fallen opponent. The enraged zhulong didn't give him the chance. The moment he got a hand around the grip, he was gored by a massive tusk through the hip. Blood sprayed, saturating the already dark sands as the great beast shook him from side to side.

The zhulong acted with murderous intent. Nobody stopped it. Eventually, it flung him against the wall, and if he wasn't dead, he would be soon.

"But he won!" Mahraveh shouted, not concerned with the timbre of her voice.

"Boy, he will fight until he kills us all or dies trying," Rajeev said. "That is our destiny."

"And what, the zhulong wants to be afhem of al-Tariq?"

"No," Rajeev said. "That was just for fun. To weed out the weakest of us."

Mahraveh scanned the upper decks, and in the middle, spotted Babrak laughing and eating like he was watching a play and not the death of good warriors who could help in the fight against the Glass. All Afhems were equal under the eyes of the God of Sand and Sea, but he comported himself like a caleef.

"This really is your first time here, isn't it boy?" Khonayn said.

Mahraveh nodded.

"Muskigo's throwing out a prayer. Dracir and Amoud were the final two out of a bout of ten," he explained. "Each of the seventy-nine Afhems has presented a champion, as well as a single markless volunteer."

"Right." Mahraveh knew that much. There were seventy-nine Afhems and always would be—one for each of the islands dotting the Boiling Waters, as the first Caleef dictated millennia ago. Their followings and holdings were not equal, but if one afhemate ever fell in totality, another rose to take his place on these very sands.

Until now, it was always a he. Mahraveh aimed to put an end to that.

"Why help the child?" Rajeev said. "He won't last a second."

"I prefer to beat the best," Khonayn said. "The winner, if he survives a beast of the sand or sea, then rests while a fresh ten battle."

"And the winner?" Mahraveh asked.

"The same. After everyone fights, the surviving victors must face each other. Only he who stands in the end will be crowned, and al-Tariq will have a new afhem."

Or she, Mahraveh thought. She could feel sweat building beneath her helmet. She looked at the ranks within the bunker. Twenty men at least. Some were bloodsoaked and gravely injured.

"Four have survived their beast so far," Khonayn said.

"Poor Amoud," Rajeev said. "I'd fight in every round if I could, and still kill all of you."

"Pride is a warrior's downfall," Mahraveh said.

Rajeev chortled. "Who said that?"

"I believe it was Afhem Muskigo before he routed your leaders' people on the sands." Khonayn threw Mahraveh a nod of acknowledgment.

"I just don't want to cheat myself out of any glory," Rajeev said.

"Nor I," Mahraveh said.

Of course, she didn't mean it. She enjoyed the thrill of battle as much as the next, but the thought of needing to slaughter so many men—plus worthy beasts—didn't feel like the battle she'd signed up for. However, she didn't honestly know what the battle she signed up for was, not really. She only knew what she'd win.

She'd been so lost within her own head that she hadn't realized names were being called.

"Usef," said the ugly man with huge earlobes standing by the weapons. A soldier that must have been from the Usef Afhemate stood and approached the weapons wall, selecting a fauchard.

Mahi watched as man after man heard their names and did the same before lining up at the portcullis.

"Jalurahbak."

"May the God of Sand and Sea be with me," Khonayn said. He spat into both his hands as was customary among Shesaitju warriors—to surrender some of their salt and water to him. Then he slapped Mahraveh on the back. "Wish me luck." Just as Mahraveh turned to watch him line up to enter the arena, she heard the final name called, and the chortle from Rajeev which followed.

"Ayerabi."

XXV

THE KNIGHT

Torsten felt the warmth return to his limbs, and all around, over the ringing of the church bell, he heard people start whispering that the monsters had disappeared.

"My Queen?" he rasped. He couldn't hear her anymore. His body felt like it had after battling Redstar atop Mount Lister, broken. Freezing to the core.

He planted a hand on the stone of the courtyard and felt cool liquid run over it. Finger's quaking, he brought them to his mouth. It was water, bubbling forth from the broken fountain. He sighed in relief.

A cacophony of whispering broke out all around him, all blending. He could perceive none of it over toll of the bell or the deep ringing in his eardrums from hitting his head.

"Oleander…" Torsten said.

He crawled further, until his knuckles brushed against hair, soft as velvet. He patted along it, finding her face. His palm covered a patch of mottled, scarred skin, finding the smooth side as he stretched his fingers across. Her skin was colder than the stone beneath him.

"Oleander?" He said, drawing himself closer, wrapping his massive hand around the back of her neck and lifting her head with no resistance. With his other, he patted for her chest, desperate to hear a heartbeat, but instead, he found the shaft of an arrow sticking from the center.

Suddenly, form came to the whispers closing in all around him.

"She's dead."

"The Queen's dead."

"By Iam, the monsters did it."

Fear caught in Torsten's throat and made him feel like he was drowning. He pulled her closer and pressed his ear against the top of her chest, scratching his cheek against the arrow as he did. Blood filled his earlobe, still leaking from a pair of fang-marks on her neck—marks, which Torsten shared.

"Sir Unger!" Lucas called out. "Sir Unger!"

Torsten could hear the boy's injured foot dragging along the stone but didn't care. Guards barked for citizens to get out of the way, and nobody dared resist this time.

"Sir Unger, Sir Hystad will make it, he—" Words got stuck on the tip of Lucas's tongue as his voice grew nearer. "By the light of Iam… What…"

Torsten felt hands on his shoulders. He shook them away and pressed Oleander closer.

"Oleander…" Torsten whimpered, strands of her hair stuck on his bloody lips. "Oh, my Queen." He squeezed her face against his, feeling all the valleys and crags of her scars, and her tears running through them.

"Sir Unger, you must—"

"Don't touch her!" Torsten shouted, silencing Lucas in an instant. All the gathering crowd gasped and backed away in the face of his thunderous roar.

Torsten turned back toward his broken Queen and ran his

fingers over her forehead. Her eyes remained open, gazing upward into the darkness of the night sky. He fought his uncontrollable shaking to close them.

"Is this what she deserves?" Torsten asked in the direction of the church spire. Since he'd lost his sight, he'd found solace trusting in Iam again, knowing it'd been for a purpose, that it was the cost for his shattered faith when he lay locked in the dungeon of his own kingdom, branded a traitor.

"I couldn't save you…" he whispered. Now, that was all he knew. Whatever had happened, he'd been tossed aside by her killers like a blind, old, useless man. "For all my words. All my promises."

"Is that Codar?" Lucas said.

"He tried to save her," answered a nearby guard, voice gruff like his was severely injured.

"Nobody could save her," Torsten said. Slowly, he rose to a single knee, then another. He ignored Lucas's attempts at helping him, until he stood upright, Oleander's body draped across his arms. Her head lay over his arm, that long, slender neck which had inspired so many songs of beauty, hanging limp.

More gasps sounded from the sight of her denuded body as he turned, beaten, bloody, and broken. Torsten trudged toward the streets, again refusing Lucas's help. He felt like he was wading through white rapids.

"Iam save us all," someone said.

"Look how frail she is," said another.

Torsten heard the nervous footsteps of citizens backing out of his way. He listened to their shock. From guards to the very men of South Corner who'd rioted and caused so much chaos, bound and restrained against the cart they'd flipped. Few loved her, many hated her, they all feared her, but there wasn't a soul who'd ever seen weak. The towering beauty who could turn men's hearts to ice was cradled in Torsten's arms like a hunted fawn, not just weak, but gone.

Torsten didn't cover her. He left her exposed for all to see, their true queen. And all those citizens who might've doubted the parts of the stories about how she'd sacrificed her beauty to save Pi and the Kingdom, suddenly could deny it no longer.

From every angle, Shieldsmen and soldiers arrived, begging to help. Torsten ignored all of them. He carried Oleander one heavy footstep at a time back up the road toward the castle gates. He knew the way. All he had to do was follow the chiming of the castle's warning bells, which drowned out that of the church's all too late.

"Open the gates!" Lucas shouted ahead.

"It's too dark. Who is that?" a guard called down from above.

"Open the gates, you sorry sod!" Lucas shouted. "It's the shogging queen!"

A portcullis cranked open, then heavy doors swung, the hinges screeching like angry specters. Torsten never stopped. He continued his march, hearing the flood of footsteps at his back as, suddenly, hundreds who would have cringed at the sight of their wicked Queen, followed behind her.

Men of the Glass approached from all directions, desperate to figure out what happened while they were holed behind the castle walls in defense of the Crown. Lucas struggled to keep them at bay, but still, Torsten waded onward. His fingers dug into Oleander's flesh, bracing against the onslaught of curious and confused hands, against the heat of torches brought close by men to see her with clarity as if they didn't believe it.

"Torsten," Sir Mulliner's voice carried. "Torsten, is it true, is it… Shogging exile… Back away from him, Marcos, or you'll be on the streets by morning! Let him through."

Suddenly, Torsten found himself pushing through less confusion. He waited until the frantic voices and clattering armor began to echo in the Castle's grand hall entrance, reverberating amongst the glass spires above. Then, his impossibly weakened legs finally gave out and collapsed to his knees.

"Torsten!" Mulliner and Lucas said at the same time. They grasped his shoulders to keep him from face-planting, Torsten's nails clinging into Oleander as he'd once seen Pi clutch his orepul. He couldn't help it. He didn't want to let her go.

"Sir Unger, we'll take her from here," Lucas whispered.

"When Iam kills me, you will!"

Sir Mulliner squeezed Torsten's shoulder. "I should have been out there. Yig and shog, I should have been there!"

Torsten managed to pry his left hand loose from the Queen's supple thigh and clutched Sir Mulliner's jaw. "Is the King okay?" he said. "Is Pi, okay?"

"He's fine, he's—"

"What's happening?" Pi's small voice filled the hall. All at once, every guard, servant or noble in the castle was rendered silent. Torsten could only imagine the way they regarded him then. Like a wounded deer.

"Your Grace, you should return to your room," some new member of the Royal Council said.

"Out of my way," Pi demanded.

"Your Grace, please."

"Out of my way!"

The boy's tiny footsteps were all that could be heard over the distant bells. They grew faster and faster until their cadence became a run and Torsten heard his labored breathing.

"Sir Unger," he squeaked, his voice trembling. "What happened?"

Torsten turned his blind face toward the sound of him. Torsten's blood-drenched face was streaked with sweat that felt like the tears he was unable to produce. Finally, both his hands came loose, and the Queen's body rolled across the floor. There seemed no better place for it then on that cold marble, icy as the frozen dirt of the lands from which she hailed.

"What happened!" The boy broke down and ran to her. "Mother… mother? Someone fetch the Royal Physician! Help her!"

Nobody answered. Everyone merely backed away, giving their king space as he wept uncontrollably. Everyone but Torsten. He crawled toward the boy and wrapped his arms around him. He didn't care about being appropriate. He didn't care about any of it. All he felt in his embrace was the heaving of a crying boy who'd lost his mother; who'd already endured more than any man, woman, or child ever should.

"She's gone, Pi," Torsten whispered. "Your mother is dead…"

Speaking the words out loud made his chest sting, but he forced them for Pi. Whatever the king said next was indiscernible through his tears.

"I—I failed her…" Torsten said.

He held Pi tight, not fighting as the boy's tiny fists beat against his chest in agony until he no longer had the energy. Torsten never allowed his grip to lessen. He held Pi upright, and nearly as much, Pi kept him from collapsing from sorrow and exhaustion.

The 'Flower of the Drav Cra' was dead, and there wasn't a thing he could do to stop it…

XXVI

THE THIEF

Grass rustled beneath them, and mud sloshed as they snuck back through the graveyard toward the other side of town where the Drav Cra were still capturing everyone unfortunate to have been in Fettingborough. Whitney knew stories about the raiders, every Glassman did. They usually burned and looted, but they'd barely caused enough stir for anyone to have a chance to run. Judging by those dead, they'd silently eliminated the town's few guards, then dragged everyone out of their homes and taverns before a soul could fight back.

Whitney had to wonder why they didn't just kill them all and be done with it.

Celeste burned somewhere bright above, but she was cloaked in a blanket of storm clouds. Rain drove at their necks and lightning flashed in every direction as it often did in this area of Pantego. Thunder rumbled as if Iam was tossing boulders. The conditions were better for sneaking than Whitney could have hoped for, but he thought the description of them "sneaking" was generous since Rand's sword sheath kept clanking against his boots like a bell tower.

Grint waddled behind. The dwarf was surprisingly quiet,

given the dwarf's typically loud nature. The dwarf was still grumbling about how Rand had untied Whitney, but Whitney wasn't listening. All he could think about was Darkings, and Gentry, and Aquira, and Sora.

He longed for the days when he didn't care about anyone or anything other than himself.

"Here it is," Rand said. He lifted the slain Drav Cra scout's bow and held them out for Whitney.

Whitney snatched it and slung it over his shoulder, then took the man's quiver. He turned and nudged the body with his foot.

"Think you can carry it, Grint?" Whitney said.

"Ye flower pickers think yer sooo much stronger because ye can see over a horse," Grint groaned. He stopped alongside the body, bent over, and started to lift it. Rand offered help, but the dwarf swatted him away. "We dwarves are built for…" He drew a deep breath, then heaved the corpse over his shoulders with a loud grunt. "Power."

"Quiet," Whitney warned.

Grint's face went redder than ever, but he balanced the body and started moving. "Quiet," he grumbled. "I'll give ye quiet." He was surprisingly strong, carrying the dead Northman warrior over his shoulder like a sack of flour. Grint was so short that the Drav Cra's head up front and toes behind practically dragged in the dirt.

"I still don't get the plan," Rand said. "Are you sure *you* understand it?"

"I've killed a goddess," Whitney said.

"No, you didn't," Rand snapped. "You were part of a *team* who supposedly killed a giant spider, and I am positive the whole team understood the plan before going bare-assed into the middle of a Drav Cra horde."

Whitney spun around. "Why are you bare-assed?" He smiled. "We just need to thin the ranks a bit. Twenty to three aren't good odds no matter how many cards you have shoved up your sleeve.

Can Darkings fight if we get him out or does he just flap his arms around like a little girl?"

Rand had fire in his eyes but said nothing.

They continued, passing unmarked gravestones and makeshift Eyes of Iam made of twigs and wilting vines.

"Okay, in there." Whitney pointed to another alley he guessed to be close enough to the Drav Cra without being fully visible.

The walls on either side of them were nondescript, but from Whitney's explorations, he'd placed them between the cobbler and a coin bank. Another time and Whitney might have found himself drooling over the opportunity to slip into the vaults and relieve Fettingborough of their stored wealth.

A loud grunt pulled Whitney from his thoughts. Grint threw the warrior off his shoulder.

"Meungor's axe," Grint said, stretching his shoulders. "I can't believe I'm trustin ye."

"You know better than any you can trust me," Whitney said. "I stole the crown just like you asked. This is nothing."

"And ye lost it just the same."

"And I believe that was mostly *your* fault, wasn't it scragle-beard?"

"Ye take that back!"

"Okay, okay," Rand said. "Stop it. Are we just going to bicker with one another this whole time? Besides, it was me who stopped you after you broke the crown."

"And who do you think had the other half?" Whitney said. "And I took it from him too."

Grint snorted. "Yeah? Don't see it on ye no more."

"It's uh…" Whitney paused. He realized he had no idea where it was. To him, it seemed like years ago when he and Sora had been toying around with it on a ship bound for Panping before Kazimir arrived and they vanished. It didn't join him in Else-where, which meant that Sora was the last to have it as far as he knew. And knowing her, she probably tossed it into the sea just to make a point.

"None of this matters," Rand said. "Can we focus? The sooner we figure a way out of this, the sooner we don't ever have to see each other again."

"Took the words right out of me mouth," Grint said.

Whitney let out a grunt and then a sigh. He said, "Well, just follow *my* plan, and we'll be fine." He stepped toward the front of the alley, which was now close enough that he could see without needing lightning for aid, not that it relented anyway.

In the square ahead, a Drav Cra warrior spat orders. Two sides of a long, braided mustache hung on either side of his bare chin. His muscles bulged, each bicep bigger than a normal man's head.

Closer now, Whitney had a better sense of things. Twenty or more Northmen stood around, unconcerned and confident. They were imposing, all with battle axes or warhammers, draped in furs, matted and mottled from the heavy rains that had barely let up in weeks. From there, thankfully, Whitney couldn't see anyone painted or with bones rattling from their robes, which meant they didn't likely have a warlock with them. That would have complicated things even further.

One wagon, filled with those in Whitney's troupe, was already loaded and being sent off with half the troops. A dire wolf snapped at zhulong heels, keeping them moving briskly despite their proper owners being absent. For a moment, Whitney considered ducking and running after it, taking his chances alone against a dozen Drav Cra. Those odds weren't much worse, and he could easily leave Barty to the wolves.

Before Whitney could decide, Grint hocked up a wad of spit and rubbed it between his palms.

"Gross," Whitney said.

"Ready?" Grint asked.

Whitney and Rand nodded. Then, together, Grint and Rand

hefted the Drav Cra corpse into a standing position as Whitney moved to the back end of the alley and drew an arrow. The warrior's head lulled to his chest, lifeless, but it was stormy and dark. Plus, they were still a fair distance from the gathered Drav Cra horde. When the man was upright, Rand turned back to Whitney. Whitney urged him with a nod. Rand shook his head in resignation.

"This is for you, Siggy," he muttered, then lifted his chin. "I'm done with the wench," Rand shouted in his best Drav Crava accent—which was terrible, but it was still far better than Grint's earlier attempt when they'd decided Rand would do it.

The body's butt rested on Grint's head. Whitney stifled a laugh. It was what the little bastard deserved. *Steal from the King...*

"This girl's ripe. Who's next?" Rand called, waving the dead man's hand around to make him seem alive.

Whitney could only pray his plan would work. Problem was, he had no idea who to pray to about a scheme involving a dead man coaxing a bunch of warriors into an alley to rape a woman.

"There you are, Gorvan," one Drav Cra replied, apparently having wondered why their scout never returned. "Let's go!"

"What's the rush?" Rand said. Grint made his best impression of a woman screaming.

"Go on," said one warrior. "We'll catch up." Several comments in Drav Crava followed. Whitney assumed they were lewd, which made the next part even easier than it already was. The sounds of the wagon pulling out of town and its zhulong mewing carried on the air. It was better than Whitney could've asked for.

Together, Rand and Grint pulled the warrior back into the alley a bit until they were out of sight, then dropped the body and ran back toward Whitney.

"How many are coming?" Whitney asked, but it was too late.

A few warriors already appeared in the mouth of the alley. As Whitney let the arrow fly, he realized it was the first time he'd shot an arrow since the day in Troborough when the Black Sandsmen attacked. In truth, that was only half a year or less, but to him, having endured time in Elsewhere, it was more than half a decade.

To his surprise, the arrow found purchase in a neck—but there were so many of them, he would've had to have tried in order to miss. Whitney had another arrow nocked before the warrior could raise alarm. Another shot later and the second one was down. But it wouldn't be enough. Whitney was disgusted by how many of the warriors had shown up for a chance at some poor young girl. Then he remembered… it wasn't just *some poor girl*. It would have been Franny.

"Bastards," he said before he let off one more shot, not even looking to see if it would connect before enacting the next part of the plan.

Rand and Grint were already hidden in the high grass behind town when Whitney tossed the bow aside, fell back, and joined them. They crawled in opposite directions, then waited for the opportunity to strike.

By now, Drav Cra voices cried out in warning, but Whitney could hear the snorting zhulongs and their hoofs against the mud just audible over the sounds of the wagons already on the Glass Road.

"Shog in a barrel," Whitney whispered to himself. Then louder, "Plan doesn't change!" They were hoping to be able to take at least one of the wagons in town before they moved out.

They used the cover of rain and the veil of grass to keep them hidden as the Drav Cra warriors stormed through the alley. With the direction of the wind, they'd planned it so that rain would beat against their faces and worsening their vision on top of the darkness.

With the crude blade in one hand and his dagger in the other, Whitney listened carefully to the sounds of the warriors. At best guess, after the two or three he'd shot in the alley and those who would have chased after the zhulong caravan, there were still six warriors remaining.

"Oni'zdest, u kostakah u kludbish del!"

The voice was close. Then lightning flashed, and Whitney made out a leather boot, top lined with fur, inches from having stomped on him. Whitney popped up and frantically stabbed forward with his blade. The Northman must have seen it coming. He deflected the blade. Vibration coursed through Whitney's arm but the warrior sucked in a breath, telling Whitney he'd still made contact.

Growling, the Drav Cra lowered his head and tried to smash Whitney with his elbow and missed. Whitney didn't wait, he slashed with both blades, foregoing all defense. His first strike was deflected again, but the Northman neglected the dagger that raked across his abdomen. When the warrior flinched and looked away, Whitney darted back, saving himself, and fell into the grass.

All around him, he heard battle. Rand and Grint would be delivering similar sneak attacks, hopefully to much deadlier effect.

"Quit hiding, devil!" the warrior growled.

Whitney had made his way behind the man and drew his blade along the warrior's exposed hamstrings. With immediate vengeance, the Drav Cra reached down and snagged Whitney by his hood, lifting him to eye level. The tall man was rage-filled, evidently not considering the position the move had left him in.

Whitney kicked out and caught his opponent in the groin. The man went down, and Whitney landed atop him. Without wasting time, Whitney stabbed his dagger into the warrior's chest. A gurgle of blood bubbled from the dying man's mouth but not before he grabbed Whitney's wrist and yanked it with whatever remaining strength he had left. Whitney shouted, giving away his position. A smile played at the man's lips just before the air evacuated his lungs.

In a panic, Whitney stood, but ducked just as quickly, narrowly avoiding an axehead as it hummed through the air above him. But the move left him vulnerable. A hard knee rose to meet his face. Whitney reeled back, then felt another punishing his gut. Doubled over, world spinning, Whitney saw the axe coming at him again. He fell aside, avoiding it once more. Whitney grasped for his dagger, but it wasn't there—still lodged securely in the first man's chest.

His new attacker pursued him. Whitney weaved between gravestones, fighting back the gags as he tried to catch his breath. The Northman didn't hesitate to turn the giant stones into pebbles.

"That was someone's loved one!" Whitney heaved as another stone crumbled.

"Takostchivo entr'zt, bareese!"

The man swung his axe again, but Whitney caught it by the shaft. It surprised even him, having never been much of a fighter. The raw wood splintered into his palms, and the Drav Cra gnashed his teeth like a rabid wolf, but Whitney let the man's momentum carry him, pulling him close. With a scream, Whitney drove his forehead into the bridge of the Drav Cra's nose. Blood poured freely from both of them, and the man relented his grip on his axe to cradle his nose. Whitney brought the shaft-end of the axe around and drove it into the man's temple, knocking him out cold.

Whitney stood, stumbling, feeling the contents of his stomach —which he realized was little more than a bucket of ale—roiling around, his brain swimming. Locating the body containing his dagger, he snatched it and shoved it down into its sheath. He had no doubt another attack would come imminently, but he leaned against the lone tree in the center of the graveyard to catch his breath.

In the distance, Rand was engaged in swordplay with a Northman. Ex-Shieldsman or not, he moved like a dancer and his opponent with the power of a ram. Whitney would have appreciated the skills of both men had he the time, but one of the savages now charged him, crude blade high above him, mouth open in a roar.

Whitney put aside his weariness and advanced on the man who was a good head taller and had the reach. But Whitney was no weakling anymore—no longer just a pretty face with dextrous fingers. He slid to the right, keeping distance and drawing a semicircle in flattened grass to keep from being skewered into the tree like a meat stick in Winde Port.

The Drav Cra warrior lifted his foot twice, each time placing it down just a fraction of a span from where it had started. Whitney couldn't tell if he was feinting attack or planning one. One thing was sure: the man showed restraint, likely due to the presence of two of his ilk, dead near Whitney's feet.

"Are we here to fight or dance?" Whitney taunted, pointing his blade.

The warrior growled and swiped down. Whitney lashed out with a punch to the man's inner arm. It wasn't meant to do much damage, but to continue to anger his opponent. The angrier someone was, the dumber they'd become—yet another lesson Sora might never learn. But this one was smart; he spun his sword with a flick of his wrist and gave a half-hearted swing, just to create distance once again. Whitney stepped back, playing the game. Then the warrior drove in, fast as lightning, elbowing Whitney across the face, sending him spinning back into the tree.

Whitney ducked on instinct just in time to hear the metal sink into the wood above him. He kicked out, catching his opponent in the gut, then looked up to ensure the blade was still wedged into the tree before turning to grab hold of the man's head. Whitney punched him several times until his knuckles hurt. The problem was, Whitney could needle away at the man all day and make little progress, but the Drav Cra needed only one solid hit to end the whole thing.

"Je'zt u bet, bareese," The man shoved Whitney away, then said, "You will die, quim licker."

Whitney didn't know what a quim was—but he was sure he didn't want to lick one no matter what.

The Northman circled Whitney. He was a moving wall of corded muscle, flexing and contracting with each step. Whitney leveled his blade but kept his off hand by his dagger sheath. He waited patiently while the Northman sent fast, compact jabs, then brought his sword around. Whitney rolled with the first punch, letting the others glance by. He dodged the sword strike and weaved, but the bigger man continued his assault. Whitney managed to deflect the blade with his own, but it sent him reeling, and the Northman had the upper hand.

Just then, lightning struck the plains somewhere behind them. Judging by the flash, and the deafening *crack*, it was close. The Northman, who Whitney realized probably wasn't used to thunderstorms, froze momentarily. His eyes went wide with fright.

Whitney smelled the opening and charged. He dodged a half-assed attempt at a swipe as the Northman came too, forced himself inside the man's reach, drew his dagger, and shoved it hard between the warrior's ribs, twisting it in a half-circle.

The weight of the soon-to-be-corpse dragged Whitney down. Whitney scrambled to rise, unwilling to get caught off guard again.

"Drop the weapon," said a thickly accented voice as Whitney stood.

Whitney spun to see Rand squarely in the grasp of a Northman, blade tight against his neck, but Whitney didn't drop his sword... didn't even flinch.

"Drop it or I death him."

A quick glance around told Whitney it was just the three of them. Whitney had killed two of the men. How many Drav Cra had Rand taken down by himself—three, four? Where was Grint? Already dead? Whitney imagined the stumpy little dwarf, headless in the grass.

"Well?" Whitney said. "What are you waiting for?"

"I'll do it. Bareese, mutek, I'll do it."

"I trust you will," Whitney said, stumbling forward. "But I don't give two shogs in a dirty barrel about him. He tried to kill me. So, please. It'll save me the trouble."

The Drav Cra warrior looked puzzled for just a moment, then said, "I will not fall for your bluff—" The man stopped talking as the edge of an axe blade tore through his face. When the man fell, Grint stood behind him.

"I told ye we should've woken up the twins," Grint growled. He spat on the body, then rubbed the blood off his blade on the man's furs.

Rand let out a lungful of air. "Thank you," he said to Grint. Then, turning to Whitney, he said, "How'd you know he was there?"

"I didn't."

"You—what?" Rand asked, still out of breath.

Whitney shrugged, then turned back toward Fettingborough. "Great job everyone."

"Where are ye goin?" Grint asked.

"We're going to need horses if we're to catch up to the zhulongs," Whitney said.

"That's yer plan? Get horses and chase down the wagons? The rest of them Northmen'll be waiting with bows ready."

"Well, then we'll just have to have our bows readier, won't we?" Whitney was several strides ahead of the dwarf, nearly back in town.

"Wait a yiggin minute!"

Whitney whipped around and stretched the crude blade out straight. The tip grazed the dwarf's red mustache, and the flat of it rested against his big, round nose. "You can do whatever the yig you want, but I have friends on that caravan, and I'm going to rescue them," he said. "The only reason I don't skewer this sword straight through your rock-filled head is that somehow, by luck or destiny designed by some god, you saved my life by kidnapping me. This is the last kindness I'm going to show you. Is that understood, dwarf?"

Grint bit his lip. Then he pushed the blade away with the side of his hand, snorting as little mustache hairs tickled his nose. "This isn't worth it," he said to Rand. "We did our best."

"Use your head, Grint," Rand said. "If we don't get you-know-who back, we're dead anyway. I swear to Iam, if he's dead already…"

"Then it's yer head. I'll be vanished in the Dragon's Tail. I'm tired of the sky anyway."

"This is your fault! We should have been with him."

Rand threw himself at the dwarf, tackling him and driving a fist into the side of his furry cheek. But Grint had a low center of gravity and flipped the tables. His thick elbows pounded Rand in the gut. Whitney grabbed him by his hair at the back of his head and tore him off.

"What are you two on about!" Whitney said. "Trust me, Barty Darkings isn't worth any of this, but if you help me save everyone, maybe I'll just bruise him up instead of killing him."

Grint spat up blood and wrang the mud from his beard. Rand stood, panting wildly.

"Right then," Grint said. "Well, that about settles it. No amount of gold is worth dyin for, lads." Grint bent down to pick up his axe. He turned specifically to Rand. "Good luck, Langley.

Anywhere's better than with that thievin fruitcake. I hope ye get yer sister back, so ye stop complaining."

With that, Grint Strongiron turned and walked toward the darkness and the endless plains of grass.

"My sister is worth it, you ingrate!" Rand shouted. "Sigrid is worth it! Get back here." He picked up his sword and ran after him, but Whitney grabbed him by the back of his collar and yanked him back.

"We don't need him," Whitney said. "Go on, coward!" he called after Grint. "Go pout your way back to the Dragon's Tail like the sad sack you are."

"Dammit!" Rand roared. He threw his sword against one of the gravestones, the *clank* masked by the rumbling thunder. Then he fell to his knees and ran his hands up over his face in frustration, covering his cheeks in mud.

"Oh, get up," Whitney said, kicking him in the heel. "We're better off without him slowing us down."

"You don't understand," Rand said. "I made a deal."

"Oh, I understand. You think I enjoy helping a man like you? But a bunch of savages have people we need to save. Shieldsman or not, that should be enough. Now wipe your face, and let's get after them so you can do whatever you need to do and save your damn sister."

Rand's hands balled into fists, mud and blood squeezing through his fingers. He exhaled and grabbed his sword. "Too many lives have been lost due to my cowardice," Rand whispered, head drooping like he was talking to himself. He peered up at Whitney through the rain. "We can't let all those folks die, too. Let's save them all."

XXVII

THE KNIGHT

"It's been too long, my King," Torsten said. He knelt before Liam Nothhelm's grave, deep beneath the Glass Castle in the Royal Crypt. It was one of the few times he preferred being blind. With sight, he'd see all the stuffed corpses' frozen eyes watching him, belonging to king's both famous and infamous—heroes and monsters those above wished to forget.

He wondered how future knights might think of Oleander when they saw her in the family crypt, if she'd be remembered for a streak of failures and brutality brought about by fear and loneliness or for helping Torsten rid the kingdom of her brother's curse when all seemed lost.

Torsten imagined the former. People seemed to remember the bad more than the good, especially when it came to anyone but Liam. He who built the mighty Glass—the greatest power in Pantego, raised high atop the rotting corpses of a thousand enemies. Oleander's family among them.

"You were more than a mere man to me, my King," Torsten said. "I saw you as I saw Iam Himself, but perhaps that was the problem. All the women who snuck into your tent in Shesaitju, the North, and especially in Panping… I should have said something. Uriah was right about a great many things, but he wasn't right about that. Oleander nearly drove the Glass into Elsewhere after your mind went, and it's all because you kept her in the dark."

Torsten's fist ground into the stone floor. Down where spring's lips couldn't touch, it remained cold as winter. A shiver ran up his spine, and Torsten slid closer to Liam's grave, where the warmth of the torches on either side could kiss his frigid cheeks.

"It took many years for me to understand why you chose her, my King," Torsten whispered. "The world gave her that name, but the truth was, you didn't want a flower, did you? You wanted an axe."

He imagined a tear falling from his now-useless eyes, splashing against the plaque denoting Liam's name and many honored titles. Torsten gathered his breath.

"At least you thought you did until you watched the blade sharpen," Torsten said. "Why couldn't you share your kingdom? Why couldn't you share your light with any but those we conquered?"

Torsten swallowed against a dry throat. He pawed at the floor for his cane and used it to rise. His entire body remained sore from dealing with the assassins... *Rand's sister,* he reminded himself. Redstar was gone, but monsters remained in his wake, made from the darkness he wrought. Torsten just hoped that same unforgivable fate of being turned into a bloodsucking fiend hadn't fallen upon Rand as well.

"I've learned something, my King," Torsten said, his head hanging. "As much as I love you, I know now that we're all just... men. Even you. Few will shed a tear for your wife; many will fake them. They'll say she got what she deserved. I had the honor of seeing her, the real her—I didn't need eyes to do it."

Torsten lifted his head. He knew from experience that if he'd had eyes, he'd be staring straight into what had been preserved of Liam's, frozen open for all of time.

His mind brought him back to those streets where the citizens Torsten had sworn to protect did nothing to protect him, nothing to protect their queen. He thought about the feeling of helplessness as he lay buried beneath Iam's church, listening in frustration to the Queen's pleas.

"She thought of me as her knight," he said. "Sweet, loyal, Torsten," he repeated the words he'd heard her speak so many times before. "Loyal." He let out a disgusted breath. "Loyal!"

He punched the wall next to Liam's sarcophagus.

"Loyal to who? The man who stole her from her people? Made her suffer under the hate of so many so he could treat her like a rag? Did you even know what you had in her? No, of course, you didn't."

"They'll all say Pi is better off, but we both know that isn't true," Torsten said. "I hope he has the best of *both* of you in him. You opened so many eyes, Liam Nothhelm, but perhaps Pi can help them actually 'see. Truly, feel it."

Torsten tapped along the wall, then pressed his lips against the glass lid which sealed Liam's mortal body away for eternity.

"May you see her again in the realm of light," Torsten said. "And this time, know what you have before it's lost. Goodbye, my King. Perhaps you would have hated this, but I vow to stand at Pi's side and make sure that when the great Kings of Glass are remembered, his is the first name that comes to mind. Over King Autlas, over King Remy, over you…"

He kissed the tomb a final time, then turned and headed for the exit. It was easy to locate. The stale air in the crypt only flowed in a single direction. It made the skin around his eyes itch worse than usual.

Days had passed since Oleander's murder, and this was the first time he'd been able to drag himself from his quarters. With

Lucas injured, Torsten needed to borrow one of the scribes. Desperate to learn more about the Dom Nohzi and the upyr, they pored over every scroll and tome that even mentioned them in passing. But even the new Master of Rolls could locate very little on the subject. Most throughout history didn't even think them real.

"Sir Unger," Lucas greeted as he entered the tunnels.

"Lucas," Torsten said. "I told you, you could spend another few days in the infirmary."

"I'll be fine." Lucas took Torsten's arm, and he didn't fight it as the young man led him through the castle's undercroft. Lucas's every other step lurched as he withheld putting weight on his injured foot.

Torsten exhaled. "How frightening we'll be, a blind knight and his hobbled guide."

"I couldn't listen to Lord Jolly groan about burning Brekliodad to the ground for another night."

"He should be happy he's alive," Torsten said.

The Lord from Crowfall had to have his left arm amputated just below the shoulder after his wound got infected. Torsten cursed himself every time the thought that the man deserved worse crossed his mind. He'd only been trying to help.

She'd have been safe in the castle without his brand of help, Torsten thought.

"So, is it true?" Lucas asked, stirring Torsten before his thoughts turned darker. He knew Lord Jolly had to feel guilty, even if he wouldn't admit his role in exposing Oleander while she was drunk and helpless.

"Is what true?" Torsten said.

"That the killers were the…" He lowered his voice. "…Dom Nohzi."

"It seems so."

"But why would they make a move like this after so long? I didn't think they were even real."

"A question Valin Tehr's man Codar might have known before he died so frivolously."

Lucas slowed "You think Valin had something to do with this?"

"I don't know what to think, but I do know that Codar knew the killers personally. Even called one 'grandfather.'" Torsten didn't mention that he knew one of them as well. In fact, he hadn't yet told anybody about Rand's sister's involvement. Rand's redemption had provided hope to a hurting kingdom, and Torsten didn't want to destroy that before knowing exactly what was going on. The Sigrid he knew was no fighter, at least not with anything but words, and certainly not a supernatural assassin for hire.

"That doesn't make sense," Lucas said. "To be his grandfather, no way he'd be able to move like that. Or even be alive. Codar wasn't that young a man."

"Well, *men* don't drink blood either. The killers were upyr, Lucas. None have been sighted in generations. Yesterday, Master Caspar—the new Master of Rolls—had his assistant read me a few legends in which their presence is noted. Not since Liam's Great Grandfather are they discussed."

"I know you don't trust Valin but… assassinating the Queen Mother. That's too public for him."

"All I know is that the Queen Mother is gone. Someone will pay for it, yet the Breklian Oligarchy will deny involvement as they always have with the Dom Nohzi. Condemn their actions, yet do nothing. All we can do for now is be there for Oleander's son, our king. There's a funeral to plan, and we'll have to secure it. Apparently, against monsters of legend and lore."

Lucas sighed. "And I thought everything was getting better."

"What a pleasant dream that was."

Lucas continued leading Torsten through the tunnels. Groans and mad screams sounded as they passed the hall leading to the dungeons. They were quieter for a time after Redstar fell, but troubles in South Corner had them filled again, especially after the riot. Torsten longed for the simpler days when the men slammed behind bars were simple like Whitney Fierstown, when they were thieves and greedy nobles—men with clear reasons behind their delinquency.

"Sir Unger!" a courier greeted them as they ascended the stairs into the castle proper.

"What is it?" Lucas questioned.

"A galler just arrived with word from Sir Nikserof and the Glass army."

"Give it here." Lucas snatched it and shooed the man away. Wi'th everyone on edge since the attack on Oleander, Torsten didn't blame him. Deserving or not, when royals started dying, that meant anyone could be a target.

"What does it say?" Torsten asked.

Lucas unfolded the letter. Torsten listened as he spread it flat across the castle walls.

"Sir Nikserof says, uh." He cleared his throat. "He says 'the siege is beginning to break. Afhems throughout the Sands have ceased throwing their support behind Muskigo Ayerabi, instead choosing to focus on a new tournament in Latiapur to decide on new afhemate leadership. He says the siege is breaking, and some of Muskigo's men have begun to sneak out of their fortifications and surrender, both on sea and land.'"

Torsten's hand involuntarily balled into fists. A wave of emotion came over him, and once again felt tears welling in the corners of ravaged eyes but knew they weren't really there. Taking a deep breath, he extended one arm to the wall to steady himself.

"Sir," Lucas said, dropping the scroll to grab him. "What's wrong. Isn't that good news?"

It took Torsten a few seconds to gather himself enough to respond. "It is."

"Then… I don't understand. You look like you've just seen a —been touched by a ghost."

"It's just, all these times I come close to doubting Iam remains with us, he shows his hand. Oleander freed me so I could defeat Redstar. Now as even her memory fades from this world, news arrives of an end to the war which plagues us. I lose my sight, and he sends me you."

"Sir, with all due respect, I don't think Iam has anything to do with me."

Torsten followed Lucas' voice so that he could take the young man by the shoulder. "I may not be the easiest man to serve, but your presence has been a blessing Lucas. Just know that. To have eyes I can trust in a time like this… Pi's future is bright thanks to men like you. You will make the Order very proud one day."

"Sir, I…"

"You needn't say anything," Torsten said. "Circumstance brought us together, but in this castle, friendship is a rare thing."

"I know it is likely grief talking, but thank you, Master Unger. I never wanted to be a Shieldsman, but—"

"Nor did I," Torsten said, smiling. "Nor did Sir Uriah. But for the best of us, all we can do is answer the call. Now, wear a brave face, my friend. We must bring this good news to the King."

"Sir." Lucas tugged on Torsten's arm. "There is something I need to tell you."

"Can it wait? His Grace can use this news."

"I… yes, it can wait. This way."

Lucas took Torsten's arm and led him toward the Great Hall where they could find passage to the tower up to Pi's private quarters where he'd remained in mourning since his mother returned to the castle.

They reached the side aisle of the Throne Room where for days, susurrations of all sorts could be heard. The haunting aroma of Oleander blossoms assailed Torsten's nose. Oleander's body was presented in the center, tidied for preservation by Abijah Pymer, the new Royal Physician, until the time of her burial. Without any priest's present, considerations were still being made for how it might be done.

Torsten was glad he couldn't see her so stiff and lifeless; her face uncharacteristically calm. Whether driven by passion or rage, her façade had never been one for such banality. He attempted to rush through to avoid the scent of flowers fueling his grief, but the moment they entered the room, Lucas' grip tightened, and the young man stopped.

"What's wrong?" Lucas asked.

Torsten didn't have to answer. The moment they and the rattling of their armor stopped, he heard a voice from the other room saying, "She truly was a remarkable woman."

"Tehr, what in Iam's name are you doing here?" Torsten asked. He veered toward the sound of the man's voice so fast he left Lucas behind.

"Paying my respects, if that's all right with you," Valin said.

"Respect? That's a new word, coming from you."

"I have great admiration for those who rise from nothing. Her, me… you. We all have a lot in common, don't we?"

"We have nothing in common," Torsten said. "Now, who let you in here?"

"I did," a thin voice answered. Torsten heard the clatter of King Pi's Shieldsman escort approach from the Great Hall.

"Your Grace," Lucas said, bowing.

"Your Grace," Torsten said as well. "Is everything all right?" He hadn't heard from the boy since they'd embraced in the Great

Hall. Torsten knew he should have checked on him more, but he couldn't.

"I merely wished to convey my condolences to Lord Tehr," Pi said. "I have heard how his friend and supporter Codar gave his life in an attempt to save my mother."

Valin shifted his cane aside and fell to his knees out of respect, playing the part of loyal subject as well as ever. Torsten even heard him force a snivel before he spoke. "Your generosity knows no bounds, Your Grace. Codar, he… he fell in love with this kingdom after I took him in. I can't imagine any other way he would have wanted to go than standing up for it against monsters of his own people's making."

"*His* own people's," Torsten remarked. "Your Grace, we can't trust outsiders right now."

"I know how people felt about my mother, Sir Unger," Pi said. "Especially in places like South Corner. And still, Codar sacrificed his life for her."

"Your mother was merely misunderstood, Your Grace," Valin said.

"How dare you speak of her!" Torsten growled. He stomped toward the man, but Pi promptly stopped him.

"Sir Unger, stop," he demanded. "We've all suffered enough here. Lord Tehr has offered his help in getting justice for my mother."

"There is no justice to be gained in fighting shadows," Torsten said.

"Codar taught me a great deal about the Dom Nohzi," Valin said. "About who they are, what they want… where to find them. If we strike fast, we can end their wicked games."

"And how do we know he wasn't one of them? Playing you all along."

"Because my friend is in the grave!" Valin snapped in an uncharacteristic display of emotion. He drew a long, beleaguered breath, gathering himself. "Forgive my outburst, Your Grace. Codar long claimed the rumors about the Dom Nohzi being men and women tainted by Elsewhere's touch were true, and now we know they are. You were there, Torsten. Witnesses say a woman as slight as a handmaiden tossed you like a child's doll. Those… things that killed your queen were not human."

Torsten bit his lip. He desperately wanted to say that the woman wasn't just any woman either, but he couldn't. Not with Valin around. He needed to get Pi alone. "They weren't," Torsten admitted.

"Exactly."

"So, what—we send another army after them? Your Grace, we spoke of peace, what use would that do to us?"

"What if they come for His Majesty next?" Valin asked.

"Someone had to summon them," Torsten reasoned. "Make a blood deal, or whatever they call it. Certainly, Codar taught you about that. Your Grace, all we need to figure out is who offered Oleander to their heathen gods. Put me in charge of it, and I will not fail you." Torsten approached the king, him being the one to fall to his knee this time. "I will not fail her."

"I trust you more than any other in this castle, Sir Unger," Pi said. "But you were too close to her to see clearly. Look at what they did to her in our very streets." Ever since his freedom from Redstar's curse, Torsten had known Pi to be composed, but his voice began to quake. "In front of everybody…"

Torsten turned toward the scent of flowers. "I can't," he said softly.

"How can there be peace when my mother could be murdered like that?" Pi said. "Her blood spilled like a goat sacrificed to the Buried Goddess."

"Your Grace. Now is not the time to lose yourself in vengeance." Torsten slid forward on his knees. All the battling of egos, he'd forgotten the very real truth. A troubled boy, not a king, had lost his mother after already losing his father. He slowly extended his hands and wrapped them around the boy's slender shoulders, feeling them heave.

"You don't understand," he cried. "Your parents left you to the streets. You didn't care about them; you've told me yourself."

"There is more to being a parent than blood. Your father was as the same to me. He was all I ever needed."

"My father is dead too!" Pi shouted. Torsten released him and backed away. "People think I don't remember things, but I do. I remember him lying in front of me. I barely recognized him any longer he grew so thin. Now her? Why would Iam take them both so soon… Why!"

Torsten's chest tightened upon hearing the heartbreak in the boy's tone, but he didn't back away further. "Your Grace, I think you need to rest," he said softly.

"No. Every time I show even the smallest hint of something other than complete composure, you people tell me to rest! The time for resting is over. Lord Tehr has promised to help."

"Help with what?"

"A galler has been dispatched to Governor Nantby in Yaolin City," Valin said. "The finest mercenaries in the region—Glass, Panpingese, the best—will be sent after the Dom Nohzi before they have even a chance to react. It will be Codar's last gift to this kingdom."

"Already?" Torsten said. "Your Grace, I am your Master of Warfare. I should have been consulted. We have no idea who in that order are related to Breklian nobility. We could ignite another war."

"Good," Pi whimpered.

"Good? Your Grace, I want justice for your mother as much as anybody, but we need to focus our efforts on ending the war in the Black Sands! I only just received word that Muskigo is on the brink of defeat. We can't afford—"

"I have agreed to pay for the campaign," Valin said. "Reparations of South Corner will need to slow, but the people will understand. A cowardly act such as this can't go unpunished."

"Oleander died because of rioters from South Corner," Torsten said.

"Misguided fools. Now they will see—"

"My mother died because all she had to protect her was you, " Pi said, so softly it was as if his mouth merely formed the consonants. Torsten strained to hear him, but when he did it felt like he'd been stabbed through the chest.

"Now, now, Your Grace," Valin said. "Codar was trained by the finest swordsman in his lands, and even he fell. Iam's enemies are strong, but now we must be stronger. We must stand together."

"Together?" Torsten rose and stalked in the direction of Valin. "There is no together. Pay for what you will. Lie to our King, but all you'll ever be is a gangster."

"Actually," The way he said the word… Torsten could practically see the smirk spread across his gaunt face. "It has been decided that I will soon be ennobled and sworn in under the Eye of Iam as the Kingdom's Master of Coin. All I've ever wanted is to serve my kingdom, and now my wealth can be the Crown's wealth. No strings attached."

If there were a blade in Torsten's chest, now it felt as if it were twisting. "Your Grace, is that true?"

"Lord Tehr has proven his love for this kingdom, and his skill at handling autlas," Pi said. "He grew up here in Yarrington, not away from it like Yuri Darkings. And thanks to him, we have a chance at finding the Caleef before our enemies do, at fixing our city. At vengeance for my mother."

"Your Grace, he can't be trusted!" Torsten shouted.

"I trust him. I do. I discussed the idea with Lord Jolly this morning, and he agreed that attacking the Dom Nohzi was crucial in proving our strength. That with Lord Tehr unhindered by who owes what, we can move fast."

"I should have been consulted," Torsten resigned.

"We sent Sir Mulliner for you, and he said you dismissed him."

Torsten felt foolish. He'd been so deep in research, he barely remembered Mulliner trying to pull him from his room. The only reason he went to visit Liam's grave was that his research brought him to a passage about a Black Sands assassination attempt on the great king. The very attempt which Torsten had incidentally thwarted as a boy, earning him a place as a King's Shield squire upon Liam's recommendation.

I should have been with Pi. But even being near him had made Torsten feel like more of a failure. And his oversight had allowed more whispers into Pi's ear from unworthy men.

"Your Grace, please—" Torsten began before Pi interrupted him.

"Stop. Nothing can be done without gold. Father taught me that, and we lose more and more every day. We need Lord Tehr who has been nothing less than gracious, and if you can't accept that, then perhaps there is no longer a place for you here."

Torsten could hardly speak. His throat felt like it was closing off.

"Torsten, you're grieving," Valin said. "We all are. This kingdom is lesser without you here. I know we've had our differences, but please, find peace with your loss and then together, we can do great things."

Torsten couldn't contain himself any longer.

"What is your game, you wretch!" he roared. "You did this somehow, didn't you? What do you want with him?"

"Sir Unger, you will calm down this instant!" Pi ordered.

Torsten didn't answer. Before he knew it, he was stomping toward Valin and then felt strong hands on his back and arms.

"Sir Unger," Sir Mulliner said. "Please." Torsten was transported back to that day outside of Winde Port when Redstar drove him to kill one of his own men, and Sir Mulliner had to stop him. His whole body went weak, and he staggered back. Lucas was there to keep him from tripping over Oleander's funeral arrangement, but not before he felt a few of her flowers crunch beneath his boot.

"Sir Unger, you—" Pi began before Valin cut him off.

"It's all right, Your Grace." Valin cleared his throat. "None of us are thinking clearly. No man in this world cares for the Glass like Sir Unger here. I know that with all my heart. So, do you. This loss has been hard on both of you. Trust me, I know what it's like to lose both parents."

"Is every word out of your mouth a lie?" Torsten said. "Everyone knows you grew up the bastard son of some harlot you didn't know."

"Loss is loss, no matter the circumstance," Valin said. "Now, I may not be formally on the Royal Council under the light of Iam, but I think there's no better place for me to start than to help plan a funeral for the Queen. Something quaint and inexpensive, to help the people remember her in a fairer light. I have some ideas for the Master of Masons for a statue to add to the courtyard in which she and Codar died as well."

"I think she'd like that," Pi said. "Would you mind discussing it in my quarters? I can't smell these flowers any longer."

"Of course, Your Grace," Valin said. "Sir Unger, differences aside, will you be joining us? If I'm certain of anything, it's that the Queen would have wanted you there at the end."

"I—I think I should get some rest, actually. I haven't slept since… Your Grace, if I could have stopped them…"

"I know, Sir Unger," Pi said, then sniveled. "I'm sorry, I didn't mean what I said. You saved my life, saved this kingdom, and I am forever indebted. Mother cared for you. I should have consulted with you on moving against her assassins, but I understand you want answers more than anyone. With Lord Tehr's help, we can get them ourselves."

"And we shall, Your Grace," Valin said. "First, we bid farewell to the fallen. Then, we discover why they fell and make sure it never happens again. Now, after you." Pi stepped by him, and Valin slithered closer to whisper to Torsten. "And Sir Unger, my offer remains. The care of the Vineyard is yours, whenever you might need it." He clacked away before Torsten could reply.

"Get a hold of yourself, Torsten," Sir Mulliner said after Valin, and the King moved on. "This is why Shieldsmen should leave their swords in their pants."

Mulliner marched by, along with a few other Shieldsmen, to escort Pi back to his quarters. Valin clicked along behind them, seeming like he was purposefully tapping his cane harder than necessary as a taunt.

"Ah, I forgot to tell you, Your Grace," Valin said on their way out of the room. "I was able to speak to a friend at Hornsheim. They paused deliberations to send a member of the priesthood to help guide Oleander's soul to the light. They're using their fastest horse. I know the Crown didn't wish to make such a request and sour relations."

"Thank you, Lord Tehr," Pi said, now distant. "This kingdom owes you a great deal already."

"Nonsense, Your Grace. If I were born anywhere else, I'd have died on the streets without family, without a home, and without purpose."

Torsten knelt as he listened to them go and rearranged the mess he'd made of Oleander's flowers. His heart paused as his hand grazed hers which was draped off the glass pedestal on which she was arranged. His forefinger rubbed hers, and for a moment, he thought about taking her hand, but with so many potential men of the Glass watching, he merely lifted it and lay it back across her chest.

"At least a priest coming is good news, right?" Lucas asked.

"Because delays to their decision are all this kingdom needs," Torsten grumbled, satisfying the itch below his right eye.

"She'll need all the help she can get."

Torsten didn't scowl at the boy, but he didn't have to.

"Sorry," Lucas said. "I just meant—"

"Relax. I'm not a fool, I know what she's done, but she won't die in vain." Torsten didn't wait for Lucas. He didn't even find his cane before he swept off toward the exit. He knew the way back to his quarters, after all.

"What are you thinking?" Lucas said as he caught up.

"Valin Tehr is connected to all of this, and I plan to find out how. He can flash his wealth around our young king and outsiders like Lord Jolly all he wants; the truth will come out."

"He and Codar were like brothers, Sir Unger. Everyone knows it. Those monsters killed him too. I know you don't trust Valin, and you shouldn't, but maybe he really does want to help."

Torsten whipped around. "One of those monsters was Sigrid Langley," Torsten said through clenched teeth, ignoring all the murmurs from the sycophants filling the Great Hall.

"What?" Lucas asked, incredulous.

"You heard me. Dom Nohzi, upyr, or not, she was Sigrid."

"How do you know?"

"She told me," Torsten said.

"She lied," Lucas said, matter-of-factly.

"I am blind, not dumb."

"The legends about upyr say they're known for illusion magic. What if it was a trick on your mind."

"It barely sounded like her anymore, but it was her. I know it. Valin Tehr said she left with Rand, but she hadn't."

"Sir Unger," Lucas said. Torsten could tell by his tone that he didn't believe him. It was Winde Port all over again, liars and snakes making him seem insane. He no longer wondered why Oleander seemed the same in this place.

"I didn't know her or Rand, but I'd seen her plenty at the Maiden's Mugs," Lucas said. "She wasn't a pushover, but she wasn't a warrior like that. You couldn't see. The way the killer moved… And her hair. It was white as snow, her skin the complexion of uncooked dough and her eyes were gray, not green."

Torsten's lip twisted. All these days since, he'd never thought to ask what she looked like. Plenty talked about the male assassin as if he were death incarnate, but the woman they simply said looked similar. He'd imagined they'd just meant how she was dressed.

"I don't care what you saw," Torsten decided. "It was her. She knew me, she knew Rand, and I knew her." Torsten shoved him away and continued on his path toward the stairs.

"Sir, what are you going to do?" Lucas asked.

"What I should have from the start. Valin Tehr is many things, but he truly is exceptional with gold. Men like that keep records of everything. Yuri Darkings did—even had records of his traitorous dealings found in his Old Yarrington mansion. Something in the Vineyard will prove Valin's guilt."

"Guilt of what?"

Torsten didn't bother answering. He could feel it in his veins, Redstar happening all over again. Only this time, the man wasn't foreign or a wielder of blood magic, he was a Glassman. Easier to trust, charming, manipulative—Torsten wasn't sure when or how the man had won Pi over, but it seemed it had already happened. He wondered what messages passed through the castle that he'd missed to make it all happen so fast. All the things his handicap hid from him.

Using the railing, he reached the floor of his quarters. He

knew which door it was. Only a few doors closer, in Lord Jolly's chambers, he heard the man weeping. He pressed his ear against the door.

"I should have never pushed her, Abijah," he whispered, pausing every few words to weep.

"Just lie still, my Lord," the Royal Physician said. "You must take this lest we risk further infection."

"I failed Liam. I failed to keep his family safe."

Torsten considered entering, but if Lord Jolly had supported Valin, he was no longer sure who could be trusted. Perhaps he was just too broken to care what he'd done. Just as Pi was too hurt to think of anything but revenge.

For most of his life, Torsten wasn't privy to the inner workings of the castle. He wished he'd spent more time paying attention to the sort of enemies that could dwell within it and not only those from foreign, conquered lands.

There's still one of them left to protect, Torsten thought. *And I won't fail him again.*

Torsten retired to his room. He reached out and allowed his fingers to graze the broken part of the wall where it was said Redstar threw Rand, and where he'd hung Oleander up and left her to die. He stopped there, then one by one removed the pieces of his armor. He paused as he removed Liam's own sword, Salvation, from his back-sheathe.

"Where I go, you can't follow," he whispered. He kissed the hilt, shaped like a dragon with the Eye of Iam at the pommel, then placed it in the center of his bed. Then he followed the wall over to his desk within which he kept a small dagger he used to open scrolls. It was an old thing without an extraordinary story of how it came to be, and it had never done anything special. In a way, it reminded Torsten of himself. For that reason, he strapped it to his belt, then headed back for his door, looking more like Whitney Fierstown, 'the world's worst thief,' rather than a proud Shieldsman and once-Wearer of White.

His leg got caught on his bedsheets, causing him to stumble a few steps.

"You should have this," Lucas said, reminding Torsten that the boy was there. He softly tossed something Torsten's way, and his hearing was good enough for him to catch his cane.

"Thank you," Torsten said.

"Sir Unger, what are you planning on doing?"

"Nothing you need concern yourself with."

"Sir Ung—Torsten, please."

"I meant everything I said earlier," Torsten said. "You'll be aa fine a Shieldsman as any. But this is something I have to do."

"Then let me come with you."

Torsten shook his head. "I don't need eyes with me to see the truth. I'll find it even if it kills me. Just listen to Sir Mulliner, and you'll do fine. He's a grump, but I can tell he likes you." Torsten extended his cane to the floor and moved for the door. Lucas stepped in his way.

"What did Valin do to you?" he asked.

"Move, Lucas. I won't let another snake whisper lies into the king's ears."

"Please, just tell me!"

Torsten had never heard his young aide raise his voice in such a way. It stunned him for a moment. Then Torsten remembered Winde Port again, how nobody had believed him. He recalled how the Shieldsmen treated him like a cripple after he'd lost his sight, despite having just saved the kingdom from Redstar.

Lucas was still there. He didn't run when Torsten claimed the killer was Sigrid, something Torsten knew nobody would believe. Only then did he realize that was why he hadn't told anybody. It had nothing to do with Valin.

"Please," Lucas said again, voice cracking.

Torsten sighed. He backed up slowly until his legs bumped his bed, then sat. "I was young," he said. "It wasn't long after I'd made the climb to take the vows of a Shieldsman. A very high noble whom Liam had an interest in protecting had gone missing, and Taskmaster Lars—a young man then—assigned me to investigate it. The nobleman's wife hadn't seen him in days. So, I followed the trail. I'd been so used to fighting in wars after the campaign against the Drav Cra. It was hard not to focus on violence."

Turned out, the noble liked to frequent Valin's Vineyard. So much so, that one day he couldn't pay for his infidelity. Valin said they kicked him out, but a few days later the body turns up floating in the docks, beaten half to death, parts chopped off him and..." Torsten buried his head in his hands, "...stuffed into his own mouth."

Lucas winced audibly.

"Everyone said he must have been robbed. You know, the kind of things that happen in Dockside. But I knew; I could tell just looking at his bloated body that it was more."

Liam and Sir Davies advised I drop it—that Valin's emergence and the Vineyard's existence had kept South Corner in check after decades of lawlessness—but I didn't. After unshaming the man, I took his body to the Vineyard. Not a soul said they'd ever seen him before except the young girl he fancied. She loved him, you see. Loved that lecherous man. And she had a different story to tell about what happens when patrons of the Vineyard are late on their payments too many times. A story about a rumored arena below Dockside and the 'volunteers' who fight there.

"I'd never seen fear it someone's eyes like when I asked her to come with me to the castle. All the men I'd killed in battle, none of them looked so scared. I promised her nothing would happen to her, but on our way back to the castle, we were stopped by soldiers. The nobleman's wife had proclaimed her guilt that she killed her husband because she found out what he'd been doing, then cut her own wrists. I left the girl outside and went into their home to look. When I got out, the girl was nowhere to be found. Not at the Vineyard, not floating off the docks—nowhere.

"Valin claimed he'd had nothing to do with it. I pushed for us to look deeper into his underground arena, but apparently, South Corner wasn't worth the trouble. I obsessed over it. Sir Davies was finally going to give in when the Panpingese mystics attacked Builders' Cairn in the east. Then we marched off, and all was forgotten."

"Why didn't you go after him when you returned?" Lucas asked.

"Dealing with rogue Mystics has a way of making you forget men like Valin. I thought about what happened from time to time until I saw more horrible things and lost more people I promised to protect. Until, eventually, like all the others, it simply felt like South Corner wasn't worth the trouble. And then Valin stepped into the Great Hall last week like Iam had forgotten his sins as we had. Suddenly, him helping save me seemed less like protecting his interest and more like a play for my support."

"Of which he apparently didn't need."

"Valin Tehr taught me that the worst of us aren't those we fight against on the field of battle, but the ones sleeping in the shadows right by our feet. The monsters under our beds."

"I… Sir," Lucas stuttered. "I get it. But what if all those years ago, he really was telling the truth? What if you were wrong and the wife did do it?"

"Please, Lucas. You said you fought in his arena before. You're telling me every man down there fought of their own free will?"

"Every man I talked to did. Sometimes events were private though, for only specially selected patrons to watch. Men with enough gold to have a mansion in Old Yarrington."

"Exactly," Torsten said. "He keeps the rabble tame and the lords entertained. Sometimes, you don't need to see proof, Lucas. Sometimes, you just know, deep down in your soul, that something is off. I knew it with Pi when he was cursed. I knew it with Redstar. And I could have killed that wretch the moment I laid eyes upon his birthmarked face, but I didn't. I won't make that mistake again."

Torsten stood to walk, but Lucas clutched his wrist.

"Sir, I know he's not a good man," Lucas said. "He's not even a bad man. He's downright awful. But why would he kill the Queen now? If it was over something she'd done while in control, he could have had her killed months ago. But she was unpredictable, flashy. He has a stake in half the clothes-makers who dressed her, not to mention the parties she threw. I know it—my parent's provided cakes, and he always got a cut, thanks to his protection."

"He's Master of Coin now, isn't he?"

"And his closest friend in the world is dead."

"A Breklian, killed by Breklians he knew. Ones who'd taken in Sigrid, who they also knew. It's all connected, Lucas, and I will find out how. Now, out of my way."

"Sir, don't do this!" Lucas grabbed at him again, and Torsten's hand fell toward the grip of the dagger at his waist. That was when he realized what Lucas thought he was about to do. Walk into the King's chambers and slit Valin's throat.

"Don't worry, I'm not going to kill him," Torsten said. "Despite what he says, he and I are nothing alike. I seek only to bring his misdeeds into Iam's light this time. He invited me to enjoy the Vineyard. It's time I take him up on his offer."

"Fine. Then you'll need eyes you trust with you."

XXVIII

THE DAUGHTER

Mahi stood with her back facing the portcullis she'd just been safely on the other side of. Before her, all around, it was a sea of gray as the Shesaitju people gathered from all over the nation. Arrayed around the pit stood nine other warriors—all men, all larger than her, all with more muscle than her, none of them more determined than her.

Sure, they all wanted to live as much as she did—but not a single one of them had more to gain.

"People of Latiapur!" the eunuch acting as game master announced to thunderous applause. "The God of Sand and Sea provides ten more tributes. May their hands be swift, and their feet steady as the beating sea."

Mahraveh watched all the other combatants spit in their hands, then kneel to run their palms across the sand. She did the same, just like she'd seen her father do countless times before battle or sparring. It was then she noticed the shallow ring of sea-water infiltrating the edge of the arena, stained dark red by the blood already spilled. It wouldn't be cleaned out until after the tournament when drains in the dam against the cove's sea-face were opened to flood the sands and wash away impurity.

"We give honor to you, our combatants. Death comes to all, but for one of you, let it not be for years to come. May the eternal current guide you."

"May the eternal current guide me!" the combatants echoed, Mahraveh the last of them. She was too busy spinning in place, mesmerized by the sight of so many people. She'd long imagined what it might've been like the day her father won the Ayerabi afhemate, but even her imagination paled in comparison.

It was only the sight of Babrak, leaning over the high ledge and staring at her, which drew her mind back to focus. It was the first time he'd left his comfy chair the whole day. He licked his lips like he was anticipating a great feast. In the distance behind him at the highest level, sat Yuri Darkings, a hood covering his face in shadow. She couldn't believe that in an arena filled with her people, he would be the closest thing to an ally she had.

"Fight with honor!" the games master bellowed.

The volume of the crowd reached hair-raising heights. Then it grew so silent, Mahraveh could only hear the sound of sandals shifting across the sand. Her gaze darted from one wall to the other. The warriors circled each other, Mahi included, waiting for someone to make the first move.

Finally, the representative from the Usef afhemate charged his closest opponent, stabbing out with his weapon of choice, a fauchard. The blade grazed harmlessly across leather armor. Behind Usef, Sanadir's fighter brought his arm around, and a flail whipped out, catching Usef on the shoulder. Usef twisted around, now open to retaliation. Sanadir twirled, and the flail carried out a wide arc before smashing Usef in the face.

He was dead before he hit the sand.

Mahi's breath got caught in her chest. The battle had just begun, and one of them was already dead.

Sanadir moved forward to attack the next warrior, but Mahraveh didn't see any of it. She felt a hard hit against the side of her head and fought to stay upright. She hadn't adequately judged how much her helmet obscured her view and missed the attacker on her right.

When she spun, she saw a familiar face. Khonayn of the Jalurahbak afhemate rushed toward her, a round shield leading the way. It connected with her, and he shoved her backward. Still, she kept her footing.

"Sorry, Jumaat," Khonayn shouted. "There are no friends out here. I'll make this quick. The current awaits you."

Careful not to repeat her first mistake, nor the one Usef had made, she glanced behind her just long enough to be sure no one was there. Then she advanced with her spear. She struck twice, both times connecting with the man's shield and tearing off large chunks of wood.

Khonayn pushed forward. He carried a scimitar in his other hand and stabbed it once with each step. By now, Mahraveh had driven all sounds of the congregation from her mind, focusing only on Khonayn and the openings he presented. Muskigo had always advised against shields in one on one combat, claiming it slowed one down too much and hindered one's ability to maneuver correctly.

As always, her father was right. Khonayn labored behind the thing, trying to keep himself guarded while weakly trying to attack. Mahraveh waited until he got close. The curved blade came out from behind the shield, and she stepped to the side while simultaneously hooking Khonayn's wrist under her arm. Gripping it tightly, she pulled him forward, planted her foot against his shield, then pushed out, bringing her other foot up to give her even more strength behind it.

There was a sickening *crack,* which sounded like twigs breaking underfoot, as Khonayn's arm snapped. He cried out and toppled backward, slamming hard against the sand. He tried desperately to rise, fumbling to keep the shield up but stumbled over it. Mahraveh spun her spear around in her hand, hefted it above her shoulder, and was about to throw it when in her peripherals, she saw movement—another warrior trying to take advantage of her. A coward. She ducked just in time, whipped around low, and jammed the spear into her assailant's stomach. The crowd erupted as he coughed up blood and slid down the shaft toward her body.

They were cheering for her kill.

It was too loud for anyone to hear her, but she roared. She wasn't sure why. From the moment her father left for war, leaving her behind, rage had been welling within her. She hadn't recognized it until that moment, but there it was, being released in a primal scream, bubbling to the surface.

It all came crashing down when Khonayn rammed into her. She flew back over the body, her spear still lodged in the man's chest. She was able to catch her footing quickly, but by then, Khonayn was bearing down.

"Never celebrate until you win, boy," Khonayn said, broken arm hanging limply at his side. Still, she knew what a man his size could do to her even with one hand.

Mahraveh knew what she should do. The same thing she'd taught Jumaat—run. But that was half the reason she couldn't let him fight. People followed her father after his victory because he claimed so many on his own, and he was a master of black fist. Everybody had known he was the favorite and teamed up on him, but it didn't matter.

He was the Scythe.

But Mahraveh couldn't just win. She had to win the favor of all the thousands watching.

"C'mon then, coward," she shouted. "You claim you wanted to join Muskigo, but you were too frightened."

His shield sprang out, and she ducked low. But he was fast. He recovered and lashed out again, at every point in her body. Her black fist was exceptional and could help her now, but it was little match for a shield.

She slipped under one of his swipes and drove a fist into his abdomen, fast as a striking snake. Before she landed another blow that might daze him, he spun and bashed her in the back with his shield.

She hit the sand hard, scraping her knees and forearm. There was no time to recover. She flipped over as a huge foot came down and nearly crushed her. As she came to her feet, she rolled toward the fallen warrior and grabbed her spear. She pulled hard, but it didn't budge. She looked over her shoulder just in time to dodge another swipe. On her way back up, she pulled with every-thing she had and the spear came loose, blood spouting from the man's chest like a fountain.

"I am the snake!" she shouted as he shouldered her. She rolled to her left and punched Khonayn's ribs, then hopped back, putting distance between them. She was small; her spear was long. It gave her just the advantage she needed. Khonayn turned once more and began to say something, but before anything came out, Mahraveh drove her heel into the sand and lurched forward. The tip of her spear pieced through the fleshy part of Khonayn's neck and drove up through his mouth.

She stood still for a few seconds, too absorbed in the kill to even hear the crowd's reaction. Then she turned. Across the arena, two were still fighting while another charged her with a sword.

She wrenched her spear from Khonayn's throat, flipped it around in her hand, and launched it. It landed with a hard *thunk*, burying itself deeply into the man's shoulder. She bent, grabbing up Khonayn's scimitar as she moved toward the new enemy. With the wound, her opponent barely got his blade up before she gutted him.

She was breathing heavy as she approached the remaining

two. The one with his back to her stabbed forward with a scimitar just like the one she now held and spilled his opponent's entrails out onto the sand. Mahraveh dug deep in the sand. This one was massive enough to knock her out with a single punch. Adrenaline coursed through her, but she'd never fought like this. The real thing made her arms far sorer than training. Her father had been holding back.

She'd put on enough of a show already. Now she had to survive.

Just as the warrior was about to turn toward her, she dove forward and slashed with her scimitar. The blade drew a deep gash along her opponent's neck from his ear down to his collarbone. Blood gurgled from the wound, fear burst from his eyes, but he didn't go down.

He wheeled around, hefting a one-handed hammer she hadn't seen. She deflected his weight with her parries, just like her father taught her, but he never went at her with all his might. The hammer struck her sword on the flat, sending her, and it, flying back.

The man stomped toward her, raised his hammer high, then fell to a knee. The deep wound she'd inflicted took too high a toll. The hammer slipped through his fingers, cracking against his skull, and he crashed face-first into the ground.

The arena cheered. Mahi exhaled. She'd learned from Amoud's mistakes not to celebrate. Instead, she looked up to where she knew the eunuch game master would be standing.

"Jumaat," he said, "of the Ayerabi! Victor!"

Behind him, Babrak, seated again in his oversized chair, stopped laughing, turned to his fellow afhems. "Coward!" he shouted, loud enough to hush the boisterous crowd.

"Have you something to say, Afhem Babrak?"

"My apologies to the games master. Perhaps I spoke too soon. I can't say I blame him. Of course, he would want to separate himself from that fool, Muskigo Ayerabi, who thought these sands merely a place to show off."

Mahraveh seethed beneath her helmet, breathing heavy and not just from battle. She squeezed the grip of her sword so tight her knuckles went white.

"By all means, do not hold back, Afhem Babrak," the games master replied.

Mahraveh was sure the eunuch was being facetious, but Babrak was too stupid to know the difference. With the warmongering afhems left in charge of Latiapur, the eunuchs back at the palace couldn't have been happy with their Caleef missing. Babrak rose from his seat and made his way down the walkway.

"The rebel who thought he knew better than the Caleef." Babrak shook his head, looking down at Mahraveh. "The only thing worse than a foolish afhem who brings unwanted war upon us is one of his afhemate who was too cowardly to follow. What have you to say?"

Mahraveh knew the only reason Jumaat hadn't gone with her father was that he was too young at the time. Babrak knew that as well. But she didn't dignify the fat pis'truda with a response. Instead, she stood and lowered her head in reverence. She wasn't sure why she'd done it, but her father taught her that if she wasn't going to respond to him, it was best to at least still show respect.

"Very well," the games master said, stepping in front of Babrak. "We honor your brethren. May his soul find it's way along the eternal current. But the Black Sands and the Boiling Waters are not won only with the blood of men. For you, we've chosen not just one beast, but three!"

The portcullis opened to Mahraveh's left, and then another to her right, and yet another behind her. The first of the three appeared at her left, and then the other two. Pit lizards, bigger than any she'd ever seen in Saujibar, and they looked starved.

Mahraveh backed up and forced the three lizards to align

themselves in front of her. They weren't close to one another, but at least now she could see them all without turning her head. Pit lizards were dangerous creatures. It wasn't just their bite that was to be feared. It was the bacteria in its saliva that, once in its victim's bloodstream, functioned like venom. It acted fast, furiously eating away at the skin and flesh.

A flick of her wrist sent her scimitar spinning in her hand. Around and around, making sure her wrist was nice and loose. It was more for sedation than anything else. Everyone knew a bow and barbed arrow was the best method for taking down pit lizards, but a bow wasn't an option for the arena. They were getting close. The one on the right hissed, then the one next to it hissed and snapped its massive maw at the one first, teeth clattering against teeth.

That gave Mahi an idea. Quickly, she darted to the far right, causing the beasts to turn sharply. They moved fast when running straight, but turns were tricky for the short, squat creatures. And these, in particular, were long. Man-sized at least.

As the front one turned, its tail whipped against the one behind it, and its into the third. Mahraveh continued in the circle, the lizards following. When she reached the other side, the same thing happened but in reverse. This time, the back one snapped at the middle one's tail.

She did it one last time, and the desired effect took place. The back two lizards turned on one another, snapping hard and drawing blood. When the front one saw it, he joined in. The crowd got quiet, unsure of what to think. Mahraveh watched as the three reptiles tore into each other. The middle one had the rear one by the throat, and the thing thrashed wildly.

The front one, clearly confused, mounted the middle one and was abruptly thrown aside. The rear one stopped thrashing, dead.

The Mahraveh's surprise, the crowd cheered.

Now the remaining two fought, claws and teeth slashing and

digging. Mahraveh slowly closed in, careful not to draw too much attention. The middle one, worn out from the fight, soon lost the advantage and found itself belly up with the largest of the three atop it, biting and tearing.

When Mahi was sure the beast was near death, she made her move and leaped forward. She lifted her scimitar high, then brought it down, driving the blade through the largest one's eye—its most vulnerable spot. Its tail continued to whip. She knew those scales were sharper than any weapon in the arena, so she gave it a wide berth. Finally, it went still.

The last one wasn't dead, but it was dying. Mahraveh worked her sword loose, back and forth. Blood dripped from the tip as she stalked toward her prey. The lizard groaned and hissed, but its back appeared broken.

Mahi turned toward Babrak and pointed her sword at him, then she brought it down in a wide slash down at the lizard, slicing the soft underbelly. Blood poured out in a deluge against the black sands.

The arena exploded, the onlookers standing and cheering in ovation.

Babrak just stared at her helmeted face. She had just bent over, hands on her knees to gather her breath.

"Rest, warrior," the eunuch said. "For tomorrow, your story is written upon the sand."

The portcullis back to the undercroft caverns slid open. Mahraveh took a few short steps toward it before realizing how wobbly her legs were. It wasn't killing that was difficult. She'd done that to those rotten Glassmen and felt nothing.

She'd just never before feared death. All those years learning from her father, she knew she was safe.

Now she knew why he didn't want her to march at his side.

XXXIX

THE THIEF

"'T*hievin fruitcake*,'" Whitney said, mimicking Grint. "He's got some nerve, running like a scared cat."

Rand didn't bother responding. Together, they climbed a hillock overlooking a plain with a single road cutting through—the Glass Road connecting Yarrington to the Panping Region in the far east. Above them, the sky was beginning to lighten, but a thick fog rolled in with the early morning, and the air was still crisp. The Drav Cra were headed back west, away from Panping, away from Sora.

Still, Whitney followed.

He and Rand quickly searched through Fettingborough before setting after the Drav Cra on horses stolen from the stables. The savages were sloppy. Dozens of citizens were left behind; their families broken apart. Some beaten, others sleeping. They found Grint's guards, Zane and Dorblo, throats cut in their beds. Aquira and Gentry were missing from his room. The whole place was covered in scratches, and the bed was little more than cinders, with the roasted corpse of a Drav Cra beside it. But there was no sign of Aquira, which meant either the wyvern had flown off after putting up a fight or had somehow been captured. Or… Whitney shook his head, refusing to think that thought.

Hours later, he and Rand left the horses a good distance off once the Drav Cra horde was within earshot. They didn't bother to tie them up in case they never returned.

"So, what possessed you to get caught up in Darkings business? After all, they say you *saved* Torsten and redeemed yourself." Whitney said as they climbed. Anything to draw his attention away from how sore his thighs were from trudging through mud and wet grass.

"Valin Tehr," Rand said without emotion.

That was a name Whitney hadn't expected to hear. As he'd said the other night with the troupe, he knew him. Anyone who'd spent time in Yarrington's darker corners would. Whitney didn't ever care about stealing for the wealth. He never saved much of it anyway, and most treasures he took, he did so for the thrill, to prove he could. He'd bury priceless things around Pantego just in case, and use any gold to enjoy lavish nights like a proper noble. But, occasionally, fences approached him to take things they desperately wanted. In Yarrington, most of those shady types worked for Valin Tehr. He always shrewdly negotiated the lowest possible price.

"What in Elsewhere and Exile does that cheap shog-licker have to do with any of this?" Whitney said.

"He has *everything* to do with *all* of it," Rand said. "It's true: the rumors. I did save Torsten, but I didn't do it alone. Valin Tehr helped me do it, in exchange for me helping him. He stole my sister to make sure I couldn't say no and has been holding her at his brothel… keeping her locked up like a dog. He threatened her life, basically said she'd be his personal whore if I didn't do this. I had no choice."

"Gods and yigging monsters, there's always a choice," Whitney blurted. Then he thought about every bad decision he'd ever made… then he thought about what he would have done to save Sora, what he *had* done: played nice in Elsewhere for six shogging years, and stayed true to her in hopes that he'd return and have his happily ever after. "She's my sister," Rand said. "What was I to do—"

"You're right," Whitney interrupted. "There was no choice."

"No need to get smart," Rand said, resigned.

"No, really. You did what anyone with half a heart would've done, and rightly so. But why does anyone care about Barty anyway? Enough to hire you and Grint. I met his old man, and even Yuri knew he was a screw-up. Didn't seem like he'd go through all of this to relocate him." Whitney stopped for a breath and blew out a raspberry. "But what do I know? I've got enough father issues."

"As I've said, Bartholomew Darkings isn't who I'm concerned about."

Whitney gathered himself and continued along a few steps before turning back to Rand. "Well, don't leave me hanging like this," he said. "Who's down there that's worth the money of Valin Tehr?"

"Sorry, thief. I can't tell you."

"We fought Northmen together! In certain lands, that'd make us close as brothers… or, blood brothers… I don't know. I was an only child."

"Trust me, you'd rather not know. But I promised to get him somewhere for Valin. If he dies, if these savages kill him, they kill Sigrid as well. Bartholomew is just along for the ride."

"Mmmmm, right. It's the Caleef, isn't it?" Whitney said, matter-of-factly.

"It's not the Caleef," Rand protested a little too quickly.

"I may have been away for six years, but I've heard things."

"Six years… What?"

Whitney ignored him. "And I know Yuri Darkings broke him out and joined the rebels."

"It's not the Caleef!" Rand snapped, clutching Whitney by the collar. "Trust me, you don't want anything to do with this. So just worry about your own people."

"Iam's shog in a barrel, fine." Whitney pulled free and straightened his shirt. "I'm just trying to make conversation. So, you won't mind if I have words with Darkings then?"

"Go crazy. He's half the reason I'm in this situation."

Whitney grinned and rubbed his hands together. "In that case, we're in luck." He nodded toward the top of the low hill. In the light of the coming dawn, they could now see the Drav Cra they were tracking.

They were pulled over on the side of the road, the zhulong eating muddy grasses. Two dire wolves played tug-of-war with a chunk of meat. Whitney shuddered to imagine what kind of meat it was. All he knew was a few Drav Cra warriors stood nearby, chuckling, exchanging trinkets as if they were betting on which of the beasts would win the meal.

Inside the rearmost wagon, Barty Darkings sat, face pressed against the bars. The corner of Whitney's lip curled up at the sight of him. He saw his mouth moving, begging the savages; claiming his wealth. Whitney couldn't think of a better man to suffer so. A part of him considered joining the band of Northmen just to make sure they treated the Darkings with "proper care."

Beside the former constable, a dozen more from Fettingborough were stuffed into the wagon whose names Whitney might never know. And in the carts ahead, he knew were more towns-folk, as well as the friends he cared about.

Dawn's light bloomed across the plains, and the rain started up again. Whitney could see where the wagons were headed. Where there were only twenty or so Northmen in Fettingborough, that was just a small raiding party. A couple hundred warriors had set up camp in a low valley. Fur-covered tents, more beasts of burden, and covered campfires dotted the countryside.

"Shog, that's a lot of heathens," Whitney said, dropping down into a prone position. Rand joined him.

"Heathens? Maybe you really are friends with Sir Torsten?" Rand commented.

"Best friends."

"Looks like they're tearing down camp," Rand said. "But why? A low, guarded position out here in the plains, hidden from lightning, they could go on raiding for months before the Glass has the men to end this.

"You'd have thought they'd've just settled down Fettingborough," Whitney argued. "Nice beds. Roofs."

"After what happened to them in Yarrington and outside Nahanab, I doubt they're eager to settle down in more Glassmen homes."

"Look over there," Whitney said. To the east, buried behind a veil of rolling fog, separated from the others, two Drav Cra stood, apparently taking a leak. "Thin the herd?"

"I don't think killing two out of two hundred will matter much," Rand said.

"Two less trying to kill us," Whitney said. "We can steal their furs. Might come in handy sneaking in."

"Yeah, because we're both towering, pale savages."

"Trust me. People never look close enough until it's too late. Everybody sees what they want to see, even them."

Rand lowered his hand to his longsword. "It can't hurt, I suppose. But we aren't going any further without a proper plan."

"You're killing me, ex-Shieldsman," Whitney sighed. "I'll get the ugly one." Then he laughed softly. "Both ugly. The one with the big… uh… codpiece?"

"Just get the one on the right. We can hide behind those

bushes and wait 'til they turn around and head back toward the wagons."

At that moment, Whitney felt something large press against the back of his neck, and the ground pulled away from him—or rather, he rose from the ground. With the force of one of the zhulong, Whitney was thrust around to face the biggest, nastiest Drav Cra he'd ever seen. His hair came to a sharp point in the front and was pulled into one long braid. Across his neck, he wore a grisly scar. The giant Northman glanced back and forth between Whitney and Rand, who he similarly held by the scruff of the neck. Whitney felt as if he was going to black out and couldn't even manage to find a weapon his hands were so preoccupied with trying to pry the man's hand off.

"Looky, looky," the beast of a man said. "Look what Drad Mak found." Without warning, he pistoned his arms outward and sent them both flying through the air.

Whitney's stomach did flips. It felt like he soared an eternity, and his whole body clenched in preparation for impact. He landed a long way down the hill, bounced several times and then rolled to a stop only a few meters from a grouping of warriors. Whitney coughed, chest heaving, lungs looking for air.

"We have to run," Rand said, also breathless. He yanked on Whitney's cloak, but it was no use. He barely got to his knees before they were seized once more by Drav Cra warriors.

One said something in Drav Crava, then laughed.

"Time to join friends," said another, accent harsh as the Latiapur summer sun.

Rand drew his longsword and gripped it with both hands. "Stay back!" he shouted as he swung it in a broad arc.

"Put that puny thing away," Mak said, stomping down the hill, battle axe still on his back and laughing like Rand was merely an amusement. Good thing, as his battle axe had a socket made out of a skull and blades the size of a giant's thumb. Anyone with a weapon like that knew how to kill with it, and took themselves too seriously.

To the big Northman, the sword Rand wielded must have been like being attacked with a sewing needle. Mak kept walking until its tip neared his chest. Whitney could have sworn the metal bent under the pressure. Mak slapped it away with the back of his free hand. Rand seemed too exhausted from the fall to hold it. The sword splashed into the mud, and Rand slipped to join it.

Whitney glanced from side to side. He could make a break for it, but warriors waited in every direction. And while one of the dire wolves enjoyed the meal it had won, the other stalked nearer, its massive paw stretching over a small round stone, flaunting drooling fangs as long as Whitney's fingers.

"I think you have the wrong people," Whitney said, coughing. He rose to his hands and knees but promptly earned a boot to his gut. He rolled over, the air knocked out of him.

"You don't realize the mistake you're making," Rand wheezed. "Do you know who I am? The Glass will wipe you away."

Mak clutched Rand by the collar and heaved him off his feet. "They already tried," he growled.

"Do you think we're alone? We're scouts for the Glass army. Villages, way stations, fine, but now that you hit a place big as Fettingborough they'll come for you."

"Let them send their best then."

"Who's that?" one of the Drav Cra stationed by the wagons asked.

"You don't recognize this one?" Mak said, holding Rand a little higher. "Wearer of White for a moon."

Rand punched at Mak, even hitting him in the face a couple of times. The Northman hardly reacted.

"Thought I didn't recognize you?" Mak asked as he cast Rand aside like a spent sack of flour.

Rand landed near two pairs of furred boots, and the warriors they belonged to wasted no time snatching him, one at each arm.

"And this one." Mak turned and stalked toward Whitney. He knelt before him and poked him in the center of the forehead, knocking him back onto his rump. "Who are you?"

"Do you want the long answer or the short one?" Whitney said. All the strength he'd gained in Elsewhere worked amongst the strongest of the Glintish, but the Drav Cra were a different breed.

"Fierstown!" Barty screamed from within his cage, grabbing the bars. His outburst was met with the flat of a sword cracking against his knuckles. Mak then slapped Whitney across the face with the back of his hand.

"Hey! There's no need to be rough," Whitney said, spitting up blood.

"Leave him be in the name of the King!" Rand demanded.

"Long way from home for a failed Shieldsman. *Keo'lzt mech far.*"

By now, the whole of the heathen army was looming, watching the show. Even the Fettingborough citizens peered through the bars of their prisons. As two parted, Whitney noticed Gentry huddled in the corner of one, crying. Aquira was next to him. Her mouth was muzzled, and she wore a metal, spiked necklace like you'd see being used to force someone to the gallows. That explained why she hadn't torched them all.

"What are you going to do with all these people?" Whitney asked. Suddenly, his natural inclination to try and get under the Drav Cra leader's skin faded. He knew he had to be careful, for their sakes. It wasn't only his neck on the line.

Mak reached through the bars and grabbed hold of Talwyn's hair. He smiled and said, "Each one will serve a... unique purpose."

Talwyn whimpered, and Lucindur said something in Glintish.

But it was Conmonoc who sprang to action. One booted foot lurched out and smacked against Mak's massive forearm, crushing it against the metal bars. Mak roared, rage painting his pale face pink as a sunset. He shook the bars so hard the wheels lifted on one side and the zhulong took a few steps forward out of trepidation.

"You dare lay hands on me, filth?" Mak reached through the bars, grabbed Conmonoc's neck, and with the force of a god, bashed the man's head into the metal.

Whitney cringed, the girls shrieked, and Gentry sobbed louder, but it was Benon's agonized cry that stirred the Wildlands to silence as Conmonoc's face exploded into a misty gore, dead in a second. The guy might have been a pile of day-old shog, but even Whitney wouldn't have wished such a fate for him.

Aquira lunged at Mak's arm, but the chains holding her in place snapped tight. The spiked collar dug into her scales, her blackish blood running down through the gaps between them. Her squeal made Whitney's heart plummet even further.

"No!" Benon screamed. "No! No! No!" The cage rattled under Benon's kicks, and his screams turned into low moans.

Mak laughed, shaking out his arm.

"Why are you villains always such sociopaths?" Whitney asked. A few of the Drav Cra stood around, but none touched him as if waiting for the command of their leader first. That was when Whitney again noticed the dire wolves pacing just beyond the wagons. The second, larger one, had finished its meal now and licked its chops. A scar ran down one half of its long snout from the nostril and up to a half-missing ear.

"Did you think you and the Mad Queen's hangman would show up and save the day?" Mak asked Whitney. "Maybe the pretty one might fondle you a bit in thanks? All you southerners are pitiful with your women. Those of us who didn't choose the warmth of the south *take* what we need to keep us warm."

"You know, no one's stopping you from going back," Whitney said.

Mak glared Whitney's way. "Bring that one here," he told his compatriots, still looking at Whitney but pointing at Rand.

They complied, dragging Rand. He didn't budge without a fight, but the two easily overpowered him.

"You will all suffer for the mistake your former-Wearer made in killing our Arch Warlock and ending our alliance." Mak closed his fist around a patch of Rand's hair and wrapped his bicep under his chin. Rand's face turned purple.

"That's what this is about?" Whitney asked. "Redmoon? All this over him?"

"Redstar!" Mak snarled, jerking Rand's neck. Rand struggled, spittle flying from his mouth.

"Not now, Whitney," Rand gurgled.

"So, you just want revenge?" Whitney said, ignoring Rand. He was talking fast, watching Rand's eyes lose life under Mak's grip. "You think killing or enslaving all these innocent people will somehow make up for Torsten killing Redstar? That's ridiculous. Why don't you just go after Torsten?"

"The Glass Castle is the most secure place in the realm," Mak replied. "When we take control over the White Bridge, those responsible for murdering Redstar and slaughtering my men in the south like ants will come to me!"

Whitney floundered for a lie, something to make the Drad ease up on Rand. Drav Cra closed in around him, all of them, eager to tear into another southern flower-picker.

"Why make things harder? I can get you into the Glass Castle," Whitney said. I've done it before."

Mak eyed Whitney curiously, eyes narrowing just a bit. His men, however, didn't stop nearing. Whitney could smell their foul breath—raw meat or blood or whatever it was savages ate.

"Do you know who I am?" Whitney said. "Whitney Fierstown, World's Greatest Thief and the first to be acknowledged by the Glass Kingdom itself—at your service. Just let up a little. Let the whelp breathe."

Mak's arm loosened up just a bit, and Rand pulled in a sharp breath. "Why would you…"

"Don't listen to him!" Barty yelled. "He's a liar and a thief."

"A fact he just willfully shared," Mak said. "If you speak again, you will lose your tongue."

"You can keep that one. He's the son of the former Master of Coin. Worth a lot dead or alive—but the rest of these people are worthless to you," Whitney continued. "If Torsten Unger comes out here, he brings an army with him. But if you go to him… you can take the castle with hardly any effort, even if it's just you and me. As you know, most of Torsten's army is out dealing with the uprising in the south."

Mak appeared to consider Whitney's words before saying, "That ingrate is right about one thing. You are a liar. All these people, they will help draw Torsten to me. He will watch his people suffer as mine have."

"I don't know if 'watch' is the best term…" Whitney muttered.

"Throw them in with the rest of them and start packing up! We leave shortly."

"Drad Mak, my men are tired," said the Drav Cra with the long mustache Whitney had seen in Fettingborough.

"Drad Ugosah… Are your men so weak?" Mak said. "Tell them they can sleep when they visit the bosom of the Buried Goddess." He shoved Rand at the man. "Let's go."

Fur-clad savages shoved Whitney and Rand toward the wagon with Bartholomew Darkings in it. Whitney couldn't help but smile. Maybe he didn't have a plan to escape this—yet—but an afternoon with old Barty was worth the diversion.

"What are you grinning at, pretty boy?" Whitney's escort asked, prodding him with one of his sausage fingers.

"Nervous twitch," Whitney said.

"Whitney, what do we do!" Gentry shouted from the troupe's prison. Whitney saw the small boy's tear-streaked face, Aquira clutched under his elbow. Whitney had never seen such sorrow in her big, yellow eyes. Talwyn and Lucindur were behind them, and they leaned forward upon noticing him as well.

Whitney stuttered for a response. The Drav Cra guarding their wagon promptly silenced them all with a bang on the bars with his hammer.

Then the door for Whitney's own cage swung open, and the men stuffed him in. Rand put his legs up and fought it.

Once a stubborn Shieldsman, always a stubborn Shieldsman, Whitney thought.

"Just get in," Whitney whispered, defeated. He gave Rand's ankle a whack and broke his balance. He flew into the cage and smashed shoulder first against the bars. Right next to Barty, who was visibly shaken, but tried to act cool.

"Fierstown," he said. "I'd hoped we'd never see each other again after I spared you in Winde Port."

"Oh, don't worry," Whitney said. "You won't be alive to see me for very long."

"Mister Langley, how is it you allowed this ingrate to travel at your side?"

"I'll give you ingrate." Whitney charged—or rather crawled as the cage was so confined—for Bartholomew, but Rand recovered and restrained him. Whitney stretched his leg as far as it would go and kicked the former constable.

"Enough," Rand said, seething.

"We are both caged like Panpingese servants," Barty said. "Can we dispense with the childish threats?"

"I've been asking all the gods to put me in a cage with you,

you shog-eating bastard," Whitney said. "Do you know what you did to me!" Whitney only stopped resisting when a dire wolf propped up on the side of the cage and growled. Slobber sprayed onto the side of Whitney's face.

"I said, settle down, both of you!" Rand ordered. He shoved by a woman and positioned himself between Whitney and Bartholomew. "It's bad enough we're all here, but if we want any hope of getting out, we'll need to work together."

Whitney drew a deep breath, then unballed his fists. He hadn't even realized he'd been squeezing them so tight. Seeing Barty up close, in all his grotesque, plump glory, it brought back memories of the years in Elsewhere, real as ever.

"That's a good boy," Barty said.

"This isn't over," Whitney retorted. "You're going to wish that Kazimir got to me before Torsten did."

"Never trust a foreigner to do a Glassman's work. This time, your luck has run out."

Whitney bit his lip in frustration, glaring at Darkings, who glared back. Now, Whitney regretted not asking Kazimir to put a blood pact or whatever it was back on Barty before they left Elsewhere—or, whatever happened to the upyr.

"Where's that insufferable dwarf?" Barty asked.

"Ran away like a coward," Rand said.

"Now Rand, don't be like that," Whitney reprimanded. "I'm not sure anyone could call what Grint did running. It was more of a... a waddle."

"You still haven't learned to shut up, have you, *Blisslayer*?" Bartholomew asked.

"I take pride in never learning," Whitney said.

"Any idea where they're taking us?" Rand questioned.

"Yes, they told me personally while they imprisoned me," Barty replied.

"Mak said something about the White Bridge while you were

face down in the mud, Rand," Whitney answered, not taking his eyes off Darkings.

"That place is the gateway to the kingdom," Rand said. "North through the mountains is treacherous, and not every dwarven kingdom remain loyal allies. The southern waters, well… we all know. But the tower is fortified. It would be suicide for a force this small."

Whitney shook his head. "I was just there. Couldn't have been thirty armored men posted. Didn't you just pass through?"

Rand swore. "Yeah, but we stayed in the carriage, dirtied up. Grint thought I might be too recognizable, and his old mercenary company passed through there plenty, so he did all of the talking. They're probably light with the war going on in the South. Others must be searching for these raiders."

Whitney gestured to the cage. "Some job they're doing. Didn't they think to post a few in Fettingborough?"

"They're probably dead," Rand said. "The White Bridge isn't a posting any good soldier wants."

"You Shieldsmen really do hate protecting your people, don't you?"

"We're stretched thin thanks to men like you."

"Like me?" Whitney said, aghast. "That bastard you're protecting… he and his father helped cause this war!"

"Please," Barty scoffed. "Liam, his impetuous wife, and son caused the war. We're trying to end it, whatever side may win. Isn't that right?" Barty extended his arm to the side and shook the bony shoulder of the only gray-skinned man in the cage.

At first, Whitney thought it was the Shesaitju warrior who ran with Grint, but as he peered through the frightened people of Fettingborough, he realized it wasn't. The man didn't reply or say anything. But Whitney turned his stare upon him. The man's eyes appeared like saucers against his taught, emaciated skin, but they seemed somber.

"By Iam, I was right?" Whitney said to Rand.

"What are you talking about?" Rand said.

"You really did it? You helped take the Caleef, didn't you?"

Murmurs from all the people stuffed into the cage broke out.

"Don't be a fool. He's just a prisoner of war with critical information," Rand said. "We need to get him to the Wearer as quickly as we can."

While Rand continued his lie, Whitney kept staring. The ex-Shieldsman could spew zhulong shog all he wanted, but Whitney was the king of spewing shog. He saw right through him. Whitney had missed a lot while in Elsewhere, but he'd pieced together plenty from stories heard while traveling. He knew that the Darkings traitors had freed the Caleef and that the Shesaitju god-king had then vanished.

Whitney had never seen the Caleef—they didn't let just anybody into the Boiling Keep, where he and his tongueless guards lived—but Whitney'd heard about him, how his skin was always painted black, how he always wore gold. This loin-clothe-wearing man looked like a starving slave if anything, but the way the upper half of his face twitched when Whitney said, "Caleef." There was no mistaking it.

XXX

THE MYSTIC

Freydis returned a few hours later, escorted by dire wolves. Her hair was braided, intertwined with vines laden with small silver discs that resembled those hanging from the temple. Her face was no longer streaked with the blood of the Glassman from Gold Grin's ship, but now it was fully red with two dots of black on each cheek and one on her forehead. She wore a thin, hooded robe, gray with no fur. It dipped low in the front, revealing her cleavage and even her navel.

Sora watched from within her own body near the edge of the Earthmoot pit. A body which was now bound at the wrists and ankles, and chained to a tree. Sora knew because Nesilia knew, that the enslaving ties couldn't actually hold her. The tree itself would bend to the Buried Goddess' will if need be. Even the hemp of which the ropes were hewn—though dead—would return to life with only a whisper.

"My Lady," someone whispered from just behind Sora as Freydis approached. Nesilia turned to see a Drav Cra man, naked and covered in flaking white paint. He was younger, no older than sixteen. He was indwelling for the first time, one who might rise as a warlock, or die attempting.

"It truly is you, isn't it?" he said. "I can see it in your eyes. I felt it… from the first moment, I felt it."

"What is your name?" Nesilia asked.

"I… I do not feel worthy to speak my name in your presen—"

"Wvenweigard," she said. Sora knew the man's name as well.

A grin didn't just spread across Wvenweigard's face, it over-whelmed it. "You know me?"

"I know all my children," Nesilia said.

"Why do you not just tell them all? You've barely spoken since your arrival. I'm sure just a word and they'd all bow. Prove it to them."

"Wvenweigard, do you truly believe I am she—the Lady Nesilia, the Buried Goddess?"

"I do," he said. "With all my heart, I feel it."

"Should an immortal goddess need to prove anything to mere mortals? I could snap my fingers," which she did, "and all of you would open your eyes in Elsewhere."

Very real terror cast itself over Wvenweigard's face, and Sora knew Nesilia spoke the truth. The thought of her hands being responsible for sending anyone else to that awful place was too much for Sora to bear—even if they were Drav Cra savages.

"I can see the Earthmoot isn't all that you expected it to be," Wvenweigard said. "I am sorry for your bindings."

"Do not be fooled, child," Nesilia replied. "I have been present at every Earthmoot. Since Rathgorah indwelled my first the Arch Warlock."

Nesilia turned back to the pit and the prepping warlocks. "That one," Nesilia said, ignoring the question. She nodded toward Tihabat of the Dagson clan, one of the listeners, children who put their ear to the earth to listen for the warlocks buried beneath while they were indwelled. She was Kotlkel's own niece, which Sora now knew. The girl was finishing painting his entire body red.

"She will lead you all astray," Nesilia said.

"Lady?" Wvenweigard said.

"Something dark stirs within her. It should be cut out."

"That is Tihabat Dagson—" Wvenweigard started.

"I know who she is!" Nesilia snapped. She turned back to Wvenweigard and was about to speak when Freydis arrived and demanded, "Leave us."

Knowing her reputation, Wvenweigard wisely did as she asked. "I'm still not sure this is worth the risk, My Lady."

"You must learn to trust me, daughter," Nesilia responded.

"I do. Always."

Sora struggled, every bit of her willing herself to move, her heart to stop beating. Anything to prevent this from continuing. It was no use. Even Nesilia seemed to tire of the constant opposition. She forced Sora's neck to crane and sighed.

"Is everything all right, my Lady?" Freydis asked.

"This vessel's resistance grows tiresome," Nesilia said.

A hopeful gleam caught Freydis' eye. "Take me then," she said. "Forget all of this nonsense. Why would we ask the earth to choose, when its master is here among us?"

"You would die, Daughter. You are strong, but not nearly strong enough."

Freydis' chin sank.

"But don't worry," Nesilia continued. "You have your place. You will lead your people into a new era. The Second God Feud is coming, and there will be a great shifting."

Freydis continued to appear deflated, but there wasn't enough time for her to process the thoughts before Tihabat crossed the clearing to meet her.

"Are you ready?" she asked Freydis. Even her small face was stained by animal blood.

Freydis reached out and brushed the side of the girl's face with the back of her hands. Sora felt more unnerved than ever watching Freydis act so tender. "As I've ever been, young one," she said. "May you indwell many times in your future."

"I hope you never rise," Tihabat said softly.

Tihabat led a stunned Freydis to the edge of the pit then continued on to meet with another warlock prepared to indwell.

While she did, Oracle Rathgorah approached the pit, covered in more tokens and bones than before. "It is time," he said, to the hundreds of warlocks gathered around the pit, all of those from around the tundra. It was their calling as warlocks to indwell at the time when Nesilia was cast underground to end the God Feud, not a choice.

On the opposite side of the pit, the dozens of listening children sat in a straight line. Sora heard Nesilia's thoughts and realized they were being trained to be Drav Cra warlocks. Only a year before, Wvenweigard had been among them. Each one had a single bar of paint across their foreheads.

Seated on the benches surrounding Sora, still drinking, joking, and carousing were men and women—Drav Cra from every clan throughout the tundra who had traveled here for this sacred ceremony. It wasn't only to find an Arch Warlock, but those former Listeners now old enough to indwell would have a chance to become warlocks themselves... or suffocate trying.

Amid those waiting to be indwelled, Kotlkel Dagson stood. The scowl on his face made Sora want to smile. Or were those Nesilia's feelings? Things were growing fuzzier now, the lines between their thoughts blurred.

His robe, like Freydis', was unadorned, but his face was painted elaborately. Behind him, Sora recognized none of those present, but Nesilia knew them all. A flood of names poured into Sora's mind, and she fought to breathe.

Freydis stepped to the edge of the pit. Kotlkel's glower threatened to draw blood.

Oracle Rathgorah made his way around the pit and took a seat amongst the people. He nodded his head.

Kotlkel let his robe fall around his feet. The child, Tihabat, scampered over and tied a rope which dangled from the branches above around one of Kotlkel's ankle. He stood naked, exposed like all those Sora had seen carousing in the woods and still, Nesilia didn't look away.

One by one, the warlocks followed, nude but for their paint, until finally, Freydis let the robe she wore fall from her shoulders. She stood staring at the pit of shallow blood and dirt, pale skin rising with goose pimples. Tihabat took no care when tying the rope around her ankles, the frayed ends scratching her skin.

Nesilia eyed Freydis with something… approval? Love? No, it wasn't love. Yet, part of Sora yearned for what they shared in that moment. Although Nesilia was bound along with Sora, together, she and Freydis stepped before the pit in faith.

Sora noticed the woman who'd kissed Freydis earlier, Sahades, not far from her. Her eyes gleamed. She ignored everyone but Freydis.

Above the warlocks, human bodies, Glassman all, were strung up and dripping blood. When Sora had first arrived, she was surprised at the lack of death and darkness—but now she knew the savages were reserving it for this abomination.

"Again, with that term," Nesilia said, reading her thoughts. *"Of all people, I thought you'd be more accepting."*

"Even I have limits," Sora replied.

It stank. Death surrounded them, but the warlocks acted as if they were enjoying a picnic in a meadow.

Oracle Rathgorah's voice stole everyone's attention. He stood and declared, "People of the North, today, long ago, our Lady was buried but not forgotten. This ceremony, so old there is none living with any recollection of its origin, even me, is sacred. From above, the blood pours, and below, our Lady stirs."

"*This is barbaric*," Sora thought.

"*This is beauty*," Nesilia responded.

"Before you stands one who will rise in glory, many who will rise to continue serving our Lady, and others who will never breath again," Rathgorah went on. "Bare as the day they were born. From the womb into our Lady's awaiting arms."

In unison, the people surrounding the pit stood. They were warriors and hunters, men and women, dradinengors of their clans and children—all equal today. All present to bear witness to the glory of their goddess. Sora felt again like she was in the church of Troborough watching the Dawning ceremony led by Father Hullquist, the town's priest of Iam, but understanding none it.

But this was a church out of a nightmare.

"As has been done for generations, our Lady's servants will lower themselves into her presence, surrounded by her dirt and the blood of life," Rathgorah said. "Each will call upon their strength and faith to rise before the dirt fills their bellies and lungs. The Lady will choose warlocks to survive, and one to rise last and lead her people."

The gathered crowd cheered. Sora unintentionally recognized a few of them as dradinengors, hollering for warlocks of their own clans to earn Nesilia's highest blessing. Haral of the Dagson clan, however, Sora couldn't find amidst the faces. She hadn't shown herself since arguing with Kotlkel and storming off.

Sora had to give the Drav Cra credit for something: in other places, those warriors would simply murder one another to determine who would be Arch Warlock. It reminded her of what history taught about how the Caleef of the Black Sands was selected. When people would volunteer to throw themselves into the Boiling Waters until the God of Sea and Sand granted one the lungs to survive and serve as his voice on Pantego. Though, at least they got to choose the risk of death.

"My brother never was very original," Nesilia remarked, responding to Sora's thoughts. *"Stole that from me. Just look at how Caliphar's people refer to him. So literal."*

"Brother?" Sora asked, hating herself for being intrigued by anything Nesilia had to say. Putting together the pieces of Nesilia's extensive history was difficult, but when she heard the name, she saw the truth.

"Not if I had a choice. But he so hated Iam for stealing my attention. Never could take his eyes off me. So, I drowned him when Iam wasn't looking."

"I will not fail you, my Lady!" Kotlkel shouted. "The traitors shall reveal themselves." His glare toward Freydis didn't leave any question to whom he was referring.

"The traitors are in the south, not here," Sahades replied.

"Freydis, how are you alive?" a common woman behind Oracle Rathgorah hollered.

"We left you rotting in a Yarrington dungeon!" called out another.

More angry chatter broke out, mixing with the rattling of tree boughs until Sora could understand none of it.

"Brothers and sisters!" Rathgorah announced. "We mustn't fight amongst ourselves. The earth is the realm of our Lady, and so it shall reveal all."

"So, it shall," Kotlkel said, smirking.

"It will, when you never breathe again," Freydis hissed. "All you deserve for abandoning your Arch Warlock."

"There will be plenty of time for answers if our Freydis rises," Rathgorah interrupted. "Until then, we might as well count her amongst the dead. That goes for all of you."

The din of the crowd rose again.

Rathgorah struck the ground with his staff until the people

quieted down. "Now, Nesilia's chosen hands, will you bless this pool?"

The warlocks around the pit spoke no words, but each extended a palm. The Listeners pulled knives from their belts and slashed each of the warlocks' palms. Tihabat cut Freydis' so deep that the warlock bent over and gasped in pain. By instinct, she raised her hand to slap the girl, then noticed the judging eyes all around and lowered it.

The sight made Sora want to wince, remembering all the times she'd done the same to herself, drawing on Elsewhere's power before the mystics taught her otherwise.

"Buried but not dead," the warlocks and the Listeners all chanted in unison as they extended their hands over the pit and squeezed, so their blood trickled in. Wolves howled in the distance.

"May the earth encase your lungs and filter the air," Rathgorah said. "May you be remembered if you never rise."

"Freydis," Nesilia whispered to her chosen servant. There was great distance between them, but Sora was sure Freydis heard. "Redstar proved unworthy of my favor. You can't."

Sora watched Freydis draw a deep breath. If she was afraid, she hid it well.

"I feel her presence in the air," Sahades said to Freydis. "Be with her now."

Then they all stepped forward and into the pit. The ropes around their ankles went taut. No sooner had the warlocks' feet hit the blood-stained soil than Rathgorah raised his staff. Fresh blood dripped down from his freshly-cut forearm and onto the gnarled wood. From all around the pit, particles of dirt swirled into the air. They mixed with the blood of the bodies strung up above, twisting about until they filled the pit over the warlocks, burying them alive.

When finally, the last of their heads disappeared, the Listeners all spread equally across the pit and fell to their knees.

"Children, listen for the breath of life," Rathgorah said, wheezing. That last act of blood magic appeared to have exhausted him, barely able to keep his eyes open. Two men helped him to his seat. "Remember, you are one with the Lady."

"Yes, Oracle Rathgorah," they all said. Then they dropped prostrate to the ground and pressed their ears to the hard, packed dirt. Tihabat was in the area where Freydis, Kotlkel, Sahades, and at least a dozen others had gone under.

Whatever magic and power the buried warlocks could draw on, they were on their own to survive. That was when Sora realized it wasn't like the Black Sands' Caleef at all. There was no blessing of survival. Only the most powerful lasted longest.

"What if it isn't Freydis?" Sora asked Nesilia, remembering now that if that were the case, she was meant to be crucified and hung to bleed like the desiccated corpses hanging above.

"Then, we test all of their faith," Nesilia replied. *"The world is chaos, my dear. Unstructured, ebbing and shifting like the very earth. I wonder, who among those out there would forsake tradition for faith?"*

"You'd kill so many of your own people?"

"The weak must be purged, like an injured fawn caught by wolves. This is nature."

"I won't let you," Sora thought, and Nesilia heard.

"How could you deny it? Of all the hosts to appear in Skorravik—my realm of Elsewhere, it was you. A girl capable of slaying that insufferable witch Bliss. A girl capable of burning an entire city to ashes, and of banishing an immortal upyr from the mortal realm. Strength begets strength; the chaos of nature gave me you."

"I don't care who they are. They don't all deserve to die!" Sora argued.

"Then pray Freydis is as strong as she seems, for only she looked into your eyes and saw the truth of what lies beneath."

"I'm going to get out of here," Sora threatened, *"and I'm going to destroy you."*

Nesilia's cackle filled Nowhere, Elsewhere, and beyond. The trees seemed to dance gleefully on the wind, but the smell carried upon it was death. And all around the pit, the Drav Cra eyed Sora as if they too heard it.

"There is no out of here," Nesilia said. *"I am you, and you are me, bound in Elsewhere and Pantego. You are a goddess, Sora. In time, you'll embrace it, or you'll wind up drowning in darkness like my brother and all those who opposed me long ago."*

XXXI

THE KNIGHT

"Torsten, are you sure about this?" Lucas asked as they delved deeper into South Corner. The stench was even worse than it had been days ago. The crisp night air only seemed to augment it. And with all the construction, even more citizens had been displaced to cluster together in group-homes, churches, and worse.

"How many times are you going to ask?" Torsten said, scratching his brow.

"Until we turn around," Lucas replied.

"If I didn't know better, I'd think you were protecting our friend, Mr. Tehr."

"I'm not, I swear… I just…"

"Relax, Lucas. I'm only joking. Yes, I am capable of jesting."

Lucas exhaled in relief. "Well, I know what he's capable of too. Everyone here does. He had enough support before the cultists. Now, he feeds and houses them. Rebuilds homes and shops. Every eye in South Corner is his."

"There is only one Eye we need be concerned with."

"Can't we just think this plan through? My parent's place is around the corner. They aren't only bakers. My mother could whip up a stew for supper that would change your life."

Torsten stopped. "Do you see what I'm wearing, Lucas?" he asked. "I am not your commanding officer today. If a warm dinner and the love of your parents is what you want tonight, then by all means. But it was men like you who saved them and so many others the night of the cultists' riot. Not Valin, *you*. And I think it's about time we dug his claws out of this place even if only a little, don't you?"

"I…" Lucas sighed. "I do. I only hoped to live long enough to be a Shieldsman—"

"And see you parents' faces when you tell them?" Torsten finished for him. "You will yet, my boy. Iam is with us tonight. Can't you feel it?"

"How do you know?" Lucas asked.

"Because he has to be. Now, come on, it's this way, isn't it."

"It is."

Lucas took his arms, and they turned down another street. Torsten had no doubt Valin continued to provide for the needy, not out of kindness, but because the needy were his weapons. Torsten knew the man could influence a riot against the Crown at any time with nothing but the promise of richer foods. In fact, Torsten was convinced Valin had inspired the one by the markets.

They passed by the clamor of the Grove Street Church, not far from the Vineyard. It was so alive with commotion, so packed with refugees it sounded like a tavern. Torsten guessed the place had never seen so many occupants for one of Father Bristol's sermons. Now, the man was off in Hornsheim, and his humble chapel stunk like Elsewhere. Torsten battled the urge to vomit at the smell of shog, rotten food, and body odor.

"It seems the wickedness of the Buried Goddess will never fade," Torsten said.

"It could've been my parents in there," Lucas said.

"It could have been any of us. Sir Davies, Liam, they were all right. South Corner needs a man like Valin Tehr to keep the order, but also to keep it down. A purging fire destroyed this place, and maybe it's time everything changes."

Lucas stepped in something squishy before he could answer, and gagged.

"What is it?" Torsten asked.

"Feel blessed you can't see," Lucas replied. "C'mon, the Vineyard is just ahead."

A few steps away from the crowded church, the smell didn't get any better. Silence filled the air, and all that could be heard was trash and refuse blowing along the streets. Outside, people crowded the streets, begging for scraps from Valin's table before they were ordered away.

"Ey, you!" a guard barked at them. "Off the streets. There's a curfew in place."

Torsten knew that, of course. By order of the King's Shield, not even the cleanest of beggars was permitted to sleep on the streets. It was a mandate he himself had sanctioned. He didn't blame the poor souls of South Corner who'd rioted for getting Oleander killed—they couldn't have known Dom Nohzi assassins would arrive—but he did know the violence angry groups were capable of, especially under the influence of a man as powerful as Valin Tehr.

"Ah, my apologies," Torsten said. "My friend here was just taking me to his house to have a night under a roof."

"You spent too long in the castle, Danvels?" the man said. Only then did Torsten recognize his voice as belonging to the guard captain of Dockside. They hadn't yet had time to look into replacing him. "Your folks' place is the other way."

"Oh, that's right, sir," Lucas said. "So much training, my brains been in a fog."

"Sir?" Captain Henry chuckled. "You're going to be a Shieldsman for Iam's sake. You know, I was in training for it once. Under Sir Unger, actually. Apparently, I didn't have what it takes, so you lot shoved me into this foul, shog-stained place."

Torsten honestly couldn't remember that. At the height of Liam's reign and constant warring, many passed through the Order. Even more weren't worthy of it. "The King's Shield isn't for everyone," Torsten said.

"Hey, I'm not complaining. There's always something to do in Dockside. Up in the castle all day, I think I'd go mad from boredom. Well, until lately that is."

"The Crown thanks you for your longtime service, Captain," Torsten said. "Now, if you don't mind, we really must be going."

"Try to be quick about it, aye? There are more muggings these days than ever before. And killings, it turns out."

"Thank you," Torsten said. "Good to see you again."

Lucas tugged on Torsten's arm, but they only made it a few steps before Captain Henry shifted back in front of them.

Captain Henry grabbed their wrists together. "You both were there when the Queen was killed, weren't you? Any idea what in Iam's name happened?"

"We're still trying to figure that out," Torsten said.

"Oh, c'mon. I've heard rumors about monsters. Others say it was the Black Sands."

"Captain, just walk away," Lucas said under his breath.

"Why is it everyone always asks me to walk away when things start to get interesting?" Captain Henry said. He released their wrists and circled them.

"Captain, please," Lucas said. "We need to go."

Torsten raised an arm in front of Lucas and stepped forward.

"You ain't headed to mum and dads, are ya?"

Neither answered.

"You're heading down to the Vineyard again, aren't ya?" Henry said.

"It is not your business where we're going," Torsten said.

Captain Henry wound his way back in front of them. "C'mon, is the Shield finally making a move on Valin Tehr? That bastard's been shogging on us for so many years I've lost count."

"I only seek to meet with his friends…" Torsten swallowed back the lump in his throat. "In private."

Captain Henry snickered. "Well, why didn't you say that from the beginning? You wouldn't be the first Shieldsman wanting a taste of the Vineyard."

"Valin offered me a deal," Torsten said. "It's only right to look into it."

"Well, the worm's up in Old Yarrington right now, but his place is fuller than ever."

"How do you know that?"

"Valin Tehr watches our every move. We watch his. It's the way of things down here."

"Well, Captain, you can do the Crown a favor and keep an eye on this street," Torsten said. "Make sure nothing out of the ordinary goes on while we're inside? Oh, and I think it's time we reconsider having a loyal man like yourself in the Shield."

"Me, a Shieldsman?" Henry said. "I gave up that dream a long time ago."

"The kingdom needs more loyal men."

"Well, Sir, in that case, I'll keep this street as clean as our virgin king." Torsten's jaw dropped upon hearing a Glass soldier speak like that. The captain must have noticed because he quickly said, "Sorry, Sir. Only way to get people to tell us a damn thing down here is to talk like them."

"That's all right," Torsten said. It wasn't, but he didn't have time to scold soldiers. "Thank you, Captain. Keep up the good work. And I'd appreciate if you didn't tell anybody you saw us down here."

"Saw what?" Henry laughed, then pounded his chestplate in salute.

Torsten offered an appreciative grunt, then pulled Lucas along.

"Oh, and Danvels," Henry said before they were gone. "I still haven't paid your parent's a visit like I've been meaning to. You know what, maybe I'll head over there, see what she has in the oven."

"It's night," Lucas replied. "They'll be closed."

"Oh. Right. Well, maybe in the morning. Enjoy, gentleman." He strolled away, whistling.

"I don't trust him, Sir," Lucas said to Torsten. "As I told you last time, I always got a bad feeling from him. I should've looked into replacements sooner."

"Do you think he's in Valin's pocket?"

"If he's not, he spent way too much time patrolling this street trying to be. Let's go to my parents and come up with something else. I swear, they can be trusted."

"Are you really worried about Captain Henry?" Torsten said. "We'll be fine, Lucas. Valin can watch us all he wants, but so long as he seeks the favor of our king, he can't kill me yet.

"Sir, you know he's capable of anything!" Lucas raised his voice and yanked back on Torsten's arm. "Please, you aren't thinking clearly."

"No, boy, for the first time I am. I won't let evil fester any longer." He pulled free of Lucas and used his cane to climb the steps up to the Vineyard's front door himself. "Now are you coming, or not?"

Lucas exhaled, then followed.

As Torsten pushed through the doors, a wave of sweat and infidelity washed over him. It sounded much like the church inside, with the altruistic Valin Tehr offering so many homeless a place to lay their head.

"Hold it," a thug said almost immediately. Torsten recognized the voice as belonging to the one named Curry, who'd shouted for Abigail so crassly. "What do you want?"

"Kind sir, I was wondering if the Vineyard was still in… *business*," Torsten lowered his voice to utter the word.

"Not tonight, we're a bit crowded if you can't see."

Torsten reached up and drew back his hood to reveal his seared eyes. "Ah, my apologies."

"By Iam, rotten luck that is." Curry took a step back, and Torsten heard another of Valin's men muttering. Even some of the homeless men, women, and children scattered throughout the place whispered.

"Do you know who that is?" the man said, so low nobody else would've been able to hear him, but Torsten's hearing seemed to get better every day.

"Sir Unger, Mr. Tehr isn't here right now," Curry said.

Torsten put his arm around the man and led him aside where they could use hushed tones. "I'm not here for Valin. I was hoping I could…" He exhaled slowly. "Spend the night?"

"Spend the… oh." Curry snickered. "A Shieldsman like you?"

"Please, I need it."

"Well, Mr. Tehr says the Vineyard's rooms are only meant to be used to house the people of South Corner for now."

"You would deny the slayer of Redstar and our Master of Warfare?" Lucas said, entering the conversation.

"Hey, it's not my rule," Curry replied.

"Relax, my friend," Torsten said. "Forgive my aide. We're all on edge after what happened. Mr. Tehr offered me a night here to help relax. I've recently lost a very close friend, and I'd love to take him up on his offer so that I can think about anything else for just a few hours."

"I don't—"

"Look, I know nobody wants to get into trouble with Mr.

Tehr," Torsten said. "But, if it helps all the same, I happen to be from South Corner."

Curry sighed. "I suppose that's true."

"I'm sure there's more than enough room, 'downstairs,'" Lucas added.

"Wait right here." The two guards left and argued a bit in hushed tones. Torsten couldn't hear what they were saying, but he waited calmly. He could hear Lucas nervously tapping his thigh with his thumb.

"You're doing well," Torsten said to him. "Just keep playing along."

The guards returned. "All right, we'll make an exception, just for you," Curry said. "Nobody wants the Master of Warfare to be angry with us."

"Ah, thank you," Torsten said, feigning relief. "I will make sure to let Valin know how helpful you've both been. With the position he's about to be named to, I'll be spending a lot more time with him."

"What position?" Curry asked.

"You'll find out soon enough."

Again, Torsten heard the men whispering to one another, this time sounding gleeful. It seemed even Valin's own rotten followers were left in the shadows when it came to his affairs.

"All right, come on inside," Curry said.

Torsten stepped forward and found himself being patted down.

"You do you realize who he is?" Lucas questioned.

"Sorry, everyone gets checked now," Curry said. "Thanks to… well… you know."

"It's okay," Torsten said. The guards eventually found the dagger sheathed in the back of his belt and removed it. "Ah, sorry about that. I thought I told Lucas to change my belt."

"No good help out there these days," Curry said.

"Sorry, Sir," Lucas muttered.

They checked Lucas next, then ushered him and Torsten further inside. The fire crackling at the hearth was the only thing that masked the stench. Torsten didn't blame Valin for desperately seeking quarter in the Glass Castle. The place was a pigsty. Torsten didn't need to see it to know it.

Lucas had to help Torsten step over a few sleeping citizens. Others coughed, hacking like they were diseased. Torsten actually preferred the brothel as it used to be. This just reminded him of the kinds of places he'd slept in as a boy when his parents were too drunk to know where he'd gotten off to. Or after they'd died, leaving him without a bronzer to his name.

"So, what's your fancy, Mr. Hero?" Curry asked. "Jubila's Glintish like you. Gotten enough men under her spell, she could probably raise an army."

"No," Torsten said. "I was hoping you might have someone fair and blonde...Tall. Someone with a northern look?" Torsten felt grimy just asking, but he had to play the part of a nobleman off to live his wildest fantasies. He had to play to the rumors about him and Oleander which so many likely had heard but never spoken of.

"Like the late queen, eh?" Curry asked.

The other guard snickered. "What's it matter what she looks like?"

Torsten didn't answer. His throat went unexpectedly tight.

"Ignore him. Course we do," Curry said. "Here at the Vineyard, we got every vintage your heart desires." He stopped and whistled up toward the second floor. "Ey, Abigail, get your ass down here."

Torsten followed the direction he shouted and heard the soft, gentle voice of Abigail helping a sick, homeless boy drink stew. Even in such a place, she found a way to be kind. Torsten knew his plan to have her help him one last time was a good one.

"Abigail!" Curry shouted.

"All right, I'm coming!" she yelled back. "There you go," she whispered to the boy. "Just try to finish this, all right? I'll check on you as soon as I'm done."

"I swear," Curry groaned. "If these girls wanted to be mothers so bad, Iam knows why they came here."

Torsten grunted in agreement but clenched his fist. He knew what it was like to have a mother from a brothel. The Vineyard was still a tavern, but she frequented places just like it, sold around by her father and happy to do it so long as they could get their hands on manaroot and forget the world. Torsten was probably pushed out in the basement of somewhere just like this before he was a forgotten urchin.

"Well, she ain't the Queen," Curry said as she approached, "but she'll have to do."

"What is it, Curry, you fat slob?" Abigail asked.

"We've got another special circumstance," Curry said. "So how bout you put on a smile and show our royal guest a good time."

"I… Torsten, you're back?" she said.

"I am," Torsten replied.

"The slayer of Redstar wants a night to remember," Curry said, taking no efforts to mask his delight.

Torsten cleared his throat. "I…" He couldn't fake it. He had no idea how men came to the Vineyard and did what they did without feeling the mark of sin on their souls forever.

Abigail sauntered closer and ran her fingers along his arm. "Don't worry, Sir Unger. I'll be honored." She took Torsten's hand and slowly wrapped it around her waist, pushing so he could feel the shape of her supple thighs. He bit his tongue and went along with it, feeling ashamed. But it was his only option.

"Your friend will have to stay up here," Curry said.

"It's my sworn duty to look after him," Lucas said.

"Even as he gets his jollies off?" Curry chortled. "You Shieldsmen and your honor. Just sit down at the bar. Someone'll fetch you a drink. And try not to give any of these leeches any."

"I must insist," Lucas said.

"It's fine," Torsten said, nodding Lucas along. Not having Lucas join him was going to throw a wrench in the plans, but if he argued too much, the thugs might start to get suspicious. He would have to improvise. He'd have to be like... *Whitney Fierstown*. The thought nearly brought bile to his throat.

"Sir?" Lucas said.

"I'd rather be all alone with her," Torsten lied.

"Sir Unger, you can't see," Lucas said. "I don't think—"

Torsten pulled him close. "Don't let another soul get down there," he whispered. "I don't care what you must do."

"All right, let's go, my Lord," Curry said.

"You won't need this, my Lord," Abigail stole the cane from Torsten, then took his arm and led him around the bar. Torsten banged his shin on a stool but didn't let the pain show. Someone behind the bar worked some keys, and a door opened, then Curry led them downstairs.

The stench of shog was promptly replaced by one more familiar to the Vineyard—sweat, sex, and shame. But that wasn't all. It had been over a decade since Torsten's investigation took him anywhere near the Vineyard's basement, where lewd fantasies came true, but the metallic tinge of dried blood was unmistakable.

"It's been a while since we got any Shieldsmen in here," Curry said. "But Mr. Tehr is always happy to show the protectors of our kingdom a good time. He always says, 'stress is the bane of civilization.'"

"Like you know what that means, Curry," Abigail remarked.

"Better than you do, girly."

"Oh yeah, what then?"

"Well, I ain't know what a bane is," Curry said, "but it means that men need the touch of a good woman. Wait." He stopped at the bottom of the stairs, earning a curse from Abigail as she bumped into him. "I thought Shieldsmen weren't supposed to lay with anyone? That's why they always sneak around while here."

"We aren't priests," Torsten said. "We are simply betrothed to the Crown."

"Well, I won't tell her you're cheating." Curry laughed at his own joke.

"They sneak here because this place is filled with vermin like you," Abigail said.

Curry clutched her hard by the wrist, earning a wince. "Careful, Shieldsman," he said. "This one's got a mouth on her. Good for this line o' work, but that's about all."

"I think I can handle her," Torsten said.

"Let's go then," Abigail said, grabbing Torsten's arm and pulling him along.

As they followed Curry, Torsten focused on every sound around him, no matter how minute. The way air passed through openings, footsteps within one of the rooms, the sound of wine pouring into a glass. Somewhere along that hall was Valin's office and quarters, buried underground like a rat. If he kept records of anything, they'd be locked up in there.

Curry greeted a handful of Valin's thugs along the way. Not too many. If Torsten had his eyes, handling them would've been no problem. In fact, he recalled from all those years ago that Valin never was one for over-securing anything. He preferred to flaunt what he did to those who cared to look hard enough; show how untouchable he truly was.

The confined nature of the corridor opened up, and the ground suddenly shook.

"Quiet down, Uhlvark!" Curry shouted across a vast room they entered.

The giant's feet slid on what sounded like sand. Chains rattled, then snapped, and the dim oaf moaned in displeasure.

"Foooood?" he said.

"Maybe next time make the cow last a week, numbskull," Curry said.

"Be nice to him," Abigail snapped. "I'll find you something in the morning, honey!" she called to the giant.

Uhlvark clapped his hands, the bonds on his wrists clanging together. "Thank youuu, pretty Abigail. Pretty as a daisyyy."

"You keep sweetening up to that thing, he'll wind up snapping your back like he did poor Lenny," Curry said.

"Oh, that was an accident," Abigail replied.

"Accident? He nearly made his head pop off."

"Valin warns everybody not to bother Uhlvark while he's eating. That was Lenny's yigging fault."

"Excuse me, but are we in Valin's fighting pit?" Torsten asked.

"What pit?" Curry said.

"I was the Wearer of White. You think I don't know about Valin's other businesses?"

"Valin don't pay me to think," Curry said.

"That's for sure," Abigail remarked.

"One more word out of you, you'll be pleasing the pigs who walk in," Curry said.

They wound their way around a curved path, then Curry stopped. "Got another special guest for the box," he addressed someone. After a few exchanges of small talk that got Torsten's skin crawling, the new thug pulled aside a curtain of beads.

"Mind if I go take a leak then, Curry?" the thug asked. "You can look after him for a bit."

"Make it quick," Curry said. "All right, in you go Shieldsman. It ain't as luxurious as upstairs, but 'the people come first,' and all that shog. Enjoy a taste of the bitter North. Sweeter than the 'Flower of Drav Cra' herself."

Torsten froze for a moment upon hearing the title. But Abigail towed him along through the entry. Now he knew where the stink of sex came from. He heard it too. Rooms on either side of him were occupied by Valin's women and their 'guests.' He heard them faking moans, others whipping the men and getting them to howl. He dared not imagine who among them he might know, who among them might occupy the very same floor of the Glass Castle as him.

It was no wonder nobody ever shut the Vineyard down. It was difficult for him to imagine that Liam himself hadn't ever visited its filthy halls, with all that Torsten now knew about the man's vices. The Vineyard hadn't always been the only brothel in Yarrington, but Valin had long since put all the others out of business. His girls were exotic, catering to man's every sinful desire. Places like Westvale and Winde Port offered depravities as well, but they couldn't compete.

Glinthaven, where Torsten's ancestors were from, was known for such decadence. But their bodies were said to be treated like mere housing for their auras within, and they treated them like such. Watching his parents' decay in such places as the Vineyard probably had a lot to do with why Torsten had never visited the place of his ancestors. He'd gone a lifetime struggling to care about anything but his kingdom and the king who'd raised him from the filth. Never had he even felt tempted, until…

"Right here," Abigail said softly. Her words came out like a purr, and her breath was hot on his neck. She yanked on his arm and drew him through another set of beads. Another push and he fell backward onto a bed. Considering everything else, it felt like lying on a cloud the sheets were so soft. One might even think it luxurious if not for the pounding and forced moaning from the couple in the next room.

"Sorry about the noise," Abigail said, chuckling. "Tough times, these are."

"That's all right," Torsten replied. He sat up, and before he knew it, her foot found his groin and pushed, ensuring he remained where he was.

"We'll make enough noise to get them back for it."

"You don't—" he started, but the next thing Torsten knew she was straddling him. His mind reeled back to that night with Oleander when she threw herself at him. He'd needed every fiber of his being to fight temptation then, and he feared tonight would be the same.

"No need to be shy here," she whispered directly into his ear, then she nibbled on the lobe. A shiver slithered along his spine like a snake carved from Winter's Thumb. "I want this. You deserve this. You saved my life… twice. All you need do is relax, my knight."

Torsten could hardly recall precisely what she'd looked like, but thanks to Curry, he knew who he imagined sat atop him. And her own words, "my knight…" she sounded exactly like Oleander. From her voice to the attitude behind her words. Like there wasn't a soul on Pantego who could touch her.

"You've saved me more than you know, Torsten Unger," she said, her hand grazing along his inner thigh, playfully swerving back and forth. "You know what those savages did to us girls when they came through? You deserve a goddess."

"Please, I need to—"

Her lips pressed against his, silencing him. She ran her hands over his bald head. Her legs closed on his hips, squeezing tight. He tried to push her away, but she'd already hiked up her dress, and his massive hands clenched her legs instead. They were long, supple, just like…

"Oleander, stop," he managed to squeeze through his lips.

Abigail drew her head back slightly, but still so close that the warm breath she exhaled became what he inhaled. "So that's who you want tonight?" she said. "I can be her. Take me, Sir Unger. Take me, or I'll hang you over the walls like the others!"

Before he could answer, she kissed him again. Her long nails dragged along the back of his head and down his neck as she pulled him in. Her long hair framed his face, silken and nearly silver in his mind's eye. For a moment, he lost himself. He kissed her in return, flipping her, so her back was now on the bed.

He pawed at her chest for the laces, and she helped guide his hand, all while loosening his belt with the other. Passion overcame him—a year of denying himself because she was the wife of his king. Denying himself because the whole world saw her as a monster, and for so long he had too.

The dress lifted over her head, and his palm came down between her breasts. Her skin was cold, but it was what lay beneath it that finally stirred him.

A heartbeat.

Oleander's corpse, lifeless beneath him filled his mind, and he staggered back, falling off Abigail as he tumbled from the bed.

"Sir Unger, are you okay?" Abigail shrieked.

She groped at him, trying to help him up, but he crawled back. "I…I'm fine."

Abigail chuckled. "Perhaps less queen is in order. I know you Shieldsmen deny yourselves so much. We should start slower. Perhaps some manaroot to help ease your mind?"

"No." Torsten shook his head, then aggressively scratched at the still-tender flesh around his eyes.

"That's fine. Just come back." She patted the bed. "Let me do the work."

"No…" Torsten stammered. Using the curtains, he pulled himself to his feet. "No, Iam forgive me, no." He wiped the phantom tears he imagined trickling down the scorched skin at the top of his cheeks, which only made it itch again.

"Iam can't see you here," Abigail said. "It's just Oleander, and you."

"You're not her!" he snapped.

"I thought this is what you wanted?"

"You're not… I know. I'm sorry. I didn't really come here for this."

"Well, you came here for something." Abigail stood, moseyed toward him and ran her nail along his cheek. "So just tell me what you want. I promise, I'm so happy to see you."

"This life," Torsten said. "Do you enjoy it?"

"What?"

"This," Torsten repeated. "Do you enjoy this?"

"It's fine, I suppose. With good company. Keeps me from having to sleep on the street or move somewhere far worse."

"What would you do if you didn't have to stay here and keep Valin Tehr's pockets full?"

"Honestly?"

Torsten nodded.

"I s'pose… I always wanted to see Panping," Abigail said.

Torsten gently clutched her face. "Then go there," he said. He reached into his pocket, pulled out his pouch of autlas, and placed it in her hands.

"Iam's shog," she swore, then covered her mouth. "S-sorry."

Torsten wasn't wealthy by any means, but his new position on the Royal Council left him considerably better off than most of Yarrington. He'd gone so long not realizing how good he had it. Liam hadn't only given him purpose. He'd saved Torsten from becoming a dishonorable lecher like nearly everyone from South Corner he'd ever met.

"My Lord, I can't accept this," Abigail said, shoving it back. Now Torsten knew with no doubt he wasn't with Oleander.

"You can," he replied. "My aide is stuck upstairs, and I cannot see. But you can help me."

"I'm not…" She swallowed loudly. "I'm not sure I can anymore."

"You can. All I want you to do is run out screaming that I hurt you, I'll do the rest. I need to get one of Valin's men to take me to his private office, and I fear that unless I get the jump on him, I won't have a chance."

"But… but you wouldn't hurt me."

"I know. And I know this sounds bad, but what happens next can decide the fate of this kingdom. You helped me once before, Abigail, and nothing good came of it. But this time, we can change everything."

"But Valin—"

"Won't know a thing. You take that gold, you hop on a wagon, and you go wherever your heart desires. Can you help me, one last time, Abigail? Will you once again serve your kingdom?"

He listened to her throat bobbing as she dressed herself. Silence passed between them, and the pace of her breathing hastened. "You saved my life from the Black Sands murderers," she said softly. "Then all of us from savages. I'll help you with anything, Sir Unger. Grab here."

Abigail took his hand and placed a piece of fabric in it.

"What's this?" Torsten asked.

She yanked on the other side without answering, and her dress tore down the front.

"It will look more believable this way," she said.

"Clever girl," Torsten said.

"That is the arena back there by the way," she said. "It's one big circle, crawling with Valin's boys. You might be seen attacking one of them. They're used to us girls running out in a frenzy."

"I'm sure they won't be able to look away from you."

"You're too kind, my Lord. But I think I can distract them a little longer for you."

"How?" Torsten asked, wary.

"You'll see."

She turned away, but Torsten quickly turned her head back to face him. "Abigail, the last thing I want is for you to get into any trouble."

"I'll sneak around just like in the Fellwater Swamp. I'll be fine."

Torsten sighed. "Just be safe, and you will be. Iam clearly favors you. Thank you, Abigail. I hope that, should we run into each other again, it will be on better terms."

"Last time you saved me, I was shoveling shog for murderers. Now I'm here. Next time, I'll be the queen of somewhere… for real this time."

"What a lucky place that would be. Now, are you ready?"

"I am. Just one thing first."

A response was on the tip of Torsten's lip when she kissed him. Only this time, it didn't feel like she was doing a service or forcing passion. In fact, Torsten wasn't sure he'd ever been kissed like that in his life—not even by Oleander.

"Sorry about this," she said. She pulled away, and again, before he could respond, she slapped him across the face.

"What did you just call me, freak!" she squealed. "Don't touch me like that. Ouch!" She threw herself through the beaded curtain, and out into a wall.

"Hey, what's going on!" the thug posted outside shouted.

"He… he… he cut me!" Abigail yelled.

"Get out here!" Curry yelled at her, and then his voice drew nearer. "Hey, *Sir* Unger. I don't care who you are. Nobody damages Mister Tehr's property."

Torsten found his footing as he listened to the sound of fingers on leather—Curry's grip tightening on a club just outside the room. Torsten breathed out slowly, focusing every ounce of his energy on his hearing.

"I'm talking to you!"

The curtain swung open, beads rattling. Torsten ducked to the side, then drove his elbow into Curry's gut. The man doubled over, and Torsten raised a knee into his head to daze him, then wrapped his bicep around Curry's head and covered his mouth with his enormous hand to muffle any screams.

Torsten patted Curry's sides, searching for a weapon more efficient than a club. He gave the man's ankle a kick and discovered a knife tucked into his boot. Curry wriggled to get free as Torsten bent to retrieve it, but Torsten shoved him against a wall. Dragging the dull side of the blade along the back of Curry's head he stopped when he found the soft spot at the base of his neck.

"Quiet," Torsten whispered. "Or I'll gut you like a fish. Understood?" Curry shook his head and attempted to shout. Torsten dug the point of the knife in until it drew a spot of blood. "I said, do you understand?"

This time, Curry nodded.

"Good, I'm not here for you," Torsten said. "You're going to lead me to Valin's office. Can you do that?" Torsten let off his mouth a bit.

"You think I have a shogging key?" Curry asked.

"I don't need a key. Let's go. Slowly. And you try anything, it's death or the Glass Castle gallows, your pick. The Shieldsmen have business with your employer tonight."

Torsten felt the lump in Curry's throat as he swallowed hard, then the thug led Torsten out of the room.

"Everything's fine," Curry said, likely to some other patrons who'd heard the disturbance. "Enjoy your time. Just a bit of a misunderstanding."

The air grew fresher as they emerged from the makeshift brothel of draped fabric and beads. Curry turned Torsten the wrong way, but Torsten promptly forced him back and made another show of force with the dagger. He may not have known which door belonged to Valin's office, but he could feel the flow of air from the exit to Valin's expansive cellar.

"Don't even try it," Torsten warned.

"I didn't mean—by Iam." Curry froze. "Who let him free!"

"Uhlvark, huuuungryyy," the giant said. Chains no longer rattled as his footsteps made the very ground shake. A cow began to whine, the sound of metal bending causing goosebumps all over Torsten's body.

Abigail, you genius, Torsten thought.

"Back to your chains, oaf!" another of Valin's thugs shouted.

"Huuuh?" It felt like an earthquake struck as the giant spun. "Ouuuuch!" Uhlvark roared. Torsten couldn't see, but he heard wood snapping, then the distinct tones of a man being launched across the pit.

"Whoooopsieee," the giant rumble. "You okaaaay?" The injured man howled in protest as the giant grabbed him. He must have attempted to use a weapon to break free because the giant yelped, then the man's screams echoed as he flew across the room in the other direction.

Canvas and wood scaffolding crunched from the direction of the underground brothel. Women and visiting patrons shrieked in fear. More of Valin's thugs shouted at the giant, pouring toward the arena from every direction.

"Get that giant in order!" one shouted.

"Get the chain whip!" said another.

"Let's go," Torsten whispered into his captive's ears.

Another jab of the knife got Curry moving as chaos erupted all around them. Guards tried to keep the clientele and their women from fleeing, promising it was under control. Uhlvark stomped around, sounding more frightened than menacing. As they reached the hallway, Torsten couldn't help but feel a pang of pity that they put the creature through such duress.

It's Valin's fault, keeping things where he shouldn't.

"H-his private office and quarters are up this way," Curry said. "There's men outside. One's bigger than you. Just leave now, and maybe you'll get out of this thing alive, Shieldsman."

"I'm not the one who should be worried," Torsten growled, nudging Curry to continue.

"You think we fear the Crown? They can't touch Mister Tehr."

"Maybe. But I can."

"Eh, Curry, what's going on back there?" someone hollered from down the hall.

Torsten reminded Curry there was a knife placed against his neck. "Quiet," he said. "Walk normally, and tell them about the giant. You're just leading me out."

"Uhlvark broke free again and tried to rip open the meal pen," Curry said, fast and nervous. "Threw Ludwig clear across the stands."

"And you ain't helping?"

"Got a very important guest here who we can't let get hurt," Curry said. "You two are welcome to go down and help chain him back up though."

"Mister Tehr says never to leave his door, we never leave. Go on then, get him out of here and then get your ass back down there to help." He and the man next to him laughed.

Torsten stayed behind Curry, knife at his back. He tilted his ear toward the guards they neared, trying to get a read on both their positions. The one he assumed was 'as big as him' breathed raggedly. It stunk worse than the brothel, too.

Torsten figure he'd take him down first. A jab to his throat, get him off balance, then throw him into the other. Curry wouldn't be a problem if...

"He's after Valin!" Curry shouted.

The man pushed off without warning. Torsten slashed blindly as he stumbled and caught Curry somewhere fleshy. The big guard came at Torsten, who stabbed out, but the man grabbed his arm and struggled to free the knife. He leveraged Torsten, shoving him against the wall and bending his elbow until the blade fell toward him. Torsten frantically stamped, trying to find the man's ankles but missed.

You're a Shieldsman, he told himself as his arm bent further. *You are the shield of this kingdom. Sight is for the weak. Only Iam needs guide our path.*

Torsten had always fought with honor, but he was in a place without any, where giants were slaves and women something far worse, where the only god was coin and whatever it took to fill your pockets with more.

He drove his knee up into the man's nether regions just before his own arm gave out. The blow caused the knife to merely scrape Torsten's ribs on the way by. The big one keeled over and Torsten spun around him. He somehow heard the third guard taking a swing at him with a club and ducked just in time. The club smashed into the big guard's back, and before the third one could apologize, Torsten swept with his massive leg and knocked him off his feet.

He drove a fist square into the man's forehead, knocking him unconscious, then rolled over his body as Curry took a swipe. Torsten found the floor and prepared to spring up. Something raced toward his head. He caught Curry's foot and flipped him ass over teakettle, but a second foot caught him across the jaw as the man floundered.

Torsten recovered quicker and pounced, driving blow after blow toward Curry's fat face. Curry had his guard up, so none landed, but Torsten was large and powerful. Curry's forearms were likely broken and splintered inside.

A sudden bloodcurdling howl from back in the arena echoed loudly.

"Nooooo!" Uhlvark roared, making even the mightiest beasts of Pantego sound puny and pathetic.

The distraction broke Curry's block, and Torsten's fist drove through his face. As the man's arms fell limp, the big guard grabbed Torsten from behind. Torsten's arms were wrenched backward as he was heaved off his feet.

"Come after Mister Tehr, will you?" the bulky guard growled. "This is his city you fools let rot. His!"

Torsten pushed one of the guard's arms away and got an elbow or two in, but his blows met a bulging stomach and accomplished nothing. The guard's arm wrapped his throat. Torsten shoved off the wall with his feet, driving them both backward and into the other guard. Torsten thrashed like an angry zhulong, but it was no use. His throat started closing, his hearing muddled, he felt the energy draining from his limbs. Then, in an instant, the fat guard's grip went loose, and he collapsed, dragging Torsten down with him.

Torsten lifted a weighty arm off himself and rolled free, gasping for air. He groped to find a wall, anything, with which to find balance. Instead, a familiar hand found his.

"Sir, you're all right?" Lucas said.

"Lucas! I'm fine," Torsten said.

"I don't know what you did down here, but they left me with one man."

"Easy enough to handle for a former brawler like you?" Torsten said, smiling but out of breath.

"I faired better than you. C'mon." Lucas needed both hands to heave Torsten to his feet, groaning the entire way. Torsten couldn't blame him. He'd put on a few pounds since he'd been unable to train in any sort of meaningful way.

Uhlvark yelled again, only this time it sounded like they were getting control of him. The floor rumbled louder than it had yet as if his entire body had fallen like a one-hundred-year-old oak in the Haskwood Thicket.

Lucas's muscles tensed. "So that's what you did," he said.

"I had help," Torsten said. "Valin doesn't have his claws in everyone yet."

"Keys." Lucas released Torsten and lifted a key ring off the fat guard. Then he started trying them on the door.

"Hurry up, will you?" Torsten asked. One of the guards groaned, and Torsten kicked toward the sound, cracking him in the jaw.

"Shog." Lucas dropped the key ring. He went to pick it up, but Torsten quickly clutched his wrist.

"Breathe, Lucas," Torsten said. "We'll be fine."

Lucas retrieved the key ring and followed Torsten's advice. A few seconds later, the door clicked open, and they entered. Torsten could picture it from over a decade ago. Walls adorned with riches no lowborn from Dockside should've ever even seen. Though underground, he had windows in the form of exquisite paintings from around Pantego. All bought with blood money, flesh money—sinful money.

"Check the desk," Torsten said. "Look for a ledger, scrolls. Any gods-damned thing that might have Valin's seal on it."

"It won't be in here," Lucas said.

"What are you talking about?"

"This room, it's all for show. He, uh… He brings the winners of every fight in here to congratulate them. Tells a story about one of these trinkets to make us think we can have this wealth." Lucas lifted something heavy off a table then let it clank back down.

"He does like to flaunt," Torsten agreed.

"That door, it's always locked. I think it's his private quarters."

"Where?"

Lucas knocked to show Torsten where. He fumbled with the key ring and tried every key he could until Torsten stopped him.

"If that's his real office, I guarantee nobody but the man himself gets in," Torsten said. "Check the desk while I open it."

He moved Lucas aside, then patted the area of the door. He found the handle, the hinges, then set his shoulder against it. For a long time, Glass soldiers had joked that Torsten had the blood of giants in his veins. He knew it wasn't true. He came from as common of Glintish stock as there could be.

He reared back and rammed his shoulder against the door. Pain radiated across his side. Whatever wood the thing was made with, it was reinforced. But he found that without the hindrance of sight, he could drive his body forward with reckless abandon.

He stepped back and smashed against it again. This time, the slight crackle of wood splintering was obvious. So, too, was the burning sensation as Torsten's shoulder popped from its socket.

"Nothing in here, Sir," Lucas called over.

"Keep looking," Torsten groaned.

"No, that's just it. Every drawer is empty. Every single one."

"Not a thing about this man is real." Torsten grunted and threw himself against the door again. The crack deepened, and Torsten's head flashed with agonizing pain. If his shoulder wasn't dislocated before, it was now. He didn't wait to let the shock settle. He ground his teeth and charged forward one last time.

The door blew off its hinges. Torsten burst through, hitting the floor hard and rolling over, clutching his shoulder.

"By Iam," Lucas said. He rushed in and tried to help Torsten up.

"No," Torsten shooed him away. "Find Valin's records so we can get out of here."

Torsten had sat idly by while too many wolves and snakes infested Yarrington. He knew he might not leave this place alive, but it no longer mattered.

Shouting from down in the arena had ceased echoing so loudly, which meant they didn't have long before their mess was discovered. Torsten wasn't sure what they might find, but he knew anything would help prove Valin wasn't fit to serve the Crown. It had to. Iam hadn't placed Abigail in Torsten's path for no reason. Iam himself was serving as Torsten's eyes, leading him toward justice.

"There are personal letters on his desk," Lucas said. "Loads of them."

"Take them too," Torsten said. "But inside. Look inside for records."

Lucas jammed something into the desk drawer and pried it open. He rifled through the contents. "Here we are!" He thumbed through pages. "There are amounts, dates. By Iam, this has to have something."

"Well done. Now, help me up. I think it's time we get out of here."

"Right away—what in the name of Iam?" Lucas' tone went grim, like he'd found a skeleton. Valin probably had left plenty of those in his wake, but they wouldn't fit in a desk drawer.

"What is it?"

The ledger dropped on top of the desk. Lucas unfolded something.

"Lucas?" Torsten said.

"*'The Caleef still hasn't reached me in Latiapur,'*" Lucas read.

"What is this?"

"A letter dated yesterday," Lucas said. "'*You made promises, Valin. You said the deserter Rand Langley wouldn't fail after you took his sister. I expect results when I pay enough to make you the wealthiest man in Yarrington. I need the Caleef to develop a foothold here. The rogue afhem's daughter alone isn't enough. You may think you're powerful, but the Darkings family has been*" *around for centuries, and we will endure long after you're dead. Get him here!* Signed, Yuri Darkings.'"

No pain could keep Torsten from putting together the truth of what he'd just heard. "That was the price..."' he muttered. It all made so much sense now. Rand Langley and Valin Tehr worked together to free Torsten from Redstar's prison, and now Torsten knew the true cost. A cost that helped Valin earn enough gold to pay for all the help he'd been providing the Crown with ease.

Valin was using Rand to escort the escaped Caleef back to his people. All in the name of protecting a sister Valin apparently also controlled. A sister that had murdered Oleander for the Dom Nohzi.

"T... Tor... Sir, what do we do?" Lucas stammered.

"Lucas, you need to get that back to the castle," Torsten said. "I'll only slow you down."

"Sir, there's something I need to—"

"King Pi needs to know before it's too late," Torsten interrupted. "Sir Nikserof needs to know. I know Rand. He'll do the right thing and turn the Caleef over if we can get to him."

"Sir—"

"Lucas, go!"

"Go where?" a familiar voice said. Armored men filed into Valin's office, and judging by the clattering of their armor, they weren't merely Valin's thugs.

"Captain Henry?" Lucas said. "What are you doing here."

"Heard a disturbance only to find men of the Crown, breaking into and robbing a lawful citizen of the Glass Kingdom?" Henry said. "Oh, this is too good."

"Lawful?" Torsten said. He attempted to stand, but pushing against the floor with his injured shoulder had it burning. "You will let Lucas pass, Captain."

"Not sure I can do that."

"Whatever Valin is paying you to protect him, know that the

Crown will have it stripped from you if you don't heed my orders."

"Who said anybody is paying me? I'm doin my job. Just protecting the rights of our citizens."

"I am the Master of Warfare and a King's Shieldsman. You will do so, or you will hang!"

"Are you? I don't see any armor on them," Henry said. "Do you, boys?" A few more guards agreed with him. "Could be anybody breaking in."

"Captain, please," Lucas said. "This changes everything."

"What, you thought you could come down here, get Valin thrown away and then nobody would ever find out how you stood atop the gate that day and let Rand leave?" Captain Henry asked.

"I didn't know who they had with them!" Lucas insisted.

"Oh please. You were supposed to keep the gate closed so we could work them over. You knew Bartholomew Darkings was in there. Did he ever tell you that, Sir Unger? Did he ever tell you the real reason he was stationed at the South Gate that awful day."

"Lucas, what is he talking about?" Torsten asked.

"I had a feeling. You thought you were better than us, boy. But nothing comes from shog, except for shog."

"You knew?" Torsten said, breathless.

"Sir, I swear, I only knew Rand left with Darkings," Lucas said. "I figured that was the payment for saving you. I had no idea the Caleef was in there."

"Letting a known fugitive like Darkings leave the city?" Henry said. "Tsk tsk."

"I was following your orders!" Lucas shouted.

"Were you? And I suppose your parents' shop wasn't the first Valin helped repair after the riots. I suppose his men didn't keep them safe, just like my wife and kids."

"I didn't ask for any of that."

"You never had to," Captain Henry said. "Now, I'm *asking* for you to hand that letter over, and they'll continue living on in blissful ignorance."

"If you touch them!"

"They're fine, for now. Now, hand it over!"

"Don't," Torsten said. Pain no longer mattered. He forced himself up to his feet and stalked forward. Eyes or not, meager members of the city guard would have heard of his exploits in Liam's war. A few of the guards even backed away a few steps.

"Captain, this is the last time I will ask," Torsten snarled. "Step aside, or you will be punished as a traitor."

"Sir, I swear I had no idea," Lucas said. He sounded on the verge of crying. "I don't even know why Valin would want the Caleef."

"Because controlling kings is the true path to power," Valin Tehr said. The guards silenced, and the clack of his cane as he limped into the room echoed. "Crowns are just heavy headwear. Well done, Captain."

Captain Henry used the distraction to seize Lucas and rip the letter out of his hands. Then he threw Lucas against the wall. "Maybe now you'll start trusting me," he said, out of breath.

"I think that could be arranged," Valin said.

"Valin," Torsten spat. "You dare sit with *our* king after what you've done! I'll have your head." Torsten didn't think twice. He charged in Valin's direction but didn't make it two steps before someone smashed him in the side of the head with the blunt end of a weapon.

"No!" Lucas shouted. He threw himself over Torsten. "Don't hurt him!"

Captain Henry laughed. "All this for some paper. Whoops." The letter tore once, then again, and again, before Henry sprinkled the shreds on top of Torsten and Lucas.

"Think about your family, Lucas," Valin said. "You will face justice for this insolence after all I did to help them for you, but they don't need to."

"I... I..."

Torsten was too dazed to respond, but he felt Lucas being peeled off him. Torsten struggled to his hands and knees and grasped at wherever Valin was. Captain Henry's boot slammed down on his arm.

Torsten groaned.

"You Shieldsmen are all the same," he whispered in Torsten's ear. "You forget where you come from."

Torsten spit up a gob of blood while Henry cackled. He had no vision to become fuzzy, but that didn't stop his brain from experiencing fuzziness in every other conceivable way. All he could picture was being back in Winde Port the last time he'd failed his kingdom when Sir Mulliner had to put him down like a crazed boar. Only, that time the men were confused and deceived by a heathen. This time, they were betrayed by men of the Glass who'd turned their backs on their own people.

A fist rushed toward his head, but Torsten heard the movement and snapped into action, catching it. His injured shoulder burst with sharp pain, but he ignored it. He grasped, and his hand fell upon one of the soldier's belts where he seized hold of a knife. With swift movement, he sliced upward at the place he knew Captain Henry to be.

All he heard before a mass of fists and boots beat him unconscious was gurgling. All he tasted was blood, his own, and that of a traitor.

XXXII

THE THIEF

Whitney's cheeks went hot. His head rolled back on his shoulders, then slipped by Rand on his hands and knees and punched the Caleef straight in the nose. Blood poured down, people gasped, and the Caleef grabbed his face, but he didn't protest. He couldn't protest. Whitney shook out his hand.

"What the yig are you doing!" Rand demanded. He grabbed Whitney and threw him back against the bars.

"That gray bastard was responsible for the murdering of hundreds, including my own hometown," Whitney said. *Hometown.* Before Elsewhere, Whitney barely cared, but after building a new life there, the thought of it hit harder. It was like his timeline had been reversed. All thanks to Bartholomew Darkings, the Caleef, Grint, the list went on.

"He had nothing to do with that," Rand said. "This is not the Caleef."

"Tell yourself whatever you need. I know what I see. Swear it. Swear to Iam on your sister's life it isn't him."

"I wouldn't dare use our Lord's name in vain," Rand said softly, unsure.

"Because it's him!"

"You've really done it this time. Langley," Barty groaned.

"The Caleef," someone said. "Here?"

"Trying to sneak through these lands," spoke someone else.

"You monster!" The man who shouted that had a foreign look to him, like a mix between Sora and Torsten. He lunged at the Caleef and clasped his hands around the skinny man's throat. "My brother died at Winde Port!"

"Get off him!" Rand delivered a blow to the attacker's gut and sent him reeling.

Chaos erupted. There were nearly twenty terrified people stuffed into the low cage, and all of them smelled blood. Fists and legs thrashed. The Caleef shuffled into the corner, cowering. There were no more god powers in him than the bars at his back. He was a lie.

Darkings shoved a woman in front of himself for protection and joined the Caleef in being a weakling. Whitney felt his blood boiling. He'd spent a lifetime never getting close to anyone or anything, even enemies. Now, he was surrounded by people he hated or wanted to hurt. Rand, who robbed him of his greatest triumph, the Caleef, his childhood home, and innocence—until that day in Troborough, Whitney had stolen from many, but that was the first time he'd ever killed. And Darkings… oh, Darkings. That man's transgressions were too many to count.

While Rand was occupied holding back the wave of angry, confused Fettingboroughites, Whitney sprung for Darkings. He got a few licks in on the man's pudgy face before the entire cage rattled.

"Enough!" Drad Mak roared. He threw open the cage, grabbed the oldish man nearest inside and flung him out onto the sodden grass. Dire wolves immediately circled him, drooling and baring sharp fangs.

The fighting in the wagon stopped. Even Whitney couldn't

send another fist into Darkings' face. They all froze and watched as the wolves circled closer, then tore into the poor soul. Everyone turned away, unable to watch. Whitney wanted to tear his ears from his head just so he wouldn't hear the screams as they echoed across the plains. Soon, the screams stopped, and the awful sounds of flesh rending and bone crunching was all that could be heard.

Instead, he just stared through the bars in the opposite direction. All the Northmen were packing up, and some had even started marching already. Furs and leather armor with bone trinkets covered them all along with metal piercings so painful looking they made Whitney's skin crawl. It was an army more frightening than the demons of Elsewhere. A handful even had their faces painted white—dark bars across their eyes and lips, red dripping from their eyes, fresh blood staining the mess of sewn furs draped over their shoulders. Warlocks.

Whitney swore inwardly. He'd seen what they were capable of and this time, Sora wasn't there to save them all.

"I can't taunt the Glass if you all kill each other first," Mak said.

"You'll kill us anyway!" the strange-looking man who'd started the fight said.

Mak chortled and lifted his oversized axe onto his oversized shoulder. "Perhaps, perhaps not. But at least you won't die like that." He nodded his head toward the two wolves, tearing at what little remained of their victim.

One of the warlocks stopped nearby, kneeled and brought a finger covered in the poor man's blood to his lips. He looked up at Mak, and his eyes turned white and rolled into the back of his head.

"The Lady says it is time to move," he said, eyes still all white. "She wants all eyes on the lands of grass and trees, and away from the ice." The warlock's eyes lowered back into place, and he gasped for air as if he hadn't been breathing. He didn't stand either, and when the other two warlocks helped lift him, his legs appeared weak.

"Let's move!" Mak roared to his men. "The Buried Goddess doesn't wait."

The wagon started moving. Everyone, Whitney included, winced at the sound of wheels cranking. Altogether, four giant zhulong trudged along through the mud, pulling the two carts with ease.

"Get off of me!" Barty shouted. Whitney totally forgot he still had him pinned until the plump man's weak arms pushed at him.

Whitney was so exhausted, mind and body, he couldn't even fight it. He let off the slob and leaned back against the other end of the cage. He exhaled through his teeth—quite possibly the only part of him that didn't burn with pain.

"You'll pay for that," Barty sneered as he rose back up. "You shog-licking excuse for a—"

"He won't," Rand said and shoved him back down. "Sounds to me like you had a lot worse coming to you."

"How dare you lay your hands on me," Barty spat at Rand.

"You're lucky we have a deal, or I'd gut you myself for all you've done."

"Says another traitor."

"Being a traitor is one thing," Rand said. "Being a sniveling, backstabbing, coward is another. Now, sit back, shut your mouth, and let us figure this out."

"What he said," Whitney agreed.

Barty's face went the color of one of Farmer Branson's plums, then he sank back down. Like always, he was all talk until someone tougher got in his face. And Rand may have been many things, but he was the most intimidating person around, Drav Cra monsters excluded.

A lengthy silence passed through the cage until finally the

Caleef leaned forward and said, "I'm sorry for the loss of your home." His voice was soft, weak, nothing like what one would expect for a god-king.

"Congratulations," Whitney remarked.

The Caleef's lip twisted. His dark eyes appeared earnest, but Whitney was tired of the affairs of nobles and kings making the world a mess—especially since he was done thieving, it helped nobody.

"I swear to you this: I had nothing to do with the rebellion," the Caleef went on. "I wanted, and still want, peace. Ever since Liam showed us that fighting for our space on the Great Shores didn't mean us ravaging each other, I wanted it. Not all of my people agree, and so I am sorry. But these men can help me change that."

"Bah, that ain't the real Caleef," one of the prisoners said.

"About as godly as my grandmother," said another.

The skinny, gray-skinned man seemed almost ready to cry as the entirety of the prisoners dismissed him as a fraud. A man like him probably wasn't used to even being talked to, let alone talked down to. That very fact gave Whitney a sense of satisfaction.

"Look, Fierstown, this isn't where any of us wanted to be today," Rand said after another long bout of silence. "But for all of our sakes, we need to find a way out of this."

"Ain't no way out of this, boy." the man with the foreign appearance said as he hastily shoved something toward his mouth.

"What is that?" Rand asked.

"None of your business," he said, chewing.

Rand grabbed the man's wrist and shook. Manaroot fell to the carriage floor, and the man scratched desperately for it. Although a sensory amplifier, the plant—more like a drug—was highly addictive, and made the user a danger to those around him. Rand snatched it from the ground.

"Give it here!"

"Stop this, friend! We're going to get through this," Rand said. "All of us. We just need to stay focused."

"You can keep lying to yourself," the man said. "I hope you've said all your prayers. I know I have."

Whitney rolled his eyes. He'd had enough talk of gods for one lifetime.

Rand, however, turned his head toward the man. "It's going to be okay…"

"Javaud," the man offered.

"Javaud… a strong name. Your mother was Glintish. Father Panpingese?"

"How'd you know?" Javaud asked.

"Your skin tone… amber like someone from Panping, but your ears… Excuse me, but no one will be calling you a knife-ear. Your hair… tight, curled. If your father was of the Glass, it would be straighter."

Javaud smiled.

The wagon rumbled as it reached the top of the low hill Whitney and Rand had been caught upon. Whitney noticed the large footprints in the mud leading up behind them, no idea how the giant Mak managed to sneak up on them.

I'm losing my touch.

"And you…" Rand turned to another prisoner. "I saw you in town. You run the… what was the name of the tavern?"

"The Five Round Trousers." She was the server who'd taken to Whitney that night. Without as much ale in him, he realized she was a lot older than he'd previously thought—gray hair, but still pretty in her own right.

Rand went on to talk to someone else, and Whitney recognized what he was up to, stupid as he thought it was. Rand was trying to give hope to these people. But he wasn't going to do that by talking to them about what… where they were from? Where they worked? What he needed to do was give them some *real* hope.

"Let me tell you all something," Whitney started, standing as tall as the squat cage would allow. He stumbled a bit as the wagon rocked and bounced, then smiled.

"What are you doing?" Rand whispered.

"I've been locked up in the Glass Castle," he tilted his head as if thinking, "twice… maybe three times. I've lost count. I've been imprisoned in a dwarven ruin by Redstar 'the Deceiver' himself. You know that name, right? He leads these ugly ice lovers… or, led, I suppose."

One of the Drav Cra glanced over but stayed silent.

"Shortly after, I was tied up in the web of a massive spider queen. Some call her Bliss, some the One Who Remained. You people want to discuss gods and goddesses? That was the closest thing any of us have seen to a deity, I can assure you of that."

"Oh, sit down," Barty said. "You're giving us all a headache."

Ignoring him, Whitney continued, kicking Rand's boot. "I've been captured by the King's Shield, city guards… spit and shog, you name it. There's some other things you wouldn't even believe if I told you. Upyr assassins, demons of Elsewhere, and worse."

"Please, pray tell," Bartholomew said. "Why does that matter to any of us?"

"My *point*, Barty, is that you are all in the presence of the World's Greatest Thief, and there's never been a cage that could keep me locked up." He expanded his chest, taking in a deep breath.

"My name is Whitney Fierstown!" Whitney pronounced. "Yes, yes, the same Whitney Fierstown of Westvale fame. He who stole the Sword of Grace from right under Lord Theroy's nose while the right bugger slept face-down in a puddle of his own spit. Had myself a throw with his lady daughter that evening as well."

It had been years since he made this speech, but it rolled off his tongue like only yesterday. He could give it in his sleep.

"The Mischievous, Master of Mayhem, the very same credited for single-handedly delivering the Splintering Staff out of the hands of the Whispering Wizards," he went on. "You know them, fine folks of Fettingborough? Whitney Fierstown, dispatcher of Drav Cra heathens. Hope of the hopeless and helpless. Thief of all thieves. The Filcher Fantastic himself. If you think for one second some ice-eating, snow-shoveling, shog-smelling horde of cousin-husbands is going to keep me locked up, get ready for a show."

A loud, sharp crack of metal on metal sounded just behind Whitney and the mustached Drav Cra warrior Whitney'd heard called Ugosah shouted, "Shut up in there!"

Whitney raised his hands in placation, then took his seat again next to Rand.

"What's the plan?" Rand whispered, hopeful.

"Yes, please, enlighten us," Barty said, rolling his eyes.

He's just jealous his home wasn't included in my finest moments, Whitney thought. Then he shrugged and said. "No idea. Let's think of something."

A collective groan rose from the wagon's inhabitants.

"Hey, Don't worry," Whitney said. "I didn't have a plan any of those other times either. Something will come to me."

I hope, he thought.

He glanced out of the wagon, seeing the zhulong which dragged his friends along in their own prison. They were performers, not fighters. None of them deserved this.

Hours passed, and no plan had presented itself. Whitney was exhausted but found himself unable to rest. Plans usually came quicker to him. Thanks to Grint, he hadn't a proper night of sleep to help him think straight.

Instead, he sat watching Bartholomew with intense focus, waiting for the moments the despicable man started to drift off to sleep before kicking him and jarring him back to consciousness.

"When we get out of here, you're finished, you hear me?" Barty said. "I'll make it my life's work."

"Going to grab another Dom Nohzi?" Whitney asked.

"Clearly, they're not all they're talked up to be. I'll find something worse, don't you worry."

"Worse than Kazimir?" Whitney paused and pictured the white-haired devil of a man sitting on the well in Elsewhere-Troborough, contemplating life like some murderous philosopher. Like Torsten, he wasn't so bad when you looked beyond the surface. Whitney had a knack for finding strange friends: a blood mage, an all-too-stubborn knight, and a blood-sucking immortal who pushed the leniency of his deities too far.

I really need to meet some new people.

"When I'm done with you, you'll be wishing for Kazimir," Darkings threatened.

"Huh?" Whitney asked. He'd completely lost his train of thought regarding the conversation with Barty. Looking at the wisp of fur above his chapped lips made his stomach roll every time.

Bartholomew grumbled under his breath, then kicked one of the other weary prisoners. "You, switch with me," he said. The man barely had a chance to respond before Barty was shoving himself into the other man's place and out of Whitney's range.

Whitney smirked and let his head roll to the side. It was sunset. The eyes of dire wolves stood out like brilliant topazes against the coming darkness from the west.

"Say, Barty," Whitney said. "Don't those eyes remind you of something? Maybe that hideous amulet of your mother's I stole?"

"I know what you're doing, thief, and it won't work."

"Hmm," Whitney mused.

Rand sat by the cage's door, fussing with ways to get it open. The Drav Cra marching around them barely even paid attention any longer, except the occasional banging on the bars to wake everyone, followed by a collective laugh.

Whitney had taken a crack at the door earlier, but it was no use. They'd wrapped the chains to keep it shut, and used a Shesaitju lock that dangled down near the wheels, far out of reach unless Whitney tried dislocating his shoulder, which even still would have been a stretch. And fiddling might work, but the Drav Cra kept a close enough eye that that wasn't a real option.

"You're never going to cut through the chains," Whitney said.

Rand glanced back, frustration twisting his features. He had his belt buckle in one hand and had been quietly grinding it against the chains for over an hour, as if that might work. *Maybe if he had a year.*

"I don't see you coming up with any ideas," Rand snapped.

"I don't come *up* with ideas," Whitney said. "They come to me."

Only they aren't, Whitney admitted only to himself.

He wasn't sure if it was his time in Elsewhere or his new life of being thought of as a hero by ladies like Talwyn, but he had nothing. Breaking chains was impossible with the tools they had. The lock was out of reach. The Drav Cra were *ungoadable.* Most didn't speak more than a few words of common now that Mak and his commanders were way out in front leading the march.

Whitney's head fell back against the bars. If he listened carefully, he could hear the sounds of Gentry's crying, of Aquira's muffled squeals. Eventually, his heavy eyelids shut. He battled them as best he could, but he was so tired…

XXXIII

THE KNIGHT

Torsten still hadn't gotten used to waking in total darkness. Every new morning felt like he was floating, formless. He'd panic and nearly fall from his bed. This time was no different. Only, as he groped through the darkness, he realized he wasn't on his bed. His fingers found the cold, damp stone, moss growing through a series of cracks.

Valin, he thought, fists clenching as he remembered what had happened.

He crawled along until he found a wall—more stone. His entire body was sore, making standing a chore. His head rang like church bells on the morning of the Dawning. He skirted along the wall, patting it to keep from falling until eventually, his hands fell through an opening.

Excitement overtook him. He thrust his entire arm through, but the rest of his body fell against metal bars, somehow even more frigid than the stone. He grabbed for the next bar, then the next, all the way down until he found another stone wall.

Another dungeon, he thought, all the energy fleeing his limbs. He fell against the metal, a few rats scurrying as his heavy knees hit the stone. Then a deep itch set upon his scorched brow, always worse when he was irritated.

"You're awake," Valin Tehr said. "Finally. I should have you cut to pieces for killing Captain Henry. You know how hard it was to coax him to my side?"

The news that he'd killed a captain of the city guard settled into Torsten's heart like a boulder. Visions of tossing Sir Havel Tralen to his death at Winde Port.

"You with us, Sir Unger?" Valin said.

Torsten's head searched, turning his ear this way and that. Valin's voice carried in the stone-walled dungeon, bouncing here and there, making it impossible to pinpoint him.

"You traitorous scum. I'll kill you too!" Torsten found the bars again and gave them a violent shake.

"Always the rush to violence with you," Valin said. "Isn't that what allowed Redstar to shove you into a place just like this? If I remember correctly. Won't you ever learn?"

"You saw what happened to him," Torsten said, seething.

"With your sight, and my help."

"You used Rand! A man from these same streets. And you turned his sister into a monster."

"Trust me, I had nothing to do with her. As far as I knew, she died the night of the riots. An… unforeseen complication."

"Because you needed her to control Rand," Torsten realized.

"Very good."

"He has no idea about her, does he?"

"I suspect only Codar knows… knew enough about the Dom Nohzi to understand what happened to her. This far west, they're little more than bedtime stories to frighten children."

"And Codar summoned the blood pact upon Oleander's head?"

"He did."

Torsten's grip tightened, his nails digging into his thumbs. He couldn't believe Valin would admit it with such impunity.

"Oh, calm down." Valin whacked the bars above Torsten. The *clang* made him wince, and the vibrations in the metal had his bones chattering. "We did the kingdom a service. Do you know what it means to make a blood pact with the Sanguine Lords?"

"It means you're a coward!"

"It means that if they reject your offering, your own life is forfeit. They haven't assassinated royalty in centuries, in any kingdom. They are beings of the shadow, and an attack like this? I forbade Codar to pursue the pact, told him there were other ways, but he went behind my back."

"And he died anyway," Torsten said. "I only wish I was the one who'd done it."

"He wasn't supposed to be anywhere near that church! But proud Codar… He left me a map showing the region of the Dom Nohzi's hideout, then left."

"Maybe he realized the kind of man you are and tried to stop it."

"You aren't the only one who lost a friend!" Valin roared. Before Torsten knew what hit him, the man's cane pressed against his fingers, crushing them against the bars. He pushed, harder and harder, until they were on the verge of breaking, then let off. Valin drew a deep, calming breath.

"You were there when he stepped between the monsters and their prey," Valin said. "Did you hear anything he said? Any reason why?"

"So that's why I'm still alive. Your dear old friend is dead, and you have no idea why?" Torsten sneered. "How does it feel to be left in the dark? Lied to?"

"I gave you so many chances!" Valin said. "I offered to work together all those years ago and again, right upstairs, only days ago.

Time and time again you proved the stubbornness that allowed this kingdom to rot with that witch behind the throne. From the Drav Cra to the Black Sands, even Liam's death. You tell me there isn't a part of you that doesn't wonder if she poisoned him."

There was a time that thought had crossed Torsten's mind, but no longer. He'd come to know her well enough to know how much she truly did love her husband. She just struggled to show it, as she struggled with so much.

"She didn't," Torsten said assuredly. "And maybe she wasn't what this kingdom needed, but she was *our* queen regardless. She was the mother of a boy who needs one now more than anything."

"Oh please," Valin scoffed. "He'd be better off with one of my whores. Or me."

"You don't deserve to even breathe near him!"

"At least I know what I am. You're so quick to judge, but I hear every rumor from the castle. How you stared at Oleander while she swayed her hips. How you panted in lust while she took you in her room. Lust destroys kingdoms, Torsten, and you are guilty of it—of letting it cloud your judgment—no matter how much you pray to Iam."

Valin paced in front of the cell, dragging his mangled foot behind him. Torsten didn't respond. This time, he couldn't. He hated that there was truth to the snake's words. Oleander may have found the light, but Torsten knew that if she had been tossed into a cell after Liam died until her spell of insanity waned, the kingdom would have been better off.

But Pi may never have returned without the orepul and Redstar's influence, Torsten reminded himself. *Without her, the Nothhelm line, chosen by Iam so many ages ago, may have died off.*

"All those years amongst nobles has made you soft, Torsten," Valin said. "You forgot this place. You forgot what it means to claw for every breath. And these people are the Glass

Kingdom. Oleander, Liam, to them we are men to wield swords; fodder for the so-called enemies of Iam. It took a man like Redstar to open your eyes for Skorravik's sake, even as he closed them!"

Valin banged on the bars. Then he exhaled slowly. "But Pi is still young. He can still be taught what the Glass Kingdom is, not the fantasy you parade around that infernal castle. Fighting wars over nothing while your people starve. You're so afraid of another Redstar because his rise was *your* failure; you can't see that I'm more savior than scourge."

"Look around your own brothel, Valin," Torsten said. "Look at the sins you peddle. If you really think yourself a savior, you're even more mad than I thought."

"I merely know what the people want when they aren't too busy hiding from Iam's gaze. Soon, the Caleef will either be found, and I'll be hailed a hero, or he'll find his way back to his people, and the war will worsen. Either way, my position strengthens."

"You're insane."

"Then the Dom Nohzi will face our wrath for what they've taken. South Corner will be rebuilt, made to flourish with the support of a king who sees more than those beyond his own borders."

"No. The world will find out what you've done, and you'll pay, for all of this. You'll pay for everything you've ever done. Shieldsmen will come looking for me."

"And they'll find nothing. A blind, grieving man goes walking off to South Corner for a bout of pleasure in a brothel, anything can happen. Now, I have a royal funeral to attend to, and as the soon-to-be Master of Coin, it's only right for me to be there. Take your time to think about what Codar said. I can make your death a lot less painful if you play nice."

"You think I fear pain?"

"No," Valin admitted, "but I've watched you a long time. You hate watching others suffer and well… my audience craves it."

Valin's cane tapped as he hobbled away. Torsten was so angry he could barely breathe. His entire body felt like it was going to come undone. He could almost feel the fire searing his eyes out again.

"Oh, and Torsten," Valin said, voice now echoing from further away. "Do try and forgive Lucas. He truly did know very little, and he'll need it for tonight. I think the fool really wanted to be a Shieldsman. It's easier without family holding you back, isn't it? We both know." Valin released an exaggerated sigh. "Youth. Don't mourn too hard for your beloved Queen. You'll see her soon in Elsewhere. You and I know you both deserve it."

"Get back here!" Torsten roared, slamming on the bars. Stone dust fell from the ceiling covering his head. He shook, and he shook until his arms gave out.

It was no use.

He was trapped once again, and this time, Rand wasn't around to save him. Or Sora for that matter. The blood mage seemed to show up in his gravest moments. So much so, he'd believed she'd been guided by Iam's hand despite her depraved powers; that he was using something wicked in order to spread His light, if only she'd open her eyes.

Neither of them arrived. He wondered if all this time he'd seen divine intervention, but it had only been coincidence. If now his luck had run out.

He sunk back against the wall. In the Glass Castle dungeons, he had his sight, and supporters even if he didn't know about them. People like Rand who knew where he was. If Valin was right about one thing, it was that it wasn't hard for him to vanish. He wasn't a king. He was a worthless knight kept around in a position out of courtesy for prior service. He'd be forgotten as soon as Pi moved on to a new mentor.

Only Lucas Danvels knew where he was. A boy who'd kept far too much to himself, and if he wasn't dead yet for trying to undermine Valin, would very likely be soon.

Torsten let his head fall back against the wall, a screen of cobwebs breaking against his bare skin. He aimed his face toward the ceiling.

"What now?" he asked, hoping Iam was still listening. "I've done everything I thought you wanted. What did I miss?"

All that answered was the rustling of more rats and the distant drip of water somewhere outside the cell.

"If the boy had only told me what he'd seen, we might have figured this all out!" Torsten punched the floor, cracking open the skin of his knuckles. Then he sighed. "It's not his fault. He was scared for his family, I know. Everyone here is, and we all should be. *I* should have done more. I should have put Valin away decades ago instead of charging off to war."

Torsten raised his knuckle to his lips and licked off some of the fresh blood. The feel of Sigrid's teeth in his neck... Oleander's cold corpse... the taste of copper washed across his mouth.

"What now?" he said softly. "Liam, Uriah, they never taught me how to handle men without honor or fear. They only taught me to fight what I can see. I hoped Redstar was the end of the usurpers, but Uriah was right... Ill kings did bring circling wolves. They merely came from within."

Torsten clutched absently for the pendant of the Eye of Iam which once hung from his neck—that which was given to him by Liam. In so many battles, it had renewed his hope when all seemed lost.

"Is this truly what you want?" Torsten asked. "Tell me that it is, and I'll stop fighting. Show me something..."

"Valin's got something on you too, eh?" a gruff voice asked from the other side of the cell. Torsten nearly leaped out of his skin.

"Who are you?" Torsten questioned, now crouching and ready for anything. "Have you been in here the whole time?"

"I suppose I have." He burped, and Torsten could smell the liquor on his breath from across the cell. "Funniest thing. Most men snore when they fall asleep drinking. I go down, silent as a crypt."

He slapped the stone and Torsten flinched.

"Right, you asked who I am too," the mysterious stranger said. "I guess Father Morningweg will have to do. I can't recall when I was called anything else."

"You're a priest?" Torsten asked in complete disbelief.

"Don't you see my holy blindfold?"

Torsten didn't answer. The man clearly didn't know who Torsten was, and he didn't want to reveal his condition and surrender the upper hand.

"Yes, I am indeed a Priest," Morningweg said. "Wouldn't be if I could help it, but what can we help?"

"What?" Torsten replied.

Morningweg groaned. "It's a long story and my head's pounding. Valin gives me the run of the place, any girl I want, but now all of a sudden I'm tapped out and tossed in here to sober up, so I can go be a priest again for the kingdom." He blew a raspberry.

"Of course. The priest Valin got 'relieved by the convent' is just a sham." Torsten sunk back into his spot.

"A sham?" he said, sounding insulted.

"Priests don't smell like you. You reek worse than the brothel."

"I'll have you know I served in the church of Fessix for thirty years before the savages burned it to the ground on a raid. All I hear are those peoples' screams when I'm sober, so forgive me if I'd rather not be scolded by a man who finds himself in Valin's dungeon. He's a cruel lump of shog, but the men who wind up down here usually deserve it just the same."

"I…" Torsten's throat went dry. He remembered hearing about that attack on the village when he was Wearer of White before Liam died. He remembered being in the Shield Hall and sending out relief rather than troops because securing a foothold at Crowfall was more important than one small village. "I'm sorry."

"It isn't your fault, whoever you are," Father Morningweg said. "Sorry, it's been a while since I could think so straight."

A minute or so went by in silence until Torsten's brow began to itch again.

"So if you're a priest, why aren't you in Hornsheim?" he asked.

"I don't suppose anybody cared about a priest without a church or flock," Morningweg said.

"You could have returned there years ago, or been placed somewhere new. There are traveling missions throughout the East. People that desperately need to hear the word of Iam."

"Nobody needs to *hear* it," he scoffed. "They need to feel it, deep within. What can I possibly say to anyone when I stopped feeling anything? All my friends, dead, over nothing."

"'Iam cannot protect against all evil, only illuminate it, so we may drive it back into the shadows,'" Torsten said, quoting scripture.

"Yeah, some god," Morningweg scoffed.

"The echoes of the God Feud linger. Not all men have seen the light yet."

"I thought Liam was supposed to fix that?"

"Some evils take more than a single lifetime to erase. You should know that."

"And trust me, I do. Huddled, locked in my church so many countless times, my arms wrapped around children when the savages came. And every time I thought it was faith that guarded us until Redstar and the Drav Cra finally broke in."

Torsten sat up. "Redstar was part of that raid?"

"He led it," Morningweg said. "Turns out, it wasn't faith that protected us so long. It wasn't the fortress of Iam's light that was our church. The savages simply didn't care whether we lived or died. We were worthless to them. Our food and clothes though, like gold."

"I understand, Father," Torsten said. He edged along the wall to get a little closer. "Trust me, more than anyone, I do. I have seen more evil than you can imagine. My faith has been shaken too many times to count. But every time, when the world seems darkest, He shows me the way."

"Are you a priest, too?" Father Morningweg asked. "You sound like one."

"A Shieldsman."

"Well, Shieldsman, Iam hasn't met Valin Tehr yet."

"He's a flea compared to Drad Redstar, and I stopped him."

Father Morningweg seemed to choke on his next breath. "You what?"

For a moment, Torsten was surprised. Everyone in Yarrington had come to know how he delivered the final blow to Redstar after turning the Shield back against him. "Forgive me," Torsten said. "I forgot to introduce myself. I'm Sir Torsten Unger."

Father Morningweg didn't answer. Instead, he scampered across the floor and wrapped his hands around Torsten's cheeks. It happened so fast Torsten nearly punched him. Morningweg patted his face, feeling the form of it until he reached the mess of scarred tissue across his brow that left his eyes useless.

"By Iam, it really is you," he said, incredulous. Before Torsten could answer, the priest broke out into hysterical laughter. Torsten got a faceful of alcohol-coated breath that might have been enough to leave him inebriated.

"What is it?" Torsten said, shoving the man's face away.

It took Father Morningweg a few seconds to settle himself. "I helped Rand Langley break you out so you could face Redstar."

"You helped Rand, too?" Torsten promptly seized the priest's shoulders. "Do you know anything about what happened to him. About his sister?"

"I only helped him sneak into the crypt, nothing more." Again he chuckled. "By Iam, of all the places to be thrown today, here I am with the man who avenged my town."

"I did—"

"I know, I know, a priest shouldn't want revenge, but I did," Father Morningweg interrupted. "Oh, I did. If I could have been there when you drove your sword through his heart... I don't think there's a girl in Valin's field that could give a man such pleasure."

"Father!" Torsten whispered sharply.

"Sorry. I'm not used to anyone caring. So, it's true then, that Redstar took your eyes with him?"

Torsten nodded, then realized he made the same mistake Pi always had with him. Father Morningweg was blind as well. "It's true," he said.

"A shame. You'd have made a far better priest than I. At least you might have been able to protect my people against those monsters."

"I've failed mine too many times to count."

"Such is life under Iam." Father Morningweg exhaled. "Maybe you're right. Maybe he is still watching over us to place us here together after we helped each other get what we wanted without even knowing."

"And perhaps it is a coincidence," Torsten remarked.

"Either way, I thank you, Torsten Unger. Thank you for giving me closure. I only wish we didn't have to meet like this."

"Help me get out of here, Father. Whatever Valin has on you, we'll make it right."

"Alas, I'm not a fighter. Wretched as Valin is, without him, my altar boy, Devlin Boremater, would be a worthless street urchin. I owe him."

"Who doesn't." Torsten's lip twisted. "Then pray with me, Father?"

"I haven't prayed since that day."

"Then it can't hurt to try, can it?"

Torsten held out his palms. He knew Father Morningweg couldn't see them, but still, he waited, silently. The slow pitter-patter of water from the distant leak sounded repeatedly. Then, finally, the Father took his hands.

Clearing his throat, Father Morningweg began. "Father of light, within you there is no darkness—I can't do this, Sir Unger…"

"Yes, you can. It's fine. Please, Father?"

"Father of, light, within you there is no darkness. No shifting or turning of shadow. It is here in our own darkness that we beseech you for guidance. Would you reach down your hand toward us, two broken men, blind but not without sight?"

"Blind but not without sight," Torsten repeated.

"We've come to the ends of ourselves, and without your grace, we fear this is truly the end. If not for us, then for your kingdom we've come to love. Show us the way, oh, Holy Iam."

Father Morningweg cleared his throat again and released Torsten's hands.

"I'm sorry. It's been a long time."

"No, no. That was perfect. Thank you, Father," Torsten said, his heart full. He'd been so busy with the kingdom and learning how to navigate without sight. It took being thrown into a dungeon for him to have a quiet moment to look deep within and listen.

"Would it sound ridiculous if I said that actually felt good?" Father Morningweg asked.

"It's always nice to be good at something." Torsten laid a

hand upon the man's shoulder. "I'm sure you brought a great deal of hope to your people. I'm sorry about what happened to them, but maybe one day you'll find more people to give hope to. Don't lose sight."

"A tough thing to say, for us." He snickered as he drew up his blindfold slightly.

"Morningweg, it's time to go!" Valin's man Curry barked, followed by a swift kick to the bottom of the cell's bars.

"And so, it is," Father Morningweg said.

"One last favor, Father?" Torsten said. "Ignore the rumors about the Queen, true and otherwise. Offer her soul a chance at the light, and maybe Iam will take a chance on her too."

"I'll do my best. I'm a drunk, homeless priest; who am I to judge?"

Father Morningweg stood, and Torsten found himself doing the same. He wasn't sure why, but just being around the man lifted his spirits. It didn't matter that he stank like sewage. Torsten couldn't help but feel there was something special about the Father, or had been before he'd forgotten it all.

"Let's go Morningweg!" Curry ordered. "Enough playing with the guests."

"Give me a minute, Curry, you insufferable bastard," Father Morningweg snapped, again sounding nothing like a priest.

"I hope you find your way out of here, Torsten Unger," Father Morningweg said to him. "Actually, here."

Torsten listened as the priest untied something, waiting patiently. Then a damp cloth draped over his palm.

"Sorry, though I sleep like a corpse, I tend to sweat like a dog," Father Morningweg said. "There's still a bit of blood on it from that raid too. I call it good luck. Anyway, Wren the Holy blessed this worthless strip of cloth when I was confirmed into the House of Iam. He wanted me to serve as his second in the Yarrington Cathedral of Iam, to groom me. The young fool that I was wanted to *help* people and went off to Winter's yigging Thumb instead."

"I…" Torsten swallowed. "I can't accept this." He pushed it back toward Morningweg's chest.

"Please. You should wear something anyway. It helps with the itch from the burns. Hopefully, it serves you better than it did me." He took Torsten's hand and wrapped the cloth around it. "Farewell, Slayer of Redstar."

Torsten was left speechless as Morningweg stumbled off toward the exit of the cell.

"About time," Curry said as he unlocked the gate to let him out, then quickly relocked it.

"Oh, shog off," Father Morningweg said.

"By Iam, you still smell like a grave," Curry groaned.

"Well then, it's a good thing I'm off to a funeral. Now, do you plan to take my arm and lead me, or to stand around smelling my breath all night?"

Their verbal spat continued until they were out of earshot. Torsten found himself standing at the bars, listening all the way. In all his life, he'd never met a priest with such a mouth on him.

He carried the blindfold back to his spot against the wall and sat down. Then he stretched it out in front of him, running his thumb along the bumpy weave, feeling where the bloodstain had left it rigid. He brought it slowly toward his nose and took a whiff, regretting it immediately. Apparently, the stink of alcohol was carried through sweat.

"Blessed by Wren the Holy," Torsten said to himself, then laughed meekly. "If only he were here right now to help guide us all."

He placed the blindfold down and tried to relax. Now that he was alone again, he realized how hungry he was, and thirsty. If Valin wanted to break him, he expected that he wouldn't be fed until he was on the precipice of death. Shieldsmen training prepared him for such things when Uriah had him climb Mount Lister in the dead of winter with nothing but the shirt on his back.

And now that he was alone again, he was left with the same question. *What do I do now?* He had no idea how to escape on his own, especially now that all Valin's men knew to look out for him. He wished he hadn't told Abigail to run as far as she could. He wished, against every fiber of his being, that the thief Whitney Fierstown had been locked up with him.

Torsten opened his mouth to call out his name, just in case, but stopped before he did. Instead, he scratched the sudden itch burning under his right eye. As he felt the grooves in his seared skin, he gave in.

"Let's see," he said. He scooped up Father Morningweg's blindfold again. Torsten's head was far larger, as it often was with most men, so it was a tight fit once he got it tied. The front had folded over during the struggle. He shoved his finger beneath to straighten it over his cheekbones.

"Still…" Torsten lost his train of thought as his head turned, and he saw the vacillating glow of a torch outside his cell. And another, smaller one down through a tunnel. A tunnel that had form, arched with a keystone running down the center.

A tunnel, that somehow, Torsten could now see.

XXXIV

THE THIEF

"Hello!" Whitney shouted. A bit of hay blew by him, fresh out of the stable by the smell of it.

He spun. Celeste and Loutis shone on the horizon, down a dirt trail lined by familiar, wood and thatched hovels. He turned again and saw the Twilight Manor, bright with activity. The usual drunks of Troborough stood around. He spotted Hamm through the window, yammering on to the guests about something. Alless dodged a pair of groping hands on her way to serve a table. She was pretty as ever, fair skin and her hair pulled into two braids.

Whitney turned back toward the brighter of Pantego's moons. The things he would do for a proper drink, but he felt compelled in the other direction. He couldn't help it. He stumbled through the town square like he was sleepwalking. The blind priest of Troborough's face tracked him from amidst the churches ruins—Torsten once again.

"Torsten," Whitney said, snapping to. He ran up to him and said, "Torsten, what's going on?"

The hulking mass of muscle aimed his useless eyes over

Whitney's head, silently turning toward the trail. Before Whitney knew it, he was walking back along, compelled once more.

Branches rattled. Mrs. Dodson shooed some troublemaking children off her property. They ran by, laughing and pushing one another.

Whitney kept going until he reached a crude wooden fence. The gate was open, creaking in the light breeze. Through it and down a dirt path stood the home he'd grown up in. His cherry-faced mother stood in the lighted entry, waving him onward, wearing her infamous apron stained from various fruit pie fillings. His father stood behind her, arms crossed and wearing an expression equally cross.

Whitney stopped walking.

"What are you waiting for?" Kazimir's unmistakable voice asked. Whitney nearly jumped out of his shoes he was so startled. He turned to the upyr who sat on the fence, staring at an apple, turning it over in his hand. I wasn't eating it, never did. His eyes were like a coming storm, his hair silvery as a northern wolf's.

"Oh, it's just you Kazzy," Whitney said, clutching his chest. "Couldn't stay away from me, could you?"

Kazimir tested the apple with his front teeth, made a disgusted face, then tossed it over his shoulder. Just as he did, two children blew by Whitney, nearly knocking him over.

"Hey, watch i—" The words were stolen from him when he realized that it was his younger self who'd done it. But he wasn't alone. Young Sora was with him, her ears still too big for her head. Her hair was a mottled mess from whatever troublesome adventure they'd gotten themselves into in the forest.

Young Whitney darted ahead, his mother and father waving him along. Sora stopped, picked up the apple, and searched behind her. But it was as if she saw straight through Kazimir and Whitney.

"C'mon!" Young Whitney shouted. "Pie's gonna get cold."

Sora stared up at Celeste as she let the apple roll off her fingertips. She didn't seem happy and thoughtless like a child should be. Instead, her features, her posture… she seemed troubled, crushed under the weight of the world. Her gaze passed across Whitney's and he reached out to her. For a moment he thought she noticed, then she took off to join Young Whitney.

Big Whitney hurried toward the fence to watch. Young Whitney raced into the house, but as Sora tried to follow, the door slammed in her face. The sight made Whitney's heart sting.

"Sora…" he whispered.

She turned, tears in her eyes, then plopped down on the doorstep. There, she continued to stare at the night sky, eyes wet. Whitney fell to his knees, wanting to join her in crying.

"Why am I back here?" Whitney asked, voice shaking.

"Now that is a good question," Kazimir replied.

"Is this Elsewhere?"

Kazimir hopped down from the fence. He bent down, picked a bunch of grass and sniffed it. Then he opened his palm and allowed it to be caught on the wind. "Does it matter?" he said.

"Well, then why are you here?" Whitney said, nearly shouting without meaning too.

"I closed my eyes for but a moment. Or perhaps I've made another mistake and earned the punishment of the Sanguine Lords. I'm done asking why."

"Let me in!" Sora's scream echoed. Whitney's gaze snapped back up, only now she was no longer a child, and it was daytime. She was the Sora he knew now, more beautiful than the Queen of Glass herself.

Sora banged on the door to Whitney's childhood home, only now it was overgrown with vines, destitute. Her hands and arms were covered in fresh wounds, her blood staining the long grass which covered the front step.

"She's locked out," Kazimir said.

"I can see that!" Whitney snapped.

"You see nothing, fool." The upyr's strong grip found the back of Whitney's head and forced him to stare. "Look closer. An entire childhood of wanting your family for her own, she's still there, begging. Why don't you let her in?"

"I did, I…" Whitney let out an exasperated sigh. "What the yig are you talking about?"

"I can feel it on her. Smell it. The struggle, like she's neither here, nor there. Like me. She's terrified."

"She's nothing like you."

"She shouldn't be, but she is." Kazimir released Whitney's head. Then, in a flash, he was by Sora's side. She ignored him, continuing to pound on the door. He sniffed her neck, eyes rolling back into his head as if he'd taken a mouthful of manaroot. He licked his lips.

"You promised to stay away from her!" Whitney shouted. "You promised." He jumped to his feet and ran toward them. As he did, darkness crept over the ruins of his home like tendrils, or the shadow of giant hands. He heard a woman's laugh, and the sound chilled him to his core. He knew that laugh. He'd heard it from the demon claiming to be the Buried Goddess when he and Sora were both torn from Elsewhere and thrown to opposite sides of the world.

Kazimir looked to the sky, darkness turning his pale face and hair black. "You can't have her," he said.

"Kazimir!" Whitney screamed. The house seemed to grow more and more distant. He was exhausted. "Kazimir, you promised."

Kazimir breathed in slowly through his nose, lower lip trembling with desire. "I may have conquered death…" He turned to Whitney, and for just a moment a wave of sadness passed across his features. "But I am only a man. I'm sorry." He bore his fangs and plunged them into Sora's neck.

Her scream shook the earth as if the Buried Goddess cried out with her. Flames erupted from her hands and swirled around both her and the upyr. Kazimir didn't flinch, only wrenched her head to the side and drank, even as the fire had the flesh flaking off his face in embers.

"Sora, no!" Whitney screamed.

———

"Wake up."

"No!" Whitney sprung up, sweat pouring down his face, searching from side to side. "Kazimir, no… no…" he panted.

"It's just a dream, Fierstown," Rand said.

Whitney's eyes blinked blearily. His heart-rate seemed to slow. He held his hand to his face, just to test if the world was real. It didn't matter, that dream felt real too. From Sora's cries to the sense of cold which emanated from Kazimir's body.

Just a dream, he reminded himself. *Elsewhere is far behind you.*

He drew a deep breath and scanned his surroundings. The darkness was all-encompassing. The last thing he remembered before falling asleep was driving over bumpy, rocky terrain. Now the moons, Celeste and Loutis both dangled in the sky like eyeballs in the Webbed Woods.

Whitney felt a finger against his lips.

"Don't talk. Shhhhh," Rand said. "Something is wrong."

It was quiet, still, uncomfortable. The only sound was a gentle sobbing coming from somewhere to his left. Everyone in his carriage had passed out from exhaustion except Rand, and now Whitney. On both sides of the wagon, a tall, white structure stretched toward the sky and beyond that, merely darkness.

"We're on the bridge already? How did… did they kill all the guards?" Whitney asked.

"No, that's just it," Rand said. "You ever been on this bridge without getting stopped first?"

Whitney thought back to just a few days ago when he and the troupe had passed through. They'd not only been stopped, but a heavy tax had been threatened for use of the pass. He shook his head.

"I've been awake, watching," Rand said. "Not one guard. No resistance, like the bridge has been abandoned. Something is wrong."

"Think things heated up in Shesaitju? Maybe they were all called down to aid?"

"No. Something else," Rand whispered.

Straightening his back, Whitney looked through the back of the cage. Just the empty White Bridge and the towers marking its portal could be seen. There's no way anyone could have passed without being questioned by guards, least of all, foreigners with cages full of prisoners.

Drav Cra savages walked alongside the wagons like zombies from legends of the Culling in Brekliodad's dark past, their little trinkets, and tokens jingling with each step. It was an unnerving sound amid the silence. Their wagon was now side-by-side with another for the first time since their imprisonment began. The one holding his friends.

Whitney sighed. As much as he fought the belief in gods and goddesses, he couldn't help think that it was all a sick joke, like Iam, Nesilia, or some other unnamed deity sat upon a throne of skulls and bones watching as Whitney was thrown into captivity over and over again. As if Fake Troborough hadn't been enough.

Even in the darkness, Whitney could still see Conmonoc's spattered remains. Behind his mangled corpse, Gentry slept, gripping Aquira tight. Beyond them, Whitney now saw where the sobbing originated. Crying softly into her mother's chest, Talwyn's shoulders bobbed.

As Whitney watched her, a tall tower passed by, casting them in shadow. It looked normal, blue and white flags flapping lazily, the Eye of Iam emblem in their center always watching. Whitney's eyes never left the mid-point tower as it shrank into the distance. Then something glinted in Celeste's light.

"There!" Whitney whispered. "Did you see that?"

Rand silently warned Whitney to keep his voice down, then whispered, "What?"

"Something—" His words were cut off at the sound of bowstrings snapping. Small flames coursed through the sky and all around them, and fire rose from grand basins, illuminating the darkness. Anyone who was asleep slept no longer. Who could with dire wolves barking and Northmen swearing?

"Halt!" The voice carried on the open air like Iam himself. All sound stopped except for clinking jewelry and the drawing of blades.

"Ik tarvoo!" came the reply in Drav Crava.

Every heathen took up arms and shields, but it was useless. From the towers on either side of the bridge, Glass soldiers emerged with their bows trained down at the horde. And on the sides, more soldiers climbed up ropes onto the walls, having been hiding, hanging beneath it.

The Drav Cra formed a tight circle, hoping against hope to be able to stop a barrage of bow-fire if it were to come down to it. They had the numbers, but not the position.

Typical, brainless savages, Whitney thought.

"Drop your weapons, surrender the prisoners, and fall to your knees," a deep voice commanded. "Only then will your lives be spared."

"Sir Reginald," Rand remarked.

"You are nothing, puny Glassman!" Mak shouted back. "Where is Unger?"

"Come now, heathen. You didn't expect the leader of the

King's army to drop everything to stop a minor inconvenience such as yourself?"

Whitney could no longer see beyond the backs of the Drav Cra warriors and their raised shields, but he could picture Mak's face reddening at the insult. Beyond that, Whitney had to admit, it was a well-planned ambush. Torsten himself couldn't have done it better. The Drav Cra army was far more substantial, but out on the seemingly abandoned bridge, where there'd be nowhere to run, numbers hardly mattered—especially since Sir Reginald and the Glass soldiers had the high ground.

The only problem, judging by the lack of their firing, was that the Drav Cra had prisoners and the Glassmen on the bridge didn't want to die. The savages didn't seem to share that fear. They so loved being buried.

"Lower your bows, surrender the bridge to us, and we will not crush every Glassman and woman in these cages," Mak said.

"I say again, drop your weapons, and we will not litter you full of new holes," Sir Reginald retorted. Bowstrings pulled tauter. "Truly you don't believe I'd hesitate to put down rabid dogs, do you?"

Just then, the ranks parted. Drad Mak approached the wagon and began working the lock. Then the door swung open. Everyone receded from the big man, but one poor soul wasn't quick enough. The Drav Cra leader snatched him and dragged him out.

"Please, no," the man stammered. "Please!"

The circle parted, and Mak pressed himself and the prisoner through, then the circle closed again.

"I said surrender the bridge, or we kill them one by one," Mak warned.

"You say surrender. I say surrender. Can we not do this all night? There has been enough bloodshed," Sir Reginald said. "On both sides. Release the man, lay down arms, and we discuss you and your people returning home peacefully. Final warning. None of us wants to see another battle.”

“Of that,” Mak said. “You are wrong.” There was a scream followed by the distinct sound of a body hitting the hard bridge floor, then the creak of bowstrings tightening again.

“Hold your fire!” Sir Reginald said.

“Oh, but I thought it was your final warning?” Mak chortled. “I’ve learned your ways, frail man. I watched as Torsten Unger had chance upon chance to kill Drad Redstar. Saw his loyalty to— what, honor? That is why, in the end, he has lost. There is no honor. Just the mighty and the weak. Bring me another.”

Rand swore as more savages approached.

Whitney pushed his way toward the cage door, and Rand edged with him. Finally, a plan popped into his head. *Took long enough.*

“What are you—”

“Shhhh,” Whitney said.

“You’re going to get us all killed,” Barty complained and elbowed Whitney as he went by.

“Shog in a...” Whitney spat, rubbing his shoulder. After sending a sharp glare, Whitney pushed forward.

“If we get out of here,” Barty warned. “I will have you hanged.”

“Because that worked so well the first time.”

Whitney sat in the spot the unlucky Glassman had been in, directly across from the Caleef. The god-king sat cross-legged, eyes closed as if deep in meditation. If nothing else, he looked holy, but Whitney saw through the farce.

The cage door sprang open, and all the prisoners panicked. They shoved, kicked, screamed… anything to survive. All the talk of working together and learning about each other went right out the window.

Ugosah, the mustached Drav Cra, reached in and at the same

time, the Caleef's leg stretched out. The savage's hand wrapped the Caleef's delicate ankle. It was dark, but Whitney thought he saw a smirk touch the corner of Sidar Rakun's lips at the last second.

"No!" Rand screamed, lunging at the savage. Another one of them punched him square in the jaw as he did. Barty made a half-hearted attempt to hold onto Sidar, though he looked more like he didn't want to dirty his fingernails.

"Let go of him!" Rand yelled, but it was too late.

The Caleef was dragged out onto the bridge. As the cage door swung shut, Whitney pressed his cloak into the spot where the latch should've caught.

"This one's a gray skin," one of the Drav Cra said.

"Bah, they're all the same, covered in mud," the mustached Drav Cra said.

Whitney turned, looked to Rand and grinned. "I'll get the other wagon," he said. "You get this one. You get those beasts moving, and they won't stop."

"The Caleef..." Rand stared longingly out of the caravan as the Drav Cra lifted the Caleef. They took a while to do it. The man was so skinny and weak, he could barely stay upright.

"Do something, deserter," Barty snapped. "This is the only reason you were brought along."

"It's time you choose, Rand," Whitney said. "All these people, or your sister." With that, Whitney pushed the door open and hopped down. The Drav Cra were preoccupied, and he did his best to ignore the ongoing shouting feud between Sir Reginald and Drad Mak.

Whitney crouched low and snuck along the perimeter of the wagon. Looking over his shoulder once, he was relieved to see Rand was down now too. How the Shieldsman would manage to keep Darkings from following was up to him.

"Stop this madness, Mak, and we can discuss terms like men," Reginald said.

"Like you people discuss with us before you slaughtered my army in the night?" Mak shouted.

"Blame Redstar for that!"

What came next was a sound Whitney hadn't expected: laughter, in great heaps, from all the Northmen.

Whitney shuddered and ducked between the two wagons. Looking under, he could see the furred boots and hairy legs.

Then he saw even hairier legs—four of them, then eight.

Two dire wolves paced only yards away. Whitney held his breath but worried his thumping heart would be loud enough for them to hear. If not, he was sure they would smell his fear. He looked up to see Gentry gazing down as he passed, Aquira's big, sad eyes shining beside him. Whitney lifted a trembling finger to his lips and kept moving. He could only hope none of the Northmen turned around, that none of the dire wolves would notice as he climbed up to the bench overlooking the whole scene.

Two giant zhulong stood, yoked together at the necks. Whitney almost felt bad for the gentle creatures. They looked tougher than they were—but those tusks were sharp nonetheless. Grabbing the reigns, he risked giving them a light tap. Nothing happened.

"Come on," Whitney whispered. "Come on."

A snarl from his right nearly sent him reeling from his seat. One of the dire wolves stood, front paws up on the bench, back paws still on the ground. Standing erect, the thing must have been two meters tall if it was a yard. Its yellow eyes pierced the night and drool dripped from black lips.

"Good boy," Whitney said. "Good—"

The dire wolf snapped its great maw, and Whitney slapped the reigns hard against the zhulong backs. The pig-dragon beasts lurched forward, and he slapped them again. Northmen in front turned just in time to be either run over or gored by thick, sharp tusks. Blood sprayed, and the carriage jolted back and forth as the wheels bounced over the fallen Drav Cra. The chaos must have confused everyone because arrows started pouring down from above, and Northmen started chucking spears and shooting arrows of their own. A fireball from one of the warlocks traced across the night sky and blew a group of Glass soldiers off the side of the bridge.

Whitney looked back. "Everyone okay?" he said through the bars. He didn't wait for any answers. "Good. We're going back!" He turned the wagon around. It was a tight fit, but the wagon circled, and the zhulong charged back into the mob. "Hold on!"

It was like driving over boulders beyond the bridge in the Jarein Gorge. Screams and crunches echoed. More than once, Whitney had to dodge arrows, and one even landed next to him, nailing his cloak to the bench. One hand on the reigns, he used the other to tear himself free.

"My cloak!" Whitney complained. When he looked back at the road ahead, he immediately jerked the reigns, narrowly avoiding Rand running after a Drav Cra who chased after the Caleef in the chaos. Another second and Rand would've numbered amongst the dead.

"Forget him, Langley!" Whitney called.

Whitney then spotted Barty, crawling and covering his head like a coward. He was off to the side, and one yank on the zhulongs' reins and Whitney could've ended the pathetic man for good. He could get vengeance against the man responsible for sending him to Elsewhere.

His hands clenched until his knuckles whitened. Anger coursed through him. Six years without Sora only to lose her again. Six years with a murderous upyr as the only thing he could call a friend. Whitney cursed. Glass soldiers fought in a line behind him, striking out at anything in the chaos. A turn that fast might flip the wagon and damn them all to a worse fate.

Whitney glanced back at Gentry's terror-stricken face, and then he held his breath. He had to just to silence his brain. Keeping their course straight and safe, Whitney growled as the wagon raced by Bartholomew Darkings, and he lost his chance.

He'll get his, Whitney told himself. *They always do.*

Just the act of sparing the man made every part of Whitney feel numb. But he managed to keep hold of the reins and spur the zhulong toward freedom. Arrows still rained down all around, but they were nearly out of the thick of it. Toward the center of the bridge, a circle of painted Drav Cra stood hand in hand. Warriors surrounded them. Their shields were arched overhead, guarding the warlocks against arrows. A small fire began to grow in the middle of the circle, but Whitney didn't see anything else. A scream from behind him drew his attention.

"Whitney!" It was Gentry, and Aquira was growling, the sound muffled by the manacles around her snout.

Whitney turned around just in time to see a blade thrust toward his head. He dodged the brunt of it, but it still took a chunk out of his arm. Having no choice but to let go of the reins and climb to his feet, Whitney turned. He had no weapon, the Drav Cra had seen to that. A crude blade bounced off the wooden seat, and Whitney blocked another attack. It was now clear Ugosah, glorious mustache and all was determined to kill Whitney and stop the carriage.

"You're going to die, thief," the man said, jumping down onto the wagon driver's bench.

"I have a plan for that day," Whitney said, weaving away, "and today isn't it."

The man sliced downward again, and Whitney pinned the man's arm and blade to the wooden frame of the cage. The blade fell, leaving the Northman in an awkward position, but that didn't stop him from punching Whitney in the face. Two hands gripped Whitney's collar and lifted him, then slammed him down onto the top of the cage.

Whitney groaned and rolled over, awkwardly trying to find a way to stand on the metal bars. The warrior balanced himself with one hand and shoved Whitney down with the top of his axe. Whitney squirmed, but Ugosah was too big for Whitney to break free.

"Now, you die!" Ugosah said. Just as he did, Aquira flew as far as she could with her chains within the cage and dug her claws into the Northman's hand. Ugosah squealed like one of Mrs. Dodson's pigs.

"Thanks, girl!" Whitney said as he used the opening to kick out at Ugosah's feet. He successfully swiped the legs out from beneath the man and watched as Ugosah's face bounced off the bars, blood gushing from his mouth where his teeth were forced down his throat.

The Drav Cra were tough, Whitney had to give them that. The man rose alongside Whitney as if nothing had happened, sneering and licking the blood from his lips. Suddenly, the vehicle lurched as it passed from the stone bridge onto the road and Whitney almost lost his footing. Then, he did, slipping just as the warrior lunged at him. The man sailed overhead, off the wagon, and down to the hard, red rock.

Whitney coughed and wheezed, legs inside the carriage on either side of a metal bar. He laid there for a minute, listening to his friends beneath him cheer. He didn't feel like cheering at all. Eventually, the wagon came to a halt. The battle sounds were distant now. Slowly, Whitney rose and looked back, choking against the pain.

The other wagon, Rand, Barty— they were nowhere in sight. There was just a blaze of orange light emanating from the bridge, not so different from Sora's fire, and screams filling the air.

Whitney's eyes drifted down to the cage filled with the Glintish troupe and some others from Fettingborough. The tears he saw were welcome—something he hadn't seen in far too long... Joy.

Whitney stepped down to the bench and watched as the two zhulong which were supposed to be pulling them had stopped to eat shrubs on the side of the road. He hadn't saved everybody, but he knew from stories that sometimes heroes had to make choices. That not everybody could be saved.

Aquira clattered to the edge of the cage and nestled against his hand. Gentry cried happily. By the sounds of it, Talwyn, Lucy and others did the same. Rand's fight wasn't over yet, but they—Whitney's people—were safe.

XXXV

THE DAUGHTER

Mahraveh knelt in the shallow water on the floor of her warrior's chambers cavern, washing the blood from her hands and forearms. She scrubbed hard at her fingernails with a bit of sponge from the Intsti Reef.

Suddenly, she heard a gasp. She turned and saw Jumaat finally coming to. He'd been out so long, she'd been worried she gave him too much laca leaf.

"W… what happened?" he groaned, rubbing his head.

"The Ayerabi champion advanced."

"The what?" He looked down, and when he realized he was wearing nothing but a loin-cloth, and that Mahraveh was wearing his armor, covered in fresh dents and drying blood, his voice raised an octave. "Mahi, what did you do?"

"Something drastic." She couldn't believe she was repeating the words of Yuri Darkings, of all people.

"You didn't—"

"I'm sorry, Jumaat. I couldn't risk it."

"I… you… How?"

She turned fully to face him, then she reached to the side and lifted the helm over her head to show how it concealed her. "No

one questioned a thing. It's fortunate you're as skinny as a girl."
She flashed a smirk; his features darkened.

"This is not a joke, Mahi!" He went to stand, but was still
faint and fell against the bed. "I swore before the sea, like all the
tributes, to fight with honor. Before the God of Sand and Sea. It's
sacred!"

"I know you did. But I swore to my father I would find a way
to help."

"So all that training. You were lying to me the whole time?"

"I wasn't lying. I just couldn't—"

"Risk me dying like a fool?" He turned away and crossed his
arms. "Don't worry. I get it. But what do you plan on doing when
they realize who you are?"

"I was hoping they wouldn't."

"You have never been here for the crowning of an afhem.
How would you know? When they strip them down and shave
their head into the sea. Are you some sort of mystic who could
replace yourself with me on a whim?"

"I don't know, Jumaat. But I know I can win."

"And I can't," he said, punching the floor where he still sat.
"Got it."

"That's not what I'm saying."

"Yes, it is, even if you won't say it out loud."

"I didn't think—"

"That is right! You didn't think! It does not matter that you're
a woman. They cast men who break sacred vows into the Boiling
Waters. They'll kill us both when they find out, especially with
Babrak running things."

"I can convince them not to."

"You can't do the impossible. You have to let me fight in the
final round, Mahi. It is the only way."

"So you can be afhem?" she said. "Because a woman
can't be."

"That is not my decision."

"Neither is this." She turned to him. She pictured the size of Rajeev and all of the others. She didn't know who'd advanced before or after her, but she could only imagine. They'd crush Jumaat into the sand.

"I'm fighting," she said. "Whatever happens after, that's in our God's hands. You have to trust me."

"I did," he said softly. She noticed him staring at her hands before she realized she'd half dropped into black fist stance.

"Jumaat." She approached the bed and went to take his hand, but he pulled away.

"I hope you win, Mahi," he said. "For all our sakes."

"I will. I'll make all of this right, and then we'll sail off to save our fathers together. I promise you on the Black Sands and the Boiling Waters, and all that lies in between. I told you, I refused to lose you."

Silence passed between them until finally, he regarded her. "And you never will." He exhaled and took her hand. "I understand, my lady. It should have been you from the start. I just…"

"I know. And I'm sorry I poisoned you."

"You know me too well. I would have never let you go out there otherwise, even if it meant my certain death."

"My protector." She lay down in the bed, her weary limbs making it easy. Jumaat joined her, so they were side by side, hands still clasped.

"At least now, if things go wrong, we'll die together," Jumaat said.

"We'll be old and gray by the time that happens."

"Yeah? How do you know?"

"The sea told me," Mahraveh said, nestling her head into the crook of Jumaat's neck.

"She's wise as she is deadly. She told me I'd never win, and it turned out true." He rolled onto his side, facing her. His free hand ran across her cheek. Mahraveh thought about answering, but the warmth of his hand coupled with exhaustion from battle, she had already started to lull.

All it took was one close of her eyelids, and she was out. Jumaat never left her side.

"Ayerabi!" came a voice accompanied by a knock at the door.

Mahraveh sprang up, toppling off the bed.

"Why is your door barred?" the guard outside asked.

Mahraveh froze, then Jumaat said, "I did not wish to be bothered before the fight." She glanced up and found him beaming from ear to ear. "I have been praying."

"Is that what they call it?" Mahi whispered.

Jumaat put a finger to his lips and gave her a stern look.

"Of course," the guard said. "Well, I bring a meal prepared by the Caleef's own chef. Eat, then report to the weapons stand."

Mahraveh waited a few seconds before cracking open the door. She snatched the clamshell plate and barred it again.

"Thanks," she said.

"Mmhmm," Jumaat replied. "That looks good."

Mahi slapped his hand away. "I need my strength."

Her final meal did smell delicious—roasted pit lizard and rock crab curry. It was a Shesaitju staple, drawing on both the sand and sea and as vivid in its red color as the reef itself. She hadn't realized how starving she was until then. She started shoveling into her mouth when Jumaat crouched beside her.

"Careful, I might have poisoned it," he said.

"I'll take my chances," she said, mouth full.

"I suppose I should ask you if you're ready this time," he said.

"No," she answered. "But I have to be." She devoured the last bit of food, scraping her finger along the bottom and sides of the shell. She wished there was more, but knew a full belly was dangerous in battle. It would just slow her down.

"They have no idea how strong you are," Jumaat said.

"I just hope that bastard Rajeev made it," she replied.

"Don't be vengeful."

"I need to put on a show," she said. "Otherwise, like you said, Babrak will have me killed the moment I'm revealed. When the people see that his best man died to a woman—"

"He'll have to save face. Always a step ahead of me, Lady Ayerabi."

"Just do me a favor."

He grasped her hand. "Anything."

"If I die out there, and they realize who I am—or I win, and Babrak can't be swayed—and come for you… Get out of here."

"I will not run."

"I'm not asking you to. Find the Glassman, Yuri Darkings. Our fathers don't have long, and he has the wealth to make a deal. Use it to convince Babrak to help, or to make a deal with the Glass Kingdom. Do whatever it takes to save our fathers, so they may live to fight another day."

"You have my word." He spat in his palm and extended a hand. She did the same before shaking it. But he didn't release. He pulled her into a tight embrace, their foreheads touching. "But you will win, Mahraveh Ayerabi. And throughout the Black Sands, the people will sing the name of the first female afhem, champion of the Tal'du Dromesh. Then we'll save our fathers."

Mahraveh choked back tears. "For Saujibar," she said.

"For our home."

She closed her eyes, breathing in his scent. It reminded her of that home, and she would let that memory fuel her. When they released, she stood, and without another word, she headed out the door, ready to do what needed to be done.

Guards met her and led her to another gate leading into the

sand pit. She stood alone this time, her spear resting against the wall. She gripped it and held it up, remembering all those years of training beside her father. She wished he could see her now.

A rumble and the metallic clanking of chains was her first warning as the gate began to rise. The next was the roar of the audience.

The sun sat high, warming the top of the arena for the finale, while the sands and all the bottom were bathed in the green of the tremendous nigh'jel globe hanging overhead. From smaller gates all around the circumference of the arena, her opponents were let out one at a time. She didn't recognize any of them except for Rajeev—of course, he'd made it—but counted four others. That meant the beasts had slain two other warriors, including Amoud.

"Latiapur!" the eunuch shouted. "Enough games!" Beastmasters prodded a growling desert leopard into a caged entry. Others cleared the corpse of the pit lizard it had apparently battled. Mahraveh had wondered what the crowd was clamoring over before she was let out.

"Honored combatants, the sea swells for your mighty performances," the eunuch went on. "But only one of you will claim afhemdom. I wish it could be you all, but that is not the way of our people. Only the mighty may endure the whipping sands and crushing waves."

The other combatants spat in their hands and ran them through the sand, and this time Mahraveh joined them at the proper time.

"We give honor, to you, our combatants. Death comes to all, but for one of you, let it not be for years to come. May the eternal current guide you."

"May the eternal current guide me!" the combatants echoed, just as they had last time. Between then and when the fight was signaled to start, Mahraveh closed her eyes and breathed in. The sea was near. She could smell the salt. And she could smell the stink of death and rotting corpses filling her home. All because the leaders of her brave people had taken a fondness for cowardice.

By the time her eyes re-opened, the others had fanned out. Rajeev broke rank and charged, relentlessly attacking another combatant. Metal sparked, but Mahi couldn't watch. A reedy looking warrior stalked toward her. His tattoos were distinct against his bare arms, and so were the many scars.

When he was close enough, he feinted a thrust with one thin sword only to stab upward with the other. Mahraveh saw it coming and knocked it aside with the shaft of her spear. She recognized the ruse right away. The man expected her to block and anticipated her trying to use the advantage to attack, but she didn't. Instead, she leaned back and brought her spear vertical, spear tip directly in front of her face.

These were the best of the combatants. She couldn't extend herself without studying them first. The way his hands gripped his weapons. The way his hips moved when he stepped into a stroke.

He smiled, approaching again. Their weapons play lasted for several minutes, Mahi deflecting every attack. He wasn't overly strong in comparison, so using his weight was easy. She waited until frustration of not being able to pierce her defenses mounted, then finally saw the opening she needed. She sliced the warrior's hand, causing him to drop one sword.

"You are a warrior, not an artist," she remembered Muskigo tell her. *"Do not look for the one-hit kill. Slice them a thousand times if need be and watch them bleed out."*

She lashed twice more, drawing two deep gashes on his arm before he recovered. His stance didn't allow a strike at anywhere more vital without her leaving herself vulnerable to his remaining sword. Blood flowed freely down the warrior's arm, but he didn't relent. The scars were proof he was no stranger to battle. Unfortunately, Mahi was. She'd trained with the best, but actual combat was new to her.

The warrior raked his weapon around and caught Mahraveh on the hip. It wasn't deep but it stung. He swiped again, but she was ready this time. She allowed his blade to slide along her spear pole and cut her hand, but he extended his arm too far. He was off-balance for only a moment, but it was enough for Mahraveh to dig her spear tip into the side of his neck. She removed it, and his lifeless body dropped.

She wiped the blood from her brow and saw Rajeev still fought on the other side of the arena, two corpses at his feet

Mahraveh began to make her way toward him when she noticed another man to her right. He'd killed an opponent and was closer to her. The three of them exchanged glances, then Rajeev grinned and bowed, and invited Mahraveh and the other to fight each other.

"Don't let me interrupt you," he said.

The other warrior didn't. He gripped a spear from his fallen foe and threw it at Mahi as hard as he could. She wasn't used to dealing with such speed. She spun, the blade grazed the side of her helmet on its way by. She landed on her hands and feet like a cat, then sprung back upright. The crowd seemed delighted by the display.

The third man charged her, wielding a sickle-blade. She flipped backward as he swung. Her back heel strung on the landing, but she pushed forward, following beneath another of his swipes and gashing the side of his torso.

She was about to spin to face him when she realized Rajeev was done waiting. His axe raced toward her head, and she evaded it just in time, but not enough to avoid his massive frame. She slammed into his hip and twisted, earning an elbow to the gut that sent her to the sand.

Rajeev could have crushed her beneath his foot if the other didn't come at him. His sickle-blade cut and slashed. It was a rare warrior who could master such a weapon, but the unpredictability made it proficient in one-on-one combat. Rajeev parried, but he was on his heels, his back to her.

Mahraveh caught her breath and prepared to make her move, but as she stood, a bellot pelted her in the helmet. The crowd booed a patron who'd decided to interrupt the fight. Guards stormed down the stands to arrest him. All Mahraveh noticed was Babrak up above, a smirk smeared across his face. She couldn't imagine what he'd paid the man to defy honor like that.

She turned back to the fighting and saw Rajeev get close enough to daze his opponent with a head butt. The man staggered, tried to strike, but Rajeev caught his arm and pulled him into the waiting tip of his blade. Rajeev heaved the man over his shoulder, blood showering him before the man slid off like meat from a skewer.

Rajeev puffed out his chest and roared, breathing in the adoration of the crowd. Again Mahraveh saw her opening and took off. She was only a couple of meters away when she stabbed at him, but she was overeager, like a sand snake must never be if it wishes to survive.

Rajeev spun, deflecting her spear just to the right of his torso, and he elbowed back, catching her in the nose-piece of her helmet. She landed with a thud on top of the other warrior, the air evacuating her lungs as his knee dug into her back.

"My apologies, boy," Rajeev said as he stepped down on Mahi's fighting hand. Her fingers released the grip of her spear, and he lowered the tip of his axe blade to her throat. He looked up to Babrak and the others—an opportunity to gloat. But it was also the opportunity Mahi needed.

With her other hand, she grabbed a fistful of bloodied, black sand and threw it into Rajeev's eyes. Instinctively, his hand went to his face, his foot backed off her hand, and she was able to roll to her feet.

The crowd stood in anticipation.

Her spear still lay on the ground at his feet, but she didn't need it.

"You filthy, pis'truda!" Rajeev barked. "Fight with honor!"

"You tell me to fight with honor, yet you fight for that sack of zhulong shog?"

With that, Mahraveh dropped back into the black fist stance. She took a deep breath, and everything around her seemed to vanish except for the sounds of battle. They played in her ear like music as she closed her eyes. The gentle beat of footfalls. The sound of steel cutting the air. She bent her knees and felt the wind of Rajeev's axe slicing above her head. She rolled backward, then sprang up, extending her feet. They connected with his ribs, and she heard a crunch. Small as she was, black fist taught its wielder how to focus strength to a singular point.

"Impressive," Rajeev said, clenching his jaw. "But there's no way a child will best me."

She didn't speak. Didn't move. Remained steady and calm in her black fist stance.

"Black fist?" he said. "In a fight between fist and steel, I'll take my steel."

Rajeev came forward, driving his axe downward. Mahraveh spun aside and punched Rajeev under his arm. The force was like that of a battering ram. She'd once seen her father kill a zhulong with one punch, and she was sure the other afhems weren't as graced in the ancient martial arts as he.

Rajeev grunted and swung again, this time in a horizontal plane directed at her neck. She easily ducked and punched again, this time connecting on the other side. She could tell Rajeev was getting angry, which was precisely what she wanted.

A fighter who's judgment was clouded by anger was a fighter who made mistakes.

She noticed Rajeev tighten his grip on the axe handle as he moved in again. This time, she didn't wait for him to strike.

I am the snake.

She kicked twice, each one like a horse hoof into each of the man's shins. He doubled over, and she drove her fist down on his head. The followthrough left him sprawled out in the sand, cursing. He tried to get up, but he swayed as he did and staggered to the side.

Mahraveh kicked his axe aside and didn't bother looking to the crowd for approval before she straightened her hand, clenched her fist, and drove it straight into Rajeev's chest. The bones crunched, piercing his heart, as he flew back onto the sand.

Mahraveh couldn't hear even her own heartbeat over the cheers of the crowd. She looked around, her vision red and unfocused. The bodies of her opponents lay all over. Some headless, and some just a frayed mess of ligaments shredded by many cuts.

In the distance, she heard the game master's voice. She expected another round with some foul beast, although she knew she'd never be able to survive it. It took every bit of her focus to punch Rajeev in a way that would affect the mountain of muscle. He lay on his back, lips trembling as he struggled to speak. The eternal current would take him soon.

"Jumaat of the Ayerabi," the game master roared, and the crowd shouted back.

"Jumaat! Jumaat! Jumaat!"

Mahraveh stepped forward, looking up toward Babrak, then at the games master. By now, he was a tall silhouette against the blinding sun. The crowd continued to cheer, and for once she didn't feel like waiting for something to happen. Waiting for her father to come back. Waiting for the Glass to attack. Waiting to help.

She reached up, grasped her helmet, and tossed it aside. The collective gasp of the crowd as her dreadlocked hair fell to her shoulders and beyond made even the cheers seem like gentle whispers. Babrak and the other afhems leaped to their feet. Far behind them, Yuri Darkings stood as well. She thought she could see the smile across his face before he stood and headed out of the arena.

"What madness is this?" Babrak demanded, clamoring to the end of the walkway. He shoved the games master aside, nearly sending him off the side of the walkway. It bolstered Mahi's resolve, reminding her of what he'd done to Farhan. "You are not Jumaat," he said.

"I am not," Mahraveh said.

"Deceiver!" an afhem cried out. "Cheater."

"What is the meaning of this?" the eunuch asked.

"Jumaat took the oath on the sand and sea, but he is no warrior. I am. Trained by my father, Muskigo Ayerabi. The Scythe —who won his name on these very sands.

"This is an outrage!" Babrak shouted.

"Afhem Trisps'i," the eunuch said. "You will calm yourself."

"Quiet, you!" Babrak grabbed the man by the robes and shoved him further behind him. "This cannot be allowed. You have deceived us all, and taken a place not meant for you.

"What? Have I not done what is required of any warrior?" Mahraveh paced the sand, looking up at the crowd as she did. "Have I not defeated the same number of foes as any other who won their afhemate through this hallowed place?"

"You are a woman!" Babrak said.

"Are women disqualified? Or are you embarrassed that the greatest warriors in the Black Sands fell to someone who should be fanning you and stuffing your fat belly?"

"You will watch the way you speak to me—"

"Are we not equals now, oh, mighty Babrak?"

"We are nothing! Can't you all see how the progeny of Muskigo is so like him? They don't respect our customs, our laws! Because of them, our Caleef is missing. Our enemies are at our doorsteps. Have you not heard about how Saujibar was raided by Glassmen? Enemies, brought by her father's lack of trust. You would hand the great al-Tariq afhemate over to this... this... this ingrate!"

Many other afhems came to Babrak's side as if supporting him. But not all. She recognized the head of the Jalurahbak afhemate as well as the Avassu. She'd fought and killed one of their champions with honor, and watched the other fall.

"A woman has never fought upon the sands," Avassu said, "nor lead an afhemate. But no law forbids."

"And what of broken vows made in the name of our God? What would the Caleef say if he were here?"

Afhem Avassu stroked his long beard but said nothing.

"Would we declare no victor then?" the eunuch asked.

"Quiet, you sackless piece of shog!" Babrak grabbed him and threw him against the wall of their viewing box. "It does matter that she's a woman!" Babrak shouted to the crowd. "It matters that her family thinks they are above our laws."

"Then throw another of your champions at me!" Mahraveh shouted. "I'll kill him, too. I'll kill anyone you send in here until all of you realize we don't have to be lap dogs to the Glass any longer. Liam is dead, and my father proved our strength at Winde Port!"

"Before the gods punished him with fire! Sent him crawling to the city of Afhem Calidor, one of those poor fools who thought to support him. He's probably dead now."

"Had you stood with him instead of hiding here, maybe that wouldn't be the case."

"Silence!" A powerful, matronly voice filled the arena, striking silence into everyone. Sand swirled about the center, revealing the shape of a woman covered in seaweed, shells, and coral—one of the Sirens. Mahi didn't know much about the Tal'du Dromesh, but she'd never heard stories of the Sirens at one of the tournaments.

Mahraveh wasn't sure why but she fell to one knee. If all the dealings with fighting and Babrak hadn't done it, her skin was now coated in goosebumps. Even the grand nigh'jel globe grew brighter, painting even the sky a sickly shade of green.

She dissipated into a puff of sand, then appeared beside Mahraveh. Her bumpy fingers ran upon her cheek. "Your story does not end here," she whispered.

Mahraveh couldn't even think of how to respond.

"A sacred vow was made to our realm!" the Siren then said, her voice now carrying. "To fight with honor to the death and the eternal current. This daughter of the sands and matron of the sea has broken nothing. We see in her heart that she would have upheld this vow but for the chance to make it."

"Holy Siren, if I may—" Babrak began.

"I said, silence!" Her voice thundered. Mahraveh couldn't tell if it was herself shrieking, or the crowd. "But a vow was broken, as the waves against the cliffs, and the God of Sand and Sea doesn't abide weakness." The Siren reappeared directly in front of Mahraveh and stared at her. Her dark eyes churned the deepest blue like the Boiling Waters during a typhoon.

"Mahraveh al-Tariq, she will be," the Siren said, floating in a circle around Mahraveh. She could hear Babrak's groan of disapproval along with his gaggle of sycophants. "But the sea will have its payment."

The Siren vanished again, and Mahraveh spun, following a trail of black sand floating to the center of the arena. When the tempest calmed, Mahraveh saw that Jumaat stood in front of her, stripped bare.

He searched from side to side, face contorted by terror. Then his gaze froze on Mahraveh.

"No!" she screamed.

His eyes were glued to Mahi's as the Siren pressed her lips against his. The gray drained from his face until it was white, his veins popping out like the strands of a spider web. His cheeks shriveled, eyes, still on Mahi's, bulging. When the Siren backed away, his desiccated corpse turned to ash and fell in a pile to the ground.

Mahraveh did the same, sliding on her knees as she cried out. The Siren faced her, then the crowd. "The sand and sea are just," she said. "But they are not merciless." Then, as quickly as she'd appeared, the Siren was gone, black dust dithering around where she'd been.

All noise in Tal'du Dromesh stopped. Mahraveh crawled to the gray mound of ash that was Jumaat. She lifted her hands, dust sifting through her fingers. Then, looking upward, she let out a cry of anguish. The only sound in the whole arena.

XXXVI

THE DESERTER

"It's time you choose, Rand," Fierstown said. "All these people, or your sister."

Rand felt his heart drop as the words reached his ears. He'd gone so far for her already. Sided with men who may as well have been devils, all to free her from the fear of savages like the ones about to murder these innocent people—Whitney Fierstown and Bartholomew Darkings excluded.

Before he could respond, Fierstown opened the cage and slipped out.

"Langley," Bartholomew said. "Rand."

Rand ignored him. "Iam, help me," he whispered to the sky, though he didn't imagine that after all he'd done, Iam would care to listen at all. Then he followed Fierstown out onto the bridge, staying low. The Drav Cra were busy handling the Caleef while Mak and Sir Reginald played their game of *who wants to die first?*

Rand Langley's heart raced. He'd been in battles before, but never with such dismal chances of survival. Never this outnumbered. It didn't help that he was following a mad fool who only seemed out for himself.

What did I do to deserve this? He remembered the bodies swinging in the dry, cold air thanks to Queen Oleander's cruelty. He remembered running as masked cultists turned the city where he'd grown up into a nightmare. He remembered his own disgust when he discovered that Valin Tehr had Sidar Rakun in his clutches, before signing up to deliver the Caleef home to the Black Sands.

Rand knew what he deserved.

The thief paused by the two zhulong pulling the other wagon. "Fierstown," Rand whispered, but heard no answer. Rand's gaze darted back toward the Caleef. The savages had him upright and dragged him along toward Mak. That gray man was everything, the key to Sigrid's life. And the savages didn't even care that he wasn't a Glassman, as covered in mud as the prisoners were, it was hard to even tell the color of his skin.

Barty was at the back of the cage, fingers wrapped around the bars and staring with that haughty expression he so often wore. Nothing would've made Rand happier than finishing this quest and never having to see the traitorous lech again.

"Fierstown," Rand repeated, harsher this time. When he turned back, he saw the thief in the wagon's driver's seat, holding the reins. Goose pimples coated Rand's arms in a flash. A dire wolf gnashed at Fierstown, ready to tear his head off in a single snap.

Rand rushed to help, pushing his boots off the stone as hard as he could, but Fierstown smacked the reins, and the zhulong pulled. The canine beast's razor-sharp teeth tore a chunk out of the side of the wagon before the heavy wheels knocked it aside.

Rand was certain Whitney didn't plan it, but chaos ensued. The growling wolf and the cracking reins frightened the zhulong, and they took off at full speed, crushing whatever stood in their way. The Drav Cra panicked and attacked. The Glassmen did the same.

Arrows and spears soared while armor and shields *clanked*. Rand might've panicked too. However, he could lose all his titles, all his self-respect, but nothing could take away his Shieldsman training.

He spun back in the Caleef's direction. The savage had tossed him aside like spoiled meat and drew his axe. In Rand's peripheral, he saw a warlock pull a knife and slash open his hand. Rand shot forward and barreled into the man just as he summoned a fireball to launch at one of the defense towers. The brilliant, orange orb of death sailed harmlessly over the bridge as Rand stole the knife and plunged it straight through the heathen's painted forehead.

He'd learned what they were capable of using blood magic, so an instant kill was the only option.

A screeching drew Rand's attention. Behind him, the thief had turned the wagon hard to head back east into the Wildlands—Iam knows why—and it nearly tipped over before slamming down. Then, shooting forward behind the power of two frightened zhulong, it crushed a dozen men.

Rand also saw the Caleef rob one of his captors of a boot dagger and ram it into his back. The frail god-king didn't even knock him over, and the savage whipped around, smacking the Caleef in the face and kicking him to the ground. Then he brandished his axe, and stalked toward the fallen Caleef.

Fierstown's wagon raced along the path Rand needed to take to save Sidar Rakun. Meanwhile, Bartholomew Darkings had climbed out of the other cart and crawled like a beggar looking for crumbs. An arrow clattered next to him, and he looked like he was going to shog himself. The other prisoners wisely stayed in the cage where they were safe from arrows.

"Stay strong, Sigrid," Rand said under his breath. Then, ignoring Darkings, he bolted toward the Caleef. The thief's wagon swerved, just missing him. Rand could feel the wind of it rushing by against the back of his wet neck.

"Forget him, Langley!" Fierstown called out.

Rand glanced back to see the dastardly thief taking one hand off the reins to salute before scrambling to grab it again. In that second, Rand realized that Bartholomew wasn't far off the path. He wasn't exactly sure why the thief hated him so—though it wasn't hard to imagine. With only the slightest veering of the cart, Fierstown could've flattened him. Only, he didn't.

The heartless bastard who plucked the Glass Crown right off the head of a dying King Liam turned down vengeance to keep his friends safe. After all that happened, Rand was having a difficult time keeping faith. As he, Grint, and Bartholomew traveled across Pantego with their royal quarry, stopping in taverns and hearing citizens bemoaning the kingdom and war, it was more difficult every day having faith in anything. More and more, it seemed that monsters like Valin Tehr were primed to take over, that the time of honor and nobility was crumbling in the hands of queens like Oleander.

The sight buoyed Rand's spirits as he turned back toward his mission and slammed into the Drav Cra warrior just before the man's axe split the Caleef's skull. The weapon clattered out of his grasp, and Rand tangled with him on the ground. The hulk of muscle flipped Rand over and drove a fist into his cheek. Rand absorbed the beating and stretched his hand, clawing with fingers, bloody and hurting, until they found the axe's shaft.

He could only brush it with the tip of his index finger until the Caleef managed to compose himself and kick it closer. An instant later, the blade sank in and out the savage's skull, and Rand rolled free, now armed.

"Sidar, get to me!" he shouted.

The terrified Caleef remained on the ground, eyes wide and white as Loutis. He'd probably never seen so much blood, let alone been in a battle—pampered his whole life. The entire journey, every time they heard a wolf howl in the night or a galler *caw,* the man would flinch like an explosion went off.

Rand hurried to him. One of the Glass soldiers who'd been hiding under the bridge leaped out. Rand ducked left, a longsword humming by his head.

"I'm not—" he said, but the man took another slash and Rand hopped back, getting his axe up just in time to parry the next strike. With a horrifying snarl, a dire wolf crashed into the Glassman's side and sent him hurtling off the bridge. An arrow from the towers struck the beast as it glared over the side, barely piercing its thick hide. Its head turned, yellow eyes and blood-stained fangs like something out of a nightmare.

"Let's go!" Rand grabbed the Caleef's hand, heaved him to his feet, and pulled him along into the fray, heading east off the White Bridge. Arrows continued *clacking* down from above and *thunking* into flesh. Drav Cra dropped like so many flies. Rand understood the strategy. He hated it, but he understood. The Glassmen on the bridge were fodder to keep the Drav Cra occupied while arrows tore the Northmen apart. Sir Unger was never so cruel as to sacrifice lesser soldiers, but Torsten was no longer in charge.

The Caleef yelped, then yanked so hard on Rand's wrist that Rand went down too. As he dropped, the dire wolf leaped over them, its massive body blotting out Celeste for a moment.

The wolf's claws shot up sparks as it skidded to a stop and reared back, sights set on the two of them.

"S... S... Sir Langley," the Caleef stammered.

Rand squeezed the axe until his knuckles throbbed, rose to his heels, and prepared to take the beast on. From the side, a Glassman thrust a spear into the dire wolf's belly and garnered its attention. The roar pierced through all other sounds, and a mighty swipe left four massive gashes across the soldier's chest.

"C'mon!" Rand lifted the Caleef again and ran. The wagon was ahead of them now, the prisoners crying, terrified. One got too scared and tried to run, but was immediately struck in the throat by a stray arrow. One of the zhulong drawing the wagon had been riddled with arrows and collapsed in front of the other which struggled to try and drag the wagon forward over its corpse.

"Help us!" the prisoners inside yelled.

Rand and the Caleef raced by it, and then he heard Whitney Fierstown's voice in the back of his mind. *It's time you choose, Rand.*

Rand cursed, stopped, and yanked the Caleef toward the cart. He shoved him down, under cover of one of the wheels, then turned and sliced the yoke free from the dead zhulong and rammed the other with his shoulder. The beast was dumb, and he needed it to stop struggling to climb the corpse of the other and go around.

Rand sh

outed at it to move as he pushed to try and free it. It was no use. He paused for a moment to catch his breath, then noticed Bartholomew, lying beneath the corpse of a Drav Cra warrior, furs stretched to help hide him.

"Help me!" Rand yelled.

The cowardly traitor held his finger to his lips then shooed him away.

"Darkings, you bloody, yigging coward!"

Rand cursed again, louder this time, then continued to push the zhulong to help free it. He was about to give up when Javaud, the man Rand had caught sneaking manaroot, appeared at his side and pushed with him. The zhulong backed up a bit with their combined strength.

"Just a little more," Rand strained to say through his teeth.

"Thank y—" Javaud's response was cut short when an arrow

jammed straight into the center of his back. Javaud fell flat against the side of the zhulong. An onslaught of arrows, more than any time earlier in the ambush, filled the sky like a swarm of angry bees.

"Take them down!" Sir Reginald yelled from somewhere.

"No!" Rand screamed. He turned to cover Javaud, then saw why the Glassmen had unleashed such a barrage. In the center of the bridge, four warlocks stood in a circle, blood draining from their wrists so fast they wouldn't survive long. Flame wreathed them, turning every arrow aimed at them to ash before they struck.

"Now!" Mak the Mountainous thundered.

"The Buried Goddess watches from below," the warlocks all chanted in sync. Their voices carried on the air, ripples of distortion making every word echo.

"The eyes of all the world shall fall upon the White Bridge," one voice said, louder than all the rest. "Your sacrifice here shall not be in vain."

In one smooth motion, the warlocks threw up their blood-covered arms. Flame consumed them, swirling about their bodies and coating their skin. They became the fire itself, and then like four snakes they shot forward toward the towers on either side of the White Bridge. The tops of each tower exploded. Glassmen flew off, into the Jarein Gorge and on the bridge.

The deafening *bangs* were enough to startle the zhulong more than arrows or clanging steel could. It pushed free of the corpse, knocking Rand and Javaud's body free as well. One of the wagon's back wheels hit the tusk of the dead animal and snapped off, bouncing over the edge of the bridge. The other cracked in half.

The wagon nearly tipped, but the zhulong, so filled with adrenaline, dragged it along even with the back wheels broken. Rand didn't have long to come to grips with the fact that their one ride to safety was now destroyed, or that all those poor souls in the cage might have lost a chance at survival.

Stone and other material rained down in every direction, pelting Rand's back as he continued to cover Javaud's body. All that was left where the warlocks stood chanting was a circle of bones. Their ash filled the air like heavy snow, concealing the light of the moons.

"Slaughter them all!" Mak roared.

Rand tried to stand, but his ears rang from the explosion. The smog of smoke, soot, and ash made it impossible to see clearly. He could feel the heat in his lungs. He could taste the warlocks' disgusting flesh. The sounds of battle amplified, and though he couldn't tell who was screaming or grunting, he knew that the warlocks' blood magic had turned the tide.

Someone coughed beside him. Rand squinted down and saw the Caleef, almost invisible with all the ash matching his skin tone.

"Sir Langley…" he wheezed. "What now?"

"When I say run, you run," Rand replied. "Don't stop for anything. I didn't go through all of this for you to die on this Iam-forsaken bridge."

The Caleef nodded.

Several seconds passed while Rand watched for an opening. "Run!" Rand lifted the Caleef, and they took off through the smog. All he could see was shapes and motion; sparks as metal collided. But the arrows had stopped flying, which provided an opening.

An axe swung at Rand's head. He evaded it, ducking and punching up at the wielder's face. Then he brought up his blade and slashed the man across the chest. He tossed him aside and continued running, the Caleef right beside him.

Another Drav Cra warrior charged through the smog at the Caleef. Rand veered to intervene and was about to spear the man with his shoulder when someone yelled, "Langley, help me!"

A hand snagged Rand's ankle. He tripped and was only able to gash the Caleef's attacker on the leg with his still-drawn blade. The warrior lost his footing and smashed into the Caleef at full speed, knocking him off balance.

Rand glanced back and saw Bartholomew, still huddled beneath furs and so soot-coated he looked like a Shesaitju himself. Darkings grasped frantically at Rand's ankle again, completely overwrought with fear like a drowning man pushing down on heads to survive. Desperate.

Rand kicked Darkings in the jaw and broke free, lurching forward and narrowly avoiding losing his head to the injured warrior's axe. Instead, the thick blade scraped Rand's shoulder as Rand slammed the Drav Cra's head against the stone on his way back to his feet.

"Sidar!" he yelled, coughing on the acrid air. "Sidar!" Rand spun and saw a pair of gray hands gripping the bridge's railing to his right. The Caleef angled over the gorge, a hundred meters above the rapids which emptied into Trader's Bay further south.

Rand lunged forward and grabbed the Caleef's forearm just as his fingers gave out. He heaved the god-king up, safely draping his torso over the railing until the brunt of his weight was on the bridge.

Out of the corner of his eye, he saw another weapon rushing at him, this one a longsword belonging to a Glassman. He left the Caleef where he was and got his dagger up to deflect the strike. Then he swung in a wide arc to build distance between himself and the attacker. Only, another attack never came.

"R... Rand Langley?" the man said. Rand squinted to see clearer and realized that it was Sir Reginald. They'd trained together, what seemed like a lifetime ago. A few times, the Shieldsman had even joined him and the other trainees where

Sigrid worked at Maiden's Mugs. Rand didn't know him well, but he didn't have to. The bond of Shieldsmen ran deep.

"Sir Reginald," Rand said, breathless. "Sir Reginald, please, you have to help us get off this bridge."

"They say you saved Sir Unger, they…" His eyes darted over to the Caleef who was busy pulling himself the rest of the way over the railing. Shieldsmen were trained to look deeper, to see the world. It didn't take a genius to put two and two together. Sir Reginald had likely been there, months ago when the Caleef visited the Glass Castle for King Pi's coronation and was subsequently imprisoned.

"Is that…" Reginald said, now equally breathless. "That word you were yelling. 'Sidar…'"

"It's not what it looks like," Rand said. "Please, just listen to me."

"It was you. Traitor!" Sir Reginald screamed and charged. Rand barely had time to defend himself. Killing Drav Cra in the name of saving his sister was easy, but a Shieldsman was a different story. He slid left, pinned Reginald's sword with the forearm, kicked, and then pushed him away.

"Sir Reginald, listen to me!" Rand pled.

The Shieldsman clenched his teeth and rushed Rand again, but a *whoosh* of air sent him sprawling back. Rand heard that distinct sound of an arrow sinking into flesh and sinew. His entire world went silent.

He looked right and saw the Caleef standing, and Glassman's arrow buried deep in the side of his chest. He didn't look in pain. No, he seemed surprised though, like even he wasn't sure if he could get hurt that badly.

"The sea calls for me…" the Caleef rasped as he staggered backward. Rand turned his attention away from Sir Reginald and tried to grab him. His fingers grazed the Caleef, but Rand watched in abject horror as the most important man alive flipped over the railing, plummeting over the south side of the bridge and into the Walled Lake.

"No!" Rand screamed, his throat nearly raw. He raced to the edge to see if, by stroke of luck, the Caleef had managed to grab hold of a part of the bridge, but his gray body was lost in the darkness.

Rand's own body went hot. His heart throbbed against his rib cage. He turned and saw Drad Mak standing amidst a wave of embers. The savage looked curiously at the Glassman, short bow in his hand as if he hadn't expected it to fire so straight, as if there were no consequences to what he'd just done.

Mak sneered, then tore another arrow out of the corpse at his feet. Rand charged. Mak fired, and the arrow soared over Rand's shoulder and struck Reginald, who remained too stunned to dodge it.

Rand leaped and brought his dagger screeching toward Mak's face. The mammoth of a man didn't even bother drawing his axe. He caught Rand's arms and flung him aside with ease. His dagger flew from his grasp, but Rand caught his balance and snapped into a low fighting stance.

"Do you know what you've done!" Rand screamed. "You damned her."

"The only lil' girl here is you," Mak said, laughing. He flicked the furs off his shoulder, then drew a battle axe from his back. The thing was as tall as Rand, with two arced blades set on either side of a human skull.

Rand looked around frantically and spotted an axe not far off. Taking two full steps, he snatched it up and roared, "You'll join Redstar in a grave." Rand slashed at Mak from up high, then down low. He came at him from every angle, just as he'd learned in training, but the man's reach was too great. Mak parried each attack, then dodged one, shifted to the side and smashed Rand in the nose with his elbow.

Rand's back hit the stone so hard it knocked the wind out of him. Mak cheered for himself and stretched his back like he was working out a kink.

"You think some pink-skin like you could beat me?" Mak said. "Grew up down here, warm and fuzzy. The Great North would spit you out like chewed fat."

Mak raised his axe high and brought it crashing down. Rand was able to roll out of the way just in time, but the blade broke through stone as easily as rotting wood. Rand slashed as Mak pulled it free, slicing a bit of the Northman's leg and leaving a shallow cut. It was superficial but seemed to infuriate the Drad beyond control.

He swung with all his might. Rand blocked it, but the strength sent him staggering. Mak didn't stop. A flurry of powerful blows rained down upon Rand. His arms felt like they were going to break, but the shaft of his axe did first. He flew back and landed against the dead zhulong, Jaraud's glassy eyes staring at him.

Rand could hardly breathe now, hardly raise his arms he was so battered. He let the two halves of the axe fall from his grasp, then rolled off the beast to his hands and knees. He panted as he tried to get to his feet, watching Mak's fur-clad boots stomp closer, stirring up ash and dust.

"You killed her!" Rand screamed. He punched at Mak, but the savage grabbed his hand and wrenched his arm to the side. His boot slammed into Rand's gut and sent him soaring into the bridge railing.

Every part of him burned with pain. He groped for the rail, anything to provide purchase so he could get back to his feet.

"Die!" Sir Reginald screamed and ran at Mak, a broken arrow still sticking out of him. Mak hopped out of the way, clutched the Shieldsman by his head with two hands, and squeezed until Reginald's skull popped like a melon.

Rand threw up, then rose to his wobbly legs. As his face rose over the stone railing, he could see the black depths of the Jarein Gorge. Somewhere down there was the Caleef's body. Somewhere down there, was Sigrid's only chance of survival.

"You don't give up, do you?" Mak said, stalking forward. Blood drenched his pale face.

Behind him, the Drav Cra horde began to cheer. The last of the Glass resistance had either been killed or surrendered.

"Unhand me you filthy animals!" Bartholomew shouted as two of the savages lifted him and tore apart his fine tunic, laughing the entire time. "You'll all pay for this."

"What could you people and your false god possibly have to fight for?" Mak said. "The Buried Goddess isn't defeated, her plans are merely delayed. Soon, she will free your world from the bindings of civilization."

Rand steadied himself against the railing. Pain pulled at his side with every breath. It took every ounce of him to get words out. "Family," he growled. He charged again, and Mak swung his mighty axe.

Rand hit the ground as the flat of the blade connected with his temple. His head rolled to the side, and he found himself staring into the eyes of a woman; the barmaid from Fettingborough, who, apparently, wasn't lucky enough to escape.

"Siggy," Rand said as his consciousness faded. She was all he could picture, tied up in Valin's playground, used like cattle. He'd failed her. He'd failed everyone. Tessa, the Order, Sigrid... everyone.

"Lock them all up," Mak said. "We need a present for when Sir Unger arrives."

Rand felt people lifting him by his shoulders. "Sigrid..." He mouthed again as he was torn away from the woman. "I failed you..." Then his world went dark.

XXXVII

THE KNIGHT

Torsten pulled down Father Morningweg's blindfold and again found a world of darkness. He quickly drew it back up, and glimmers of light filled in. There was no color, even to the fire on the nearest torch. Only shades to give form to his surroundings. He could see the spaces between the cell's bars, the gaps in the stone walls, though not the little imperfections like rust or moss. But it was something.

Torsten held his hand out in front of him and rotated it, watching as his fingers wriggled, the light of the torch bouncing off each one. It was like he and everything beyond were drawn in the deep blacks and white of Glintish charcoal art.

"It can't be…" Torsten stammered. He still couldn't cry, but he felt like he could. Instead, an ecstatic laugh slipped through his lips. His bruised limbs experienced a surge of energy, and he sprang to his feet.

He patted along the wall, taking everything in. He never imagined he could marvel at the way stone blocks fit together. Or the joint where a metal bar met a fastener.

Torsten laughed again and ran to the other side of the cell, amazed that he didn't have to take care with every step or worry about slipping on a loose stone. He shook the prison bars, watching as they vibrated, the torch-light playing off them. He wondered if this was how the artists or the Lightmancers of his ancestral homeland saw the world, then remembered.

"Iam is still with me," he said. He looked up, seeing the gentle shimmer of water pooling within a crack in the ceiling. "You're still with me."

"Would ye quiet up down there!" someone shouted from the other end of the dungeon. "Fight's about to start!"

As Torsten regarded his own hands again, grasping the bars, he finally realized what it meant that he wasn't in chains. A blind man like him, they'd have little trouble controlling him. One bang of metal with a club and he'd be too disoriented to accomplish much.

The one time Valin shows mercy, Torsten thought, sneering. *He forgot that even down here, Iam sees.*

"Who's fighting?" Torsten called. No answer. He banged on the bars again. "Hey, who's fighting?"

"That's none of yer business," the guard finally answered.

"Well, I'd like to say a prayer for them."

"How about ye say one for yerself."

"Oh, don't be such a…" Torsten paused. Being in this awful place was affecting the looseness of his tongue, "…shog."

"What did ye call me?" A chair slid, and the man lumbered down the passage toward Torsten's cell. He was a big one with a belly so large he looked about ready to give birth if he could. Torsten imagined this had to be the guard who he'd knocked out in order to break into Valin's office, now sent down to the dungeons for his failure.

"Oh, I recognize your voice," Torsten said. "You're the one—"

"I went easy on ye, cripple," the man interrupted. "I won't make that mistake again."

"I suppose it's my fault you're down here?"

"Yigging right it is." The man leaned against the bars and Torsten backed away. With the torch eclipsed, he couldn't make out the man's features behind his bulbous silhouette, but he could imagine the expression he wore.

"I'm sorry about that," Torsten said. "Why don't you let me out of here and I'll put a word in for you with the city guard. Get you a nice post topside."

"The only man ye'll be putting a word in with is Iam."

"If you say so," Torsten said. "That's my last offer. When I get out of here, you'll join Valin in the gallows."

"Get out of here?" he chuckled. "Ye and that boy should have run when ye had the chance. Ye'll rot in here."

"And you right along with me. You already failed him once. Where do you think Valin will throw a slob like you if you fail him again? Straight into the pit, then float your body out into the Torrential Sea when you can't keep going. I've seen it before."

"Well, ye won't see it ever again, *Shieldsman*. Won't see nothin'."

"Fine by me. I can only imagine your ugly mug. It's hardly the last thing I'd want to see." Torsten couldn't believe the words coming out of his mouth. He felt like Whitney those nights in the Glass Dungeon when they'd first met, goading and prodding for weaknesses. He hated admitting it, but a part of him understood why Whitney enjoyed what he did so much, playing people.

This place is ruining me, he immediately countered the thought.

"Got quite a mouth on ye for a Shieldsman," the guard said.

"Amazing what the mouth can do when it's not full of food," Torsten replied. "You know, I'm glad you said no. The city guard would take one look at your belly and laugh. I can hear it jiggling from here."

"That's it." The big man fumbled through his keys and found

the lock. "Valin said to make things hard on ye, so how's about I get started." The gate swung open, and the man stomped in, gripping a wooden club.

"Ye just couldn't make things easy," he said. He banged the club against the bars. The sound was grating, and Torsten wasn't faking as he covered his ears and staggered backward.

For a moment, he forgot he could see, but then found the source of light from the torch again. His back foot slid against a wall, and there, he found his bearings.

"Not so mouthy now, aye?" the guard barked. "This oughta shut ye up until Valin gets back."

He reared back and swung at Torsten's head. Torsten ducked beneath it, feeling the *whoosh* of air against the top of his head. The light played across the guard's face, revealing his eyes spread wide in shock. Then he growled and swung again. Torsten evaded it, sliding right. The man whipped around, remarkably fast for his size, but Torsten dipped again.

"How're ye—" the guard grunted in frustration. "Get over here!"

He unleashed a flurry of mad swings, and Torsten dodged each of them in turn. So long out of practice, it still felt like he'd been in Shieldsman training only yesterday. His weary muscles remembered everything.

He backed up against the metal bars. The guard took one last swing, throwing every bit of energy into it. Torsten slid right and drove a fist straight into the man's fatty necks. The guard coughed, heaving for breath as he folded over, allowing Torsten to catch the club and bring the handle down on the back of the man's skull in one smooth motion.

The floor rumbled as he landed, out like a candle between clenched fingers. Torsten grabbed his keys, closed the cell door, and worked through them until the lock clicked.

Whitney would be proud, Torsten thought, again having to shake away the notion.

He checked the two cells on either side of his. He couldn't help but wonder if Lucas was in one of them, but each was empty. He imagined the poor kid was back at the castle, meant to eventually be used as Valin's pawn in the King's Shield.

Valin's Shield, Torsten thought grimly.

Torsten's grip tightened on the guard's club, and he continued down the tunnel. Even with his semi-returned sight, it was difficult to see. The darkness was oppressive, with only a few torches dotting the path.

He reached the corner and peeked around. He saw nobody, but the ceiling shook violently. He winced until it quaked again, then stuck out a palm. Motes of dust coated it, becoming invisible as they merged with the shape of his hand. The ceiling continued to vibrate like feet were pounding above, and he thought he heard chanting.

"I guess Valin's arena is back up and running," he whispered. He took one step, then was forced back behind the corner by voices.

"Mister Tehr says to strap some rocks to her and ditch her in the harbor," a thug said.

"It's been weeks since a fight," another said. "I wanted to watch."

"Wanting to risk his bad side right now, with all the traitors around?"

"No, please." The voice was soft, pleading. "I'll leave. You'll never hear fro—"

It was Abigail.

"Shut up, wench," said another. Then Torsten heard the explicit sound only a slap across the face made.

"Just tie her up. We'll do it after. He won't know the difference."

Torsten threw the door wide and charged in, screaming. The two didn't even stand a chance. Torsten grasped one by his neck and bashed down with the club. The thug's neck snapped and Torsten dropped his corpse, then turned to focus on the one futilely beating on Torsten's shoulder. The crowd thundered above, which helped to keep the man's screams and garbled pleas unheard as Torsten strangled the life out of him.

"By Iam... Abigail?" " Torsten said as he knelt by her side.

Her arms wrapped around him, shaking.

"Thank you," she cried. "Thank you. Oh, Iam, thank you."

"You need to get out of here. Now." Torsten reached down with both hands and cupped her face like a child. She was beaten, bruised, barely recognizable. But she was alive, and that's all that mattered. No one else would die thanks to Torsten's failures. "You're done with this life, clear?"

She nodded. "Yes. Thank you."

"Now hide here," Torsten ordered. "Don't make a sound. I'll clear a path. Then you run. You run damnit, and you don't look back."

Torsten unconsciously found himself standing in the doorway, squeezing the club so hard his knuckles lost color. All the rage from his run-in with Valin Tehr decades back returned in full force. He panted wildly until he was able to find focus again.

"I'm so sorry," he whispered to Iam. "But that man is going to pay for what he's done. Even if it means Exile."

He hurried out of the room, drawing deep breaths as he moved, struggling to calm himself. He didn't dare look into any of the next rooms he passed. He had to stay focused.

Above him, the crowd grew louder. Darkness closed in on him once again until he could see a grated gate at the end of the way and the light filtering through. Another guard stood, face pressed against it. With the guard's back exposed, Torsten barely had to creep. His muscled arm closed around the man's throat, and in no time, he was unconscious.

A leg, literally the size of a tree trunk, slammed down in front of the gate. The crowd erupted as someone inside screamed the name, "Uhlvark!" Whatever the fight was, it seemed the giant was involved, fresh off the incidental chaos caused by Abigail unlocking his chains.

Torsten studied the arena. It was nowhere near as grand as the Tal'du Dromesh in Latiapur, but that only meant everyone was closer to the action—more a chance for unintended injuries. Stands carved out of the rock wrapped the cavernous space on two sides, and the others were wood and canvas scaffolds. A whole section was destroyed from the day's early activity in the room, but the rest was filled with grimy faces of Yarrington's commoners but for one area that was separated by guards and rope, where exquisitely-clad nobles attended. Torsten hoped to Iam he wouldn't recognize any of them.

Although he knew, as Liam had, that sometimes people needed to unwind. It was better not to know how.Up above the stands were carved apertures through which he saw beaded curtains, and a few men watching over the arena with near-naked women draped over them. Torsten imagined that's where he'd been earlier with Abigail, in the private viewing boxes now being used for Valin's brothel.

It was suiting that the riot had inspired Valin to realize that blood and perversion need not be separated. The very thought gave Torsten a shudder.

"Me no waaant to fight," Uhlvark said, barely audible over the voracious crowd.

"You don't fight, you don't eat," someone snapped at him.

"But I huuungry. Eat first?"

"You know how it works." Whoever the man watching him was, stabbed him with something. Uhlvark stumbled, holding a fresh wound on his shoulder. Chains rattled, still attached to his wrists, and Torsten now saw the spikes in them that dug deeper whenever the giant pulled.

"Make a mess of that man, and you get your pick from the box of a nice, juicy bovine," Uhlvark's keeper said. "Or would you rather go another week without eating."

"No, no no," Uhlvark whined. "Me fight, me fiiiiight."

Torsten had difficulty focusing on the rest because when the giant moved, he spotted his opponent. Lucas stood across the sunken pit, face bloodied. He gripped a rusty halberd with two quaking hands, the shaft broken to cut its reach in half.

"Now, try not to kill him too fast," the keeper said.

"Kill fast, eat sooner," Uhlvark replied.

"Kill fast, piss off Valin. And you don't want to do that, do you?"

"No, never make papa mad!" The fear in the giant's voice was unmistakable. Torsten could only imagine what Valin had put him through to make him his own personal killing machine. Despite their size, giants were known for being docile and kind-hearted, more apt to crush a man by accidentally stepping on them than outright murder in a fight.

"Hands up," the keeper said.

Uhlvark did as requested, like a toddler stuck in his shirt. Locks clicked, then the cuff's fell free from Uhlvark's wrists. The giant groaned as he rubbed them, the stench of blood, both fresh and dry, impossible to mistake.

"Today, on this day our gracious host reopens this time-honored tradition, he brings you a grand spectacle!" The speaker was none other than Curry. "Today, a traitor to Dockside shall face down our undefeated champion. May Iam have mercy on his soul."

"Go!" the keeper demanded. "Kill the bastard slow, and I'll throw in a chicken."

Uhlvark smacked his lips, then squealed again as the keeper prodded him. The dance began as Uhlvark lumbered forward, and Lucas stumbled back. The latter's weapon slipped from his fingers, and he scurried to pick it back up, earning roaring laughter from the crowd.

Torsten was furious with the young man for keeping things from him, but not a soul deserved this. No Shieldsman training would prepare someone for facing a giant.

Torsten grabbed the lever to the gate, pulled, and ran out. There was no time to think. No time even to ask for Iam's guidance. He knew his God was with him, and that was all he needed.

Surprised gasps sounded all over as Torsten came into view. Everyone but the giant heard or saw him coming. Torsten charged Uhlvark full speed, then smashed him in the anklebone with the club he'd stolen.

It felt like hitting a pillar of stone. Uhlvark cried out, then hopped on one foot. The shockwaves sent Torsten staggering before he could attack again, once nearly stumbling beneath the giant's foot.

"This *is* a surprise," a guard in the crowd said. "The blind knight is back."

"Guess Valin didn't want to make it too easy."

Torsten found his balance and brandished the club. Uhlvark stomped down.

"You huurt mee," the giant said. The features of his oafish face slowly contorted until anger was written all over it. He stuck out his lower lip, saliva spraying, then slammed his foot down again. Again, to the delight and laughter of the crowd, Torsten lost his balance.

"Sir Unger, what are you doing here?" Lucas asked, voice quavering, as he finally gained the courage to step up beside Torsten.

"Saving you, apparently," Torsten replied.

"Sir, I'm so sorry. I didn't mean—"

"Save it for confession. We have work to do."

Lucas swallowed back a retort. "Valin said the Queen Mother's funeral is tonight," he said instead. "It was them, I think. Just as you thought."

"I know."

"I'll d…"

Uhlvark stomped again, and both of them winced.

"…distract him while you climb out," Lucas said. "You can grab one of his men, make them lead you to the exit."

"I don't need guidance anymore," Torsten said.

"What are you talking about, Sir? Just go. Leave me. It's what I deserve."

"Would you be quiet and listen!" Torsten seized Lucas by the shoulders and hurled him out of the way just before a large chunk of stone tossed by Uhlvark squashed him like a bug.

Lucas rolled over, and his gaze darted between Torsten and the enraged giant, who suddenly didn't seem so dumb and innocent. Torsten stared straight in Lucas' direction. No words needed to be said.

"How…" the young man marveled.

"Ours is never the place to ask how or why," Torsten replied. "We are the right hand of Iam. The Sword of his justice and the Shield that guards the light of this world. And right now, Lucas, I need you to forget everything else."

Uhlvark roared, causing the very ground to rumble and the crowd into eerie silence. Then he charged.

"What do we do?" Lucas asked, clutching his halberd tight.

"Stay away from his hands, and for Iam's sake drop the weapon, you'll only make him angrier."

Lucas threw the halberd aside without asking. "Now what!"

"Move, you fool!"

Uhlvark's boar-sized fist slammed toward Lucas, who

snapped out of his state of terror and rolled aside a beat before being crushed. The crowd groaned in disappointment. Lucas didn't have time to rest. Uhlvark moved slow, as would be expected of anything his size, but his attacks came with incredible range. A flat hand slapped down, a giant pinky clipping Lucas and knocking him into the wall.

Torsten quickly studied the pit. There were three gated passages out, including the open one where he'd emerged from. He couldn't be sure whether or not he'd missed a stairway out of the dungeon area through there, but the risk wasn't worth it. If they escaped through there only to find dungeons and torture chambers, they'd might as well hang themselves. The other two were locked. A fourth and larger one had two rows of retractable metal bars behind which a few cows roamed, constantly taunting Uhlvark's stomach.

The pit wall was high, even for Torsten, and spikes capped it. He might've been able to climb out, but in the time it would take, he'd be caught by Valin's men if the giant didn't get to him first.

Motion in his peripherals stirred him, and he ducked. Uhlvark's tree trunk arm swept overhead.

"Get over heeeeeere," Uhlvark's deep voice sounded. "I'm huuungry."

He grasped at Torsten, who sidestepped. But a second hand promptly followed, and Uhlvark hooked his index finger around Torsten's heel. He lifted, Torsten's legs slipping out from beneath him like he'd been rammed by a zhulong.

At the same time, Lucas shouted, "Stop!" and rammed into Uhlvark's hunched-over frame.

Torsten slipped free and sprinted for the open gate where Uhlvark's keeper stood atop it, sneering. Promptly, the gate crashed back down. But Torsten wasn't looking to escape just yet.

He skidded to a stop before the pile of Uhlvark's chains. Each iron link was the size of Torsten's head, and far heavier. But Iam had grown him abnormally large for a reason, that much was clear.

Torsten peered up and saw Lucas struggling. The young man dove through the giant's legs before he was crushed. Uhlvark leaned over, peeking beneath his loincloth. He grasped outward for Lucas, but couldn't find the angle and nearly rolled heels over head. If he had, Lucas surely would've died. Lucas could barely stand, so exhausted he was from throwing his body around.

Torsten had to gain the giant's attention somehow.

"Coward!" someone in the crowd shouted at Torsten.

"Help him!" yelled another.

A chunk of bread pelted Torsten in the shoulder. "Thank you," he whispered toward the ceiling as he snatched up the debris.

"If you're so hungry, eat this, beast!" Torsten shouted. His aim with projectiles had never been his strength, but without being distracted by the details of his surroundings, it felt easier. Uhlvark was too gargantuan a mass of light and shadow to miss. The bread pelted him in the side of his mangy, balding head. By then he had Lucas lifted by the heel with two fingers. He turned toward Torsten, nostrils flaring.

"Mean man dies fiiiirst," Uhlvark said.

He flicked Lucas aside like nothing, then barreled at Torsten. Every crash of Uhlvark's enormous feet made it difficult for Torsten to stay upright, but he dug his feet in, bent at the knees, and wrapped his hands around the links in the heavy chain. He watched the unsightly giant closely, looking for where his muscle's tensed. Torsten could feel the anxiousness of the crowd hopeful of satiating their blood lust.

Uhlvark punched down with both fists. It was a clumsy move, but it was clear the giant had never been trained to fight. He was all bulk and no skill.

Torsten waited until the last moment, then dove out of the way, heaving the chain with him. His shoulder apparently hadn't been dislocated earlier, but it still burned from the weight, and as Uhlvark's fists cracked against the wall of the arena, Torsten wrapped the chain around one wrist. The giant screamed and smacked Torsten with his other hand, sending him flying.

He rolled to a stop, dizzied from the blow. The pain in his shoulder from bashing down Valin's door flared up worse than ever. The taste of blood filled his mouth. He fought to focus and saw Uhlvark's fingers clenching, just out of reach of him as the giant yanked on the chain which wrapped his other arm.

"Let me go!" Uhlvark shouted as if the chain could respond.

Torsten yanked again and a few links grated, providing enough slack for the tip of his fingernail to scratch across Torsten's face.

"Die!" Lucas yelled. At some point, he'd retrieved the halberd and slashed Uhlvark in the back of one thigh. Giant skin was tough. It had to be to endure the bitter cold of their homes in the Pikeback Mountains. The blade drew blood, but didn't pierce deep, nor did Lucas' second slash. It did, however, earn Uhlvark's attention.

The giant kicked at Lucas, who abandoned the weapon and leaped onto Uhlvark's horse-sized foot. Uhlvark shook his leg like he'd stepped in shog.

Torsten darted forward, ducking under a thrashing limb. He grabbed the heavy chain, gritting his teeth as he lifted it. He waited until the giant's arm swung his way, then caught it with the chain. The force sent Torsten skidding back, but he stayed upright and wrapped the links around the limb, then yanked the end beneath through the giant's legs, not daring to look up.

"Huuuuh?" Uhlvark moaned. He bent over to look back, then fell forward, his arms crossed and the chain so tight he wound up stuck. Torsten ripped Lucas free of Uhlvark's death-clutch on the boy's leg and pushed him aside. Then, snatching up the halberd, he leaped onto Uhlvark's back and raised it high, with every intent on stabbing it down into Uhlvark's neck and severing his spine.

But Torsten had fought in too many battles to remain blinded by the fog of war long. He noticed all the faces in the crowd, their tide turned, desperate for him to land a killing blow. Fickle as the seasons.

"P… p… please no hurt me no more," Uhlvark muttered. "Pleeease."

Uhlvark glanced over his shoulder, unable to break free. His eye went bright with fear. Tears even welled in its corner, and Torsten remembered that the poor being was forced to fight; turned into a plaything by greedy, salacious men.

Torsten lowered the weapon. "Lucas," he said, turning to the boy. "Let's go." He extended a hand, and it took a few seconds for Lucas to gather his wits enough to take it. He climbed up using the giant's thigh, and Torsten heaved him up.

"Get offs me!" Uhlvark roared, his back heaving. Torsten grabbed a clump of the giant's withering hair, using it to steady himself.

"You'll be free soon enough," Torsten said to him as he grabbed Lucas' wrist. Together, they stepped on the back of Uhlvark's head and leaped into the stands, Torsten leading Lucas for once.

Gasps sounded. Every patron nearby jumped from their seat and backed away. A few of Valin's cronies were present, including Curry, who'd allowed Torsten inside in the first place.

"How in Elsewhere…" Curry stammered. "You're blind."

"So are any who would feed the existence of this place," Torsten said. He raised the halberd and pointed it at Curry, so there would be no mistaking he now saw him. "Move aside, or Iam help me, suffer the fate of the enemies of the King's Shield."

One of the thugs laughed. "You're outnumbered Shieldsman."

"Am I?"

"Lucas, stop him," Curry said. "Stop him, and all will be forgiven. Think of your poor parents. Think of how Valin so generously rebuilt their world for you."

Lucas stepped forward, glanced at Torsten, then back at Valin's men. Lucas' hair was matted to his forehead by glistening sweat. Exhaustion seemed to plague every inch of him. For a moment, Torsten was unsure, not confident his aide was truly on his side. His lead foot slowly rotated toward the kid, but then Lucas dropped into a fighting stance and faced back toward Curry.

"I know what they'd want me to do now," Lucas said.

Torsten flashed a grin.

"Take this." He tossed the broken halberd to Lucas, then turned toward the rock wall where Uhlvark's chains were attached using a colossal pin. Nervous chatter broke out in the crowd. Lucas swung the halberd to keep Valin's men at bay, who had only clubs and daggers. More, however, fought through the stands toward them.

It took every ounce of Torsten's already near-depleted energy store, but he finally lifted the pin free. Uhlvark promptly collapsed on his side, the metal links clanking against the opening in the wall through which they had been secured by his keeper.

"Ouuuch," he mumbled. He went to scratch his nose, and the chains slid free. "Huh?" He turned around fast, and though the other end of the chain remained around his wrists, the back side whipped up and slammed against the stands, sending rock fragments flying.

A large chunk hit Uhlvark's keeper, pulverizing his head in an instant. The crowd broke out into a frenzy of fear. Screams echoed all around. Abigail had tried to use the giant to get Torsten out earlier, and now he cleared a path for her freedom by doing the same.

"Let's go!" Torsten hollered.

He and Lucas took off. Curry was the only one brave enough not to abandon his post, but Lucas dodged a swing of his club and jabbed him hard in the gut with the snapped shaft of his polearm.

Getting lost in the chaos that ensued was easy. Valin's men, nobles, Docksiders, streetwalkers—anything with a brain got caught up in the frenzy. Torsten and Lucas flowed with them, cramming down the tunnel and back upstairs into the Vineyard. Torsten was lucky for his size. Otherwise, they'd have been stampeded like some of the poor souls he heard howling in anguish behind.

They burst through the front doors, out into the cool, salty breeze of a Yarrington night. Dockside city guards converged on the street in a hurry. Without their former captain alive and in Valin's pocket, Torsten wasn't sure what to expect. Considering his experiences with Redstar, however, he figured the worst.

Torsten pulled Lucas out of the mob and into an alley. A blind beggar rested against the wall, a small fire burning beside him.

"I can't believe..." Lucas paused to catch his breath. "Sir that was... That was incredible!"

"Not for those who failed to escape," Torsten said.

"No, but we did."

Torsten permitted himself a sigh of relief. War was about planning, layers of strategy that allowed one to react to the enemy in an informed way. It wasn't improvising, like how Whitney Fierstown lived, yet, from the moment he left the castle to invade Valin's Tehr's domain, Torsten had barely a plan to run with.

"We did, indeed," Torsten said. "And now, it's time to end this."

"Sir." Lucas took Torsten's arm. His features darkened. "I should've told you about Rand, Right from the start, I should have—"

"Yes, you should have. And you should have told me how Valin threatened your parents. We could have protected them."

"I know…"

"But second chances are the way of Iam. You will be disciplined accordingly; however, now is not the time."

"No, we have to stop Valin. Look." Lucas reached down and pulled a tiny shred of paper from within his boot. He held it up for Torsten to read.

"I can see, but not that well," Torsten realized, seeing only the shape of it.

"It's Yuri Darkings's signature and the last bit of the letter, *'Get him here!'*. I'm pretty sure Valin burned the rest, but I managed to hide this. It's not much."

"Let's pray it'll be enough," Torsten said, taking it from Lucas. He clasped the boy by the forearm and shook. "Faith will handle the rest. Good job. I knew you'd be a fine Shieldsman one day."

"I hope so, sir. Now, let's get it to the King."

"No. I'm going to stop Valin, and you're going to get your parents to safety so they can never be used against you again."

"What?" Lucas asked, incredulous.

"Go to them, Lucas. Valin might still have them under watch as insurance. Get them to the castle, and we'll find somewhere new for them. Perhaps Troborough or Oxford, somewhere in need of fine food to brighten their spirits."

"But Sir, what if you need my help?"

"The Glass Castle hasn't forgotten me yet. I'll be fine. Now go. That's an order." Torsten gave the boy a shove back toward the street. Lucas staggered and stared back. Torsten hated to be ungrateful for the modicum of sight he'd received, but he'd give Salvation itself if only to recognize the gratitude in the boy's eyes.

"Iam bless you, Sir Unger," Lucas said, breathless, then he scampered off.

Torsten squeezed what tiny shred of proof he had about Valin's worst crime as he gazed up toward the Glass Castle's spire casting its false light across all of Yarrington. Beneath it, the funeral for Oleander was being held; a sham designed by the man who'd caused her death.

"Not tonight," Torsten whispered, a harsh edge entering his tone. "Not tonight."

XXXVIII

THE THIEF

It took most of the day, but Whitney and his wagon full of refugees finally made it back to Fettingborough. None of them had planned for the return trip, it just seemed the most logical thing to do. For one, there was very little chance the Drav Cra would escape the bridge *and* decide to go back to Fettingborough. Whitney and his crew were worthless after being used to make the Glassmen hesitate.

The other reason Fettingborough made the most sense was it was one of the final communities until Panping. The Wildlands still stretched out before them, and although Whitney didn't expect to find anything worse out there than a Drav Cra army, there would undoubtedly be the regular manner of beasts: lions, bears, your occasional goblin horde. Just like anyone in the Glass Kingdom, Whitney'd heard all the stories about bloodthirsty humanoid goblins living in primitive villages at the base of the Dragon's Tail and sacrificing virgins to the sun and stars—but he was one of the few who'd encountered them in person. They were little more than scaly little lizard creatures that stood on two legs most of the time. They didn't speak. He questioned whether they even thought. And they certainly didn't wield spears or wear armor. They were, by far, the least threatening predator in the Wildlands.

For most, being back in Fettingborough conjured up bad memories, but no one complained at the opportunity to stretch their legs. The Drav Cra had left the village mostly intact. Now in the daylight, it was clear that about half the population of the place was left alive to grieve for those lost and others maybe never to return. They were all just tools for taking the bridge and making threats. The Five Round Trousers looked mostly the same as it had the night before, and the basement was still stocked with food and ale. The Drav Cra had been hasty and sloppy in plundering supplies.

Whitney felt a little bad, like he was stealing from the barmaid he'd met in his cage, but he was sure she'd have wanted the escapees to get a bit of respite.

The thought of her brought a pang of guilt. Had he left all those people to die back on the bridge? Would Rand actually try and help them? Whitney thought for sure the man had decided to grab the Caleef and high-tail it as soon as he'd stepped foot onto the bridge.

Whitney found a new room at the Five Round Trousers that wasn't scorched by Aquira, and Gentry got his own since there weren't many travelers left to take the rooms. There was nobody to pay for them either.

Gentry hadn't spoken much since the return. He'd been through a traumatic experience and needed some alone time to process it all. They all would. Aquira wouldn't leave Whitney's side. He practically had to beg her to stay with Gentry so the boy would feel safe and promised if she did, he'd find a way to remove her crude muzzle as quickly as possible. There weren't any locks so he wasn't sure what to do yet.

Benon and another man Whitney didn't know were off in the fields behind town burying Conmonoc alongside many locals.

Some of the others joined them to say words, but most stayed in town, eating their fill and resting. A priest of Iam would've been nice to ease emotions—Whitney didn't believe in much, but those eyeless weirdos always knew just what to say—but they were all still off in Hornsheim playing house. The church itself was empty but for a local woman and her kids, kneeling before the Eye of Iam and asking "why."

He'll never answer, Whitney thought as he passed them on his way to the stables.

Most of the Pompare Troupe's stuff—tents, cooking wares, wagons, and the like—had been recovered by the stables, still hitched to their horses. The Drav Cra didn't bother to take a thing. Even the Pompares' fancy carriage hadn't been ransacked. Francesca was already in the kitchen, grateful everyone had made it back alive. She was working hard to produce something hearty to give the people a morale boost.

Talwyn and Lucindur cared for the horses and the two massive zhulong they now owned. The poor things were mighty spooked, and Lucindur played her salfio while Talywn brushed them.

"So, where are the Pompares?" Whitney asked Lucindur, nodding toward their empty carriage. He'd barely finished his sentence before Talwyn was hanging on his neck, showering his face with kisses.

"You saved us," she said. Then, in his ear, whispered, "You deserve a reward." He felt the distinct feeling of her warm tongue on his earlobe. He let out an uncomfortable laugh followed by an involuntary shudder.

Whitney gently pushed her back and said, "It was nothing," then looked to Lucindur. "The Pompares?"

Their trip and subsequent unloading had been hasty, and Whitney had failed to take a proper roll call.

"They weren't in the other cage?" she asked.

Whitney shook his head and swore. "Did you see them at all after they went upstairs last night?"

"No."

Whitney jogged back to the Five Round Trousers and checked the Pompares' room. It was private, all the way at the end, so he hadn't looked yet. He quickly turned away and retched at the sight of Fadra Pompare naked in a puddle of his yig and shog.

Gentry called from down the hall, and Whitney turned. "Stay there."

"What's wrong?" Gentry asked. The boy stroked Aquira, her mouth still held shut in the metal muzzle. She slithered out of his grasp and tried to run to Whitney, but her injured wing was attached to her left leg, and she stumbled, squawking in pain. Whitney scooped her up.

"Nothing. Just… It's empty. No need to…" His voice trailed off as he closed the door and met Gentry down the hall. "Let's go figure out how to get Aquira free. What do you say?"

Gentry nodded.

"All right, find a table for her, and I'll be right back," Whitney said, and gingerly handed her to him.

Outside, Whitney found a couple of townsmen and told them what he'd found. "Could you discreetly get rid of the body? Don't want the boy knowing just yet. He's been through enough." They nodded, and Whitney said, "He's going to be heavy." They groaned but did as he asked. Considering all he'd done for a few of them, and their relatives, they couldn't deny him.

Lucindur sat on a stoop by the general store. Whitney took a seat next to her and said, "You okay?"

"Fine. You?"

"Fadra's dead," he said softly.

"What? How?"

"Throat is slit. Did you know he slept naked… unless they

were… blagh." He shook the thought away. "Modera isn't there. We should have someone search for her."

Lucindur closed her eyes for a moment, exhaled. "I'll handle it."

"Thanks," Whitney said. "Oh, and don't tell the boy yet, huh? Let him deal with what he's already dealing with before adding more to his load."

"Right. Talwyn too," Lucindur said as she walked, then approached another group of men, presumably sending them out to sweep the town for any who might have avoided being captured in the first place.

Back inside, Gentry must have noticed Whitney's concern expression. "The Pompares will be fine," he said. "They always are."

Whitney wasn't sure who the boy was trying to convince. The sad truth was that lords and ladies—and no mistake could be made, that was how the Pompares behaved—were rarely *fine* without those who cared for them.

Whitney forced a nod of approval and a meek grin, then took a seat with Gentry at the same table they'd all gathered around just a few nights before—though it felt like a lifetime ago. Aquira lay prone on the table as they worked on removing her muzzle. It was a crude design, certainly not designed for a wyvern since nothing was designed for a wyvern.

For an hour, Whitney tried with very little success, and he was getting frustrated. Aquira kept trying to fly, but one of her wings was cut, and the contraption held the other in place against her body. It didn't help that she kept screeching and jerking her head away. For a creature that was supposed to be smart, she didn't seem to understand that Whitney was trying to help. That she felt he was hurting her on purpose pained Whitney beyond words. It felt like he was hurting Sora…

"Please, Aquira, I'm not trying to hurt you," he said. "I need to get this thing off. You'd like that, wouldn't you?"

The words soothed her for the moment, and Whitney was able to continue. There was no lock, nothing to pick. Once the ring snapped closed, it was designed to stay that way. Small spikes dug into Aquira's frills. If not for her glaruium-strong scales, they'd likely have killed her already.

"Come on, come on, come on," he demanded under his breath. Whitney had been using the sword Ugosah, the mustached Drav Cra man dropped during their fight on the wagon, prying at the seam and hinges over and over. He threw it down in frustration when, for the third time, a shard of the weapon broke off in the muzzle.

"Shog in a barrel," Gentry said.

"Hey, don't say…" Whitney started, then waved his hand. "Shog in a barrel is right."

"What are we going to do?" Gentry asked.

Whitney shook his head. "I don't know."

Aquira snorted, and a puff of smoke rose from her nostrils.

"I wish she could talk," Gentry said.

"Would make this whole thing a lot easier, wouldn't it?" Whitney said.

Aquira perked up. She stood now, gesturing in a way that seemed a lot like she was nodding her head. She puffed smoke again and tried to fly, but her injured wing had her moving in tight circles. Puff. Puff.

"Lay down, Aquira," Whitney scolded. "We've gotta get this thing loose."

She puffed again, and Whitney tried to force her to lie down.

"Are you trying to tell us something?" Gentry asked.

Puff. Puff.

"Stop it," Whitney said again.

"I think she's trying to say something!" Gentry insisted.

Whitney let out a breath and said, "Okay, fine. I've been trying to get her to talk to me for months. You think you can figure her out? Be my guest."

"Really?" Gentry asked.

"Pick her up," Whitney said. "Careful of her wing."

Gentry carefully lifted the wyvern.

"Do you have an idea how to remove your muzzle?" Whitney asked Aquira, feeling stupid even as he said it.

Aquira... *nodded.*

Whitney smiled, then cleared his throat. "No."

She nodded again, and Gentry smiled this time. Ear to ear. Unapologetic.

"What do we do, girl," Gentry asked.

She shook her head.

"See, she's just moving around," Whitney said. "That thing is making her uncomfortable. Can you blame her?"

"No, I think she's still telling us something," Gentry said.

Aquira shook her head harder. Then her big eyes looked around the room. She shook her head again.

"Nothing... or... Not here!" Whitney exclaimed, then realized he was shouting. Nobody in the tavern was in the mood for that kind of excitement yet, troupe, locals or otherwise. "Somewhere else?"

Aquira extended her neck in the direction of the exit. She squeaked as the contraption dug into her scales.

"Walk?" Gentry asked. Then he turned to Whitney and said, "Walk. She wants us to walk."

Together they started toward the door. Whitney still felt a little silly, but he couldn't deny that Aquira was acting funny.

"Aquira, tell us where to go, One puff for right," Gentry instructed, "two for left. Let's see how smart you really are."

They went outside, passing by Lucindur and the others.

Puff.

They went right, and Whitney wondered if the wyvern truly guided them. When they reached an intersection, Aquira did nothing, leading to more suspicion. Had Whitney so desperately wanted some kind of connection to Sora that he'd imagined her pet was talking to him?

When they didn't move, Aquira flapped her injured wing and nudged them forward. About a block later, she puffed twice, and they turned left.

"Aquira, where are we going?" Whitney asked just before she screeched and flapped wildly. "Here?"

Aquira nodded.

Gentry would have put her down, but she could still barely walk.

"The blacksmith?" Gentry asked.

Aquira nodded again.

"Aquira, you're brilliant!" Whitney exclaimed, grabbing the wyvern from Gentry's arms. He threw off all restraint, thinking he'd figured out her plan. He remembered back in Winde Port, in all the fire and chaos, how Aquira was zipping through the white-hot flames like they couldn't damage her.

"What? What did I miss?" the boy asked as he followed Whitney.

The front door swung open, and the shop was empty. Dust motes carried themselves in the sunlight, dancing like Talwyn on stage. The town blacksmith was nowhere to be found, and his entire stock of goods had been pilfered. Apparently, it was worth something to the marching savages.

"You sure you can handle it?" Whitney asked Aquira.

She didn't respond except to flap her good wing in a frantic attempt to move forward.

"What are you talking about?" Gentry asked.

"I hope I'm right," Whitney said as he threw open the curtains over several windows, flooding the place with more light. In the center of the room stood a wide, brick forge already filled with coal as if the blacksmith had been getting ready for the day when he was taken—although that couldn't have been true since the raid happened at night. Whitney tenderly placed Aquira down, then made his way to the side of the forge and, using a bit of flint and steel, struck up a flame.

"On the bellows," he told Gentry, pointing. "Squeeze then release, slowly. Let the flame build."

"How do you know about this stuff?" Gentry asked as he pumped, forcing the flames higher.

"You pick stuff up when you travel the world," Whitney said, then realized how stupid he sounded telling a kid who had spent his entire life on the roads of Pantego about world travel. In reality, Whitney had learned what to do in Elsewhere Troborough, helping the blacksmith make farming tools for his parents and the other farmers.

Smoke started to fill the room, burning Whitney's eyes. Gentry started coughing. Waving his hands around to clear the air, Whitney said, "Flue. Gotta open the flue."

Gentry reached up and threw a lever and immediately the smoke began evacuating the room.

"Guess you don't learn everything out in the world," Gentry said, laughing. He stopped the moment he looked down to see Aquira's sad eyes and still-muzzled mouth.

"All right, girl." Whitney lifted Aquira to eye level. "You sure about this?"

Puff. Nod.

"Wait. What are you going to do?" Gentry asked.

Without answering, Whitney placed Aquira down on the warm brick. The wyvern looked back before lowering her head into the flames, hot as the magma in the bellows of the Dragon's Tail where only the bravest and greediest dwarves mined.

Whitney winced, and Gentry screamed, "What are you doing!"

"Don't worry," Whitney said. "She's impervious to the stuff… I think."

As they watched the metal turn yellow, the fire started to die. Whitney looked up to see Gentry had stopped pumping the bellows, enraptured by the sight before him. A beat passed before Gentry's eyes met Whitney's and Whitney offered an assuring nod.

"Oh, right. Sorry."

"Good. Good. Keep doing that." Whitney said as he quickly spun a circle, looking at the tools at his disposal. He found a pair of gloves and slipped them on, then snatched up a broken hammer and chisel and placed them down near the anvil.

"Okay, that's enough." At Whitney's words, Gentry stopped pumping. Sweat glistening on the kid's forehead. Fear twisted his features.

Careful only to touch her with his gloves, Whitney lifted Aquira from the flames and placed her on the anvil. Despite having a fiery hot ring of steel around her snout, Aquira never looked better, as if she were somehow revived within the flames.

"I'll try to be careful, but you have to try not to move, you hear?" Whitney said.

Puff.

"I guess that means 'yes.'" Whitney drew a deep breath, then coughed from the smoke rapidly filling his lungs. "Okay." He coughed again. "Here we go."

Gentry closed his eyes as Whitney placed the sharp end of the chisel against the glowing steel right at the hinge, then gripped what was left of the hammer's shaft and drove the head down. It *clanked*. Aquira groaned. The muzzle didn't move.

"Those spikes," Gentry said. "They're going to kill her."

"They won't. Her skin is strong as glaruium. Try not to worry."

The hammer came down again and again.

"A little more. Almost got it."

Finally, the clasp popped and half the manacle clattered against the anvil. Whitney hadn't noticed the bit that was stuffed far down her throat. He pulled, and it took Whitney's full strength to pull it out. The poor wyvern gagged, Whitney nearly threw up, and then the whole, white-hot contraption clanked to the floor.

Aquira shook her head and stretched her neck. When she opened her jaw, a plume of smoke escaped.

"You did it!" Gentry said as he reached in to pick her up.

"She's hot as heated steal!" Whitney grabbed him. "Don't touch."

Aquira recoiled slightly and bobbed her head.

"You really can understand me, can't you?" Whitney asked.

Aquira didn't respond.

"We need water," Whitney instructed.

"Where can I—"

"Try the stables. There's gotta be a trough still full."

When Gentry left the building, Whitney turned to regard Aquira. She continued to cough up a mixture of phlegm, smoke, and liquid fire. A chunk of the table beneath her melted away. Whitney stared at her and remembered the first time he and Sora had met her in Winde Port. He remembered how Sora had marveled at the creature like she was the most amazing thing she'd ever seen.

"Do you…" Whitney swallowed. His throat was insanely dry from the heat. "Do you know where Sora is?" he asked. "Is she still in Panping?" Saying it out loud gave him goosebumps. He couldn't believe he didn't think of asking earlier.

Aquira made a clicking noise and slowly shook her head. Her double set of eyelids blinked closed, and she hung her head.

Whitney's chin sank to his chest as well. "We'll find her, girl," he said. "I promise we will. She has to be there still. It's all she wanted."

A moment later, Gentry returned grasping a large bucket with both hands, staggering with every step. Water cascaded over the sides as it swung between his wide-spread legs.

"Put it down over there," Whitney directed, voice cracking. Thinking about Sora took him to dark places.

Still wearing gloves, Whitney carried a squirming Aquira to the bucket. She nipped at his hand but didn't bite down.

"You've gotta cool down, Aquira," he said. "If we're going to carry you, you... can't... be... so..." He fought with her and then finally, a sizzle of steam lifted from the bucket as she splashed in.. "There you are."

She flopped around until the bucket overturned, and she crawled out, still using only one front leg. Gentry bent and scooped her up, and they set off toward the Five Round Trousers.

"Why don't you take Aquira upstairs and get some rest," Whitney told Gentry when they stood before the inn. "I'm going to help square things away out here for a bit so we can get moving." That had been the last thing on Whitney's mind. Everyone needed a rest. But Aquira reminded him of the only reason he was traveling in the first place: to reach Panping and find Sora. There'd been enough distractions and playing hero.

"Whitney!" Lucindur called, walking toward him. "They found her."

Whitney bit his lip in frustration and thought, *Another distraction.* Out loud he said, "She okay?" wondering why he cared about a woman so vile in the first place.

"Let's just say the Drav Cra are no respecters of persons."

"What does that mean?" Whitney asked.

"She was ravaged and left for dead. She's still alive. Barely."

"Where is she?"

Lucindur led Whitney to a house with high grass where a garden once was. They passed one of the fortunate townsmen on the way through the front door. "She's upstairs," he said.

"Thanks, Jahn," she said, and the man waved and gave a solemn smile. The whole scene reminded Whitney of his time in Elsewhere when his father, Rocco, was gravely injured.

Upstairs, Modera laid in a bed with blankets up to her neck, shivering. Her eyes were barely open, but she said, "Whitney Fierstown."

"Modera Pompare," he said, not knowing what else to. He and Lucindur started walking into her room, but Modera stopped them.

"Not her," she said. "Just you."

Whitney turned to Lucindur, ready to argue for her, but Lucindur put up a hand and turned back into the hall.

"You're going to be fine," Whitney said to Modera after closing the door.

"Don't be such an idiot," she replied. "I am dying."

Whitney was taken aback by the honesty.

"I need you to do something for me…" she went on.

Whitney leaned in. "What?"

"Care for Gentry," she said. Then she pointed at the door behind which Lucindur would've been. "Not her. Not Franny. No one but you. Do you understand?"

"I…"

"Are you stupid? It's simple," Modera said with such vigor Whitney questioned how injured the woman even was.

"Fine. Yes. I'll care for the boy. Why?"

"Because he's a fly-in-the-clouds fool and needs to learn how the world works, but he's our youngest, and a troupe is only as strong as its weakest member. Even if our illustrious Pompare Troupe is dead."

"He's not weak."

Modera blew a raspberry. "Teach him all that you know. The boy is quick, just blind to the realities of the world in which we live. Whatever you are, Whitney Fierstown, one thing you aren't is naive."

"I suppose... Yeah," Whitney said, puffing out his chest. "I suppose that's true."

Whitney thought about the life Gentry could have. Free of this troupe and the money-hungry control freaks who ran it, he could really soar.

"He deserves better," Whitney whispered.

"No need to insult," Modera said. "Besides, not everyone is made for greatness, Fierstown. Just give the kid the tools he needs to survive. It's not like he's going to be one of the swinlars of Glinthaven. He likes you. Gods know why. He likes you."

Whitney reached for Modera's hand. The woman shoved it away.

"Just because I'm dying doesn't mean I like you any better," she said. "Now, get the yig out of here and let me die in peace."

Whitney backed away a few steps before turning toward the door.

"Fierstown," Modera said.

Whitney turned back.

"Give my husband a proper burial?"

"Both of you," Whitney said, then returned to the hallway with Lucindur.

As the door shut behind him, he heard a sound downstairs like glasses clinking.

"Lucindur?" Whitney called.

"Come here," she replied.

Whitney raced downstairs, expecting trouble. Instead, he found her in the kitchen going through the cabinets. "Have a drink with me?" she asked.

"Do we have time for that?" Whitney said.

"The caravans are still being prepared. What can we do? There's some fine Breklian brandy here, and it shouldn't go to waste. Come. Sit."

Whitney glanced through the window at the busy members of the troupe passing by. He sighed. "A drink sounds perfect, but if anyone asks, you used your magical wiles to trick me."

Lucindur slid a short glass over and sat down opposite him.

"She told you to take Gentry with you, didn't she?" Lucindur asked.

Whitney was stunned. "How did you…"

"It wasn't magic if that's what you're thinking." She laughed. "Truth is, before you showed up, Gentry was different. He rarely spoke. Hardly ever came out of his tent. Then you and that wyvern showed up, and it was like new life blossomed in his chest. None of us speaks of it for fear of bringing attention to it and him reverting. She's right, they may have taken him in, tried to treat him as a son, but Gentry should be with you. Perhaps it's you who has the magic."

Whitney took a sip of the brandy. "Iam's shog, this is good."

"Nothing in the world like Breklian brandy," Lucindur agreed. She cleared her throat. "So, you'll do it? Take him with you to Panping, and wherever your quest for Sora leads you next?"

"I don't know," Whitney said. "He's a kid. I don't know what I'm doing with a kid."

"You don't know what you're doing with a wyvern either. Think of it as having a caretaker for your little reptilian friend."

"I can barely keep myself alive." He took another sip. "Panping… I don't even know if Sora is there. This could be a giant waste of time."

"If I have learned anything in this troupe, it is that we are all stronger together. No matter who we are."

"Only when you have a silver-tongued hero like me to save your skins," Whitney said, smirking.

Lucindur chuckled. "Do you remember what we discussed the other night?" she asked.

Whitney squinted, thinking. Then a light went on in his brain, but it died just as quickly. "But you said you couldn't locate Sora in the… what did you call it… the Red Tower?"

"I said it would be difficult, but not impossible. And while I wish you could remain with us as we try to revive this troupe, I owe you all the help I can offer in your quest." Lucindur downed her drink, winced from the taste, then slammed the glass down. Whitney couldn't help but be impressed by her style. "Now, do you have anything that belongs to Sora?"

It wasn't the first time Whitney had been asked that, and it saddened him knowing he had nothing. "No."

"Nothing? Are you sure? Nothing she touched or carried?"

"Shog and spit. Aquira!" Whitney said, standing from the table.

"There you go," Lucindur said. "With Aquira, we might be able to find her."

"I'll go get her now," Whitney threw back the glass of brandy and started toward the door until Lucindur stopped him.

"No, not now," she said. "Later. After everyone is asleep, bring her to the cemetery."

"What, will we be communing with the dead? Ghosts. I don't like ghosts."

Lucindur smiled warmly. "No, we just need somewhere wide open where we can be alone. Under the stars."

"If I didn't know any better, I'd think I'd figured out where Talwyn got her aggressive nature."

"What's the saying? 'The apple doesn't fall far…' But no, don't flatter yourself, Fierstown. I prefer my men dark and brooding."

"I think I know just the man for you," Whitney said. "We should get back. I'll bet Franny's cooked up something nice.

Maybe you could play a little bit for everyone. Get their spirits up?"

"No, I'll need to save my strength for this evening if I'm going to have any chance of finding your friend," she said. "It's been a long time since I attempted a lightmancing this complicated. Perhaps too long. We should both get some rest. Come see me when Celeste reaches her zenith."

"I don't know how to repay you," Whitney said.

"We'll think of something."

XXXIX

THE DAUGHTER

Mahi's face was cold stone as she stared across the Boiling Waters. Little droplets of rain pinged against her bare arms. She was cold but refused to shiver, refused to show any emotion at all. A drop hit her cheek, just below the eye, but she didn't even blink.

Upon her finger, she wore a ring made of polished gold, signifying her position as one of the seventy-nine afhems. A new tattoo, stark white against her gray skin, was added to her neck. They'd shaved half her head and added the ink that was customary for afhems. Where the reed of her father's house rose up behind her ear, a crashing wave branched out and onto her skull—the mark of the al'Tariq afhemate.

Her afhemate.

No longer was she Mahraveh Ayerabi, daughter of Muskigo Ayerabi. Sure, she would always be his daughter, but now she was his equal as well. Mahraveh al-Tariq, conqueror of Tal'du Dromesh. She clenched her fist as she heard Yuri Darkings pass by on her right. She remembered the day, not so long ago, after Babrak had thrown Farhan through the Sea Door, when she'd stepped out into the courtyard of the Boiling Keep and cringed under his stare. Now, he and his mass of wealth answered to her.

With the Caleef still missing, Mahi was forced to endure Babrak's passive ridicule of Muskigo as he presented her with the ring and stood nearby, as was custom, while the eunuch marked for the al-Tariq placed it upon her finger.

Babrak couldn't say much. No one could. Mahi had won the afhemate fairly to become the first female afhem in history. She knew it was going to take a miracle for her to keep it—jealous men throughout the Black Sands would continuously take shots at her—but she would fight each battle as it came.

"Can I get you anything, Afhem Mahraveh?" The voice was distant and hollow, same as every other had been since she'd watched her best friend sift through her fingers like sand.

"Huh?"

"Any way I could serve you?" the voice asked again.

"Nothing," she managed to squeeze out. Footsteps retreated. "Wait."

"Yes, Afhem."

"What is your name?" she asked.

"Bit'rudam." The man was young, good-looking. He reminded her of Jumaat with his skinny but firm frame. But unlike Jumaat, he looked as if his brain barely functioned beyond merely following the commands of his superiors. Unlike Jumaat, he was alive.

Bit'rudam was assigned to her along with all the warriors sailing this ship. Warriors of the al'Tariq afhemate, who'd watched the tournament but weren't brave enough to risk their lives in it. She'd have them risking their lives soon enough.

And it wasn't only them. Three Serpent Guards had abandoned their posts at the Latiapur Palace in the dead of night to join her, intent on helping her save her father and find the Caleef rather than passively waiting for his return. They stood directly behind her, without her asking. Their ragged breaths made her skin crawl, and the glare of the beady eyes behind their nightmarish masks was even more terrifying. She was glad to have them, though she wished she'd have been able to see Babrak's face when he found them missing while he made himself comfortable in a palace not meant for him.

"Bit'rudam," she addressed her new follower. "How many ships do I have again?"

"Enough."

Mahi turned to him. His expression was blank, and she couldn't tell if there was a hint of disdain or respect. "Am I not your afhem?" she asked.

"You are."

"Then when I ask a specific question," she said, "I expect a detailed answer."

"I would give one if I could, ma'am. The storm which took your predecessor damaged many of our ships. I have been in Latiapur since. However, repairs are ongoing. We will be the blight of the Boiling Waters again soon."

"I have no plans on staying here."

"Mahi!" Yuri Darkings called from down on the main deck, screaming over a gust of wind which had just caught the ship's ruffled sails.

"It's Afhem Mahraveh," she replied.

"Whatever it is, we are approaching."

He gestured ahead, and Mahraveh's gaze followed the sweep of his arm toward a break in the mist. Sunlight broke through, shining bright atop a cashew-shaped island. Homes made of hardened mud coated the cliffs on the southern side. Others were carved into the very rock itself. Hanging, wooden walkways with impossibly long fishing lines plunging through them and into the sea zigzagged up the rock face.

The other half of the island wore a sheet of black palms and green leaves. An oasis lay in their center, with a massive, stone temple to the God of Sea and Sand erected upon it, half within the water.

Mahi had never seen a paradise so beautiful. It was a place far superior to the dead black sands and the beasts and armies which roamed there. But none of that was what stole her attention. For moored within the islands central inlet were at least two dozen warships of varying sizes, each with uniquely carved and painted bows. The fleet of the al'Tariq afhemate which had guarded the western reaches of the Boiling Waters against pirates and invaders for decades now it all belonged to her.

"Portside approach!" a warrior shouted as he swung down from the top of the sails.

Before Mahi knew what was happening, Bit'rudam grabbed her and led her down the stairs toward the captain's quarters. She shook him off of her when she reached the main deck. Her hand reached for the spear latched to her back.

"What are you doing?" she asked.

"A ship approaches." Bit'rudam pointed. Without an eye for the sea, as these men had, Mahi didn't notice the shadow of a ship off their left side, heading straight for them. She hadn't even needed to give the order. Every warrior aboard the ship arraigned themselves along the port-side and aimed their bows toward the unidentified vessel. More held ropes up on the masts, scimitars in their mouths as they prepared to swing across.

"We must get you to safety," Bit'rudam said.

"Yes, Afhem, he's correct," Yuri Darkings said. He lay his hand upon Mahraveh's shoulder this time and tried to lead her to the secured cabin, but she stood firm.

"I stand with my people," she said. Then, drawing her black-wood spear, she slammed the butt of it against the deck. A few of the warriors glanced back at her but dared not stare long with enemies approaching. Yuri slunk back into the shadow of the captain's quarters and peered around the corner.

"They fly white!" a warrior hanging from the mast shouted down.

Mahi peered through the wall of warriors as the approaching sail came into view. She recognized the symbol painted upon it: a sea-snake wrapping a trident belonging to the Jalurahbak afhemate.

Mahi hurried forward, shoved through the ranks and propped herself up on the rail. A few warriors begged her to step down, but she ignored them.

"Afhem al'Tariq!" a basso voice echoed across the water. "Afhem al'Tariq, please lower your bows. We mean no harm!"

The ship abandoned its course to ram them and instead, turned its side to them. Mahi's men still didn't lower their weapons, and she didn't blame them. But as the Jalurahbak ship's deck came into view, she saw no warriors lined up to face them, only a single man waving a white scarf.

She recognized Afhem Tingur of the Jalurahbak afhemate from the crowd in Latiapur, and the few times he met with her father when she was young. He'd been Afhem for longer than Mahi was alive, rare for those in their position. Surprising, since he was the least intimidating Afhem she'd ever seen.

Babrak may have been fat, but he was massive like a zhulong. Tingur wasn't fat, but he wasn't fit, just soft like he hadn't exercised in ages. His bald head was lumpy and his beard too wispy even to be braided. Mahi had never heard a legend of one of his victories or exploits in all her life, yet still, he ruled his small, nomadic afhemate. Smart enough never to be wiped out or seen as cowardly enough to be usurped.

"Afhem Mahraveh, I am Afhem Tingur!" he called out. "I watched you on the sands." A wave rocked the man's ship and caused him to lose balance. His afhemate roamed the northern Black Sands where the grass was plentiful and life was easier. "Khonayn was my second for years. You fought him with honor."

"What do you want, Afhem?" Mahi said. They had lowered their sails to half to keep pace with Tingur, and every minute of wasted time was the longer her father suffered under the Glass's siege, and by now, their food stores had to be running low.

"I… I should have supported your father from the start. He saved my life long ago in the war with the Glass. I know it's probably too late, and we don't have much to offer, but the Jalurahbak afhemate stands with you."

Mahi grabbed a hanging rope and leaned out over the sea, feeling the salt spray her cheeks. She wiped her face. She knew she hadn't aged much since her father left for his rebellion, but her hands were now calloused.

All those months ago she may have hated Tingur for rejecting her father, only to come crawling to his support when everything seemed lost. She may have cursed him. Now, she lifted her spear, then pointed it in the direction of her new isle, and the dozens of black ships floating beside it. Mahi pulled herself back, dropped the spear—a sign of peace. Then she spat in both hands and raised them toward Afhem Tingur.

"Then I welcome you," she called out. "*We* welcome you! For too long we have suffered beneath the boot of the Glassmen, afraid of a king whose time has come and passed. But that was our fathers' and their fathers' loss. It is time we stop fighting over scraps and show the Glassmen the wrath of the God of Sand and Sea!"She hadn't spoken to her new followers much since they left Latiapur, nor they to her, but each of them spat into their open hands in response, giving salt before erupting into cheers. All those upon the island must have noticed the symbol of their sails and heard their cheers, as they joined in. It echoed so loudly all around her, it was like a terrible storm brewing. Even Yuri Dark-ings stirred from his hiding place and marveled at the commotion.

A chill ran up Mahi' s spine. Farhan was dead because of her. Jumaat was dead because of her. And aboard her ships were hundreds of men who may soon suffer the same fate. But she shook away the thought. Muskigo "The Scythe" Ayerabi, was worth every last one of them. He alone had possessed the testic-ular fortitude to stand up to the Glass when nobody else would.

"Bit'rudam, direct our new allies into the inlet," she ordered. "When we arrive, I want every able ship to be prepped and ready for battle immediately. Tomorrow, we sail for Nahanab" "Yes, Afhem." He bowed before turning and rushing to fulfill her wishes.

"Mr. Darkings," Mahi said, turning to him and purposely leaving out his true honorific. "Dispatch gallers. Any man or women, Shesaitju or not who locates the Caleef and brings him to me alive will receive ten thousand gold autlas."

"Ten thousand?" Yuri replied, incredulous. "I've placed my support behind your family, but that is all I have with me. Your lower decks are filled with many fine weapons purchased with my coin before leaving Latiapur!"

"And I am grateful for your service, but I won't ask again. If he is found, Latiapur will surely reimburse you. Then you can either crawl back into whatever hole you came from."

Yuri bit his lip, then bowed excessively low. "As you command, my lady."

Mahi still wasn't used to people jumping to obey her, but they would now. All of them. If she ordered her warriors to charge without shields into the swath of Glassmen, they would. At least until her leadership failed them. She would have to be smart.

She would not lose them.

She could not.

The God of Sand and Sea was with her. The Siren had practically blessed her, and as her new army became clearer, Mahraveh daydreamed of little, pink-skinned heads on the sharp ends of blackwood spears.

XL

THE KNIGHT

Torsten stood before the gates of the Glass Castle, left open so any man or woman of the kingdom might bid farewell to a member of the royal family. He'd expected that custom might be abandoned in consideration of how Oleander died, but it was better not to show fear. He only hoped Pi was adequately protected.

Shieldsmen at the gate watched who came and went. There were few visitors compared to other royal wakes. Most citizens passed by and offered little more than a cursory glance toward the castle. Braver ones entered the bailey for a better view but went no further. At least they were honest.

As Torsten delved across the open grounds and into the Great Hall, he felt sick. It seemed any noble who hadn't been there in Valin's playpen was filing in, appearing jovial and without a care. They picked at the food offered by castle handmaidens and gossiped amongst each other and with members of the Royal Council.

Torsten had guarded enough of Oleander's parties and other royal funerals to know the faces. Very few among them came from beyond Yarrington for this momentous and solemn occasion.

Lord Eveliss, Duke of Fort Marimount, was there and some others Torsten knew to be loyal houses of the Crown, but most were like the Darkingses or the Jollys. Landowning families with respected names, sycophants waiting for their time to rise up the ladder, or those eager to earn enough favor to sit comfortably right where they already were for the rest of time, growing fat.

"Torsten?" a gruff voice asked. Torsten spun and saw Lord Kaviel Jolly approaching. An empty sleeve hung from his left shoulder, no arm there to fill it. "Torsten, where in Elsewhere have you been?" he asked.

Torsten leaned up on the balls of his toes to see if Lord Jolly was alone. "Busy," he muttered as he continued toward the castle entry.

"Busy?" Lord Jolly sounded appalled. "We were forced to plan the public viewing entirely without you. Sir Mulliner was left to handle all of your affairs. He may be the most experienced Shieldsman here, but he has little experience securing events like this."

Torsten paid him no attention, still craning his neck, scanning the crowd.

"Torsten." Lord Jolly pulled on Torsten's shoulder and turned him around. "I understand grief, but as a member of the Royal Council I must remind you of our duty to the King *and* his family."

"Don't dare talk to me about duty!" Torsten seized him by the collar. Lord Jolly winced, and Torsten quickly loosened his grip. "That's all I'm thinking about. Where is Sir Mulliner?"

"Beside the King; at the throne," Lord Jolly said. "Where you should be."

Torsten grunted in frustration. He pushed Lord Jolly aside and stormed toward the grand, arched entry of the Throne Room.

"Master Unger," Lord Jolly implored, moving back in front of him. "You smell like you slept in a sewer. Please, if you cared for

Oleander like I thought you did, go to your quarters. Draw a bath, clean yourself up and look presentable. There's… is that blood on your blindfold?"

Torsten stopped and regarded the West Tower. Lord Jolly was right. Torsten did look and smell like he belonged in a dungeon. More importantly, lying on his bed was Salvation—the sword Liam had carried into battle so many times—the sword which had slain Redstar.

There's nothing clean about what I must do, he reminded himself.

"No, Lord Jolly," Torsten said. "If you care for Oleander as much as you claim you did. If you truly moved down here to honor your brother and serve your king, then you will step aside so I can do what must be done."

Lord Jolly went to say something, then his throat caught. Torsten took it as an invitation to shove by him and into the Throne Room. Oleander petals were sprinkled around the Queen's coffin, still right where he'd left it. Citizens cycled through, stopping beside her to pay their respects, or curse her cold corpse. They were meant to offer prayers, though most stopped to stare like she was a curiosity. They wanted a chance to see their shrew of a queen up close and find out if her beauty was overstated.

It wasn't.

Last time Torsten couldn't see her, but now he did. She wore her favorite azure dress, the bottom draping down from her pedestal and across the floor like cascading water. Even with his limited sight, Torsten could perceive the frilled ends, coated in flecks of diamond. Her long, silvery hair tumbled over her shoulders the way it would when she'd made Torsten check the back of her dress, or clasp one of her many necklaces though she had handmaidens to do it. A milky, crystalline mask covered the burnt half of her face, skin powdered at the edge, so it was impossible to see where she'd been damaged.

Torsten's heart began to race. He had to lean against a column to gather himself. He hadn't seen her in a month, and now she looked like a porcelain doll.

This is all too perfect for her.

He drew a deep breath, then pushed his way through the line of citizens, earning scowls and grunts of disapproval. He struggled to merely glance at her as he passed by, struggled not to kneel by her side and remember all those times he was appalled by her, or feared her, until the moment he saw the true Oleander atop Mount Lister. The lioness who would do anything to protect her cub.

"I'm glad you made it," a familiar voice said. Father Morningweg stood by the Queen's head, tracing his burned-out eyes in prayer with each passer-by. Torsten hadn't noticed him before he'd spoken. The man actually looked like a real priest, with his head shaved, an Eye of Iam pendant hanging from his neck atop a white robe.

Father Morningweg flicked his nose, face aimed straight at Torsten. "I could smell you coming from the entry," he said.

Torsten offered him a nod, wondering if the man could still see, and continued along. The Glass Throne lay ahead, fit for a king twice Pi's size. Shieldsmen lined the exquisite carpet which unfurled from its dais. Members of the Royal Council were its foot, including Lord Jolly. Among them was none other than Valin Tehr—the apparently-already-appointed Master of Coin. He whispered something into Pi's ear while the boy sat, chin in his palm, a thousand-meter gaze aimed toward his mother's corpse.

"Sir Unger," one of the Shieldsmen saluted. Then another. None of them stopped him as he approached, and he was only a few meters away by the time Valin looked up, and the subtle grin was wiped off his face.

"Torsten?" Pi said, sitting up. He slid to the edge of the over-sized throne. "Torsten, where have you been?"

All the color left Valin's cheeks. "S... Sir Unger, we've missed you," he said.

Torsten bit back a response. He fell to a knee before the throne and lowered his head. "Your Grace, I'm so sorry I wasn't here for you," he said.

"Mother trusted you," Pi said. "I trusted you, and... and you weren't here."

"A mistake only Iam can forgive."

"Have you been drinking, Sir Unger?" Valin said. "This isn't the—"

"You will be silent, snake!" Torsten roared. His voice echoed down the hall, casting a hush upon the crowd. He looked toward Valin, through the blessed blindfold that gave him sight. Valin couldn't have known Torsten's eyes now saw and were focused on him, but the way he squirmed and shifted his cane from one hand to the other was satisfaction enough.

"Torsten, that is enough," Pi said. "This isn't the time. Lord Tehr provided all of this for mother, and I'm grateful."

"Your Grace, it's clear Sir Unger is still in too much pain," Valin addressed Pi. "We should fetch someone to escort him to his quarters quietly."

"Your Grace." Torsten turned his attention directly toward Pi. The king's head tilted as if he too felt that he was being looked at. "Do you remember the dream you told me about?" he said. "Of peace unlike even that which your father dreamed of."

Pi nodded meekly.

"It's never too late," Torsten said. "It wasn't for your mother. It wasn't for your father. He'd just... he'd lost the truth of Iam's light. I don't know when it happened, but we shouldn't have let him lose sight."

"Your Grace, I know you care for Sir Unger, but he's rambling like a drunkard," Valin said. "Please, I insist we have him removed and finish this discussion later. This is your mother's funeral, not a council meeting."

"I warned him of the same," Lord Jolly said.

Torsten could tell Pi wanted to say something, but he didn't. He couldn't.

"Sir Mulliner, come here," Torsten requested. The Shieldsman stood directly behind Pi, with a watch over the entire room. He looked from side to side, confused. "Please, I need your help getting up."

Pi and the rest remained still and silent for a long moment until Pi raised his hand and offered a slight wave. His expression showed pity for Torsten, the man he'd thought was his mentor—for what he now believed to be a cripple without a real place any longer.

"I don't know what happened to you, Sir Unger," Mulliner said. "But you look worse than you did after Winde Port." He took Torsten by the arm and lifted him. Torsten clutched his arm in return.

"Si… Austun. Do you trust me?" he asked.

"I thought I did."

"Humor me one last time."

"What is it?" Mulliner asked.

Torsten exhaled slowly through his teeth. He knew there would be no going back. It was now or never, and he couldn't allow himself to make the same mistakes he'd made in the past. Redstar lived and brought ruin to the Glass. Torsten could not allow Valin to do the same.

"Iam forgive me," he said. Then he tore the longsword from Mulliner's sheath and pushed him aside. Lord Jolly threw himself in front of Pi, whose eyes went wide with fright. But not as wide as Valin's.

Torsten didn't give him a chance to say anything and spread his poison. With one fluid swipe, Torsten slashed the blade and cleaved the head of South Corner's biggest and only crime lord clean from his shoulders. Valin's cane fell first, clanking against the marble even as his body dropped. Then his head landed with a thud and rolled to a stop at Torsten's feet, tongue hanging out like he'd just missed his chance to get a last word in.

An instant later, Mulliner tackled Torsten to the ground as he had too many times before. Swords and spears of a dozen Shieldsmen pointed at his neck. Torsten didn't fight this time. He just looked up at the king, who gaped in horror at Valin's headless body. Lord Jolly tried to shield him, but Pi didn't let him. Then, the fray caused Torsten's blindfold to be ripped off his head, and his world went dark again.

"It was him, Your Grace," Torsten said, calm as a lamb to the slaughter although he had to speak loudly for his voice to carry over the terror of Oleander's crowd. "Rand, the Caleef, the Dom Nohzi… he was behind it all. I couldn't let another deceiver steal your ear, no matter how rich."

"You've truly lost it this time!" Mulliner shouted. "Take this traitor away to the dungeons for good."

"There is proof, Your Grace!" Torsten said. His previous calm allowed a quick movement to free him for a second so he could breathe. "I saw it myself."

"For Iam's sake, you *can't* see," Mulliner said. "Get him in cuffs before he murders someone else!"

"I've never seen more clearly. Your Grace, I would never betray you. I swear it on your mother and father. I swear it on my own life." Torsten wrestled free again, removed the shred of Valin's letter, with Yuri Darkings' signature emblazoned across the parchment, and slapped it down on the floor.

Mulliner and the others then yanked Torsten backward, gaining full control of him. He'd somehow managed to find the blindfold and struggled to get it over his seared flesh. Through the mess of legs and limbs, Torsten saw Pi leap off his throne and pick up the fragile piece of paper.

"Wait!" Pi said. Torsten heard the boy's light footsteps near him, then the sound of fabric creasing as he knelt before him. "What is this?"

"The truth," Torsten fought to say.

Torsten found himself staring into the eyes of the king. He couldn't see color, but he knew how they matched Liam's. Only, now that he wasn't blinded by the brilliant shades of amber, he now saw Oleander's in them too. Fierce and unyielding as the wild tundra from whence she came.

Torsten reached out and grasped both sides of Pi's face. "I see them both in you so clearly."

Pi patted Torsten's scorched eyes over the blindfold. He appeared dumbfounded at first. Then his confusion turned to marvel. Torsten knew Wren and other priests long enough to understand how it was different when a blind man faced you, how no matter how close they were to looking at you, they were always slightly off. But Torsten's focus never wavered.

"How?" Pi whispered.

"Iam is with us again," Torsten replied. "Perhaps, he never left. We only needed to close our eyes and let him in."

XLI

THE MYSTIC

A day and a half had passed since Freydis descended below the muddy, bloody soil. Sora still found herself chained to a tree in the Buried Hollow. Her wrists burned and ached from the restraints, but Nesilia didn't seem to care. She'd slept there, eaten there, relieved herself just beyond the borders of the pit—which was more than most of the savages did.

The ceremony, which was supposed to be something sacred and beautiful, had turned into an orgy some time ago, and the Drav Cra had only become more drunk and belligerent. Sprouts rose from the dirt as warlocks surrendered and used their magic to send themselves up. They were then yanked to the surface by their ropes, and not punished, but celebrated. Dragged into unspeakable celebrations of their people.

Listeners called out when they no longer heard heartbeats underground, their warlocks having pushed too far and suffocated alone. Nobody dug those failures up to check; they merely trusted the Listeners and sliced the rope. The dead were left to feed the earth and the maggots until they were no more than pale bone.

By now, of the many who went under, only four remained

buried and alive. Kotlkel, Sahades, Freydis, and young Wven-weigard were all beneath the plot of dirt Tihabat had listened to from the start, though now all the other listeners were in a circle around her, ears to the ground. Their ropes had tangled by then, now making it impossible to tell which line belonged to which warlock.

Presently, a vine sprouted from the earth. It took a handful of Listeners to grab it and heave. Nesilia perked up to watch the body surface, and Sora couldn't help but watch from Nowhere with great interest. Wvenweigard coughed on dirt and was revealed. He lasted long for one so young and was greeted with congratulations.

Like he did with all those indwelling for the first time and becoming warlocks, Rathgorah greeted him personally.

"You have lain with the Lady, and now drink of the blood of her first creation," Oracle Rathgorah said. He held the bowl filled with his own blood and dripped a bit of it onto Wvenweigard's tongue. "You are her warlock. Her hand upon this realm."

More cheers sounded. Other surviving warlocks, young and old, greeted Wvenweigard, bringing him food and drink. He smiled, but Sora could tell it was forced. Out of the corner of his eye, he watched Sora—no, not Sora, Sora's body. He seemed glum when he should've been ecstatic.

"He could've lasted longer," Nesilia said within, as if Sora were asking. *"But he believes."*

"Then he's a fool," Sora answered. She said, but she couldn't deny the anxiousness she now felt. Nesilia wasn't feeling it alone. Only three remained, and only one could ensure nearly everybody in this forest wasn't slaughtered by their own goddess for doubting her.

"Unhand me, scallywag!" shouted a gruff voice. It was in such opposition to the overwhelmingly celebratory sounds surrounding the pit, impossible not to hear.

A moment later, a towering figure stumbled through the dark of the woods and into the clearing: Grisham "Gold Grin" Gale, wearing half of King Liam's Glass Crown stolen by Whitney what seemed like ages ago. A dire wolf walked at his back, snarling and keeping him briskly moving forward. He was an infamous pirate, scourge of all the seas, and his eyes were bright with terror. It was an unnerving sight. Behind them were what remained of the other pirates from his ship and a small army of Drav Cra warriors.

"What is the meaning of this!" Oracle Rathgorah exclaimed. He was still weary, requiring his staff to stand. "On this most sacred of days!"

Haral, dradinengor of the Dagson clan stepped in front of Gold Grin. She was now dressed like a proper warrior. Her hair was a nest of golden sunshine. Tight leathers hugged her massive frame beneath furs, and she carried a long spear.

Nesilia shifted in a way that spoke of discomfort or confusion —not an emotion Sora was used to feeling from the goddess. Sora, however, felt hope rise.

"That quim licker lied to us," Haral said, pointing to Sora. "Just as Warlock Kotlkel prophesied."

"Haral, explain yourself." Oracle Rathgorah rose to his full height, which had somehow become impressive. He trod across the filled pit. The Listeners didn't flinch, didn't even move from their spots listening to the soil, but nearly every man and woman present had stirred from their carnal revelries, lurking in the shadows of the trees, wearing furs or nothing but blood and dirt, the risen warlocks among them.

"Before Kotlkel Dagson indwelled, he gave orders for us to find out what the Panpingese witch was up to," Haral said. "He suspected there was foul play afoot, that the Glass were unsatisfied with driving us out of Yarrington and slaughtering our great, unified army, but sought to taint this sacred place as well."

"Seize her!" Haral shouted. Immediately, the warriors with her began to approach Sora.

"Stop," Rathgorah said softly. They all did. "She is chained to a tree and bound at the wrists and feet. What more do you want?"

"These *flower pickers* were found waiting off the coast. Tell me that is a coincidence?"

All eyes pointed toward Sora now, mouths whispering.

"We mustn't rush to judgment," Rathgorah said.

"I am dradinengor of the Dagson clan!" Haral shouted, now spinning to address the entire gathering. "I may not be a warlock or a hand of our Lady, but Drad Mak will die in the south, and our army did not join him to die for Redstar. Only we can keep the Glass from invading again!"

Voices all around echoed their agreement, and many unburied warlocks even drifted toward her in support. More armed warriors accompanying Haral flooded through the darkness. She wasn't exaggerating the size of her army. They had dire wolves, axes, thick armor… everything those at the ceremony didn't.

"How dare you bring weapons to this sacred place!" Rathgorah barked.

"You've made it necessary," Haral said. She then plucked the broken crown off Gold Grin's head and shook it. "Look at this. This man is Glass nobility, traveled here with them to destroy us!"

"Nobility?" Gold Grin laughed. "I be a pirate who raids the Glass same as ye. I be a friend, and that there be my treasure!"

He snatched back the crown, but the dire wolf nipped at Gold Grin's rear. Haral grabbed Gold Grin and flung him down the hill. He skidded to a stop at the edge of the pit, in a pool where the blood of the bodies above had gathered. The glittering crown bounced, then fell flat at Tihabat's foot. The girl momentarily lifted her ear from the ground and crawled closer to look at it, but Rathgorah bent down and lifted it. He spun it in his hands, examining it from every angle.

If Whitney could only see where that thing is now, Sora thought.

"What is—" Gold Grin spat and wiped his blood-covered tongue. Then, as his head rose, he noticed Sora for the first time. "Sora?" he said.

"See!" Haral said. "He calls her by her true name. She is no goddess, only another deceiver."

The whispers of the crowd turned into full-voiced murmurs. Rathgorah turned his attention from Haral and examined the irate mob. Fear rippled across his face. They were drunk, lustful, distracted—all the ingredients necessary for a riot. And Sora didn't need Nesilia's memories to recognize that the relationship between warlocks and Drav Cra warriors who provided all the food and supplies for their people by raiding settlements wasn't always harmonious.

Rathgorah hooked the crown to his belt. "Bring her to me," he commanded, pointing his staff at Sora.

Once again, Sora was grabbed, unshackled from the tree, and hoisted to her bound feet. Rough hands shoved her toward the Oracle. Nesilia could have freed herself from the bonds and turned them all to ash if she wanted, but like Sora, she waited, watched.

Sora's thoughts drifted to the orepul—said to have encased part of King Pi's soul. She felt like that, like her body was nothing more than a doll.

"What do you have to say?" Rathgorah asked.

Nesilia said nothing, and Sora was buried too deep in Nowhere to do anything.

"Answer him, foreigner!" Haral demanded.

"Do you still not understand to whom you speak?" Nesilia said through Sora's parted lips. "This whole ceremony—is it not meant to honor me? For generations, you people have begged for my spirit to bless you, yet now I am here in physical form, and you scorn me… tie me up like an animal."

"It is the Buried Goddess!" came a voice from the crowd. It was Wvenweigard.

"Shut up, *bareese*!" another cursed at him, but Nesilia only looked straight ahead at Rathgorah.

"Some would still believe your very presence here stains this sacred ritual," Rathgorah said. "A foreigner from a foreign land."

"And you?" she asked.

Sora couldn't help wonder why Nesilia didn't yet fight back. She knew her opinion on non-believers, and she was more than capable. Sora had seen her command the vines, the ocean, the wind. They were surrounded by the Buried Goddess' own creation. The words she'd spoken to Wvenweigard were true. A snap of her fingers and death would collapse upon them all—Sora didn't even believe the finger snapping was necessary.

"Sora, what's goin on?" Gold Grin asked. "I stayed moored and waited just as you asked, then their longboats surrounded us." The sounds of fists against his huge body met Sora's ears and silenced him.

"See, he did come with her. Let us end this!" Haral shouted to Oracle Rathgorah. "Dig up the traitor, Freydis, and crucify them both like we should have done from the start. Then Kotlkel and I will protect our world from the foreigners who have so scorned us!"

"We mustn't taint the indwelled," Rathgorah protested. "We will know who remains in the end."

"Already they are tainted, just sharing the earth with her."

Several cries of agreement rose until a small voice broke through the crowd. "One has died!"

Everyone turned to see Tihabat Dagson pointing to one of the three tangled ropes still with a body on the end. Two large warriors walked over to the corresponding rope and pulled.

"No!" Rathgorah shouted. "They feed the earth. The dead mustn't rise from the Earthmoot."

"Move aside!" Haral said, pushing him. Rathgorah reached for his dagger but stopped. Her warriors would easily overwhelm him, and with warlocks scattered throughout the crowd, it was impossible to guess which side they'd take.

The warriors unwound the ropes and pulled the one to which Tihabat gestured. Sora saw a leg burst through. She found herself hoping it wasn't Freydis and she didn't understand why. Then she realized her thoughts and feelings were Nesilia's and not her own. In that moment, she also realized Nesilia wasn't strong enough to resist. Like when they were drowning in Ice Deep, she felt fear, real fear, not just using it to taunt Sora.

"*Stop it, girl,*" Nesilia said within. "*You don't understand the powers you trifle with.*"

"Oh, I believe I do!" Sora shouted internally, and it came out through her physical lips as her own self broke through momentarily. It stole the attention of everyone present as the dead warlock flopped onto the dirt, lifeless, and no one even noticed. It was not Freydis, but Sahades.

Across the pit, roars of violence coalesced with yowls of anguish, tipping Sora off that Gold Grin had made a move.

Nesilia reclaimed control of her body and spun to watch the battle, but she didn't move. Sora focused with all her might to try and drive her legs toward the pirate, but they merely shook.

"*Do something,*" Sora said within. "*You owe him for forcing him here.*"

"*He came of his own volition.*"

"*That's a lie.*"

Gold Grin stole a blade off one of the Drav Cra, and his men had done the same with similar weapons. One got the jump on the dire wolf and split its skull. They fought with the bravery and skill Sora had come to know.

"Stop this!" Rathgorah shouted. Nesilia turned back, and Sora saw the blood pouring from a newly-opened wound on the Oracle's arm. Immediately, everyone fighting—Drav Cra and pirate alike—froze just as Sora had in the Webbed Woods so long ago under the influence of Redstar's magics. "Enough is enough."

Rathgorah flicked his hand, and all those fighting floated over the pit and to a spot before him. Sora stood amid it all. If the Oracle released his hold on them for even a heartbeat, Sora was sure she'd have been run through by a spear.

"This is Earthmoot, and you have all desecrated it!" Rathgorah roared. His voice was louder, enhanced somehow.

"Oracle Rathgorah, it was she… this knife-ear… this witch." Haral spoke through a clenched jaw, forced shut by Rathgorah's magic. "She ruined it, and it was Freydis who brought her here. Let us end Redstar's foolish influence once and for all."

"One of the indwellers has died, and you were all so blinded by ambition that you tore her from the Lady's loving womb. How will we expect the Lady to care of her passing if we cannot even muster the respect to do so ourselves?"

"Would that it have been her!" Haral exclaimed, clearly referring to Freydis.

"But it was not. Only Kotlkel and Freydis still breathe." He looked to the children as if seeking confirmation of his words. When none protested, he continued. "And if she wins, she is rightfully our Arch Warlock."

"Then dig her up now and put her to death, or else she will bring about the death of us all," Haral pleaded.

"And further mar this holy day?" Rathgorah scolded.

"It is this mystic keeping her alive with her dark magic. Otherwise, our Lady surely would have made Freydis the first to swallow dirt."

"Do you claim our Lady to be so weak that one of the

Panpingese could control the fate of her hand?" Oracle Rathgorah asked.

"Rathgorah, let them go," said one of the watching warlocks, an older man with knotted gray hair.

After a nod, he lowered his hand, and they were all released of the power. "If any of you moves a muscle toward one another, you will be dead before you can explain," Rathgorah said.

Sora was relieved to see that Gold Grin and his men obeyed. The stout pirate straightened his beard and cracked his knuckles. "I'd like to see ye try," he said but made no move.

"The one they call 'Sora,'" Rathgorah said. "Now that the truth is revealed. Tell us, why are you here, and why are these men accompanying you with a crown of glass?"

"This vessel is Sora," Nesilia said. Hearing her name spoken allowed made Sora want to cringe and recede fully into the nothingness of Nowhere. "She is the daughter of the Ancient One, Sora Sumati, and the former king of Glass, Liam, the one they call conqueror. I am not she."

Haral laughed, and her warriors joined her. "If this tiny thing is the daughter of Liam the Conqueror, then I'm a goddess too."

Rathgorah clamped his fingers in Haral's direction and her lips sealed. "You still claim to be the Buried Goddess," Rathgorah said. It was not a question. When she didn't answer, he raised his bloody hand. With it, Sora felt her feet leave the ground. "Then allow me to kill a god."

"Chaos it is," Nesilia said. She stretched her wrists, and the bindings there and on her ankles turned to ash. She fell back to the earth, breaking Rathgorah's magic. The warriors holding her gasped, but Nesilia raised a fist, and the trees above came to life, snatching them off the ground and crushing them in their boughs.

"Sora!" a voice called suddenly, familiar, but distant. Hearing it caused Nesilia to miss a step and stagger, and a spear thrust forward, gashing her side. Nesilia grabbed it, and the weapon erupted into a flame so hot, it consumed its wielder.

"We are deceived!" Rathgorah yelled. He pointed his staff, and his powerful magic again manipulated the muscles of Sora's body.

"No, it is you all who have been deceived by your own eyes!" Nesilia shouted. More branches from above extended toward Rathgorah, but they stopped before wrapping him.

Nesilia's fear returned in full force when the Oracle's magic wasn't broken, and she was lifted higher off the ground. Again that familiar voice echoed in Sora's mind. When she blinked and reopened her eyes, light bloomed all around them. The warlocks were gone, and she thought she saw...

"What mystic power is this?" Nesilia asked, her voice now bound to Nowhere as well. *"Stop resisting!"* The light dissipated and again the Drav Cra reappeared. The scars in the Oracle's body seemed to glow, and all the warlocks and warriors were arrayed against her. Gold Grin and his men were on their knees, at their mercy and unable to fight.

"I'm not doing this," Sora answered.

"The light... it can't be you..."

Nesilia struggled against Rathgorah's power, but she couldn't break it. Sora could feel the Buried Goddess willing her to help, now unable to speak, like Sora had been during her blackouts on their journey from Panping. Like Nesilia was now buried deep in Nowhere.

Gold Grin's voice warbled through the confusion, calling Sora's name. Then, in a sudden and jarring shift, Sora found herself in Nowhere once again, pushed out entirely. "No! No! No! No!" she called.

She was alone. Nowhere enveloped her, snuffing out any sense of her surroundings. There was no more sight or sound.

"Gold Grin!" Sora yelled.

"Sora?" that familiar voice came again. Now, with Nesilia's fear not clouding her own thoughts, Sora realized who it was. "Sora!"

"Whitney!" Sora screamed.

"Sora!" she heard again.

There was a loud slamming sound, followed by a brilliant white light. It was bright, impossibly bright, like she was staring at the sun. She squinted, putting her palm up in a futile attempt to block it out. Then, Sora saw something that conjured up tears.

"Aquira!" Sora breathed, the word barely coming out she was so overwhelmed. She became even more stunned when her eyes shifted down and saw Whitney collapsing to his knees, hands wiping away tears. He started crawling, then got up and ran at her. She watched as he ran but didn't move, she couldn't. Rathgorah's power still overwhelmed her muscles.

"Whit. Oh, Whit," she said. "Is that really you?"

XLII

THE THIEF

Whitney had a fitful rest, tossing and turning in his bed. It was hot, and his blanket had long since bunched itself at the bottom of the mattress. His mind raced, telling him that if he fell asleep again, he might return to that awful, hopeless dream of Kazimir and Sora.

Still unable to beat the heat or his rampant thoughts, Whitney tore his shirt off, balled it, and threw it against the far wall, then flipped his pillow and punched it a few times before lying back down. After a moment, he groaned and scooted out of bed to open the curtains, hoping a bit of air would drive away the stuffiness of the room. The problem was, it was still daytime. He didn't understand how the entirety of the refugee party seemed to be fast asleep while he just rolled around in sticky sweat.

It wasn't even hot out. The constant rains had brought in cool air, but his mind wouldn't stop turning. Thoughts of Sora coursed through his mind like a theater play. Them together in Yarrington, Winde Port, even memories from Fake Troborough and seeing her playing with his younger self by the river. Then the awful dreams. All these thoughts and more ensured Whitney would remain miserable.

Shutting his eyes tight, he said, "Iam, if you're real, if you're listening…" then he groaned again. "Shogging exile, forget about it." He stood, opened the room's window even though rain sprinkled in. Then he flipped over and squeezed the pillow around his head.

He must have fallen asleep, because the next thing he knew, the smell of night-blooming jasmine hit his nostrils. He opened his eyes and nearly leaped from his skin when he saw someone standing there, just paces from his bed.

"T-Talwyn?" Whitney stammered.

She wore nothing but a smile, and her smooth, dark skin glowed like polished bronze with Celeste's light pouring in through the open window. She stepped forward and pushed her long black hair over her shoulder.

"Hi. Um. What are you doing?" he asked.

She continued her stride, hips seeming to draw circles in the air. Whitney blinked, turned away, turned back, blinked again. He didn't know what to do, what to say. Instead, he merely pushed himself up on his elbows, suddenly aware of his own body. As hot as he was, he pulled the blankets up to cover himself.

"I told you, you deserve a reward for your heroics on the bridge," she said.

"Most people just give out ribbons, or autlas," Whitney said, flustered. "This… Talwyn—"

"Shhhhh," she said, now so close Whitney could feel the heat of her skin. She grabbed his hand and moved it toward her navel, but Whitney forced it to her hip.

"Listen, I'm flattered, really," he said. "I'm honored. I'm… many things. But, you don't want this."

"Trust me, I don't do anything I don't want to," she said, pushing against his hand. Strands of hair tickled his chest as she lowered her face toward his and said, "And I want this."

Whitney squirmed and slipped around her, coming out the

other side. She turned, glanced down at him in naught but his underwear, and then, smiling, said, "Whitney, I know you want this."

"I—I—Talwyn, just listen to me for a moment…" he said.

But she already had her hand against his chest and pushed him backward. "It's been a long… hard… journey and we are all ready for some relief. Maybe we could help each other?"

"I don't…"

"You can make believe I'm her if you need to."

Whitney's eyes went wide. "How…"

"I'm Glintish Whitney. This, all of this, life at its rawest. It's all art."

"Art." Whitney chuckled. "Yeah."

Whitney pushed Talwyn back and onto the bed. She was smiling, but her grin quickly left when she noticed he wasn't following. Instead, Whitney grabbed his shirt and pants from the floor and threw open the door. He hopped down the hallway on one leg, getting dressed and said, "This is not right," to no one in particular.

Gentry's room wasn't far, and Whitney didn't bother to knock.

"Huh," Gentry said, half asleep as Whitney swept in.

Whitney clicked his tongue, and Aquira's head popped up. "Just going to take Aquira out for some fresh, rainy air. Don't mind me. Keep sleeping."

"Mmmmhmmmm," Gentry said and then rolled over.

Whitney scooped up the wyvern and placed her on his shoulder. She blinked lazily, then draped herself like a warm, reptilian scarf around his neck. With Gentry growing so close to Aquira, Whitney hadn't spent nearly as much time with her as he'd become used to. Probably because every time he saw her, he thought of Sora.

He also hadn't realized how heavy she'd gotten. When they'd first met back in the Winde Traders Guild, she'd been barely larger than a house cat. Now, her head hung to Whitney's chest on one side and her tail even lower on the other. She must have doubled in size.

He softly shut the door and passed Talwyn on the way downstairs. "Excuse me," he whispered. "Sorry." She still looked utterly stunned, like she'd never been rejected before in her life—which she likely hadn't. He couldn't believe he was doing it either.

Whitney said he was sorry, but he wasn't, not really. He'd never have thought Lucindur had meant this when she said they'd figure out a way to repay the debt. What was she thinking, that Whitney would just throw himself at her daughter in order to find Sora? The Glintish people were obviously loose with their sexual exploits, and although Whitney could've been found in many a bed over the years, things were different now, and he thought Lucindur knew that.

"Lucindur!" Whitney shouted as he reached the Fettingborough cemetery grounds. Aquira lifted her head, then put it back down again just as fast. Grass was still matted from where he, Rand, and the cowardly Grint Strongiron had battled the Northmen. Drav Cra bodies were sprinkled about, the last to be cleaned out. They all deserved to be burned, or worse.

Lucindur didn't respond, but Whitney could see the candles burning softly next to the old undertaker's shack.

"How dare you!" Whitney growled.

Lucindur didn't even twitch. She sat on a cushion no doubt stolen from the Pompares' carriage, legs crossed, lightly plucking at her salfio. A stream of smoke billowed from a pipe pressed between her lips. Around her, Fireflies rose and fell, softly glowing like magical energy.

"If I knew this would be the cost—"

"Shhhhh," Lucindur cut him off.

"I am tired of being shushed!" Whitney shouted.

Lucindur stopped played and turned her head. Just her head. "What are you prattling about?"

"Your daughter. You expected me to, what, *pleasure* your daughter in return for finding the woman I love? What kind of sick, twisted, Glintish—"

"Pleasure my daughter?" Lucindur laughed. "Whitney, I assure you, I have no idea what you're talking about."

"Then how did she know about Sora!"

Lucindur stood and laid her salfio to the side. She took a quick puff of her pipe and said, "I didn't say a word to her about Sora. She said Sora?"

Whitney thought for a moment. Talwyn hadn't said a name, he didn't think.

"Not exactly," Whitney admitted. "She said, '*You can make believe I'm her.*' What was I supposed to think?"

"It's not exactly a secret that you're pining after someone, Whitney Fierstown. For a thief, you don't mask your emotions very well. At least not during this season of life."

Whitney ran a hand through his hair. "Former thief. So, you didn't send Talwyn to my room in exchange…" He let his words trail off. "I'm sorry. It's been a rough night."

"For us all," Lucindur reminded him, smoothing the wrinkles in her dress absentmindedly. "And how is my daughter? Did you turn her down gently?"

"Not exactly."

"You will right that wrong when we are done here, yes?" Lucindur asked. It wasn't a question, although it was posed as one.

"I'm sorry."

"My daughter cares for you, Whitney. Gods know why. She's not used to being turned down and is never shy about her wants. She's not weak either, but I will not have her sulking. There's a long trip ahead of us and today has been difficult enough. Now, give me Aquira, and take a seat."

Whitney handed the wyvern over, then looked around for another cushion. When he didn't find one, he looked back to Lucindur, but she was seated again with Aquira curled up in her lap. Lucindur's eyes were already closed, and her fingers were moving along the fretboard, strings vibrating beneath her fingertips. They slowly began to glow blue, like the nightcap mushrooms that shone in the forest of Troborough where Whitney grew up.

Whitney lowered himself to the cold earth. The ground was squishy and wet, but he settled in and cleared his throat.

"Just relax and let the song wash over you," she said.

"Mmmmmkay?" Whitney closed his eyes and tried to focus, but he didn't know what he was supposed to be focusing on. "Like this?" he asked."

Lucindur didn't answer. She just began singing, slowly at first, the pace picking up gradually.

> *Let your mind be opened,*
> *eyes be opened.*
> *Let the winds of eternity*
> *bring upon them clarity.*
> *Your eyes can't see*
> *but your mind is free*
> *to travel Pantego*
> *wherever she may be.*

Lucindur continued playing the stringed instrument, notes echoing in the still of night. As time passed, Whitney grew uncomfortable, then discouraged.

"I don't see anything," he said.

Light upon stars
dancing afar.
The nameless, the lost
Forgotten at great cost
Upon song and light
give us sight.

The fireflies began dancing around Lucindur in an unnatural fashion, and Whitney realized they weren't fireflies at all. Lucindur kept singing, but Whitney didn't hear the words. He just watched as the streaks emanating from the light specks grew in size until all that could be seen was an ever-moving bright spot. Aquira purred—a sound Whitney'd never heard her make.

The salfio chords were so loud now, Whitney wondered how anyone in town wouldn't hear and come running. But Lucindur's voice still cut through, and she hardly projected at all.

See what you came to see.
See with your soul, not with your eyes.

Instantly, the light died away; the sounds died away. Pressure built around Whitney's ears as if he were underwater. Whitney tried to open his eyes but found that, despite the utter darkness, they were already open. He began to panic. Everything was gone. There was no sky or stars. He couldn't feel the wet grass beneath him. It was just emptiness, and he was terrified he'd fallen into Elsewhere again.

"Hello?" he called. His voice echoed like he stood at the bottom of the Jarein Gorge. "Lucindur!"

Nothing.

Whitney's heart beat in his throat, horse hooves driving him deeper and deeper.

"Oh, Gods, not again," he said. "Not again. Please, Iam, not—"

"No!" shouted a voice Whitney knew. "No! No! No!" It was distant and hollow, but he knew it well.

"Sora?" he said. "Sora!"

"Gold Grin!"

Gold Grin? Whitney thought, then yelled, "Sora!"

A moment passed, and Whitney still couldn't see anything, but he felt something: hope.

"Whitney!"

"Sora!"

They shouted each others' names back and forth while Whitney pumped his legs. He had no indication he was moving at all, and her voice came from every direction at once, but he refused to stay still. He spun circles, desperate to find the source of the sound.

A sudden, loud *boom*, like a massive metal door slamming shut, buried Sora's voice, stopped him in his tracks. He turned, and his eyes were met with a blinding light not unlike what he'd seen in Elsewhere, pulsating from the top of Mt. Lister.

"Gods, no. Not this place again," Whitney said aloud.

Then, within the light, he saw Aquira's shadow, flapping no-longer-injured wings and heard her trilling her tongue.

"Aquira…" Sora whispered under her breath.

Even in silhouette form, Sora was unmistakable. All breath fled Whitney's lungs, and he collapsed to his knees. As soon as enough strength returned to his members, Whitney began crawling, then pushed himself to his feet, and he ran to Sora. But as much as he ran, he didn't seem to draw closer. He called her name again. She turned, staring in his direction, through him more than anything.

"Whit," she said. "Oh, Whit. Is that really you?"

"What you don't recognize me?" He smirked through his tears. "Sora, where are we?"

"Nowhere."

"Sora, are you okay? What do you mean 'nowhere'?'" Whitney asked.

"I don't… It's awful." Sora tried to grab Aquira who flapped in front of her, but her hands passed through. "Whit. It's awful. How did you find me?"

"You're the one who understands magic." Whitney shrugged. "I think Lucindur…"

"Lucindur?"

"Don't worry, she's only a friend," he snickered.

Neither he nor Sora may not have been able to approach each other, but she smiled and shook her head. It was the same look she gave Whitney every time he told her something ridiculous. The look he'd go through anything to see again.

"And I thought you only worked alone?" Sora said.

"You changed me." He reached out as if to touch Sora's cheek. She closed her eyes like all she wanted was to feel the warmth of his hand. But he couldn't draw any nearer.

"You can't," Sora said. "I think… I think we're in my mind or, somewhere between Elsewhere and our world," Sora said, unsure.

"Your…" His lump in his throat bobbed as he swallowed hard. "Between?"

"Whitney, the things I've done. The awful things." Something happened, and Sora dropped to her knees, then clenched her stomach and curled up. Aquira lowered herself and nuzzled at Sora's arms, unable to physically touch them.

"What's wrong?' Whitney asked, trying to approach. As soon as he got close, he was far again. "This isn't making any sense. Is this real?"

"I've been asking that question since it started," Sora replied.

"Light of Iam, Whitney. The things I've done." Sora sat up, and the terror in her expression rocked Whitney to his core. He'd never seen her like that before, even the first time she encountered Kazimir. "Nesilia. She—"

"Nesilia?" Whitney interrupted. "What are you talking about? Sora, where are you?"

"She's using my body, Whit! She's done all horrible manner of things with it."

"Where are you?" Whitney asked sternly. "I'm coming to find you in Panping. Whatever the mystics did to you, I'll stop them."

"*The mystics are mine!*" a deep, sultry voice echoed all around them, making Whitney's very bones chatter.

"Who is that?" Whitney asked, spinning.

"No… no… get out of here." Sora reached for her head and squeezed. "Leave him alone!"

"So, after all this time the thief still cares for you?" The being formed in the shape of a shadow behind Whitney. Dark fingers wrapped over his shoulder and he spun, but whatever demon it was turned to mist and appeared back in front of him.

"Leave her alone!" Whitney shouted.

The demonic woman laughed. "You never should have escaped Elsewhere, foolish mortal. Sora banished you there because she knew she didn't need you anymore. You're worthless. She didn't need love. She has me."

"No!" Sora screamed. "No, Whit, don't listen to her… She's trying to… pull me away. Argh, I can feel her taking back control. She's so strong."

Whitney ran through the demon's incorporeal state and to Sora, now able to approach her. He couldn't touch her, but he kneeled to stare straight into her amber eyes. She was more beautiful than he ever remembered, like a queen out of a children's story.

"Whitney, wherever you are, you have to hide," Sora said. "I can… feel her anger that you intervened. Our connection weakens her hold of me… it…"

"Nothing weakens me!" The demon's voice thundered. The blackness of her form enveloped them, set to swallow them whole. Aquira cowered between them, and Whitney had never seen such dread in the wyvern's eyes. She lowered her head and squealed.

"Sora… Sora… tell me where you are," Whitney said. "If she's in your head like with King Pi, I'll get her out. I'll go to Torsten. He'll know what to do."

"No, it's more than that. I'm in between… we're both of us…" Sora squeezed her head with her hands and her eyelids shut. "If you care about me, find a way to destroy me. You have to destroy us."

"Sora…" Whitney went to wrap his hands around her shoulders, but they passed right through. "I do love you. You know I do. I'm going to find and help you. No matter what."

"No. Whitney, listen to me. No!"

"The only thing you will find is a grave!" Nesilia roared, her darkness now closing in and whipping around them.

Sora vanished in a blip. Whitney fell forward, then searched frantically. His heart thumped against his rib cage. He spun, and saw her behind him now, searching the darkness, confused.

Aquira rose again and unleashed a roar like nothing Whitney had ever heard from her. No longer was she the runty little wyvern. Before his eyes, she grew into a mighty dragon. Still, she retained her form, but she was massive, and the sound could have scared the skin from a zhulong.

"Settle, my pet," the demon said. "I will find you, and you will aid me in my quest."

Aquira shrunk back into the darkness.

"What is this?" Whitney said, aghast. "Where is she!"

"I have to thank you, Whitney," said the voice. "Had Sora not been so obsessed with saving you, she'd never have opened herself up to my influence. All the power of the mystics and Elsewhere. It's so lovely. Now I have it all."

Whitney heard Sora scream and searched. She appeared, staring at him, eyes wide. Then she was gone.

"She... Sora... this body... so beautiful it has men bending over backward—sometimes literally—to please her," Nesilia said. "To please me. She's so powerful she can withstand even my infinite power without bursting at the seams."

"Who are you?" Whitney demanded.

"You know the answer to that question. You've always known."

And he did. The Buried Goddess could not be mistaken. He'd felt her presence so many times before and hadn't even realized it. Redstar, the other warlocks, their power was hers, not their own. He recognized her from right before he and Sora were torn from Elsewhere, him to mount Lister, and her to the Red Tower and what he'd thought were mystics.

"*Nesilia,*" Whitney whispered with venom in his tone. "Stop this right now. Let Sora go!"

"Nothing on Pantego or in Elsewhere can stop me," Nesilia replied.

Sora cried out. Whitney turned again and saw her, now on her knees, crossing her chest with her arms, shivering. "It's so cold," Sora said. "Whitney, it's so cold. Run, please run..."

"Where are you?" Whitney asked again, accentuating each word with purpose.

"Cold. So cold"

"Brekliodad?" he said. Did Kazimir somehow find her and drag her back to his homeland? None of this made any sense. "Are you in Brek? Where are you, Sora? The mountains? Drav Cra?"

"Yes," Sora struggled to say through a clenched jaw.

"Which one?"

"My body is there... but my mind. I've—killed so many, Whitney."

"That's enough, children," Nesilia spoke, calmly now. "It's my turn."

Sora screamed and grasped her head, pulling at her hair. "Get out. Get out. Get out!"

"Listen to her!" Whitney shouted.

"She is so strong," Nesilia said. "But as you can see... as powerful as she might be, this vessel will not last forever. Even the blood of kings and queens is not eternal."

"Kings and queens?" Whitney said. "What the yig are you talking about?"

Nesilia's laugh in response made Whitney's stomach roll. "Oh, you'll find out."

Sora was on her back, seizing, a thick foam pooling at the corners of her mouth.

From the darkness, a lithe and beautiful form stepped into the light. Her skin wriggled as leaves and branches stretched out from her. Nesilia stood over Sora, then kneeled and stroked her hair, and the spasms stopped. "But fear not, I am grooming a new power."

"Let Sora go, and I won't kill you like I did—"

"Like you did my sister?" Nesilia spat. "Bliss? The One Who Remained? What a silly name. She got what she deserved. But make no mistake, Whitney *Fierstown*," she emphasized the last name. "Bliss slayer you are not. Of all those present that day, you barely escaped, barely survived. Perhaps it would have been best for our friend here had you died there, wrapped up in my sister's web."

"You know nothing!" Whitney shouted. "I will gut you."

"I know all," Nesilia said, rising. She stepped over Sora's prone frame and walked toward Whitney. "From beneath the soil, through the eyes of my loyal servants, I saw it all. You played as little a part in that as Iam did in reviving the fallen King Pi."

She disappeared as she stepped out of the light and into the surrounding darkness.

Whitney opened his mouth to speak.

"Silence!" Nesilia shouted. The black which surrounded Whitney immediately fled, and she was gone. Bright light assaulted him from all sides. "Iam is not the only one who can beckon forth light!"

Whitney's whole body burned like flame covered him. He imagined it would have been how an upyr like Kazimir would have felt if exposed to sunlight.

From the ground rose an army of pallid, sickly looking creatures. They were humanoid but definitely not human. Their oversized eyes were jet black, no distinction between iris, pupil, or sclera. Flat noses were central upon long, heart-shaped faces. The slits where the mouth should've been were too small for Whitney to imagine them being able to use them for speech, but they parted slightly, and a shrill cry filled the space. Whitney felt something warm dripping down the sides of his face and reached up to his ears, pulling away bloody fingertips.

From their backs sprouted wings like dragonflies, clear, long, and heavily veined. They all converged on Whitney, hands stretched out like they were ready to attack. He lifted his hands to block, but in an instant, it all vanished, and Whitney was left screaming in the middle of the Fettingborough cemetery, swinging his arms wildly.

"You're safe." Lucindur's voice soothed him but only just. "You're safe. You're okay." He hands wrapped his body, but Whitney shoved her away.

"What was that! What did you do to me? Where did you send me?" The questions spilled from his mouth like a thunderclap.

"Only what you asked of me," Lucindur said, panting.

Whitney noticed he was clenching his eyes and opened them. Everything looked as it had just moments ago, before he was cast into that awful place within Sora's mind. Almost. Aquira cowered behind a gravestone, peaking around at Lucindur, eyes bright with terror. Lucindur herself no longer seemed calm. She squeezed her temples between her thumb and index finger. She went to move, but fell to her knee, her leg's shaking, breathing heavy. She winced as if enduring the worst headache imaginable.

She reached into a small pouch and produced a pinch of a dark substance, then shoved it in her pipe. Whitney realized it was what he thought was night-blooming jasmine. As if she saw him looking, she said, "Manaroot. Helps the mind focus. Far better when inhaled than eaten. Far less potent."

She offered Whitney a puff, and he obliged. Immediately, he felt a sense of calm wash over him, and he could remember everything with clarity. Lucy leaned back against a headstone and stretched her eyelids, still short of breath. As she did, she retrieved a red apple from her belongings and took a bite. This, she didn't offer Whitney. He was starving now but felt too sick to put food down anyway.

"Sorry," she said, mouth full. "Doing that leaves a pit in my stomach. Feels like I haven't eaten in days."

"Whatever you need," Whitney said. He leaned up and found Aquira now at his side, growling low at Lucindur. "It's okay, girl," he said, patting her snout. "It wasn't her. She's safe."

"I've never experienced anything like that," Lucindur said. "Your friend was resisting with unbelievable power. If I held on any longer…" She gestured to her instrument. Two of the strings had snapped, and a crack ran down the bottom.

"Lucindur, I'm sorry…" Whitney said.

"Don't be, it will take some mending, but I made a promise." She took another bite of the apple. "Tell me everything."

"Sora said it was cold. Then, I'm not sure.

"Cold?" Lucindur asked. "The far north? Brek? What would she be doing there if she's with what remains of the mystics?"

"I don't know. But she's not okay. I've never seen her so terrified. Told me never to try and find her."

"The bending of mind and sight can be incredibly unnerving for those unaware," Lucindur said. "Perhaps she was confused?"

"No, it wasn't that. She knew what was going on, but we weren't alone. She... the Buried Goddess. Sora said she was being possessed."

Lucindur closed her eyes and took another drag from her pipe, then passed it to Whitney. "I feared something like this. Nothing good comes from that tower and trifling with magics beyond our mortal understanding invites demons from Elsewhere. Tricksters with false dreams of grandeur."

"No, it was her. Nesilia. I've felt her presence before, but that was in Elsewhere, this... I don't know."

"Whitney, do you realize what you're saying? You should rest, reflect on it. Lightmancing can distort perspective. It can take time for the experience to settle."

"It's like she's a prisoner of her own mind and Nesilia is in control," Whitney said, ignoring Lucindur. "She said something about being 'stuck between realms.'" His words slowed as he said them, and his gaze fixated on the half-eaten apple in Lucindur's hand.

"Ah, my apologies," she said. "That must be it. The effects can be taxing on the subject as well. You must be starving. Here." She started digging through her belongings. Aquira now felt comfortable enough to crawl right up to her a silently beg for a snack.

"It's not that," Whitney said.

She glanced up. "Are you sure?"

Whitney swallowed hard. "Stuck between realms," he repeated.

"Elsewhere *is* the realm between, where souls linger for eternity. The gods created our world to test us, and live in their own; one our souls shall never see. What the followers of Iam may call the Light, but we never get there, Whitney. No human can. Elsewhere is the eternal puzzle. Those who learned enough here in Pantego can create a place of eternal peace, and those who didn't shall imagine their own nightmare for all time."

"I've been to Elsewhere, for a long time," Whitney said. "I made peace, but this place… is so much more fun."

"You've what?" Her brow furrowed.

"It doesn't matter. But I know Elsewhere, and that wasn't where she was. She's somewhere else, between, and she's right. I can't do anything for her."

"Those who push the boundaries of our worlds too far, sometimes they cannot be retrieved." Lucindur slid closer and laid her hand upon his shoulder. "I'm so sorry, Whitney. Perhaps it's time to move on?"

"Move on? You're not listening to me." Whitney snatched the apple out of her hand and stared at the shiny, red skin. He pictured Kazimir, sitting on his parent's fence, crunching on an apple like it was a human heart.

"Whitney, I must eat."

"Oh, right." He tossed the apple back to her, forcing her to catch it unexpectedly. Then he stood and walked a few paces away. He got woozy and had to lean against a tree.

"I told you, you need rest."

I need you to do me one more favor," Whitney said, looking back at her.

"What kind of favor?"

"I need you to find one more person for me," Whitney said. "Well, sort of a person."

"Even if I wanted to, I can't." She raised her damaged instrument. "I need new strings, perhaps a new salfio entirely."

"So, we'll get them."

"These are made from the cocoons of lightnettle worm larvae. Their blood glows, and they're found only in caverns far below the Dragon's Tail. Very rare, but it takes such rarity such as that to channel my abilities."

"Where'd you get that salfio then?"

"A dwarvish curiosities trader in Panping, decades ago when I was researching our lost art."

Whitney couldn't help but laugh.

"What?" Lucindur asked, no longer amused.

"It's just that... I guess traveling to Panping wasn't a mistake. You think the trader is still there? We were planning to stop in Panping on the way to Myen anyway. It's the only reason I came along. Won't be out of the way."

"Trust me, even if we found the shop, you can't afford it. The entire troupe can't. It took all the inheritance left to me by my parents to purchase it—jewelry, books, everything."

"Don't worry about a price. I have a few things hidden in the city that should be able to fetch us some shogging, glowing salfio strings." Panping was the largest city east of the Gorge. He'd spent plenty of time there working for a fence in his younger years, then alone—enough time to hide some scores here and there for just a situation like this. Well, sort of like this. Assuming nobody else found them by now of course.

Lucindur shot him a cross glare.

"You know what I mean." Whitney bit his lip. "Look, I know this is all you promised, but Sora is in real trouble. I know someone who might be able to help her."

"Possessions are nothing to be trifled with. Maybe what you need is a priest."

Whitney waved at her in dismissal. "Not a shogging priest. Lucindur, I saved yours *and* your daughter's lives. I don't want to keep pulling that card, but it's true. Two lives, two favors. Then

I'll never ask anything of you again. Shog in a yigging barrel, you can even keep the change of what we sell and use it to rebuild the Troupe."

"What could possibly be worth that much?"

"I don't want to ruin the surprise. If I'm wrong, then it's no big deal, and we go our separate ways. But if I'm right, all you do is benefit. Get a little richer, all for practicing some magic."

"It's not just magic. Every time, I pour a shred of my essence into the song. And when I do, there are others who might hear beyond the target. Demons—like that which possesses your friend—mystics, twisted creatures of darkness might all be called to me. Lightmancers are few for a reason, Whitney. Once was a favor, and a reason to flex my powers lest I forget how. Twice so soon… dangerous."

"The mystic order is gone now. It will be fine." Whitney hurried closer and dropped to her knees beside her. Aquira hopped up atop a grave beside him and stared at Lucindur with her big, pretty eyes. "Please, Lucindur. This may be her only shot, and it's all I can think of."

Lucindur's face scrunched up in thought. After a moment she blurted, "All right, fine! If you find a way to afford the right strings…"

"And make the Troupe rich," Whitney added.

Lucindur rolled her eyes. "Yes. You do that, and I'll help you. But then I think it's time I put the salfio down for good. Demons posing as goddesses, possessed princes and mystics… it's too dangerous now."

Whitney clutched her face and planted a kiss on her cheek. Her eyes went wide with shock. Aquira jumped down and nuzzled against her leg. "Thank you!' Whitney exclaimed. "Then it's settled. We'll pack up and head straight for Panping. Better than staying in this graveyard anyway."

"Please don't make me regret this, Whitney."

"You won't. You're alive, and Sora is too. We can fix all of this."

Lucindur retrieved her broken instrument and slung it over her shoulder. "Who is this mysterious person you want me to find, anyway?"

Whitney smirked, then scooped up Aquira. "An old friend, right girl? And the only man I know who is neither of Pantego or Elsewhere."

XLIII

THE MYSTIC

"Sora…" Whitney wrapped his hands around her shoulder, and for a moment she thought she could feel the warmth of his touch. "I do love you. You know I do. I'm going to find and help you. No matter what."

She stared straight into his green eyes. He was more handsome than she even remembered, and more dashing. Like a lovable rogue out of a fairy tale, stealing from the rich and giving to the poor. She snapped out of it.

"No," she said. "Whitney, listen to me. No! You must stop looking."

"The only thing you will find is a grave!" Nesilia roared.

Sora's vision flashed back to the tundra, and she saw through her physical eyes again. She tried to call out for Whitney but couldn't. Everything was blurry and red. She was talking but had no idea what she was saying. Warlocks and Drav Cra closed in all around her. She resisted and returned to her mind, then back to the tundra, then her mind, seeing Whitney flicker as if he was little more than a silhouette.

"It's so cold," Sora said when her vision stopped tearing. She was on her knees, clutching her own arms but unable to feel them. "Whitney, it's so cold. Run, please run…"

She could hear Whitney again, but only in snippets. "Br—Br —Where—mountains? Drav Cra?"

"Yes," Sora said upon hearing the last word. Just speaking made her head feel like it was going to burst open.

"Which one?"

"My body is there… but my mind. I've—killed so many, Whitney."

"That's enough, children," Nesilia spoke, calmly now. "It's my turn."

Sora screamed and pulled her hair. "Get out. Get out. Get out!"

Aquira roared, but Sora couldn't see her anymore. Whitney spoke, but his voice blurred, mending in with Nesilia's. Nowhere overwhelmed Sora again. She screamed. She pounded her head against the ground, wherever the ground was. An instant later, she was back in Drav Cra, looking through her own eyes, Rathgorah before her.

Nesilia had reclaimed control of her body, and Sora could only watch. Nesilia's fingers squeezed the blood dirt beneath her. A grin played at the corner of her lips. She raised her hand, and Sora could feel all the power of Elsewhere—or whatever it was gods drew on—crackling at her fingertips.

Rathgorah tried to hold her down, but her rage at having been overcome by Sora's connection to Whitney was insurmountable. The skull on Rathgorah's staff cracked, then blew open, sending him and anyone else nearby flying away.

"How could you all have forgotten me!" she screamed. "Can't you feel me? Failures!"

Only rasps for air responded until Tihabat Dagson shouted, "Stop fighting!"

Nesilia hadn't bothered with the children, and the girl took it upon herself to jump on the rope connected to Freydis. She pulled with all her weight, breaking custom as her people had with Sahades. Nesilia released her grasp of the nonbelievers. They all gasped and spun toward the girl. There was silence until a shrill cry broke through.

Legs came first, then a torso and arms. Finally, Freydis screamed, "No!" She rolled over, coughing up dirt as her eyes seemed to adjust to being able to see anything. "I was not done. I remained."

"I said she would tear you all asunder," Nesilia said. She glanced toward Wvenweigard and smiled.

"Tihabat Dagson," Rathgorah wheezed. "What have you done?"

Even as Rathgorah questioned the girl, a few of Haral's men rushed to the rope to which Kotlkel Dagson was attached. At the same time, Gold Grin and his men used the chaos to quietly attempt to crawl away until a dire wolf noticed and blocked their path.

"Nice dog," Gold Grin tittered nervously.

"Stop this!" Rathgorah cried out while his people raised Kotlkel. "The Listeners have not spoken yet. Stop this!" Rathgorah's eyes snapped toward Tihabat. "And *you*!"

"Did what we asked of her," Haral said. "We could not allow Freydis, another Ruuhar to become Arch Warlock. Crucify the witch. Crucify Freydis! I'm pleading. End Redstar's corruption!" Haral drew her spear and charged at Nesilia.

Rathgorah released an audible sound of frustration. Sora felt her heart quickening, felt Nesilia stirring. Felt strength. Unimaginable strength as if Freydis' return triggered something in the goddess. Sora's body began to rise, much like it had on the *Reba*.

Nesilia crossed her arms, and a sharp crack split the ground beneath Haral, and the earth swallowed her up along with the men nearest to her. The broken Glass Crown was caught in the fissure and plummeted into the blackness.

Nesilia then softly lowered herself, as if the act took no energy. She turned and glared at the gathered crowd, her very look making them shrink away. Gold Grin stared at her, awestruck. Nesilia raised a fist, and Rathgorah and every other soul in the crowd who even thought to harm her collapsed to their knees, gasping for air as she crushed their throats.

"Don't..." Sora fought through the emptiness to tell Nesilia. All this time being trapped in her head, she'd thought Nesilia to be pure evil, but it took her reaction to Sora and Whitney's bond for Sora to realize... she was just sad. Lonely. Nesilia was that pitiable being Sora had seen through the Aihara Na's power on the first day she'd arrived in Panping. And she wasn't seducing Gold Grin to feel what sex was like for humans... she did it to try and understand the connection she'd lost. She did it to make Iam jealous, if he was anywhere out there watching, he remained silent.

"This has nothing to do with him!" Nesilia responded to Sora.

"Kotlkel is dead!" someone shouted over the gagging of Nesilia's victims. Hearing those words drew her attention, and she released them all. Wvenweigard ran to Kotlkel's half-buried body and pulled it all the way free while Haral's men struggled to breathe. The man's skin was white as Loutis. Wvenweigard pressed his ear to Kotlkel's chest, then his chin sank.

"He's been dead for hours," Wvenweigard said. "The listener lied to us."

Tihabat's gaze darted from side to side. Nesilia hadn't choked her, but her breathing was rapid as if she had. She went to run, but before Nesilia could do anything, Freydis leaped at the girl, tore the knife off her belt, and carved a hole in her throat. Tihabat crumpled in the hole left by Kotlkel's corpse.

Freydis turned to the others, panting like a wild animal.

Nobody approached her. They only watched in awe. "I remained, me!" she said. "I am Redstar's will."

"My Lady," Oracle Rathgorah said, staggering forward. "By the earth, it is you. Forgive my lack of faith." He fell to his knees at her feet. Hundreds in the crowd around them did the same, warlocks, warriors... nearly everyone.

"I should tear out your throat!" Freydis snarled. She cut her hand and darted at him. In a blink, Nesilia was between them and extended her arm to stop her.

"I can handle this, daughter." Nesilia looked down at Rathgorah. "Faith only exists for those who have not already seen the truth. I have been absent too long, and it is clear you have corrupted my hands. So, I must wash them."

With her words, Nesilia snapped her fingers as she promised she would. The trees themselves cast down sharp branches and pierced the hearts of every warlock, new and old, all those who had endured the Earthmoot and risen alive. She spared only the remaining children, Freydis, and Wvenweigard.

Sora fought but could do nothing. She wasn't sure why she cared that the Drav Cra warlocks were dead, but she couldn't stand the thought of being party to more death.

"No..." Rathgorah said, horrified as the screams continued to sound all around them. "No, my Lady, this can't be your will. It can't be!"

Nesilia knelt and traced her finger through one of the characters inscribed into the old man's body. "I created you to remember me, but it is clear you have forgotten. This haven, it made you soft."

"My Lady, I see now. My eyes... though they are, they still see. Stop this madness."

Nesilia turned to Wvenweigard, who stood, patting his chest as if he was surprised to still be living. "Your faith has saved you, child," she said. She opened her palm, and a dagger rose from the ground and flew into it. She placed it in Wvenweigard's hand. "Now prove it." She nodded toward the Oracle.

Wvenweigard regarded the weapon, then Rathgorah.

"Please, my son," Rathgorah said. "I was there when you indwelled. You drank of my blessed blood as you rose anew, a hand of our Lady."

"I am her hand still." Wvenweigard clutched the blade, and with no hesitation plunged it into Rathgorah's heart. The Oracle's eyes rolled back, and his mouth gaped, desperate to cling to life.

"You became too attached to living," Nesilia said. "But I no longer need to remember, for I have returned."

"Sora, tell them to let us go!" Gold Grin shouted. Nesilia turned and saw him and his pirate crew being held by Haral's warriors, squirming to break free. The loyalty in the warriors' expressions was clear. They'd watched Nesilia destroy their mighty leader like she was nothing, and for those who grew up in the tundra, strength was everything.

"Sora…" Nesilia laughed.

One of the warriors at the front of the others said, "My Lady, what do we do with these flower pickers? Why have you spared them?"

Nesilia smiled. "I have something special for them." She sauntered over to Gold Grin. Freydis moved up beside her.

"I say we skin them all alive," Freydis said. "Start a new tradition."

"Sora, my beautiful friend," Gold Grin laughed nervously. "Would ye mind giving me a hint at what's happenin."

"Do you trust me?" Nesilia asked.

"I… I knew ye were powerful, but I didn't know ye were capable of all that."

"That isn't what I asked." She circled him, the tip of her fingernail scratching gently around his neck. "Do you trust me?"

His gaze momentarily darted toward the horde of warlock

bodies scattered around them or skewered in the trees like meat sticks in Winde Port. He swallowed "Aye…I do."

"Good," Nesilia said. "Find Whitney Fierstown for me."

"That rapscallion?" Gold Grin said. "What's he got anything to do with anything anymore?"

"His time back on this world must come to an end."

"What?" Gold Grin asked, incredulous. The pirates argued amongst themselves.

Sora raged inside. *"You monster! I won't fight you anymore. I won't resist. Just leave Whitney out of it. I'll tell him to leave you alone."*

"If only you could," Nesilia said. *"But that is what love does. It deceives us, tricks us. Whitney won't stop trying to save you. He'll go to any length to do it; to any monster. And you won't be able to resist the pull to him. It weakens you, which weakens us."*

"I'll resist it…" Sora cried. *"I'll resist anything."*

"Don't worry, my dear. Once he's gone and the memory of the woman you were is forgotten with him, we will be unstoppable."

Gold Grin's first mate Hestor spat at Sora's face. "Enough is enough," he said. "You're a damned fool Gale. She's playin' you! We ain't killin Fierstown. He did wrong, but he was one of us for a time. And we especially ain't killin him for free. We ain't the ones gettin laid!"

Freydis didn't hesitate. She sliced her own hand, and vines grew up from the dirt, overwhelming Hestor in an instant. The warriors holding him backed away, startled. Hestor's muffled screams sounded as he was slowly carried underground.

"Ye'd let her do that?" another of the crew asked.

"Cap'n, stop her!"

Gold Grin watched his first mate vanish under the dirt, then looked at Nesilia, straight in the eye. Sora could only watch, but she could see the glint of lust. He was mesmerized by her, and there was nothing he wouldn't do. Under Nesilia's spell, or Sora's or both…

Nesilia extended her hand toward the fissure Haral had fallen into. The earth shook, and then the broken glass crown hovered out and into Nesilia's hand. She gently placed it atop Gold Grin's messy hair, then leaned in and planted a kiss on his cheek.

"Find Whitney, kill him, and when Fierstown's lifeblood soaks my earth, I will make you a king worthy of this crown." She straightened the crown on his head, then took a step back to behold him.

"The boy sank my first ship," Gold Grin said. "Consider him dead."

"Cap'n—" one of his men shouted, but he swiftly quieted him.

"Ye'll help me, or it's mutiny! All of ye. Sora here's gonna make us the richest pirates in history."

Nesilia regarded Freydis, who sneered. Then she looked to Wvenweigard, who bowed his head in reverence.

"*Your time is coming,*" Sora said.

"*Who can stop us now? Iam?*" Nesilia's laugh filled Nowhere, and Sora felt her essence fading back into the nothingness. The blackness was returning, as it had before she became cognizant in the Buried Hollow.

"*The Ancient One, the Arch Warlock… they are mine,*" Nesilia said. "*And so are you.*"

Sora fought it, but with so much faith in her renewed and Freydis returned, Nesilia's will was too much for Sora to bear. All she could think about was Whitney's face, staring at her, promising to save her. She wished he wouldn't try, but she knew he would, and it broke her heart. And then, Nowhere enveloped her, and she thought nothing…

EPILOGUE

Kazimir leaned against a column from the old Breklian Empire, older even than the Culling itself—the magical plague which reduced his ancestors to a tiny kingdom in the Far North. Older even than the Sanguine Lords—or at least the first memories of them. It stood, ancient, erected before the Lords offered Kazimir a chance at redemption, at reclaiming the blood lost in that horrible era before words were committed to parchment in an attempt to maintain history.

Snow beat against his cheeks, sticking there, piling up against his frigid flesh like a second layer of skin. He couldn't even recall what it was like to feel the cold. For that matter, Kazimir couldn't remember what it was like to feel much of anything except hunger… insatiable hunger.

It was dark, but his vision pierced through the veil and allowed him to see the cohort of Glass soldiers and Panpingese mercenaries marching through the mountain pass, foolishly thinking their weak, mortal eyes could spot the entry of the Dom Nohzi citadel even if they knew where it was.

"Damn you, Codar," he whispered. "Damn you, grandson."

Kazimir had tried, to horrific results, to create a family. After so long, his loneliness had gotten the best of him, and vacuous mistakes were made—mistakes Kazimir would never make again. Creating a mortal family, for an upyr, meant damning one or all. It meant deception, lies.

This was Kazimir's punishment, to watch as his grandson's blood dried within his heart, to feel the pangs of betrayal, and to know it could have been avoided.

Kazimir thought Codar a weak man who refused eternity, just as his father had—but it wasn't true. Codar might have been the smartest of them all.

Kazimir was the weak one. It was he who had tried claiming a powerful mystic so he might never again feel the harsh sting of the sun's light. He'd abandoned the Dom Nohzi code, not Codar. He'd spilled unjust blood. It was Kazimir who'd wound up alongside that ingrate, Whitney Fierstown, stuck in Elsewhere for six years. Even now, Kazimir couldn't escape the haunting of the man. For generations, sleep on Pantego meant waking up in various realms of Elsewhere, but now, Kazimir only found himself in that same worthless village. Sometimes Whitney was there, other times it was just him. And the worst part was he didn't completely hate it.

It was there in Whitney's Elsewhere that Kazimir was safe.

A sharp inhale pulled Kazimir back to the present, back to his place, seated high above the Vidkaru, Brekliodad's ancient capital. He regarded his young progeny, perched to his right. All the things he'd attempted in the pursuit of power; to make eternity mean something... now he understood. Ever since he found Sigrid clinging to life on the dirty Dockside streets, he vowed that he would do anything for her. But she was impossible to teach. Impossible to reason with. As relentless as eternity and Exile.

Her wild hair, now stark white instead of the fiery red it had once been, billowed like shredded threads of a standard in the strong wind. Her dark eyes gleamed like obsidian beneath the twin moons. He could see it there in her soul, just like those moons. Two sides, one beautiful and radiant, the other ugly and consumed by rage. He knew that look, the one that *knew* the world was going to suffer for her blight.

He knew too that some of that was simply coming to terms with what she now was, enduring her endless hunger; but there was more. This was why his masters had scolded him so on the many occasions when he bent the will of the Sanguine Lords, and why they themselves felt need to punish him, as he now punished her.

It pained him. His heart, if it could bleed, would.

An enchanted muzzle covered her mouth, damning her to that hunger but not allowing any satiation of it. Only Kazimir could remove it. It was only his voice which the cold metal would heed. It was her punishment for placing herself above the order, for murdering the Queen of Glass even after the accepted Blood Pact was fulfilled by Codar's death.

The irony didn't escape Kazimir. He'd done worse, pushed further. It had taken centuries between Pantego and Elsewhere for him to understand that his enduring fate upon accepting a morsel of the fetid beast, the Wianu—a creature which, too, lived in the realm between lives—was final. And it was all that mattered. His power was the Sanguine Lords' power, not his own.

Should I punish her for destroying all trace of my life before? he wondered. *For giving me clarity?*

He looked back at the proud columns leading toward the peak of the mountain like a ribcage of stone or grasping for life like great, sculpted tentacles rising to frame the door in the rock face, tall enough for giants. To the mortals below, it would only appear as a ruin. He'd heard it called many things, Forwonay, Gilly Gale, Bist'rofunis—but it was none of those things.

The men below searched, but they'd never get far. Kazimir's people would feed first.

Kazimir turned back to the pass and sighed. It was a human sound, one he had no use for any longer, but the feeling was still comforting, even after all these years. "None leave here alive," he ordered Sigrid.

She nodded once, then removed a crossbow from her back. A bolt thrummed, racing it down the snowy mountainside. His eyes followed it with perfect precision, never losing it, knowing Sigrid did the same. He missed that feeling, the thrill, the excitement when his abilities were more than a mere tool used by the Lords for their purposes.

"Reports say it's up this way!" The regiment leader's voice carried over the whipping wind. It didn't need to. The upyr could hear a fly buzz a kilometer off if they desired to. "Those murderers are finally going to pay."

"Was the Queen really worth this?" a soldier replied, shivering.

"That isn't up to us, is it?" A short period of silence went by. "Is it?"

The leader turned and saw the soldier, hand pressed firmly against a bloody hole in his neck where the bolt stuck out.

His lifeblood painted the snow beneath him, and the smell hit Kazimir's nose with the force of a thousand zhulong. Sigrid was already halfway down the hill.

"We're under atta—" He didn't finish the word before Sigrid shredded his trachea with her nails, sharp and strong as any fine blade.

The soldiers scrambled for their own weapons. Kazimir could tell by the way they shone that they were coated in silver—an old wives tale said to help kill the upyr. Effective at harming and destroying their mortal bodies maybe, and though the return path through Elsewhere was insufferable, it was not true death. There was only one way to truly eliminate an upyr, to fully wipe him from existence, and Kazimir preferred never to think of it: *Dakel un Ghastrin.* Only the wianu that turned him could kill him.

The Panpingese mercenaries wore strings of garlic around their neck. Another tall tale. The only smell that mattered to an upyr was blood, and veins pulsed all around him.

Kazimir drew two knives, two of many which adorned his chest. He threw one through the forehead of a soldier who ran at him. Terrified eyes fell headlong into the snow along with the rest of the man. Then Kazimir pulled another blade and wove through their ranks like a master seamster, gutting and rending flesh. Untouchable.

A muffled howl pierced the night. Kazimir whipped around and saw a steaming wound on Sigrid's arm courtesy of a silver blade. Kazimir felt something, strange. His heart didn't beat, but for a second, he felt like it might.

He started to move toward her, but then Sigrid grabbed the blade with her bare flesh. Steam rose, but she snapped it in half and drove the sharp end through her attacker's eye. Then, the rest of the soldiers felt the storm of her ire. A blade wasn't even necessary. Broken necks, ribs, spines; she worked through them like a battering range.

In a flash, the nearly fifty soldiers were dead—Glass soldiers, Panpingese mercenaries, and others.

"Screw the Queen!" a lone straggler shouted. He clambered over a few dead bodies. Kazimir rolled his shoulders, then removed a knife from a holster inside his coat and flung it. Sigrid slapped it down quick as lightning. She turned to him, only her raised eyebrows showing beyond that metal mask as if her face contorted into a wild sneer.

"Sigrid," Kazimir scolded.

She bent and retrieved the knife, waited for the soldier to get a little further, then threw it with all her new-found strength. From so far, all Kazimir could see was a red spray before the soldier vanished beneath the deepening snow.

The sounds of death quieted beneath the howling wind. Kazimir knew how the Glass Kingdom viewed its queen. After learning of this massacre, they wouldn't send more. Even if they did, they'd see nothing. Codar would be decided to be a liar, sending Glassmen to their deaths. Kazimir had already been punished long ago for showing his grandson the home he'd wanted for him. Now it belonged to Sigrid, his true daughter.

"Bring them to the citadel before the sunrise," Kazimir ordered. "At dawn, we feast. For successful or not, all Pantego shall know the fear of the Dom Nohzi once more."

"Yes, master," Sigrid said, her words nearly indiscernible thanks to the mask. Kazimir watched her eyes, little more than dark holes lusting over the still-flowing arteries of their victims. It'd been weeks since last she'd fed, and in her adolescence, she must have been agonizing.

"Feed first," Kazimir said. "Don't tell a soul."

He waved his hand. "Otkryt," he said, and the muzzle unlocked, falling to her chin. Her gaze darted between him and a body, then, without saying anything, she mounted a corpse and consumed.

Some punishment, Kazimir cursed himself. *All those years in Elsewhere made me soft.*

He turned and took a step. Suddenly, the snow at his feet turned to grass, one blade at a time, blooming all around him. He spun, and there it was behind him as well. A wattle and daub cabin stood alone on a field, smoke puffing up from the chimney.

"No," Kazimir said, fists squeezing. "How can I be here? I'm awake." Another step, and a familiar young boy and a girl with pointed ears rushed by him toward the cabin.

"No, I can't be back here," Kazimir said. He looked up. "I've seen your truth. I honored that Pact, it was she who—"

"Who are you yelling at?" Kazimir spun back around, drew a knife and had it at the speaker's throat in less than a second. The man didn't back away or startle. He stood, grinning from ear to ear as only Whitney Fierstown could."

"You," Kazimir snarled.

"Me," Whitney replied. "Not very nice getting snuck up on like that, is it?"

Kazimir lowered the blade. "Well if you're here, at least it isn't Elsewhere again."

"Or did we never leave?" Whitney taunted.

Kazimir pursed his lips, then blew out and walked the other way "I don't have time for this."

"No, wait. Please." Whitney ran and threw himself in front of Kazimir, hands palm out.

"What do you want, thief?"

Whitney Fierstown shifted in his stance, then released a nervous chuckle. "Kazzy, old friend. We need to talk."

END

The Buried Goddess Saga will continue in War of Men coming Summer 2019.

Thank you for reading *Way of Gods,* book four in The Buried Goddess Saga.

Being the new kids on the block is difficult and we could really benefit from your honest reviews on Amazon. It'll only take you a minute but it'll affect the life of this book forever! (Not to mention help feed our families). All you have to do is click **here** and then scroll down and write a review. HUGE thank you in advance for helping making The Buried Goddess Saga a big hit!

FROM THE PUBLISHER

Thank you so much for reading Way of Gods by Rhett C. Bruno and Jaime Castle. We hope you enjoyed it as much as we enjoyed bringing it to you. We just wanted to take a moment to encourage you to review the book on Amazon and Goodreads.

Every review helps further the author's reach and, ultimately, helps them continue writing fantastic books for us all to enjoy.

If you liked Way of Gods, check out the rest of our catalogue at www.aethonbooks.com. To sign up to receive updates regarding all new releases, visit our website.

JOIN THE KING'S SHIELD

Sign up to the *free* and exclusive King's Shield Newsletter to receive early looks and new novels, peeks at conceptual art that breathes life into Pantego as well as exclusive access to short stories called "Legends of Pantego." Learn more about the characters and the world you love.

Did you know we have a Facebook group too? All the same perks as the email readers group plus instant interaction with Rhett and Jaime! The Official King's Shield Fan Club.

ABOUT THE AUTHORS

Jaime lives in Texas with his wife and two kids. He enjoys anything creative, from graphic arts to painting. His office looks like the Avengers threw up on the walls.

Jaime has been writing since elementary school and is a bit of a grammar officer—here to correct and serve.

Rhett is a Sci-fi/Fantasy author currently living in Stamford, Connecticut. His published works include books in the USA Today Bestselling CIRCUIT SERIES (Published by Diversion Books and Podium Audio), THE BURIED GODDESS SAGA and the THE CHILDREN OF TITAN SERIES (Aethon Books, Audible Studios). He is also one of the founders of the popular science fiction platform, Sci-Fi Bridge.

SPECIAL THANKS TO:

ADAWIA E. ASAD
BARDE PRESS
CALUM BEAULIEU
BEN
BECKY BEWERSDORF
BHAM
TANNER BLOTTER
ALFRED JOSEPH BOHNE IV
CHAD BOWDEN
ERREL BRAUDE
DAMIEN BROUSSARD
CATHERINE BULLINER
JUSTIN BURGESS
MATT BURNS
BERNIE CINKOSKE
MARTIN COOK
ALISTAIR DILWORTH
JAN DRAKE
BRET DULEY
RAY DUNN
ROB EDWARDS
RICHARD EYRES
MARK FERNANDEZ
CHARLES T FINCHER
SYLVIA FOIL
GAZELLE OF CAERBANNOG
DAVID GEARY
MICHEAL GREEN
BRIAN GRIFFIN

EDDIE HALLAHAN
JOSH HAYES
PAT HAYES
BILL HENDERSON
JEFF HOFFMAN
GODFREY HUEN
JOAN QUERALTÓ IBÁÑEZ
JONATHAN JOHNSON
MARCEL DE JONG
KABRINA
PETRI KANERVA
ROBERT KARALASH
VIKTOR KASPERSSON
TESLAN KIERINHAWK
ALEXANDER KIMBALL
JIM KOSMICKI
FRANKLIN KUZENSKI
MEENAZ LODHI
DAVID MACFARLANE
JAMIE MCFARLANE
HENRY MARIN
CRAIG MARTELLE
THOMAS MARTIN
ALAN D. MCDONALD
JAMES MCGLINCHEY
MICHAEL MCMURRAY
CHRISTIAN MEYER
SEBASTIAN MÜLLER
MARK NEWMAN
JULIAN NORTH

KYLE OATHOUT
LILY OMIDI
TROY OSGOOD
GEOFF PARKER
NICHOLAS (BUZ) PENNEY
JASON PENNOCK
THOMAS PETSCHAUER
JENNIFER PRIESTER
RHEL
JODY ROBERTS
JOHN BEAR ROSS
DONNA SANDERS
FABIAN SARAVIA
TERRY SCHOTT
SCOTT
ALLEN SIMMONS
KEVIN MICHAEL STEPHENS
MICHAEL J. SULLIVAN
PAUL SUMMERHAYES
JOHN TREADWELL
CHRISTOPHER J. VALIN
PHILIP VAN ITALLIE
JAAP VAN POELGEEST
FRANCK VAQUIER
VORTEX
DAVID WALTERS JR
MIKE A. WEBER
PAMELA WICKERT
JON WOODALL
BRUCE YOUNG

www.ingramcontent.com/pod-product-compliance
Lightning Source LLC
Chambersburg PA
CBHW031602180726
48284CB00005B/1372